The Champions of Talamh

By Ian and Rachel Clancy

First paperback edition August 2025

Illustrations copyright © 2025 by Summer Allen

Follow us on Twitter @ClancyAuthors

ISBN
979-8-9999055-0-5

For Charles Clancy
A True Champion

Table of Contents

Animus

A small wooden puppet, barely a foot tall, walked across a worn stage with the perfect illusion of life. There were no strings connecting her hands and feet, and yet she followed every movement of the puppeteer's gnarled fingers. She was dressed in red armor, and a silver sword gleamed in her hand.

Jeza, Endring thought sullenly. *Justice*.

The old puppet master flicked his wrist upward, and the puppet threw her sword then caught it again with a flourish that brought a gasp from the children that crowded around.

Then the puppeteer began in a rolling tone that echoed out farther than it should.

"'Bring me the beast!' Jeza cried as she held Adalci aloft. She would slay the primordial hydra and make the world safe once more!"

The puppeteer reached down and pulled an unseen lever. The stage split to the sound of grinding gears as smoke billowed out. As he raised his hand again he stretched his thin fingers wide, and five heads lifted through the mist on spindly necks.

"Jeza attacked the beast, pouring all of her strength into every stroke of Adalci."

The puppet leaped at the hydra, bringing down her sword and severing one of its wooden heads, and the children cheered.

"The battle was fierce, lasting from Rending to Feasting, and again, and again! Three full weeks they fought. In the end, the goddess fulfilled her oath and slayed the beast! But it was not enough. No. More hydra would rise, and the world would be overrun!"

Several more heads appeared in the fog that hung around the stage, slithering up like snakes as the puppeteer wiggled his fingers.

"The eight gods knew they needed to banish the beast to a new realm, a realm not yet created. And so it was-" Jeza lifted her sword above her head "-with the power of the mighty Adalci, sword of justice, the eldest of the gods drove her might down upon the world and shattered the realms!"

The sword slammed down as the puppeteer flipped another switch, imperceptible to the children, but Endring saw. The stage rumbled back into place as a burst of light exploded. When it was gone, the smoke had cleared, and three orbs hung above the stage at the whim of three long fingers.

"And so she broke the world into three. Las, Erimos, and Suntara."

Endring glanced up. He could see Erimos now, nearly centered in the night sky, a dim brown disc. Beside it, Suntara hung like a blue marble, half its size. The clouds were thick over Suntara, as though a great storm was stirring the oceans.

"And the realms she split into three," the puppeteer continued. "Talamh, realm of man. Sbarga, realm of the gods. And Nyx, realm of the dead, resting place of the great primordial hydra, so that it may never again trouble mankind."

Endring had seen this puppet show before. Every cycle the old puppeteer set up his stall near the bottom of the temple steps, on the edge of the sprawling fields of the Gods' Mount. Tonight, the fields were filled with tens of thousands of celebrants, endless stalls and vendors. The yellow clad monks of Desita sent fireworks into the sky that showered sparkling light over the people, and throughout the celebration, hazy blue pockets of Nyx hinted at a mighty horde of spirits in attendance.

He sighed.

Every cycle it was the same, nine straight days of endless excess and revelry, culminating on the last and greatest night of feasting. Tonight. But the revelry would soon end. This wasn't a night for celebration, but for mourning. They just didn't know it yet.

Endring let his eyes wander down to the city of Arrajin at the base of the Gods' Mount - more of a hill really, but that didn't sound divine enough. Across the river Arrtris, the city sprawled to the horizon, teeming with nearly a hundred thousand souls, hemmed in on all sides by thick jungle. Up and down the path to the Mount there strode thousands of pilgrims clad with togas or chlamys that bore the colors of devotion upon their sleeves. He let his eyes drift to his own robes, the purple of Bei'ai, and he felt ashamed. He slipped a hand in his pocket, and it rested on cold metal.

Endring glanced up. Suntara had started to overtake Erimos now, half of it cresting the brown disc behind. It wouldn't be long. A twinge of fear forced his eyes away from the spectacle. Did the gods know?

He drew his hand out from his pocket, clutching the cool metal disc. As he opened his fist, he stared at the symbol engraved on the surface - a crude face. The left half was the face of a man with wavy hair and a sharp eye. The right was the face of a beast with sharp fangs and the eye of a hawk. He turned it over in his hand, and a flash of his guild seal, black against his palm, caught his eye. A single tear - the seal of the monks of Bei'ai.

The puppeteer's boisterous voice drifted back into focus. "That is the tale of the Shattering and the eight gods of Sbarga!"

Endring flipped the medallion over one last time and stared at the awesome countenance of the beast. "Nine," he muttered.

A form suddenly ran into his hand. One of the children hadn't looked where he was going, and the medallion rattled to the ground at Endring's feet.

"Sorry, mister!" The youngster said.

Endring's gaze searched the ground frantically for the medallion, but before he could spot it, the boy scooped it up.

"Here!" He didn't mean to sound harsh. "Give me that, boy!"

He held out a hand, but the boy stood frozen, his eyes wide as he stared at Endring's countenance in the flash of a firework. Endring pulled at the corner of his hood, trying to hide the marred flesh that covered the right side of his face.

"That's mine," he said more softly, pushing his hand toward the boy.

The boy quickly dropped the medallion into his open palm and ran off into the crowd.

A deep, rolling sigh pulled his focus up to where a man approached, holding two glasses of wine, and he closed his fist around the medallion. Sammel. Perhaps the only one in all the worlds he considered a friend.

"You're back."

Sammel nodded. He was casually taking in the temple grounds, his mouth an unreadable line. He was the kind of man that would be lost in a crowd - plain features, a square jaw, and dull gray hair - but for the way he dressed. He favored bright patterned tunics and fine pants. And his boots. Always the most outlandish he could buy. Today's choice was a pair of purple wyrm hide with gilded trim. And at his hip was coiled a relic, the whip of Iyanu. It was a braided whip of bright orange with a faint glow. A relic was a rare enough thing to make anyone stand out, and yet he wore it openly.

He stood in stark contrast to Endring - his dark purple oracle's robes, so dark they were almost black, and the full hood pulled close to cover his face despite the humid heat of the jungle. He'd spent his whole life hiding himself, wishing to be that person that blended in so well.

"I understand this is custom," Sammel said, extending one of the wine glasses toward Endring.

Endring took it hesitantly.

"I've never been to the festival before," Sammel said.

"I assumed as much."

"It's been a fascinating experience. The devotion people hold to the gods seems to be a small factor for most of them. I wouldn't have guessed that."

"People like to celebrate, Sammel."

"True."

"Don't you have any festivals out in the desert?"

"Liberation day."

Endring let his gaze fall to the crimson wine. The glass felt heavy in his hand, and his thoughts became turbid. The champion's loved ones would be in attendance tonight. He pushed that thought aside and turned his focus back to the festival.

"And what is liberation day?"

"Every year we celebrate the day we broke away from the gods and their boons. The party is not so lavish as this, but there is pie."

Endring smiled. He turned his eyes back out toward the festival field. A table was being set in front of the main stage where the champions would feast. All eight of them hadn't been gathered together at the temple in months, and a host of monks of Uthando and Desita were rushing around preparing the area as the red clad guardians of Jeza strolled around the perimeter.

"It won't be long," Sammel said, matching his gaze.

How could he do that? Endring thought. Sammel stayed so cool through it all. The weight of what they were doing threatened to crush Endring, and yet Sammel watched the festival with simple curiosity.

Sammel turned toward him again, clearly aware of the turmoil on his face. "Killing them is the only way."

Endring hushed him sharply, clenching the now warm medallion in a hand slick with sweat.

On one hand, the coldness with which Sammel managed this whole affair was repulsive to Endring, but if he admitted the truth, he was also jealous. Sammel could see the bigger picture so easily and do what needed to be done.

Sammel turned back toward the temple grounds with an easy tone. "How many times have you attended the festival?

"This is my fourth." He pushed at the thoughts assaulting him and tried to recall his first time. "I was so excited as a boy. My parents traveled all the way from Suntara. It was the first time I rode a chariot."

"I enjoy chariot rides. There's something comforting about the cold dark."

Endring let his eyes drift up to Suntara where it slid across Erimos, and then down to the pylat tether. Three large chariots were anchored there, their golden pylats flapping wings like sunlight.

"And the festival? Did it prove as exciting as you thought?"

"No." Endring let his free hand brush his mangled face. "The other children weren't kind."

"Children are many things, but seldom kind. You should have anticipated their response."

"I was five, Sammel. You don't anticipate that when you're five."

"I believe I would have."

Endring flipped the medallion around in his hand. He hated waiting, and as much as he tried not to look up, he found his eyes darting to the two worlds overhead. "My parents kept me away from other children. I had never thought about how they would respond."

"And how did you respond?"

"I ran away. I ended up there, in the sanctum." He pointed behind him to the temple. Its wide portico rose up on either side, and massive stairs ran up the middle past the columns of the Champions. He'd lived here since he was eight years old, and still it had lost none of its grandeur. "I remember seeing the statues of the gods for the first time. I stopped in front of Bei'ai's shrine. She seemed smaller than her siblings. Weaker somehow. Like she might understand. It was almost like her statue was watching me."

"Which is absurd, of course. Statues can't see anything."

Endring bit his lip. He didn't appreciate Sammel tainting this memory with his practicality. "Maybe. But the gods can. They see and hear, and call to us." He was once again keenly aware of the mark of Neveri pressed against the seal of Bei'ai in his right hand. "It felt like she could see me, like she understood somehow."

"So you weren't surprised to be guilded to the order of Bei'ai?"

Endring shook his head. "I'd known since that night. It was like she never stopped calling to me."

Endring could feel a weight bearing down on his soul. Maybe it was his own conscience. Or maybe she was still watching. He'd spent countless agonizing hours wondering if she could ever forgive him for his part in what they were about to do. Could he find a place in the Midding?

He didn't want to think about it again. Not tonight. He'd made his choice, and he would see it through. He pointed up to the sky. Suntara was easing across Erimos, nearly to the zenith of the Shattering.

"Have you ever seen this, Sammel?"

He shook his head. "No. I've always been on Erimos during the Shattering. I've been very excited to see it myself. It seems fitting, doesn't it?"

"What does?"

"Us. Here. Tonight. The world being remade as we remember the moment it was undone. It's like the old stories of the changing seasons. The dead leaves fall away, and you watch as the new blooms."

The changing of seasons. Endring slipped the medallion back in his pocket. He liked that image. It was simply a barren tree, but what they hoped would bloom next would bring life back to Talamh. Life as it was meant to be.

The crowd was growing restless now, watching as the planets slowly slid into place overhead. Endring imagined what it must be like for those on Suntara and Erimos, watching for the same moment, people on three worlds all celebrating the same thing at the same time. And somewhere in Sbarga, were the gods watching too? Did they know what was about to happen?

The crowd began shouting now, some attempting to count down, others calling a premature start to the new cycle. And slowly Suntara rolled into place, perfectly aligned with Erimos, and above the planets the Eye of Kisandin pulsed brightly. The crowd erupted in cheers and the clink of thousands of glasses and goblets.

Sammel lifted his glass. "To new beginnings."

Endring lifted his own glass, but his eyes were locked on the table of the Champions. They were drinking, all eight, downing the wine as they toasted the new cycle.

Endring's hand trembled. "To new beginnings."

He drank down the wine, warm and sweet, and he watched as the champions set down their goblets. In front of them, a player burst onto the stage, hands extended, and called up a magnificent display - an illusion of pegasus glowed around them. They swooped and dove, shimmering with moonlight and running through a conjured cloud as they circled the champion's table. But just as suddenly, the light faltered as a horrified scream tore through the night sky. Endring pulled his eyes away, reminding himself that it had to be done. Still, he would not watch them die.

"Come, Sammel. It's time."

He spun toward the temple and started up the marble stair. Behind, he heard chaos erupting, small at first, the cries of the monks as the Champions began to vomit blood. Slowly the news spread, and the crowd became restless as fear and tension filled the air.

Endring ducked through the doors of the temple, vaguely aware of the sanctum and the towering statues of the gods.

They hurried through the door at the back and into the hall of trees, and Endring felt a catch in his throat. Stained glass windows were set into the walls on either side, and in front of each window stood a tree, eight in all. He had seen the soft brown trunks and bright red petals a thousand times. But now he watched as the red petals pulled away from each tree in droves, swirling in an unfelt wind as they spiraled down into piles at the roots. No sooner did they settle on the ground, than they choked to a dead brown.

Sammel let out a sharp whistle. "It's true then? When a champion dies, their tree dies?"

Endring's voice came out a reverent whisper that still felt too loud. "They'll blossom again when new champions are called." He set his eyes on the end of the hall. "We should hurry."

He set off at a quick pace and his robe stirred the petals as he marched past. At the end of the hall a set of stairs descended into the ground. The walls of smooth stone were hewn straight out of the solid gray rock. The passage was narrow, but not so much as to be uncomfortable, and they made their way single file down to the ancient stone door at the bottom. He took a breath and stepped inside.

"Incredible!" Sammel said.

The room spread thirty feet on either side. There was nothing soft here, just cold carved stone with runes and swirling images. It was ancient, seamless, constructed by the gods themselves. A railing ran along the edge of the balcony that curved inward around a massive bubble of deepest black. The depth of it could never be measured or guessed, like staring into the endless sky. And all along the black, little spirits danced like blue flames.

"That's Nyx?"

Endring nodded as he stepped forward, then stopped a couple feet from the Veil.

Sammel walked closer as though entranced, and lifted a hand toward the rippling black.

Endring grabbed his wrist. "Don't touch it."

Sammel raised an eyebrow as he pulled his hand away. "I wouldn't have. I've heard the stories."

Endring's gaze wandered from Sammel to a statue of Bei'ai, standing just beside the Veil. Her arms were outstretched, beckoning weary souls toward Nyx. She was slender and strong, and her cold stone eyes seemed to bore into his soul. He dropped his gaze to her seal on his palm. It was too late to turn back now.

"Those lights," Sammel said. "They're the souls of the dead?"

"Yes." Endring let his eyes wander the dancing spirits that flitted curiously back and forth, as though gauging the men's intentions.

"Fascinating. So close, and yet a realm away. Can you call them out?"

"Another time, perhaps."

"Yes, of course."

Endring stepped toward the dark mass, and the blue lights swarmed to his presence like a moth to flame, causing the Veil to bow outward. He lifted his hand, pressing in against the black. The cold was sharp against his sweaty palm. The soft surface gave way at his touch, and his mind was bombarded with a thousand voices all vying for his attention.

"I'm not here for you," he muttered.

The spirits persisted, swimming in between his fingers and throwing themselves against the barrier.

"I said begone," he said sternly, and a few flitted away.

"How does it work?" Sammel asked. "You simply call to him?"

"Not simply."

He pushed his attention past the clamoring sounds, stretching his mind into the endless abyss beyond. He felt his stomach flip as the empty void threatened to suck him in, and he tried to focus on his feet against the solid stone lest he lose himself in the empty black of Nyx. His lips parted as he leaned toward the Veil. And he whispered.

"Neveri."

His voice was so low, the word barely slipped from his tongue, and still the dark stretched out to swallow it up. His mind was reeling as he stretched further into Nyx, league after league into the abyss. The empty dark closed in around him, and he felt adrift, his instincts begging him to pull back. But he pressed on until a single voice filled his mind, a presence so powerful it made his knees weak. He called again, inaudibly.

Neveri.

The presence rushed toward him, and a golden light filled his senses. He pulled back, listening for Sammel's breathing, the hum of the lanterns, anything to anchor him to the realm of the living. The golden presence followed him as the void of Nyx faded and his mind passed through the Veil, once again grounded in Talamh.

The blue spirits had scattered into the dark and now only the golden spirit remained, hovering on the other side, close enough to touch. A familiar awe fell over him at the powerful presence, and even Sammel was reverently silent as the light took shape, slowly morphing until it resembled a man, and from within the dark Endring heard - or rather felt - a low voice rumbling through his chest, words only he could hear.

Well done. Even now I feel their souls entering this realm. You've performed a great service for your people, Endring.

A pang of guilt shot through him. "May they find rest in the Midding."

They will have a hero's welcome tonight. And we shall begin our work upon Talamh.

A flash of golden light shot out, pushing toward where Endring's hand rested against the Veil. It was so swift and powerful, his instinct was to pull away, but he found he couldn't. His hand was held fast against the light as it burned against the black.

Too long has Talamh been without balance, but tonight, I break free of my long imprisonment. We set right what my brothers and sisters have broken, and we stand again as nine gods!

A sudden rumbling started from somewhere deep. But was it deep within Talamh or Nyx? Endring couldn't tell. His hand was still stuck firmly against the Veil. Or was it pressed against the light? The Veil seemed to recede and he felt heat throbbing in his palm. He was suddenly gripped by horror of the whole Veil tearing open and all of Nyx spilling into Talamh, or all of Talamh spilling into Nyx, and he trembled.

"Endring?" Sammel's voice sounded unsteady as the ground began to rumble beneath their feet.

"It's alright," Endring answered. "He's breaking through. It'll be alright." He hoped he sounded more confident than he felt.

The shaking became more violent as the light of Neveri's form intensified. Endring could sense a growing urgency from within the Veil, and it swelled outward threatening to swallow him up, but still his hand was held fast.

"The temple! It won't hold!" Endring yelled.

It will hold!

He heard something clatter from the passage behind them, and Neveri suddenly lunged into the Veil, bowing it outward like a bubble ready to burst, but its soft, black surface held fast.

Endring could hear Sammel scrambling backward as Neveri lowered his shoulder and charged again, thundering into the inky black and sending shockwaves rippling through the floor. The room shook violently, and the stone slab overhead began to chip and shatter as pieces crashed into the floor, spraying debris across the ground.

He felt Sammel steady himself with a hand against his shoulder as he yelled over the noise. "What's happening?"

"I don't know. He should have been able to break free."

Again Neveri drew back, throwing himself furiously against the Veil. The ground lurched and Endring's knees slammed into the floor. His arm wrenched as it stayed stuck fast. He could hear sounds of destruction from somewhere above, and he was gripped by the fear that the entire temple would be brought down.

No! NO!

"Stop!" Endring yelled, desperation filling his voice.

Neveri threw himself into the Veil again and again, each time the quakes becoming stronger. Sammel was on the floor now, bracing himself, as Endring desperately tried to pull free. The ceiling shook and trembled as if it would give way.

"Please! You must stop!"

Suddenly, he felt the Veil begin closing over his hand again.

Neveri let out a roar that shook Endring to his core. *I will not be denied! I will have my power upon Talamh again!*

He turned to face Endring and his golden light pushed back the dark with unfathomable will, splitting Nyx and reaching Endring's palm once more. For a moment, he thought Neveri would tear his way through, but instead an intense pain gripped Endring, like he had dipped his hand in flame. It spread up his arm until a warmth filled his body, and the pain subsided.

As the warmth dulled, Endring felt Nyx closing back in. The shaking had stopped, and Sammel was on his feet, standing ready with his hand on his whip and his eyes wide.

Find the crook!

"The crook?"

The crook of Bei'ai. It's the only way!

Neveri pulled away, and Endring felt his hand release. His arm dropped limp, and he sat panting for a moment, but the voice of Neveri lingered in his mind.

Do not fail, my Champion!

The golden form of Neveri disappeared into Nyx, and the murky Veil sank back to its original shape as the weight of the light receded.

Endring slumped back, breathing heavily.

Sammel walked close and placed a hand on his arm. "What happened?"

He shook his head, still feeling a lingering burning in his right palm. He lifted it, and in place of the seal of Bei'ai, he saw the golden sigil of a Champion, a face half man and half beast.

Sammel leaned closer, staring at the symbol.

Endring was shaking. His mind reeled as he tried to understand. "This wasn't meant to happen. It wasn't meant to be me."

"Champion?" Sammel stared at him. "What do we do now?"

He shook his head. None of this was the plan. Neveri was supposed to be free, to retake his place in Sbarga, to call a champion, someone else, and Endring was supposed to serve as the Oracle of Bei'ai the rest of his life.

He turned and locked eyes on the statue of Bei'ai. He was no longer hers. He was something altogether different. He could feel it. The boon that coursed through his veins was pulling at his bones and his flesh, inviting him to test its limits.

"The crook of Bei'ai." He looked up at Sammel. "Have you heard of it?"

"No."

"I think it's a relic. And we need to find it."

Justice

Eight massive stacks of cut granite sat slowly baking under the Erimos sun. They were lashed together by chains of iron and placed on broad sleds. Around them, forty men stood - the quarrymen of Govere. They were a sweaty bunch, hearty and sun-dark, and each pair of eyes peered out from a hand sized swath wiped from a layer of grime.

Sweat poured off Voske as he drank down a gulp of precious water from his canteen. He was proud of every one of them. He'd worked hard to shape this ragtag group of laborers into what they were - the best rotting quarrymen in the realm - and he would take any one of them over any smooth-handed, slackboon on the three worlds.

"One last task, boys," Voske called as he dropped his canteen in the sand. "We load these stacks on that skiff-" he pointed to the large sand skiff that idled beside the stacks "-and we can all head to Lorhk's for a cold drink and a hot meal."

It was hard work. Loading days always were, but the men squared their shoulders and gathered round.

Voske hopped on the deck of the skiff overlooking the sandy wastes. Behind them, the Govere quarry stretched in a wide pit of reddish brown rock and a few shrubby plants too stubborn to die. At its center a pillar rose, carved in the crude form of a sword.

Voske locked eyes on it and touched three fingers to his forehead, muttering. "Water's low. We could use your help." He let out a breath and looked back at his men. "Alright," he called to the weary workers. "Ten on the ropes. The rest push. One at a time, and be quick about it. First round at Lorkh's is on me."

That last phrase put a lighter step in their tired legs, and they strode into position, bracing against the first titanic load.

Voske walked to the end of one of the ropes and grasped the coarse fiber in his calloused hands, noting the hammer seal on his right palm that marked him as a laborer. He was a burly man, head and shoulders over any other, with a thick blond beard and a short ponytail. His shirt was off and draped over his neck, long since drenched by sweat. He called up his boon and felt his muscles ripple with fresh strength.

"Klief," he called to his side. "Call the time."

Klief was second in command at the quarry, a jovial type with a friendly smile and, somehow, a rotund belly. He drew himself up and his clear voice rang out through the open air. "Ready and pull! Ready and push! Ready and pull!"

They heaved in time, and slowly the sled slid upward, rising from the red sand of the wasteland to the deck of the skiff.

A sudden cry and a thud drew Voske's attention and he glanced to his side. The young man on the end of the alternate line was a recent addition named Barles. His face was clean shaven, as was his chest. As he told it, he'd been a coconut picker on Suntara. Whatever he'd done to enrage the aristocrats there had been bad enough to get him exiled to the armpit of Erimos.

He won't last, Voske thought with a sigh.

"Barles!" He yelled. "Get out of there and get some water."

The young man looked grateful and quickly relieved himself of the lines.

Klief paused in the call until Voske reached over and grasped the second line in his other hand, then gave him a resolute nod.

"Ready and Pull! Ready and Push! Ready and Pull!"

They heaved the stack onto the deck of the skiff and over to the far side, then transferred the ropes to the second stack and did it again. It was back breaking work, and by the seventh, some of the men were spent.

Voske eyed the last remaining stack with resolve. It represented nearly a full day's work of cut stone and it would be folly to leave it behind, but the men were growing faint and the water was well and truly spent by now.

"Spit and swill," a man named Rix whined. "Let the smoothy do it. He's been sitting pretty for half an hour."

Voske followed his gaze to where Barles sat, sipping a squeezed flask and still looking red-faced. The rest of the men weren't much better. There were at least twenty still on their feet, but many were sitting down breathing hard, and several more lay on their backs panting. The cloudless sky overhead showed no signs of relenting.

"Make your call, Foreman," Klief said, ambling to him. "Normally we get six. Gods know the coin counters'll be happy with seven."

"I'm not leaving a full stack in the wastes."

"It's not going anywhere. We'll be back next week for it."

Voske shook his head. If they left it now and did as many stacks next week, they'd have the same problem. "It's going. Round up everyone still standing to push. You and I can pull. And get Rix to start binding down the stacks."

"Just two on the ropes?"

"We can manage."

Klief looked uncertainly at the stack. "Sure you aren't biting off a bit much?"

Voske rolled back his shoulders. "We're the rotting Govere quarry, Klief. There's nothing we can't do."

Klief nodded reservedly and gave a sharp whistle. Immediately every man that could shuffled into position. Twenty below and just two above, guiding the load.

"One more, boys!" Voske yelled out. His body ached, but he called up the last reserve of his boon and let the strength of it fill his muscles. "Put your backs into this one, and I'll buy everybody *two* rounds!"

A haggard cheer rose as Klief started up the call. The men's feet sank into the sand, but once they had it sliding, the load started up the ramp without much trouble.

"Ready and pull! Ready and push! Ready and pull!"

Steadily it rose, and Voske could hear the timber of the skiff groaning under the incomprehensible weight. He strained against the ropes, and he could hear Klief huffing with every agonizing step. Three planks, four, foot by foot they crawled forward until the bulk of the weight settled onto the deck.

All of a sudden more hands were available, and even Barles was eager to join in sliding the payload into position.

Klief laughed and slumped down against the railing of the skiff. "You're a madman!"

Voske smiled and gladly turned the load over to the fresh hands. "Just stubborn."

"You know this is going to be a problem though don't you?"

"Oh?"

Klief pointed to the eight stacks, now orderly positioned along either side of the skiff. "Once those coin counters know we can chisel out eight, they're gonna be hounding us for it every week."

Voske took a deep breath. "You may have a point."

"Better to keep expectations low."

"Mmhmm."

"That reminds me…" Klief let his voice trail off and gave Voske a nervous look.

Voske felt his heart sink. "Tell me this isn't about Feasting."

Klief held his hand up in a conciliatory motion. "I'll make it up to you."

Voske wasn't sure he could stand one more dinner where Klief's well meaning wife thrust a potential mate upon him. "Klief." He sighed.

"She means well. I told her to stop meddling, but you can't tell women anything. They're more stubborn than a gryph guarding its nest."

Voske slumped over the side of the skiff. His boon was spent, and he felt fatigue rushing through his body. He just had to hold on until they got to town, and then they would rest.

He glanced sidelong at Klief. "Set my expectations low then?"

Klief shrugged. "I'm sure she's got a good heart."

"Gods and Chosen. Does your wife think I like ugly women?"

Klief smirked.

"Stacks are set!" Rix yelled.

Voske straightened up against his sore muscles and glanced over the stacks. "Spin up the shunts, and give it full sail. Feels like a northern wind to me."

Rix yelled out the command, and in quick order ropes were wrapped around the four shunts at each corner of the deck. The men yanked back on them in tandem, and the whirling blades came to life, gently raising the deck just a hand or two above the red sand of the wastes.

"Full sails!" Voske yelled. "The light won't last forever."

With that they were off, the full complement of laborers breezing across the wasteland like a ship over the high seas.

Soon they could make out the farthest edge of Govere, buildings shimmering and waving in the heat. The entire village was devoted to the quarry, and appropriately, everyone in the quarry lived in the village. Truth be told, there wasn't another town for miles. Out here in the wastes, it was just Govere. Even Barles was staying with Klief until he could build a home for himself. Voske would be well and truly shocked if he lasted long enough for that to happen.

He licked his lips. He could almost taste the cool cactus nectar and gryph steaks from Lorhk's tavern, and slowly he could feel the muscles in his arms loosening with the relief only evening could bring.

The skiff started a long, slow turn and the entire deck tilted ever so slightly to the side, following the well worn path to the village. Voske felt a sudden pain in his hand and winced. It stung like fire ants. He looked down, shaking his wrist.

"You alright?" Klief asked.

"I'm alright," Voske answered. He turned his palm over as the strange prickling sensation continued, and his mouth dropped open. The brand of the laborers was closing over, the skin healing back and reforming the lines of his palm. He shook his head, watching with disbelief. He'd seen this before, but he had asked for it. He didn't want to lose his laborer's boon, and he couldn't fathom why he would. What had he done to anger Jeza?

"What is it?" Klief asked, moving toward Voske. "You look like you've seen a spirit."

No sooner had the brand disappeared than his palm erupted in pain. He grabbed hold of his wrist and gritted his teeth as a new brand was seared into his flesh.

"Voske," Klief urged. "What in Nyx is it?" Klief grabbed Voske's wrist and turned it toward himself, staring down in wonder as the lines of the new brand were drawn. They curled upward and around, forming the pommel of a sword that stabbed downward, into the earth. Beneath the usual black mark glowed a golden light.

Klief found his voice first. "That's-"

"Quiet, Klief," Voske snapped, still staring in disbelief.

"That's the mark of Jeza," Klief hissed. "That's the rotting champion sigil! You're... You're the-"

A sudden snapping sound seized their attention and both men's eyes darted for the source. One of the stacks had broken free. It slid down the deck with a heavy grating sound and three men leaped aside, narrowly avoiding the crushing weight.

The entire scene felt surreal, and it took Voske a moment to even understand what was going on.

Rix was yelling. "Smoothy! What in Nyx did you do?"

Quickly Voske's instincts rushed back in, and he ran forward, waving to the men near him. "Stop those shunts, and catch hold of the tie!"

Several men grabbed the rope but their feet slipped on the smooth deck, and they were dragged toward the low rail behind it. The stack pummeled into another on the opposite side, and the entire skiff shuddered at the impact.

For a brief moment it was over, the deck leveled out, and the fallen men regained their feet.

"That was the smoothy's fault," Rix whined loudly. "I told him to double strap it!"

Klief's voice answered angrily. "Don't give me that mire! It was your job to check his work!"

Voske ignored them for the moment and kept his eyes on the front. The shift had pulled their course ever so slightly off the path and now the bow of the skiff was barreling toward a standing stone. A red column, nothing overly impressive and one that he'd never noticed before. It jutted out of the ground like the finger of a mountain, ready to rip the shunt apart.

Klief was still chewing Rix down the other side. "Of all the pig-headed, guildless, idiotic, things to do. You know better than to leave a rotting coconut farmer-"

"Brace yourselves!" Voske yelled.

Moments later the pillar crunched into the skiff like a pick into limestone. The shunt exploded in a spray of metal shards, and a dozen men were launched over the railing, tumbling into the red clay.

"Get hold of the lines," Voske yelled, but no one had the footing to stand, much less stop the shunt's from spinning.

The skiff lurched like a bull, sending a spray of red clay and rocks in all directions.

Voske could see Barles, somersaulting toward the railing. His head slammed into the hardwood before he toppled over, landing on the red ground like a sack of flour.

The wood of the railing groaned and splintered, and the titanic stack of granite loomed ominously over the young man.

"Barles!" Voske yelled, but there was no time.

In one swift motion Voske lunged from the skiff and slammed into the ground beside him. He could hear the deck groan just behind him, and in an instant he knew he was too late. He felt the hot stone crash into his back, punctuated by the desperate yell of Klief.

Time felt like it stood still. The weight of the granite pressed into him, and he felt the bones in his back begin to break, but at once a new strength surged within, coursing through his back like fire. It rushed through his shoulders and down his arms and legs, bolstering his back until his bones burned like iron. He stiffened under the titanic weight of the stones, then, beyond comprehension, began to push back.

"Mire and Nyx!" Rix yelled, from above.

Voske kept shoving, lifting the stone slowly with his legs and finally bracing his hands against it.

He could hear the shunts shutting down one by one, until the only sound was his labored breathing.

He let out a yell and pushed upward. The ground around his feet cracked and split under the weight, and every fiber of his being burned at the effort, but his arms didn't break. In the back of his mind he became aware of the cries of awe and terror from the men behind him, but he just kept pushing until the stack reached the deck, then he turned and shoved with his shoulder. The granite scraped across the wood planks until it was steady, and he left it, turning to Barles. He stooped down and gathered the boy in his arms before turning back around. The skiff was lost, the shunt destroyed. The eight stacks remained on deck, but no one was looking at any of those. They all just stared at him, like he was a god himself.

Or a champion.

Vigilance

Folds of golden light wrapped themselves around Illeri, kissing her cheeks and glowing against her skin as her long brown hair swirled down from where she floated, buoyed by the light. Her arms were stretched out to her sides, and her brown eyes stared into the star-speckled black, taking in every detail, tracing every constellation. Around her, the sounds of the chariot had faded. Here in the radiant field there was only her slow and steady breath, only the pulsing stars and the familiar pull of her boon. She could feel the field flooding out of her chest, swirling up her arms and spreading across the sky beams, enveloping the chariot. She was all that stood between the passengers and the cold dark.

She took a deep breath that swelled in the stillness around her. The blue skies of Las had melted away nearly an hour ago, and with the closeness of the worlds it left precious little time to see the stars. With her mind's eye she traced the Fist of Skard, six stars with the thumb pointing toward the tail of Xavesh, the Divine Dragon. From there her eye moved to Ravthere, the brightest star in the night sky. Most people knew it as the Eye of Kisandin, ever vigilant. In Doveth it marked the beginning of harvest season. In Tajerim it guided sailors into port. Yesterday it marked the zenith of the Shattering on Las.

Are you watching? She thought. *I am.*

She swallowed hard and stared into its brilliant light, looking for any sign of movement. She kept watching until her eyes began to water and her neck ached, but she refused to look away.

The voice of the guide called loud enough to drift through the field and call her focus back. "Fifteen minutes to Suntaran skies!"

Illeri's eyes finally wandered from the star and back down to the chariot deck, taking a much needed break for her neck.

Two pylats bobbed in the dark, wings flapping along the starlight as their bodies moved in unison. The crew held their lines firm, steering the creatures through the expanse, and the guide stood just behind them. Across from her she could see her fellow radiant, floating within the aura of golden light.

Behind the wayfarer's dais was the traveler's deck. They had one-hundred and three today. Most were returning from celebrations of the Shattering. She'd paid them little heed. She'd carried thousands of souls back and forth across the cold dark on countless voyages. It never mattered to her who they were or where they were headed. Her eyes were on the stars.

She turned her focus back up, sighting Ravthere again.

Where are you?

Maybe Kisandin was mocking her. Maybe he had turned his eye toward her one time, knowing it would unravel her. She'd waited years for this moment, for the worlds and stars to line up again, to hopefully catch a glimpse. It had nearly driven her mad, all these years of watching and waiting.

The memory replayed in her mind. She was a radiant on *The Archon's Grace* at the time, and above her shone the Eye just like tonight, only that time a pupil was in the center, and it stared directly at her.

She frowned at Ravthere.

Where is it now?

"Prepare for descent," the guide called.

Illeri stayed focused on the star, unmoved. She wouldn't get this chance again for a long time.

I'm still watching, Kisandin. Do you see me?

As though in response, the light wavered. It was barely discernible, but she'd watched the star enough to notice the change. Slowly it bowed outward, as though a lid was closing over it, then, for a split second, a dark black shape appeared in the center of the star, like the pupil of a god.

She drew in a sharp breath. There it was at last!

Suddenly the chariot wrenched violently. *The Wandering Maid* was an old vessel, and it sometimes shook like a wet dog when it reached the blue skies.

"Steady!" The guide called, looking at the men on the chains. "We're pitching skyward!"

The pylats winged their way toward the blue of Suntara, sailing on rays of sunlight. From her position, she could see a line of golden dust from the smaller pylat, streaming off of its lower wings and passing over the radiant field.

She glanced at the guide. He was middle-aged, dressed in a blue himation with a golden cloak and his foot tapped rapidly against the green spruce of the dais.

"It's rubbing," she called.

"What?" He said, raising an eyebrow.

"The right side underchain. It's too tight."

"I know the chains are tight." He scowled. "This one's a juvenile, we give him more leash, and he'll snap the lines."

"He can't stretch his wings if he's too constricted. You're gonna roll the chariot if you don't loosen them."

The chainmen hesitated, looking from her to the guide.

"If I want your input I'll ask, *radiant*."

The way he said the word with such contempt. She had half a mind to tell him she could have been a guide at one cycle. By all rights, she should be a pathfinder by now. She'd been asked enough times. But how could she give up the field and the cold dark?

The ship shook again, more violently, and the passengers gave a startled cry.

The smaller pylat strained against the chains, and the golden sparks showered over the chariot until they were clear to everyone.

The guide held out a moment longer with a clenched jaw until the chariot started to pitch hard. "Loosen the under chain!" He snapped.

The chainmen braced themselves, letting the chain ease loose, relaxing the strain on the young pylat's wings. It gave a jolt forward, and the guide gasped, but the lines held, and the pylat flapped its wings with relief as the chariot steadied.

The guide gave one last look toward Illeri, and she scowled. She knew it was silly to be angry. She could just take a position as a pathfinder and be respected by them all. Still, what did she have to do to prove herself? From his contemptuous look, she didn't expect an apology from the guide. He probably thought radiants were beneath him.

"You're welcome," she called coldly.

No sooner had the words left her mouth than pain ripped through her arm. It started in her hand and burned across to her shoulder. She cried out and collapsed to the deck as the radiant field around her dissolved. The cold of the wood was jarring, and the pain in her hand tremendous.

She felt someone grab her and turned to see the white haired pathfinder. He bent over her. "Radiant?"

"Jurdan," the guide called. "Take her place! Make it quick."

"Are you hurt?" The pathfinder pressed.

It was a grievous offense for a radiant to leave the field unannounced, but she heard more concern in his voice than criticism. She stared back at her vacant post until a young man jogged into position and the field warmed around his figure, lifting him into waves of gold.

She glanced up beyond the field. Ravthere was there, but the pupil was gone. The star stared at her with a steady light.

"What happened?" The guide snapped.

Illeri met his eyes. "I don't know."

"Don't know?" He sounded incredulous.

"I had a pain in my hand, then the field collapsed."

"Pain is no excuse. What if Shavra was taking a break? You could have killed us all!"

"Peace!" The pathfinder scolded.

He took her hand gingerly in his own and turned it over, revealing the freshly charred sigil of Kisandin, the ever watchful eye. It was pulsing with golden light. She stared at the mark, too stunned to speak. Overhead, Rathvere pulsed silently. Was this a joke? Did he still mock her?

"By the eight," the pathfinder breathed. "Pull the chains up, we're diverting back to Las!"

The guide scoffed. "Are you serious? We're about to land. We have passengers on board who've paid for a trip to Suntara. And what do I tell them?"

The pathfinder stood, helping Illeri to her feet. His voice was sharp. "Tell them, *guide*, that we are headed back to Las, and we will compensate them for their trouble. We have the honor of delivering Kisandin's chosen to the temple." He held Illeri's hand up, palm out. "Not one of them will complain about that."

The guide's face went white as fresh snow. He stared in disbelief for a moment and then bowed low. "Champion."

Passion

Hikari held his right arm out straight, and his smooth olive skin glistened in the warm light of the inner sanctum. He turned it over, still getting used to the sigil of Desita on his palm, a brand of golden light in the form of a rising sun. It was similar to his player's boon, the manipulation of light and shadow, but his old boon had been an illusion. This? This was the real thing. He wasn't tricking people into seeing something that wasn't there. He was actually commanding the light. He could see it like threads woven through the beams that filtered through the windows above. He could pull on them, bending them toward a single spot to illuminate it, or bending them away and leaving shadow in the void.

He steadied himself with a serious expression and looked at his captivated audience, all monks, mostly women. They stared at him with adoring eyes and blushing cheeks. He smiled, extending the moment.

"Tell us more," one young monk said, a boy of about twelve wearing the yellow robes of Desita. "What happened next?"

"Has no one ever taught you the art of the dramatic pause, darling?" Hikari winked at the boy whose comment drew a few scattered chuckles, and then he was back in character, his face serious and his body tense.

"And so I stood," he continued, "high on the Shattering stage, surrounded by the majestic sight of a conjured team of Pegasus." He fixed his attention on the light from the stained glass windows. Several panes had been shattered in last night's earthquake, and golden beams of sunlight glared through the gaps, glinting with motes and specks. He felt his new boon at his fingertips, as though the warmth of the sun had filled his hands from the inside. He grabbed at a few strands of the light and wove them together until he had it shaped like several glowing pegasus, majestic wings flapping as he tightened and released the strands of light. His old boon could have given him more depth and color to play with, but these pegs felt real. They scattered heat around them like living creatures of sunlight, like some equine version of a pylat.

He smiled.

"It was then that a sound reached my ears. Not a pleasant sound, mind you. It was the dying call of a Champion, a horrid cry that made my blood turn to ice, as sure as Kissandin sees!"

He pushed out his hands, dispelling the sanctum light until he stood in gray shadow.

"I looked, and there they were, drowning in their own blood. All eight of the gods' chosen. My heart was stricken. What madness, what treachery had brought such injustice?"

He crouched low, locking eyes on the enthralled young boy.

"What did you do?" He asked, nearly breathless.

Hikari kept his expression sorrowful and his tone somber. "All that I could. I leapt from the stage at once, rushing for the table. Already the monks of Jeza were closing in, and the people shouting and crying. But as I neared the champions, I was again struck, not with a sound, but a searing pain-" he held his palm aloft and gave it a thoughtful look "-as if I had dipped my hand into the very heart of the burning sun!"

He stood again, and turned his palm toward the crowd. "I stumbled forward onto the grass as the pain overcame me. There was no time to worry about my own predicament. The champions were in trouble!"

He let the threads of light go, and they fell back around him, dispelling the shadow. "I leapt to my feet and hurried toward them. A monk turned to face me, but when he did he saw something in the darkness… the golden glow of my new sigil. I had been chosen. I hadn't the wits to check my own palm after the pain, so I followed his gaze and saw the mark of Desita. I was aghast! How could such an honor be bestowed upon me? I was unworthy of the goddess' favor!"

"What did the monk do?" The boy asked eagerly.

"Well, he offered to take me at once to the temple, but I would not have it! I sent him back to assist the others. It was the champions who needed help, not I."

Hikari smiled as he looked over the crowd, met with wide eyes and warm smiles. The feeling of holding their attention never lost its charm.

One monk was watching him with a nervous expression. He wore the red and white robes of a judge, and he had a shock of curly hair in dusty brown atop his head. He was young, barely eighteen by the look, with sharp features. He strolled forward awkwardly.

"That was… quite a tale, Champion."

Hikari glanced nervously at his robes. He assumed everyone was nervous around judges. The idea that someone could tell when you were lying wasn't exactly a comfort. He dropped his voice for only the young monk to hear. "Had I known there was a judge in the audience, I may have been more forthright."

The monk's eyes widened. "I… I won't say anything."

Hikari smiled. "I thank you for that. Getting called two hours later while sitting alone washing makeup off my face doesn't have the same ring. However, I really did jump down to help."

"I assume the monks of Jeza stopped you."

"Quite right, darling. I suppose I couldn't have been much help anyway."

"You are Desita's chosen?"

"So I am. And who might you be?"

"Gillis," he said nervously. "My name is Gillis."

"Hikari." He gave his signature bow, one arm behind his back and a slight tip of the head. He'd spent years perfecting it, just like every other aspect of his persona. "Perhaps you've heard of me? Player of Rel'van, heralded as the greatest master of illusion on the three worlds."

Gillis grinned. "Of course I know you. I've seen your plays a couple times. It's little wonder you were chosen so quickly."

Hikari smiled. "And you are a judge?"

Gillis straightened up dutifully. "No. I mean, I was guilded as such, but I am the liaison here at the temple."

"Liaison to whom?"

He looked up awkwardly, as if Hikari should know. "The champions."

Hikari raised an eyebrow. "Ah! Very well." He snapped his fingers, calling the attention of the group, and raised his voice to address them. "Perhaps we shall continue the retelling of my glorious calling another time. I feel Master Gillis and I have much to discuss."

There was an audible groan, especially from the women, but they all dutifully shuffled back toward the exit of the sanctum.

Hikari turned his attention back to Gillis. "Now then, as liaison, I presume you'll be the one in charge of having my belongings transferred to the Gods' Mount?"

Gillis tugged at his collar. "Yes, Champion."

"Wonderful! I have four estates on Suntara, and two on Las. I'll need a portion of my belongings brought from each, namely the awards that I received as a player, the many gifts bestowed upon me by various archons - I'll see to a detailed list, of course - my harvest wardrobe - it is rather stifling here, isn't it, darling? Then there's the satin couch from my Northern Las estate. Just wait until you see it, Gillis! Crafted by the tailors of Je'Ramth, the most exquisite blue satin!"

He took a breath and looked at Gillis who was staring wide-eyed like a spooked deer.

"You can retrieve them, can't you?"

"I-I'll try, Champion," he stammered.

"Very good. If I think of anything else, I'll add it to the list, and of course I'll send word to my groundskeepers at each property to have them ready for your arrival. Well not *you*, naturally, but whomever you send. Tell me, how large is the staff here?"

Gillis took a deep breath, and Hikari guessed that a stiff breeze might blow the poor man over.

"Are you alright, darling?"

"I'll… See it done. Of course. You… you can count on me, Champion." His voice cracked at the end.

Hikari narrowed his eyes. The position of liaison was one of great responsibility, yet Gillis looked like he might crumble at the request of only one champion. Only the gods knew how he'd survive when the other seven arrived.

"How are you holding up?" He asked.

"Is it so obvious?"

"I'm afraid so."

Gillis sighed. "Apologies, Champion. I will try not to show my discomfort. When your predecessor was slain, may she find the Midding, so was mine."

"Yours?"

"The liaison to the Champions." Gillis seemed to muster his courage and held his chin up for once.

Hikari smiled good-naturedly. "By the gods. Why didn't you say so?"

"It's not your concern, Champion. I assure you, I can carry out my duties."

"Of course you can, Gillis, but to go from apprentice to master in the midst of all this?" Hikari motioned to the damaged sanctum. Several windows were shattered overhead, and a long crack ran the length of the floor down the center. "It's got to be like sailing a ship for the first time in a squall. I'll tell you what," he said, clapping Gillis on the shoulder, "forget everything I said. I'll make arrangements to have my things transported. Just make sure they're handled carefully upon arrival. Especially the satin couch!"

Gillis nodded thankfully.

"And don't worry, Gilli. Things are going to get smoother from here on out. We'll learn together."

Gillis smiled. "I certainly hope you're right."

"Of course I am. I'm Hikari!"

Mercy

Burz stood beside the thick wooden planks of a corral. His eldest son, Orin, stood on the lowest rung, leaning out over the top. He was smiling broadly as he watched a herd of pegasus stamping around the grassy yard, grazing and lounging in the midday heat of Tajerim. Their wings were tacked by soft leather harnesses that kept them on the ground, all but one small foal. It was a little paint horse, white coat and wings dappled brown. The youngster trotted around the mares nipping at flanks like it was trying to start up a game, and largely being ignored.

"When do they learn to fly?"

Burz looked toward his son. Orin was only seven years old, but he already had Burz' strong jawline, and steady hands. In that moment, he looked grown, and in a few weeks he would be guilded and off on his own to be trained. The thought was bittersweet, and Burz put an arm around Orin's shoulders.

"It depends," Burz answered. "Every foal is different, but that little one's almost ready, I'd say."

"It's a shame they have to wear the harnesses."

"I used to think so too, but here in the city, they're safer if they do."

Burz looked behind them. They were on the outer edge of the bustling port of Tajerim. It was the only home Burz had ever known, guilded to the local soldier's guild, married in the temple of Desita. He could see the shimmering tiled roof of the temple from here and beyond the port and the glittering Larimar Sea. The mighty River Arrtris cut straight through the heart of the city, splitting the docks in half and spilling into the bay. He could even make out the statue of Kisandin that watched over the port. He couldn't count how many times he'd touched the worn down feet and asked for a blessing as he headed down to the docks.

As a soldier he'd known every flowering garden, every grand terrace, every den of lowlifes, and he'd grown accustomed to the rhythm of Tajerim. It was just a short boat ride upriver to Arrijan, and every major festival clogged the ports, but he'd never seen it like this. Ships were crammed along the waters of the dirty brown Arrtris and spilling out along the docks by the sea.

Orin caught his gaze and turned toward the crowded river. "Is that why you have to fly?"

He nodded. "No passage upriver today, and I've got to get to the Gods' Mount."

"And what about us?"

He looked down at the boy and mustered a smile. He hated the thought of being apart. He'd spent one night away from Hadris their whole marriage, and none since the boys were born.

"Just a night or two," he said softly. *Two weeks*, he thought. *That's all you get before he's off and guilded.* He hated losing a single day of it. "The temple's gonna see that you and your brother and Ama make it safe and sound as soon as the river is clear."

"Why are there so many boats, Ada?"

"It was the festival of the Shattering. It only happens once every twelve years."

"But I heard the monks say they've never seen it like this. Not even on the Shattering."

"True." He frowned. "It's bad during the festival, but this is worse. People are in a hurry, some to get to Arrajin, many to get away."

"But why?"

He looked at Orin's eyes. He was old enough now. He knew when something was going on.

"You know that for a champion to be called, the old champion must die."

He nodded, giving a glance toward Burz' right hand. "That's why you were called. The old champion died."

Burz slowly lifted his hand off the fence until the golden sigil of Uthando peeked out, a cluster of yarrow flowers. "Not just this one. All the champions died." He could almost hear Hadris scolding him for scaring Orin, but he was old enough for the truth. "They were killed. So eight new champions will be called. That's never happened since the first Champions."

"That's why there's so many people?"

Burz nodded. "Many are headed to Arrajin to see the new Champions. And many are fleeing the city, afraid of what might happen now."

"Why are they afraid?"

"Well, they think the gods are angry with us."

The quivering voice of a man broke in. "Which isn't true, of course."

He looked up to see the head monk of Uthando approaching with a mortified expression. Beside him, the rancher led a black pegasus by its reins. A couple more monks strolled behind them, and at the back…

"Hadris."

She met his gaze and smiled. Her brown skin was lighter than his own, and her dark hair fell in waves behind her shoulders. She was walking with their youngest, Kyren, clinging to her arm. He looked much more like his mother than Orin, but he had Burz' bright blue eyes.

"Right, Champion?" The first monk pressed, trying to keep his own doubts out of his voice. "Only wild rumors about the gods turning their backs on Talamh. Nothing more than rumors."

Burz straightened up. "If the gods were angry, they would not be calling new champions."

He sighed his relief. "Good. Yes. Of course."

"Champion," said the rancher, coming to a stop.

Burz cleared his throat. That title was going to take some getting used to.

"This is Hevsaba," the rancher said as he extended the reins toward Burz. "He's the finest stallion I've got. I raised him myself from a colt. Used to be a racer, and he can make the flight to Arrajin and back in one go, more even."

Burz took the reins, feeling the familiar grain of the leather. It hadn't been so long since he'd last ridden. The peg blew out a breath as it stamped closer, stopping obediently by Burz' side.

"He's magnificent," he answered.

"That he is. He's a gift."

Burz raised an eyebrow. This was something he would have to get used to as well. His instinct was to refuse, but he knew what an insult that would be, so he nodded kindly. He could see in the man's eyes how proud he was of this steed. "Uthando bless you for your generosity."

"Uthando has blessed my herd. It's my honor to give back to his champion." The rancher gave an unpracticed bow, then excused himself as the lead monk stepped forward.

"Is there anything else you require, Champion?"

Burz glanced at Hadris. She was forcing a smile, but he could see the tension in her eyes. "Nothing," he answered. "Make yourselves ready, and I'd like a moment to speak to my family."

"Of course, Champion."

They bowed with a more practiced ease, and it was all Burz could do to keep from stopping them. All his life he'd been the one to serve, and the idea of being served instead made him very uncomfortable.

Once they had walked away he breathed a bit easier, and he looked toward Hadris, still at a loss for words. "Quite a change," he finally croaked.

She brought Kyren over, and Burz looped the stallion's lead around the fence post. He wasn't going to rush this moment. He settled in beside Hadris as Kyren climbed up beside his brother.

She frowned at the sleek black steed. "Are you going to be alright?"

"It's a one hour flight. I'll be fine." He flexed his knee, feeling the familiar report of pain through his left leg. It hadn't fully healed, and he wasn't sure it ever would.

"The monks have arranged an honor guard," he said sullenly.

"Soldiers from Tajerim?" Her voice was tight with tension. "Well, tell them no!"

"And insult them? I think a champion should be more diplomatic than petty."

Hadris scoffed, turning her eyes on the field of pegs. "Petty? Please, Burz! After what they did to you?"

He rubbed at his leg. "They followed orders. I used to follow orders just as blindly."

She caught his eye. "You *never* would have followed an order like that."

He dropped his gaze. He knew it was true, but he didn't want to spend his last moments in Tajerim dwelling on bitter memories.

"That's all behind us now. We have a chance at a new life."

Kyren walked between them, looking up at Burz. "You're leaving without us, Ada?"

"Only for a little while."

Hadris rested her hand on the young boy's shoulder. "We'll get there." She glanced up at Burz. "We just have to wait for the port to clear."

"Just don't be long in coming."

"We'll be there as fast as possible. I promise. Kyren's excited to see the temple."

Kyren looked up with wide eyes. "I heard they have fireworks!"

"He's especially excited about the fireworks."

Burz grinned and tousled Kyren's hair. "I'm excited to see them too. Maybe they'll let us ride a peg together, see them from the air, huh?"

Kyren's grin widened. "Really?"

"Maybe."

Hadris was frowning now, and Burz' smile faded. "If your Ama says it's alright."

"I worry about you being up there by yourself, let alone with the boys."

"Please," Kyren said, grabbing hold of Hadris' leg. "Please, please!"

"Maybe when you're older."

He frowned, but Burz caught his eye and grabbed his chin.

"Don't you worry. There'll be lots to do at the temple. We'll make sure they have the biggest fireworks in the history of Talamh."

"Really? You can do that?"

"Of course I can. I'm a champion. Now, how about you go talk to your brother for a minute, hmm?"

Kyren nodded and wandered away, leaving Burz and Hadris alone.

"I've been healing long enough, you know," Burz said with a sigh. "I used to ride Sauri every day. It hasn't been that long."

"Four weeks ago you were having trouble getting out of bed."

"And I've been getting stronger ever since."

"Standing up straight and spending an hour in a saddle are not the same thing. I don't see why you can't just wait for the boat."

Burz turned to face her, softening his tone. "The hardest part is getting in the saddle. If I can do that, I'm halfway there."

"And if you fall a thousand feet out of the sky?"

"Then Uthando will have to pick a different champion."

She drove her fist lightly into his shoulder, but he could tell her eyes were slick. He reached out and pulled her into an embrace.

"I won't fall."

She let some of the tension drain as she wrapped her arms around him. "Just promise you'll be careful?"

"I promise."

"I already thought I lost you once."

He kissed the top of her head softly. "I know."

They held each other for a minute before Hadris pulled away, letting out a long breath. She would be fine, he had no doubt of that. She was the strongest woman he knew.

"So nothing crazy. I heard enough stories about you and Sauri."

Burz chuckled as he recalled his old dappled peg. The other soldiers had called him a flying menace, but there was no pegasus that could match him. He missed that peg.

"I promise," he said again.

He looked away toward the West. Somewhere beyond the trees Arrajin was waiting, and he could see a few monks gathering on the far side of the field to greet the honor guard, four soldiers bearing the banner of Tajerim. He was relieved that he didn't recognize any of them. No doubt that was intentional.

"Ada! Look!"

Orin was pointing toward the pegs in the field with a smile. The young foal stretched its wings and bounded away from its mother, and her wings twitched against the soft straps that held them down. The youngster lifted, gaining a couple feet with wide spread wings before tumbling back down into a pile of soft hay.

"He almost did it!"

Burz smiled as he walked to the boys. "They'll have to tack that one very soon."

They watched as the mare caught up, nosing at the little foal who was strutting proudly.

Orin beamed. "Soon he'll be flying like the rest."

"That's right," Burz watched as the paint spread his wings again, rushing around the mares in a wide circle.

He felt antsy suddenly. He knew he had to go, but he didn't want this moment to end. He wanted to stay in this field, in the warm sun of Tajerim, watching these pegs. Once he left, this life was behind him forever. That should have made him very glad, but he still longed for his oldest life, before everything had changed, when he was still a soldier, and Tajerim was his city. He'd thought often of going back into that, but never of stepping out into something altogether new.

"You'll be expected there soon," Hadris said, as though reading his thoughts.

He nodded and looked at his sons. "Orin, Kyren, come over here."

They dutifully strolled over, and Burz went down on his knee, embracing them, then he dragged Hadris down as well, and they all huddled close, saying their goodbyes. Burz kissed them and blessed them, and warned the boys to mind their mother. It felt too swift, and then it was over, and he straightened up and headed for Hevsaba. He lifted his good leg into the stirrup and swung himself atop the black pegasus, and his old instincts came back to him in a rush. He gave one last look at Hadris, smiling against the pain in his knee so she wouldn't know. She watched as he clicked his tongue and nudged with his heels, and the peg started forward at a trot toward the monks and soldiers. They were mounted and ready by the time he got there.

"After you, Champion."

He could feel Hevsaba tense, eager and ready, muscles tight in his flanks, and his wings fluttering. He eased the reins and let the peg run, and at once he spread his wings wide and with one mighty thrust of his hooves, he broke from the ground and soared skyward.

Burz could hear Orin and Kyren yelling after him and he glanced back, waving, and once more glimpsing the city. It was bittersweet watching as it faded into the distance. Here was his history, his memories, all of them wrapped up in the cobbled paths and turquoise water, but here was also the sting of betrayal that left a wretched taste in his mouth. Uthando had given him a chance at a new life, one where the pain of the past could finally heal, and he would never have to taste betrayal from those he considered brothers again. This is what he'd prayed for.

He gave no more than a sidelong glance at the soldiers behind him and the banner of Tajerim before turning his gaze toward the jungles of Las and the brown line of the Arrtris below. They would follow its course to Arrajin, and the Gods' Mount, where his family's new life awaited.

Prudence

Three thousand miles from the city of Tajerim, on the other side of Las, snow drifted softly across the Shinoam Mountains. It settled to the frozen ground like a woolen blanket and covered the sparse trees until they looked like an army of spindly snowmen. Weylyn marched past their ranks, picking her way carefully toward the peak. At nearly sixty, she was starting to feel her age on the long, cold treks, but her violet eyes were still sharp and her ears sharper. Her long gray hair was woven into a single braid that ran down to the small of her back.

The cold bit at her red cheeks, and she pulled her fur hood up tight. She could have taken a position hunting the tame lands to the south - most hunters her age had moved south years ago - but instead she'd spent the last two weeks tracking a pack of snow wolves through the mountains. It wasn't about the money, though the tailor's guild would have paid a fortune for their velvety furs, and it wasn't about the prestige. The air here had never been breathed before, the waters never drunk. There were wonders in the unknown places of the world, and her feet had tread paths that only the wolves and the gods knew. She wouldn't trade that for any soft life in the southern plains.

She scrambled up the final rise to the peak and paused there, sweeping the surrounding land with a discerning eye. The Northern cliffs dropped into an icy fjord, and an ancient sea-serpent's bones jutted out of the snow-covered ice like talons of the sea.

Weylyn held up a hand to shield her eyes and stared south. The falconers would have their birds out today, watching for flares. She smiled, thinking about their expression when they found out the pickup wasn't a stack of furs or the scales of an ice wyvern, but a hunter.

Out of instinct she tried to tap into her old hunter's boon, to reach out and feel the skies above and know if the falcons were already on the wind, but as she drew on her boon, a different sensation coursed through her, like heat at the back of her eyes, and the flash of a vision filled her mind. The ice of the mountain evaporated into a slope of wildflowers and the barren trees blossomed with the vibrancy of life. She looked back at the fjord and saw the serpent bones, now resting on the stony beach of a fast-flowing river. She sucked in a breath, staring wide-eyed at the vista until the bitter wind swept it from her sight, and the world returned to the moment. She'd never seen anything like it before, and she couldn't fathom what kind of magic could turn the foothills of the Shinoam green.

She pulled a heavy glove off her right hand and stared at the pulsing golden light of the sigil of Strah, a coiled serpent.

"Alright then," she said, turning an eye skyward. "That'll take some getting used to."

She grabbed the bow from her back and strung it, then selected a silvery Desitan arrow from her quiver. She couldn't be sure the falcons were on the wind, but now was the normal time, and it was either a pegasus ride to the closest town or a week-long hike. Every child of Talamh grew up knowing that if you were called by a god, you sped to the temple of Arrajin as fast as you could. To do otherwise was heresy. Not to mention, she was cold and low on food, and had no desire to walk another week.

She loosed the arrow and watched until it exploded into a red plume that could be seen for miles. That done, she pulled her fur trappings close and brushed the snow off a stone to sit down. An agonizing twenty minutes passed, and the frozen wind of the peak picked up, howling through the fjord, till at last she heard the cries of a falcon.

She smiled and waved her arms overhead, watching as it swooped her direction. A pegasus ride it would be.

Ambition

The sound of the Arrtris rushed ceaselessly over the hum of the boardwalk. It was a pleasant enough place, running the length of the river between the Trade and Sacred Quarters. The boardwalk itself was made from cool stone slabs green with moss, and the city side was lined with vivid flowers in mahogany beds. But the morning sun was bright and the jungle air stifling. Zengin never imagined he would miss a thing about Tajerim, but what he wouldn't give for a sea breeze.

At its heart, Arrajin was just another large city, teeming masses of people swirling around each other, vying for space and control, pursuing their base desires. No different than Tajerim. Pristine white buildings marked the wealthy neighborhoods where the streets were relatively clean and well cared for, and the rest of the city wallowed in filth as the ceaseless ambitions of the people drove them to fight for their chance to get out, to live in the white washed homes with the beautiful ones.

The river banks were crowded. He would have expected more people to be put off by the unbearable humidity and the relentless, biting mosquitoes. Not even the smell of wet soil and decaying plants kept them at bay. People had an astounding ability to tolerate the intolerable. Today, they had another reason to stay away. The unfathomable offense at the desecration of the sacred. And yet it seemed to be drawing an even bigger crowd.

He had heard the rumors early in the morning when the stars still clung to the fading dark. An insurrection in Arrajin's Sacred Quarter, and a bloody scene down by the river that *chilled men to the bone*. Or so it had been told to him. He also found people had an astounding ability to exaggerate. The only thing he was sure of was that there had been a gruesome and bloody defiling of the sacred site known as the Gods' Home.

Zengin held up the end of his toga, a fine green cloth gilded in a geometric pattern along the hems that made him look two inches taller. He wasn't short, by any means, but nor was he tall. The extra couple of inches gave him a more commanding presence. He had short brown hair, neatly kempt, and his form was trim and fit. He always kept his face clean shaven, and his toga was clasped with a gold pin in the form of a pelican.

He stepped carefully over the puddles on the street, his sandals making a quiet scuffing noise, barely perceptible. He still wore his gloves. He told himself it was a choice, but it felt entirely wrong to take them off. He'd spent so many years this way, why not do the same now?

He carried on until he could see the river's edge where crude barricades were propped along the boardwalk. Here a crowd of several hundred had formed, no doubt attracted by the same spectacle that drew his own interest. They spoke mostly in hushed whispers, though several of the women were sobbing at an irritating volume, and a couple men yelled idle threats like 'Just let me know who did this,' and 'Try that on this side of the river, cowards!'

He slipped in behind the crowd, to the porch step of one of the waterfront homes. The Gods' Home was among the oldest and most revered sacred sites in all of Talamh. He had seen it before, a modest home of rough stone and statues of the divine parents and the eight children playing in the front yard. Each child was the likeness of a god, ranging from two to about twelve in age. It was a key stop along the pilgrim's road that squirmed its way through Arrajin in a winding, illogical path.

And then his eyes fell on it, across the river in the Sacred Quarter, lit by the golden light of the early sun. Lifted on a pike, towering over the divine family, there was the body of a man stained with blood. A pair of wings had been sown to the naked flesh of his back, and horns from a bull were pressed into his head and tied on with harsh wire.

Zengin studied the face of the man, twisted in a pained expression, and traced with dry blood. He could taste it. That metallic tinge. Warm, thick, sticky.

A memory surged to the front of his mind, a young boy lying in a pool of blood. It spilled out from his head over a plush woven rug that depicted an idyllic pasture. Fine wool from the Geris highlands. It was the kind of rug you would find in the home of a stuffy merchant or Bureaucrat who had never been in a pasture in their life.

The blood was still pouring out. It wouldn't stop. And Zengin's hands were slick with it. He wiped it futilely on his toga, annoyed with having to replace the rug and clean up the mess. *Rotten boy*, he'd thought, *If he'd walked in any other time…*

But it wasn't his memory. They never were. They were memories forced upon him. Memories he never wanted. He clenched his right hand into a fist and shoved the memory down, focusing on the present. The sound of the coursing river, the smell of the decaying plants… and the mosquitoes. He smacked at a bite on his neck and recentered on the Gods' Home.

The arrangement of the mutilated body was obviously intentional. It lorded over the gods, whose hands had been painted with the dead man's blood. It dripped from stone fingers to the hard packed dirt below. And the way the body was modified, it was meant as a message.

Zengin's gaze wandered to where a man was leaning against the side of a nearby home. He was the only other person who didn't seem troubled by the site and was studying it with great curiosity. Zengin recognized him at once, the unmistakably garish clothing, ornate boots, and that orange whip at his side. He wasn't soon to forget him.

Zengin blinked as he studied the man. He had been searching the city for him for two days, ever since he ran into him at the festival, but he hadn't expected to find him here. He tugged the glove over his right hand up, assuring it was snug, then folded his hands behind his back, and strolled casually over.

As he approached, the man gave him no more than a passing glance before turning his eyes back across the river.

"That's a gruesome sight," Zengin said coolly.

The man nodded.

"What do you think it means?"

"It's intriguing," he said in an equally cool tone. "But what makes you believe it means anything?"

Zengin looked the sight over. "I see intent. Don't you?"

The man pointed to the bloody corpse. "Of course. The way the wings are placed. Carefully. Deliberately. The stitching is fine work. A surgeon I'd say."

Zengin let a bare smile curl his lips. "I'd agree. They didn't defile the statues themselves, tear them down or break them. They chose a body to set up as lord over the gods, to lower them. Dishonor them. But who is the message for? The gods themselves? Or perhaps someone more local."

They locked eyes, and this time the man studied Zengin more carefully.

"Have we met?" He asked.

"No." *He recognizes me*, Zengin thought. He couldn't blame the man for not placing him. Their encounter had been brief, a simple touch on the night of the Shattering, barely enough for Zengin to glean a memory. It happened sometimes when his boon was accidentally used on some stranger, usually a meaningless memory he quickly forgot. But he would never forget the sight of this man poisoning the champions' wine.

They both stayed silent. Normally Zengin could use prolonged silence to his advantage, but the stranger seemed completely unbothered by it.

Zengin began again. "I heard a report of heretics across the river. Has that been confirmed?"

"Very much so," he answered. "The city guard has shut down all the crossings into the Sacred Quarter. That's why no one's on the other side."

"And do we know what they want?"

The man shrugged. "Do *we* know? An odd way to word it. Perhaps you should simply have asked if *I* know."

Zengin pursed his lips. "Perhaps I should have. Do *you* know what they want?"

"No. I can honestly say that I don't."

He was good. He said much without saying everything. He really didn't know what they wanted, but he knew something.

Zengin took a moment to assess the man's peculiar countenance. His hands were gloved, likely unguilded. His clothes were garish, and there was no sweat along his brow, meaning they were likely enchanted by a skilled tailor to keep him cool, something Zengin wished he'd thought to do. That made them very expensive. Finally, the golden whip at his side was clearly a relic of the gods. There were very few people in all the realm who personally owned a relic, let alone an unguilded. He found himself wondering how someone with no boon could acquire such wealth.

He decided to try a different approach. "My name is Zengin."

"Sammel." He turned, expecting the traditional greeting of a displayed boon, but his eyes fell on Zengin's own gloved hand and he nodded in understanding.

"And where are you from, Sammel?"

"Erimos."

"That's a long way to travel for a religious festival, especially for someone the gods passed over."

"There are many different reasons to attend such a momentous festival."

"Quite true. Some to honor the gods, some to eat the food, and at least one to take vengeance on the divine."

Sammel coughed absent-mindedly. "Do you refer to the defilement of the sacred site, or the death of the gods' chosen?"

"Doesn't it seem they're connected?"

Sammel cocked his head to the side. "On the surface, yes, but that doesn't mean they're connected at all."

His voice carried a tinge of discomfort, and Zengin decided to press the point. "They're both a message, different in form but not in kind. A slap in the face of the gods, the kind carried out by an extremely bitter soul with a lifetime of grievance."

"That well could be," Sammel answered, instantly relaxing. "I imagine the realms are full of bitter souls."

Zengin furrowed his brow. He'd probed the wrong direction and his mind scrambled for a different explanation. Of all the times to lose his scribe's boon. A quick glance at Sammel's current memory would, no doubt, be illuminating.

But he had another option he was eager to try, the champion's boon of Metnadur. The honey of Metnadur was said to sway minds and open lips. He had felt it since he'd been called, and he pulled on it now, warmth coursing through him from his palm until his mouth was filled with it. It tasted sweet on his tongue.

"Why do you think the champions were killed?"

Sammel furrowed his brow and seemed to be at odds for a moment, then he cleared his throat and started talking. "The champions weren't killed out of vengeance, nor by a bitter soul. That was necessity."

"And this?" Zengin pointed at the scene across the river.

"I would guess this was done by a completely different person. An angry one, with an insatiable bloodlust."

"What makes you say that?"

Sammel pointed at the body strung up above the statues of the children. "Do you see the marks on his body? The bruising? He was killed slowly, and with great malice. And I suspect they began mutilating him before he was dead."

"And yet they were done for the same purpose?"

Sammel grimaced. "No."

"There is *some* connection between the two. Tell me what it is."

"Neveri." He looked at Zengin warily as the word left his mouth, shocked he had said it. He would be much more on guard now.

Neveri. The word tickled at a memory somewhere in the depths of his mind, but he couldn't place it.

Sammel shifted. He wouldn't stay now, and Zengin was running out of time.

"Do you know what I think?" He turned to face Sammel, looking him square in the face. "About the person who killed the champions?"

Sammel matched him, squaring up. His shoulders were tense, and his arms hung ready at his sides.

"I think he believed he was doing what was necessary, to serve a greater purpose. I believe he didn't work alone, but had help in the temple. He crept inside, escorted by a monk, perhaps young and open to their cause?"

He watched as a single bead of sweat formed on Sammel's brow.

"He was let into the kitchens, to the wine barrel set aside for the champions. I hear the poison he used was swift and brutal. Of course it would have to be if you didn't want to risk any recovery. Am I right?"

Sammel's jaw tightened and he winced as if in pain. "Yes."

"What does *Neveri* mean?"

"A… name." His hand strayed to his whip.

"Your leader?"

"Yes."

"And why was it necessary to kill the champions?"

Sammel blinked hard, groaning. "To weaken the barrier between realms. T-to make the Veil thin enough to break."

"And why would one want to do that?"

"So he could pass through."

"Neveri?" He guessed.

Sammel nodded with a jolt as though against his will, and he grabbed his whip, holding it tightly. "No more questions," he said. "For your own sake."

"Just one. After that, you're free to go. Who is this Neveri?"

"The god of Animus."

A god? This was madness, and yet Sammel's eyes were sharp and lucid. Whatever the truth, he believed it. But what god would dwell in Nyx? And why would he need help to break free? As far as Zengin knew, no one had spoken to a god in two thousand years. And there was certainly no god named Neveri.

"Animus?" He mused.

A sharp voice pierced through the grim quiet, "Alright! Back to your homes!"

The city garrison had sent a dozen men. It was shameful it took this long. They strolled along the boardwalk with intent, driving off the gawkers, dressed in light leather with the seal of Arrajin, a stalking jaguar, on their chests. The one in the front wore a simple leather cap. He seemed to be in charge.

"I'nt safe!" Their leader called. "Had those rotting usurpers shooting arrows up on Peldrin street. Nearly had a casualty! Come on. Back up."

Zengin glanced back to see Sammel was gone. The crowd was dispersing, and he stood his ground, flexing his right hand against the stiff leather of his worn glove.

"What's the meaning of this?" He said strongly as the guards approached.

"For your own safety. 'S wrong to be gawking at that anyhow. Let that poor sap find the Midding in peace, gods willing. Now I order you to go!"

"Do you?"

"Yeah!"

Zengin smirked. "I don't take orders from people like you."

A small crowd had stopped now, gawking at this new scene.

The guard grew stern, pulling out a club from his belt as he nodded for the two men behind him to do the same. "Then we're gonna have a problem."

"Yes," Zengin peeled the glove from his fingers one by one and slipped it off his hand, holding his palm up for them to see. The golden sigil of Metnadur, a solitary mountain, shone out clearly, and the man's jaw went slack. "We are."

"Champion! Forgive me!" He dropped his club back in its holster and knelt on one knee.

"All is forgiven. You couldn't have known. Now, I need four of your men as an escort to the temple."

"Of course!" He stood and snapped for four guards to come up to the front.

"It's time I get to the temple and make myself known. Tell me, do you know how many champions have arrived?"

The guard stood and tucked his hands sharply behind his back. "Two that I've heard of, but we've been on patrol all night. It could be more by now."

Zengin nodded quickly. "I'm sure it is." He motioned to the four guards. "You two lead, and you two follow. I want no heraldry in the city. Keep this quiet until we're inside the Gods' Mount. I will make my own introductions when I'm ready."

"Would you like a horse, Champion," the commander stammered.

"My sandals will suffice," he answered. He looked back at the Gods' Home one last time. He still had a thousand questions, but they would have to wait. He'd already put off Metnadur's summons long enough.

"We should be quick," he said. "Lead on."

Ingenuity

Two rotting days. It had been two rotting days since the black eyed bandits took over the Sacred Quarter. The morons apparently didn't know how banditry was supposed to work. You come in. You loot. You leave. But these pools of mire had set up camp. Their ranks patrolled the streets, scaring the residents who were trapped here spitless, and their leader had taken over the shrine of Metnadur, a hideous building near the center of the quarter.

But Locin had a plan. She always had a plan, like any good thief. She pushed at wild curls that shot out all over her head like coiled springs, fighting them under the hood of a dark green cloak she'd stolen. It was so long it hung nearly to her ankles - or maybe she was just so short - and it bore the same mark she'd seen popping up in crude graffiti all over the quarter - some kind of beast man. Currently she was crouched in a miserable little alleyway rubbing at the skin around her eyes with a piece of coal she'd nabbed from a spent fire. The only way out was through them, and the only way to do that was to look like them.

"Easy haul," she grumbled. "That's all this was supposed to be. Rich nobs leave for the festival, we break a window, grab some jewels. *Easy*. These dumb cultists have some great rotting timing." She dropped the coal on the rocky alley and picked up a pair of rough leather gloves, smiling for a moment at the golden sigil of Iyanu, a never-ending knot, on her palm. "How do I look?"

Her cheeks grew hot, like someone was laughing at her, and she wrinkled her nose.

"Yeah, well, what do you know anyway?"

She summoned her new boon and instantly she could feel the wooden walls of the alley. She focused on a small clod of mud by her foot and willed it upward until it floated in the air beside her, then she tossed it where she imagined Spark was standing. It splattered against the wood.

"That's what you get." She stuck out her tongue, then traipsed to a puddle and looked in. Her soft brown skin was covered by a wash of dark freckles and her eyes were smeared with wide black circles. "It looks fine, Spark! You're just jealous that I'm prettier than you."

She flashed a smile and felt a sharp pinch in response.

"Ow! You know you're a real pain sometimes. It's good enough. We're getting across that rotting river. I don't want to spend another minute here!"

A twitch in her right hand told her Spark agreed. The longer these fanatics held the Quarter, the more dangerous everything was becoming. Not to mention, Locin was a champion now. She was eager to get to the temple and rub the stuffy monks' noses in that.

"Me," she smiled. "Gods and Chosen! I thought the gods were dumb as stumps, but Iyanu picked me. At least one of them has some sense. Can you believe it, Spark?"

The spirit was pressed in close, just as excited as Locin. She'd never tell Spark, but she had gotten so used to her presence, she couldn't imagine life without her. The moment she'd lost her thief's boon, she'd been terrified of losing their connection, and not even being called as a Champion made her as happy as realizing Spark was still there.

"Alright. Enough of this nonsense. Time to see how good this disguise is."

Locin rolled her shoulders back, then sauntered out of the alleyway and onto the bridge road. It curled around in a long arc until it dead ended at the North river crossing. When she'd first come to the Sacred Quarter, on the night of the Shattering, she'd been able to simply walk across. Now the bandits had it barricaded like the river was their mote and the quarter was their fortress.

"Alright," she rehearsed as she walked. "Let's say you're a bandit. I walk up to you and I say, 'I've got a message for the scum over there.' Then I stroll across like I own the place."

She felt a pinch in her left hand. Spark apparently thought she was already dead.

"That's not the *whole* plan," Locin protested.

Another pinch told her Spark didn't care what the rest of the plan was. It didn't have a hope in Nyx of working.

"You're not being helpful."

She pressed on down the main road until she reached a point where it narrowed, and the jettied levels of the buildings hung over the road until it felt like a tunnel.

She quickened her pace, eager to get clear of the suffocating section until she spotted a door. It had an unassuming design, though its stone construction set it apart from the wooden buildings around it, and it was hanging wide open, as though it was inviting her in for a quick peek.

She slowed to a halt and craned her neck around the doorframe. "What do you think?"

Spark's answer felt like a shiver up her spine, a warning signal.

Her shoulders hunched at the sensation, but her curiosity was piqued. "Anything good inside?"

A twitch in her left hand.

She edged forward, staring into the yawning dark. "You worry too much."

She stepped a foot through the opening and the dirt of her sandal ground against the stone floor. There were no windows to be seen, just a chair on one side behind a desk, and a trunk resting on the floor next to that.

"Found ya," she said, eyeing the trunk. She opened the door a bit wider, letting in as much light as possible, then cast one more furtive glance down the road before slipping fully inside.

The trunk ended up being a collection of old tools. A couple daggers and a broken set of reigns that looked way too big to fit any horse she'd seen.

She slammed the lid shut with a huff and wandered to a rear door that stood ajar. There was a tunnel down, bored into the ground like a mine shaft and lined with thick timber. She'd seen smuggling tunnels like this before, but this one was way bigger, and it'd been ripped to shreds. Giant gouges were torn into the walls and floor, and several of the thick supports looked like they'd been burned to char, then snapped like kindling. The bottom of the slope was clearly collapsed, sealing the tunnel closed.

"What in Nyx," she muttered, and she edged out of the tunnel. Maybe coming in here was a bad idea after all.

She headed back to the road and swung the door closed. She could feel the warmth of Spark across her back, and she was grateful for the spirit's touch. "What was that?"

Before she could gather her thoughts, a gruff voice pulled her from her contemplation. "You!"

She looked with a start.

A big brute was standing just outside the narrow portion of the road. His eyes were ringed with the black ink of the cultists, and he was staring toward her.

"Did Borroka send you?" he asked, pointing her direction.

Locin recovered her wits and folded her arms over her chest. "Who wants to know?"

"Just get in here. We got a visitor."

She raised an eyebrow. "I'm headed to the river."

"You'll get in here now," the brute growled, "Or you'll be headed to the noose."

Locin stiffened and walked after him, emerging onto the broader stretch of road, and he led her toward an old building that had an unpleasant odor about it.

"Spark," she hissed. "Are there more inside?"

A chill ran up her spine, then another, then a third.

"So we're dead."

Spark didn't reply. Normally that meant she was out scouting, hopefully for a way out of this mess.

Locin wondered what the hierarchy was here. There had to be one. They were too organized to be without rank and file, and the way this oaf spoke to her told her she must be pretty low in the pecking order.

As she neared, the brute waved for her to hurry. "Come on then," he growled. "Someone's come through the tunnels. Says he's got business with Borroka, and she wants him brought straight away."

Another tunnel? That was it then. Her way out. She quickened her pace as a smile pulled at the corners of her mouth. "What's the matter? She afraid he'll get lost?"

The brute reached out a fist and grabbed the collar of her cloak. "Borroka says, we don't question. Got it?"

"Gods!" She clawed at his hand with her fingers, which felt like a feather clawing at an oak. "Fine! I was just asking."

The brute let her go. "You must be new. You're gonna learn not to ask real quick." He made a face like he smelled something foul, and he pointed to the rough coal around her eyes. "What in Nyx happened to your face?"

Locin frowned, and pulled her hood a bit lower. Spark was back, and laughing again, and Locin ducked down and scurried in as fast as she could. Inside, the unassuming gray walls were covered by pictures, roughly drawn with black paint. Most were that same face she'd seen all over the quarter, half man and half beast, but others were beasts of legend, hydras, cerberus, giant serpents, and cockatrice. In the center of the stone room, the floor sloped downward to a large square opening in the floor covered by a thick grate.

Three men were standing close to the opening, bare chested and aggressive looking. One of them had the face of a half-man painted on his chest, and they all watched the opening expectantly.

She snuffed at the thick stench inside. "Rot it! What is that smell?"

"Sewage."

She grimaced. Not exactly the tunnel she'd been hoping for.

"And yellow alyssum," a second man added.

She felt herself tense. Spark wouldn't come with her. She would have to find her way alone.

She felt a soft brush on her shoulders. It would be okay. Spark was letting her know they would meet up on the other side.

"They send you to escort him?" The first man growled.

"Yeah, sure." She strolled forward as casually as she could, resisting the urge to pinch her nose, and stared down at the sewer entrance. "I'm assuming this runs to the Arrtris?"

A scuffing sound from below interrupted her question and the first man heaved the grate open, letting it clang loudly against the stone floor.

She leaned in as an old man pulled himself up from the dark hole. He looked strong, but worn, his drab clothing and satchel were smudged with dirt and his legs were soaking wet from the knees down. He held a torch in his right hand and when he turned toward her she saw the flesh of his face, twisted up like tree bark.

"The first man sneered at him. "Borroka's expecting you."

"Good."

Locin looked around frantically. There was no way in Nyx she was taking this old man to Borroka. Besides, whoever this Borroka was might see through her flimsy disguise. She had to go now.

"You," the brute said, commanding her attention. "You will take our *guest* to the shrine of Metnadur." Contempt dripped from his voice. Whoever the old man was, he wasn't exactly one of them. But he was welcome here, which meant he wasn't exactly on the other side either.

Locin snapped to attention, trying her best to look like a proper hooligan, but her eyes kept darting around the room. She needed a diversion, and quick.

"I'm perfectly capable of getting there myself." The old man protested.

The Brute sneered. "You don't really think she's gonna let you just walk around, do you? You made your choice, old man. You ain't one of us anymore."

The man held his head high in proud defiance. "I never was." He turned his attention to Locin, looking over her ridiculously long cloak and smudged eyes. Luckily, it didn't seem to faze him. "Let's hurry then. I don't have long."

Locin smiled uneasily. "Anytime now, Spark," she whispered through clenched teeth.

Suddenly one of the brutes gave a wild yell and started slapping at his trousers. The other men all looked with alarm toward the commotion.

"What in Nyx is wrong with you?" The Brute growled.

"Something was crawling up my leg."

"Up your leg? Really Grimes?"

Locin took the opportunity to summon her boon. This time she focused on the satchel over the old man's shoulder. She could feel the supple leather, it felt expensive, and the fine thread. She traced it back behind him until her mind registered the cold metal buckle. It was different than she was used to. She missed the feeling of her hands, the practiced twist that uncinched the strap and broke the satchel free, but she reached out with her mind and fumbled around until she felt the buckle loosen. She directed her boon to push the satchel toward the hole as it fell away.

The man felt the shift and lurched to catch the bag, but it was already moving too quickly and it slipped through his fingers, spiraling down into the grimy sewers below.

"By the eight!" The man yelled. He spun back toward the putrid hole, and Locin seized her chance.

"I'll get it!" She yelled and she sprang toward the ladder before anyone could object. "I'll just take that torch."

The man handed the torch over, still shaking his head in disbelief. "Try to recover it intact."

Locin scrambled into the darkened passage. The satchel had landed half in the waterway and she snatched it up. "I think I see it," she yelled back to the top. "Just give me a minute."

"Make it fast," the brute yelled after her.

Locin rolled her eyes and started walking quickly back in the direction that felt like West. If this actually did bring her to the Arrtris, then she was free.

A thin smile spread on her lips and she quickened her pace. "Nice work, Spark."

Nothing greeted her but the stillness of the dank sewers, and she snorted at the smell of the putrid yellow flowers. She couldn't see them, but that rancid cheese smell was unmistakable. No wonder spirits avoided it.

She heard yelling back through the tunnel, and she tucked the satchel securely under her arm and took off at a run. She was free, and Spark would find her on the other side.

1: Broken Ties

Nestled in the heart of the Sacred Quarter, the shrine of Metnadur was akin to a miniature palace. Murals of the god of ambition adorned the walls of the great room, watching over the white cushions and low mahogany tables that ringed the perimeter. High windows above them were curved to direct the sunlight so that it always shone on a basin of fragrant oil at the very center of the room.

Endring wrinkled his nose at a foul smell. Yellow alyssum had been set around the edges of the room in stone pots, no doubt to ward off spirits, and the usual offerings around the basin were gone.

Endring eased into the room and shut the heavy doors behind him. His sandals squished lightly from the sewers, and he felt uncomfortable in the scratchy commoner's garb. Adding that to the loss of his satchel had fouled his mood, and by the time he saw Borroka, he was regretting coming.

She was a head taller than most of her sex, with tan skin and a strong build. Half her head was shaved bald, with a tattoo of a hydra along the scalp in dark green ink, and mousy brown hair fell past her shoulders in braids on the other side. Her leather tunic was a grimy green and her left arm was banded with rows of teeth that looked sharp enough to cut. On her right arm she wore a peculiar golden bracer, sown with emerald thread. Endring had seen it before in an illustration. The bracer of Neveri was said to control the beasts of animus, but those had died out millennia ago. Now it was just a useless trinket.

"Endring," she said. Her arms were crossed and her lip curled. She looked at him as though he was an inconvenience, as though he was the one who needed *her* and not the other way around.

"Borroka."

"What do you want?"

He hesitated. The real reason for his visit was the Crook of Bei'ai, but asking her directly was bound to make her suspicious. While she claimed to serve the same god as he, they were *certainly* not on the same side.

"Why do you think I'm here?" he snapped. "All the Gods' Mount is ablaze with the news. A band of brigands attacks the Sacred Quarter, sets fire to the bridges, and defaces the holy sites? I should have known you were responsible the moment I heard, but I held out hope I was wrong. Until I learned of that little *display* at the Gods' Home. By Neveri, when he walks again you shall be held to account for this bloodshed!"

She sneered and withdrew a wicked looking bronze shotel from the basin beside her. Had she really been oiling her blade in the sacred basin of Metnadur?

"And what are you here to do Endring," she chided as she wiped the blade clean with a rag, "chastise me?"

He stepped forward, his anger still brimming over his fear. "That man you impaled was a servant of the temple."

"Was he?" She said in mock surprise. "How uncomfortable for you."

His voice darkened. "You don't know just how much danger you're in. When the temple comes for you, and they will come, there will be no quarter given. They'll purge the world of every faithful that follows you, and you will have succeeded in nothing more than sullying the name of Neveri."

She licked her lips. "We'll see how far they get."

"You have what? A thousand men?"

She sneered.

"Two? Fool!" He pointed back toward the gods' Mount. "The city garrison numbers higher, and you can add to that the monks of Jeza. I'm not sure if you've ever faced one, but they are fierce. Your men are unguilded, no match for a warrior's boon. And they're armed with what? Wood axes and sickles?"

"You've underestimated me before, *Oracle*."

Borroka didn't bluff. He at least knew that. If she thought they could defeat the entire garrison and the forces of Jeza, she had a plan.

His eyes drifted to the bracer again. Why wear it if it was worthless?

"Don't tell me you think *that* will save you."

"Why don't you stay and watch?" Her eyes were cold and hard. "How long did you say until the garrison arrives?"

"Your hubris ill suits your position."

"And your cowardice ill suits a faithful of Neveri."

"Cowardice?" He turned and paced toward the wall where the putrid smell of the alyssum clung. "I have risked more than any man to see this come to pass. Do you think there is no inquiry at the temple into the deaths of the champions? I have risked my title, my good name, my very life. Does all this make me a coward, or is it my lack of revelry in bloodshed?"

She tucked her sword into a black sheath on her belt, then paced away from the center of the room. "I've told you before. You don't have the stomach for what needs to be done. Do you think change, real change, has ever come through peace?"

He sighed. He knew she was right, but he didn't care. This was different. This was not a revolution, or a man made endeavor. This was divine, and it *would* be different.

"My sources said you would release him on the night of the shattering. So you failed?"

He turned from his pacing and stared at her. She had made her way to a bench at the side of the chamber and was seated, crossing one leg over the other as though she was an archon and this was her palace.

"We took the Sacred Quarter to present as a gift to Neveri, the very heart of worship of those usurpers. But apparently we put too much faith in the Oracle of Bei'ai. Are you incompetent, or does she still hold your allegiance?"

He rubbed idly at his right palm through his glove. "Had you bothered to run your plan by me, I would have warned you off." The idea that she had sources, someone among his people who reported on his actions, rankled him. "But I suppose you stopped listening to me a long time ago. You defiled the Gods' Home. *You.* I've been down to see it. I'd know your handy work anywhere."

"You should. I stitched you up a time or two."

Endring crossed his arms. "So your plan was to butcher an innocent man and defile Neveri's birth place? He means to reconcile, to rejoin his brothers and sisters in Sbarga. You think this would please him?"

Borroka cocked her head to the side. "You never really understood who Neveri is. He's not like you. He's not weak."

Endring charged across the room and stopped right in front of her. She sat unflinching as his wrath bubbled over. "I alone have spoken with the god of animus! *I* found him in the depths of Nyx. *I* have orchestrated this whole plan. Without me, you would have nothing but your empty belief!" He felt the boon of Neveri trying to ride the adrenaline in his veins, burning through his palm and wrist, but he suppressed it. He could not let her know.

She stood, facing him down. "And how sad it is that after all that you don't understand. This is why when he is released, *I* will be chosen as his champion." She held up her own right hand, bare palm. "I will have the power of animus, and no more need of you."

"You?" He scoffed. "You agree Neveri is a god, and yet you have no respect for the divine. I followed your goons through the Sacred Quarter. Shrines are torn down, or defiled. They've looted the temple of Uthando, and I've no doubt many more sites! And what of the relics?"

"What of them?"

"They could be useful. Tell me you haven't destroyed them?"

Borroka sneered. "You care so much for trinkets of the old gods?"

"Of course I do! They're powerful tools. But you know that." He took a step back and glanced toward the window. "Most of the relics in Arrajin were kept in the House of Dusk. If your men-"

"You really do think I'm a fool."

"I think you're willing to throw away everything sacred, with no regard for consequence. You've let your bitterness consume you, and it will bring us to war!"

She snarled. "Maybe a war is exactly what this realm needs."

Endring curled his right fist tight, shoving down the surge of power he felt. "And that's why you'll never be champion. You don't want to restore what was, you want to destroy what is."

"Only that which dies can be reborn."

Like a tree. He thought back to Sammel's words. *But not like this.*

"The relics, Borroka. Where are they?"

"Safe." Her eye twitched as she spoke, it wasn't much, but it was enough for him to notice.

"I hope you're right," he answered. "If I were you, I'd get them out of the Quarter before you're overrun."

She raised her chin in defiance. "I said they're safe, and I keep my word, unlike some."

He feigned a scowl. "Your idea of *safe* was to come marching in here like you owned the place. You're going to have to do better than safe. They need to be untouchable."

"They need to be useful," she countered. "You fools at the temple have such reverence for power that you've forgotten how to wield it."

Safe and yet within reach. Endring ran through his knowledge of the Sacred Quarter. Where had she hidden them?

"They're here aren't they," he accused. "In this palace?"

She laughed derisively. "I have no need for such trinkets."

"But your men do. They would never stand a chance in a fight, so you armed a group of common criminals with the relics of the gods." He shook his head with dismay. "You're insane."

"We'll take what's left for us," she answered. "And soon we'll take what's due us."

"And when the temple comes, you'll lose it all."

She snarled and took a step forward. She was nearly his height and they stood face to face. "If they think they can reach that high, let them try."

Endring kept his face unmoving. *The tower! That's where she's hidden them.* "And your thieving men? Who's going to keep them from just walking away with the spoils?"

She lifted her chin. "It's my turn to speak."

Endring took a deep breath. "Let's hear it then."

"We took this wretched Quarter because of our faith that Neveri would emerge during the shattering."

There was an edge of malice in her tone, and Endring could feel the boon of Neveri, bristling again in response. "And?"

"We can hold, but not forever. Troops will come from other city-states and temples. I will give you one week to fulfill your duty and free Neveri."

He laughed. "One week? Then what, you kill me? Need I remind you, I am your only access to Neveri." He was sure if she knew the truth, she would strike him dead here and now. He had lost his access, and they were blind.

"One week, and I move against the temple."

She couldn't. Her forces couldn't be enough.

He scowled and for a moment his voice sounded deep and guttural, as though he was more animal than man. "If you move against the Gods' Mount, you declare war on the gods themselves. All nine. And who do you think will save you then?"

Her eyes narrowed with suspicion, but he turned and stalked out of the room before she could reply.

He rejoined his escort, and they turned toward the entrance to the sewers, but as he walked, his eyes wandered to the Gambit of Iyanu, the tallest tower in the Quarter. It rose over the surrounding buildings, straight as an arrow with a wide, flat top. A ring of metal circled the peak with the green glow of a thousand sparks. It was a marvel of the ancient world, centrally located in the Quarter, and a virtual fortress. As he watched, he felt his boon flood his eyes, and his vision sharpened like a hawk. He could clearly see the rim of the tower high above, great dark wings flapping over the sides. Far too big to be a bird, and all wrong for a Pegasus. His chest tightened. She wasn't bluffing. She had something more powerful than the monks and the garrison could comprehend, and he had one week to stop her. He couldn't do this alone.

2: Champions

Voske had seen some beautiful architecture in his life, from the sandstone library of Evr'ai on Suntara, to the towering Kerata arena on Erimos, but none of it compared to the Gods' Mount. Rolling green fields of perfect grass covered the sloping hill, stretching from the main road up and away toward the temple. He could see the wide portico with its columns formed like the first champions guarding over the entrance to the sanctum. West, the square, stone barracks and stables stretched across the grounds, and East, old brick buildings with arched windows and glass domes sprawled. But his eyes rested most of all on the spires. Eight of them surrounded the temple, circling around the grounds near the edges of the jungle, towering over temple and trees alike. Each was formed exquisitely, though different to honor the different gods.

Voske had dropped his meager belongings with the monks as soon as he arrived at the temple and set out to wander the outer yards. The monks had looked mortified by the idea of a Champion just wandering the grounds alone on his first day, but none of them objected, and Voske wanted to get the lay of the land. He didn't need an entourage to accomplish that.

He'd made his way to one of the two spires that flanked the entrance road from Arrajin, the spire of Jeza. It rose in a great spike, contoured at the edges until the stone appeared sharp. It was made from one solid piece of smooth rock, as if it had naturally formed here. He brushed his fingers along the stone, looking for seams, the barely detectable imperfections where an architect had melded the materials together. He had been all around the base of this spire and had yet to find a single one. He couldn't remember a time he had ever seen such flawless workmanship.

He stepped back, taking it all in. "Impressive."

"Is it?"

He turned to see a young girl watching him, hands on hips. She had soft brown skin and a face full of freckles. Her hair was a wild mass of curls sticking straight out all over her head, one stray curl drifting wildly across her face. She blew at it to no avail.

"It just looks like a big rock to me."

He crossed his arms defiantly over his chest, sour for the interruption. "I suppose you don't appreciate fine craftsmanship, then."

"Uh, yeah. That's not it." She sauntered closer, staring straight up at the spire's imposing height and poking it like one might poke at an unidentified spot on the floor. "I just don't consider a pile of stones impressive. Now, a finely crafted Beinot, or a vintage bottle of Girdea 'ai don. Nyx, you can even make a case for a man who's both good looking and intelligent. But that?" She motioned with disdain to the towering structure.

Voske stared down at her. "Thanks for calling me impressive. Who are you?"

She turned her gaze from the tower to him. "Of the two, you're definitely more impressive. Gods! They told me you were big."

"Call me Voske," he said.

"Name's Locin." She flashed her right palm where the sigil of Iyanu was charred into her skin. "Gillis said you were down here."

"Hm." He looked her over. She seemed young for a champion. "You're what, a cycle?"

"Seventeen." She scowled as she stepped back, kicking out her hip. "You're what, four cycles?"

Not even close. But she knew that. "Did you want something?"

"Nope. I heard some monks talking about some giant new Champion of Jeza, so I had to come check it out. Skard! They really didn't do you justice." She turned back to the spire. "So, these are full of dead people?"

He raised an eyebrow. "If you're referring to the sacred ashes-"

"I don't see what's so sacred about them. I mean, it's just old dust in jars."

"You might want to remember, you'll be one of those piles of dust in a jar one day."

She drew her lips in a line as she scowled at him. "Yeah, and I'm pretty sure I'm not gonna give a rot about my ashes."

They stood there, both with their arms crossed, staring at one another. She was opinionated, he'd give her that.

"I'm forty," he finally said.

Locin tried to hold her serious expression, but her lips started to curl in a smile, and soon she was laughing. "Gods! You really couldn't let that go, huh, old man?" She turned and walked a few paces to the plain wooden door that led into the spire. "Wanna see what's in there?"

"Good luck," Voske said. "I tried."

"Maybe you didn't try hard enough."

He was not going to take that insult. He made his way over and leaned his full weight into the door. It didn't budge. "Satisfied?"

"Okay." Locin stepped up, swatting at his arm until he moved aside. "Let me try."

He looked over her small frame. "Right. You're gonna open-"

A creak interrupted him as she pushed the door inward. "How?"

She smiled at him, her hands behind her back. "Ingenuity!"

Voske stared at her skeptically before he snatched hold of her arm and pulled it forward.

"Ow, hey! Watch it!"

He held her hand up and saw a thin iron pick tucked between her fingers. "Turns out ingenuity looks a lot like crime."

She smiled. "Sometimes. You coming in or not?"

He stood hesitating, leaning forward to try and see through the open crack of the door. "Jeza is the goddess of justice. You expect me to condone this?"

"It's entirely unjust to keep you out of your own tower," she said. "I mean, think about it!"

"It's not my tower. Not until I'm dead."

Locin pushed the door all the way open, keeping her eyes on him. "Suit yourself. I'll tell you what it's like." She winked and then spun around and bounded inside.

Voske glanced around for a moment, but no one appeared to be watching them. "Mire and Nyx." He ducked inside.

If the tower was impressive from the outside, it was breathtaking from within. A central pillar ran the height of the spire, and buttresses spiraled over the wooden stairs that wound their way to the top. The buttresses were smooth, solid white stone, each carved in a geometric design, no doubt as seamless as the rest of the spire.

"You coming, big guy?"

He could see Locin already a good ways up the stairs.

He let his hand rest on the wooden handrail. It was carved in similar fashion to the buttresses, seamless wood that curled around and up. Beside the stairs, stone shelves lined the spire all around the walls. The shelves were empty here.

"So, where are the dead guys?" Locin asked.

Voske hurried until he caught up to Locin, and they walked side by side up the wide passage. "Further up."

They continued on for some time, winding around the tower until Locin lost the bounce in her step.

"Gods! Why in Nyx couldn't they have put these things at the bottom?"

"Tired already? Some champion you are." Voske smirked.

"Hey! I'm the Champion of Ingenuity, not stair climbing. Sorry we can't all be in the shape of a…." She stopped and glanced at him.

"God?"

"I was gonna go with gorilla."

Voske rolled his eyes. "So you were what in your past life? A thief. Unguilded?"

She chuckled. "You're naive."

"What is that supposed to mean?"

"Thieves are not unguilded."

"The thieves guild?" He scoffed. "That's not a thing. The gods would never condone that."

"Jeza wouldn't, that's for sure." She pointed ahead. "Oh, look!"

They could see the urns now, just up ahead. Voske glanced down over the rail. They'd traversed almost a third of the tower.

Locin whistled. "So these are Champions?"

He strolled up beside her, stopping in front of the lines of urns, each one unique, representing the ashes of that Champion. Each jar was immaculately clean and well maintained. He was glad to see the temple monks gave such care and respect to honoring the fallen Champions.

Locin reached out and grabbed one, pulling it off the shelf. "Let's open it."

Voske quickly grabbed the urn away, carefully nestling it back in its spot. "You touch another one, and I'll break your arm."

She scowled at him. "That sounds excessive. Has anyone ever told you you're no fun?"

Gods, if she only knew.

"I'm going to the top," he said. "Are you coming?"

She leaned out over the rail and stared up at the impressive amount of stairs left. "Nyx it! You're really going all the way?"

"I didn't come this far to turn back now."

He started climbing again, letting his eyes follow the rows and rows of urns. He saw one painted with the image of a man holding up a boulder as people huddled underneath. Another depicted a woman placing a tree across a turbulent river. He would never belittle these exploits, but it had been several generations since a Champion had done anything truly outstanding. There were no exploits like the old days, no grand deeds that were sung about, no legends passed on in story.

"So, all these were champions?" Locin asked, letting her fingers lightly brush each urn as she passed, which greatly frustrated Voske.

"Yes. Only Champions are laid to rest in the spires."

"And, uh, the ones that just died…"

"After the exaltation."

They were getting close to the top now. Locin was falling behind, stopping to catch her breath.

Another urn caught his eye. Heimris. It was gilded with gold and it depicted his battle with the last hydra in the days before they disappeared. A little ways beyond him, he spotted the urn of Saelin depicting the battle of Torja where she killed more than a thousand men.

Locin caught up again now that he had slowed down. She bounced up the remaining steps to the top where a ladder led up through a door in the ceiling.

In a place of honor on its own shelf was set a large, stone urn.

"Skard," Voske said as he stepped up to the shelf. "First of Jeza's Chosen." He let his fingers hover just over the surface of the urn for a moment before pressing his hand against the image of Skard.

"You told *me* not to touch them."

"That didn't stop you."

"Not the point." He heard the hatch creak open. "I'm going up."

By the time he turned she was halfway up the ladder. "Wait! You shouldn't-"

And she was gone. Voske turned his eyes back on Skard, trying to ignore her, but there was no telling what trouble she could get into up there, and being he hadn't stopped her coming in, he felt responsible, at least in part. He carefully made his way up the ladder and out into the fresh air. The sun felt unreasonably bright after the dimly lit spire.

"Now *this* is impressive," she said.

The top of the spire was a flat circle with a bronze railing around it. In the center, the Great Basin of the exaltation fire stood, nearly as tall as Locin and wide enough to fill most of the space. It was already filled with piles of wood, and more was ready in stacks against the far wall. Locin leaned over the rail, gazing south toward Arrajin.

"What are you doing? If you fall, it'll be *your* ashes in a jar." He peered over the rail and felt his knees grow weak. "Gods."

"Don't tell me you're scared, old man!"

"Of course not. Just taking it all in." He grabbed the rail with a shaky hand.

"Uh-huh."

He pried his eyes away from the ground and looked out over Arrajin. The Arrtris glinted with sunlight as it cut between the smooth green hill and the multicolored tile roofs of the city. He could get used to those colors. Nearly everything on Erimos was brown or red. Maybe it had been too long since he'd been any place more alive. Maybe that's why he felt so stodgy.

Locin looked over at him. "You ever been to Arrajin?"

He shook his head.

"Good, because I'm gonna show you the ropes."

Voske smiled. "The ropes, huh?"

"Yeah, you know, the good places. I know all the best watering holes, good places to throw knuckle bones." She smacked his arm. "Nyx! I could get you into some fights, if that's your thing."

Voske took a deep breath. "Why do I get the impression these places are less than savory?"

She smiled. "Because you're not as dumb as you look."

"I thought you said I looked impressive."

"I said you were huge."

"Impressively huge?"

"Don't push your luck."

Voske stepped back from the rail. "Knuckle bones, huh?"

She smiled. "I knew you were a gambler!"

"I don't gamble," he protested. "I win."

"Yeah. We'll see."

Voske laughed. The biting humor was all too familiar, but it made him feel at home, and he started to think maybe Las and Erimos weren't all that different after all.

Inside, the temple of Arrajin was as extravagant as the outside. The main temple was a labyrinth of corridors and balconies overlooking grand stone rooms bedecked with carvings, statues, and tapestries that moved, replaying the artist's vision of great stories past. There were numerous courtyards where the flowers never ceased to be perfectly in bloom and wellsprings bubbled up with sweet water.

Illeri had spent the better part of the morning exploring the grounds, avoiding crowds and anyone who referred to her as 'champion' or 'chosen' or even 'favored of Kissandin'. It was all too much. She was Illeri, a wayfarer from the middle of nowhere. She'd spent her life invisible, suspended in a radiant field, and she'd liked it that way.

But here in the temple she was seen. Everyone wanted to speak to a real Champion. And they wouldn't stop touching her - grabbing at her hair and touching the edge of her garments far less subtly than they supposed. It was worst on the commoner grounds where pilgrims still flocked to the temple despite the murder of the eight and the damage to the sanctum. Perhaps that part was her fault. She intentionally left behind the monks of Jeza who were trying to guard her. They made her uncomfortable too, in their own way. If she needed protecting, she was important, and she didn't want to be.

So it was she found herself hiding away in a small nook of the temple scrollery, reading. She let her fingers grab at the corner of the page. She'd spent the last twenty minutes reading three pages of a book about Kissandin and his champions. She was so distracted, she'd read every line six times, and she still didn't think any of it was sinking in.

She sighed. Who was she kidding? She could read a thousand books on Kisandin and his champions, and it would never be enough. She clenched her fist against the golden sigil. She could feel the warmth of her new boon, but every time she tried to reach for it, it seemed to flow through her grasp like water.

"You look vexed."

She started at the intrusive voice, glancing up to see a man watching her. He wore a bright chlamys of orange, yellow, and pink. It looked like petals of a flower draped around his deep olive skin. He had a charming smile and perfect white teeth, and even the tousled black waves of his hair looked effortlessly flawless. He looked familiar.

"I admit," he continued in his smooth tenor, "I didn't expect to find anyone else down here. Quite an unused corner of this place, isn't it?"

Hikari.

She felt her cheeks flush. She'd seen him at least half a dozen times in various plays, but seeing him here, up close, talking to her was a whole different thing.

"Have I managed to embarrass you already?" He asked, noting the flash of red on her face. "Are you mute perhaps?"

"No," she stammered, staring down at her book.

"Very good," he said amiably. "So not mute, just shy? Shy I can work with." To her chagrin, he sat down beside her, stretching his arms. "I'm hiding, truth be told. When I first arrived, I was informed that even my fame as a player could not prepare me for the renown of a Champion! Naturally, I brushed off such nonsense. I could handle it."

She tried to roll her eyes while looking away.

"Ah!" He sat up suddenly. "But I haven't properly introduced myself." He flashed his palm, and the seal of Desita glimmered in the dim alcove.

Of course she knew. When someone as well known as Hikari became Champion, it created quite the buzz around Talamh. She'd heard shortly after she arrived the previous night.

"Merciless. That's how I would describe them. If I have to fight off one more adoring pilgrim, I might-"

He must have spotted her irritated scowl because he stopped mid thought and widened his eyes. "Embarrassed *and* angered you? My gods, darling, I beg your forgiveness! I'm making a horrible first impression."

"I know who you are." She tried to keep any irritation from her voice, but she heard some seep in any way. "Both as a player and a champion. And I am sure it's quite a burden that you must bear." The sarcasm did more than seep into her voice. It swarmed over her words and left him looking hurt. She sighed. "I'm sorry. That was mean."

He waved it off. "It's only mean if you don't deserve it. I'm most certain I did."

She looked back to her book. She hadn't meant to offend him, but she was at least grateful to be done with the conversation. But after reading the next line three times, she noticed he was still there, reading over her shoulder, and she tensed, glancing back up at him.

"Rather dense, isn't it? I'm sure I could suggest a more thrilling book. Have you tried *Amid the Sands*? Or anything by Telving - his plays especially. He has a masterful way of infusing so much life into his characters they almost leap off the page of their own accord."

She tried not to wrinkle her face. "It's a history of Kisandin. It covers his time in the One Realm, as well as his champions and relics."

Hikari forced a yawn. "Well, that's settled. We have to get you better reading material."

Before she could react, he snatched the book from her lap and stood, slamming it shut with a thud.

"Hey!" She stood to her feet and grabbed for it, but he deftly moved it away with a boyish grin. She felt a quiet rage simmering as she straightened up and turned to march away. She had no patience for immature games and people who thought they knew best. She might have admired Hikari of Rel'van once, perhaps even been smitten with him like every girl in Talamh, but he was little more than an arrogant, self absorbed child.

"Oh come now, darling," he said as he chased after her. "I meant no harm."

She refused to slow down until he stepped in front of her, holding her book out to her.

"Take it. Go on. No hard feelings. Besides," he resumed his boyish smile, "it can't be so bad to be teased by a champion, can it?"

She crossed her arms angrily. "You're very proud of that, aren't you?"

"Well of course, darling! Only eight in the realm are chosen."

"By a god who picks as much on their whim as any merit. I've read of some of the past Champions. A few more than earned the title, but not all. Who's to say the gods didn't shut their eyes and point, like some sort of cruel joke? Being a champion is meaningless if you don't live up to it."

When she finished her tirade, she saw he looked truly wounded now. His shoulders slumped, and his frown was quite genuine.

"I'm sorry."

He held the book out. "No need to be. You're right of course." He straightened back up and smiled, but his eyes still looked hurt. "I will, of course, prove my worth, my lady, and more than earn my title."

"I wasn't talking about you."

"Of course you were. I'm the only champion here. I may have been blindly chosen, but I will bring Desita honor through my actions." He shoved the book toward her again.

Illeri sighed. "I wasn't talking about you." She unclenched her hand and showed him her own golden sigil. His eyes went wide, and she saw some relief there.

"Gods and Chosen! The Champion of Kisandin, as I live and breathe!" He bowed and then gave a second look at the book she held. "I suppose that explains this."

"I thought it could help."

"Well, it certainly can't hurt."

She took the book. "Thank you." But as she went to step around him, he blocked her.

"I regret we got off on the wrong foot."

"It's okay."

"No. It's not. I shall endeavor to make it up to you."

"Really-"

"It's settled." He smiled at her. "I'll introduce you to my personal chef, and he shall ravish you with tastes so exotic all other food will be ruined for you."

"That's not-"

"And what is the name I should give him?"

She took a deep breath. "Illeri."

"Illeri. Perfect."

He twirled away and disappeared around a corner. She stared the way he'd gone, back to the temple, and the monks, and the other champions, and finally decided to retreat to her bench. She nestled back down and found her place in the book again, reading the same lines over and over as her mind drifted into aimless thought.

Later that evening, Voske had been summoned to a feast at the temple. He wasn't required to attend, but he'd been told the rest of the champions were also invited, and he was keen to meet them. Truth be told, now that he was a champion, he didn't think anything would ever be *required* again. He could pretty well do as he pleased.

He stared at the monks of Jeza, clad in deep red, who stood just outside of the feast hall. One had a bo staff slung over his back while the other carried a sword on each hip. It was a strange sensation having monks around waiting on his every need, guarding him. The thought made him smile. Guarding *him*? He was head and shoulders over the tallest monk he'd seen, and he could feel the strength of Jeza saturating his veins. It wasn't that different from his old boon, but the power was immense, like his body could hardly contain it.

The monks stood on either side of a set of gilded mahogany doors. From within he could hear a low chatter and he hesitated, motioning to the doors.

"The others are in there?"

"I believe so, Champion."

He nodded. "Good."

It was ridiculous to feel nervous. He had already met one of them, and if the rest were anything like Locin, they would get along fine.

"It's not that I don't want to meet them," he said, as much to himself as the monks. "I'm sure they're fine people. It's just, once I step through this door, it's real, you know. I'm a Champion."

Wasn't he already a champion?

He stared down at the sigil on his palm. It didn't feel real yet. He still had one foot in Govere. But once he stepped through this door, that life was well and truly behind him. He would be a champion for the rest of his life.

Probably.

He laughed out loud, and when he looked up, the monks were averting their eyes. He cleared his throat and glanced around the room.

The walls here were covered with bright tapestries, depicting scenes that moved and changed. He had seen enchanted weaving before, but never anything this detailed. One such tapestry caught his eye, the colors slowly shifting and changing as the image of Skard raised his axe and rushed into battle over and over again. He brushed a calloused hand across the soft threads. Was he *that*? He lifted the corner of the tapestry and glanced at the seamless stone behind. The delicate threads felt like they would unravel in his hand.

"Champion Voske."

He turned at the intrusion to see a young monk with sharp features watching him. He had been introduced to him on his arrival.

"Gillis?"

"I was on my way to dinner. I thought you would be there already."

"You're eating with us?"

The young man looked scandalized. "Attending you. I would never presume…" He shifted uncomfortably and his gaze wandered to the woven pictures that draped the walls. He motioned toward the tapestry of Skard that Voske was holding, and his voice was high and tense. "Do you, er, like the artwork, Champion?"

Voske looked back at the tapestry scrunched up in his hand. "Oh, sure."

"That one is named *The Battle of Fauld.* It's… almost two thousand years old… and very delicate." He visibly cringed.

"Right." Voske pulled his hand away, then brushed at the wrinkled corner of the fabric.

Gillis sighed his relief and motioned to the door. "Are you ready, Champion?"

Voske nodded and strolled back to the double doors. He was Voske, the best rotting foreman in Talamh. He'd gotten that position because he never backed down from something new or challenging. He threw open the doors, and the handles banged into the inside walls. He winced before strolling into the dining hall.

Inside, a host of servants flanked the perimeter, and the center of the grand room was set with one large round table. The table was covered with the most outrageous feast Voske had ever seen. At the center was a roasted boar and two plates of lamb. There were platters of fruit, exquisite baked pies, cakes, and breads of all kinds. Each place was set with two gilded plates, a tankard, and a goblet. Even the utensils gleamed gold.

The other champions seemed to be making themselves at home. Six of them sat around the table. Well, five. Locin sat *on* the table with her feet dangling, drawing glares from the man beside her. He wore an ornate toga of black and gold, pinned with a golden pelican.

"You are aware you have a chair, aren't you?" he said drably.

She stuck out her tongue at him, then waved to Voske. "Come on, old man. We've been waiting for you."

Voske smirked as he moved to an open seat and Gillis took his position dutifully by the table, smiling. "Apologies for my lateness, champions,"Gillis said, "but I see the monks have gotten you settled."

"This really all for us?" Locin asked. She leaned back and grabbed an apple from a platter of fruit. "This could feed a whole village!"

"Or him!" An olive skinned man stared wide eyed at Voske. "My, but you are large."

"I'm the Champion of Jeza," he said proudly.

"Of course you are!" The man laughed and then displayed his palm. "Chosen of Desita, Hikari of Rel'van."

Voske raised an eyebrow. "I know that name."

"Doesn't everyone, darling?"

"I don't."

Voske turned toward the voice to see a woman. Her age was hard to guess as she looked fit and youthful, but her hair was gray, and her face held the lines of age.

"Weylyn," she said, holding up her right hand. "Champion of Strah."

"And you've never heard of me?" Hikari mused.

She shook her head.

"Well, not much for the theater, I presume?"

"Never been to a theater. I spent my life in the northern mountains."

"Mire and Nyx!" Locin swore through a mouthful of apple.

A sharp cough sounded from a dark skinned man across from Locin. He was glaring her direction.

"The mountains?" Locin pressed, and she swallowed hard. "Nobody goes to the mountains."

"Hunters do." The woman smiled.

"Which mountains?" The dark skinned man asked. He had a bald head, and he was covered in blue and white tattoos that ran in lines down his arms and over his scalp. He sat straight, watchful. Voske had seen men like him. Soldiers. You could always tell by the way they sat or carried themselves.

"The Shinoam," Weylyn said. "North of Karanth."

The brooding man next to Locin spoke again, his keen eyes on the soldier. "And you're from Tajerim. I would recognize that accent anywhere."

The soldier turned his eyes on the man with a dark look. "And you don't hide your accent as well as you think."

He smirked. "Most people think I do. But yes, I am also from Tajerim. Zengin."

The soldier pointed to the pelican pin he wore. "House Torvel. That makes you what, the Archon's son?"

"Perceptive."

Voske stabbed a huge chunk of boar and jabbed it toward the bald man. "And what's your name, soldier?"

"Burz."

Hikari leaned in. "You were a soldier?"

"Third regiment, guards of Tajerim."

Zengin laughed lightly. "You're *that* Burz? I should have guessed."

Burz scowled deeply.

"Amazing!" Hikari glanced at Voske. "How did you know he was a soldier, darling?"

Voske wrinkled his nose at being called darling. "He's stiff." He shoveled some boar in his mouth, and pressed on as he chewed. "Soldier's are always stiff, like they're just waiting for a battle to start."

Burz folded his arms. "The term is *disciplined*."

Voske looked at the last champion, a quiet girl who had been staring at her plate and arranging her silverware in different patterns. "What about you?"

When no one else answered, she finally looked up, mortified that everyone was staring at her. "Illeri. of Tor. I was a wayfarer."

"And now?"

"Oh." She awkwardly displayed her palm barely long enough for Voske to make out the sigil of Kisandin. She quickly turned her attention back to the silverware.

Weylyn was reluctantly poking at some fancy cakes shaped like seashells. "What are these exactly?"

"Truffle cakes," Gillis said emphatically. "Truly one of the most decadent morsels you will ever eat. Try one!"

She looked skeptical.

Locin laughed. She leaned out across Zengin and grabbed an apple, tossing it to Weylyn. "Just eat the normal stuff."

Zengin let his fork fall with a clatter, and he sighed in disgust. "Do you have no manners?"

She grinned. "Do I make you uncomfortable?"

"My dear, you would make a barbarian from the Selcat Downs uncomfortable."

Locin took a slow, deliberate bite of her apple, making a loud snap, then crossed her legs, pulling her short toga even further up her thigh as she leaned toward Zengin.

He wrinkled his nose. "I should expect such behavior from a thief."

She froze in the middle of another bite.

"What's that?" Hikari asked.

Locin spit out the apple. "Rotting son of a serpent! How did you know that?"

"I should expect such vulgarities as well."

"Oh, I can show you some vulgarities you rotting-"

Voske shouted over the din. "Or we could all be civil. Just eat some food, and be grateful the gods took a liking to you."

That at least got them to quiet down and even Locin plopped into her chair, though she was still glowering at Zengin.

"A thief?" Hikari exclaimed. "Has an unguilded ever been chosen before, Gillis?"

Gillis opened his mouth to answer, but Locin broke in.

"Woah! Nobody said I was unguilded."

"Apologies, darling. I only assumed-"

"I was a thief alright, and a rotting good one. Had the boon to prove it."

Hikari's eyes went wide. "A boon? What is a thief's boon?"

Burz scoffed. "Folklore, nothing more. They like to make us think they have boons, but what god would gift a thief?"

Locin smirked.

"They call on spirits." They all turned at the quiet voice of Illeri. "I've read about them."

"Thank you!" Locin said. "Finally, someone who's heard of the thieves' guild."

"I imagine all of Talamh will know soon," Gillis said with a smile.

"What?" Locin's countenance dropped.

"The history of the Champions is recorded in great detail," he continued. "I've no doubt scribes have already been sent to your places of birth to find any information they can. And there will be interviews of course."

The room grew terribly quiet. None of them seemed keen on having their pasts delved into. Only Weylyn looked unfazed where she sat eating some lamb. What could they dig up on her? The northern trees weren't likely to talk.

Voske glanced up. "You should join us, Gillis."

"Oh, I couldn't."

Locin straightened up and pointed to the empty seat. "We got room. And more than enough food."

"Speak for yourself." Voske stabbed his fork across the table, securing a large leg of lamb for the top of his plate.

Hikari stood, his chair legs scraping the marble floor as he backed up. "We insist, darling! If you're to attend us, we should get to know you."

Gillis reluctantly strolled over as Hikari pulled out the empty seat. He sat down, stiffer than Burz, and smiled politely.

A sudden coughing and gasping brought their attention back to Weylyn. She held up half the seashell truffle and had her lips puckered like a fish. "How does it manage to be so sour and yet sickly sweet at the same time?"

Hikari laughed. "Isn't it wonderful?"

"No." She set the thing down on the edge of her plate.

Voske laughed before turning his attention back to his own meal, shoveling in a mouthful of roasted vegetables that tasted like Sbarga.

"That leaves you," Hikari said.

Voske stiffened as he looked up at the room. "Voske, foreman of the finest quarry on Erimos."

"Laborer?" Gillis looked surprised. "I could have sworn-"

"And what about you, Gillis?" Voske poked his fork across the table in his direction. "A judge, huh?"

"In boon only," he said quickly. "I was never trained as such. I was chosen quite early for the duties of liaison. It has no boon of its own, and so those deemed suitable are taken from among the servants of the temple and trained for the position. Usually until they are two and a half cycles." He added the last part bitterly.

"I agree," Zengin said condescendingly. "You needed more training. You were second in line for the job. Tell me, what happened to the other?"

Gillis stared wide eyed. "Gevrin? He ran off three months ago with a… monk of Desita. Quite a scandal in the temple, well, until the feast of shattering."

"He would have been more prepared," Zengin continued. "But I suppose you'll have to suffice."

"There's no need to be harsh," Burz said.

"It's fine," Gillis stammered. "He's right. Gevrin had been trained nearly a cycle longer than I. I was meant to be a backup, in case anything happened to him."

Locin was scowling toward Zengin. "You seem to know a lot about all of us, pelican boy. How in Nyx do you know everything about everyone?"

"Because it's my business to know," he answered. "In case you haven't noticed, we're going to be stuck with each other an awful lot for the foreseeable future. Am I the only one who bothered to ask a few questions before now?"

"Well next time you want to know something, ask me to my face." Locin snapped.

"True enough," Weylyn said. "We'll spend the rest of our lives together. Perhaps that's an incentive to get along."

Voske scanned the rest of the table letting the thought sink in. This was his new life. This was his new family. The gods had made the decision for all of them, for better or worse. His eyes traveled to Zengin and he took a deep breath. Hopefully it wasn't for worse.

They all settled back in, and Locin looked at Gillis. "So, you have the judge's boon? You can tell when we're lying?"

"Yes. Don't worry, I wouldn't betray anyone's confidence." He shot a noticeable glance at Hikari, who winked in response.

Locin pushed back from the table, smiling. "Shall we test it? I haven't stolen anything since I got to the temple."

Voske laughed. "It doesn't take a judge's boon to know that was a lie."

She scowled at him. "I could change, old man." She nodded to Gillis. "Well?"

He stared wide eyed and gulped down some air thickly. "That is a lie, Champion."

Voske laughed, and she smirked.

"Fine. Something harder."

"I'll have a go!" Hikari said eagerly. "My first performance was *A Kiss on Midding*."

"Yes," Gillis answered cheerfully.

"Okay," Locin chimed in. "Let me try another one. I have a rather *well hidden* birthmark." She winked at one of the young monks nearby. The boy's cheeks flushed, and he stared at his feet.

"Um, yes," Gillis responded warily. "That - that is true."

"It's not a parlor trick," Burz snapped. "It's a gods given boon. Leave the man be!"

"Oh, it's alright. I don't mind."

"The gods might," Burz continued. "As Champions, we should show more respect."

Locin laughed. "For the gods? A bunch of prigs off in Sbarga throwing their magic at us to keep us happy? I don't think they give a thought in Nyx about how we use our boons."

Burz looked like he had more to say, but he clenched his jaw and stayed silent. Voske could feel the tension building again, so he pointed to Gillis' seat to change the subject.

"Where are they, by the way?"

"The eighth?" Gillis sighed, grateful for the change of topic as well, it seemed. "No one is sure. We haven't received any news about Bei'ai's chosen."

"It's taking a while then?" Hikari asked.

Zengin glanced up. "Metnadur called me a day after the festival."

"Me too," Illeri said. "Kisandin, I mean. A little over a day."

Voske smiled proudly. "Ha! Six hours for me. Jeza must have had her eye on me for a while." He leaned back with a grin on his face.

"Six hours?" Hikari mused. "She must have indeed!" He was smirking a bit too much.

"What?" Voske let his grin drop. "When did you get called?"

"Oh, it matters not."

"When?"

Gillis cleared his throat. "Champion Hikari was called less than two hours after Champion Veshri's death."

"Two hours?" Voske scowled.

Illeri pointed to Gillis' chair again. "And Bei'ai still hasn't chosen a champion?"

"She's chosen one," Zengin said coolly.

"Gods," Locin said sharply. "How do you know?"

"I went by the hall of trees as soon as I arrived. Her tree is blooming."

Gillis nodded. "Yes. A champion has been chosen, but none have come forward."

Voske crossed his arms and stared at the eighth seat. "Well then, where in Nyx is he?"

Lost Souls

Rasa hunched in the rafters of an old tailor's shop. She was a waif of a girl, thin limbs, long, stringy red hair, and skin like ivory. She was dressed in an oversized tunic and loose fitting pants, ragged clothing clearly not made for her, and her right hand was wrapped in strips of linen.

The shop had been abandoned for years, but the structure was in decent shape, wooden rafters, high windows that let in a lot of light. Four mirrors stood against the far wall from where she was. They were full length mirrors, and most likely pricey at one time, though now they had faded around the edges, and one was shattered. The rest of the old shop consisted of a counter, empty shelves, and several long-abandoned bolts of unenchanted fabric. Enchanted fabric would never have been left behind.

The most curious part of her surroundings were the hazy blue shapes that danced and shimmered in the light streaming down from the windows. She had been seeing them for three days now, ever since that golden mark had shown up on her palm. She clenched her fist around the scraps of linen, pushing the thought from her mind. It couldn't be right. The goddess wouldn't have chosen her. No one would choose her.

She shut her eyes and then opened them again, but those misty blue figures were still there. She had the sense that if she stared at them long enough, they would take form, fully fledged people with faces and stories. But she couldn't bring herself to look at them for long. She grew uneasy whenever they came too close.

She pressed her back into the rough wood of the wall, stretching her legs out along the beam she was seated on. She had definitely lived in worse places. Like the old tannery outside of Nibs. It took weeks to get the smell out. She could remember being so hungry, she tried eating some of the old hides. That place might have been the worst. Well, the worst since she'd been on her own. She shoved that thought down.

She caught a glimpse of three little blue mists standing together on the floor of the shop. She had the sense they were talking. About *her*. Why would they do that? She shoved her chin down into her shoulder in an attempt to get comfortable. It was late afternoon. She had managed to trade a bolt of the old cloth for a loaf of bread, warm and fresh. It had settled in her stomach some time ago and she could feel it pulling her toward sleep. But she hated sleep. It brought dreams with it.

She shook her head, deciding to stave it off, but when she looked down, the three spirits had become four. She glared at them.

"Go away," she whispered.

She turned away from them, but kept glancing back out of the corner of her eye. She had heard stories about the champions. Everyone in Talamh knew their boons. But hearing that the Champion of Bei'ai could communicate with the souls of Nyx sounded more glamorous somehow. Or maybe ethereal? Mystical? All she had were these hazy figures stalking her, and she couldn't even make them go away. She shut her eyes fast, hoping to forget about them. But the bread was waiting. And the afternoon sun was drifting through the tall windows.

Rasa's eyes bolted open. She'd woken from a dream of being buried under the hot sand of the Pellin Desert. She could still taste the burning grit that had flooded her mouth and dripped down her throat.

Rasa.

As she shook sleep away, she felt a strange sense of urgency. Someone, or something, had woken her on purpose.

She sat up, nearly toppling off the beam. Moonlight was streaming through the windows, flooding the shop with a silvery glow that bounced off the mirrors and shimmered along the walls.

And there in front of her on the beam squatted a blue figure rippling in the silver light.

"What do you want?"

She had a sense tickling at her mind, like a long buried memory. She needed to look out the window. But why?

The blue haze stood, tall and lean. And moved… floated maybe… to the window just below. She needed to look out *that* window.

Rasa grabbed the beam and quietly slipped over the side, feeling with her foot for the lowest arch of the rafter in the corner of the room. She found her footing, then swung down, lowering herself to the floor.

The spirit was pressed against the window. She knew it wanted her to look outside, and the urgency of it tugged at her. It was upset. What did a spirit have to be upset about?

Rasa sidled warily to the window and peeked out at the city street. She could see lights up and down the road. Most of the shops and taverns here were still open, and a few people still traversed the street. It couldn't be too far past sundown, though she had no real sense of the time.

The spirit urged her again. She needed to look at the guild house. She tried to remember where it had been. She'd been staying here for a few days, and she'd passed it a few times.

"The merchant's guild?"

The spirit seemed excited. Yes. That was it. It was vital that she look at the merchant's guild.

Rasa leaned against the glass, cold on her cheek. She could just make out the sign across the street. The guild hall should have been closed by now, but a light could be seen shining out of one window, the wavering orange light of a candle.

The spirit urged her again. To go outside.

She felt her heart start pounding.

"It's not safe," she whispered.

She could almost hear a pleading voice. It was important.

She tiptoed her way across the room without a sound, pressing her hands against the solid oak door until it opened barely a crack. The front of the guild hall seemed vacant.

"There's nothing there."

Watch.

She focused on her breath, slow, controlled. It helped. She quieted her fears and waited. She didn't have to wait long. She could see a couple of figures coming up the road, one larger, a man. The other was a girl, no bigger than Rasa. They were dark silhouettes against the night sky, but she could tell they wore togas, not the usual laborer's garb. That meant they were wealthy. Maybe merchants from the guild.

Not merchants. How did she know that? Was it the spirit? Was it speaking to her?

The girl was in danger.

As they drew closer, it was unmistakable. The pair stepped into the light of a tavern window next door to the guild hall. It was enough for Rasa to make out the girl's features. She was young. Her face was done with makeup and her hair was pinned back behind her ears. She wore silk gloves over her hands and in her left ear she had an earring. It started at the top of her ear and ran by chain down into her lobe, dangling toward her shoulder. If she could see it better, she would be able to make out the color and design, the mark of her varlet. It was too familiar a sight.

Rasa shut the door and pressed her back against it. Her heart was racing, and she couldn't seem to control it. She let her fingers drift to her own ear lobe, rubbing the mark of her old life away.

"I can't!"

The spirit was frantic now, but she shook her head. It was all crashing back in, like waves threatening to drown her. She wouldn't go back to that life. She wouldn't go near it.

But the spirit was begging. Sobbing?

With sudden fierce clarity, she knew the girl was only thirteen. This would be her first.

"Gods. I can't leave her."

The spirit leapt with joy at the hope extended.

Rasa took a couple deliberate breaths then turned back around, pushing the door open enough to slip through.

The pair had made it to the guild hall now, and the varlet was knocking, one hand on the girl's wrist. She seemed to be pulling away, resisting him. He gave her a firm slap across her face and Rasa could swear she felt the impact. She'd felt it a hundred times. Desperation started to well up inside. The girl was crying, her tiny form rising and falling with sobs. The guild door creaked open, and Rasa was out of time.

She ran for them. She didn't have a plan, but she could feel the spirits cheering her on. They were with her, for what little that meant.

She was small, but she had momentum, and the varlet didn't see her coming. She threw herself into the back of the man. He cursed as he stumbled, and his grip on the girl loosed. He fell toward the door just as it opened inward, and he landed on top of the merchant, a frail looking old man.

Rasa grabbed the girl's gloved hand. "Run!"

The girl looked terrified, but as Rasa pulled she quickly rose to follow. The tavern seemed the best bet. Taverns were always busy on Erimos.

Rasa reached the door just as the varlet righted himself, screaming murderous threats after her. He was headed their way, clearing a terrifying amount of ground with each stride.

"Come on!" Rasa yelled.

The girl had regained her wits and seemed to be resisting Rasa. She understood the hesitation all too well. She yanked her through the tavern door and they both stumbled into a very crowded room. There was a hum of noise, laughter and conversation. The people of Erimos were generally kind, but a tavern was hardly a safe place. She was kicking herself for not thinking this through. She pulled at the girl and they bumped into a tall, gray haired man with rosy cheeks.

"Woah! Can I help you ladies?"

Just then the door burst open and the varlet came storming in, mad as Nyx. She could see him clearly for the first time. His round face was red, and he had greasy black hair pulled in a tight ponytail. He was panting from his jog over to the tavern until he spotted them.

The girl began profusely apologizing and trying to break free from Rasa's grip. But she wouldn't let go. She grabbed the girl's wrist with both hands.

"Stay here," Rasa insisted. "He can't take you from-"

But the man took two quick strides and snatched the girl away, then tossed her aside before turning his wrath on Rasa. She threw her arms over her face, but he slapped them aside. By now the commotion had roused the whole room, and people were craning to see what was going on. The varlet struck her hard across the face, and she scampered back and braced herself for another blow. But it never came. The kind man had gotten between them by now, and was shouting that the varlet best leave. He sneered and backed up, then grabbed the wrist of the other girl as he headed for the door.

"Wait!" Rasa cried. "He can't take her."

The girl shook her head violently. She didn't want Rasa's help. She would be the one beaten for it.

"Let her go," Rasa yelled again.

Suddenly a yelp sounded from someone nearby, and a middle-aged woman made her way to Rasa, grabbed her right wrist and held her hand up for all to see. In all the commotion, she hadn't realized the linen strips had fallen away, and the sigil of Bei'ai, a moon and three stars, was glowing in the dim light of the tavern.

Within moments the whole room had erupted, but Rasa had her eyes on the varlet, who was now edging toward the door, still tugging the frightened young girl.

"Stop!"

The room quieted when she spoke.

"Let her go!"

The varlet tightened his grip on the girl's arm until she cried out in pain.

Rasa felt helplessness overtaking her until a burly hand settled on the varlet's shoulder.

"You heard the champion, rotter."

The varlet turned straight into a powerful punch from the burly man, and within moments, five large men had grabbed the girl away and tossed the unconscious brute out the door. The whole tavern erupted in a cheer, and Rasa felt relief as she headed toward the girl.

"It's going to be okay."

The girl looked around, startled, but Rasa let a finger trace her own left ear, showing the girl the marks in her upper ear and lobe. Showing her she understood.

The girl relaxed, finally letting herself believe it was over, and a kindly woman took her to a table and settled her down with a glass of water.

The next several minutes were a blur. The crowd pressed in around Rasa, with reverent whispers of 'Champion'. The entire tavern swore on their livelihoods, children, and the gods that they would keep the young girl safe, and then they turned their attention to her. She was handed the finest foods the tavern had to offer, a jug of sweet wine, and cool, clear water. She had a room available, if she were willing to honor the tavern keeper by staying the night, and sixteen different people offered to take her straight to the Pylat tether in the morning. Everyone seemed to be closing in on her, and her breath grew haggard.

Somewhere in the back of her mind she felt something comfortable and dark, some place quiet where the voices faded and the feel of a dozen hands touching her arms and her hair melted away. She closed her eyes and drifted into the dark, and a kind voice whispered in her mind through grateful tears.

Thank you.

3: The Exaltation

On the roof above the Champion's Wing of the temple of Arrajin, a sprawling slab of marble spread out in a wide vista, rounded on all sides with an ebonwood railing that was woven like cords. At either end of the roof stood a bulkhead in the shape of a great pair of wings, and six large statues of pegasus were spaced around the perimeter. Their wings glowed softly like starlight, and their outstretched wingtips touched. In the wide spaces between them, each of the eight spires was perfectly framed against the jungle beyond, and the setting sun painted the sky behind in vivid hues.

Burz leaned on the rail, staring at the spire of Uthando. It rose up against the sky like the long bare trunk of a gnarled oak. He missed his family, and he was still uneasy about this life. His leg throbbed from the long day of walking around the temple and being introduced to everything the attendants thought might be important. He was grateful for the somber atmosphere which gave him time to meditate and pray. This was a new beginning, and one he hadn't expected. It was a blessing, to be sure, but he was also desperate not to take it for granted. And if he was honest, some part of him was afraid to be too excited. Had the tides really turned, or would it all fall apart again?

He sighed as he locked eyes again on Uthando's tower. "I was angry with you," he whispered. "Perhaps Jeza also, but you most of all. It sounds foolish to say. I know you don't control the actions of men, but… I still blamed you for them, as though you might have reached down out of Sbarga and pulled me out, spared me… this." He reached down and pressed a fist against his leg. He lifted his hand again and opened it, staring at the golden sigil. "I guess in a way you did."

His voice trailed off as he heard someone moving behind him. He glanced back to see Voske making his way over. The mammoth man rested his hands on the railing, but kept his back straight so that he towered over Burz.

Burz straightened up to his full height.

Voske still towered over him.

The big man nodded. "Nice night."

"It is." Burz turned his eyes back toward the spire of Uthando. He wasn't in a talking mood.

"These statues are something, huh?" He motioned to the massive stone Pegasus on either side.

"Yes."

That was it. Nothing more to be said. And yet, Voske settled in, staring out over the temple grounds. Burz thought about leaving, but that seemed rude. He just wanted to be alone.

Not exactly *alone*. He glanced over his shoulder at the door that led below. No sign of his family yet, but he'd been assured they would arrive today.

Hadris was always the talker. At functions like this, he would escort her around on his arm while she charmed the people, and he avoided small talk.

"So, you were a soldier?"

He glanced back at Voske who was watching him with a goofy smile. "Yes."

"Nice."

Voske started drumming his hands idly on the railing. And not in time with any rhythm. It was a haphazard, grating sound that echoed across the smooth marble.

Burz gritted his jaw as the poor rhythm slammed against his ears over and over. Finally, he decided talking was the best way to make it stop.

"You were a laborer?"

Voske stopped drumming and pressed his hands back into the railing. "Yep. Just like I said. Just a laborer." He shifted awkwardly.

"That must have been interesting."

"Oh, sure. It was."

Burz let out a breath, content to let the conversation die. But almost at once, the slapping sound started up again.

"What did you do?" Burz asked.

"What?"

"The interesting labor work? You mentioned you worked in a quarry?"

"Oh yeah. It was, uh… interesting." He cleared his throat. "I carried rocks."

"Rocks?"

"Granite, mostly. Big slabs of it, and I would, uh, carry them. Yep. I carried a lot of big, heavy rocks…"

Silence engulfed them again, and Burz resigned himself to the slapping ruckus. It turned out the talking was actually worse.

He was just planning an excuse to slip away, when he heard Kyren yelling for him.

"Ada!"

He smiled as he turned around. They'd just emerged through the far door, and Kyren and Orin were rushing toward him. Behind them, Hadris sauntered across the roof. She was dressed in a new toga he'd never seen. It was a deep blue and draped her form from one shoulder. Across her chest were studded bright star-like specks and the same specks sparkled throughout her hair, and she wore a copper colored shawl that draped her shoulders. Even the boys wore small, neat togas in the same blue, trimmed in the copper of Uthando. Clearly something the temple had provided. It was nothing he could have provided…

Before he had time to let that thought take hold, Kyren rushed at him, and Burz grabbed him, scooping him up for an embrace.

"Is this your family?" Voske asked.

Burz mussed a hand through Orin's hair, then pulled him close as he set Kyren down. "My boys, Kyren and Orin." He pointed to Hadris as she strolled up. "And Hadris." Their eyes locked, and he felt a wave of relief as she smiled at him. He was whole again.

Orin's eyes rose to Voske, and he stared agape as he pulled free of Burz. "Wow. You're huge."

"Orin!" Burz said.

But Voske just laughed. "It's alright. I *am* huge." He stretched his impressive arms out and flexed. "That's why I'm the Champion of Jeza!"

Even Kyren had moved over now and was poking at Voske's leg. His voice was low and awestruck. "The Champion of Jeza!"

"Boys!" Burz pulled Kyren back. "Give him some space."

"Oh, they're fine, Burz. You and I are practically brothers now." He set his hands on his knees and bent down to address the boys. "That means you can call me Uncle Voske."

"Nope," Burz said. "Don't call him that."

"How strong are you?" Orin asked.

And Kyren yelled, "Can you pick up a whole house? Or an ocean?"

Hadris shushed him as they drew a few looks from the reverent crowd.

"Sorry," Kyren whispered harshly. "Can you pick up a whole, entire ocean?"

Voske winked at the boy. "Give me a bowl big enough, and we'll find out!"

Burz rolled his eyes until Hadris moved close and slid her hand in his. He met her gaze and smiled. At least she wasn't enamored with Voske.

He squeezed her hand gently. "You look amazing."

"Thank you." She leaned in against his arm, and he relaxed.

"This is the wife?" Voske had straightened back to his full height. "I don't get it, Burz. Where does an old stone skin get a girl that pretty?"

Burz felt his chest swell with pride. "Voske, Hadris. Hadris, Voske."

She smiled politely. "Champion of Jeza, huh?"

"At your service!" He gave her a gracious bow.

"I bet he could lift a mountain!" Kyren said in an attempt at a whisper that was still way too loud.

"Well," Voske said. "I could at least lift the two of you!" He snatched up the two boys and curled them over his arms, then started spinning in circles.

Burz scowled. He took a step forward to stop them, but in his haste he twisted his left leg, and a sharp pain shot through it.

"Boys!" His voice was sharp. "This is hardly the place!"

The three of them came to a sudden stop. Voske froze awkwardly mid-spin and the boys looked disappointed.

"Everything alright?" Voske asked.

Burz held his chin up, and ignored another flash of pain. "This is a solemn gathering. It's not the time to be playing around!"

Voske smirked. "It's just a bit of fun, Burz. I doubt the previous champions will mind."

"I mind!" He knew it had come out more sharply than he meant, and he felt Hadris squeeze his hand.

Voske raised an eyebrow and slowly uncurled his arms, letting the boys drop back to the roof.

They let out an audible groan, but they obeyed. They were good boys.

"Maybe next time," Voske said. He kept this tone even, but he glared at Burz.

What did he know? He wasn't a father.

But as the boys sulked back over, Burz felt a twinge of remorse.

"It was good to meet you all," Voske said cordially, but his tone was stiffer now. "I'm sure I'll see you again soon."

He wandered off, and Burz gathered Hadris and the boys to himself.

"What was that about?" Hadris whispered.

Burz shrugged. "Nothing. I just don't like that guy."

More and more monks were filing up to the roof now, and the space was quickly becoming crowded as the bright orange of sunset was fading to a deep purple, and the first stars glittered overhead. He could still just make out Suntara hanging near the western horizon, half shrouded in the silhouetted tops of trees.

"I'm glad you're here," he said, pulling the boys in as he slipped his hand free from Hadris. "See that? That's the Spire of Uthando. And he's chosen *me* as his Champion." Burz smiled proudly as the boys let out quiet sounds of admiration. "He's given our family a new life here at the temple."

"We saw our rooms," Orin said.

"Yeah!" Kyren bounced up on his heels to see better over the rail. "My room's as big as our house was!"

"It's not *that* big," Orin protested. "But it is really big!"

Burz was just letting the warm, happy feeling of family overtake him, when Orin darted to the side, eyes searching the temple grounds.

"Which one's Jeza's spire?"

Kyren gasped. "I bet it's even bigger than Uthando's!"

Burz winced.

"And much more stronger!"

Orin rolled his eyes. "How can a tower be stronger?"

"I don't know." Kyren shrugged. "But I bet it is!"

"Okay," Hadris grabbed the boys gently and turned them back toward the view. "We'll have plenty of time to look at the other spires later." She shushed them and then continued in a whisper. "Right now, it's time for the exaltation."

Atop the tower of Uthando, a small pinpoint of a candle shone, carried through the dark toward the pyre. The crowd around them quieted as more people noticed the motion.

"What's a exaltation?" Kyren was back on his tip-toes.

Burz grabbed him up and lifted him so he could see. "We're honoring the old Champions by burning their bodies. The fire represents the shining light of their life, the brightness they brought to Talamh for the betterment of all people. It burns all through the night until dawn."

"Then what happens?" Orin asked eagerly.

"Rebirth. The symbol of the new champions. It will be their turn to shine." He felt a catch in his throat. He was Burz, the dishonored soldier. How was he supposed to shine?

Hadris must have seen the way his shoulders slumped, because she reached out her arm and slipped it around his back, leaning her head close to him.

He breathed out as the candle was set into the pyre, and soon the whole top of the spire was ablaze. All around the grounds, the other seven burst to life as well, as the last fading dim of twilight gave way to the black of night.

"Are they going to the Midding?" Orin asked, his voice somber.

"Yes," Hadris said softly.

"Do all the Champions go to the Midding?"

Burz and Hadris exchanged a glance, and then he answered. "I don't know. I hope so."

"Will I go to the Midding?"

Burz stiffened. He'd often considered the afterlife, but it was still a mystery in many ways. "As long as you do what your mother says," he finally managed.

It was the best answer he could give. Everyone knew Strah looked favorably on those who honored their parents, and to be admitted to the Midding, you only had to catch the eye of one god.

Orin nodded, satisfied with that answer, but Burz felt tense. He knew so little about all of this. That wasn't to say he knew any less than others, just that the gods were often cryptic and distant.

He locked his eyes on the tower again, feeling unsettled. Did Uthando really have some grand purpose for him, or was he chosen at random?

"You'll tell me about it later?" Hadris whispered, sensing his tension.

He nodded, but what would he say? That he was a failure, and was worried he'd be one as a champion too? She would draw it out of him, eventually. She saw through him like no one else ever would, but he was grateful for that. He was grateful that he wasn't alone.

He knew that when dawn came, the atmosphere would change. The Ceremony of Rebirth would bring with it music and dancing, a celebration to honor the new champions. To honor *him*. But for now, he was glad of the reverent stillness as the whole of the Gods' Mount stood as one watching the flames of exaltation brighten the horizon.

There was nothing better than Suntaran wine. Well, maybe the Suntaran men, the beaches, the smell of the sea, the luxurious estates, the fashion… gods, Locin missed Suntara. She tipped up the goblet, admiring the etched glass that was shaped like a flower, tinged pink, each petal incredibly detailed. These were the kinds of things she used to find in the estates of the richest nobs, but now they were hers. She laughed, and she felt Spark bristle.

"Nothing," she muttered. "Just thinking how we used to make fun of nobs and their fancy glasses. Who needs a glass shaped like a flower?"

Spark laughed.

A deep voice broke in from behind. "I agree."

Voske stood watching her with arms crossed, and Hikari stood beside him with a similarly fancy goblet.

"I rather like them," Hikari said. "It's like drinking from a piece of art."

"Maybe a bit soon." Voske crossed his arms over his chest and nodded to Hikari's wine. "To be serving wine to the champions."

Locin smirked. She wasn't afraid. "That why you're not drinking, old man?"

He wrinkled his brow. "Nope."

Hikari held his goblet out, trying to look sure, but his eyes went a bit wide. "They have tasters. I checked with Gillis."

Locin laughed. "You checked on that?"

"Well, forgive me, darling, but it seemed like a wise precaution."

Locin looked back toward the party. The fires of exaltation were still burning bright. The whole roof of the temple was covered with monks and Oracles, and a few honored guests. All stuffy and somber.

"How long does this thing last anyway?" She groaned.

Hikari smiled glibly. "Straight on until dawn."

Locin and Voske groaned in tandem.

"What? Are you two not enjoying this? It is, after all, a timeless ceremony to honor our forebears. Someday crowds will pile on this very same roof to watch your body burn."

"Gods," Locin moaned. "I'm glad I don't have to sit through that one."

"Look at the bright side," Voske said. "They all had the decency to die together, so we don't have to go through this again."

Hikari coughed. "For a while hopefully."

The three of them all stared at each other for a moment, the awkward implication setting in.

"Well," Voske spoke at last, "maybe I'll just go first, make you two have to sit through this nonsense while I skip through the Midding eating Sbarga food off golden plates."

"Sbarga food?" Locin laughed. "What in Nyx is Sbarga food?"

Voske shrugged. "I don't know. I always imagined they had food light as clouds and thick as a roast, tasted like pure bliss."

Hikari raised an eyebrow. "You did?"

Locin laughed. She felt Spark laughing too, and soon Hikari and Voske had joined in. She hadn't been sure what to expect from the other champions, but these two were alright.

She felt a nudge from Spark. She liked them too.

"Alright." She set her empty goblet down. "I'm bored, and I'm sure as Nyx not standing up here sulking all night over some dead folks I never met."

Hikari looked taken aback. "Well, it is tradition."

"Yeah, and we're champions. We can come back later. They'll burn all night. So?"

Voske furrowed his brow. "So what?"

"So are you coming with me? Look, everybody in the rotting temple is up here. Probably a few guards left inside, but more or less we've got the place to ourselves. And we're champions. No one's gonna stop us. We can go wherever we want, do whatever we want."

Hikari set down his goblet. "You know… there was this particular relic room I was dying to see. The monks steered me away yesterday."

Locin grinned. "Now you're talking."

He sighed. "It'll probably still be guarded though."

Spark bristled.

"Oh, I can get us in."

"Fine," Voske said. "But we leave it like we found it."

She smirked. "Sure thing, old man. I won't bother a thing."

"Good." He smiled. "Then I'm in!"

"This way, boys."

"Men," Voske corrected, flexing his hulking arms.

Locin rolled her eyes and headed toward the stairwell. The rooftop was crowded, and more than a few mourners glared at the trio as they shoved their way through toward the door, Hikari at the back apologizing profusely as they passed through. Locin wasn't worried about it. She was a champion now. No one was allowed to be offended at her. She smiled. She'd been the underdog her whole life - the small girl, the unguilded, the thief - but now, she was on top. She squared her shoulders and shook her curly mane with pride, but she was so caught up in her self adulation that she walked straight into a man in the purple robes of Bei'ai.

"Nyx it!" She swore. "Watch where you're going."

She glanced up. He was no monk. He wore the purple robes of the Oracle, clasped with a golden pin that bore the tear of Bei'ai. When she jostled him, his hood slipped. The right side of his face was mangled lines of red flesh. She would recognize that face anywhere, and from the way he stared wide eyed at her, he recognized her as the dirty cultist that ran off with his satchel.

A shiver ran up her spine.

She stood frozen, unsure what to say or do. What had the Oracle of Bei'ai been doing with the cultists? She opened her mouth to speak, but Hikari pushed into her from behind as he forced them onward.

"Apologies, Oracle. It's quite crowded up here. May dearest Bei'ai guide their souls to the Midding."

This seemed to break the Oracle's focus away from Locin, and he pulled his hood up, casting shadows across his face as he nodded. "May they find rest in the light of Sbarga."

Locin kept looking over her shoulder as Voske and Hikari pushed her along until they stood by the door to the temple. Voske pulled it open and warm yellow light washed over them, but Locin kept her eyes fixed on the hooded form. She could tell he was watching her too, though all she could see was the darkness under his hood.

"Come on, darling! I have relics to try out."

She turned to see Voske glaring at Hikari.

"That is, relics to view without touching at all?"

Voske nodded.

Locin cleared her throat, then smiled. "I hear the helm of Jeza's there."

Voske perked up. "The… helm of Jeza, you say?"

Hikari winked at Locin. "The helm? Gods, could you imagine? I hear if you wear that, you can see through the eyes of the goddess herself, catch a glimpse of Sbarga!"

Voske squirmed.

"Gods and Chosen!" Locin slapped the big man on the arm. "You might even be able to taste some delicious Sbarga food. Who knows?"

"Fine!" He broke. "But everything goes back the way it was."

Hikari gave an excited cry as he rushed through the door. Voske was close on his heels, and Locin stopped for only a moment to glance back at the Oracle. He had turned away now, and she could see him by the rail, staring out across the temple grounds. That mystery would have to wait. She ducked inside and let the door slam shut behind her.

Suntara and Erimos still glowed in the night sky, but the divide between them had slowly spread as Erimos fell further and further behind. Within weeks its dusty visage would be obscured by the sun, and a few weeks after that, Suntara would fade from the sky as well as Las outpaced them both. Endring quietly watched the worlds drift apart as the music of the exaltation rose and fell around him.

He stood near the middle of the roof, holding a goblet of wine and wrapped up in his thoughts. On his left the Oracles were gathered near the edge of the roof. He could hear them speaking in hushed tones as they watched the horizon, no doubt awaiting the Ceremony of Rebirth that would accompany the first rays of sunlight. On his right, some of the champions laughed and toasted, barely seeming to remember the somber reason for their gathering. And here he was in between. No longer an Oracle, not quite a Champion.

He let his eyes drift back to the horizon. A pale line seemed to be fighting against the black, and he knew it wouldn't be long. He was eager to leave this place. There was too much happening all at once, and he didn't have time to sit here drinking wine in quiet contemplation.

Soft footsteps on the stone behind him drew his attention, and he turned to see Aurilis. She wore a copper sash over her pure white toga as an homage to Uthando and her skin was a ruddy complexion. Her eyes were a sharp gray despite her age, and her white hair was done up in a simple braid that rose like a crest and spilled down to her shoulders.

"High Oracle," he said with a bow.

She fell in beside him, staring out at the horizon. "It was a beautiful ceremony. Did you see any of it?"

"My presence was required elsewhere." His eyes wandered to the smoldering pyres, and he shoved down his guilt.

"It often seems to be of late. I would think the Oracle of Lost Souls would be more attentive in the wake of such a tragedy."

He nodded, tense. Aurilis was barely disguising her suspicion, and he wondered if that was intentional.

"You've put yourself in a difficult position, Endring."

"Have I?"

"Come now, don't tell me this comes as a surprise. For a cycle you've been telling us about Neveri, claiming he existed, urging the oracles to take the matter seriously. And now these heretics show up and attack the Sacred Quarter."

Endring felt his hackles rise. "So after all these years, you're finally listening?"

"What I'm doing is warning a friend. Very few could have tampered with the Champion's wine."

Friend? He thought. *It's been years since we've even shared a meal.* "And you suspect me?"

"Some of the Oracles do."

He risked a glance toward them, all lined up in their pious procession as they skirted the roof to view each pyre.

"Would you say they're justified in their accusations?"

Endring scoffed. "You think I had some part in this attack? You know me better than that."

"I'd like to think so. But you can't deny you've been acting strangely. You've hardly been seen since the Shattering. You wear gloves, which you know is an affront to the gods. It's concerning."

He flexed his hand, feeling the supple leather. How long could he keep up this charade? Sooner or later he was going to arouse too much suspicion, and he still had too much to accomplish. He needed more help. That was it. Maybe these new champions? Already one had seen him yet hadn't said anything to the temple. Could they be open to the truth?

"Are you even listening?"

"I am."

"The Shattering shattered everyone," Aurilis whispered. "We all have to pick up the pieces and keep moving."

They fell silent and for a moment Endring caught the faint smell of wild orchids drifting on the breeze. He could remember the first time he smelled them. Eight years old, freshly guilded to the order of Bei'ai, and eager to throw himself into the Veil. Would that he could feel that way again, before the heavy years of adulthood had settled over him like a shroud.

"If it helps," Aurilis said, "the situation in the Sacred Quarter will be brought to an end soon."

Endring glanced at her. "Oh?"

"Eprim is planning to retake the Quarter with the help of the city garrison."

"When?"

"Tomorrow."

He'd known this was coming, but he hoped to have more time. He couldn't shake the image of those wings atop Iyanu's Gambit. Whatever Borroka had, she was confident. "I'm not sure that's a good idea."

Aurilis frowned. "Honestly, Endring. Are you trying to make yourself seem guilty?"

He sighed and spoke truthfully, "Those cultists are monsters. I don't care about protecting them, but I do care about innocent lives. I'm afraid Eprim might be treading on a viper's nest."

"He's the Oracle of Jeza. It's his decision."

"Of course it is, but you can overrule him."

"I will not use that power without good cause." She looked warily at him. "Is there good cause?"

What could he say that she would believe? "There are… rumors."

"What kind of rumors?"

"Creatures," he tried. "Great winged beasts."

"Go on."

"I'm not sure," he said, and she shook her head. She wasn't listening. "Nothing like anything we've seen. Beasts of legend."

"Beasts of legend?" She scoffed. "Preposterous."

"Don't be so quick to dismiss this."

"Listen to yourself! No beasts of legend have been seen in two thousand years."

"Times are changing." He clenched his right hand into a tight fist as he watched the pale morning light spread up toward the tree line. "Who knows what shadows might wake from the deep places of the worlds?"

Golden light burst through the sky as the sun rose.

Aurilis stared at him a moment longer with eyes full of accusation, before turning to watch the ceremony.

Endring followed her gaze over the tree line to where a small cloud formed over the jungle, just the barest dark spot that slowly swelled in size. The phoenix. As the flock drew close, their normally fiery feathers looked dull in the morning light. They rushed toward the temple like fleeting shadows. There were hundreds of them, and they circled just overtop the spires of the gods, crying out their sharp calls as they dipped into the fires of exaltation. The flame spread along their wings, and their feathers glowed in the light, until the sky looked like a wheel of fire. They swooped through the smoky trail, forming a whirlwind of ash and flame until Endring could no longer tell where the fires of exaltation ended and the phoenix began. They spiraled up into the sunlight and shed their smoky covering, glowing like embers of Sbarga as the crowd on the rooftop cheered.

"There's so many," Aurilis said, but her voice was still solemn.

Above them the final wisps of smoke curled out of sight on the tails of the phoenix, and the lilting music of the night gave way to a lively tune. The people let out a cheer for the new champions, and a wide circle was quickly marked out for dancing.

Several of the champions leapt into the ring alongside monks and other guests. They were joking and dancing, poorly mostly, and over it all Endring caught one more whiff of wild orchids blooming somewhere in the jungle beyond them. He savored the scent until it faded, and the smell of the smoke choked his senses.

4: Arrajin

The Ceremony of Rebirth lasted well into the afternoon, and when it was done, everyone slipped off to sleep the rest of the day away. At least that's what Locin did. By the next morning, she was still feeling groggy, but she couldn't stop thinking about the Oracle of Bei'ai. She grabbed his satchel and headed out into the common area that connected the Champion's chambers and formed the centerpiece of their wing.

The room had a large round table with eight fancy gilded chairs, a few couches around a hearth - Locin couldn't imagine that was used often - and a few benches on the side wall in front of high arched windows and a view of Arrajin.

The sun was just up, and the others were eating breakfast at the table or lounging around, but Locin was sprawled on a bench with the leather satchel. She hadn't thought much of it, but after seeing him at the exaltation, her interest was piqued. What was an Oracle doing with the cultists, and what had he been bringing them?

She rifled through it. Most of it was a mess of soggy pages. She wished she'd had the foresight to dry them out right away, but how could she know they'd be so intriguing? The only other items were a small pouch of jerky, several quills, a pot of ink, a hefty purse of marks, and a crystal looking glass. She held it up to her eye several times, but as far as she could tell it simply made small things look bigger, and that was it.

She set these random bits aside and carefully started peeling the soaked pages apart, setting them in the sunlight. They were hand written in a rough script. Maybe jotted down in a hurry? Most of them were too washed out to read, but a few words could be deciphered. The word 'Crook' was included several times, as was the phrase, 'Cross over, cross over.' Of course there were a thousand other words around them so faded that it was impossible to make sense of.

She sighed and laid out another page to dry. She was running out of space in her patch of sunlight and her back was starting to hurt from hunching over.

She glanced toward the table where Voske was shoveling in a whole egg and sausage pie. He saw her watching and motioned to a second pie.

"Hungry?"

She wrinkled her nose. He ate like a pig. "Who can have an appetite after watching you?"

"I've been testing out my boon," Voske said defensively. "Makes me rotting hungry."

Locin smirked. She spotted a suitable pillow on the couch and called on her boon, feeling it flood her senses. It was like the air around her was an extension of her body. She felt the softness of the couch, the wood grain of the table, the smooth glass of the window prickling cold against her. She lifted the pillow and hurled it toward Voske. He was midway to his mouth with a fork full of pie when the pillow caught him in the shoulder, and his food splattered onto the table.

"Hey!"

Spark laughed. Locin felt the cadence of it in her cheeks.

"What?" She said. "You're not the only one who's been trying out your boon."

He grumpily snatched the bite off the table and popped it in his mouth, scowling at her the whole time.

She grinned as she looked back at the stack of pages, then sucked in a breath. The next page was near the very bottom of the stack and seemed drier than the rest. The top was still mostly ruined, but in the center of the page, three lines of writing were clearly legible.

> *In the hands of an old soul, a vice to lay them low,*
> *a splintered reed within a red horizon.*

> *In the hands of the flourishing, a trial to lay them low,*
> *a crown upon a frontier yet unbroken.*

*In the hands of a guide, a sight to lift the spirit,
an end to ward away the final fate.*

She leaned over the page, racking her brain to make sense of any of it. Old Souls? Endring was an old soul. Or maybe he thought he was a guide. Certainly he wasn't flourishing. She shook her head. This was pointless.

"What are you doing?"

She looked up with a start and quickly flipped the page over. Voske was standing over her, looking down quizzically.

"Nothing."

"Mmhmm. You were writing poetry weren't you."

She made a face. "Gods no. I hate poetry."

"Looked like poetry to me."

"That's right Voske," she quipped. "I wrote a bunch of poems then dunked them in water."

He folded his arms. "Alright, then what is it?"

She looked back down at the sodden pages, kicking herself. "You know what, you got me. It's poetry."

He frowned like he was trying to decide if she was serious.

Fortunately, at that moment the main door opened and Gillis strolled in. He looked just as awkward and nervous as yesterday - maybe more.

"Ah, good," he said, looking over the room. "You're all awake. We have a busy day ahead of us."

"We have things to do?" Voske asked.

Burz looked up from his place at the table. "Did you think champions just loafed around all day?"

"I didn't mean it like that. I meant planned things."

Gillis smiled. "Well, there are the festivals."

"Festivals?" Locin perked up.

Illeri craned her neck to look at her. "They hold one every time a new champion is chosen."

"Yes, Champion," Gillis said. "Though in light of the *unique* circumstances of your choosing, the Oracles have decided all eight of you should attend each festival in a grand tour. They hope it will give you time to get to know one another."

"So, parties?" Burz said with an edge of disappointment and a wary glance at Voske. "That's what we have planned?"

Voske laughed loudly. "So we will be loafing around."

Zengin sighed. "Where are these festivals to be held?"

"Each one will be held in a city relevant to the god and champion honored. We'll start the tour on Erimos with a festival honoring Iyanu's Champion."

"Yes!" Locin felt Spark's excitement too.

"And when do we leave?" Hikari asked.

"Four days. The High Oracle wants to give time for the champion of Bei'ai to arrive and for the proper preparations to be made. As liaison, I'll be taking you to Arrajin today to procure things you'll need for the tour - clothing, armor and armaments. Things of that nature."

"Shopping?" Locin hopped off her perch and started stuffing the pages back into the damp satchel.

"Yes," Gillis answered.

"Excellent!" Hikari said, brushing at the blue silk chlamys he wore. "These old things are fine, but I must look like a champion!"

Voske groaned. "We don't have to go, right?"

Burz stood, smiling, and Voske gave him a sidelong glance.

"He did say more than clothing," Burz said defensively. "Arms and armaments."

Voske stared blankly and Locin snickered. "Pointy sword. Big hammer. You know, weapons."

It finally sank in and the big man clapped his hands together. "Well, why didn't you say so?"

Gillis laughed, and turned for the door, but then turned back again, as if remembering something. "Ah, one more thing, Champions. You may notice extra guards around the temple. There's been a lot of chaos, extra pilgrims… I mean what with the deaths of the Cham-" he gulped "-other champions, and the state of the temple-"

Zengin rolled his eyes. "Get to it, Gillis."

"Ah yes, sorry. We've had things going missing lately."

Voske glanced at Locin, hardly for a moment, but she caught it. "What kind of things?"

"Offerings from the sanctum. That's actually more common than you would think. Other things too, personal effects from some of the monks, a relic from the reliquary."

"A relic?" He didn't look at her this time, but his tone of voice said it all.

"The sandals of Iyanu, to be specific."

Hikari waved his arms around dramatically, also giving the briefest glance toward Locin. "Don't worry, Gillis, darling. I've no doubt those things will turn up. It's a big temple. Things get misplaced."

Gillis frowned. "I'm not so sure-"

"Come now. There's shopping to be done!"

He wrapped an arm around Gillis' shoulders and led the man back out the main door. Soon the others were all following.

Locin gathered up the Oracle's satchel and ducked into her own room, tossing it safely beside an old trunk before turning back to the common room. But Voske was standing in her doorway.

"Mire and Nyx! You scared me."

"We should talk."

Locin frowned. She felt Spark pressing in close, curious to see how this would go. "I'm not much of a talker."

She moved to go around Voske, but he put his hand against the doorpost, blocking her exit.

"Then I'll talk. I used to be a lot like you, you know."

She stared at the hulking, fair-skinned man. "Small? Curvy?" She kicked out her hip.

"Reckless. I didn't care much what happened tomorrow, as long as I was having fun today."

"Good philosophy! Now let's go before Hikari buys out every piece of cloth at the tailor."

"I mean it!" He said sharply. "This road doesn't go anywhere you want to be."

Spark knew better than to chime in, but Locin could almost sense her struggling to keep from pinching her. Locin ducked under Voske's arm.

"Thanks for the warning, old man. I'll take it to heart."

She didn't give him time to answer. She just headed out the door, jogging to catch up with the others. She had better things to do than listen to someone tell her how to live her life.

Spark drew close, pulling at her.

"Rot off, Spark! I'm nobody's kid, and I don't need advice from a big, dumb ox."

Spark withdrew, and Locin was content to leave it at that.

Weylyn adjusted her pack as she followed the other champions across the temple grounds. She must have looked silly with her pack, bow, and quiver. She knew this because of the looks she had gotten from Gillis, the other champions, and even passers by in the field. She hadn't even considered whether she should take them or if she would need them. For fifty years, this had been her life. Pick up her pack and bow and set out each morning. She was sure if the others could see her personal chambers they would be shocked. She hadn't filled a single drawer or laid a personal item on a table. Everything she owned was in this pack.

She strolled along beside Illeri, conversing pleasantly.

"How long were you a huntress?" Illeri asked, looking her over.

"It would have been fifty-one years next season."

"That's a long time. I was only a wayfarer for eighteen, and I don't even know what to do with myself now. It's like my whole life has been upended."

Weylyn had lived long enough to have her life upended more than once. This certainly wasn't the worst one, but it might have been the most dramatic. "I do miss it," she said.

"The hunting?"

"The stillness, perhaps. I've barely set foot in a city in thirty years. Certainly not one as big as Arrajin."

"I've been in plenty of cities, but I always liked being in the cold dark best."

Weylyn glanced at the blue sky overhead. "Somewhere I've never been."

"Never?"

She shook her head. "I was born and guilded in the Shinoam Valley. I've never had the opportunity to leave Las. What's it like?"

"Sbarga." Illeri stared wistfully at the sky. "It's quiet, nothing but stars in every direction, and the golden pylats."

"I'd never seen a Pylat before flying here. I always imagined they looked like birds."

Illeri chuckled. "More like butterflies."

Weylyn smiled. "You know, I'm glad I was chosen. I think I'm looking forward to all the new things I can see and do."

Illeri bit her lip, looking unsure.

"You aren't?"

"I miss the old things. And what if I'm not any good at the new ones?"

"People usually aren't. But we learn."

She nodded, though she hardly seemed reassured.

"Ah!" Hikari yelled as he came strolling up beside them. "*This* is more like it!"

They were nearing the edge of the temple grounds now, and apparently news had spread that the champions were coming into the trade quarter. The banks of the river were lined with people, swarming out over the path and sitting on the low stone wall that lined the bridge into town.

"Stay close!" Gillis called, and his voice was nearly drowned out by the roar of the crowd.

A path had been cleared through the sea of people, held back by Jeza monks that lined the road on either side. The champions made their way leisurely toward the bridge to the beat of drums and the blast of horns.

"Is it always like this?" Weylyn asked, looking toward Hikari.

He laughed. "Would that it could be. Exciting isn't it?"

She looked over the crowd, feeling suddenly very ridiculous in her tattered hunting garb, but the people didn't seem to care. She heard someone shout her name, and she turned to see a woman wearing the cobalt blue of Strah and waving excitedly.

Ahead, Voske scooped Locin up on one arm, waving with his free hand as she blew kisses to the crowd, and they erupted in wild shouts and applause.

They were at the Arrtris now, a wide brown river that separated the Gods' Mount from the city.

"Gillis," Weylyn called forward. "Where are we going?"

Gillis fell in beside her, speaking so they all could hear. "The Lion Agora," he answered. "It's the oldest and most prestigious in Arrajin, and it's been cleared for our visit today. I thought we would stop at the Desitan Sash first."

"Perfect!" Hikari said. "It's been years since I've been to the Sash. Does Tailor Revee still weave there?"

"She does. Though I'm not sure if she'll be there today."

"Gods, I hope so. That woman could make a nag look like a warhorse."

Weylyn looked at her own stained clothing. She was sure if she weren't a Champion, the Desitan Sash is the kind of place she'd be asked to leave.

Hikari leaned over. "Don't be nervous about a new look, darling. The Sash is the best tailor shop on Las, and there's only a few better on Suntara."

Weylyn raised an eyebrow. "Why would I be worried?"

"Oh come now. You may have lived alone in the woods for a while, but you're still a woman."

Weylyn smiled. "I dare say I'm like no woman you've known."

Hikari laughed. "I don't doubt it, but do you mean to tell me you had nothing you thought was beautiful? Pretty even? No?"

"I had a wooden hair pin. It kept my hair from my eyes, but I thought it looked nice, so I strung some owl feathers on it."

"There you go!" Hikari answered.

"I wove the string out of yak hair."

"Getting weird, but still fine."

Weylyn stepped onto the bridge, but as soon as her foot hit the stone, she felt unsettled. She looked around. The crowd was still cheering, and the other champions marched on, but she couldn't shake the strange feeling that pulled at her. "Fashion isn't what concerns me, Hikari. I've had little need for it."

"Then what does concern you? You seem troubled."

She shook her head. "I'm not sure." She felt on edge, the way she had when her old boon sensed a predator near her camp. Everything in her said, 'be alert!'

They rounded the top of the stone arch, giving her a better view of the city. On the far side, hundreds of children stood on the gently sloped rooftops throwing flower petals that drifted down to the rocky road below and banners stretched across the street, welcoming the chosen of the gods.

She scanned the crowd. In the shadows of the waterfront, hidden behind the brightly adorned devotees, a few mangy faces could be seen, rubbed with soot, scarred and gaunt. They stared out through peep holes in the throng.

Hikari must have followed her gaze. "Do they have you worried?"

She shook her head. "I'm not sure. Who are they?"

"The unguilded," came a voice from behind them. They turned to see Zengin looking at Weylyn intensely.

"The unguilded?" Weylyn said with surprise. "There were unguilded in Karanth. They were good folk, hard working."

"That's in smaller villages. Here they're considered unclean. They scrub the sewers and stock the furnaces. You'll eventually learn not to see them."

She looked back at the sorrowful faces. "Why don't they leave? Make a bow and head into the wilds?"

Zengin smirked. "Not everyone has your particular skill set. No. They help maintain the town and in return they're allowed to scratch out a living, provided they keep out of sight."

"That's terrible."

He shrugged. "No one said it's desirable. It simply is."

They were nearly across the bridge now, and the unsettled feeling still followed her, tugging at her mind. After all the time she spent in the wilderness, she'd mastered her old boon. She could sense every beast around her, where they were, what species, how large, what sex. It was a sixth sense she had honed to a fine point, and this new boon felt similar, but more elusive.

They stepped onto the far shore, and suddenly the light over the crowd grew dim as a small sun formed over the champions where Hikari held his hands high.

"We only get one first impression," he called cheerfully. "And by Desita, we might as well make it a good one!"

Locin stretched out her arms, and the flower petals all around the street stirred and rose into the air, swirling around the small sun and casting long shadows over the crowd. She nodded to Hikari, and they both flicked their wrists, sending an explosion of light and flower petals through the air. The crowd erupted in cheers and began surging toward the champions and it was all the Jeza monks could do to hold them back.

Weylyn only half watched the display, looking around for any swords or drawn bows. The unsettled feeling had started to fade, but something told her not to let it, to push in and follow where it led. She turned back toward the bridge and leaned into the feeling. Her eyes started to burn, and she blinked. Suddenly the crowd was gone, and she was staring into mist. It rolled off the Arrtris as its surface roiled and churned, and heavy drops of rain slapped the stones around her.

Something in the mist rumbled, not like thunder, but like the low growl of a beast, and she became aware that something was lying at her feet at the end of the bridge. She looked down to see her own body. A giant hole was torn through her chest, and the ground was red with her blood.

"Weylyn?"

Hikari's hand on her shoulder pulled her back, and suddenly the light of early morning pierced the clouds of her vision and the cries of the crowd replaced the rain.

"Are you alright, darling?"

She turned to see the others, still trying to make headway through the adoring mob. She nodded. "Yes," though she wasn't sure that was true.

"Well then, come on! The agora is just here."

5: The Lion Agora

The Lion Agora was a sprawling plaza filled with every kind of shop imaginable. There was a cobbler, a carpenter, a forge, and a dozen more, and in the center a massive lion statue stood with its mouth open as if it were roaring over the city.

The Desitan Sash was the agora's tailor, a cheerful shop with wide glass windows and a sign with delicately scrawled script. Inside, the champions were quickly led to two rooms, the men to one and the women to another, where several attendants were eager to assist. They were shown drawings and designs and piles and piles of fabric until Illeri's head swam.

She was currently staring into a full length mirror draped in a silky fabric. Her shoulders and arms were exposed, and her fair skin was smooth and flawless. She'd never seen her skin like this, without a single blemish or freckle and shimmering slightly in the light. She leaned into the mirror, staring hard at her reflection. The dark circles under her eyes were gone. And was her hair really that straight, or was that an illusion too? It was hard to tell.

"You can change this much?" She glanced at the attendant, a young woman with perfect blonde curls.

"That and more, Champion. We have the finest enchanted fabric in all Talamh. We can make you smaller, taller, change your eye color or hair color."

Illeri looked at the five garments draped over the young woman's arm. Part of her was enjoying this, if she was honest.

The Desitan Sash was nothing short of decadent. The private area had three grand mirrors set in front of low platforms, a long velvet couch with a swooping wooden frame, and walls covered in designs and artwork. Around the edges of the room, wooden crosses were draped with luxurious garments of all types, and a central table had been set out with cakes and a pitcher of wine.

The curtain that divided this room from the main shop split and Weylyn and Locin made their way in, followed by two more attendants. Weylyn had a few pieces laid over the tattered sleeve of her hunter's garb, and Locin was carrying a massive pile of fabric that nearly covered her whole face. Behind her, the attendant had an equally absurd pile.

"This place is amazing!" Locin said, dropping her pile on the couch and rifling through it. "Can you guys believe we get to just buy whatever we want? Gods! It's good to be a Champion."

Weylyn set her own garments down beside Locin's mound. "Are you purchasing all those?"

"Not *just* these," Locin answered. "But it's a good start. Nyx it, I'm gonna look good!"

"I'm certain you will, darling," called a distinctive male voice.

Illeri paled and glanced toward the curtain where Hikari was just poking his head inside.

"Everyone decent?"

"Hikari?" Weylyn sounded as surprised to see him as Illeri was. "Don't you four have your own dressing area?"

"Oh, Weylyn, come now," he said, quickly slipping inside. "You can't leave me out there with those cretins! No sense of style. Not one of them. I at least had hopes for Zengin, but no, he just wants everything dark and drab and…" His eyes fell on Illeri and he brightened at the sight. "And that's more like it. You look breathtaking, darling."

She blushed and looked down, brushing her hair back behind her ear.

"Ah but perhaps something in green," he said, and before Weylyn could object he scurried over to Illeri's attendant and snatched a silky green chiton off her arm. "Just look at the pleats along this sleeve, such beautiful lines, you must try it."

Illeri took the garment from him and cast a nervous glance around the room. The other women didn't seem overly bothered by Hikari's presence. Maybe she was being too self-conscious.

"Come on then," he said, motioning toward the garment. "Let's see it."

She held the green fabric awkwardly up to her neck. As it touched her skin her reflection changed, adjusting to the new enchantment. Her straight hair grew a bit wavy, and her eyes shifted color from deep brown to bright green.

"They're… green?" She looked at the smiling attendant. "My eyes."

"Do you like it?" Hikari asked, studying the garment.

"I… I don't know."

Locin hopped up on the platform beside Illeri wearing a short pink toga that had streaks of bright teal running from the hem to the waist.

"It's nice," she said, giving a quick glance at the garment before locking her eyes on the mirror in front of her. She gave a low whistle as she ran her hands along her curves. "What do you think, Hikari? Green eyes suit her?"

"Well, they certainly match the chlamys." He stared at her eyes thoughtfully, and she dropped her gaze. "Weren't they brown before?"

"Yes."

"I'd go green," Locin said, looking over her own brown eyes in the mirror. "Brown is so boring."

"Oh, darling," Hikari strolled forward and took Locin's chin in his hand, studying her eyes. "No eyes are boring! Brown eyes can look like warm fall leaves, or smooth, velvet chocolate. I've seen eyes like the bark of a weathered oak, eyes like a pair of shining hazelnuts, or sparkling tourmaline!"

Locin stared wide eyed as he held her chin. "Huh. Which are mine?"

He looked deeply in her eyes. "Deep, velvet chocolate with flecks of sunlight."

She smiled as he let her chin go, brushing at her cheek lightly. "I see why the ladies love you." She fanned at her cheeks with her hands as Hikari hopped back down, smiling.

Locin cleared her throat as she tore her gaze away and pointed to Illeri. "Enough about my eyes. What about her?"

Hikari stepped up on the platform behind Illeri, studying her eyes in the mirror. She sucked in her breath as he reached around and took the chlamys from her, moving it aside until the old illusion returned with the sleek, straight hair and her own brown eyes. He narrowed his gaze, drinking in their color, and then smiled, brushing a hand gently along her cheek.

"A golden sunset shimmering on amber glass."

The whole room stayed silent as Illeri's cheeks flushed a shade darker.

Hikari hopped down. "We should find something similar, but without the eye color change." He snapped his finger at one of the attendants, and Hikari and the attendant disappeared back through the curtain.

"Well," Weylyn said as she slipped on a pale blue toga. "He's charming."

"No kidding," Locin breathed out as she hopped down and grabbed another garment, slipping it on. "Gods, he's dreamy. Too old for me, though. Too young for Weylyn."

She smirked. "Very thoughtful, Locin, but he's not my type."

She waved Weylyn off. "He's every girl's type."

Illeri stepped down and grabbed a glass of water, taking a long sip until Locin glanced her way.

"He's about your age."

She spluttered, spraying water over the floor.

Locin laughed. "Nyx it. He really got to you, didn't he?"

"No," Illeri said defensively. She set down her glass and looked around the room. There was nowhere to go. She wanted to crawl into her toga like a turtle shell and hide.

"It's no wonder he's got the reputation he does," Locin continued, hopping back up to the mirror. The attendant stepped onto the platform to help her situate the toga. When they got it in place, her waist seemed narrower, and her breasts were definitely larger. "Yes! More like this, please."

Weylyn raised an eyebrow. "What reputation?"

"You know. With *the ladies*." She winked. "Gods, he's probably got women throwing themselves at him on every world."

Illeri felt angry. Jealous? Gods, she couldn't be jealous. She wasn't interested in Hikari. Sure he was charming, but that was it. Nothing more.

"Okay, darling!" He came bursting back through the curtain with a similar chiton, this time in a deep blue. He handed it to Illeri. "Go on then. I won't look." He turned his back to her and waited.

Illeri hesitated for a moment as Weylyn and Locin watched her, and then she turned to face the wall and slipped out of her toga, slipping on the new garment. It fit perfectly, draping over her skin, and the blue color was a good match for her complexion.

"Okay."

Hikari turned and smiled at her. It was everything she could do to hold his gaze and not blush like a hopeless guildling at her childhood crush.

"Much better," he said. "Take a look."

He held an arm out toward one of the mirrors, and she stepped up. She had her hair, straight but not too sleek, and her brown eyes. Her skin was still a bit too flawless, though. "It feels like such a lie doesn't it?"

"Not a lie!" Locin said. "An *illusion*. And a good one." She was turning to the side now, checking out her profile.

"Everyone lies," Hikari said as he looked Illeri over. "The trick is to make it look believable. Too much change and everyone's going to know it's fake, but just a pinch here and a tuck there, and there's the idea in the back of everyone's mind that it could be natural."

"Maybe natural is better," she whispered.

"Of course, of course." He propped his chin on his fist as his eyes slid down her form. "Can we do anything about those hips?"

The warmth in Illeri's chest quickly dissipated. "What's wrong with my hips?"

He fussed with the folds of fabric at the top of her thigh. "They're just a bit wide for the cut of this chlamys."

She gathered the folds of her garment and stepped off the platform, setting her back against the wall. "I think I'm done being examined." It came out more coldly than she intended.

Hikari frowned. "What's wrong, darling? Did I upset you?"

Locin jumped down off her platform and stared at Hikari. "Gods. I had hope for you, Hikari; I really did. But you're as dumb as the rest of them."

"Rest of who?"

"Men."

Weylyn grabbed Hikari gently by the shoulders and spun him around, walking him to the door.

"You can't mean to send me away? It's misery over there, darling. All they'll talk about is troop movements, and how sturdy the temple is."

Weylyn stopped by the curtain. "Hikari, I've lived alone in the woods my whole life, and *I* know better."

"Better than what?" He pleaded. "Is this about her hips? I only meant they were a little wide for the silhouette of that garment. Personally, I love a woman with curves."

"Out!" Weylyn gave him a shove through the curtain and then turned back to face the other two girls. "Well, that should be more peaceful."

Locin laughed. "Based on his reputation, I'm assuming he never takes his women clothes shopping."

Illeri was grateful he was gone. She felt flustered, and angry, and she climbed back up on the platform, but all she could see were her hips. She pulled the chiton off roughly and threw it on the floor. "I don't want that one."

After a couple excruciating hours at the tailor, Voske was relieved to move on to the smithy. He stared up at the impressive forge near the back corner. He was standing a decent ways off, and still sweat beaded on his brow. There was only one smithy in Govere, and it was nothing like this. It was a rundown little place. The smith wasn't highly skilled in plying his boon, but the forge was hot enough and the work, mostly horseshoes and picks, got done all the same. And the locals respected him. He worked hard, like a proper Goveren. Everyone around here had soft hands and smooth skin, like they didn't know what hard work was. Voske had been just like them once.

The forge was the centerpiece of the shop. It was an immense stone cut from a single block, and it had to weigh several tons. It hung from massive iron chains, and the roar of the flame inside could be felt in the floor below. The front of the shop was ringed with practical goods, horseshoes and picks, but also sickles, brackets and hinges. All of these were sturdy and well-crafted, but couldn't compare to the private stock displayed behind the counter. It caught Voske's eye as he strolled over. Weapons of polished gold hung on the rear wall, radiant and adorned with all manner of jewels. The swords, axes and spears glimmered like the crowns of kings. These were the weapons of champions.

Voske let his eyes trace the form of the armaments, each one more astounding than the last. If one blade had a hilt of pure gold then the next had diamonds set into the pommel. The most outrageous example was a large spear in the very center. The tip looked like it was formed out of a single diamond that transitioned into a pure gold socket, the shaft was wrapped with brilliant red wyvern leather and the butt of the spear was a golden spike, embedded with rubies.

"Champion," came a voice from beside him.

He glanced to see an old man standing next to him, covered in liver spots. He was skinnier than Voske imagined a smith might be, but his soot stained leather apron was a dead giveaway.

"You must be the smith," Voske said, extending a hand.

The old man gripped it with firm, well calloused fingers. Voske smiled. Here was someone who knew hard work.

"Atrius," the smith answered, holding up his right hand. A black hammer and anvil was charred into his palm, the seal of the smith's guild. "It's my privilege to serve you, Champion."

Voske held up his own palm. "Voske will do nicely."

"The Champion of Jeza? I should have guessed!"

Voske placed his hands on his hips and smiled broadly. "The one and only!"

Atrius nodded to the weapons behind the counter. "Those are the weapons of your predecessors. They've been forged here for the last thousand years. That spear you're admiring belonged to your forebear, Alavinsian."

"I'd almost be afraid to fight with something so…" He motioned to the spear, at a loss for words.

"Exquisite?" Atrius guessed. "Not to worry, Champion. To my knowledge he never had to wield it in battle."

Voske raised an eyebrow. "No causes worth fighting for?"

"It's a blessing to live in an age of peace."

Voske's eyes alighted on an axe that looked out of place among the rest. It had a double head made of worn bronze that folded down in the shape of wings, the haft was covered in plain brown leather and the bronze head was still stained with age-old blood. He'd never seen anything so magnificent in all his life. He made his way over, nearly in a trance, and picked it up off the rack.

"You have a fine eye." The smith hurried over and held out his hands for the axe. "That's Straznik Bram."

Voske's eyes went wide. "The axe of Skard?" He carefully handed it to the smith who hung it back in its place.

"It's not as lavish as its newer counterparts," Atrius said, almost apologetically, "but it's priceless for its history."

"How old is it?"

"Almost two thousand years," Atrius answered. "The haft has been replaced a few dozen times, but the bit has never dulled. It's been in this foundry for over twenty generations."

Voske let his hand brush the tip of the blade lightly, and it drew blood. "I bet it saw some battles."

"Many." The smith brushed his hands down along his apron and motioned toward the sidewall where several suits of armor were on display. "Weapons will come soon enough, champion. First, armor! You'll be expected to wear the ceremonial armor of Jeza, of course. There's some traits that are required, the engraved sword upon the chest, the crimson color and the oak wreath that encircles the helmet, but the style is left to your discretion."

Voske clapped his hands together. He'd never even considered trying on a suit of armor and the prospect sounded exciting. "Where do we start?"

Atrius motioned for him to follow to the counter. Burz was already standing there, looking at the armor with a trained eye, and Voske fell in beside him, placing a hand over his mouth and trying to figure out what Burz was so intent on.

"Wait here," the smith said, before ducking behind the counter.

Voske looked at Burz, then back at the armor again. Just like the weapons, they were all intricately made, studded with pearls and rubies and plated with precious metals. One had an intricate leaf design that made it look like a forest of woven gold and silver, another had the faces of lions roaring from the shoulders.

"What do you think?" Voske asked, nodding to the suits and passing Burz a sidelong glance.

"They're fine costumes," Burz answered.

Voske looked back at the armor more critically. "Costumes?"

Burz pointed at the leafy armor, "The breastplate is too long, you'd never be able to bend over."

"I'm sure they can modify that."

"They'd have to."

The voice of the smith called their attention. "Modify what?"

Voske looked back to see him holding a large book. He set it atop the counter and motioned Voske to join him.

"These are the armors of every champion of Jeza that came before you. They've been cataloged and illustrated. Of course, we can design something different for you, but this might serve as an inspiration."

He flipped the book open to the back pages, to where the more recent work was featured.

Voske immediately recognized the leafy armor from the display and thoughtfully tapped his finger against the page. "Breastplate's too long on this one," he said. "I wouldn't be able to bend over."

"I remember this one," the smith crooned. "I crafted it myself. Not the most functional, granted, but the artistry was exquisite."

"What good is artistry if it gets me killed?"

The smith made a double-take. "As I understand it, the last champions were poisoned. It was no fault of my armor."

"Of course, but what if I got into a fight?"

"Forgive me, Champion, but It's been two hundred years since any of these armors have had a taste of battle."

"But they could."

Atrius shrugged. "Very well, any of them could be modified to suit your wishes."

"Good." Voske flipped the page backward to reveal the showy costume with the lion faces. He cleared his throat and glanced over at Burz, who was watching from a distance. "This seems… different. What do you think, Burz?"

Burz stepped closer and scoffed at the illustration. "Tell me you're not considering that."

"I didn't say I was. I just said it was different."

"Good, because those shoulders are ghastly."

Voske looked back at the illustration. "They look angry. It's intimidating."

"It's not about intimidation," Burz said with a sigh. "Think about how heavy those would be."

Voske straightened up and broadened his shoulders. "I'm the champion of Jeza. They could be ten times that heavy, and I'd be fine."

"Of course," Burz said. "It's your choice. Like you said, you're the champion."

Voske looked back down at the shoulders then back up at Atrius with a musing expression. "Then again, they might make it harder to see."

Atrius shrugged. "If it's a concern I could lower them down to shoulder height."

"Bah," Voske waved him off and kept flipping back through the pages. The next few were women's armors, then an open chested armor that Burz absolutely hated, then a big bellied breastplate that made the champion look more like a piece of pottery.

Voske sighed in exasperation. This wasn't exactly what he'd expected. When he thought of champions, he didn't imagine smooth-handed layabouts decked in useless gold. It was a soft metal. He at least knew that. It wouldn't be any good in a battle. When did champions become something to parade around? They used to be heroes.

He looked up at the wall again, looking over the glittering weapons. He didn't want to be paraded around Talamh to curry favor for the temple. He wanted to be knee deep in battle, or lifting whole bridges that collapsed. He wanted to live the old stories.

Like Skard.

His eyes darted back to Straznik Bram. It was a sturdy weapon, made for calloused hands. And it had to have a match in this rotting book. He flipped all the way to the front, to the first page, and pointed a rough finger at the illustration.

"This!"

It was a simple design, bronze scales and pauldrons that folded down from the shoulders forming wings over the arms.

Atrius looked mortified.

"What? I want this."

"B-but that's Skard's armor, champion."

"Rotting right it is. Make it red if you have to. Add the symbols of Jeza. But this is what I want."

Atrius stared like his eyes were stuck, and he'd forgotten how to blink. Voske slammed the book shut and pushed it toward him. He took it, and rushed off toward the far side of the forge.

"Bold," Burz said.

Voske shrugged. "It's practical, useful."

"The people may hate you for it," Burz said coolly. "If you take such legendary armor as your own, they may see it as you putting yourself equal with Skard."

Voske tensed. "And why not? We're both champions. We both have the same boon, the same strength of Jeza in our blood!"

Burz laughed. "You really think we're anything like the heroes of old?"

"Don't you?"

"We're just people, Voske. People who were given a gift, and gods willing we can use it for the betterment of the realm."

Voske pounded a fist bitterly on the counter. "They were people too, Burz. They just weren't afraid to be more."

Burz tensed, his voice going low and stiff. "I'm not afraid, Voske."

Voske realized the other champions were all looking their way now. He unclenched his fist and breathed out. "The gods can choose us, but only we can make ourselves champions."

Atrius returned, carrying a measuring stick. "I need your measurements for the armor, Champion. If you'll follow me."

Voske followed him toward the back of the forge, looking one last time at Straznik Bram.

Locin ran her fingers over rows of daggers. She'd held several, each perfectly weighted and sharp as Nyx. This smith knew his stuff. But she kept coming back to the same one, a curved blade, a little long for a dagger, with a simple leather hilt. The blade was silver on the outside with a jagged sharp edge, and the inside half of the blade was a deep blue like cobalt. She picked it up and smiled.

"I wish it had a mate."

She felt a brush against her right arm. Spark liked this one too.

She spun it around in her hand a few times, flipping it in and out, and then she tucked it surreptitiously in her belt.

"We are here to shop, darling."

She glanced at Hikari who stood nearby, watching her.

"You can just purchase it."

"Less fun that way." She winked, and he rolled his eyes. "What about you? Any weapons for the champion of Desita?"

He smiled broadly. "A fine blade. Atrius helped me design it."

Burz laughed. "What are you going to do with a blade, player?"

"Well, fight of course. If the need should arise. Every hero needs an iconic weapon, and I assure you, mine is that."

Locin pointed to the gaudy golden things behind the counter. "Tell me it doesn't look like those."

Hikari scowled. "It has some gold, some flare, but I assure you it is quite fashionable and functional."

Burz strolled over. "All you're going to do with a sword is hurt yourself."

Hikari looked indignant. "I'll have you know, I played more than a few swordsmen on stage."

"That's hardly the same thing."

"We even had training, an old soldier. He helped us learn."

Burz picked up a saber and deftly flipped it around, extending the hilt toward Hikari. He took it confidently.

"Show me what you've got, player."

Hikari turned the sword in his hand a few times to get the feel of it and then slashed at the air ahead of him. "It's so light. Gods, what I would have given to have a sword like this in the *Battle of Fear's Height*."

Burz grabbed a sooty rag from the side of the forge. "You mean in the play, *Battle of Fear's Height*."

"Of course. The actual battle happened five hundred years ago."

"On the slopes of Wursinglass on Erimos. I'm aware."

Hikari smiled, "You're a student of history?"

"I was a soldier. It was required reading."

Hikari flipped his sword toward the rag in Burz' hand. "Planning on doing some cleaning?"

Burz walked just in front of Hikari, twirling the rag into a knot. "Not really."

Hikari took a step back. "Well don't tell me you're planning on snapping me with that."

"Afraid you'll get dirty?"

"Not really, but this toga cost seven thousand marks."

Burz let the rag go slack. "What?"

Hikari was bouncing from toe to toe now, brandishing his sword like a player. "It's fine, darling. Just grab a sword if you really want to teach me something so badly."

Burz shook his head. "Too dangerous."

"Afraid you don't have enough control?"

"Afraid you don't. Now try and hit me."

Hikari hesitated for a moment and pursed his lips. "Shouldn't you be wearing armor?"

Burz smiled. "I'll let you know when I need it."

"Your choice." Hikari lunged forward as he spoke and swiped at Burz with the flat of his sword.

All the sword found was air and Burz quickly snapped the rag back at him, landing a sooty black mark right in the middle of Hikari's chest.

Hikari looked down at the black smudge and then up with a sheepish grin. "That's me dead then?"

"It is."

"This hardly seems fair though. If I really were trying I could hit you."

"Afraid you'll hurt me?"

"Of course. The swords we used on stage were blunt as a rolling pin."

Burz squinted an eye as he appraised Hikari head to toe. "Don't worry." He answered. "If I get hit, you deserved to hit me."

"And what would I tell your wife and children?"

"Tell them I died at the hands of a sword wielding thespian in a seven thousand mark toga."

Hikari frowned. "You say that like it's a bad thing."

Burz shook his head. "I only meant to say it's a thing. Nothing more, nothing less."

Locin laughed. "Now this is entertaining."

Hikari brandished his sword once more. "Alright then. Ready?"

Burz nodded.

He swung again, and again he was met with a sooty slap from the rag, this time on his stomach. Another swing brought about a snap to his shoulder, then one on his right arm.

He paused his attack and dusted himself off, leaving a tell-tale streak of black smeared down his sleeve.

"Hopefully it washes out," Burz said.

Hikari pushed his tongue into his cheek, studying Burz for a moment. "That's not what's bothering me."

"Oh?"

"What's bothering me is how a forty-year old man with a limp manages to stay so spry."

Burz frowned back at Hikari. "What makes you say I'm forty?"

Hikari bit his lip. "You're what? Older?"

"Gods, no. Why would I be older?"

"You just look… mature."

"I'm thirty-three. And I don't limp."

"My mistake."

"I have two young boys," he said. "They age you quick enough. Have I proved my point?"

Hikari relaxed, dropping the sword to his side. "What was the point, again?"

Locin took the sword from Hikari and hung it back in its place. "That you shouldn't have a sword."

Hikari looked wounded. "Well, certainly it's different on stage. We had to exaggerate every motion." He swung his arm in rounded arcs. "For the people in the back, of course. But you could teach me!" He locked eyes on Burz.

"No."

"Oh come now, one champion to another! I won't call you old ever again."

"No."

Locin laughed as she looked back out over the agora. The sun was high, and the monks of Jeza that had accompanied them were lazily sitting around on stone benches.

The voice of Gillis brought her gaze back. "Well, I believe that's it."

All the champions had wandered back over, though Zengin was suspiciously missing.

"That's it?" Locin asked.

Gillis nodded. "Our shopping. The agora is set to open back up in a few minutes, and we are due back at the temple."

"But the day is young!" She protested. "You're really gonna bring the champions to the trade quarter and only show them the Lion? There's so much more to see."

Gillis gulped down air and stared at her nervously. "Such as?"

She smirked. "The Pig."

She felt a pinch from Spark. Sure, she had enemies there, but not too many, and there was something she needed.

Gillis went white as a ghost. "You can't be serious."

"What's the Pig?" Weylyn asked.

"The Squealing Pig," Gillis said. "It's a… um… a rather disreputable place."

"My kind of place!" Locin said. "Besides, there's plenty of reputable shops between here and there. So who's in?"

"I'm up for it, darling."

"Me too," Voske said.

Soon the others had agreed to come along as well, and Gillis seemed to be on the verge of a panic attack.

"We don't have enough monks!" He protested. "And… and I haven't cleared the streets. It's not safe." He looked from champion to champion. When he spoke again, his voice was fraught with worry. "Where is the champion of Metnadur?"

Voske clapped the young man on the shoulder. "We're champions, Gillis! We'll be fine!"

"Has anyone seen him?" Gillis continued.

Locin smirked as she skipped out toward the waiting crowds. "Come on, this way!"

6: The Squealing Pig

The Squealing Pig. Locin knew it well. It was *her* corner of the Trade Quarter. Meaning, not *hers* specifically, but her kind of people. Home to thieves and assassins and vagabonds of all kinds. This was where you came for the things you couldn't buy anywhere else. This was home. The buildings were much more worn than the Lion Agora, dingy gray things with back rooms you could get into if you knew the right words - and she knew the right words.

By this point, they'd lost most of the other Champions, and only Voske and Hikari were with her, strolling along looking out of their element. She gave Voske credit. He seemed more at home than Hikari. The latter looked on with wide eyes at the dirty streets and shady characters strolling by. But it wasn't wide-eyed fear. It was more like wonder. The wonder of a little kid excited for something new.

He stuck his nose in the air and breathed in, wrinkling it against the stench. "What *is* that smell?"

"Smells like a bit of everything," Voske replied. "Waste, rot, death."

"It's the monkeys," Locin said.

The streets were full of them, skittering under foot, hanging from buildings, trying to grab food from carts.

"The rich neighborhoods hire people to keep them away," Locin said.

"Truly?" Hikari smiled. "Their whole job is to - what? Chase monkeys around?"

She shrugged. "They chase them, trap them, clean up any food to stop them coming back. So they all end up here." She stretched her arms out wide, motioning to the Pig. "In the areas where no one can afford to hire monkey chasers."

"You know a lot about Arrajin," Voske said. "You from here?"

"I'm from everywhere. Mostly Suntara though. That was probably the closest place I had to home."

Voske laughed. "*You* have a home on Suntara? What is it? A shack on the beach?"

"A bit bigger than that."

"Fine. A cottage on the beach?"

She pulled her finger across her lips, sealing them shut, then smiled and flicked her hair back as she turned her eyes ahead.

A monkey was wandering toward them now, greedy little black eyes searching to see if they had any food. Locin hated the monkeys. They were a constant reminder that rich people took everything for granted, foisting all their problems on the poor. The monkey took two little leaps forward, reaching dirty paws out toward her leg, and she gave it a swift kick. It scurried off with a yelp.

Hikari gasped. "Poor thing!"

"Yeah, right." Locin said. "Those things are nothing but pests."

"So you say," he said as he knelt down. A few of the monkeys had taken notice at the yelp and were watching them warily. "Come on now, we aren't *all* so cruel."

"I wouldn't," Locin warned. It was just like a smoothy to come to the Pig and act like he knew better.

Hikari ignored her warning and held a hand out to the nearest one, making a clicking noise with his tongue.

"Come here, little monkey. Come on. I won't hurt you, darling."

The monkey took a couple nervous steps toward him, sniffing at his hands, a hopeful gleam in his eye, but he quickly realized there was no food, and his expression soured.

"There we go. Not so bad as the lady says, are you?"

Suddenly, the rotten thing leapt through the air, screeching like a banshee, and attached itself to Hikari's shoulder. He screamed and started flailing about as the monkey scurried across his back, reaching in his toga with greedy paws to see what it could find.

"Get it off!" Hikari yelled with desperation in his voice.

Locin was laughing so hard she could barely speak, and she felt Spark's laughter hot in her cheeks. "I warned you!"

"Gods and Chosen!"

Voske was laughing too, a deep rolling laugh. He reached one hand over and grabbed the monkey by the scruff of its neck, then threw it across the plaza into the dust. It stood up, screeching at them with a fist in the air like an angry housewife before turning tail and disappearing into the crowd.

"I told you. They're horrid, dirty monsters."

Hikari was busily brushing at his hair and adjusting his toga, but he still looked disheveled and entirely out of sorts.

"Well," he said, "I won't be doing that again!"

Voske was still laughing heartily, but he gave Hikari a friendly clap on the back as they started walking again.

"We have nothing like that on Suntara," Hikari continued.

"Sure you do," Locin said. "You just don't go to those parts of the city. Ever been to Nordev?"

Hikari brightened. "Beautiful city. They have the most amazing wall that runs along the northern edge, formed out of pearl. When the moonlight hits it, it's absolutely breathtaking."

Locin scowled. "Exactly my point. If you ever ventured to the South docks, you'd know they're entirely infested with rats. Rotting things are a plague down there."

Hikari's smile faded and he looked a bit sheepish. "I had no idea."

"Yeah, I know."

"We didn't have anything like that in Govere," Voske said. "But then, not much can live out there in the desert."

"I imagine not," Hikari said. He straightened himself up and turned back to the Pig with wide eyes once more. "Well, I for one have learned an important lesson."

"What's that?" Locin asked.

"Always trust your tour guide." He gave her a little bow and a charming smile. "So, where to, my lady?"

Locin turned her gaze back to the agora. In front of them was a tavern, ugly thing painted a putrid shade of green. It stuck out of the ground in a dome shape like a half buried turtle shell.

"See that?" She said. "That's the Copper Kettle. Agrid runs the place. After the first few drinks, she cuts 'em with water. Figures you'll be too drunk to notice."

"You learned this how?" Voske asked.

"Hey, I can hold my liquor. But she knows better than to cut mine anymore."

She pointed to a shop beside the tavern with some garments displayed in the window and a set of rickety double doors that were propped open with big rocks.

"And that's the Silk River. You can find stuff there you can't get in the Lion Agora."

"Oh?" Voske said sarcastically. "Like what? Clothes that are stitched wrong? Maybe a toga that smells like monkeys?"

"Nice try." Locin rolled her eyes at Voske. "More like clothes with hidden pockets, or that make you less… conspicuous."

"Great." Voske frowned. "A whole shop for thieves."

"Not just thieves. Other people use that stuff. Assassins for one."

"You know some assassins?" Hikari could barely contain his excitement. "That's fascinating!"

"How is that fascinating?" Voske exclaimed. "How is it not just horrifying?"

"Relax." She smirked. "The assassin's guild would never sanction a contract on a Champion, at least that's what they tell me."

Both men stopped and exchanged worried glances.

"She's kidding, darling. In poor taste, considering recent events, but a joke nonetheless."

Voske just grunted disapprovingly.

"Keep up," she called without slowing down.

She could see her destination ahead, a singularly shabby building. The stone walls had multiple cracks running up the surface, and vines were sprouting out of the fissures, climbing up the outside like it was a natural cave. While most of the buildings in Arrajin had sweeping beauty, or at least some interesting character, this one was just an ugly square of gray. Its arched red door had faded to a rusty brown and a sign painted in the window simply read, 'Curiosities'.

"Ilum's place." She stopped in front of the door and turned to face them.

"Listen, let me do the talking in here. This is not your world." She shot a glance toward Hikari with his smooth chest and high bearing. He stuck out like a torch in a mudder's den.

"Don't look at me, darling. I learned my lesson with the monkey, remember?"

She turned her eyes on Voske. "Same for you. Keep your head down and don't draw attention."

Voske crossed his arms over his chest. "And what do they sell here? Secret weapons you can hide easily?"

"Anyone can hide a weapon easily. That just takes practice."

He eyed her questioningly.

"Don't touch anything, and don't cause trouble. You may be Champions, but these people aren't going to care. Actually, it's best we don't tell them."

Hikari laughed. "That may be difficult. Surely they'll recognize me, darling. I mean, I am Hikari after all."

"Look around. Do these seem like the kind of people who go to fancy plays?"

He let his eyes wander the sparse crowd of bedraggled misfits. "You may have a point."

She bit her lip and looked him up and down. "You do look too fancy though." She grabbed some mud from beside the door and wiped the grime across his face.

"Ack!" He jerked backward, looking aghast. "Is that really necessary?"

"From now on your name is Pit, and your name is Scar," she glanced at Voske. "Got it?

"Why does he get to be Scar?" Hikari protested.

"He looks like a Scar, and you look like…" her voice faded. He still looked way too clean. "Just keep quiet and follow me, okay?"

They both nodded.

Locin took a breath and turned, pushing the door open. The inside was filled with a variety of goods, from books and instruments to games and toys, a few pieces of furniture that looked like they had seen better days. There wasn't much Ilum wouldn't try to sell, and usually for much more than it was worth. Locin counted three guards, though two of them were milling about and attempting to look like shoppers. The third, a man easily Voske's match in size, was standing near the door with his arms crossed and a serious expression on his face. He had long hair, a flat nose, and half his face was covered by a deep black tattoo.

And Ilum. As soon as he heard them enter, he'd made his way out from the back room and was standing by the counter on the left side of the shop, frowning deeply at Locin.

"Look who's back."

She smiled, throwing her arms out wide. "Ilum!"

"Don't give me that, Locin. What do you want?"

She glanced back at Voske and Hikari. "Why don't you boys do some shopping." She lowered her voice. "Remember, lay low."

Hikari was already headed to the back wall where several lutes were hung on rusty hooks.

Voske just grunted and turned to eye the large man with the tattoo warily.

Locin sighed as she watched them, then made her way over to the counter.

Ilum was scowling. "I'm not in the mood for your games, girl."

"Hey, don't forget who it was that got you that lot of original De'rans. Hm?"

"That favor's long spent. You want something from me, you're going to need to do more."

She crossed her arms. "Okay. Turns out I'm not here for a favor. Or information. I'm here to shop."

"Since when do you shop?"

A horribly off tune strumming sounded, and Locin glanced to the back wall where Hikari held a dusty lute that was missing a string.

"And what in Nyx is this you brought in my shop? Since when do you hang out with nobs?" He let his eyes drift to Voske, and he grunted.

Voske was standing face to face with the large man. Both had their arms crossed over their chests and were exchanging deep scowls.

Locin pulled a coin purse out of her pocket and dropped it on the counter.

Ilum arched an eyebrow. "What do you want?"

"A piece I saw when I was here last. Old. Looked like a small statue."

"I have a lot of small statues."

She leaned over the counter, speaking as low as she could while still being heard. "I didn't give it much thought last time, so I don't remember exactly, but it was like a man... with feathers."

His eyebrow stayed up as he stared at her.

"Nyx it, Ilum. Can we just go look in the back?"

He grunted, then shuffled to the door and waited as she hopped the counter. She gave one last look back to see Hikari had moved on to a row of trinkets, and Voske was now pretending to shop, but he kept his eyes on the tattooed man.

She ducked through the door, and it softly closed behind her.

The back room was where the real goods were, walls of priceless pottery and paintings, the glint of jewelry and endless oddities. There was even one life size statue of an old naked man that she thought was supposed to be Metnadur. It looked older than dust, cracked and worn down.

She headed to a shelf of smaller figurines and glanced over them. As soon as she had seen the markings in the Sacred Quarter, she'd remembered this piece, but where was it?

"Mire and Nyx! I know it was here. Rotting thing."

But it wasn't. It wasn't anywhere. She knew she hadn't imagined it. But maybe Ilum had sold it. "Gods! Why can I never catch a break?"

She felt Spark's presence tugging her, and she wandered in the direction of the motion. Spark led her down a row of antiques to a shelf near the back wall. There, haphazardly laying in a heap of other trinkets, she saw it. A small figure of a feathered man, large wings wrapped around his body, and a horned head bowed. This was it. She could see it plain as day in her mind. A horned man with wings scrawled across the white marble of an old wall. *Neveri*, she thought. That was the word written below the image.

She grabbed up the small figure and clutched it with a smile. "Yes!"

"Not just yet." Ilum said. "We haven't discussed price."

"I left twenty marks on the counter. That's more than enough."

"Not for this."

She was kicking herself. In her enthusiasm she'd made a novice mistake. She let him know how much she wanted it.

"It's not even worth twenty, and you know it."

He was smirking now. "Forty marks."

"I only brought twenty."

He held his hand out, nodding to the figure clutched in her hands. "Then I'll take that. And you can come back when you have forty."

"You rotting pool of-"

A loud crash from the main shop interrupted them, and they both looked toward the door.

"Oh no," Locin muttered.

And then they heard yelling. Angry yelling.

Ilum rushed for the door, and Locin quickly tucked the figure in a discreet pocket. Then she was close on his heels.

As she burst into the main shop, she heard Hikari yelling. "Well, that's not what your mother said!" He was dodging away from the two smaller guards, and the light in the shop was going crazy, flaring around their eyes, then dropping to pitch black. A huge shelf of merchandise was knocked over on the ground near the front, and Voske was tussling with the large tattooed man.

"Gods!" She yelled. "I told you not to touch anything!"

"Sorry, darling," Hikari yelled as he danced away from another blow. "Things seem to have gone sideways."

Just then, Voske lifted the large man and threw him straight over a shelf into the back wall to the sound of scattering, out of tune lutes.

For a moment everything was still, and all eyes were on Voske. Then the large man scraped himself out of the rubble, and all three men drew swords.

"Ah, that changes things," Hikari said. "Time to exit stage left."

He ducked for the door.

Ilum turned to Locin and reached a grubby hand out to grab her, but she easily dodged him and flipped herself over the counter.

"Let's go, old man!"

Voske turned at her voice, and took two big strides to the door. He barreled through it, sending faded red splinters cascading outward across the Pig.

Locin and Hikari were right on his heels. She could hear Ilum and his men yelling profanities after them, but they didn't slow down until they were a safe distance away. They slowed to a walk, all out of breath, but Hikari was beaming.

"That was exhilarating!"

"Gods!" Locin said. "All you had to do was shop quietly for a few minutes."

"He provoked me," Voske said in a sulking tone.

"Well, I did shop, darling." Hikari produced a green, gilded deck of cards. "Perhaps we can play later?"

Locin shook her head. Hikari was right. It was exhilarating. She glanced back one last time to confirm no one was following, then she started to laugh.

"Did you see the look on Ilum's face? Gods, that was probably worth it."

Hikari was laughing now too. "It was certainly the most fun I've had in a long time."

Voske grabbed the cards from Hikari. "I warn you, I'm pretty good."

"Is that so?" Hikari said. "Well, never let it be said that the magnificent Hikari shied away from a challenge!"

"Count me in," Locin said, and she snatched the cards away from Voske. She lifted the deck and looked them over. Looked like fancy nob cards. "What I'd like to know is when you had time to pay for these." Hikari smiled sheepishly and Locin placed her hand against her chest, feigning shock. "Don't tell me you *stole* them."

"Much to my shame, darling. In my defense, it was difficult to find my coin purse with a ruffian swinging a candlestick at my head."

Locin clicked her tongue disapprovingly. "My, my. What would the champion of justice have to say?"

"He'd say you'll pay for them tonight," Voske answered. "When I skunk you both."

Locin smirked as she felt Spark's tap on her hand. "You can try," she said, tossing the deck back to Hikari. "But I have to warn you, I'm feeling lucky today. Like everything is coming up gryphs."

7: Creations and Contrivances

Illeri peered around at the bustling plaza she found herself in. She was well beyond the Lion Agora, and far from the empty streets that had been cleared for the Champions. Here, the endless ebb and flow of the crowd jostled her along an intricate stone street. She had somehow managed to lose the group of Champions, the monks of Jeza, and even Gillis by this point, and panic was setting in. She tried taking in a deep breath to calm herself, but a large man who smelled like rotten meat bumped into her, and she gagged as she nearly lost her balance.

She turned around, thinking she could backtrack to the Lion Agora, but everything behind her looked just as unfamiliar. How was it she could navigate by the stars and follow an unseen path through the vast expanse of the cold dark, but she was lost here?

She stood on her tiptoes and took note of the buildings. They all looked the same, cold white stone, hanging wooden signs, brightly colored doors. But then one caught her eye. It was tucked away in a corner of the plaza, out of the flow of travel. It had a rundown gray facade, and the whole thing looked tilted, like a strong wind might knock it over.

She decided to use it as a landmark and made her way closer. Its wooden sign read *Yzod's Creations and Contrivances*, and an inventor's Spark burned behind the letters so that they pulsed green to blue and back again. The door, once a bold blue, was worn and scraped down to the original brown wood, its previous color only deduced by the chips of paint still clinging hopelessly to its marred surface. She tried peering in the windows, but they were thick with dust, and so many baubles and oddities were piled inside that her view was utterly obscured by the murky stacks.

She was about to turn back and try to orient herself when a flash of metal caught her eye in the dusty window. It looked like an antique oculus stuffed in the corner of a high shelf. She'd never seen one so old before, but she couldn't guess its condition through the dark glass. She wanted a closer look. Gods knew her feet were already sore from walking, and maybe a quick break would help her clear her head.

As she ducked inside, a music box beside the door started scratching out a melancholy tune. She could see the faint green glow of an inventor's spark from somewhere within the rusted drum, and several tines of the comb were missing, leaving stark gaps in the melody until the light flickered off and the drum ground to a halt.

"Hello?"

She looked around the cluttered room, which seemed more like a workshop than a store. Inventions and contraptions were piled on every surface or hanging by ropes from the ceiling. Most were lifeless and even the few that blinked with the green glow of their spark looked unfinished.

A commotion caught her attention, and she looked to the side of the room where something scurried across the counter, a small dark shape. She carefully made her way over, scanning the shelves of paper and scrap metal as she approached. In a flash, the thing leapt off the counter and lifted into the air above her.

She let out a quick yelp before her eyes fixed on it. It was a little wyvern with white scales that glittered turquoise at the tips. It flicked its tail and spun once in the air before crashing down and spitting a tiny puff of fire out toward her that fizzled as soon as it left its mouth. Illeri stayed still, watching as it righted itself, shaking its head.

"A wyvern?" She moved closer and held out a cautious hand. "It's okay, little guy. I won't hurt you."

Again it tried to take flight, and again it spun wildly and crashed down on the counter with a whimper. This time, Illeri noticed its left leg and wing were composed of wire, leather and small metal pins that vanished in the mangled skin of its side. She leaned closer, observing the same eerie green glow seeping out from the cracks in the mechanism. It flapped the constructed wing a bit, with little effect and with great difficulty, and then gave up the efforts and made a cooing sound.

She reached out, gently brushing its side, and the wyvern nuzzled its face into the palm of her hand gratefully.

"What happened to you? Poor thing."

"Ryshi," came a gruff voice.

She startled and spun around. There was a man standing behind her. He had short brown hair that was starting to gray and a face full of stubble. His eyes - one blue and one violet - were dark as if he didn't know what sleep was, and he wore a strange open wire gauntlet on his hand that glowed green against his palm.

"His name," he repeated, but his eyes were still focused on the gauntlet as he poked it with a thin metal rod. "It's Ryshi."

He twisted the rod into the glowing center of the gauntlet and a zap sounded with a bright flash of light.

"Nyx it!" He yelled as he ripped the gauntlet off his hand. He let it clang to the floor as the light faded, and he rubbed his injured palm.

"Ryshi?" Illeri turned back to the wyvern.

Its head perked up at its name and it gave another soft coo.

"What happened to him?"

"Who?" The man picked the gauntlet back off the floor and stared at the inner workings with a look of mild disgust. She caught sight of his right palm, charred with the image of two fingers alight with fire. The seal of an inventor.

Illeri scowled. "Ryshi."

The man set the gauntlet aside and looked up. When he spotted Ryshi sulking, he made a clicking noise with his tongue, and the wyvern stumbled across the counter toward him, half dragging the damaged leg. He picked Ryshi up, and tightened a screw on one part of the leg, then another. He spun a gear around until it clicked into place, then he set Ryshi back on the counter. The wyvern cautiously lifted the leg and set it down twice, then walked about in a little circle. Confident the leg was working properly, he took off at a run and plunged off the other side of the counter to the sound of a loud thump and a scattering of bolts.

"That was cruel." Illeri crossed her arms and glared at the man.

He scowled back at her. "Fixing his leg was cruel?"

"Why make him come to you? He could barely walk."

"And you clearly know what's best for him."

"I know you could have easily walked to him."

He sighed and set down his tools, giving her his full attention at last. "Trappers."

She stared at him, wondering if she was supposed to understand.

"You asked what happened to him. Trappers. They catch the wyvern in the jungle to sell as pets. If the trap injures the creature, they leave it to die."

"So you didn't…"

The man laughed. "What? What did you think? I ripped off his leg and wing so I could invent something?"

"No, I just-" Illeri felt suddenly ashamed and she dropped her gaze. "I don't know what I thought. It just looks painful."

"Less painful than having no leg."

She looked up at him. "How did he end up here? With you, I mean."

"I found him on the edge of the jungle. Trappers had thrown him out and left him for dead. I've seen it a dozen times."

"Have you saved others?"

"Nope."

She looked toward a slight skittering noise that told her where Ryshi was, and a few seconds later he poked his head around the bottom of the counter.

"Then why did you save him?"

"Because he was crawling after a big, fat cicada. Most of them lay around cooing until they die. But not him. He decided he was hungry. He comes to me when he needs help. That's our deal. Because without that fighting spirit, he'd give up and die - even with the new leg."

"Can he fly?"

"Not yet. I figured out the leg, but that blasted wing…" he sighed. "I'll get it. I just need more time."

The man turned his focus back on the gauntlet, opening it up and pulling out gears, as if Illeri were no longer there. She glanced around the workshop again, her eyes fixing on a metal orb on the counter nearby. It was opened up, and she could see a tangled mass of wires and gears.

"So… you're an inventor?"

He shot a glance at her that made her feel terribly stupid - which it was supposed to, she was certain. She cleared her throat and winced.

"I mean, obviously you are. I've just never actually met one. I've been in shops that sold inventions, but most inventors aren't actually there."

He stared at her blankly as she grew more uncomfortable. "Did you come here to shop or talk?" He turned around, grabbed his gauntlet and pulled out another gear, turning it over in his hands.

She turned to survey the shop, picking up a dull silver orb that blinked at her touch with a purple light. She felt silly pretending to shop, and she wasn't sure this was any better than the noisome crowd outside. She set the orb down and turned back to where he was still pulling gears out of his gauntlet and laying them in order on the counter in front of him.

"Actually, I'm lost."

"And you wandered into my shop? Lucky me."

"I was with… some people. And we got separated. I just wondered if you could tell me how to get back to the temple."

Maybe he was too busy with his invention, or he didn't know how to get to the temple. Whatever the reason, he didn't answer.

She heard a rustle and looked to see Ryshi peeking at her from behind a stack of messy books. He tilted his head like he was studying her.

She held a hand out toward him. "Feeling better?"

Ryshi wandered over awkwardly as he stomped down and lifted the mechanical leg. He climbed into her palm, purring like a kitten, and she lifted him close, studying the leg and wing. They were incredible at any scale, but so small and intricate. She was sure she had never seen any invention so sophisticated, and to find it not for sale, but helping a wounded wyvern was a marvel in itself.

"Is he always so grumpy?" She whispered.

Ryshi lifted his good wing, batting playfully at her thumb.

She smiled. "At least you're nice enough." She set him back down and brushed at her toga. "I gotta go. I still have to find my way home."

She noticed Ryshi followed her as she made her way back toward the door, but a glint of old brass caught her eye, and she turned to see the oculus. She'd almost forgotten about it.

She made her way to the shelf, reaching on her tiptoes until she got ahold of it. As she pulled it down, she knocked over a pile of spare parts that scattered across the counter and crashed to the floor.

Ryshi started at the noise and disappeared underneath the shelves as Illeri winced.

The inventor came around the corner with a confused expression. "You're still here?"

She held the oculus up sheepishly. "You said I could shop."

He frowned.

"I've just never seen one this old," she said quickly. "I mean, I've used the newer ones, but this…" she locked her eyes on it. The brass was worn and tarnished, and the old silver mirrors were cloudy, but the intricacy of its design was unlike anything she had ever seen. The frame was etched with constellations and set with emeralds that could just be made out under the dust. "It's beautiful."

"You know what it is?" The inventor said curiously.

"Sure." She looked back up at him. "Wayfarer's use them to navigate the stars."

"You're one of 'em?" He glanced at her right hand.

"My boon?" She hesitated. But how dangerous could he be? She slowly lifted her hand revealing Kidsandin's sigil.

He barely reacted. "Interesting."

"I was a wayfarer. Before."

"Excellent!" He smiled for the first time since she had come in, and she noted how it emphasized the different colors of his eyes. He turned and started rifling through some papers.

"It is? I mean, it was, but-"

"Here." He held a piece of parchment out to her and she took it, looking it over.

"Star charts?" She used her thumb to measure the distance between two stars. "Current too. These are hard to come by." She looked up at him.

"You can read them."

"Of course, but-"

He laughed. "Most people don't even know what they are. Follow me." He made his way toward a curtained doorway at the back of the room, and she followed cautiously. "I've been talking to the local wayfarer guild for years now, and I have yet to find anyone who will help me."

"Help with what?" She asked as she scurried after him. "All the Wayfarers I know would be glad to help anyone who-"

She passed through the curtained door and stopped dead. They were in a long workshop that was filled with some kind of small chariot, but it didn't look like any chariot she had ever seen.

Instead of wooden sky beams it had curved metallic rods, and instead of a wooden frame, the hull was made from thin plates of aged bronze, now mostly concealed behind a foam green patina.

"A chariot?" She made her way forward and brushed her hand against the smooth frame. At the center, a complex orb shaped device sat atop a raised pedestal and hummed softly with the green light of his spark. It looked like the one she had seen opened up inside.

"A solo chariot," the man said. "Designed to sail the heavens without the aid of a wayfarer. Of course, one would need to sufficiently understand pathfinding to use it."

"H-How?" She stammered. "How does it work?"

"Ah, it doesn't. Not quite. It's close. That's why I've been trying to get a wayfarer to help. With your past in-"

"Yes!"

"That was easy."

"No one else would help you?" She glanced back at him.

He shrugged. "Most said I was crazy. *Say* I'm crazy. But I suspect they were concerned about what might result if it worked."

Illeri stopped and turned to face him. "What's that?"

"The end of the need for Wayfarers. It wouldn't be the first time an invention made a boon obsolete. As I understand it, the gods have always altered the boon to accommodate. But they didn't seem too excited regardless."

She pulled her hand back from the smooth bronze, taking in a slow breath. The thought of no one ever being able to feel the heavens around them as they sank into the radiant field gave her pause. She ached to feel it again herself, just one more time.

"Of course, it's entirely your decision." He started to laugh.

"What's so funny?"

"Gods, I just realized I almost tossed a champion out of my shop! Kisandin forgive me!"

He kept laughing. She still didn't feel much like a champion, but she understood the sentiment.

"Well? What do you say, Champion?"

Illeri slowly let her eyes wander the marvelous contraption. He eventually would do this with or without her, and one prototype was a long way from an obsolete boon.

"I'll help you."

"Ha! Excellent." He walked over to her and held up his right hand, displaying the seal of his inventor's boon. "Name's Yzod."

"Illeri."

He climbed onto the deck of the chariot and held his hand down to her. "Welcome aboard, Illeri."

She smiled as she took his hand and he helped her up onto the chariot. She felt excitement again for the first time since she'd become a champion. This was something she knew, something she loved, and here in this dusty inventor's shop, she felt like she belonged.

8: Honey and Fangs

Zengin hated the industrial quarter. He could ignore the pious holy men of the Sacred Quarter whose clean robes stank of debauchery, and even the slimy merchants of the Trade Quarter that would sell you their own children without batting an eye. But the Industrial Quarter would not be ignored. Every street clamored with the boons of the workmen and the stench of their trade. He pulled a cloth over his face as they passed three large dye vats, the acrid smell burning his lungs.

"How much further?" He shot a glance at the dirty urchin staying a step or two ahead.

"Right up here. Not far!" He was the kind of naive soul that would probably find himself dead in a gutter someday. Sooner rather than later if Uthando had any mercy to spare.

A crumpled message in his pocket held Zengin's interest. It wasn't long or important sounding. *Sighted at the flop house on Aelswine. Purple boots. Glowing whip. Sets in Northmost window at midday. Third story. Never misses.*

It was just the sort of correspondence he expected from a clam eye, the disreputable snitches that nobody trusted and everybody knew. Every city had them if you knew where to look. Enough marks in the right pockets had secured him the watchful gaze of every clam eye in Arrajin, and the results had been faster than he had hoped.

He pulled his tattered hood lower and glanced at the surrounding buildings. The structures here were tall and packed tightly against one another. Their white painted walls had faded to soot gray, and their polished windows glowed in the midday sun.

"At the end of the row," the youngster said. "That one with the broken windows." He pointed to a building. It looked like the rest, except the windows had no glass, and the front door was marked with a black X.

"Good," Zengin muttered. "That's all I need. Now go."

He started to brush past when the urchin's voice stopped him.

"Aren't you forgetting somethin'?" The boy held out his hand and scowled. "Half when we arrived."

Zengin squinted. Maybe there was hope for this one yet. He reached into his coin purse and let a few marks drop into the boy's hand. "Keep the extra, and your mouth shut."

The boy nodded and then scurried away down the street.

The building wasn't exactly intimidating, but it wasn't welcoming either. A large wasp nest hung in the corner of the entryway, and easily a hundred of the wretched things were clustered on the papery husk. He edged carefully through the far side of the door, tucking the cloth back in his pocket, and he crept up the stairs. The corridor opened into room after vacant room where the rickety wooden bed frames had been stripped of their mattresses and the paint was peeling off the walls. The stench in here was no better than the vats, and he fought the urge to draw the cloth back out. But he'd been in worse places than this.

He gained the third story in short order and turned down a long hallway that ran in a straight line North to South. At the far end he could see the clear silhouette of a man, standing in front of a bright Northern window. There was a large bird beside him, perched on the sill. It looked like a raven, but it was the size of an eagle. The man shifted, and Zengin caught the glint of a whip curled at his hip.

He pressed against the wall and made his way carefully down the hallway, stepping over some rubble. As he made his way, he realized Sammel was talking. The bird sat still as if listening intently.

"I did warn you," Sammel said in a hushed tone. "Desperation is a powerful motivator. But as long as she doesn't know, we have time."

Zengin stopped, content to listen as he hugged the wall.

"I'm not worried about the outcome, but I'd hate to see you-"

The bird suddenly locked its dark eyes on Zengin, and it made a loud caw. The sound was unnatural.

Sammel stopped speaking at once and turned, letting his hand fall to his whip. He locked eyes on Zengin. "Go, now!"

The bird spread its wings in response and flew off, leaving the two men alone. Sammel lifted the whip from his belt and held the coils loose in his hand.

Zengin felt his legs tense, and he stepped away from the wall, staring toward the golden cord warily. "I paid a small fortune to find you, Sammel. Perhaps we can talk first?"

Sammel cocked his head to the side as he squinted into the shadow. "Who told you I was here?"

"Does it matter? Anyone who wants to keep a low profile should know better than to dress so luridly."

"What do you want?"

Zengin reached a hand to his side where a long dagger was tucked into his belt. He didn't want this to come to a fight, but things seldom went the way he wanted. "I felt we never finished our conversation."

"True," Sammel answered. "Though after we spoke I had a violent headache for the rest of the day. I'd rather not repeat that."

Zengin kept stepping closer as he drew on his boon. "To my understanding, that only happens when you resist. Perhaps you could just tell me what I need to know."

Sammel's arm seemed to relax, and Zengin came to a stop beside the open door of an empty room. There was a smell of urine emanating from somewhere inside.

"I'd rather not," Sammel answered, and he winced as he said it.

"See there? You only hurt yourself. Besides, we all do things we don't want to do. Isn't that much of life? We do what is necessary." He looked at Sammel pointedly. "We kill when it's necessary."

"True."

"I'm certain you weren't the only one to think it necessary. There are others in the temple who feel like you did. Traitors you might call them." The honey of Metnadur warmed his tongue. "I'd like to know who they are. Who do you speak with in the temple, Sammel?"

Sammel stiffened. "I know that the leader of the radicals in the Sacred Quarter is named Borroka. She's very dangerous from what I understand." He barely winced as he resisted.

"I didn't ask for the leader of the radicals, I asked for your contact inside the temple."

Sammel shook his head, and a sprinkle of sweat cascaded to the grimy floor. "And she's not the only danger. It's the beasts she controls."

Zengin hesitated. "What kind of beasts?"

"I honestly don't know."

"And how does she control them?"

"With the bracer of Neveri."

There was that name again. *Neveri.* He had exhausted his library, finding only a few mentions in dark histories of this supposed god from the time before the Shattering. "The cult worship this Neveri?"

"Yes."

Zengin shook his head. "Wild beasts. A mysterious god. This all sounds like a child's story. Why should I believe you?"

"I don't suspect you will, but when the Jeza monks return from the Sacred Quarter, you'll know the truth."

"There are no Jeza monks in the Sacred Quarter." If they'd gone without him knowing, he would be impressed with the discreteness of the temple.

"Of course there are. They marched there today alongside the city garrison. They think they'll be chasing off a band of rabble armed with sticks. That's not true."

Zengin looked Sammel over. He sounded mad, but his eyes were earnest, and the eyes never lied. "You're forthright. I admire that."

"You're not."

"No." Zengin shifted his weight as Sammel watched him warily, but there was a curiosity in Sammel's eyes as he shifted to match. "Why tell me about the beasts? What do you gain?"

"My friend would prefer to see the monks unharmed."

Zengin glanced out the window behind Sammel. "Your friend in the temple?" He heard Sammel take a slow step toward him, and he looked back. "That's close enough."

Sammel froze in place, his muscles tensing as he tried to resist. The coils of the whip hung slack in his tight grip. "What do you hope to accomplish, Champion?"

"What do you mean?"

"It's clear you haven't told the temple about me, otherwise you wouldn't be here alone. It's also clear you know I killed the champions, though I confess I don't know how you know. What do you gain by not turning me in?"

Zengin raised an eyebrow. He didn't trust the temple. He didn't trust anyone, and the situation was exacerbated by the knowledge that one or more of the monks was a traitor. Sammel couldn't have killed the champions alone.

"My reasons are my own," he answered flatly. "Now to the matter at hand. Who is your friend at the temple?"

Sammel furrowed his brow. "Neveri."

Zengin focused his boon, pouring the weight of Metnadur behind every syllable until his lips burned like fire. "Who is your friend at the temple?"

Sammel visibly shook and his breath came in short pants. "Or… Or… No one."

"I should have given you more credit when we first met. Your resolve is strong. Who is it, Sammel? A name!"

Sammel cried out and slumped against the wall and Zengin took a step closer.

"Tell me now!"

Sammel's face was a deep red, and he held a hand to the side of his head. "Forks. Crisscross. Needles. The Champion of Neveri. The champion of Neveri!"

"His name!"

"He wants the Crook," he moved his hand to his forehead, clawing at his skin.

Zengin started to take another step forward when he saw Sammel's whip hand flick outward. He leapt to the side, safely out of range.

Clever.

The tip of the whip swung just to his left, but instead of the snap he was expecting, it rocked the hallway with a tremendous blast. Zengin was launched from his feet, spiraling backward into the foul smelling room as the walls of the hallway splintered into deadly shards of wood. He slammed into the far wall as a cloud of dust choked the air.

So that's what the relic did.

He could hear Sammel already scrambling to his feet. Clearly he had been feigning his distress. It was a good show, and Zengin had let the power of his new boon go to his head. He gritted his teeth and pushed himself off the floor. Nothing felt broken, but there was a throbbing pain in his right side and the room was still spinning.

He summoned his boon again. "You don't want to turn that corner!"

He heard Sammel stop moving, giving him just enough time to orient himself. The room wasn't as empty as he'd first thought. There was a grimy looking bed against the front wall that had been tucked just out of his view.

He sprinted to it and pushed it upright, forming a makeshift shield, then he scurried back to the other side of the doorway, where the shadows were deepest, and snatched the dagger from his belt, steadying his breath until he barely made a noise.

He could hear Sammel start moving again and seconds later his whip lashed through the opening, cracking another shockwave that sent the bed somersaulting into the far wall.

Zengin could feel his ears pop like he was in a chariot falling out of the cold dark, but he stayed low to the ground and kept his breath even. He'd only get one chance at this.

As Sammel rounded the corner into the room, looking toward the bed, Zengin slowly stood. He crouched to lunge when he saw a dark form rush through the shattered window. The bird had returned, but this time it was bigger. *Much* bigger. Its raven body had been replaced by the powerful form of a panther and its wings had grown to match. It tucked its wings into its sides as it rushed through the gap, then dug its feral claws into the floor, tearing deep gouges through the hardwood as it slid to a stop between the two men.

Sammel spun around, whip at the ready.

Zengin locked eyes with the creature, and watched with wonder as the wide pupils of a bird slowly narrowed into the haunting slits of a cat. He had only seconds to act. He chose a target and threw his dagger straight toward Sammel's chest.

The beast leapt to block the blow and the dagger sliced into its front leg, drawing out a pained yowl.

Sammel hesitated, and Zengin lunged for the door. He sprinted down the hallway as another shockwave rocked the building. He nearly stumbled on the first step, but he kept his footing and bounded down to the ground floor. His only choice was to run.

As he fled through the street, the pain in his side slowed him down, and he kept a wary eye on the sky above. Whatever that creature was, it was fiercely loyal to Sammel. That made it dangerous. It seemed to be able to change form at will, a detail he'd never heard in any story or legend, and he had read many.

When he reached the edge of the Industrial Quarter he slowed to a brisk walk and tried to gather his thoughts. Sammel might be insane, but the more Zengin spoke to him the more he was beginning to believe he was telling the truth, and the implications were frightful. What would Talamh do if there really was a ninth god? One thing was certain, if he was going to go up against the followers of such a god then he would need allies. Everyone at the temple was suspect as far as he was concerned. Any of them could be working with Sammel. Any of them could have murdered the Champions.

Any but those who arrived after their deaths.

He shook the thought from his head. They were buffoons. He'd sooner do this alone. But still, as he wound his way back toward the Gods' Mount, it became increasingly clear. The other champions might be the only ones he could trust. Gods willing, they weren't as stupid as they seemed.

9: Legends Laid Bare

Voske stared at the gilded green cards in his hand. Nothing left but a three and a lion. A miserable draw. Again.

"Come on, big guy," Locin taunted.

They had come straight back to the Champions wing after a long day of shopping and settled in with Hikari's new deck, just as promised. A decision Voske had quickly come to regret. He swore this game wasn't half as difficult on Erimos.

He sat at the large round table in the center of the Champion's common room with Locin, Hikari, and Weylyn. Across from him, Locin was smirking, her remaining cards pressed close against her chest. She laughed, and it sent her curls bouncing.

"You enjoying this?"

"We all are, darling." Hikari took a sip of water from a crystal goblet.

Burz had been smart enough to stay out of the game. He was sitting with Hadris on a couch at the side of the room and had only been keeping loose tabs, but as the end drew near, they were both paying closer attention.

"You're stalling," Burz said. He looked obnoxiously smug from his place *not* in the game.

"I am not. I'm considering my options."

"You've only got one left." Locin pointed to his undergarment. The only stitch of clothing he still wore.

Everyone laughed. Everyone but Voske. "You're bad people, all of you. Rotting awful."

By this point in the game, Hikari had lost one sandal and a belt. Weylyn had lost her leather jerkin and two boots, and Locin was suspiciously still fully clothed. Voske was trying to remember which one of these monsters had suggested they play this way. *Locin,* he thought. *It was Locin.*

"You know," Voske said. "We could have just played for marks."

Hikari smirked. "It would have been far less interesting."

"Yeah," Locin agreed. "We're Champions. We don't need marks. So why not raise the stakes?"

"Great," Voske said, and then in a mocking tone, "We don't need money, let's play for our dignity instead."

Weylyn was smiling. "He's definitely stalling."

"Gods. Fine!" He threw the three on the pile. In the end, it made no difference.

"I would have gone with the other one." Locin suppressed another chuckle, and soon the whole room was laughing again.

"I'm glad you all find such amusement in my suffering. Really. It's heartwarming."

Hikari was next, he took far too long drawing a card, as if he could somehow affect the draw by delaying it, then he took an equally dramatic pause to shuffle his cards around in his hands, one after the other, back and forth.

"Just play a card!" Voske snapped.

"Alright, darling. No need to be testy." He carefully placed a seven on top of the pile.

Nothing was going to help Voske now. Locin had her eyes locked on him with confidence. She knew it was over, and so did he. But she didn't just know. She *knew.*

"You're cheating," he said, glaring at her. "I don't know how yet, but I know you're cheating."

She was tapping her fingers on the table now, her head tilted like she was listening. "Maybe I'm just better at Bait the Lion than you are."

"No. That's not it. We choose a different game, and you would still win."

"Because I'm good at games."

"Because you're a rotting cheater."

She leaned back, lifting her cards up in front of her face so he could just see her eyes peering at him over the top. "Speaking of *baiting the lion.*" She slapped a gryph down on the pile.

The blow was inevitable, but he felt it all the same. "I told you you're cheating."

"What?" Her feigned surprise was hollow. "Do *you* have the Lion, Voske?"

He stood up, glancing around. "Hikari? Weylyn? You see it right? She's cheating!"

Hikari shrugged. "It's rather convenient the way she keeps winning, but I'm afraid you have no proof."

Weylyn was smirking at his misfortune. She had already set her cards down and had her arms crossed. They all knew it was over.

"Gods and Chosen!" Voske boomed.

But no one in the room would help him. Even Burz was staring him down with a mocking smile, and Hadris had her face buried in Burz' shoulder in a silent laugh.

"Fine. That's it. She cheats, and you all let her. I'll remember this." He laid the Lion down on the pile, grabbing his undergarment at the waist. "I hate you all."

The door burst open, and Voske thanked the gods under his breath.

"I won't even ask what you were about to do," said the droll voice of Zengin.

Voske moved his hands away, leaving his last remaining garment mercifully in place, and turned to face Zengin.

He wore a serious expression as he quickly shut the door. He looked disheveled, from the dusty grime that clung to his sandals to the wood shavings that were sprinkled across his cloak and in his hair.

"Where have you been?" Voske asked.

"Not here."

"Yes. Thank you. We did notice that."

Zengin trudged into the room, glancing around. Everyone's eyes were on him now. "I was looking into a matter."

"And do you plan to tell us about it, darling?" Hikari had laid his cards down and was leaning over the back of his chair to see Zengin.

"I do." He gave another glance at Voske where he stood with his arms crossed over his bare chest. "Assuming you aren't too busy."

"We're not," Voske answered quickly, and he sank back into his chair.

Zengin made his way to an empty chair at the front of the room and sat down with a wince.

Voske caught a look from Locin, and she shrugged. They'd never seen Zengin like this. As far as Voske knew, Zengin was just a quiet, somewhat priggish aristocrat, but here he was looking like he'd been in a brawl.

"Are you alright?" Hikari asked.

Zengin sighed deeply. "As loath as I am to include you all in any endeavor of consequence, I've been weighing my other options and found that there are none. Things are at play in this city that require swift and decisive action and you-" he looked at Voske with a disgruntled sneer "-are the *only* option I have at the moment."

Voske leaned back, furrowing his brow. Maybe he should have felt insulted, but with Zengin looking like he'd just lost a fight with a lumber mill, he figured he'd give him a pass.

"What's at play?" Burz asked from his place on the couch. "Are you talking about the Sacred Quarter?"

"That and more." Zengin leaned forward, his eyes sharp with meaning. "Tell me, have you heard of Neveri?"

Stark silence greeted the question until Locin's hand gradually rose.

Zengin's sour expression soured even deeper. "I should have figured it would be you."

She crossed her arms and scowled. "Hey, at least I've heard of it."

"Him," Zengin corrected. "I've read up on Neveri since my arrival, at least so much as I've been able. There isn't much to be found. It took some digging to find anything at all."

"Well?" Voske was growing weary and ready to get to the point. "Who is he?"

"A god," Zengin answered. "Rumored as such, at least. In Talamh there are a small minority of people that believe there were not eight divine children, but nine."

"That's heresy," Burz said, leaning forward.

"Yes," Zengin answered drably. "That's why they're a cult. Mostly they're comprised of the unguilded, those who got passed over by the gods and decided to blame the divines rather than their own shortcomings."

"Wait," Locin was leaning in, intensely focused. "We are talking about the crazies across the river, aren't we?"

Zengin nodded. "They serve Neveri, and I imagine they're not too fond of the eight."

Voske slapped his palm against the table. "Mire and Nyx. Someone needs to clean house over there."

"I'm sure the warriors of Jeza have a plan," Burz said. "They won't let this stand. Besides, they have the city garrison. That should be more than enough men."

"It should have been." Zengin answered flatly.

The air fell silent again and Voske frowned. "What do you mean *should have been*?"

"I stopped by the temple barracks on my way back this evening. You'll be interested to know the monks of Jeza paid a visit to the Sacred Quarter earlier today."

Burz sat stiffly at the edge of his seat. "And?"

"And while we were all shopping, they were getting soundly thrashed by the cult of Neveri."

"Impossible," Burz stood. "They're trained warriors with boons against unguilded vagrants!"

Zengin shrugged. "Then don't take my word for it. I merely made myself useful and gathered information while you all sat around disrobing in front of one another for sport. You truly are perfect champion material."

Voske felt a flare of anger, but it was hard to gainsay him with barely a stitch of clothing on. He clenched his fists and jaw as embarrassment crept over him.

Weylyn shifted in her seat. "And what happened to you?"

Zengin thumbed at his ear. "I was… attempting to investigate these rumors of Neveri. Things didn't exactly go according to plan, but I learned what I needed."

Burz stepped closer. "And the soldiers?"

"Retreated with their tales firmly between their legs. Those that returned, that is."

Burz sighed as he crossed toward the door to the temple commons.

"Where are you going?" Voske called.

"They'll have taken the wounded to the houses of healing. I'm going to help them."

Voske quickly pushed out from the table and hurried toward the door as Burz disappeared through it.

"And where are *you* going?" Hikari called from behind.

He turned around sharply. "Those are monks of Jeza. *My* monks. I'm going to see to them too."

"Aren't you forgetting something, darling?"

Locin held up his toga from the table and his bluster quickly faded.

He stomped back over and snatched it out of her hand, then grabbed his sandals. "I will pay you back for this, thief."

She smirked up at him. "We'll see."

He wheeled back toward the door with one last glance at Zengin. He was a champion, and this was the last time he would be caught with his pants down.

The sun was setting as Burz crossed the temple grounds toward the healing houses. Long shadows fell over the soft grass, and the heat of day was fading to a misty cool. Zengin's words ate at him as he hurried along. There was more they should be doing. Being a champion wasn't about shopping and having attendants wait on your every need. It was about serving the people.

"Hey! Wait up!"

He glanced back to see Voske now dressed and still struggling to slip his sandal on his foot as he hopped along the field on one leg.

"I'm going to help," Burz said.

"Yeah." Voske got his sandal settled and strolled beside Burz with an angry expression. "I'm coming too."

"No offense, but how are you going to help?"

"I'm not here to help. I'm here for answers."

"Answers from wounded monks?"

"Answers from Eprim. Mark my words, he'll be there."

Burz could see the houses ahead, old stone buildings with high glass domes and arching windows, each hidden in thick, creeping vines. The very air was thick with the scent of herbs.

Voske pointed. "Which one is the healing house?"

"All of them."

"How many rooms do they need for healing? I mean, don't you just touch them and they're better?"

Burz sighed, wishing he'd been able to come here alone. "Haven't you seen how many people come to the temple? Thousands come for healing each year. More than I could ever hope to heal. The monks of Uthando tend to most of them."

"Why can't you heal them? Isn't that your boon?"

He's an overgrown child, Burz thought. *Not even Kyren and Orin talk this much.*

Burz stopped in front of the main building. He was feeling nervous as they drew near. He hadn't used his boon yet, and he wasn't sure he fully understood it.

"What's wrong?" Voske asked. "Why'd we stop?"

Burz rubbed at the sigil on his palm. "Do you know how the boon of Uthando works?"

"Sure. I mean you just-" he waved his right palm around wildly in the air "-heal… people."

Burz sighed. "Every time I heal someone, I give some of my own life."

Voske dropped his arms to his sides and looked at Burz with a furrowed brow. "What does that even mean?"

"I'm not sure. The Oracle told me I can't heal too often, or I'll give too much. Apparently the fourth champion of Uthando, Taerin, healed so many that he died at fifty, white haired and bowed like a cripple."

Voske swallowed hard. "That's a high cost."

Burz stared up at the arched entryway cut into the stone walls. It opened onto the main healing house, and he could hear the groans of wounded men inside.

Voske slapped him hard on the back. "I'm sure you'll be fine." And then callously strolled inside.

Burz clenched his fist around the golden sigil. He couldn't fathom how Jeza had called such an idiot.

"You coming?"

Burz rolled his shoulders back and made his way through into a grassy courtyard surrounded by ancient brick walls. There were three more wide arched openings, one in each direction, and the glass domed roof let the moonlight filter in. A square pool stood in the middle around a bubbling spring, and the whole place was overrun by plants and herbs that covered the courtyard, climbing the smooth stone walls on the far side and sprouting from planters all along the floor. It smelled of ginger, lavender, and the fresh pine scent of yarrow which seemed to be springing up everywhere. But it also smelled of blood, rot, and death, and even the strong scent of the herbs couldn't hide that.

Everywhere he looked, monks of Jeza and soldiers were laid on beds or sitting on cushions by the walls, and the herbalists and monks of Uthando made their way around the room tending the wounded. Some sat holding mangled arms or with blood stained faces. The smell of scorched flesh filled the air, and more than a few were covered in burns. There were at least two hundred wounded, and Burz felt his chest tighten at the sight.

The Oracle of Jeza, Eprim, was there pacing restlessly. He spotted them and came over, his eyes fixed on Burz. "You came."

"We heard what happened," Burz said. "I want to help."

"Gods and Chosen!" Voske put a hand over his mouth. "This isn't a house of healing. It's a house of death. What in Nyx happened to these men?"

Eprim looked warily at them. "It might be better if they tell you themselves."

He led them toward the worst of the men, four splayed out on rough beds against the side wall. One monk lay charred fully black. A barely perceptible groan came from the figure, and Burz turned for him, but Eprim grabbed his arm with a firm hand.

"It's too late for him."

"But I can-"

"You would use all your strength on him, and he may still die. We're making him comfortable." He pointed to the soldier on the next bed. Deep gashes tore through his chest and arms.

Voske grunted. "What kind of blade did that?"

Burz walked over and looked at the wounds on the man's side. They didn't look like any weapon he'd ever seen. "This was no blade," he muttered.

He carefully laid his hand on the man's arm, feeling the slick warm blood that covered his skin. He called up his boon and felt the warmth of it rush through his arms and into his hands. At once he felt a savage pain digging into his chest. It spread along his ribs, and he clenched his teeth as his hand spasmed. His arms and legs grew weak, and he leaned into the bed to steady himself. In a moment it was over. He was left panting, leaning across the young soldier's body which was now fully healed. The gashes had closed, and his eyes fluttered open.

"That was something," Voske said in a reverent tone. "You alright?"

Burz struggled to push himself back to standing. His weak leg was throbbing now. "Yes," he managed. "I'm fine."

Eprim held out a hand to steady him as he stepped back. "Thank you."

Burz nodded but didn't answer as he tried to stay on his feet.

Voske stepped up to the young man and looked him over. "Can you speak?"

The soldier sat up, stretching his arms and smiling. "Yes, Champion."

"Tell me what happened."

He furrowed his brow. "We were ambushed, near the Dai'shron, not far from the river crossing. They came from the sky."

"Pegs?" Burz asked, but he knew this was no pegasus. He felt a sinking feeling in his stomach.

"Beasts." The boy's eyes were wide with the last remnants of his terror. "They had heads like lions with horns, great wings, and a viper's tail. And… and they breathed fire down on us."

"Mire and Nyx!" Voske said. "Are you sure you saw it right? Must have been some kind of a trick."

"It wasn't a trick, Champion. It was a-"

An unfamiliar voice broke in. "Chimera."

Burz turned toward the voice to see the Oracle of Bei'ai watching them, his cloak hiding his face in dark shadow. He had a bandage wrapped around his arm, red with blood.

"Myths." Burz narrowed his gaze. "Legends. Chimera are no more than a tale to frighten children."

"And now they walk Talamh." The Oracle strolled forward, and Burz caught a glimpse of gnarled flesh under his hood. "Word is spreading in the city. Many saw sights they couldn't explain today."

Eprim sighed. "I've heard similar reports from many of my men."

Voske shook his head. "And you didn't tell anyone?"

"We just got back, Champion."

"For that matter, why didn't you tell the Champions about this plan of yours in the first place? We could have helped!"

Eprim's jaw tightened. "With all due respect, no Champion of Jeza has entered combat in over two hundred years."

Voske leaned closer. "Maybe I'm not like those other champions."

"And how was I to know that?"

"It's protocol," Endring interrupted. "The champions aren't to be disturbed, no matter what. The High Oracle has made that clear."

"That doesn't seem like it's her rotting call!"

Burz winced. Voske was the most foul mouthed, bull headed man he'd ever met. "Maybe she has good reason."

"She doesn't," Endring said flatly. "She has a desperate need for control."

"Enough." Eprim sighed.

"I have no such need," Endring continued. "In fact, I think it's time we had the champions help. Would you speak with me? Privately."

Voske and Burz exchanged a glance, and Voske nodded.

Endring led them back to an out of the way corner where a table sat covered with various jars and bowls of clean water. Mounds of bloody bandages were piled on the table, and flies buzzed in the air above them.

He turned around and stared intently from face to face. "I know what the cultists are planning."

"How?" Eprim narrowed his gaze skeptically.

"I'm not without resources."

Voske broke in, unable to contain his impatience. "Well what is it? What are they planning?

"They're looking for something, a relic that was housed in the Sacred Quarter." He eyed Eprim. "I don't have to tell you how dangerous relics can be."

"What relic?" Eprim asked. "What does it do?"

"All I know is it's powerful, and if they find it, the results could be catastrophic."

Voske harrumphed. "Like a weapon?"

Endring nodded. "I don't know all the details, but I know where it is, and I believe we can get to it."

Eprim crossed his arms, looking wary. "What are you proposing? My men could barely get past the river crossing. These chimera, or whatever they are, could wipe out an entire legion from the air."

"Then don't send a legion. A smaller group could enter the Sacred Quarter unnoticed. There are ways in and out. Discreet ways. They could find this relic and secure it before the cultists do."

There was a glint in Voske's eye. He actually wanted to go, and he'd probably drag the rest of the Champions into this madness with him. Burz quickly preempted him.

"How do we even know this relic is still there, or that these heretics don't already have it?" He shook his head. "It's foolhardy to send anyone to their deaths on so little information."

Eprim looked pensive. "How great is the risk?"

"I believe it's great," Endring said. "If we wait, many lives could be lost."

Voske pressed his hands together, rubbing them back and forth eagerly. "We'll go."

Burz was already shaking his head. "It's too risky. We've barely been champions a few days."

"I agree," Eprim said. "I have plenty of reserves still-"

"No." Voske's tone was final. "We'll do it." He gave a pointed look toward Burz. "Any champion who doesn't want to go can stay here."

This head strong idiot was going to get someone killed. "I'm the only one of us even trained to fight. You think a player and a quarryman have a chance at surviving this?"

Voske straightened to his full, intimidating height. "I think we're rotting champions. It's about time we act like it."

Burz met his gaze, forcing himself to stand straight despite his leg throbbing in protest. He opened his mouth to speak, but Endring stepped between them, his eyes fixed on Burz.

"I know this is no one's first plan, but we've stepped into the realm of legends, and isn't that the same realm where champions live?"

Burz took a deep breath. He knew how to be a soldier. They didn't take foolish risks. They didn't act on their own. There was strength in numbers. But he knew nothing about being a Champion. He let his eyes lock on one of the wounded monks, a boy of about sixteen. Blood covered his face and matted in his hair, and his eyes were still wide with the horrors he'd seen. He might as well be looking at one of his own boys. Would a Champion condemn these boys to more horror and death?

Endring spoke again. "I can help you get into the quarter, I can tell you where the relic is, but I can't give you the will to act."

"We'll need a plan," Burz said, as he turned back to the group "and we'll need to run this by the others."

"Good," Endring said. "I'll come to the champion's wing early tomorrow."

"As will I," Eprim added, and a faint smile creased the corners of his mouth.
"Why the grin?" Burz asked.

"Today has been nothing but heartache for my men." His smile broadened. "But it might lift their spirits to hear the champions are taking up arms again."

Voske clapped Eprim on the back. "You bet we are!"

Even Burz could feel his chest swell with pride as he watched the men smiling. Maybe Voske was right. They were champions, and they'd been called for a purpose.

10: Eight

Rasa peered over the side of a chariot, her hands splayed against the golden light of the radiant field. She was on her tiptoes, her bare feet against the deck, and her stuffy, gem-encrusted sandals wherever she'd kicked them off.

Below, the low country of Las rushed past in a green blur as she tried to focus on trees in the jungle canopy. She wore a brilliant purple and blue stola, provided for her by the temple and hastily tailored to fit. She'd never had anything that fit her so well, but she hated it. It was stuffy, and shiny, and reminded her too much of her old life. Her face was clean, as was her bright red hair, twirled on her head in an intricate design like a flower. It had taken almost an hour and three women to get it that way. Her right arm was bedecked with an excessive amount of golden bracelets. She looked like the daughter of an archon. She barely recognized herself.

"You've been quite a few days in coming. I'm sure they'll be glad to see you."

Rasa looked back over her shoulder at the tall monk of Uthando. For the last hour she'd been fretting over Rasa's every whim, which was unsettling, and a little overwhelming. Four Jeza monks watched her from their position near the guide, and behind them, a single radiant hung in the field.

"I know you're going to love the Gods' Mount." The woman smiled, looking as uncomfortable as Rasa felt. "There are quite a few courtyards with fountains and gardens."

"That sounds nice," Rasa answered politely.

She turned her focus back toward the front of the chariot. The pylat was winging its way over the jungles, following the winding trail of a murky brown river toward a shining hillock that glimmered with white stone at the edge of the horizon, and spread out below it was a vast city.

All around the chariot she could see the blue wisps of spirits, darting in and out of view. They would dance over and around each other, and bound after the chariot like dolphins in the wake of a passing ship. She found them less unsettling as she got used to them, but she still tried to give them space, careful not to focus on them too much.

"Have you ever been to Arrajin before?"

Rasa looked back over her shoulder. She'd been all over the place, ferried from one big city to the next. Arrajin didn't look familiar, but she couldn't be sure. She was usually stowed below deck until…

"I'm not sure," she managed.

"You mean you were too young to remember?"

Rasa gave the monk an uncomfortable look. The poor woman seemed as eager to be done with this trip as she was.

She looked back at the Gods' Mount and the domes and spires of the city splayed out in front of it. It stood out from the jungle canopy like stone pillars in the ocean. From the westernmost part of the city, smoke rose in billows, and something dark caught her eye.

She heard the guide shout. "Five minutes to tether!" And she was sure she saw the monk sigh in relief. It couldn't be easy to be tasked with entertaining a Champion, especially one who didn't have much to say.

Rasa's eyes locked on the dark shape over the city again, darting among the pillars of smoke. It was peculiar, the wrong shape and size for a pegasus, and it was flying toward them. She could see it better now as it drew closer. Its mane looked more like the full mane of a lion, and its tail lashed through the sky like a snapping whip.

"What is that?"

"What is what, Champion?" The monk leaned her head closer to the golden field and followed Rasa's finger to where the creature approached.

Rasa squinted. "It's moving fast."

"I… don't know," the monk confessed. "I've never seen anything like it."

Rasa looked nervously toward the guide, but the wayfarer crew were already pointing to the beast and the guide looked tense.

Suddenly the spirits seemed to take notice. They started whipping around the chariot and circling the chains as though willing them to change course.

"We need to run," Rasa muttered, more to herself than anyone else.

"What?" the monk of Uthando asked.

"Turn back," she said more firmly, then, looking at the guide. "Turn back!"

The wayfarers looked at her with surprise.

"Champion?" The guide questioned. "What is that thing?"

"I-I don't know." She glanced at the spirits. They were swirling even faster now, throwing themselves into the bottom of the Chariot as if they were trying to lift it. "But it's not safe. We have to run! Get away from it!"

The guide's face paled and he looked back to the front.

The monster was close now. Its paws were easily as large as a man's head and smoke poured from its mouth, as though a furnace was burning in its belly. A savage looking man rode on its back, his eyes painted black and a bronze spear glimmering in his right hand.

"Ten clicks to port," the chariot guide yelled, snapping into action. "Two skyward, get us away from that thing!"

The chariot swerved sharp to the left, but the creature followed the motion, nearly on top of them.

"Loose the upper chains," the guide yelled. "We'll outpace it!"

The chariot surged forward, and Rasa crouched to keep her balance. She spotted two more of the creatures that rose from the smoky section of the city, rushing to intercept them as the third pursued from behind.

"In front of us!" Rasa cried.

The guide had already spotted them, and he ordered the chariot skyward.

"Protect the champion!" The Uthando monk called.

In a flash, all four monks of Jeza were surrounding Rasa, weapons drawn. But what were they supposed to do?

The chariot tipped, heading for the sky above, but the two beasts had already closed over them, and the pylats dove away from the monsters.

Rasa grabbed the Uthando monk's hand and pulled her down as one of the beasts sunk its claws into the skybeam over their heads with a deafening scrape. It roared, and the sound of it filled Rasa's senses as its back claws scrabbled against the field of light, trying to gain a foothold.

"Climb!" The guide yelled. "Get us higher! Into the cold dark!"

But the pylats held course, rushing for the Gods' Mount ahead as the men scrambled to tighten the chains. As they pulled, the chariot slowed and pitched upward, but the beast wouldn't let go. One of its razor-like claws penetrated the field of light, then another, and it started struggling up the side of the chariot, like an ominous black shadow, climbing over the surface of the sun.

The chariot rocked hard, and Rasa threw her gaze to the other side. The second beast was on them now, scratching at the hull as its rider pierced the radiant field with a cruel blade. It drove in through the golden light with some effort and he sliced at the sky beam, the wood chipping at the impact.

Rasa screamed. A sense of dread overtook her, and her breath came fast and shallow. What were these things? The blue light of the spirits circled in front of her, and she again felt their thoughts.

Where is it going?

She tried to shake the thought away, but it persisted, growing louder and more urgent as the beast overhead clawed its way toward the front of the chariot.

Where is it going?

She closed her eyes for a moment and focused on her breathing, trying to still her hammering heart before she opened them again. This time she followed the beast's path with her eyes. It was heading toward the chains.

It's climbing the field.

"The pylats!" She screamed. "It's after the pylats!"

Both of the creatures were climbing the field now, clawing their way toward the front of the chariot where thick chains held the two pylats.

Rasa leapt to her feet and leaned over the side of the chariot as the third beast roared at them from behind. She felt the frame shudder as it grabbed onto the field. They were steadily climbing, far above the ground now and the green of the Gods' Mount below.

Ahead, a swirl of spirits circled the chains as if they could protect them.

"The chains!" Rasa yelled. "They'll sever the chains!"

The guide's face paled. "Down!" He shouted, frantic. "Take us down! They're trying to knock us out of the sky."

The men pulled the chains hard, and the pylats struggled against the command, but were forced to tip down, pulling wildly left and right until the chariot rocked. One of the chimera lost its footing, sliding free of the field, scraping along the hull as it slipped away, leaving a long gash. But still two clung to the chariot, one nearing the chains at the front now.

Rasa felt a hand grab her and pull her back as wicked claws penetrated the light above her. She stumbled into the monk of Uthando.

"I've got you, Champion. You're safe!"

The chariot banked hard, trying to shake the creatures free.

"We're close!" The radiant called from his place in the field.

Arrajin was speeding by below them, and Rasa locked eyes on the green fields of the Gods' Mount. The chariot was low now, barely clearing the tallest towers of the city. But the beast was nearly to the chains.

Heat licked the side of the chariot. The third beast was back, spouting fire across the radiant field.

"Riders! Ahead!"

Rasa scrambled free from the monk's grip, and she saw them. Pegasus from the Gods' Mount, but they were so far away.

A short javelin pierced the field, landing in front of her. She traced it to one of the chimera. The rider was sneering at them, another javelin in hand. A second throw landed near the guide.

"Take us down!" He screamed.

A third javelin tore through, and the field wavered as it pierced the chest of the radiant. Rasa watched in horror as his clean white toga bled crimson, and he tumbled out of the field. The barrier shuddered and broke, and a spout of flame ripped across the deck.

The outside air crashed in like a windstorm. Her stola whipped like a flag and her red hair covered her eyes, blocking her sight. She brushed it aside just in time to see one of the beasts flipping downward over the deck. Its body crushed into the skybeam and the frame shuddered like a drum, then it pinwheeled down the wooden railing until its front claws caught hold, halting its fall. Its eyes blazed with insanity and its mouth opened with a roar, then a billow of smoke.

She started to turn away, and instantly she felt searing hot pain roasting her back and side. She watched in agony as the skin of her arm was scorched into blackened coal.

The Uthando monk screamed as she reached for Rasa. "The Champion! Help!"

In a moment, the Jeza monks closed ranks as Rasa slumped in the woman's arms. She felt the pain overwhelming her mind, and she glanced ahead. The green fields loomed, and the tether beyond, but they wouldn't make it. One of the beasts held on, wicked claws pulling at the pylat chains until they snapped. In a moment, the pylats broke free and darted for the sky above, and the chariot dropped like a stone against the fields below. Rasa felt the monks close in, a body wrapped around her own. It stung where they held her burned flesh, and she cried out. The chariot groaned and cracked as it slammed into the ground, and the impact shuddered through Rasa. She was cushioned in a tangle of bodies as they flew violently into the back rail, and she heard the sickening crunch of bones cracking and bodies breaking, but not hers. The jolt sent excruciating pain through her burned side, and everything became distant and indistinct. For a moment, everything was still, and a cloud of blue spirits pressed around her as darkness filled her mind.

Voske furrowed his brow. He'd been staring at a map of the Sacred Quarter for a few minutes now, but it told him very little. He appreciated the lines of the city, the way the newer sections had been carefully planned around the sacred monuments and shrines of old, but it told him nothing about the cultists who now occupied this corner of Arrajin.

The map was laid out on the round table in the champion's common room. The chairs were all pushed to the side, and Burz leaned over, tapping a finger on the edges of the paper. Eprim had brought the map, and he was prattling on about different landmarks while Weylyn, Hikari, Locin, and Endring watched. Zengin had taken off to do some cryptic thing on his own, and Illeri was still missing. Apparently she'd come in late the night before, and left early. Voske wondered what it would take to get all the champions in one place. If they couldn't all show up for the planning, could he count on them for the execution?

Burz laid a finger on a landmark near the east side, the Gambit of Iyanu. "You're sure the relic is here?"

Endring nodded. "Historically, it was stored in the House of Dusk, but Borroka wouldn't keep something so powerful close to the riverfront."

Weylyn stepped back from the table. "Are we sure this is a good idea?"

Voske harrumphed. "Seems like a good plan to me. No fighting, just in and out."

"I meant us going at all."

"We're the champions. Who else should go?"

"Someone trained."

Burz straightened up from the table and stretched out his back with a wince. "Normally I'd agree, but all the best trained of Arrajin already tried and failed."

"Exactly my point."

"I had a lot of time to consider this last night," Burz said. "It could be this is the will of the gods."

Hikari cleared his throat. "And what if we fail? I mean, what are the odds we succeed?"

"The cultists patrol the streets," Endring said coolly, "but their numbers are not great, and we have disguises." He pulled a small vial from a hidden pocket. It was filled with a murky black substance.

Burz reached for it, but Voske grabbed it first, turning it over in the light.

"What is it?" He held it up. It was thick like ink.

Locin plucked it from his hand with her boon and drew it to herself. "They wear it around their eyes. Gods, I coulda used some of this." She glanced at Endring, and they seemed to exchange a meaningful look. "Can't be easy to come by."

"Alright, darling. But what if we do have to fight? Don't they have chimeras?"

Voske laughed. "Still not convinced they exist."

"My men wouldn't lie," Eprim said, looking cross.

"I'm not saying they lied. Maybe they just saw wrong."

Burz shook his head. "Don't be a fool. You saw the same burned bodies as me, the same claw and bite marks."

"This isn't comforting, darling."

"Chimera or not," Weylyn said, "there are still a lot of them."

Burz leaned back over the map. "We'll be dressed as some of their own. Too many of us to question, too few to draw attention."

"Not to mention pelican boy and his honey tongue," Locin added.

"He could be useful."

Hikari threw his arms up in exasperation. "Well then we're fine, I'm sure."

"Just think of it," Voske said. "The seven of us, marching through Arrajin, relic in hand, victorious."

Hikari at least brightened at that.

Weylyn frowned. "Let's get into the quarter before we plan the celebration."

Voske crossed his arms and followed her gaze back to the map. "Here," he pressed his finger on the bridge crossing, the only one left. The cultists had burned or blockaded most of the crossings into the Sacred Quarter.

"Alright, darling. But how do we get over it without raising an alarm?"

Locin pushed Voske's hand off the map. "We don't." She and Endring exchanged another glance. "We come out here." She pointed to a building in the southeast of the map. "There's a tunnel straight to it from the People's Quarter."

"And how do you know that?"

"I've used it before."

Endring nodded. "Once you get through the tunnels, you should be able to make your way to the Gambit without any issue. As for getting inside, I'm afraid I'm little help. It shouldn't be too heavily guarded."

"Leave that to me," Locin tossed the vial in the air, and as she caught it, it seemed to disappear. "I'm a thief after all, and ingenious!"

Burz traced a finger along the map, marking the wide road that ran along the edge of the quarter toward the tower. "We should take this route."

Voske scoffed, and Burz looked up at him.

"You disagree?"

Everyone was watching him now, and Voske squared his shoulders. "Those are the main roads, probably swimming with cultists. Any idiot should be able to see that."

Burz straightened up and glared at Voske. "Exactly. Cultists will be coming and going on the main road. We have disguises for a reason. We'll blend in. It's also the quickest route, and the less time we spend in the quarter, the better."

Voske spread his hands flat on the map and leaned over, searching for a different way. "Here." He pointed out a winding path that took a lot of back alleys west through the older center of the quarter before looping back to the tower. "More obscure. Less chance of being seen."

Burz leaned in, matching his tone. "And if we are seen? How do you explain such a big group wandering narrow alleys?"

"If we don't get spotted, there's nothing to explain." Voske said flatly.

Burz laughed. "We'll do it my way."

"Like Nyx. I'm in charge here."

"What qualifies you for that? I was a soldier. This is what I did."

"That's right." Voske smirked. "I'm sure you put on disguises and snuck into cities all the time."

Burz' jaw tightened. "I was captain of the Tajerim garrison. I planned routes and angles of attack. You were the foreman of a quarry, so if we need some rocks moved, you can take the lead."

Voske grunted. "Well, now I'm the Champion of Jeza, and you're a healer."

Locin stepped up to the table as the tension swelled. "Hey, whenever you goons are done comparing sword sizes…"

The two men stared at her.

"Better. Now, I'm with Voske. Back alleys are kind of my thing."

Burz scoffed. "If you're one thief alone, fine. But where are we hiding seven champions in a back alley? We would draw too much attention."

"Burz may be right," Weylyn said.

Burz smiled smugly.

Voske glanced at Hikari, but he only shook his head.

"Leave me out of this, darling. You can find another way to settle your feud."

"We go my way," Burz said firmly. "I have more experience."

"You didn't even want to do this," Voske snapped. "Mire and Nyx! I volunteered for this, that means it's my call. You want to come along, you're welcome to, but you'll follow my lead."

Burz stood up straight and looked like he would speak again, but the doors flew open, startling them all. Gillis came rushing in leading several monks, one of which carried something in his arms. As he drew closer, laying it down on a couch, Voske recognized it as a girl, badly burned and bloody.

"Gods and Chosen," Hikari croaked hoarsely.

Voske marched around the table, and Burz was already there, kneeling beside her. "What in Nyx happened?"

"An attack," Gillis answered, sounding winded. "Her chariot was coming in, and it was struck down by…" his voice trailed off, and he looked pale.

"By what?" Weylyn pressed. She moved close, grabbing a pitcher of water on her way.

It was Burz who answered. "Chimera."

Her stola was melted to the flesh on her side, and her arm was charred black, but Voske could see her face, pale and thin, and covered in the singed ends of stringy red hair. She was barely more than a cycle by the look, and thin as a line.

"Who is she?"

"The Champion of Bei'ai," Locin said in a distant voice.

Endring made his way over, gently lifting her charred palm. The golden sigil of Bei'ai was clear.

Gillis' voice was faint. "We received word last night that she was coming."

"And I wasn't told?" Endring snapped.

Gillis just stared wide-eyed. He had no more answers.

Weylyn poured the cool water over her burns, and pulled out a knife, cutting away the fabric of the stola. Hikari made a retching noise and retreated to the far corner.

Burz slowly knelt beside her and laid his hands on her stomach, taking in a breath.

"Can you save her?" Weylyn asked.

The girl's chest rose and fell feebly.

"I'll try."

Tension filled his body as he called on his boon. He shuddered, and a groan of pain escaped his lips as the young girl's body changed. The blackened skin turned, first red and then a soft pink. When it was over, Burz' body gave out, and he slumped to the floor, but her breaths were easy now, and her round green eyes blinked open.

The girl sat up, pulling into a ball on the soft couch and staring around at them. The ends of her very long hair were singed black, and ash still smeared her face.

Voske grimaced. "Is it worth going now, Weylyn? The rotting cultists did this to her, and their gods forsaken chimera."

The girl spoke in a soft voice. "Where am I?"

"The Gods' Mount," Weylyn said. "With friends." She quickly sat beside the girl and turned her own palm over, revealing the sigil of Strah.

The young girl seemed to relax. "What happened?"

Gillis answered. "Your chariot was attacked, Champion. That's all we know."

"What about the others?"

Gillis looked back at the monks who had brought her in, but they shook their heads. "Most likely being treated in the healing houses. We'll find out right away." He motioned to one of the monks who scurried out the door.

The girl looked down at her new pink flesh, running a hand over it. "How? How am I okay?"

Weylyn motioned to Burz. He was seated on the floor, leaning against the couch to keep himself upright. He flashed his sigil.

"Thank you. All of you." She looked around at their faces.

Weylyn reached out a kind hand, brushing the singed tips of the girl's hair. "What's your name, child?"

"Rasa," she said. "I'm Rasa."

11: The Phoenix

As morning wore on, Illeri was knee deep in blueprints and spare parts. Yzod's shop was the only place that felt comfortable in her new life. The pace was slow, the lighting dim, and the company pleasant, if a little gruff. With all the uncertainty of her new life, this was an escape, and one she sorely needed.

Currently, Yzod was below deck on the solo chariot hammering against a metal cylinder and making a terrible racket. Illeri leaned against the outside of the chariot, watching as the cylinder creaked outward through a snug hole drilled in the hull.

Yzod yelled out to her, his voice mostly muffled by the boards. "We there yet?"

"Not yet," she called back, and immediately the clanging started up again.

She watched until the cap of the cylinder barely protruded past the bronze plating, bringing it in line with the rest of the cylinders that lined the hull.

"There!" she yelled.

The hammering stopped, and Illeri rubbed her ears, waiting for the ringing to subside.

The hull of the solo chariot was covered by a grid of the cylinders, they even rose up the bronze support struts and across the three sky beams, jutting barely above the frame like a tight cork in a bottle.

Each one was made of a hollow tube of bronze fitted with a tight cap on one side that could turn in either direction, but never came off. Yzod had insisted they were key to getting the chariot to work, but he was less forthcoming with exactly how.

Illeri made her way back to the rickety ladder and hoisted herself up to the deck where she spotted Ryshi on the opposite railing. He was staring wide eyed at the ceiling and looked jumpy.

She paced to him and leaned on the railing, letting him sniff her hand. "Too loud?"

Yzod crawled back out of the narrow gap that accessed the underbelly of the solo chariot. "Glad that was the last one," he said, louder than he needed. "You think that ringing's bad up here, you should try it down below."

"I offered to help."

"Bah," he waved a hand at her and sauntered to the guide's chair where a half eaten sandwich lay getting stale. He scooped it up and leaned on the back of the seat while taking a thoughtful bite.

Ryshi jumped across the railing and clung to one of the struts with his talons, craning his neck and listening.

"It looks like the noise has him jumpy."

Yzod shook his head. "He's used to it. It's something else. He's been like that all morning."

"What is it then?"

He shrugged. "Nyx if I know. He gets that way sometimes around wingers."

She stared at him blankly, trying to puzzle out what a winger was.

He chuckled. "Pegs. My father always called 'em wingers. I guess it stuck." He clicked his tongue and held out a chunk of meat from his sandwich. "Rysh!"

The wyvern hopped down to the deck, and clumsily marched over, the gears in his mechanical leg grinding softly. Once he'd snatched the meat, he looked up warily one last time before dragging his meal below deck.

"He'll be alright."

Illeri nodded. "So, what's next?"

He held up his sandwich. "This. But after that we can adjust the pitch and see if we can line it up with what you remember." His tone was curt, but his blue and violet eyes glinted.

"Pitch?"

He waved for her to follow him to the mid port strut and grabbed one of the caps on the outside while pointing for her to watch the hollow end of the cylinder. He wrapped his knuckles against the metal and she could hear a fleeting tone ringing from the plug, until he twisted the cap sideways. At the motion the inner walls of the tube constricted, and the sound rose in pitch like a wind chime.

"The wayfarer field is more than light," he said.

"I know," she answered, "it's a feeling."

He smiled. "I was going to say a sound, but you'd know better than me. The point is, we can reproduce it."

She nodded, suddenly understanding. "I'll get the tuning forks."

Yzod took another bite as she hurried down the rickety ladder onto the wooden floor of the workshop. "Where did you put them?" She called as she squeezed around the chariot.

"Check by the chisels. Should be around there."

She walked to the back corner where a spread of chisels were tucked into a leather case. Just beside them a dozen tuning forks were stuck into a small pot. She grabbed them out. He'd need a pair of tongs too.

She pawed around the cluttered shelf for a minute before checking the floor beside the tool rack. The tongs were there, fallen into the dark corner. She leaned down to snatch them up but hesitated. Just beside the shelf a burlap sack rested on the floor. There was a fine layer of dust settled on it, but she could see the faint glow of an inventor's spark emanating from within.

She lifted the edge of the bag, revealing a number of softly glowing orbs. They were made of woven bronze and stone and tapered softly on one side toward a single hole drilled in the surface. They looked very similar to the orb that was placed in the center of the chariot. She carefully lifted one out, carrying it back toward Yzod.

"Did you find them?" he called down.

"Yes, and the tongs."

"Right. You're getting too good at this."

"I'm a fast study."

She swung back up the ladder and held the tools toward him, but his eyes were fixed on the orb in her other hand.

He pointed casually at it, but his voice was deadly earnest. "I'd be careful with that if I were you."

She looked down at it quizzically. "I thought it was another chariot spark."

"It is," he said. "One of my earlier attempts."

"It doesn't work?"

"You could say that. I had made a dozen or so when I found a major design flaw."

"What was that?"

He smiled dubiously. "If you hit them hard enough, they explode. I had one send a wave of fire down the middle of the deck. Took nearly a week to clean up that mess."

She looked nervously down at the orb. "And you kept them around?"

"The spark was good, the design just couldn't hold together." He walked to the central orb and patted it with his hand. "Not like this little lady. Hums along nice and steady. She'd never explode on me."

"Right." Illeri tucked the unstable orb against the side of the railing, making sure it wasn't going to roll anywhere.

"Now," Yzod said, "How about you bring those forks over here."

She brought them to where he stood by the core, and he tapped one against the bronze surface, creating a high pitched ringing that hung in the air.

"Well?" Yzod said, staring at her. "Sound familiar?"

"May I hold it?"

He handed the implement over, and she closed her eyes, focusing on the vibrations that pulsed through her fingertips.

"This one is wrong," she said quickly.

"Too fast, too slow?"

"Too fast."

He selected a second fork and repeated the process. This time it was a lower sound, like a finger tracing the lip of a wine glass.

"Still too fast."

A third fork was much the same, but as she touched the fourth she felt her heart skip a beat. She recognized the pulses that flowed up her arm, and for a moment she could feel the warmth of the field, circulating around her body like she was a radiant holding back the cold dark.

"This one."

"You're sure?"

"Yes." She'd spent most of her life in a radiant field. She would recognize it anywhere.

"Iyanu's light," he breathed. "After all these years. Are you ready?"

She could feel goosebumps prickling her arms, and she nodded eagerly.

"Here goes something." He grasped the tongs and pinched them around the small cap at the top of the orb, then he tapped on the orb with the fork again and they both leaned down to listen.

Sound was resonating within, but it was much higher than the sound of the fork. Gradually Yzod turned the cap to the left. As he did the sound deepened. He kept going until Illeri held out a hand for him to stop. The two notes were identical.

"That's one," Yzod said.

She looked around at the metal chimes inlaid into the struts and the sky beams all around them. She felt giddy.

They started with the chimes below deck first. Illeri would lean down and use the fork while Yzod adjusted the cap. After those came the struts and then finally the sky beams, which they could only reach using Yzod's rickety ladder. It was a little tedious, and a little terrifying, but they worked quickly until they managed to adjust every last one.

By the time they were done they were both sweating like pigs and grinning like fools.

"Alright then," Yzod said as he stood by the guardrail. "There's one last thing to do."

"Start it?"

"No." He brushed his hand along the smooth teak of the rail. "First, things first. She needs a name."

She looked up at Yzod. "A name?"

"Of course. What, you don't name chariots?"

She shrugged. "Someone does. I guess whoever builds them."

"Well, that's us." He smiled meaningfully. "And I think you should name it."

She stared at him, dumbfounded. "Me?"

"Of course. I've been trying to think of a name for a whole year, but I've got nothing."

"But she's your project. I've been helping for what, two days? You've given nearly a cycle to this!"

He wagged a finger at her. "And in those two days we've made a full year's progress, maybe more." He folded his arms and looked at her sternly. "Now, I'm serious about this. You pick it, and we won't start her 'til you do."

She blanched at the thought and looked around again, trying to spot anything for inspiration. The entire workshop was a hodgepodge of tools and trinkets, certainly nothing poetic. Ryshi poked his head up from below deck, wobbling out in search of more food. He saw the rest of the discarded sandwich and shook out his tail, stretching the leather wing open and closed a few times before leaping to flight, but his wing failed and he plummeted down, crashing to the deck and rolling to a stop.

For a moment Illeri thought about going to help him, but she resisted the temptation and kept watching as he flipped back onto his feet, undaunted.

He shook out his tail, then lifted his wings again and let out a little coo. He flapped down and sprang into the air as the dust of the workshop fell away from his wings, and this time he managed to land on the rail, grabbing the sandwich.

She smiled. "What about the Phoenix?"

"Hm." He wrinkled his nose thoughtfully. "What made you think of that?"

"Ryshi."

He raised an eyebrow. "You know he's a wyvern, right?"

She chuckled. "But he's resilient. When you think he's down, he gets back up - keeps fighting."

He smiled. "The Phoenix. I like it. The Phoenix it is!"

With that he began ratcheting a lever at the base of the bronze orb and the pedestal extended upward, rising until the orb tapped the central skybeam. At the impact, a low hum reverberated outward, resonating through the brass frame and then down through the deck until the floorboards vibrated with the note.

Suddenly the spark flared with power and green light poured outward in every direction, connecting the chimes in a glowing field. It wasn't quite the same as the Wayfarer's boon, but it was beautiful and familiar. It kept flowing over and around them until they were completely wrapped in its soft radiance, then the sound slowly took its leave and only the light remained.

Illeri felt her heart leap, and she ran to Yzod's side and threw her arms around him.

"Ha!" He yelled aloud, his voice mirroring her own excitement. "It worked! Iyanu's light, it worked!"

12: Preparations

Burz spent the morning rehearsing the plan to penetrate the Sacred Quarter. He organized disguises, practiced the lowland accent, replacing every 'ay' sound with 'ah' and badly mispronouncing the word 'Arrajin', basically anything to keep his mind busy. Yet try as he might, his thoughts kept wandering back to the Champion Taerin, and the stiffness in his back wasn't helping.

He rubbed a hand against his lower back as he walked through the front door of his chambers. Being the Champion of Uthando wasn't all he'd hoped it would be. Every time he healed someone, it left him tired beyond anything he'd ever felt, and his leg was throbbing with the pain of his old wound, so his heart sank when he heard the voices of Orin and Kyren.

He'd just made it through the parlor and into the small seating area when they came running in.

"Ada! Ada! You're home!"

"Come play with us, Ada!"

"Toss me! Toss me!"

Burz held his hands up to halt their advance, trying to keep his voice cheerful. "I'll play, but you gotta let me rest first."

"I made a slingshot," Orin said. "Want to see it?"

Burz opened his mouth to answer, but Kyren quickly interrupted.

"And I swallowed a button!"

"A… button?"

"Are you rested now?" Orin pressed.

Kyren bobbed up and down on his toes. "Just one toss?"

"Yeah, one toss each. Please?"

Burz tightened his jaw. "Let me rest for a good while, and we'll do three tosses each."

He saw the disappointment on their faces, even though he was sure they understood. It wasn't that long ago he'd spent several weeks in bed. He'd just gotten to the point where he could play again, and he knew how much it meant to them.

"You can come see my slingshot." Orin's eyes were pleading. "I've been waiting all day!"

"No," Kyren insisted. "Tosses first!"

Burz was ready to cave, even though he wondered if he could even lift the boys right now, let alone toss them. But Hadris' voice broke in and saved him.

"Enough," she said kindly, coming around the corner. She was wiping her hands on a towel, her face smudged with flour. "Go play in your rooms for a while, and let your father rest."

"But Ama-"

"Go. Maybe after we can head out somewhere?" She looked at Burz questioningly.

He nodded. "I can take you to see the training grounds, and you can do more than show me that slingshot. You can show me your skill with it." They started to whoop with excitement. "*After* I rest."

"And *after* you finish all your lessons," Hadris added.

The boys scurried off, eagerly talking about training with champions, and Burz eased himself to the couch, welcoming the relief. Hadris had already watched him endure so much, and he wasn't eager for her to see him like that again. But he knew he couldn't hide it.

"What happened?"

He waved off the question as he looked around the room. Their chambers were elaborate, but not overly large. The seating room was open and airy, with four pillars at the corners, and he could see straight to the doors to the bedrooms, as well as the parlor and a small kitchen and dining area. Apparently no matter how much Hadris complained about cooking, she was loath to give it up.

He motioned to the flour on her face as she sat down. "What's this?"

She brushed her cheek and looked at the flour on her hand. "Kyren wanted some dumplings."

"Can't the temple cooks make them?"

"They brought up four different batches. He said they weren't right." She smiled proudly. "He wanted mine."

Burz smiled too. "Of course he did. They're delicious."

She cleared her throat and her face grew serious again. "Now, what happened? You look terrible. I thought you were just meeting with the others to talk."

"We were." He looked at her warily. He still didn't know how to tell her what they'd talked about. "The last Champion arrived today."

"Oh?"

He nodded. "She's a young thing, not much over a cycle I'd guess. Had burns all over her. Honestly, I thought she was dead."

Hadris leaned in. "You healed her?"

He nodded.

"What happened to her?"

"The heretics in the Sacred Quarter attacked her chariot," Burz mulled over mentioning the word 'chimera' but thought better of it. There was no need to alarm her. Not yet, anyway.

"They're attacking chariots now?" Hadris bit down on her lip, looking tense. "Is the girl alright?"

He nodded wearily. "She'll make it. Though I feel like I got trampled by a peg."

Hadris placed her hand on his shoulder and he winced at the touch. She pulled back.

"Sorry," he said quickly. "When I was healing her it was like I could feel her injuries, like I had just a taste of what it feels like to be on fire. My back, my legs, my arms. Everything felt raw and red. It's still sensitive."

She tensed. "You just healed that man last night, and now this? Don't push yourself so hard."

"I'm not exactly happy about it either, but what choice do I have? Do I let the next one die?"

"Of course not." She tore her eyes away and stared at her feet. "I know what your boon does, Burz, how it works. Just... don't give too much."

He reached out a hand, and she pulled away.

"I asked Gillis what the last Champion of Uthando did," she said. "He told me that he would heal one sick person a week. One. He knew if he didn't rest in between..."

One person a week? The number felt so insignificant, and at the same time he grew weary at the thought of going through this every week.

She sighed softly. "You need days to recover."

"I may not have that."

"What do you mean?" She looked at him sharply. "Why not?"

Burz stared down at the floor. He was going to have to tell her sooner or later, and the earlier he told her, the more time she'd have to process the idea. "We - the Champions, I mean - we're going to the Sacred Quarter."

"What? When?"

"We leave before dawn tomorrow."

She blanched at the statement. "But why? Didn't the whole army just get destroyed? Why are they sending you?"

"We aren't going to fight," he quickly clarified. "We'll be in and out before they even know we're there."

"At least you hope you will. Don't they have Jeza monks they can send for this?"

"Most of them are still recovering."

"Then city guards? Soldiers? Volunteers?"

He grabbed her hands tightly and squeezed. "We *are* the volunteers."

"They can't make you do something like this. You're a champion! It's nonsense to risk your life."

"They're not making us do anything. We really did volunteer. Hadris, listen!"

She pulled her hands away. "Then don't. Don't do it. You're not a soldier anymore, Burz. You don't have a soldier's boon. You're a healer. Let Voske go, or soldiers from Arrajin. Not you."

Burz sat up straighter. "I'm not going to let someone else risk their life in my stead. That's not serving the people of Talamh."

"But you can serve in a different way," she exclaimed. "Is giving away your life not fast enough for you? Do you have to let someone take it?"

"The plan is to not let that happen."

"Then stop inviting it!" She was scowling now, and her voice had taken on a sharp edge.

Burz narrowed his eyes. "Even if I die, the temple will still provide for you and the boys."

"You think I care about that? Will they provide a new father and a new husband?"

"Any man who dies is a father, or a son, or a brother. Is my life worth more than theirs?"

"To me? Yes! Absolutely!"

He sighed, pulling his hands back and cupping them behind his head. He took in a long, slow breath. Of course he didn't want to die, and he was sure he wouldn't, but how could he make her understand?

"When I was in bed for all those weeks, you never left my side."

She softened. "Of course I didn't. I love you."

He reached a hand down and wrapped it up in hers. "I love you too."

She glanced up at him now, and she looked worried.

"I felt helpless, Hadris. You can't know what that's like. I couldn't provide for you and the boys. I was of no value to society."

"What are you talking about? Of course you had value!"

"But I couldn't *do* anything. Uthando gave me a second chance." He pulled his hands free and held them both up, staring at the sigil on his palm before turning it toward her. "He gave me a chance to be useful again, to have some purpose beyond stumbling around the house. I can't waste that chance."

"And I can't lose you."

He sighed. "That's fair. But I need you to trust me. I won't push too far, and if I start to, I have no doubt you'll let me know." He smirked.

"I'm not worried about me letting you know. I'm worried about you listening."

"Trust me," he said confidently. "And I'll trust you."

They fell silent. He knew she was still tense, but he would give her time. It was a lot to process.

"You should rest," she said at last. "Especially if we're taking the boys out later."

He nodded gratefully.

"I'm not done with this conversation," she clarified, and for a moment he cringed, fearing she would start again. "But for now, you need to rest, and I have dumplings to finish. I think it will take some time to figure this all out, to figure out how to be the wife of a champion."

He put his hand around her neck and pulled her close, kissing the top of her head.

"I know it's not easy," he said, "but we'll figure it out together."

She nodded.

He pushed himself up from the couch and headed for the bedroom. He felt like he could sleep for a week, but he'd be lucky to get an hour, and he knew it.

He glanced back to where Hadris watched him from the couch. She looked like she had a thousand more things to say, but what good would it do? He was a husband and a father, but he was also a champion. In the end there were only two ways to make her feel better, coming back alive or not going in the first place. So he would just have to come back alive.

The morning dragged past into a weary afternoon. Rain drove against the rooftops of the Industrial Quarter, whipped by an Eastern wind that swept inland from the Larimar Sea. Streams of water ran down eaves and pummeled trees before flooding into the sewers and cascading out of the large drain pipes into the swelling Arrtris.

Endring stood by a window in the top floor of an abandoned warehouse, watching the rain beat against stone streets and churn down the river. His mind was still on the meeting with the champions, and the unexpected arrival of Bei'ai's chosen. He was at least grateful that the meeting went well, and the champions seemed determined to retrieve the crook. The only thing left was to ensure they made it safely.

He glanced at Sammel who was picking at the peeling paint of the old sill. "I know it's a lot to ask," he said. "But we need them to succeed. I know I've already asked too much of you."

Sammel peeled off a thin strip of paint and dropped it into a puddle far below. "I'm not worried about the cost," he said, "but Zengin knows my face. It could be a problem."

"Then don't let him see your face. Watch over them from a distance, keep to the shadows and only intervene if things look dire. That's probably for the best either way."

Sammel pinched off another strip of paint, rolling it thoughtfully between his fingers. His hair was streaked with more gray lately, and Endring felt guilty as he pulled his eyes away.

"Thank you for the ink," he said. "I gave it to the champions this morning."

"I can get more if you need it."

Sammel, always ready to help.

Endring sighed. "I've put a great weight on you, friend."

"These are weighty times, and weighty matters. It can't be avoided."

Endring was unconvinced. Ever since the night of the shattering, he'd questioned himself. Did they truly need to kill the champions? Could he have given that task to another? But who could he trust like Sammel?

He looked up at his old friend.

Sammel was watching him, his mouth an unreadable line. "Are you having doubts?"

Endring let out a quick laugh. "Have I ever not?"

"You believe what we're doing is best for Talamh?"

"Of course. You've seen it more than most, the stagnancy of the world. It can't endure like this. It's breaking apart. If nothing changes, the worlds will end, and no one will be left."

"There's a cost to change, and a cost to remaining the same. You picked the lower cost."

"But it was wrong of me to make you bear it."

Sammel shook his head, leaning into the window with an arm on the frame until great drops of rain splashed against his fingers. "And who else would you have bear it? They had to die at someone's hand."

Endring ran a hand through his hair. "Me?"

"I doubt you could have withstood it."

It stung to hear it, though Endring knew it was true. His heart couldn't endure the burden. But who was he to ask another man to endure something he could not?

"Sammel-"

"I've had doubts, but even then I believed in you, in the dream you had. When we met as younger men, you spoke to me of a world full of change, a place free of the bonds of decay, where no men would be outcast. He glanced back at Endring. "I'll guard the champions, and I won't be seen unless I must."

"I fear it'll come to that."

"Do you doubt the plan?"

Endring laughed. "No. I doubt the champions. They're feckless."

"Zengin seems capable."

"A few of them are, but they lack cohesion."

"You mentioned one of them was a soldier, and the champion of Jeza looks intimidating."

Endring narrowed his eyes. "When did you see him?"

"When he first arrived. I've not been a stranger to the temple."

Endring looked warily out the window and sharpened his vision, staring around the streets. "You risk too much."

"No one there knew my face, at least before Zengin found me. Besides, you're the one truly in the lion's den."

They fell silent as the downpour intensified, and a flash of lightning split the sky, followed by a rumbling peal of thunder. The wind turned against them and mist off the droplets started spraying into the open window. Sammel grabbed the shutters and drew them closed, dampening the sound and leaving them in the dim light of a single lantern.

Endring leaned back against the wall. "Do you have any word on Borroka's movements?"

Sammel looked at him curiously. "Should I? Didn't she give you a full week?"

"Those days are running out far too quickly."

"If it eases your mind, I've heard nothing."

"Not in the least," Endring smiled wearily. He held up his right hand where the sigil of Neveri shone. "If she knew what I was, she'd move even faster. Still, I fear I'll need to draw her ire away from the temple before long."

"We knew that time would come," Sammel said. He bent down to his bag and rummaged through it, pulling out a small wooden box that barely filled his palm. It was ornately carved and marked with runes. "Take it."

Endring reached for the box, brushing a hand over the lid, and he opened it. The interior was plush with deep blue velvet, and the only thing inside was a small nub of white chalk. His eyes widened. "Dare I ask how you got this?"

"You know what it is then? Good. I thought it might help with your demonstration."

Endring shut the box, feeling his heart pound at the thought. "When the time comes."

"Of course."

They fell silent again. Sammel leaned on the opposite side of the window and went back to peeling the paint, and for a moment both men were lost in their own thoughts.

Eventually, the storm outside lessened, and Endring risked cracking the shutters again, then pushed them wide, letting in a cool breeze that chased away the stale air. The rain had all but stopped now, and he looked out to where the Gods' Mount loomed between buildings on the Northern horizon.

"You'll need to be getting back," Sammel said quickly.

Endring clutched the box. He wasn't ready to give up his life as an Oracle, but that decision had been made by Neveri, and who was he to question a god?

"Soon," he said to himself. "I'll take consolation in the fact that the people of Talamh will know the truth, no longer doomed to live in darkness."

Sammel held out a hand, and Endring turned, and grabbed it.

"Be well," Sammel said. "I'll see you again when the Champions are safely back."

Endring nodded. "Be safe, old friend. Don't take more risks than you need."

"Nor you."

Endring took a deep breath and turned toward the window, setting the box on the sill as he called his boon. His bones cracked and reformed as a rush of pain shot through him. His skin tightened, and his hair grew into long feathers. His arms spread into wings, and he felt his tattered clothing slip away as he lifted into flight. He grabbed the box in his talons as he soared out of the window, feeling the humid wind fill his wings as he rose over the city. As the buildings below fell away, the Gods' Mount filled his vision, the gleaming stone temple atop its green hill.

13: The Champion of Neveri

Locin stared at the ornate door in front of her, carved wood with ancient symbols that made her stomach knot up. The Oracles' wing was almost as elaborate as the Champion's, and definitely more stuffy.

"Why is everything in this rotting temple so pretentious?"

She felt a prick from Spark.

"Hey, my rooms aren't *this* pretentious. It's not my fault the last Champion of Iyanu had bad taste."

This time she felt a fluttery feeling in her chest, the kind that meant she should hurry.

"I'm not stalling." She fingered the bird man statue in her pocket. "I just want to be ready. Is anyone inside?"

A brush against her left hand told her it was all clear, and she grabbed the handle and bent down, staring at the keyhole. She recognized the lock type. Three tumblers. Easy enough.

She called on her boon, but kept her focus right in front of her. She could feel the tiny pins inside the mechanism, smooth and metallic, and she gently raised a finger, clicking them upward one at a time until the handle turned and the door cracked open.

A shiver up her spine said Spark was nervous.

"You worry too much. If you're so scared, stay here and keep a lookout. I won't be long."

She stepped in quickly and pushed the door shut. Endring's chambers were well furnished, though less extravagantly than she would have guessed. Two red couches flanked a wooden table, and a soft purple rug greeted her feet. The walls were hung with the usual art, boring paintings of the night sky and idyllic fields, the kind of stuff she'd expect from a well off old man. She swore they all shopped from the same place. There were strange things too. Pillows from the couches were strewn around the floor, one of the curtains was ripped horizontally, half the panel missing, and purple Oracle robes lay abandoned near the window.

A sharp caw tore through the stillness and she jumped, whirling toward the sound.

"Mire!"

A large raven had landed on the sill of an open window. It tilted its head with beady black eyes locked on her, and let out another loud caw.

"Rotting bird. Shoo!" She walked over and threw her arms toward it, but the stubborn thing just stared at her without so much as flinching.

"I'll warn you, I'm a champion."

It blinked.

Stupid thing. She'd always hated birds and their creepy, beady little eyes. "Fine. Just don't tell anyone you saw me here."

Locin turned back to the room, resuming her search. She wasn't quite sure what she hoped to find, but she was sure she'd find something incriminating. She always did. Maybe another stack of papers like the ones from his satchel, or maybe a giant cauldron where he stirred up poisons.

On a shelf nearby, a form caught her eye. It was set prominently in the space as if it were important, but it was covered with a scrap of torn cloth that seemed to be the missing white curtain. She made her way over and lifted the fabric to reveal a small statue of the goddess Bei'ai.

"Why cover this?"

She made another lap of the room. Everything in this whole place was off, and it had her on edge. Something caught her eye near the bedroom door, and she knelt, running her fingers along three deep gouges in the stone floor. Her breath caught. Whatever made these was strong and sharp, and she didn't want to meet it. She suddenly wanted Spark there with her.

"Spark?" But there was no answer. She was on lookout, and that was for the best.

Locin stood back up and summoned her courage, peering into the dark bedroom. People always kept their secrets in their bedrooms.

The windows here were covered by deep purple curtains, and she could barely make out the form of a light orb, placed on a chest of drawers on the far side. She glanced back at the bird on the window sill, its cold, black eyes still following her.

"I don't suppose you have a candle?"

It just stared at her, fluttering its wings a bit as it hopped from one foot to the other.

"That's what I figured," she muttered as she fumbled her way through the darkened room. She reached the light orb and brushed her hand along the surface, brightening up the interior. Two trunks stood against the right wall and a closet of fine clothing on the left. Eight golden candle sconces were hung in a line on either side of the doorway and even the bed pillows looked expensive. But this room was more of a mess than the first. The bedding lay half on the floor, and claw-like marks slashed across the wall, cutting through a portrait of a pretentious looking man with a narrow gaze. She headed for the chest of drawers first, trying to ignore the fear creeping up, the questions her mind couldn't answer about this place.

She pulled out the top drawer and started pawing through the contents. Most of it was clothing, but there were a few keepsakes and random junk. The second and third drawers were the same and she was feeling rather gloomy about her chances of finding anything by the time she opened the bottom drawer.

Inside was a collection of loose papers and scrolls, a tattered old book, and a tarnished statue peeking out from underneath. Now this looked more like a secret stash. She grabbed the statue and pulled it out. It was heavier than she'd expected. She smiled as the light from the orb illuminated its form. It was almost exactly like her figure, half man, half beast with wings spread wide.

"Neveri?"

A wretched sound from the main room grabbed her attention. She quickly slid the drawer shut, then brushed the light, drowning the room in darkness.

She could feel her heart hammering as she listened. The sound was eerie, like knuckles cracking and something soft being torn. It made her feel sick.

She edged slowly forward, reaching out with her boon and trying to feel her surroundings. The plush mattress, the cold floor, the glass cups of the sconces. Then she tried to stretch further into the next room, the soft couches, the stone statue of Bei'ai, and warm flesh.

She froze as the sound slowly stopped and silence filled the room.

"Spark," she hissed, barely audible. "Are you in here?"

Nothing. Rotting spirit was still outside, but how had someone gotten past without her warning Locin?

She crept forward and peeked around the door into the main room. She could see Endring seated on one of the red couches, staring straight at her.

"Hello, Locin," he said.

She stood warily, her eyes darting to the front door. She could run for it, but what would be the point? He'd already caught her here. She edged around the door frame, clutching the idol of Neveri like it was a shield.

"How did you get in here?" She said.

"How did *I* get into *my* chambers?" He raised an eyebrow. "Is it really so strange that I'm here?"

"Just… unexpected," she said, then she coughed loudly, hoping the noise would draw Spark.

"Join me," he motioned to the couch across from him.

"I'll stand." Locin walked to the back of the couch. She couldn't think of a reason to feel threatened by the old man, but the strange state of the room had her on edge, and he'd gotten by Spark somehow. There was clearly more to him than met the eye.

"I see you found my statue of Neveri."

She glanced at the idol in her hand. It was bigger than the one she'd gotten off Ilum, and the furious expression on its face was unsettling. She held it up. "Kind of a weird keepsake for an Oracle."

He crossed his legs and leaned back, curling his fingers over his lips.

"I'm not surprised," she pressed. "What, with you rubbing elbows in the Sacred Quarter and all."

He smirked at her. "Were you already a champion when we met?"

"Yeah. So?"

"It explains how my satchel came loose. I don't suppose you're inclined to give it back?"

"Not really."

He watched her thoughtfully, and something about his dark gaze creeped her out. "I never would have guessed Iyanu to pick a thief for a champion, but the gods can be capricious."

"Yeah, well, I never would have guessed Bei'ai's Oracle would be a murderous cultist, so I guess we're both surprised."

His eye twitched at the word cultist, but his placid demeanor remained intact. "And what did you learn from my notes? I assume you read them."

Hardly anything. Stupid sewer water.

She smirked. "That's right, old man. I read them. I know all your secrets now. Does that make you nervous?"

He chuckled, and it unnerved her further. Did nothing faze this guy?

"And yet you haven't given me up," he said. "Why?"

She shrugged. "Authority's not really my thing."

He finally showed some reaction, a look of surprise as if that wasn't the answer he'd expected. "That's the only reason? You weren't stirred by the fate of Talamh? Not moved at all by the plight of the unguilded? I thought *that* at least might resonate. But apparently not. You simply *don't like authority.*"

She scowled, fearing he might be seeing through her ruse. "Most thieves don't." If only she'd been able to read those pages.

"And here I thought you cared about someone beyond yourself. But then, you are a champion."

She leaned over the back of the couch. "You know, if I wanted to, I could walk out of this room and tell everybody who you really are, so you might want to watch your tone."

"Was that the reason for your visit? To take that trinket and use it against me?"

She looked down at the statue and ran her thumb across the smooth stone.

"I would think my writings are much more damning than a dusty relic from a bygone era." He shifted, studying her with his steady gaze. "No. You came here because you were searching for something more. You might act like a rebel, but what is a rebel without a cause?"

"Oh yeah, and you and your murderous pals across the river have just the cause worth fighting for, am I right?" She wrinkled her nose. "You know what I don't get? Why are you dragging us into this plan of yours? Go get the Crook. Be heroes. Can't you just walk in there? I mean, you're on their side."

He snarled in response. "I am most certainly not on their side."

"Alright, I'll give you that. They didn't exactly welcome you with open arms. But they did welcome you."

"If they saw me again, it might be a different story."

Locin looked from him to the statue and back again, then slowly walked around to the front of the couch and sat down, looking him in the eye. "So level with me. Why were you over there?"

"You read my writing, you should know."

She bit her lip. "Let's pretend I haven't read quite everything yet."

"To stop any further bloodshed. The senseless violence, the defiling of the sacred, none of this is the will of Neveri."

"And who is Neveri *exactly*?"

He squinted. "Do you not know?"

She bit her lip. She was pretty sure her ruse was more full of holes than a sieve by this point. "Let's say I don't."

He smirked. "How much of my writing was ruined?"

She shrugged.

"That much, huh?" He took a deep breath. "It's a familiar story, though perhaps you've never heard it like this."

"Okay." Locin smirked and leaned back on the couch. She still couldn't decide if Endring was insane or not. "I'm listening."

He began speaking in a reverent tone. "In the beginning, when all the realms were one, when the divine parents still had breath in their lungs, they decided the only way to express their love would be to bring forth offspring, and to impart their divinity to their children."

Locin laughed. "*The Lay of the Gods*? Let me stop you right there. I've heard this one."

But Endring pressed on unfazed. "To each child they gave a piece of their divinity. To Jeza, Kisandin, Strah, Desita, and with each child their own immortality waned. Uthando was born, then Metnadur, then Iyanu, until finally they had only enough divinity left to share with one more child."

"Yeah, yeah. They would give Bei'ai their divinity and become mortal. I thought you were going to tell me something new."

Endring's jaw tightened and he squinted across at her. "Yet that was never the plan. The divine parents would give Bei'ai divinity, saving just enough for themselves. They would remain immortal."

"Hold on. That's not how it goes." Locin studied his face, but he gave up nothing. "The divine parents became the first man and woman. None of us would be here if they hadn't lost their divinity."

"May I finish?"

She sighed and waved him on.

"Imagine the surprise they felt when the divine mother birthed twins."

Locin felt her stomach flip. "What?"

"Bei'ai was born first, and blessed with divinity," Endring said. "But then another was born. What could they do? Would they abandon this final boy to a mortal life, or would they give up the last of their divinity and become mortal themselves to sacrifice for their son? And so Neveri was born, the youngest of the nine, the god of animus."

He leaned back, content for the moment to let the weighty idea hang over her head.

Locin stood, pacing behind the couch. This was utter madness. "You're insane."

He didn't answer immediately, and the room descended into silence. Locin kept telling herself to leave, but something about the idea kept her trapped in place, as though some part of her believed this rubbish.

"And where is Neveri now?" She asked, rubbing her neck. "Why isn't there any sign of him?"

"He's trapped in Nyx, banished for the crime of existing. Why do you think there are unguilded? Have you ever considered that?"

She shrugged, feeling the old shame of being unwanted and uncalled. "Because the rotting gods don't choose everyone."

"There were never unguilded in the one world, but when Neveri was betrayed, those he would call were stripped of the deity they served. Any guild which relied on animus was taken away. They cannot be called because there's no longer a god to call them."

He pointed at the statue she still clutched. "That is why I have that statue. That is why I know the cult. That is why I seek the

Crook. So that no child will ever have to look up at the sky again, and ask, 'why not me?'"

Locin felt her heart stop. She stared down at the sigil on her right palm, and the memory crashed over her like a tidal wave. She was eight years old, staring up at the temple ceiling, her tiny hand pressed against the choosing stone, slick with sweat. She could hear her father ask how long it should take, the tension in her mother's voice as she stifled a sob. Somewhere nearby children laughed and played, and Locin, tears streaming down her face, begged the gods to see her, to pick her.

She stared at the golden knot of Iyanu's sigil, anger burning inside as she balled her hand into a fist. "You expect me to believe any of this? You're cutting the line, old man." She squeezed tears out of the corners of her eyes. "There's no magical ninth god out there waiting to choose us."

"Then explain this."

She looked up, and he lifted his right hand toward her, palm open. A golden light glowed out through an unfamiliar sigil, one with a face half man and half beast.

"It's a trick," she stammered, though the words were hollow.

He stood suddenly, and he seemed taller and stronger than she'd thought. She took a step back and he held his arms to his side, shadows covering his face in the dim light. The same tearing and cracking filled her senses as before, and half his body seemed to twist. His right eye gleamed like a cat's in the dark, and his right arm was suddenly covered in fur, his hand ending in sharp claws.

She stumbled backwards into the wall, dropping the heavy statue with a thud.

In a moment, it was over. He had settled back into the gnarled old Oracle, and he sat on the couch, watching her with a steady gaze.

She reached out for Spark, but she couldn't sense her. Rotting spirit was still in the hall standing guard, and she was alone.

"Now you know everything," his voice was resigned. "You can turn me in, or I can tell you more. My fate is in your hands, Champion."

Her eyes fixed on the golden glow where his right palm lay face up on his lap, and she glanced one last time at her own sigil. She couldn't deny what she had just seen. He was a champion, just like her. She brushed the stains from her cheeks and rolled her shoulders back, strolling to the couch and taking a seat.

"Tell me more."

14: Shadows of the Past

The training yard of the Gods' Mount was more fit for a barracks than a temple. A thick layer of white sand was spread across the ground some hundred yards across and thirty wide. There were no flowering plants here, no stunning vistas, just a collection of archery targets and dummies, a few benches, and a covered portico that surrounded the four walls of the yard.

Voske's hands were covered in grit, curled into fists. He clenched his jaw and steadied his arms, feeling the boon of Jeza like fire in his muscles. He'd been out here for the better part of the evening and he still wasn't tired. He was an Erimos man, after all.

He threw one fist forward, then the other, pummeling them over and over against a massive stone pillar that stood in the center of the yard. To his frustration, it didn't budge, not even an inch. He stretched out his arms, tightening his muscles, and tried to call up every bit of his boon he could, and then he went back at it, blow after blow, his fists crunching against the raw stone. If he had the strength to lift an entire skid of granite, he could surely put a dent in this thing. He punched until sweat had lathered his muscles and his knuckles were bruised.

"Foreman." He scoffed. "I've got a better rotting chance of leading these champions than he does."

He jabbed with his left a couple more times, then leaned back and heaved his right fist into the rock so hard that the impact jarred through his body. The pillar didn't so much as quiver.

"You may want to save some strength for the cultists."

He looked back from his fruitless assault to see Eprim standing just behind him. The Oracle had replaced his customary robes with a suit of leather armor, and he had a pair of swords hanging from his belt.

Voske waved him off. "I've got plenty to spare."

He started up again, hitting different areas, searching for a weakness. The entire pillar was smooth gray stone with only one blemish, a fist-sized gouge at about chest height. He landed a couple solid swings in the dent to no avail.

"Good luck getting that to move."

Voske paused and dusted off his hands, sending a spray of white sand to the ground. "Why's that?"

"That's the Skard stone. Many have tried to leave a mark, but only he did." He motioned to the fist sized dent.

Voske's eyes widened as he pressed his own fist into the hollow of the stone. "Skard did this?"

A smile spread across his face. Now he really wanted to make a mark. He drove back his fist, tightly coiled like a spring, concentrating all his strength, and he thundered a punch into the hollow impression as he gave a cry.

The stone barely shuddered at the impact. It might as well have been a mountain.

He glanced back to see Eprim smirking.

"I'd like to see you do better."

"I don't doubt your strength, Champion. I'm no match for Jeza's chosen."

Voske relaxed, loosening his fists and staring at his aching knuckles.

"I came down here to train as well," Erpim said. "I wish I was going with you, but I'm needed here."

Voske grunted. "Yeah. I wish you were too. I'd take you over Burz any day."

"You two seemed at odds this morning."

Voske curled his hands back into fists and drove them against the pillar again. "You could say that."

Eprim drew his blades and took up a ready stance. "He's got a lot on his plate, having a family and all."

"Sure he does."

"You don't sound convinced."

Voske decided to try a different tactic and kicked the stone, which felt even less effective than his punches. He'd never been great at kicking things.

"He's too cautious," Voske said, "and stubborn."

"He's a champion. I've never known any who weren't stubborn."

"Yeah, but he's the chosen of Uthando. Isn't he all about mercy? What does he care about leading people?"

Eprim swung his blades methodically through the air with incredible dexterity. "I suppose being a soldier is a hard habit to break. He led men for many years."

"Yeah, well, so did I."

Eprim turned to face Voske, letting his swords hang at his side. "I suspect leading champions will be far more difficult. They aren't ordinary men."

Voske turned his attention back to the Skard stone, letting loose another volley of punches. He could still feel Eprim was back there with more to say though, so after a prolonged silence he sighed and turned around to see the Oracle still watching him.

"What?"

Eprim frowned. "Are you familiar with the warrior's creed? Both the soldiers' guild and the monks of Jeza adhere to it."

"Something about justice and mercy, isn't it?"

"No justice without mercy. No mercy without justice."

Voske was getting annoyed with talking. He just wanted to hit something in peace. "What's your point?"

"Uthando and Jeza are linked in more guilds than they're not. There's something about those two."

"So I gotta play nice with Uthando's stone skin, is that it? He's pretty scared of action for a fighter."

"Not scared, I think. Some men love to fight, some are loath to fight. It's important to have both sides."

Voske scowled. "Not when there's fighting to be done."

"It's my experience that when men who are loath to fight finally see that's the only choice, they fight harder than anyone. He might surprise you in the end."

Voske laughed. "I doubt it."

Eprim studied him for a moment, then nodded. "You're a natural born leader Voske. That's easy to see. But it's not enough to have a commanding presence. You've got to give them a reason to follow you. You have to inspire them."

Inspire them, he thought. But they weren't soldiers or hard working quarrymen. They were children, and nobles, and thieves.

They were each as different as the next with nothing to unify them. How in the worlds was he supposed to inspire them?

Night came swift over the Gods' Mount. The cicadas song rose and fell, as the sun dipped below the canopy and faded into black, and now the worlds were still and quiet. Rasa hunched down on a pile of soft velvet blankets and feather pillows she had stripped off the bed. She'd made a little nest between the wall and a padded bench in the parlor of her chambers. A soft lamp hung from the middle of the room, casting diffused light that melted into shadows at the end of its reach.

She could see the bedroom from here, the monstrous round bed with a rich wooden frame and soft mattress. It had four curved posts and a round canopy top, and its shadows were harsh black lines that cut through the edge of the light. She pulled her knees up into her chest and looked away, letting her eyes rest on a blue spirit that hovered close to her. It seemed to waver like a reflection underwater. She could almost make out a face, but every time it started to form, she shut her eyes tight for a few seconds. They seemed safer this way, without faces, formless shapes a realm away.

She opened her eyes again and saw it was still there.

"Are you a good person?" Rasa asked softly. "*Were* you a good person?"

A faint voice answered her. *I tried, I suppose*. It was a gentle voice that wavered like an old woman's.

She could hear them now - with her ears, and not just inside. Again the woman's face started to form, and she blinked hard.

You're frightened. But this is a safe place.

Rasa shook her head. "Safe? Maybe. But it reminds me."

Of what, child?

She opened her eyes again, and saw the spirit was closer, squatting down in front of her as if it were sitting on the floor.

"Of things I try to forget."

There, there, child! It's alright. Memories are painful, but they can't hurt you anymore.

"They can. They make me live it all again. And I have nightmares."

She suddenly felt alone, and she stared at the blue shape inches from her face. It took form unbidden, and aged wrinkles were drawn around the woman's kind round eyes.

Rasa relaxed. "Who were you?"

No one important, I'm afraid. I was a gardener in a small town on Suntara.

"And why are you here? At the temple, I mean?"

The woman smiled as she leaned back. *My great grandson. He's a monk here in the temple. I come to check on him from time to time.*

"How does it work? Do you see and hear him like I see and hear you?"

She shook her head and her eyes seemed sad. *Oh, how I wish! But no. We can see and hear some, but it's never quite clear unless the realms come close, like on the night of the Shattering. But I can catch a glimpse of him every now and then, hear a little of his voice. And there's the veil. We all wait, hoping someone will miss us enough to call us back.*

The Veil of Nyx. She'd heard stories. The thin curtain that brought the realms close enough to touch.

"The monks can call spirits through?"

Yes. Many pilgrims come to speak to lost loved ones. Her face turned downcast. *But some souls are too old to be remembered.*

"But I see you."

The old woman smiled. *Such is the gift of the goddess.*

Rasa glanced at the faces taking shape near her now. A young boy, a woman with long curls, a couple of men watching intently. She shut her eyes. It was all so much.

You can shut us out, dear. Do you want that?

"No." Her voice was muffled, her face buried in her arms, and her eyes shut fast. "I don't want to be alone."

We can watch over you while you sleep.

Rasa shook her head. The lamp light flickered, and the shadows from the bed stretched toward her like four curved claws scraping their way across the floor. She wasn't ready for the nightmares. They were always worse in a new place.

"Tell me about the Veil," Rasa said. "Is it as beautiful as I've heard, like stars in the cold dark?"

The old woman smiled again and rose to her feet. *Would you like to see it?*

"Can I?"

Of course. You are Bei'ai's Chosen.

"Take me," she said eagerly.

She stood up and wrapped her toga close, then padded out the door in her bare feet following the spirit's lead. The common room was empty, and Rasa crept across it without a sound and paced down moonlit halls before reaching a beautiful courtyard teeming with life. A huge oak stood in the center, hung with lanterns. Everything about the temple seemed sacred and wondrous.

They turned toward a high arched door and found themselves out on the great portico where the light of the moon made the great statues shine like opal.

This way, the woman said, her voice low. *Through the sanctum.*

Two monks of Jeza stood guard at the door, and they straightened up as Rasa approached. She hesitated, but the spirit drifted past them, so she plucked up her courage and dashed inside.

It was quiet and dark. Moonlight streamed through the stained glass windows above. Some of the glass was missing, and at her feet a thin crack ran the length of the room. She stepped carefully, one foot on either side as she walked, but somewhere far below she saw the blue shapes of spirits.

This way.

The spirit urged her on, down the sanctum toward the back wall, but ahead her eyes fixed on the eight shrines that curved around the expansive room. Each statue of the gods had an orb that shimmered gold in the dim moonlight. It was not unlike the light of her sigil. The orbs were placed in a different position for each. Bei'ai clutched hers close to her heart. Strah held his aloft and stared within. Jeza's orb was placed just beside her, atop a pile of skulls. She made her way to Jeza's statue. It towered over Rasa, the goddess' eyes sharp and intense. She seemed so lifelike.

"What are they?" She whispered.

The spirit cocked her head to the side. *The orbs?*

Rasa nodded.

A piece of the gods, she said reverently. *You see, they each left two pieces behind when they went to Sbarga. One here.* She pointed at Rasa's chest. *Their power, given to their champions.*

"And this?" Rasa stood on her tiptoes and stretched across the base, grabbing the golden orb and turning it over in her hand. It pulsed as she held it, mesmerized by the light.

Their presence. Given to bind the realms together. They hold Sbarga and Talamh like the tether holds the pylat to the chariot.

"A tether," Rasa said with awe.

A guard cleared his throat, and Rasa turned to see them watching her with wide eyes.

"Sorry," she whispered.

She nestled the orb back in its place and made her way to the door where the spirit waited patiently.

"I'm ready to see the Veil."

The old woman nodded.

They walked out the back doors and down a hall of beautiful red trees, with stained glass windows that colored the moon's light. Finally, they descended a set of stairs deep into the ground, where one final door opened into an other-worldly expanse.

The chamber of the Veil was dimly lit, mostly by the light of flickering blue spirits that floated in a misty, dark sheet that stretched in front of Rasa from one side of the room to the other, bowing outward toward her. A crescent balcony curved around the void that swarmed at the rail, and a statue of Bei'ai beckoned her inward. The air felt cool, and she shivered. She moved close, entranced by the lights that danced like candle flames in front of her. They seemed as curious about her as she was about them. The scope of the darkness was overwhelming, like an endless sea of souls bobbing on the black tide. Her knees felt wobbly as she stared into it, and she had a nervous thought that the whole room would tip on its side, and she would slide in.

"That's Nyx?" She asked.

An unexpected voice answered her, the voice of a man. "It is."

The voice was solid, echoing off the walls. That was no spirit. Rasa's heart was pounding as she turned to see a man in the deep purple robes of Bei'ai. He had a thick cowl over his face and an Oracle's sash across his chest, his dark eyes glinting under his hood.

"You're the Oracle," Rasa managed.

"My name is Endring." He moved slowly closer. "And you're the champion of Bei'ai."

She swallowed hard. "I am."

Endring stepped up beside her, holding his gloved hand toward the Veil, but he didn't touch it. He let his fingers hover just shy of the thick, black surface.

"Is this the first time you've seen it?"

Rasa pulled her arms in around herself and nodded.

"It's beautiful in its own way," he said.

"And a little terrifying."

"Yes. But you have nothing to fear. Those blessed of Bei'ai can touch the Veil."

"And… other people?" She'd heard the stories, people's spirits pulled through the veil into the realm of lost souls. It always sounded too outlandish to believe. But standing here, facing down the cold murky abyss, she believed it.

Endring lowered his arm and glanced toward her, and she caught more of his appearance. Gnarled pink flesh pulled at his lips and extended all the way back toward his hair and down his neck on the right side.

"I'm sure you've heard the stories. Their souls enter Nyx, and their bodies stay behind."

Rasa shivered at the thought, letting her eyes count the flickering blue souls on the other side, wondering if any had been pulled through.

"There are so many." she said.

"Desperate souls. They can't enter the Midding, and they can't come back to Talamh. They're trapped in Nyx."

She stared into the depths. It did have a certain beauty, the way the spirits flickered like so many stars against the shimmering black, like a never ending well of night. It was as beautiful as the spirit had told her and more. But it also felt sad. So many lost, desperate souls.

"Go on," he prompted, nodding toward the Veil.

She looked at him, feeling an edge of panic. "Touch it?"

He nodded. "You don't need to call a soul out, though you could. You should become familiar with it, know how it feels to reach through the Veil."

She turned to face the Veil again, though it looked less beautiful now as fear roiled within her. She lifted her hand, and with some great coaxing, forced her fingers to touch the surface. It was cold, but inviting somehow, like it was pulling at her, welcoming her to Nyx. She pressed her hand fully against it, and it bowed inward. It was oddly solid, like touching the skin of a living thing whose heart pulsed in time with the flickering of the spirits.

The veil began to tug her inward, and she felt like she would fall through. Her stomach flipped and she grabbed hold of the railing.

She could hear Endring speaking behind her. "Don't be afraid, Rasa. Nyx is all around us, as is Sbarga. The three realms are intertwined, like strands in a cord. Here at the Veil, the realms come so close you can touch the other side."

She could feel the little blue souls that swarmed around her hand. They were whispering to her, a wild, chaotic sound that swelled as more flickering lights rushed in. After a moment it became so intense, that she pulled her hand away, stumbling back.

"You could hear them?"

"Yes." Her breath came sharp and quick.

"You must never call them."

She could still feel their pull, almost hear the echo of their voices. "Why not?"

"It's as I said. They're desperate. If you answer one, they will become more insistent."

"Do they need help?"

"No help you can give. They are just poor, lost souls. You could call them out, even speak with them. But you can't free them to live in Talamh again, and you can't send them to the Midding."

Rasa nodded, but kept her eyes locked on the swarm. Many had drifted away after she pulled her hand back, but a generous cloud of souls had stayed, bobbing up and down like driftwood on gentle waves.

He's right, you know, the spirit of the old woman said. She stared at the Veil like a fish might stare at the ocean. *We're all lost, but some are more lost than others.*

Lost. Rasa felt the word mirrored in her own soul. "I understand," she answered.

"Good," Endring replied.

They fell silent and stared into the endless abyss, watching the gentle ripples that passed along its surface. Endring took a step toward her, and Rasa tensed, but she stood her ground.

"Try once more," he said gently. "This time, push past their noise. It's quieter on the other side."

Some of the dancing blue lights had lost interest by now, drifting back into the dark. Rasa lifted her hand, studying for a moment the golden sigil there. It all still seemed like someone else's life.

"It feels like it will pull me in."

"I feel that too," Endring said. "Every time."

There was some ache in his voice that she didn't understand. Maybe she would in time.

"Anchor yourself with what's around you," he said. "The feel of the stone under your feet, the sound of your breathing, the touch of the Veil on your skin. It's your life, in the end, that keeps you from sinking into the realm of the dead."

She nodded and then pressed her hand into the Veil again, the thick skin giving against the gentle push. Once more the swarm of spirits converged around her hand. She heard their frantic whispers, felt their presence pushing against her mind. It was such a jumble, it overwhelmed her. It was more like thoughts and flashes of images than words. Someone ached to see their wife again. Another longed to feel wind on their skin. And on it went in a sea of desperate pleas.

"Push past them," Endring urged. "I find it helps to fix my eyes out beyond them in the black."

She lifted her gaze to the distant black, but immediately she felt like her feet would give way and she would slip into the abyss. She gasped.

"Anchor yourself."

She let his voice hold her to Talamh as her mind drifted into the depths, and she pushed past the clamor. Suddenly she was alone in the dark. The voices had stilled, though she still sensed them, and a thousand more. She felt she could go in any direction, reach toward any of the voices. As she focused on one she saw an image of a little girl, swimming in a sunlit stream. Another voice caught her attention, and she felt cold. Her hands ached with age, and she longed for release. And then another presence caught her mind, somewhere alone in the dark. She turned toward it, and an image flashed in her thoughts. A young girl and a young boy played together in the mud. The memory nearly overwhelmed her with emotion. Sorrow, regret, pain. She felt herself drifting further into Nyx, into the deepest darkness of its void. Something was out there. She felt it, a stronger presence than the rest, and a flash of golden light. She trembled as her mind strayed from the safety of Talamh, and she was struck with the horrible thought that she would lose herself in the dark.

"Rasa?"

Endring's voice was distant, like a memory of someone she once knew. Panic started to seize her as she gasped for air. She was hovering on the edge of tipping into the void. She needed to get out.

"Endring?"

She heard her own voice as she spoke, and it sounded far away. She focused on the words as they echoed through the stone chamber. And then she felt her heart.

Thump. Thump. Thump.

She felt her hand against the cool black of the Veil, and her feet against the stone floor.

She took a deep, gasping breath as she pulled her hand away from the Veil.

Endring watched her with wide eyes. "You went deep. Are you alright?"

She was shaking, but she nodded.

"What did you see?" He was watching her keenly.

"Blackness, and spirits," she said. "And I saw memories. At least that's what I think they were. Children playing."

He nodded his understanding. "They're the spirits' thoughts. Sometimes they're memories, sometimes hopes or regrets. They can be overwhelming, but you did well." He glanced back one last time at the dancing lights against the Veil. "It's late now. Come. We should leave this place."

Rasa thought of her room, and the cruel dark shadows.

"You go," she said. "I want to stay a while and watch the lights."

"As you wish, Champion."

As he left, she turned her eyes back on the Veil. "I can call anyone?"

The old spirit nodded. *Any spirit that's passed the Veil. But they choose if they want to come.*

Rasa nodded her understanding, and then rested her hand back against the skin of Nyx. She pressed past the desperate spirits, out into the black, and she whispered, "Telal."

For a moment, she felt nothing but the empty dark and the depth of the abyss tugging her soul like a riptide. She had nearly given up, and was fixed on the sound of her breath, ready to pull back, when she saw a blue spirit drifting toward her. It came up to the Veil and started to swell and take form. She felt it rush into her hand and a flood of thought and memory burst into her mind. Flashes of laughter, tears, hope, and regrets. She saw an image of Telal sitting on the floor, braiding her own long red hair. They were young, Telal ten and Rasa eight. The year she should have been guilded.

In the memory, Telal leaned in close, tucking one last strand in place. "Don't worry, Rasa. We won't be here forever. You and me? We're gonna get out, and when we do, we'll see the whole realm, and go anywhere we want!"

The memory faded as the blue spirit passed through her into Talamh. She turned, and Telal stood on the balcony, smiling. She looked older now, almost full grown, and her eyes sparkled.

"How'd you do that?" She said with a smile.

Rasa walked over to her, reaching out to touch her, but her hand passed through. She was there, but not, a shadow given substance.

"I told you we'd get out."

Rasa choked back tears. "But you…"

Telal laughed, and it felt warm in Rasa's chest. "I got free another way. And you? Little fire head is a champion? I can't believe it!"

"I've missed you."

"Yeah. Me too."

Rasa glanced around. A few curious spirits watched. "Can you stay long?"

Telal shook her head. "Only a little while. That's how it works."

Rasa nodded. "But you'll stay a little while? Maybe we can talk."

She sat cross legged on the floor, and motioned Rasa to join her. "You bet."

Zengin stared down at gloved hands. They were the hands of a young boy.

I'm dreaming again.

He was used to the dreams, they came every night, some memory that was not his own, some horror that he had lived. But this was different. This was his memory.

He was in his childhood room, staring across the lavish surroundings toward a full length mirror. He was about ten years old, thin, wearing a long red chiton tied with gold at the waist. His room was small, with a fine armoire, a four poster bed, and a simple dark wood chest by the wall. A gilded prison.

His gaze centered on the ornate mirror again. His cheeks were tear stained, and his hands shook. He heard yelling and crashing from somewhere distant in the house - the familiar sound of his father's rage. He curled up on the floor by the foot of the bed and buried his face in his knees.

"Stop it, you baby!" He wept softly. "He'll only hurt you more."

The door opened with a soft scrape against the wooden floor, then closed again just as softly.

"Mara?"

He peeked over his arms and saw her, his old nanny. She was a lean woman with a kind face and gray hair, but at this moment her eyes looked fearful.

"I'm here," she said in barely a whisper. "It's alright, Zengin." She knelt beside him, looking cautiously over her shoulder.

"I thought you weren't allowed in here."

"I don't care," she said tersely. She was fidgeting with a hand in her pocket. "Now you listen to me, Zengin! I don't care what that monster says. He's wrong."

Zengin balled his hands into fists. He was angry. He wanted to hit something, but he felt Mara touch his gloved hand gently. She thought he was just unguilded, and his father despised him for it. She didn't know the truth. Would she recoil from him if she did? He couldn't bear the thought.

He glanced up at her. Her eyes were hard and her lips drawn in a tight line, but it was determination, not anger, and there was still compassion there. She cupped her right hand around his cheek, her own bare palm that she kept ungloved. Unguilded didn't do that, but Mara did.

"I want to give you something," she said softly. "But you can't tell anyone."

The implication was clear. Don't tell him. Zengin nodded. He wouldn't tell his father anything anymore. He learned that lesson long ago.

She smiled, drawing her hand back, then reached under her stola and pulled out something on a chain.

"There are lots of people like us," she said fondly. "But there's hope too, Zengin. Don't you ever lose hope. Things will get better."

She pushed her hand into his, and he felt something warm and metal. She smiled one last time. The noise was dying down, and she looked nervously toward the door. He would be irate if he found her here.

"Goodbye, Zengin."

That was it, her last goodbye. He didn't know it then, but he would never see Mara again after that night.

As the door shut with a soft click, he opened his hand and stared at the small idol in his palm, hung on a thin chain. It was a statue of a man in intricate detail. He had a pair of wings that sprouted from his back and wrapped around his body. Horns grew out from his head, and his eyes were narrow and cat-like. Zengin stared at it intensely until he heard footsteps in the hall outside. His father was coming.

He hurried to his old wooden chest and stuffed the idol inside, burying it beneath books and clothes, then he wiped his cheeks dry and stood his ground, facing the door.

The footsteps were close now, just outside, and his heart leaped into his throat. The door flew open and hit the wall in a fury, and a dark shape rushed into the room. It had the wings of a raven and the body of a panther, and its cold fangs dripped blood. It leapt at him with a sharp caw that pierced the air, and he threw himself to the floor with his arms over his face.

Zengin's eyes shot open. He lay in the familiar stillness of the dead of night. It was empty and dark, and the only sound was the sharp intake of his own breath. He sat up and slipped out of his bed, leaving the thin cover behind. The air in his chambers was thick and warm, and he made his way to the window, unlocking it and pulling it open. A cool breeze drifted in and caressed his skin, carrying the scent of plumeria from the gardens below. He was used to being up at night, and he didn't mind it at all. There was a pleasantness to a world devoid of people. But he could live without the dreams.

He made his way to a pitcher and dumped the clean water into a basin, splashing his face and neck before dressing, but he kept glancing all the while at a collection of boxes and trunks that were stashed on the side of the room. They had only just arrived from Tajerim, and he'd been considering dumping the lot of them in a fire. He wanted nothing from his old life. But his father knew that. That's precisely why he'd sent them.

Zengin made his way over, moving a crate aside to reveal the old wooden chest from his childhood. He opened it carefully and stared in at the remnants of his youth. There were books and toys, a wooden sword. He picked it up and felt the grain of it in his hand. He tossed it aside and kept digging past jewelry, clothes, and an old collection of globes until he spotted it, a simple tarnished chain. He pulled it out and stared at the idol. It was still here after all these years.

"Neveri," he whispered.

He ran a thumb down the cold metal, staring into the bestial eyes. Thus far his conversations with Sammel had been cryptic at best. He needed something more solid, and he knew just where to go. He had heard so much about the grand scrollery of the Gods' Mount, it seemed a shame he hadn't yet visited.

Soon he was picking his way through still dark halls, the echo of his own footsteps his only company. And it wasn't long before he found himself in front of the wide open doors of the scrollery. Inside was a cavernous ceiling, and endless rows of ancient wood shelves holding volumes upon volumes of books and scrolls. The smell of must and ink welcomed him, and he ventured in, letting his fingers brush the rows of dry parchment and supple leather spines.

He thought of the scrollery where he trained, of sunlight through large windows, and a cool sea breeze that fluttered the pages of the books. It was humble compared to this.

The Gods' Mount scrollery was without a doubt the largest and most well cared for he had ever seen. He could only assume some of these tomes had sat untouched for centuries, and yet there wasn't a sign of dust anywhere. The scribes of Strah took great care in preserving these treasures, and that pleased him.

He stopped to stare at a row of books. One caught his eye, a thick, green tome called *The Herbalist's Compendium*. He would never forget it. It was the first work he ever scribed. Endless hours of dipping the quill, the methodical noise of tapping the nib on the glass, the smell of the fresh ink, the roughness of the paper. Hour after endless hour. There was a beauty to the mundane nature of those simple tasks. But it reminded him, too, of the rest of his life.

As he opened the book, he was eight years old again, using his boon for the first time. His father needed to know what happened on a rival Archon's trip to Helain. And the memory was right back fresh in his mind. The knife driving into a pale woman, over and over into her chest to the sound of ripping flesh and gurgling screams. It was the first time he felt fresh blood, warm on his skin, the first time he felt the thrill of murder warring against his own horror. He'd cried after, and his father beat him for it. So he waited until he was gone, and he cried more. It was the first night he hadn't slept, and he hadn't slept through a night since.

His anger boiled inside, and he looked down to see his nails dug into the pages of the book. He grabbed the torn pages and ripped them out, the sound of it filling the scrollery.

"H-hello?" Came a voice from the darkness. The shy voice of a woman. "Is someone there?"

He made his way toward it, coming out from the rows of books to see Illeri nestled on the wide ledge of a massive arched window. She sat with a book in hand, the glow of the moon lighting the pages.

"Oh, Zengin. I didn't expect anyone else to be up at this hour."

"Nor did I."

"I don't sleep much at night."

She motioned to the window, and he moved closer to see the night sky overhead, endless stars against ominous black.

"Isn't it beautiful?"

"I suppose," he said. He let his eyes flit down to the book in her lap, a hand written journal of some kind, certainly not the work of a scribe.

"You couldn't sleep either?" She asked.

"I seldom do."

"I had to hold the field at all times day and night. I never settled into much of a routine, so I stay up at night sometimes to see the stars."

"I've never given them much thought, I suppose." He looked back up, noting the differences in each one now, some silver, some golden, one shining a soft pink, all different in their size and brightness. Suntara was visible beside a crescent moon, watching over the stars like their king and queen.

"They were my life."

He let his eyes drift back down to her. She was staring up at the stars with longing as the moon showered its light across her pale skin.

She looked at him. "What keeps you up?"

He shifted, sitting down on the ledge. "If beauty keeps you up, it's the opposite for me."

She frowned, scrunching up her face. "How so?"

"I've seen the worst parts of our realm. The most vile impulses of men. The ugliest things there are to see."

She let out a thoughtful 'hm' as if she didn't quite understand, but she was curious. He could see it in her eyes. He was a mystery to her, but she was shy. He knew she wouldn't press further.

"What are you reading?"

"Oh," she rested a hand on the book, covering the page. "It's just a journal. One of the previous Champions of Kisandin. Gillis mentioned they were in the scrollery."

"I recall."

"I thought maybe… I guess I hoped…" she sighed, closing the book with a soft thud. "I understand we're heading out tomorrow to the Sacred Quarter." Her voice quavered. "I thought it might help me with my boon, but it's not."

"Why do you need help with your boon?"

She shifted uncomfortably. "I haven't actually used it yet."

"And the previous champion had no great wisdom to impart? No clear explanation to help?"

"He's mostly just whining about the temple, and the people, and the other Champions. He mentions his boon, but he just says he used it. He just *altered time*. It doesn't say how."

"Perhaps another journal?"

She sighed. "This is my fourth."

It was his turn to 'hm'.

"They all make it seem like some easy thing. One described it as *feeling* time. Just *feel* the time and then slow it down. How does one *feel* time?"

"I'm sure I don't know."

"But you've used your boon, haven't you? Most of the others have."

"I have." He kept himself perfectly still and calm. He doubted she could read any subtle tells, or even overt ones, but he'd learned to never show his hand, no matter what.

"How?" She leaned in eagerly. "How do you do it?"

Zengin focused on her. He'd found Illeri to be intelligent. But he *felt*. Deeply. More than he could bear most days.

"Perhaps it is all feeling?" He said. "Maybe you're thinking too much and not feeling enough."

She slumped back against the window frame, clutching the book as if he had crushed her last, faint hope.

"I didn't mean to upset you," he said.

"You didn't. Maybe I'm just not cut out to be a Champion."

"Kisandin wouldn't have chosen you if that were the case."

She seemed to perk up a little at that, straightening her back and tipping her chin up. "I hadn't thought of it like that."

"You're a Champion now. You should think that way. No one will show you your worth. In fact, they'll try to snuff out your light so they seem brighter. Don't forget why you're here. Only a few in all the worlds are chosen to be Champions."

"Right." She pulled the journal open again, staring down at the scrawled words. "I can do this."

He rose from his spot on the ledge. He had research to do, and he preferred to have it done in the dark before the place was crawling with scribes. "I'll leave you to it."

She looked up at him fervently. "Thank you, Zengin."

He nodded and made his way back into the endless rows of tomes with one word on his mind.

Neveri.

15: Dark Eyes and Deeds

Rasa sat perfectly still. This was far from the first time she'd had someone do her makeup, but it was the first time she'd had it done by a champion, and this murky black ink wasn't exactly makeup. She stared past Locin toward a mirror on the wall. She had dark black circles smudged around her eyes that made her look dreadfully angry. She didn't like it, but if this was the disguise she had to wear to blend in, she would do it.

"There." Locin leaned back and smiled at her own handiwork.

The spirit of a young girl stood beside her, looking warily at Rasa. Rasa shut her eyes and pushed back against Nyx. She still wasn't fully comfortable with the whole thing, but she was getting used to it. She opened her eyes and avoided looking directly at the spirit, now a pale blue light hovering beside Locin, featureless and safe.

"Well?" Locin pressed. Her own eyes were the same black, and she wore the same scratchy commoner garb with a crude beastly symbol drawn on the chest. Ragged gloves covered both their hands. "It's a perfect disguise."

Rasa thought back to the riders on the chimera. It looked just like their eyes had. She nodded.

"See!" Locin stood and crossed her arms, sending her curly hair bouncing around her face. "I'm good at this."

The little blue spirit shape wobbled around, and Rasa could almost hear laughing.

Locin frowned for a moment, but then quickly shook her head. "Whatever. Let's go. The others are all ready. Don't want them to leave without us." She grabbed up her sandals and slipped them on. She'd spent most of the morning fussing over them, and they were caked in some kind of sticky mud.

Rasa slipped on her own worn sandals and followed Locin out to the common room, the blue spirit still hovering close. The others were making preparations, tightening clothes, pulling on gloves, and hiding weapons. They all looked older, and more determined. Like they knew what they were doing.

Rasa had experienced more trials than most people twice her age, and she knew it, but what did she know about fighting? She straightened her shoulders and marched out into the room. She could at least look confident.

"Gods and Chosen!" Voske yelled. He was fighting with a cloak that looked like it was trying to strangle him. He pulled at it, trying to cover his face. It was a tattered thing.

Endring stood beside him. He calmly grabbed the stray edges and pulled them loose around Voske's neck until it hung correctly.

"Rotten thing," Voske continued. "Why would anyone wear something so complicated?"

"It's a piece of cloth," Burz said coolly. He took his own cloak and hood and tossed it deftly over his head, wrapping it around his neck with ease.

Voske scowled. "They're made for people your size."

"It looks fine, old man, just stop fussing with it!" Locin swatted his hand away as he pulled on the edges.

Voske's face was smudged with dirt, and his eyes rimmed with black. He looked over the room. "All ready?"

Burz was looking over the room too, and his eyes rested on Rasa. "No."

She looked down at her own ragged stola, but she couldn't see anything wrong with it.

"No what?" Voske asked.

"No." He walked toward Rasa. "You're staying."

She felt her heart sink. "Why?"

"You were nearly dead last night."

Voske scoffed. "So were you after you healed her."

"I'm a soldier. She's a child."

Rasa edged back toward the wall. This was a familiar feeling. *Inadequacy.*

"She's a champion," Voske retorted. "She's as much right to go as you or I."

"And when she's hurt, or worse?" Burz crossed his arms and glared at Voske. "Will you take responsibility for her?"

"I will." Weylyn's voice cut through. She was dressed like the others, with her bow and quiver peeking out from under her ragged cloak. She locked her cool violet eyes on Rasa and nodded. "I'll watch over her."

Voske shrugged. "Good enough for me."

But Burz huffed, unconvinced.

"She looks capable enough to me," Weylyn said.

Rasa felt her throat catch. She was the invisible girl. She always had been. The only people who saw her, saw her as a body to be abused. But this woman *saw* her.

"Besides," Weylyn continued, turning her sharp gaze on Burz. "A god chose her. Do you think you know better?"

Burz sighed. "Of course not, but if we have to fight, what is she gonna do?"

Voske jerked a thumb toward Illeri, who was standing awkwardly by the door. "Illeri's coming, and you didn't have a problem with her."

"Illeri can control time," Burz answered.

Illeri pulled at the collar of her tunic and stared straight at the floor.

"Enough of this," Weylyn said. "I already said I'd vouch for her. Either she comes, or I stay."

They grew silent at this until Burz shook his head. "Let's pray nothing goes wrong."

Weylyn crossed the room to where Rasa stood. "Just stay close to me," she whispered. "Do exactly as I do, and don't take Burz' criticism too hard. He's a father. He's only concerned for your safety."

Rasa nodded gratefully.

"Alright," Voske said, clapping his hands together, "let's go. Monks are early risers, and I plan to be knee deep in sewage by the time they're asking questions."

"Sewage?" Hikari said, gulping. He wore the same rags as the rest of them, and still managed to look clean somehow.

Voske smirked. "Didn't I mention the sewers?"

"I'm afraid you forgot that part."

He clapped Hikari on the back. "Don't worry, smoothy, the smell only lasts a week or two."

The champions headed for the door, but Weylyn waited, watching Rasa.

"Ready?"

Rasa nodded. She felt grateful for Weylyn's presence, and even more so for the confidence she seemed to have in her.

"Ready."

The sewers were just as unpleasant as Locin made them sound. It smelled like all the worst things Voske could imagine mingled together and left to rot. He pulled his beggar's garb up closer around his neck and reached out a hand, tapping Locin's shoulder. "How much farther?"

"I'm trying to remember."

"I thought you said you were sure."

"I am. I just…" She turned, looking around uncertainly. "Everything looks the same. Rotting sewer." She glared at the yellow flowers growing near the sides. "Rotting flowers."

Voske held his torch higher and snuffed at the stench in the air. He had to give her that. He couldn't tell the difference either. They'd been walking nearly an hour past the same stone walls, the same brick patterns, and the same watery sludge. Locin claimed the flowers were part of the smell, but Voske couldn't see how that was the case when he caught a whiff of the brown mire that squished between his toes and dripped off his pant cuffs.

"It's going to be daylight before we get out of here," Burz grumbled. "We can't afford delays."

"Just give her some time," Hikari said cheerfully, trying to keep the mood light, then he passed Locin a sidelong glance. "Any minute now, right, darling?"

She rolled her eyes.

"Do you recall any sounds?" Weylyn asked from behind. "Any smells from where you entered last time?"

Locin shook her head.

Voske glanced back at the others. Hikari, Weylyn and Rasa were just behind him and Burz, while Illeri and Zengin brought up the rear. They were all dressed in ragged beggar's garb, and dark paint was smeared around their eyes. They really did make scarily good cultists. Most of them carried weapons, whatever they were comfortable wielding. Hikari had a dull bronze sword strapped to his belt, Weylyn her bow, and Voske carried a rough wooden club, something the Jeza monks normally only used for training. He was wishing his axe was ready, but such an obvious champion's weapon would have been a bad choice. Zengin and Locin had opted for more discreet weapons, and Illeri and Rasa were the only ones unarmed. Voske felt a twinge of doubt about letting them come along, but he'd made his choice. All they had to do was stay out of trouble, and they'd be fine.

"How could she recall anything *but* this smell," Hikari said in a nasally tone. He had his fingers pinched over his nose. "I've never smelled anything so putrid in all my life!"

Zengin looked at Hikari like he was an idiot, though he also had a rag over his mouth and nose to shield himself from the stench. "She means *different* smells. Although I doubt you could pick any out through this."

"Or the depth of the water," Weylyn added. "Or anything stuck to the sides. Something to break up all the sameness."

Locin shook her head. "I was kind of running for my life."

Burz sighed. "We should have gotten Endring to draw us a map. He seemed very familiar with these tunnels. I should have insisted."

Voske scowled at him, but he couldn't help but agree. Somehow he thought these wretched tunnels would be simpler to navigate. A tunnel to him was a straight shot through, but these sewers were winding with branching paths everywhere.

"We're heading south right now," Illeri said. "If that helps."

They all stopped and stared at her.

She winced. "I've been tracking the direction since we got in the tunnels. It seemed like a good idea."

"It was," Voske said, impressed.

"But, how does that help us?" Hikari asked.

Locin furrowed her brow. "It might help. I headed east. I remember getting through the grate and thinking the tunnel was heading straight toward the Arrtris."

Voske nodded thoughtfully and held his torch a bit higher. "So we watch for a right turn, back to the west?"

Locin nodded. "You do have a brain in that old head of yours."

"Very funny. Just get us un-lost, will ya thief?"

"You mentioned there was a grate?" Weylyn said.

"Yeah."

"Then there should be light coming through it."

"I guess."

"Allow me, darling!"

Hikari reached out a hand like he was clutching an invisible apple in the air, then threw his arm backward down the tunnel. Instantly the light retreated from Voske's torch, shrouding the passage in darkness.

It was a strange sensation. Voske could still feel the heat of the flame, and he swore he could still see the air rippling where the tongues of fire should have been, but the light that it cast was gone. The group grew silent and waited, letting their eyes adjust to the dark. Several pockets of starlight glowed from above them, shining down from the rainwater runoffs of the Sacred Quarter, and far down the tunnel, Voske could barely make out the orange light of a torch that wasn't his.

"This way," Voske said, and he brushed past Locin, striding toward the distant torchlight.

They walked in silence the rest of the way, as though suddenly aware of the enemies that could be standing just overtop of them.

Voske poked his head around the corner of the tunnel to see a ladder about fifty yards distant. It was leaning against the sidewall of the sewer, and led toward a faint orange glow from above. "Is that the one?" he hissed.

Locin leaned out around him and nodded, holding a finger to her lips to keep the group quiet.

Voske felt a thrill rush through him and he waved the others on toward the light. He edged forward to the bottom rung and stared up. It was at least thirty feet straight through a square shaft to a trap door at the top of the ladder. There was a heavy bronze grate over the opening, and on the other side the torchlight burned vibrantly against a dull gray ceiling.

"Three men in the room," Weylyn whispered.

Voske smiled. Already their boons were coming in handy. "Are they armed?"

"With spears. Yes."

Voske nodded in acknowledgement and placed his hand on his side, feeling the rough grain of the wooden club he'd chosen, tipped with a heavy metal knob. "I'll go first. Pile in behind me, and quieter is better."

The others nodded and he took a deep breath, then climbed upward. The ladder creaked slightly, and he steadied himself, listening above, but no one seemed to have noticed. He could hear the faint murmur of idle conversation.

He pressed on to the top, looking back to where Hikari and Locin were climbing behind him. He took in a breath, summoned his boon, and drove his fist into the grate. It flew loose and smashed into the room above as Voske leapt through after it, pulling his club loose.

The three spindly men seemed frozen in confusion. They were staring at him with wide eyes.

"Who in Nyx are you?" One of them said as they drew their spears. "We aren't expecting nobody through here."

Voske smiled as he wiped the grime from his brow. He heard Locin and Hikari scrambling up behind him, as he crossed the room and swung his club down hard against the man's spear, splintering it into kindling. He grabbed the man by the collar and lifted him off his feet as he paled.

"Don't kill me!"

"I'm not gonna kill you."

Voske turned and saw the others had scrambled up now, all but Illeri who was just peeking her head over the top of the ladder.

Burz had one cultist on his knees, the tip of his sword at the man's throat, and Locin and Hikari had subdued the third. Voske was feeling pretty confident, and he fought the urge to shout. The last thing they needed was to draw more cultists.

Weylyn moved to the window and peered out through wooden slats that covered it over. "A few more outside. Not very close, but we should be quick and quiet."

"What in the name of Neveri-" the cultists words were cut short by an Apple that Locin sent flying across the room into his mouth. He gagged for a moment, and then worked at spitting it out.

"Might want to gag them," Locin said.

"Be silent, cultists!" The voice of Zengin was quiet, but it rippled with the power of Metnadur, and an eerie stillness fell over the room. "And be still."

Burz ripped a piece of cloth from his cloak and started to gag the man kneeling before him. "Good. That will give us time to bind and gag them."

"Two of them." Zengin had his dark eyes fixed on the one near Locin. "You, come here if you want to live."

The man stood on shaky legs and marched obediently toward Zengin who still stood at the top of the ladder.

Voske kept one eye on them as he gagged and bound the cultist nearest him. The man was staring at Zengin with terror on his face.

"What are you doing?" Voske asked as Zengin circled around the man until his back was to the other champions, and the cultist stood between him and the ladder.

"We need information," Zengin said coolly. "Isn't this why you brought me along?"

Voske scowled. They didn't have time for this, but aside from a layout of the streets, they were going in blind. They could use more information about the cultists. "Fine," he said. "Make it quick."

Zengin stared at the man who was now facing him, trembling in the torchlight. "Tell me, how many are you?"

Even though his words weren't directed at Voske, he felt the strong pull of the honey of Metnadur gnawing at his mind, and he hated it.

"Twen - twenty-five hundred," the man stammered. "Maybe more by now. Borroka's been recruiting."

"Make this quick," Voske snapped quietly. Zengin's boon had him on edge, and he hated seeing this man forced in such a way.

Zengin glared at him, and then turned back to the man. "Where is this Borroka?"

"The shrine of Metnadur."

"And where are the relics?"

The man looked confused.

"The ones you captured from the House of Dusk."

"I - I think they took 'em to that big tower." He winced as if in pain, and Voske felt his stomach knot up. "Iyanu's tower with the green ring."

Burz stepped forward, seeming frustrated by this too. "We know that, Zengin."

"And now we know for certain." He stepped toward the man. "Tell me, heretic, how many guard the tower?"

The man gritted his teeth and suppressed a pained cry.

"Don't want to answer? Very well." Zengin filled his voice with his boon, and spoke again in a commanding tone. "Step back."

The man's right leg dragged backwards as if on its own, and then the left. He was standing on the brink, the back of his heels hanging over the edge of the opening, and he trembled.

"Zengin!" Voske boomed, too loudly, but he was angry.

But Zengin ignored him and pressed on. "How many guard the tower?"

"A handful of her officers, but they're armed with relics, and Char."

"Char?" Burz repeated.

Zengin spoke again, his words still pulling on the man. "Who is Char?"

"Borroka's beast, the chimera."

"Great," Locin said. "That sounds fun."

"I don't know nothing else, I swear it! Let me live. Tie me up. I won't make trouble!"

"Tell me about the chimera."

The poor man was sweating bullets now, wobbling on the edge of falling back. "They roost up there on the tower. They can see all the way to the Gods' Mount."

"And the relics?"

The man winced again.

Voske fought back the urge to snatch Zengin away and toss him on his butt. But this was why they brought him. It was good information, and they needed it.

"The relics?"

"Near… near the top of the tower. Most of them are… they're still boxed up in crates. Please! Let me go."

"Thank you," Zengin's voice droned menacingly. "You've been most helpful. Now, step back."

The weight of the words settled on the room as the man's legs dragged involuntarily backwards. Voske rushed for the man, as did Burz, but they were too late. The cultist's eyes went wide with terror and he disappeared over the edge. A sickening thud echoed back up as Voske ran to the opening and knelt, peering in the darkness below. He could just make out the man's crumpled body.

The other two cultists were horrified, struggling at their bonds as the Champions looked at Zengin.

Voske was livid. "You rotting pool of mire!" He stood and took one quick step towards Zengin.

"Stop!"

The honey of Metnadur hit Voske like a stone wall. His body jerked to a halt, and he felt his boon flood his veins on instinct.

The other champions watched in horror as Burz stepped forward. "Enough of this," he said in a stern voice. "What's done is done."

But Voske wasn't feeling so forgiving. "You rotting son of a serpent."

"Burz is right," Zengin said calmly. "What's done is done. We should hurry before more guards show up."

"You didn't have to kill him." Voske took another step with a great amount of effort until he towered over Zengin.

Zengin stared at him with a cold disinterest. "I don't have time for this." He turned toward the door, but Voske grabbed his arm, pinning him in place, and he spoke again. This time his voice seethed with anger. "Remove your hand now."

"You're not coming."

Zengin stayed still as tension filled the air. Illeri held a hand over her mouth, her face pale, and even Burz was hanging back, tense and ready for whatever might come.

"Go back to the temple," Voske said. "You've helped enough."

Zengin relaxed as the tension seemed to drain out of the room, and Voske let him go. He brushed at his sleeve. "I'm sure you'll fare well without the boon of Metnadur."

"We'll be just fine."

Voske took a deep breath and pointed down toward the sewer grate. "There's your way out."

Zengin held his gaze for another moment and then turned and started down the ladder.

Voske stayed quiet and resolute, watching as Zengin sloshed away into the dark.

An uneasy stillness hung over them as they stood frozen.

It was Locin who broke the silence as she motioned them toward the door. "As much as I'd love to sort out what just happened, the street is clear right now. It may not stay that way."

She threw the door open, and Voske could see the hazy gray of predawn. The sun would be up soon, and they couldn't afford to waste any time.

"That settles it," he said. "We take my path through the narrow alleys."

Burz scoffed.

Voske was not in the mood for another fight. "Not a word, soldier! We lost the honey tongue, so I'm keen on avoiding any conversations. And, Locin?"

She looked back at him.

"We do run into any trouble, you do the talking."

"I'm no Zengin."

"You'll do."

He strode past her and out the door, glimpsing the Gambit of Iyanu. It loomed over the dark sky like a shadow of deeper black. They weren't off to a great start for their first venture, but there was nothing left to do but press on.

"Come on," he said. "Let's get this over with."

16: The Sacred Quarter

Endring stood on a balcony at the front of the temple as the sun broke over the horizon. Golden light cracked through the dark of night and showered across the Sacred Quarter. His gaze was fixed on the Gambit, rising over the skyline, and he narrowed and shifted his eyes until the tower came into sharp focus. It was too late to worry, but he still did. Either they would succeed or not. He parted his lips to pray for their success, but would any god heed him?

"Here you are." The voice of Aurilis startled him.

He noted the sharp edge to her tone, and he let his eyes shift back to normal before she reached the railing. She stood beside him and matched his gaze.

"I gave you clear instruction," she said coldly.

"You did."

"And you think this is helping? You do realize that if the Champions are walking into a trap, I will not be able to save you."

Endring thought he could hear conflict in her tone. The High Oracle was issuing a threat, but maybe some old shred of their friendship remained.

"I should think they'd need saving, not I."

"Don't be flippant."

He glanced at her. "Do you honestly think I would send them into a trap?"

"I don't know what to think anymore." She turned to face him. "You reach beyond your station, Endring. You don't command the Champions."

"Nor do you."

Anger flashed across her face for a moment before she composed herself. "This was foolish at best, treason at worst."

"I merely offered them an opportunity to serve Talamh," he pressed. "Isn't that their purpose?"

"We're no longer in the days of Skard. It's our purpose to keep them safe."

"And in line?" Endring furrowed his brow. "Perhaps the temple has had the reins too long."

"Do you recall the last time the champions tried to rise above the temple?"

"I'm hardly suggesting a rebellion."

Aurilis turned her gaze back toward Arrajin. Golden light was shining over the temple now and spilling into the streets, shimmering across the Arrtris.

She sighed. "I can not protect you, Endring." She glanced at him with intention. "I *will* not protect you. You're playing a very dangerous game, and it won't end well for you. I told you to refocus on your duties as an Oracle, and not heap suspicion on yourself."

He matched her tone, squaring his shoulders as he turned fully toward her. "And I told you that trying to take the Sacred Quarter would fail. How many lives could have been saved if you'd listened?"

She scowled. "Enough. The Oracles have called a meeting tomorrow evening to discuss your position among us."

That stung more than he thought it would. He hadn't asked to be a champion. He'd thought to live out his life as the Oracle of Bei'ai, though truthfully he'd already lost that position before his boon was taken. Still, the thought of being shunned again bit at him, and he spoke with a bitter tone. "You've already decided, haven't you?"

Aurilis' face hardened, and she kept her tone sharp. "You've left us no choice. You have until tomorrow night to come up with a compelling argument."

He nodded tersely.

"And if the Champions do not return, all of them alive, you may have less time than that."

She stormed away, and Endring listened to her footsteps as he stared back at the tower, now bathed in warm light.

"Gods protect them," he whispered, but not to save himself. He would have to leave the temple anyway, and soon, but he couldn't bear the thought of more death on his hands.

He sharpened his eyes once more, and stared toward the tower, wondering how close they were, when something caught his eye. At first he thought it might be a trick of the light, but as he focused on it, he was sure. A dark form was soaring above the Sacred Quarter, and then another. The chimera were on patrol.

Zengin stared up the ladder at the dim light above. Voske and the others were likely long gone by now, heading for the Gambit of Iyanu. It rankled his pride to let Voske tell him off, but if there's one thing Zengin was good at it was keeping his base emotions in check. He was in control, and besides, this had worked to his advantage. He thought he would have to orchestrate getting lost and separated from the dimwits, but they'd actually sent him away.

He smiled as he dropped the torch to the damp floor, and he climbed. At the top, he found the tied up cultists working against their bonds. One of them almost had a hand wriggled free.

Idiot champions, he thought. They should thank him for coming back. If these two had gotten free, the whole quarter would know about their plans.

The man spotted Zengin, and he froze, blanching.

Zengin smiled as he made his way over. "It's nothing personal," he said kindly. "I understand your instinct to escape, run for your life, warn the others. You feel like a wounded animal fighting for life. You simply can't help yourself."

He knelt over the man, pinning him with his knees as he reached under his tunic for his dagger. He felt the ache to draw blood creeping up again, and he fought it back. He would kill them because he had too. They couldn't have anyone spoiling their plans.

The glint of steel showed as he drew the blade from its scabbard, and the man cried out against the gag. It came out a muffled, desperate whimper.

"I suppose it feels unfair," Zengin said flatly. "You were in the wrong place at the wrong time. If only another had been guarding this hole." He held the blade against the man's throat as he struggled against Zengin's hold. "But you chose your actions. You joined this rabble. You get what you deserve. Don't we all in the end?"

He drew the blade across and watched as blood pooled from the split along the man's throat and ran down, soaking his clothes.

Zengin stood, and turned his attention to the other man who had scrambled to his feet and was shuffling for the door. He tried to move too quickly and lost his footing, falling flat on his face.

"Where are you going?"

The man desperately started squirming away, using his hands to try and pull himself to safety.

Zengin called on his boon as he casually strolled toward the struggling man. "Stop."

The cultist stretched out his hand, clawing desperately at the wooden floors, leaving gouges from his fingernails as he tried to keep crawling. His body shook at the effort as he fought Metnadur's boon, pulling himself forward.

Zengin reached him, driving a knee into his back, and the man slumped to the ground, shivering with terror. Pitiful. He almost felt bad for him, but why should he? Every man makes his choices, and he faces the consequences eventually. This man faced his consequences like a coward.

Zengin grabbed his hair and yanked the man's head off the floor roughly. Leaning down, he slipped his dagger under the man and drew it across his neck.

He stood, wiping his dagger clean on the back of the man's shirt, then tucked it away in its scabbard and headed for the door. He couldn't care less about the crook, or the battle between the heretics and the temple. He was here for one reason, to find the champion of Neveri. And that's just what he planned to do.

Burz kept his hand on the worn hilt of his sword, tucked in the sheath at his side. It had been nearly three months since he'd last trained with a blade, seven since he'd been in a real fight. The sheath and hilt were stained to compliment his disguise, but the sharpened bronze showed skilled craftsmanship, much like his old soldier's sword. He hoped he wouldn't need to wield it today, but he was on edge as they made their way down a winding series of alleys. The map of the Quarter hadn't depicted the piles of clutter and barrels and crates that were stored in the tiny pass which led to delay after delay as they were forced to climb over and around. Luckily, they had only seen two cultists so far, and both had strolled past with little more than a nod.

"Just another quarter mile," Illeri said as she hopped over the latest row of crates. She'd been lagging behind for the last ten minutes, and she gripped tightly to Burz' hand as she landed on the ground.

Burz raised an eyebrow. "You really are good with directions, aren't you? I haven't seen the Gambit in half an hour."

She pulled her hand away and brushed at her hair. "The last bend turned us back north. It's not hard if you pay attention."

He glanced forward to where the others were just disappearing around a corner ahead of them. "Let's hurry. We're lagging behind."

"Mmhmm."

She sounded distracted, and he noted her looking backward.

He followed her gaze. "Is something wrong?"

"I'm pretty sure we're being followed."

Burz stared harder at the sleek walls and his hand strayed back to the hilt of his sword. "Where?"

"On the left, behind those crates. I've caught glimpses twice now."

"A cultist?"

Illeri shifted uncomfortably. "A, uh, Desitan monk I think."

He scowled. "A what?"

He didn't have long to consider it before he heard the sound of voices echoing from the alley further on. He cursed under his breath. "It'll have to wait."

He turned and hurried to catch up, feeling his frustration growing. If not for Voske's stubborn insistence that they all come, they might be to the tower by now, with far less risk of being found.

As he approached the others, Burz heard them talking with a gruff sounding man, and his heart sank at the stranger's wary tone.

"Nobody's supposed to be back here."

Burz rounded the corner as Locin answered.

"What's it to you, anyway? We're just cutting through to our post. Shortcut, see?" She had her hands on her hips looking confident as Voske towered beside her.

There were three cultists, maybe enough for them to handle, but they all glared suspiciously.

"This isn't a shortcut anywhere." He signaled with a finger to the man that stood at the back of their group. "There's been trouble makers running these alleys."

Locin chuckled. "Exactly! Borroka sent us to flush them out."

The man scowled now as his hand dropped to his sword. "Borroka sent *us* to flush them out."

Voske drew his club. "We're gonna have a problem if you draw that blade."

The man smirked. "Oh, I'm not gonna do that. If Borroka really sent you, you'd know that." He nodded to the man at the back, who lifted a small cylinder that hung on a chain around his neck. Voske surged forward, but the man leapt back and blew a sharp whistle that sounded through the alley. For a moment, they all stopped as the shrill call echoed off the walls.

Voske laughed. "Some deadly weapon you've got there."

But as soon as his words died out, the ground shook as a roar echoed nearby.

"Gods and Chosen!" Hikari yelled. "Is that what I think it is?"

The three cultists dashed out of the way, one scaling the walls as the others ducked into an alley.

Burz felt his heart pounding, and he yelled, "Run!"

Illeri ran to the side wall and pulled on a rickety wooden door. It flew open, and she waved to the others. "This way!"

A second, louder roar shook the alley as a chimera appeared overhead. The cultists whooped and cheered as it swooped toward them.

"We gotta go now!" Voske yelled.

All around them they could hear voices rising through the streets with cries of alarm.

Illeri darted through the door, and the other champions hurried after her, first Rasa, then Weylyn, then the rest.

They cut through the interior of a home, then piled out through a door on the far side, emerging into a twisted patchwork of alleyways. Here there were miniature agoras and local shops, nooks and crannies where idols of the gods could be seen, defaced and disfigured. Houses cropped up at random from snaking alleyways that wound around in oblong circles, crisscrossing each other like a man-made jungle. It would be easy for them to get lost, but also easy for them to be ambushed.

"Come on!" Illeri called, and nobody disputed.

They barreled down a back alley, then twisted to the side and ducked under a row of wash lines before emerging into a small plaza with a still fountain at the center.

The shouts were everywhere now, coming from every direction, cultists and chimera alike were searching for them. Illeri froze at the center of the plaza, staring from path to path.

"Which way now?" Hikari asked.

She shook her head. "I-I don't know."

"Well, we have to move," Voske bellowed. "We can't just stand here!"

"I know where these lead," she sputtered. "But I don't know where the cultists are."

Locin was panting now. "Everywhere. They're everywhere."

They stayed still for a moment, listening to the approaching clamor.

Overhead, a chimera flew into view above the rooftops, circling toward them.

"Mire and Nyx!" Voske yelled. "Just pick a path!"

He took off at a sprint, past Illeri and back to the south, and they all followed, rushing headlong into a stone path that gently curled around a temple on their right. Burz kept his eyes on the sky, but all he could see were the white stone statues of the gods that lined the roof above them. Hopefully that meant the actual gods were watching over them too.

"On the left," Weylyn yelled.

Suddenly a dark gray form emerged on the roof opposite the temple, as though challenging the gods. It had the full mane and face of a lion and it leered over the precipice, gouging the stone structure with its tremendous claws. From its open mouth a fiery light shone, and the air around it rippled with heat.

Burz heard Rasa scream. He couldn't blame her, his own legs felt wobbly at the sight.

"Faster!" He yelled. "Faster!"

The beast exhaled a stream of fire, scorching the air and turning the stone walls to char. Burz watched in horror as Illeri barely leapt out of the way, and Weylyn and Rasa were trapped on the other side.

"Come on!" He yelled. He waved for them to jump over the smoldering path, but before they could, the dark form of the chimera thundered to the ground right in front of them.

Weylyn lifted her bow, aiming it at the rider, and fired toward his chest.

The cultist ducked the arrow. The chimera surged toward the women, fangs bared, until its tail suddenly pulled taut. The beast's fangs snapped just short of Weylyn and a roar escaped its mouth. Voske clutched the scaled tail, crying out with the effort, holding the monster in place.

"Run!" He yelled. "Now!"

Rasa took off at a sprint, and Weylyn quickly turned after her, charging back the way they'd come, but they were separated by the beast which twisted around angrily, and Burz could see the glow of fire burning at the back of its throat. He leapt toward Voske and pushed him to the ground as another plume of flame torched the alley above their heads. Burz crouched lower, wincing at the intensity. For a moment that's all there was, pain, dirt, and flame, until a loud crash suddenly reverberated through the ground.

He rolled off Voske and stared. The statue of Iyanu had fallen from the top of the temple, and broken over the neck of the beast. It snarled and dug its claws into the dirt, scrabbling against the stony soil as it tried to wriggle free.

"Come on!" Locin yelled from beyond them, her arms still pointed toward the statue, panting from exertion.

She was standing with Hikari and Illeri near the far end of the alley. They waved frantically as the blasts of a horn sounded from somewhere close by, and the shouts of cultists drew closer.

Burz sprang to his feet and sprinted toward the others. Hopefully Weylyn and Rasa could find their own way out of this mess.

17: Twists and Turns

Weylyn and Rasa sprinted away from the chimera, back down the alley to the plaza and toward the shouts of cultists. She blinked, and she saw a flash of a vision, a cultist coming around the corner, then another on the roof to the west. She skidded to a stop and nocked an arrow, loosing it before the first man had even walked into view. The arrow took him in the chest just as he turned the corner. She nocked another, quick as lightning, and let it fly toward the roof. It caught the second cultist in the throat, and he crumpled forward and fell at Rasa's feet.

"Weylyn!" Rasa pointed up. "Chimera!"

Weylyn blinked again, feeling the foresight of Strah burn in her eyes as she saw a flash of fire running up the alley from south to north. She grabbed Rasa's hand, sprinting for the plaza until they heard the roar of the beast above. Rasa tugged hard to the East. There was a narrow gap that ran between two old stone homes. It was separated from the alley by a low wooden fence. Weylyn quickly hopped over, and as Rasa followed, she pulled her down, dodging the searing heat that scorched north along the road.

Rasa was breathing hard. "That was close."

Weylyn nodded, eyes wide. There was no use running after the other champions. They'd have to take a different route. She looked down the narrow gap. Several homes backed up to a hidden courtyard with an old well in the center.

"This way." She crouched and hurried toward the well, ducking against the stone walls of the first home. She could hear cultists shouting from the alley, but she couldn't tell how many.

"It's empty." She looked up to see Rasa opening an old wood door into one of the homes and peering in.

They stole inside and shut the door softly behind them. They could hear footsteps, and Weylyn called on her boon. Two cultists would search the alley, but they would make their way past without checking the homes. She held a finger to her mouth and gave Rasa a meaningful look. The young girl stood beside her, breathing hard, and they listened. Soon, she heard their voices outside.

"They're not here!" The first grumbled loudly.

"Musta kept moving. Come on!"

She listened until their foot falls faded into the distance and the sounds of chimera grew faint.

"We're safe for the moment."

Weylyn turned around to see Rasa had wandered deeper into the home. She stood by a small crib made of fine wood, still dressed with soft linens. She reached in and picked up a stuffed rabbit with a green bow around its neck.

Weylyn took a step toward her. "Rasa?"

"Do you think they're okay?" Rasa clutched the soft rabbit as she stared at Weylyn with glossy eyes.

"Who?"

She nodded back down to the crib. "This family."

Weylyn glanced around the home. It was a fine place, not lavish, but clean, and she could see a small vase of wilted flowers on the front sill. She felt her throat catch. "I wouldn't worry. Most of these people were at the festival during the attack."

"Her grandmother is worried. She's been waiting for them to come back." She looked up at Weylyn. "She said we can stay as long as we need to."

"Thank you," Weylyn said, glancing around the vacant room. "But we should go. We'll need to meet the others at the tower."

Rasa wrinkled her nose. "Is it safe?"

"No, but we aren't safe here either."

Rasa nodded her understanding.

"We'll just have to be careful."

Rasa leaned gingerly over the crib, not disturbing the covers, and nestled the bunny in its place. "She'll come home," she whispered. "I just know it." She turned to Weylyn and tried to stand tall. She looked even younger now.

Weylyn's eyes drifted to the crib one last time.

The soft bedding was quilted with white and pink squares, and she let her gaze linger until Rasa's voice pulled her focus back.

"Are you ready, Weylyn?"

Weylyn adjusted her quiver and set her sights on the door. "Yes. Let's go."

Voske's heart pounded in his chest as he rushed down the narrow alley. He could still hear the chimera behind him, wings beating against the sky as it roared in anger. Cultists were on their trail too, and he kept glancing back to make sure the others were with him.

"Keep up!" He yelled.

"Trying, darling."

They'd lost Weylyn and Rasa, but the chimera had chosen to follow the larger group, so he had to hope the two women had gotten away. For now, he put his focus on their own predicament. They needed to get off the streets.

Locin sprinted at the front of the group, dodging through back alleys and hopping fences. It was dizzying trying to keep track of where they were headed, but they didn't have time to slow down and ask for directions. Still, Voske was frustrated. Every step felt like it took them further from the tower and their goal.

"Locin!" Voske yelled forward. "Where in Nyx are we going?"

"I don't know," she called back. "Just follow me!"

Voske shook his head in exasperation. It figured. Illeri looked out of breath already and she had a nasty scratch down her arm from climbing a fence. They swung west, away from the rising sun and down a long, debris filled alley. It was strewn with old barrels and crates, and piles of dead branches that scraped at Voske's legs as he charged past. There was no other direction to go here, no doors, just solid stone walls. As they rounded the last corner, the alley dead ended into a sheer wall that rose twenty feet in front of them.

"Rotting mire!" Voske yelled as a gout of flame shot overhead. That Nyx beast was getting close.

"Okay," Locin said. "That's a problem."

"You don't say?"

She turned and glared at Voske. "Don't get smart with me, old man. It's not like I knew this was a dead end."

Hikari, Burz, and Illeri piled into the alley. Burz had his sword drawn, and his countenance fell when he saw the solid wall that blocked their way.

"I knew it!" He snapped. "We should have taken the main roads."

Voske clenched his hands around his club. "You want to make this my fault?"

"You did send Zengin away. If we'd had him-"

Footsteps echoed down the alley with cries of cultists as a group of them rounded the corner.

Voske rushed at them, knocking two aside with his club before they could react. He heard Burz beside him now, taking out another.

"Not to bring the mood down," Hikari yelled, "but that beast is back!"

The remaining cultists scattered as the chimera whirled around the corner and sent fire into the alley. Voske dodged out of the way, and then looked back to see the others safely huddled in the corner. They wouldn't stay safe for long, as the creature rounded for another pass. It had its eyes on Hikari, Locin and Illeri. Locin used her boon to grab a wide board at the side of the alley and pulled it in front of them like a flimsy shield.

"Rot it," Voske muttered, and then he yelled, "Over here, you mangy Nyx hound!"

He threw a fist into the side of the alley and broke the stone with a loud crack, drawing the attention of the beast. It was heading straight for him now, with nowhere to go.

He wiped the sweat from his brow, then tore a chunk from the wall and heaved it toward the chimera's head. "Come on then. Do your worst!"

The stone smacked into the beast and it screeched in anger, folding its wings as it dove toward him. He heard the others yelling, but all he could focus on was the gaping maw in front of him, white with the fire that roiled at the back of its gullet.

Voske readied himself for the blast, shutting his eyes as he threw an arm over his face. But instead of the heat of a scorching furnace, he was knocked to the ground by a blast of air over his head. As he stumbled, he looked up to see a garishly dressed man wearing an ugly yellow hat. A golden whip was coiled in his hand. He flicked it forward, and it lashed the air, blasting the chimera upward. Its fire shot wide over the rooftops, and the cultists scattered back.

"This way!" He yelled, and considering their predicament, Voske wasn't inclined to ask questions.

The man dashed back down the alley and kicked a door in, waving to the champions.

"Move!" Voske yelled as they stared at the strange man.

That seemed to shake them from their stupor, and they all rushed for the door, piling in one after the other. Once they were all inside, Voske nodded to the man and followed them.

"Straight through," the man yelled, "and out the back!"

Voske heard one last blast from the whip as he charged through the house. Out the back door they found a second alley, much thinner than the first, with awnings that stretched across from either side, effectively blocking the view from the sky. The man dashed out behind them, and Voske turned to the door and grabbed the frame, ripping it downward until a slab of stone cracked free from the ceiling and collapsed over the exit. A cloud of dust blasted through the alley as Voske stepped backward into the street. He turned to see the others were all there and seemed unharmed.

The garish man started walking casually down the alley. "Let's go."

"Not to be ungrateful," Hikari said pensively, "but where?"

"I have a home here," he said as he coiled the whip and looped it on his belt. "You'll be safe there for now."

"We follow him," Voske said, slipping his club back into his belt. "We need to get off the streets for a bit."

It was impossible to say who their would-be rescuer was, but whoever he was, he didn't seem like a cultist, and that was good enough for now.

Zengin fingered the small idol in his pocket, wrapping the chain around his hand as he leaned out around the side of a building. The shrine of Metnadur sat in the middle of a green garden with low, manicured hedges and flowering anthurium with petals that started pure white at the center and gradually turned to a bright silver, as if they'd been dipped in metal. The glistening white walls rose to gold domes, and ornate pillars supported the massive facade.

Around the shrine, the agora was a different story. Windows were shattered, walls covered with graffiti, and a pile of smoldering bits marked the end of the long night's fire. A couple dozen cultists littered the area, some on alert, others seated near the remnants of the fire drinking and eating their stolen meals.

And yet the shrine was untouched. That most likely said more about Borroka than her army. A champion needed a glorious home, and no building in Arrajin was more decadent than Metnadur's shrine.

Zengin pulled the chain from his pocket, and looped it over his head, wearing the idol open on his chest. He lowered his shoulders in a slight stoop - he'd stand out with a high born gait - and he ambled toward the shrine. His disguise was good enough that no one bothered him until he passed the golden gate into the gardens where two large men stood guard. One had a deep scar that ran the length of his face, and both perked up when they saw Zengin. He eyed the blades at their sides, wicked looking things made by an unskilled smith, but effective with curving, serrated edges like jagged teeth.

"You ain't got business here!"

The scarred man said nothing, simply staring with bared teeth that matched his blade.

Zengin called up the honey of Metnadur and drenched his words with it. No need to hold back. "I do." His voice snapped with practiced authority. It had often been enough without Metnadur's boon.

The first man lowered his sword, looking confused, but Scar held his ground.

Zengin turned his eyes to the large man and straightened his back to his normal posture. "I have business with Borroka."

But the man just kept scowling until the first guard hit him hard on the arm and waved toward the shrine.

"He says he's got business with Borroka, rotter! Take 'em. Go on!"

He smacked the big dullard a couple more times until he begrudgingly turned without a word and headed toward the wide open front door.

As Zengin passed the first guard, he mustered his boon one last time with a gracious smile. "Thank you. Now, go home."

The man nodded dutifully and strode through the gate and back into the agora. Zengin smiled as he thought just how far that man might go. Was his home even on Las?

He turned his attention to the brute ahead, now waiting dutifully just inside. He ushered him through the decadent foyer and into the main chamber where a gilded oil basin sat surrounded by weapons and stores. They meandered their way past barrels, crates, and a couple racks of the rough, toothy blades, and the man led Zengin into a lavish room beyond. It looked to be the treasure vault of Metnadur, though the heavy door sat on the ground, broken off its hinges, and the inside was nearly empty. The muraled walls glowed in the light of golden chandeliers, and a square table had been set inside with several chairs. He identified Borroka at once, picking her out of a dozen cultists who were gathered around the table. She was fierce looking, with her head half shaved and a wicked blade at her hip. She wore a bracer that shimmered with the dim light of a relic, and while her garb was as simple as the rest, her bearing gave her away. She stood with her shoulders back, and an ease to her stance. The rest of them seemed nervous around her, the way they leaned away, or the way their eyes darted to her in deference.

She looked up, and immediately ordered the rest to leave when she spotted Zengin and the large man.

As they filed out, Zengin kept his head low. He couldn't risk her recognizing him from the conflict with Sammel, not until the honey of Metnadur had a chance to work into her mind.

Once the room was clear, Borroka motioned for Zengin to approach while the brute took up a watchful post by the door.

He shuffled forward. Everything in him wanted to speak first, but he needed to keep up this charade, so he trained his eyes on the floor and held his tongue. She was moving around the desk toward him.

"Who are you? You don't look familiar."

Good, the disguise is working. Zengin let a light quaver seep into his voice, and the thick accent he'd heard often among the unguilded dock workers in Tajerim. "Geirn. I 'as stationed by the river, but they sent me with a message."

"Is that so?" She licked her lips, but her eyes flashed suspicion. Most likely her people rarely brought a message she didn't know was coming.

He chose his words carefully. "Soldiers are massin' again. Word is they'll attack."

"And?"

Zengin put a slight tremble in his nod, but he also called up the honey of Metnadur. "And they 'as wonderin', not me o' course, as I know you got the perfect timin' in mind, but they 'as wonderin'-"

"What?" She snapped.

"When the power of Neveri 'as gonna let loose."

She raised an eyebrow. It was clear she didn't understand.

"Them soldiers is rottin' cocky. Seein' Neveri's champion 'ould soil their britches."

"Neveri's champion?" She snapped. "Who said he's named one?"

He noted the edge of malice in her voice and searched for an explanation. "The men. Some of 'em says they seen him."

"*What* men? Neveri can't choose a champion until he's released."

Zengin's mind reeled and he slowly backed away. "One of them saw a shapeshifter. I don't know who."

Her eyes went wide with shock, and he knew he'd made a mistake. Not only was she not the champion, she didn't know there was one. But how was that possible?

As revelation set in, anger flashed across her face, and she clenched her right hand into a white knuckled fist. She thought it would be her, and now Zengin had unwittingly brought her word that it was not.

She stepped forward and grabbed his tunic in the middle of his chest, walking backwards as he matched her steps. Too steady. He knew he should add in a stumble, but this gambit had failed. It was time for a different tack.

Zengin squared his shoulders as they came to a stop, and her eyes lighted on the idol around his neck.

"A gift," he said softly, letting the fake accent fall away. "From someone I cared deeply about. She gave it to me after I was unguilded."

"Who are you really?"

He met her gaze. "A believer, looking for hope."

She bared her teeth in a wicked sneer, and her fist tightened around his tunic, driving her knuckles against his breast bone until it hurt. "Tell me about the champion."

Zengin ran through scenarios in his mind. To her, this champion wasn't some joyous hope for her people, it was a sting of betrayal. If the others knew, they might turn on her and follow

Neveri's chosen instead. He was in more danger than he anticipated. He called up his boon in full force.

"If you honor the name of Neveri, you will let me go."

Her face convulsed, but her grip only tightened.

"I said, let me go. Now!"

As she grimaced in pain again, a laugh broke from her lips, cold and dark.

"Metnadur's little puppet?" She took her free hand and ripped his glove off, revealing the golden visage of the mountain. She spit in his face.

Zengin twisted himself free from her grip and knocked her back, reaching for his dagger, but before he grabbed it, the large brute was on him, pinning his arms. He was more than a match in size and strength, and Zengin couldn't break free.

"Release me!"

Still the man held him fast.

"Release me now, or I will kill you both!"

The man didn't so much as tremble as he bore down on Zengin's arms.

Borroka was laughing again as she walked toward him. "My men are loyal."

Zengin shook his head. "It's not that. Even loyalty can't easily resist the honey of Metnadur."

She glanced coldly at his sigil. "A sad gift from a worthless god."

"At least I was given a gift."

She flew at him in a rage and struck him hard across the face, but Zengin only smiled. He knew her weakness, and he could manipulate her.

Borroka snatched the idol off his chest, breaking the chain. "You don't deserve to wear that."

He steeled himself, calling up every bit of his boon he could until his mouth was coated in the warmth of it, and he twisted his head to glimpse the brute. "Release me, or Borroka dies!"

The man stood unflinching, eyes on Borroka as if he hadn't even heard.

The revelation sunk in, and Zengin's countenance fell.

Borroka's cold laugh filled the room again. "That's right. Lothe is deaf. Call it a back up plan, in case the temple sent its lap dogs. And it seems they have."

Zengin gritted his teeth in anger. "I hope you have more like him. You can't hold me with just one man."

She pulled her sword without a word, and strode toward him. For a moment he thought he might die here and now, but she grabbed the tattered edges of his tunic and ripped into it with her blade until she held a long dirty strip of fabric. Zengin fought against the guard's grip futilely as she dug the fabric into the corners of his mouth, tying it around his head so tightly that it hurt.

"Let's see how well you do without your voice, Champion."

18: A Roof, a Refuge, and a Terrible Cellar

Rasa peered around a narrow road that wound through a labyrinth of stone buildings, trying to get her bearings. She'd seen few spirits here, mostly due to the yellow alyssum planted around the oldest parts of the quarter, shielding the ancient estates from the prying eyes of Nyx.

They'd gotten this far with some guesswork, and a few of Weylyn's visions, but it'd taken nearly an hour of wandering, and the alleys kept doubling back until it seemed they were lost.

Weylyn sighed in frustration. "I can't make heads nor tales of anything." She pointed at the narrow slit of sky overhead. She'd been guessing their direction as best she could, but dull gray clouds had rolled in and darkened the sky. "These buildings all look the same. Still no spirits?"

Rasa shook her head. "I think the people that lived here were superstitious."

Weylyn looked back over her shoulder, and Rasa pointed to the planters full of alyssum.

Weylyn smiled. "I suppose they keep out the living and the dead with that smell."

Rasa returned her smile and then looked up. "We can get a better view if we climb up."

"Can you manage it?"

"I like climbing."

"Well then." Weylyn secured her bow on her shoulder. "Up we go! Stay low at the top. I don't know if chimeras are anything like falcons, but I'd rather not be seen."

"I'll be careful."

They made their way to the side of a home that had decorative rows of bricks spaced along the wooden sides. Rasa hoisted her foot onto the first ledge and pulled herself up, although she almost slipped. She wasn't used to wearing shoes anymore, and the sandals for her disguise were worn on the bottom. She pulled up to the second row, wobbling as she tried to grip the stone with the clunky leather sole.

"Are you alright?" Weylyn came up beside her, climbing easily in her own worn boots.

Rasa bit her lip and nodded, and then she kicked her sandals off and let them fall to the street. That was much better. She easily climbed the rest of the tall stone face, then scurried up the roof. Weylyn soon followed, looking surprised.

"You've done this before."

Rasa beamed proudly. "Lots."

They could see the tower now, a little too far west, but they'd done alright. They could make it in another half an hour once they climbed back down.

They tucked in below the overhang of a dormer roof, and Rasa sat with her back to the window, taking a quick breather. Weylyn pulled out a canteen and handed it to her, letting her take a sip before she gave it back. It had been stifling in the alley, and Rasa was grateful for the breeze here, free of the stench of the alyssum.

"I never thanked you," Rasa said. "For convincing the others to let me come."

"It seems we all might have been better off staying behind, but you're welcome."

"Maybe."

Rasa folded her arms and shifted against the glass behind her, trying to get comfortable. Ridiculously, she felt more comfortable here than she had in the temple, and more comfortable with Weylyn than she'd remembered feeling around anyone.

She studied the older woman from behind. Something about her looked hawkish as she sat perched on the roof, her eyes scanning the skies, her bow ready at her side. She wondered what it must have been like for her to live alone in the forests all those years. Rasa couldn't imagine it, but it sounded peaceful in its own way.

"What was the forest like?"

Weylyn looked surprised by the question, but her lips curled in a slight smile. "Very different. Harsh, but not in a bad way."

"And the mountains? I've never seen one. Are they as tall as people say?"

"Some. I used to climb a peak called The Crown of the Shinoam. Snowy gryphons roost there. It's good hunting, but bitterly cold. There were moments on clear days I could see all the way past the shores of the Sea of Glass, and watch the white sails of ships from a world away."

"It sounds magical."

Her smile broadened. "At times. There were also dangers. I broke my leg in those mountains once. I thought I would die."

"Oh?" Rasa huddled a bit closer, looking at Weylyn expectantly.

Weylyn looked at her, serious at first, but then she relaxed, sinking all the way back against the dormer wall. "Fine, one story, but then we go."

Rasa nodded eagerly.

"I was hunting wolves. Some of the packs are rather large, and the wolves in the high Shinoam can be fierce. I'd been three days on their trail, and I was getting close. I was also higher on the Crown than I'd ever been. It was bitterly cold, and the snow drifts towered like mountains of their own."

"What's a snow drift?"

Weylyn looked at her thoughtfully. "I suppose they don't have those many places in Talamh. The wind drives the snow into large mounds."

"I've heard of snow. It sounds pretty terrible."

Weylyn chuckled. "It's cold, to be sure, but beautiful. There's nothing in the worlds like a fresh fallen blanket of snow, every tree branch encased in ice like crystal glass." She made a serious face that made Rasa laugh. "But it's dangerous too! I was climbing steadily toward the peak, and I caught sight of the pack at last, beautiful coats, whiter than the snow. I'd never seen so many. Well, they saw me too. They started to run, but their leader turned to watch me. He was the most majestic creature I'd ever seen. He was three times the size of the others. At first, I thought he was a white bear. Before I could loose an arrow, he let out a howl like I'd never heard. The peak shook, and the snow above me broke loose. It came toppling down the side of the mountain like a thunderstorm of snow and ice. I'd never seen anything like it."

"And what did you do?"

"I ran, but not fast enough. The snow under my feet slipped and pulled me down with it. Everything was a blur of white and gray and I felt something bash my leg. By the time I landed, I couldn't feel it at all until I tried to stand, then the pain was almost too much to bear." She pursed her lips and shook her head. "I had to make myself a splint and crawl my way down toward the valley. After two days, the falconers found me, thank the gods. If they hadn't, I never would have made it."

Rasa shivered. "It sounds awful. I don't think I'd ever go up that peak again."

Weylyn laughed, but her eyes looked into the distance, like she could see the Shinoam from here. "Oh I tried, many times. It was a treacherous climb, and so cold, but I wanted to see him again, that great white wolf."

"Did you?"

"Not yet, but I intend to try again."

"Really?"

"Why not?" She tapped her bow. "When this is all settled, and I have the time, I'll go back, reach the peak."

"But…" Rasa let her voice trail off. "You almost died."

"Almost, but when I look back, I remember the feeling of climbing toward the peak, and finding that wolf. It was exhilarating. And the good memories seem so much closer than the bad."

Rasa pulled her legs into her chest, trying to think of a good memory of her own. "I had a friend," she said softly. "Her name was Telal. She used to comb my hair," her voice trailed off and her chin sunk to her knees.

"What happened to her?"

Rasa shuddered and pushed the memory away, unsure how to answer.

Weylyn's face grew more serious as she tucked her canteen away. "It's obvious you haven't had an easy life. You don't have to tell me or any of the rest about it if you don't want to."

Rasa gulped hard. "I want to. Just, not yet." She leaned back again.

Weylyn took a deep breath. "A few more minutes rest, and we should keep moving. After all, I said I'd bring you back safe."

"Why did you?" Rasa asked. "Agree to look out for me, that is."

Weylyn's jaw tightened, almost as if the question was difficult for her.

"I don't mean to bother you."

She quickly forced a smile again, relaxing. "You are certainly not a bother, Rasa." She took a deep breath. "I met someone once. A young girl. I guess you remind me of her."

"Is it the hair?" She twisted a fiery lock around her fingers."

Weylyn laughed. "Yes. She had the brightest, fiercest red hair I'd ever seen. Just like yours."

"It's always the hair. Was she..." Rasa paused thoughtfully. "Was she like me? I mean in other ways."

Weylyn frowned and turned her eyes down to the street. "I don't know. I met her very briefly. But I sure hope so."

Rasa smiled.

The conversation died out, and she stared up at the gathering clouds rolling overhead. Truthfully, even though things were going wrong, she was glad she'd come. She'd never been a part of anything before, and it felt nice to be doing something important.

"Alright," Weylyn said, looking toward the tower in the distance. "Ready to climb back down?"

Rasa made a sour face. "It's stifling down there, and smelly."

"But less risk of being burned to a crisp."

Rasa's eyes went wide. "Good point."

"Then down we go. Hopefully we can make the tower before the storm hits."

"And hopefully the others will be there."

After the champions' misadventure, the Sacred Quarter became a hornet's nest of activity. The patrols seemed to double and then double again. There were archers overlooking every street corner, and more than once Locin saw a chimera circling the skies overhead.

She had her hood pulled close over her face, sulking along behind the others, but she kept her eyes fixed on their guide. He seemed to know every nook and cranny, every back alley and unlocked door. He may have dressed like a gaudy player, but he followed the shadows like a seasoned thief.

"He's not a thief," she whispered, and she felt Spark tap her right arm in agreement. He wasn't graceful, but he was quick and strong, and she was impressed. But could they trust him?

They wound their way south for nearly half an hour before sneaking around the edges of an empty plaza to a weathered home that was set back from the road. The yard was overgrown, and the door nearly hidden behind a bushy kumquat tree. Here the foul smell of yellow alyssum tainted the air again, which soured Locin's mood even more. The putrid flowers were growing in bunches around the tree and the sides of the house.

"Mire and Nyx," she spat at the stupid flowers. "Does everyone in the whole rotting quarter grow these things?"

She felt the familiar brush of Spark that told her it was okay, and they would join back up later.

But she hated it. It always set her on edge when Spark wasn't around, and especially now in this hostile place with this stranger. It felt like walking blindfolded.

She slapped at the branch of the kumquat as she followed the others inside. A long narrow hall ran the length of the home with doorways branching off on either side and stairs at the end that headed down into the larder. She eyed the man as she entered, and he shut the door behind them with a soft click.

"Second door on the right," he said.

There were three doorways on either side of the hall, though none of them actually had a door. The first two rooms were a dining room on the left and an odd looking gallery on the right. The walls of the gallery were covered in crudely drawn paintings that looked more like smudges than actual artwork. Her eyes locked on a large canvas tucked against the wall with something resembling a woman's face painted in obscenely bright hues. It was amateur stuff, nothing that could fetch a price, but it made her wonder at their mysterious rescuer. He moved like a thief, was comfortable in a fight, and even painted? But he wasn't particularly skilled in any of it.

The others were heading into the room ahead now, and Locin hurried her pace to catch up to the next pair of doorways. There was a kitchen on the left and a sitting room on the right. The other champions were in the sitting room, and Voske and Burz were drawing deep blue curtains across the windows. The room was cluttered with an eccentric mix of odds and ends, and seven mismatched chairs filled the bulk of the space.

"Aright," Voske said as he drew the last curtain shut. "I want some answers."

The man raised an eyebrow as he stood in the open doorway. "You haven't asked any questions."

"Did anyone follow us?" Hikari asked.

"No," Locin said.

"Good." Voske seemed to relax a bit at that, and then he locked eyes on the man again. "Who are you?"

"My name is Sammel." He pulled the outlandish yellow hat from his head revealing a dull gray mop of hair. "Is anyone hungry?"

They all looked at each other, exchanging perplexed glances. Most of them still looked shaken, and Locin sauntered to the window, peeling back the corner of the curtain, and peeked out at the side yard.

"I suppose we owe you some thanks," Burz said. "You saved us back there."

"True." Voske rubbed his chin. "That still doesn't explain *why*."

"You needed the help."

"And you just happened to be walking by?"

"No," Illeri said softly. "He was following us."

Everyone was taken aback by that, and none more than Locin. She felt frustrated that Illeri had spotted something she had missed, but consoled herself with the fact that she had only seen him because she was trailing so far behind. Locin shook out her legs against the dull burn in her thighs. It wasn't her fault she was in such good shape.

"I saw you," Illeri continued more boldly. "Well I saw your hat. It's quite… unique."

Sammel held the droopy yellow petasos up and examined it, but Locin saw what looked like the barest hint of a smile on his face.

"Hm," he said. "I'm not usually spotted."

But Voske only growled. "Why were you following us?"

"My intention was to watch for any trouble, and help you out of it if need be."

"Why in Nyx did you do that?" Voske said.

Burz was tense now, and he stepped toward Sammel. "More importantly, how did you know we were even in the Sacred Quarter?"

Sammel glanced from Burz to Voske, as though weighing his words carefully. "A mutual friend asked me to watch out for you."

"Who?"

Sammel shrugged. "This friend would prefer to remain in the shadows. Suffice it to say, I will continue to ensure you're safe and that your purpose here is fulfilled."

Voske leaned forward, rubbing his temples.

"That's all fine, darling," Hikari stood up and began pacing, clearly agitated, "but what about Weylyn and Rasa? They're still out there somewhere!"

"I saw them run off when you were separated."

Illeri sat up in her chair. "So they're safe?"

"I have no way of knowing," Sammel said. "I only know they were alive the last time I saw them."

"Great!" Hikari threw up his arms. "Of course the last time you saw them a chimera was roasting the street!"

Voske suddenly moved for the doorway, but Sammel stepped in his path.

"Can I assume you plan to look for them?"

Voske scowled. "What else would I be doing?"

"Every cultist in the Quarter will be looking for you."

"And if they find me, they'll regret it."

"Slow down," Burz called from behind, "Getting yourself killed isn't going to help."

"I agree," Sammel said. "It would be safer to wait here until nightfall."

"And what about them?" Voske snapped. "Every cultist in the Quarter is looking for them too. I'm not going to just leave them out there to die."

"And we won't," Sammel said. "You have my word."

Voske seemed to hesitate at that.

"Your name is Voske, correct?"

"That's right."

"Well Voske, might I offer my services again? I can look for the Champions of Strah and Bei'ai. I won't be recognized, so the risk is minimal.

"And what about us?" Illeri asked nervously.

Locin peered out the window again. There were several hours left until nightfall. "We wait until dark, and then we get the crook. That is why we're here."

Hikari looked at her nervously. "Even after all this? Won't it be much more difficult now?"

"Sure, but that just makes it more fun."

Sammel nodded. "Good." He slapped the yellow hat back on his head and turned to leave.

Burz grabbed his arm. "What if you're caught?"

"I won't give you up."

Burz shook his head. "I meant for your own sake."

"I appreciate your concern," Sammel answered. "Though it's unwarranted." He pulled his arm free and turned for the door. "Stay here, out of sight. You can help yourself to anything in the larder. With any luck, I'll have the champions of Strah and Bei'ai back by sunset."

"And if you're not back by then?" Voske asked.

"Then I'm dead."

Water dripped down the wall of an old basement. The slow drip, drip, drip. The plunk as it splashed on the solid stone floor. Over and over. Zengin sat at a wooden slab with legs - hardly what he would call a table - his hands tied in front of him with thick rope, and the gag in his mouth biting at the corners until he could taste blood. He sat still, scanning his surroundings as he had for nearly two hours. He had measured the time by the shadows that came through a slit window at the top of the vaulted room, but clouds had moved in and blotted out the sun, and somewhere in the distance thunder rolled. He'd thought through every scenario, tried wiggling free of the ropes, and even tried pushing the gag out of his mouth, which had only made him bleed more.

He'd seen few guards, and very little of the shrine as Lothe dragged him down here. The hulking man was still in the corner of the room, watching him attentively. No matter how much Zengin twisted or shifted or pulled at the ropes, he never so much as flinched. Despite this, Zengin had long since given up on trying to wriggle free. Eventually the gag would come off.

He bit at the dirty cloth. He'd endured worse than this. Still, he felt anger boiling under the surface. Some part of him wanted to get free and rip the big man's throat out with his bare hands - and then find Borroka. He could feel the violent impulses raging within his mind like a wild beast beating at a door, but he held it at bay.

Footsteps echoed in the hall outside, growing closer, and he pulled at the bindings on his wrists again, trying to sit up as straight as he could. If this was his death, he would face it with his head high.

The footsteps stopped just outside the door, and it opened. Borroka leered at him.

"Why are you really here, Champion? Did you come to kill me?" She strolled inside and casually shut the door. "Word is, a scuffle broke out with my men and - did they say *seven* others?"

Idiots. It didn't surprise him they were incapable of staying unseen, but it made his plight worse.

She smirked. "I suppose I should be flattered you felt I was worthy of all of you. Are the others coming here to kill me?"

He bit down on the gag again, trying to swallow against its pull.

"Oh, that's right. You can't answer." She moved so close her face was inches from his. "I'm not afraid of your boon, Champion."

She reached her arms around his head and untied the gag, letting it slip loose.

As she pulled it away, he let his face sink down into his chest, breathing freely. Pain still lingered at the corners of his mouth, and he licked the blood from his lips.

Borroka leaned against the table and crossed her arms, her golden bracer glinting in the light of the lamp overhead. He let his eyes linger on it for a moment, so out of place among the rest of her drab garb. It was covered in runes he couldn't make out.

"I'm sure you've looted every relic in the quarter by now," he said.

She glanced down at the bracer, and then back at him. "This was mine from long ago. This is a relic of true power, a relic of Neveri."

"I've never heard of such a thing."

She reached a hand in a pocket and drew out his idol, letting it dangle in front of him on its broken chain, and he gritted his teeth. He wasn't sentimental, but he was prideful, and it was a reminder that she had bested him.

"How does someone like you come by this? It's obvious you aren't faithful. Did you even know what it was? Did the temple give it to you as part of your disguise?"

"It was mine… from long ago. I was telling you the truth."

She smirked. "Right. A gift from someone dear to you." She slipped the idol back in her pocket. "You're bold, I'll give you that. Coming right into my quarter, *my* shrine. Ambitious." She gave a subtle glance at his right hand. "I promise you, when I'm done, there will be no more temple, no more champions." She pried open his right hand and stared contemptuously at the golden sigil.

No, he thought. *Not contempt. Jealousy.*

He narrowed his eyes. "You truly hate the champions so much?"

She slapped his hand down and glared at him. "Where are the others?"

"How would I know?"

"I assume they're still in this quarter, but they haven't shown themselves."

He straightened himself up as much as his bonds allowed. "I couldn't care less where they are. I'm more interested in your choices. Why attack the Sacred Quarter? Why not attack the temple directly?"

"I'm the one asking the questions," she snapped.

"None that I can answer."

She leaned over him, baring her teeth. "I will find them."

"And what, kill us all? You did that with the last eight. And here we are."

Her mouth curled into a cold grin. "And what pathetic champions you've turned out to be."

Zengin tightened his wrists against the ropes until it hurt, using the pain to shove down his anger. She wanted him to lash out, to try and defend their titles. Whatever the others were, he was a Champion.

He let the barest drop of his boon slip into his words as he spoke again. "So you plan to kill us again? How does that serve your purposes?"

"You think I killed them?" She laughed. "No. That was your precious Oracle, I'm afraid. I simply took advantage of the opportunity."

Zengin's mind scrambled. He was certain that someone on the inside had facilitated Sammel, perhaps even an Oracle. But which one? He thought back to the night of the shattering, and the quake that spread from the Veil. It was largely believed to be the wrath of the gods, but what if the source was something more mortal?

"Endring," he mused.

The flicker of rage in her eyes confirmed his guess.

Immediately the pieces began to fit together in his mind. Endring had access to the temple. Sammel had said they needed to weaken the barrier between realms. Who better to do that than the Oracle of Bei'ai? Was it possible that the man who had helped Sammel and the champion of Neveri were one and the same?

He breathed slowly, carefully organizing his thoughts. "It must anger you to see that gnarled old man as Neveri's chosen."

Borroka sprang to her feet and drew her sword. "It should have been me," she seethed.

"You served Neveri faithfully for all these years. You understand him. And yet Endring wields such power."

Her hand trembled with anger. "When I'm done, there will be only one Champion. And it *will* be me."

He pulled on his boon again until his words dripped honey. "Let me free, and I will kill Endring for you."

She gritted her teeth as she winced in pain.

"I have free access to the temple - to him. I can get close, end his life, and Neveri will be free to call you. It never should have been him. It was always meant to be you. Now, untie me."

She lashed out, and the hilt of her sword cracked against his skull. He leaned forward as a flash of agony shot through him, and at once he felt her placing the gag back in his mouth, pulling so tightly he cried out.

She stood over him, glaring down, her naked blade held at her side. "Use your pathetic silver tongue on me again, and I will end your life."

She sheathed her blade and marched out, leaving him alone once more with the slow dripping and the pounding pain in his head. And Lothe simply stared, still as stone, at his misery.

Zengin could feel desperation closing in, and he struggled to keep the beast at bay in his mind, but it was too much. His rage overwhelmed him until he saw red, and he screamed against the gag, gnashing at the dirty cloth, and pulled his arms and legs against the ropes until his wrists and ankles bled. Eventually, he composed himself again, letting his head drop toward the table as he breathed heavily. Outside, the sound of rain hit the shrine in heavy drops, and another crack of thunder rolled. And inside Lothe watched him with placid indifference.

There was no way out.

19: Division

Heavy rain drops pelted Weylyn, and she brushed them from her eyes. She was crouched in a rain soaked alley where the storm poured off eaves that were too narrow to offer protection. She had her eyes fixed on the Gambit, just around the last corner. It was unattended, at least on the outside, and she let her eyes drift up the impossible height to where the green ring of sparks pierced the stormy sky.

Rasa's voice cut through the onslaught of the rain. "Chimera are near."

Weylyn looked back to where Rasa was pressed against the side of the alley. "How many?"

"They didn't say."

The poor girl looked especially like an urchin now, with her hair limp and the black from her eyes smeared down her cheeks. Her wet garb clung to her frame, which seemed hardly more than a skeleton.

"You'd think they'd take shelter," Weylyn said, looking back at the skies.

"What about the other Champions?" Rasa asked.

"I don't know. Hopefully we haven't missed them."

"Where else would they go?"

A sinking feeling hit Weylyn that perhaps they'd been caught, or killed. She met Rasa's gaze and saw the same thought in her glossy eyes. "For now, we'll assume they're still coming. And we'll wait."

"How long?" Rasa asked.

"As long as we can."

Weylyn peered out again, seeing a chimera darting through the rain far above. It was a massive, riderless thing, solid black with a mane the color of midnight and a tale like a black asp. It let out a roar as it circled around the tower, eventually coming to rest on a broad ledge at the very top.

"And if they don't come?"

"Then we head back to the temple for help." Weylyn forced a smile, then rested an arm on Rasa's shoulders and led her away from the corner into a shallow alcove. Here they had a good view of the front of the tower, but little else, and Weylyn leaned heavily into the wall, feeling the weight of the water.

For now, all they could do was watch and wait.

Burz held back the corner of a silk curtain, staring out at the street through the thick tangle of an overgrown shrub. The storm had dwindled to a light rain that splashed in puddles and dripped from branches. He was antsy. They'd been sitting around for hours, and the last of the light was fading now, covering the Sacred Quarter in murky gray that would soon fade to black.

"We should head out soon," Burz mused, glancing at his sigil. Hadris' words were still echoing in his mind. *Don't give too much.* It wasn't lost on him that if Sammel came back with wounded, it would be on his shoulders to heal them.

Hikari answered first. "I don't disagree, darling, but wasn't Sammel supposed to be back before nightfall?"

Voske stood from the couch and paced toward the window. "We'll give him a few more minutes."

"No need." They turned to see Sammel standing in the hallway, dripping wet, holding his soaked yellow hat.

Illeri nearly jumped out of her seat. "I was listening for the door. I didn't hear it open!"

Sammel shook a spray of water from his sloppy gray curls. "I didn't use the door."

"We'll slide past that for now," Locin said. "Any word on Weylyn and Rasa?"

Sammel shook his head. "I heard nothing, fortunately."

"How is that fortunate?" Illeri asked sharply.

"If they were killed or captured, I would have heard. Not everyone in Borroka's army is as tight lipped as she might hope."

"Not captured doesn't mean they're fine," Burz insisted. "They could have been injured in the fight."

The room grew solemn for a moment as the thought settled, but Voske quickly shook it off and strolled toward the center. "There's nothing we can do about that. We're going to assume they got away safe for now, and we're gonna head for the tower."

"There is one other piece of news," Sammel said. "Borroka has captured a champion."

"Bit of a contradiction, isn't it, darling? You just told us they *weren't* captured."

"They weren't," he said matter-of-factly. "It's the champion of Metnadur."

"Zengin?"

"Rotting idiot." Voske sighed. "I told him to go back to the temple!"

Locin sat down. "Sounds like he didn't listen."

"He's being held in Metnadur's shrine," Sammel continued. "He's alive, at least for the moment."

Burz recalled seeing the shrine on Endring's map. It was west, set in an open plaza. It wouldn't be an easy rescue. "What's in the shrine?" He asked. "Is it heavily guarded?"

"Borroka has taken it as her headquarters. There's no small number of cultists in and around it."

"Rotter got himself into this," Voske said flatly. "He can get himself out."

Burz narrowed his eyes. "You can't be serious."

"You bet your life I'm serious. I told him to hightail it back to the temple."

"And what if they kill him?"

Hikari's eyes widened. "Would they do that? To a Champion?"

Locin rolled her eyes. "Really?"

"I only meant…" he muttered sheepishly, and then blanched as the thought fully hit him.

"Fine," Voske called their attention back to the middle. "We'll get him, but we get the crook first."

That wasn't good enough. It was just like Voske to be nonchalant with a man's life.

"Zengin might not have the time," Burz insisted. "We should rescue him first."

"And risk losing the crook?" Voske turned fully on Burz now, his eyes hard as stone. "That weapon could kill a lot more than just one self important politician."

"He's still a champion."

"Then let him talk his way out of it."

Burz clenched his jaw. "It's just like you to make the selfish call."

Voske laughed. "Selfish? Selfish would be me back at the temple neck deep in a fine meal and some fine women. I'm talking about saving lives here. Lots of them."

"You're holding a petty grudge. You don't like Zengin, so you'd rather leave him to die."

"Like Nyx!"

The room was quiet now, and tense. Burz pointed at Locin where she sat looking bored. "You're telling me if Locin was captured you'd make the same choice?"

Voske took a step closer, and Burz felt his body tighten in response, which sent a dull pain through his leg.

"We'll never know, will we? Locin didn't murder a man and get herself caught like a rotting idiot!"

"Exactly my point."

Hikari cleared his throat. "Perhaps this isn't the time for such a drama?"

But Voske carried on anyway. "Sometimes a leader has to make sacrifices, but I don't expect you to understand."

That one hit differently. It was personal, and everything in Burz that had been holding him back snapped. "You're no leader. You're a thug who gets what he wants by force." He straightened up his shoulders and matched Voske's demeanor. If he wanted a fight, Burz wasn't backing down. "A stupid, petty thug."

"Better than a coward."

Burz' fist was ready to strike on its own, and likely would have had Sammel not stepped in just then, shouldering his way between the men. Voske stepped back first, waving him off as if Burz wasn't even worth the fight.

"None of this fixes your dilemma," Sammel said coolly. "So where do you go?"

Burz glanced at the room. Illeri and Hikari were staring anywhere but at the two of them, while Locin watched with a slight smirk. He suddenly felt foolish for losing his cool, and he shook it off.

"I'm going to rescue Zengin. If you want to fight your way to the relic alone, good luck."

Illeri looked mortified. "We're splitting up?"

Voske gave Burz a long, measured stare. "Looks like it."

"Look," Locin said, "pelican boy will be fine. I'm with Voske."

Hikari looked from Burz to Voske. "It seems the heroic thing to do is save the most people. I'm certain after we get the relic, we could all-"

"What if it's too late?" Illeri was scowling at Hikari. "What if something happens to Zengin?"

Hikari ran a hand through his hair, looking sheepish again. "Sorry, darling."

Burz squared his shoulders. Outside, he heard barely a drip from the rain. It was now or never. "Let's go, Illeri."

She stared at him wide eyed for a moment before nodding. "Yes. Of course. We'll go get Zengin." She glanced at Hikari one last time, then, with a shake of her head, marched toward the hallway with Burz.

"I'll be here." Sammel called after them. "Avoid the main roads."

20: A Risky Gambit

The shrine of Metnadur glistened under the moonlight, as if its walls were made of glass. The white stone facade was covered in golden vines and the last dregs of the storm dripped down on the elaborate gardens surrounding it. The place was crawling with cultists, and Illeri shook visibly as she crouched beside Burz in the shadows.

"There's so many."

Burz nodded. "They're expecting us."

"And we're just going to go in anyway? Just the two of us?"

She suddenly felt stupid for coming with Burz. He was staring at her intently now, as if sizing up her will.

She dropped her gaze. "I only meant there's a lot of them."

He furrowed his brow and pointed toward the shrine. "We head for the south gate. It's less guarded." He pulled a long knife from his belt and held the hilt toward her. "We should be able to get close before anyone asks any questions."

She took the knife with a trembling hand. It had a simple leather-wrapped handle, and looked like it was used for carving wood or cutting meat, not fighting.

"That's a last resort," he said. "Don't try to fight if you don't have to, just threaten. If you go up against one of these men with that toothpick, you'll die."

She gulped hard. If he was trying to instill confidence, this wasn't the way to do it.

"Use your boon, keep your head low, and if anything happens, run like Nyx. I mean it! Don't worry about me, you just keep your wits about you and live. Do you hear me?"

She nodded feebly. She definitely should have stayed with Voske.

"Alright, no point in wasting time. Follow my lead."

Burz stepped out confidently, squaring up his shoulders as he marched toward the gate. Illeri was frozen in place until the fear of being alone overpowered the fear of heading to the shrine, and she rushed after him, nearly stumbling across the agora. She wasn't cut out for any of this, and she had half a mind to curse Kisandin, had she not been too afraid to do so.

There were two guards at the south gate. They paid Burz little heed until he turned toward them. "Here to change the guard."

The guards looked at each other puzzled.

"We just got here!"

"Well, I was told to show up," Burz said disinterestedly. "I'd much rather find a barrel of mead and kick back if you two wanna stay here."

"Wait a minute now," said the other guard. "I ain't staying if we can go!"

The first guard looked at him sharply. "Idiot! They told us six hours. We haven't been here one! Now why do you think they'd change it up?" He looked suspiciously at them, and Illeri tried to keep her hands stiff at her sides.

Burz shrugged casually. "Didn't tell me why. Just told us to come, and we did. But nevermind." Burz turned to leave, and motioned Illeri to follow, but the second guard grabbed his shoulder.

"Now hold on! How's about you take my shift? Seeing as he doesn't want to go, I'll go grab a drink with the lady." He winked at Illeri, and her skin crawled.

The first guard stepped up, drawing his sword. "You rotting moron! How do you know these aren't some of the lot we're supposed to be keeping an eye out for?"

The second guard just looked confused, but Burz didn't give him time to think it through. In a flash, he'd pulled his sword and slashed it into the first man's gut. The second pulled his hand back, looking for his own sword, but Burz slit his throat and then turned back to the first. He was starting to yell, and Burz leapt on top of him, holding a hand over his mouth.

Illeri turned away, covering her face in horror. She listened to the man's muffled cries as he struggled against Burz until she couldn't bear it, and she pressed her hands over her ears. When it was over, an eerie stillness settled, and the air grew a little colder, as if Nyx had opened up to swallow the lost souls of the men. She'd felt it before, and her mind drifted toward a memory, a warm hand holding hers, and the same cold abyss.

She felt a hand on her shoulder, and she jolted.

"It's okay!" Burz quickly assured her, as he pulled his hand back. "It's over."

He picked up his sword. Illeri couldn't take her eyes off the line of blood that dripped from the edge of the blade, but Burz didn't even slow down, wiping it clean on the grass before turning for the shrine.

"Why did you do that?" She couldn't hide the catch in her voice.

He turned to face her. "They were going to raise an alarm."

"They were just talking."

"One of them had drawn his sword." He locked eyes with her. "These men would have killed us without batting an eye."

She let her breath slowly return as his steady eyes held her fast, and she nodded slowly.

"Good. Now, let's move."

Ahead, a row of hedges blocked their view of the side of the shrine. Burz hurried forward and stepped around the corner, but no sooner had Illeri joined him than he wheeled around and clapped one hand over her mouth, and grabbed the back of her head with the other. She couldn't fathom why until she felt a dull heat, and she looked to her left. Two large chimera sprawled lazily in a courtyard between them and the door. The one nearest had its mouth open in a yawn, and a faint glow shone from its throat.

Illeri tried to scream, which was the only sensible response, and she found herself immensely grateful for Burz' hand. He walked her backwards into the gardens by the gate, and she noticed he was breathing heavily.

"Not that way. Are you okay now?"

She nodded, and he drew his hands back.

"Gods and chosen," he glanced around the edges of the shrine. "There are too many eyes out front. We'll have to cut through the gardens."

She looked them over. They were dense, and silver fences separated each section. There was no way through there, and by the look on Burz' face, he'd come to the same conclusion.

"Maybe if we wait for the others?" She ventured.

Burz shook his head. "There's no guarantee they'll come, and I don't want to wait here to be found out. We try the front gate. Follow me."

He hunched low and skirted the outer hedges, barely tracing the tightly trimmed leaves with his hand.

She followed close, feeling fear creeping in again, and she whispered, barely audible over the night breeze.

"What are we doing?"

"Keep to the shadows. By Uthando's mercy, they won't see us."

"Shouldn't we try acting again?"

Burz quietly motioned to his side, where a wide streak of blood traced the hem of his shirt.

"You're injured?"

"It's not mine, but it won't go unnoticed."

It was all she could do to keep walking, conscious of every step. This was insane. *Insane*. She wasn't cut out for this. She was a wayfarer. The only things she was good at were holding a radiant field, reading, and staying away from people.

In another moment they rounded the corner, barely concealed from the probing light of the braziers by the front gate.

Four men and two women, all armed with the same jagged blades, were standing around the braziers. They were grimy, uncouth, and talking loudly.

"That's two marks," one of the women was saying. "You're feeling your grit tonight, Derth."

A muscular man beside her passed the two coins that clinked lightly into her palm. "Take them," he growled. "Rotting shrike."

The others laughed cruelly, and Illeri barely noticed Burz' hoarse whisper. "Illeri."

He was crouched on the ground in front of her, hands knit into a stirrup. He nodded to the stone fence beside them. "Can you make it?"

She shook her head, slowly at first, then more violently.

"I'll need you on the inside."

Of course he didn't really mean that. He needed her boon - the boon she couldn't use anyway. "I-I…"

"Hey!" Rang out a voice from beside the braziers. "Who in Nyx are you?"

Illeri felt her mouth go dry, but Burz rested a firm hand on her and stepped into the light. The cultists stared at his toga. There was no hiding the splatter of fresh blood. They drew their swords, and Burz did the same.

"Well," Derth sneered, "what do we have here?"

Illeri reached for the dagger at her side, but she remembered Burz' words. She had to use her boon. She drew her hand back and took a breath.

Feel it.

"Slow down," she muttered, and she felt her sigil warm.

"Time to go!" Burz yelled. He spun around but paused when he saw her. "Can you do this?"

Illeri's palm was burning. She felt panic grip her as the cultists rushed them, and she thrust her arm forward, as though she could cast her boon like a net. She grabbed for the swelling power with her mind as the heat drifted up her arm, but the tighter she tried to hold, the more it slipped away, like water through her fingers.

Nothing happened. Not even a hitch in the cultists' stride as her boon faded, and her palm turned to ice.

She locked her eyes on Burz and saw a flash of recognition.

"Run!" He yelled.

The fastest two men were almost on top of them. Burz shot out a foot and tripped the leader, and Illeri turned back toward the agora, but her legs were shaky, and she felt light headed.

For a brief moment all she could hear was the hammering of her own heart, and the scuff of her shoddy shoes against the stony street. She hoped Burz was alright, but she didn't dare look back.

She could see the shadowed alleys at the far end of the agora. She surged forward, thinking if she could only make it there, she could disappear into the dark city. This hope gave her a fresh wind and she picked up speed, but not enough. She screamed as a rough hand grabbed her from behind, and she lost her footing, stumbling to the ground. Derth was at her heels. He straddled her, pinning her between his knees as the weight of him crushed her.

"Do I get to kill a champion?" He said through acrid breath.

Illeri tried to snatch the dagger from her belt, but he snatched hold of her arm, ripping the glove from her hand to reveal her sigil.

"Mire and rot!" Derth leered. "Not very impressive for the gods chosen, are ya?"

He drove his cruel blade down, and Illeri felt it slice into her stomach. She gasped for breath as pain shot through her like she'd never known. He raised the blade again, but before it could fall, a sword stabbed straight through his chest from behind.

His grip faltered and Illeri started to wriggle backwards along the ground. Burz pushed the brute's body over. The leader was already dead on the ground, but the other four were closing quickly, shouting the alarm.

"Can you run?"

She looked at him and opened her mouth to speak, but no words would come.

Burz let his sword clatter to the ground, and he grabbed Illeri, lifting her with a groan, then he took off, running back through the agora.

She could see blood trickling down Burz' arm from a nasty gash. It soaked into her shirt, but she didn't object. Her own blood was soaking his.

They ducked into the alleys past the agora's edge. Mercifully the other cultists were slower. Or perhaps just over drunk. They staggered in pursuit, railing against the champions, and the gods, and each other. It wouldn't have been so terrifying were it not for the two shadowy forms rising into the air behind the shrine.

Burz kept moving until his arm started to give out and Illeri pushed out of his arms and limped along beside him, but she knew she couldn't go far. They both did.

Burz started checking doors as they moved until he found one unlocked, and he motioned for her to follow.

They slipped through the open door of a shop. It had been looted and utterly destroyed inside, but it was dark as Nyx, and they could hide. Outside, they heard the cultists cursing in the distance, and the sounds of chimera roaring overhead, but none came close.

Burz guided her to a coarse chair and had her sit, then knelt beside her.

"Hold still." He pressed a hand against her stomach, and she felt heat from his palm as the golden light of his sigil lit his face. He looked worn, and he bit down against pain as Illeri felt her own breath come easier, and the sharp pain dulled and then was gone.

Burz slumped, panting.

Illeri sat up, feeling her flesh through the gash in her tunic. It was slick with blood, but she felt no sign of a wound.

"I-I'm sorry," she managed. If she'd been able to use her boon, this wouldn't have happened. Maybe they could have even saved Zengin. She wondered what the cultists would do now that they'd tried. Would they move him? Muster more guards? Or worse...

Burz sat up. "It's not your fault." But she could see the disappointment in his eyes. "We can't stay here. They'll start searching the buildings soon enough."

"Where do we go?"

"Sammel's." He pushed himself to his feet with great effort. "Burz-"

"No time for talking. Come on."

He staggered toward the door, and she ran to his side, looping a hand around his waist so he could lean on her. It was the least she could do.

He nodded gratefully, and they ducked out into the night.

Voske fixed his eyes on the Gambit, stretching into the sky above them. The clouds overhead had hidden the moon from sight, and the only light in the sky was the green ring of sparks that spun and twisted over and around each other atop the tower high above.

"Well, that's fortunate," Hikari whispered from beside him. "No guards."

The front door was just across a circular courtyard. It seemed too good to be true, but Hikari was right. The whole courtyard was empty.

"Probably all inside," Voske grunted.

"Then let's go knock shall we?"

"You're joking, right?"

"Mostly. Though you have to admit, it would be quieter than battering down the door."

"I'll handle the door," Locin whispered. "I just need to know how many guards are inside." She started across the broad street. Fortunately, the storm had cleared out any foot traffic, and even the chimera seemed to have taken shelter. Granted, they may have taken shelter *in* the tower, but they'd face one problem at a time. First, the door.

There was a circular metal platform that stretched in a twenty foot radius around the tower, and as Voske stepped onto it, strange lines of blue light arced upward, tingling against the skin of his legs whenever his feet touched the ground.

He glanced over at Hikari, who was touching the metal disc with his hand, drawing even more of the light out.

"Rotting inventors," Voske muttered, stepping back off the plate. "We'll be seen for sure."

Hikari waved his hand and immediately dispelled the blue light. He grinned. "It feels so strange."

"There are six guards inside," Locin hissed. "At least in the main room."

"Six?" Voske stepped back on the plate. He could still feel a tingle in his legs, but the arcing light was now nothing but shadow. "Sounds like a lot."

Hikari coughed nervously. "Maybe they were taking shelter from the storm?"

"Or maybe they knew we were coming," Voske answered. "Just hold that light until we're all inside."

Voske reached the door and leaned in beside Locin. She always seemed to be right about these hunches, and he couldn't figure out how.

"Six, huh?"

She nodded.

"How sure are you?"

"Very."

There was more going on here, but Voske was sure he didn't have time to unravel it.

She shrugged, flashing him a coy smile. "I've got good instincts."

"Like Nyx it's instinct."

"Not meaning to rush you." Hikari hissed from behind, "But if we stand here long enough someone's going to see us, light or not."

"Great, then let's go." Locin bent down near the door and tested the handle. It was locked, but she quickly wiggled her fingers and tried it again. This time it swung freely, and she threw the door open, nearly blinding Voske with the bright light of the lamps inside.

The cultists were seated around a table near the front, cards in hand and drinks mostly dry. They looked startled at the commotion and one of them cried out. "What in Nyx do you think you-"

That was as far as the man got before Voske reached him and sent him somersaulting across the room.

Voske grabbed the first man's chair and swung it like a club, felling another two.

Hikari rushed up behind Voske and threw out his arm, blinding the cultist in front of him. He raised his sword with a peculiar flourish, but he didn't swing, and the cultist quickly rallied, lunging at him with a spear.

"Hikari!" Voske surged across the room, hurling the broken chair toward the attacker. It thumped hard into the back of the man's skull, setting him off balance. The tip of the spear drove into the wood paneling next to Hikari, and Voske snatched the club from his side, but Hikari had come to his senses and swung his sword, catching the cultist's leg. The cultist shrieked in pain and leapt backward, as Voske brought his club down hard over his head, breaking it in half and squashing his skull like a melon.

Locin had the last two cultists near the entrance, their pants down around their ankles, and their spears floating menacingly in front of them.

Voske took one step toward them, and they yelled in terror and started hopping out the door. If they got away, they'd bring more. He hurried after them, grabbing the spear from the wall, but as he stepped through the door an arrow whizzed through the dark and the first cultist fell, then another pierced the second. They fell flat on the metal disc and soft arcs of blue light outlined their bodies.

He felt a surge of hope and peered into the night until he saw Weylyn and Rasa stealing their way across the courtyard. Weylyn reached the cultists and wrenched her arrows free, then nodded curtly to Voske. "We should move these bodies."

"I've got it."

Voske grabbed a cultist with each arm and headed back in, dropping them by the wall.

Hikari was absently rubbing his arm and staring down at his blood-tinged sword. He glanced up as they entered and drew in a breath. "Rasa! Weylyn! Where did you come from?"

"We've been nearby, watching," Weylyn said.

"Bless Uthando! We were worried you'd been captured, or worse."

Locin was staring warily up. "We can save the heartfelt reunion for later. I thought I heard footsteps." She pointed at the ceiling far above.

Voske followed her gaze. The circular walls stretched nearly fifty feet to the second level. There were no stairs here, and the edges of the room were covered by a plethora of broken cases and ancient inventions. The cultists had looted what they could, and left the rest. Closer to the center, inventor chandeliers hung from woven cords, each just a foot higher than the last, so they seemed to spiral toward the ceiling, and in the very middle four thick chains ran from the floor to the ceiling far above.

Voske frowned. "How in Nyx do we get up there?"

"I've seen this before," Hikari said, walking toward the chains at the center. "Ah, here we are!"

He drew their attention to a lever just behind the central chains, and pulled it down. The chains creaked and shuddered in response and gradually started to move, spinning link after link, bringing down a round platform from the floor above. Voske watched with wonder as it settled to the ground floor, coming to rest with a gentle thump.

Weylyn walked closer, and tapped the stone disc with her foot. "Feels sturdy enough."

Voske poked at the chains. "You think it's going to hold all five of us?"

"It's fine," Locin said. "Just get on."

He took a tentative step onto the stone and glanced at the others. "Any idea what's up there?"

Weylyn was standing in the center of the platform staring straight up. Her body was rigid and Voske reached out a hand, waving it gently in front of her eyes. She didn't blink.

"Weylyn," he hissed, snapping his fingers in her ear.

She furrowed her brow and looked down. "There are four at the top." She said. "They heard your fight, and they're armed with relics."

No sooner had she spoken than the chains lurched to life, and the platform started slowly rising.

"Mire and rot!" Voske yelled. "No one said we were ready!"

Rasa was the only one still not on. "It wasn't me." She quickly leapt up, landing on her knees as the platform rose.

"Someone called it from above," Hikari said.

"They can do that?"

"Of course they can. No one wants to be stranded up there."

They were already rising past the glowing chandeliers, and Voske tensed, calling up his boon. "Weylyn," he snapped, "What kind of relics were they?"

"A belt," she said. "A torch, a mask, and I didn't see the last one before you snapped in my ear."

"Great."

Hikari's face lit with excitement. "The belt of Jeza perhaps? It gives the wearer immense strength. Nearly rivaling her Champion!" His smile faltered as he spotted Voske. "Not that they'd be a match for you, darling!"

Voske grunted. "And the other two?"

"I've heard of the torch of Desita. It creates dreams, if I recall. Although, I'm not sure what that means. Gods! Real relics? Marvelous!"

The platform stuttered as it neared the top.

"The mask?" Voske called.

"I'm not sure." His levity faded, and he frantically grabbed for the light of the chandeliers, bringing it rushing around them like an aura of sunlight.

Voske steeled himself, clenching his fists as the disc snapped into place on the higher floor. Here, a long, sloping stair provided access to the levels above, and the rest of the room was filled with shelves of scrolls - thousands of scrolls, small and stacked one atop the other. Here and there a few were spread out revealing blueprints of inventions. A voice called from somewhere behind one of the shelves, and Voske spun toward it.

"Welcome, champions."

Instantly Voske felt a belly laugh bubbling up inside. It was insane, but it was overpowering. He saw Locin beside him, also doubling over, and even Weylyn burst out in a laugh, shaking uncontrollably.

This is a relic, he thought. But knowing that didn't make it any easier to resist.

He heard the stomp of feet and suddenly saw a band of four cultists round one of the shelves. The man in the front wore a simple silver mask that covered his face. The mouth was curved up in an exaggerated smile. He stepped forward and spoke again.

"You're all going to die."

Voske felt anger and frustration roiling within him, but all he could do was laugh. He laughed so hard that he dropped to one knee, barely able to focus.

"Your ears!" Rasa shouted. "Plug your ears!"

Weylyn shot an arrow but it sailed wide in her shaking hands.

One of the cultists rushed straight for Rasa as she scrambled to her feet, her fingers in her ears. The brute wore a belt made of simple cloth and tied around two brass rings, but it glowed with the light of a relic.

Voske stuffed his fingers in his ears, and suddenly his laughter stopped. Nothing was funny now. He threw his body into the charging man, and managed to knock him off his feet, but his instincts took over, and he threw his hands out to catch his fall, leaving his ears unguarded. The laughter returned, rattling through his stomach until his sides hurt, and the belted cultist rammed an elbow into Voske's chest, then lifted him off his feet as easily as if he were a child and tossed him aside.

Voske's body smashed through a shelf of scrolls, sending little pieces of parchment raining down across the room. He toppled to the ground amidst a pile of paper and snatched up a wad. He had to find some way to plug his ears, but he was still laughing, even while gasping for breath.

That's when he heard the zing of metal and glanced back at the other three cultists. The final man had a massive sword that glowed with the light of Sbarga.

Of course the last relic was a sword.

21: Treasures of Sbarga

Weylyn leapt back from the center of the room, fighting to keep her hands steady as she ducked behind a shelf, overwhelmed with laughter. She could hear the sounds of a mad scrabble and a thunderous crash, but there was nothing she could do in her current state. She snatched her hunting knife from her hip and sliced into her shirt, cutting a strip of fabric, and she wrapped it around her head and over her ears, tying it tightly so it muffled the sound. Almost instantly clarity returned.

She peered back around the shelves and saw Rasa running away up the stairs, pursued by the belted cultist. She nocked an arrow as fast as she could and took aim, but the cultist stopped suddenly and pulled back, causing her shot to miss. He couldn't know she was about to fire at him. It seemed more like he was scared to go upstairs.

"Rasa!" She yelled. "Don't go up there!"

But Rasa had her fingers in her ears, and her eyes straight ahead. Weylyn leapt past the shelves and ran after Rasa, letting her bow go slack. Rasa was nearly to the door now. She opened her mouth to yell again, but a cultist stepped in front of her, blocking her path. He held a hooked dagger in one hand and a glimmering torch in the other. It was like no light she'd ever seen, soft, soothing. It seemed to pull at her soul. As she gazed into the fire, she saw a lark inside, calling cheerily from the branch of a tall poplar, and behind it, the peaks of the Shinoam. She sucked in a breath, and she could smell the cool air of morning over the pines. Snow crunched under her foot as she shifted. She was a huntress on a lonely morning, and there was nowhere else she'd rather be.

Rasa bolted to the top of the steps, her fingers in her ears magnifying the pounding of her heart. She could just make out the sounds of the other champions fighting below her, but what could she do to help? Her old instincts had taken over. Get up high and stay out of sight.

She came to the wooden beams and stone shelf that made up the floor of the third story, and she poked her head tentatively through the opening. A dozen stone pillars lined the perimeter of the room, and the cold night air rushed through the open sides, blocked partially by piles of crates. On the far side of the room she could see a long row of them, silhouettes against the darkened skyline. A few were piled up and opened, and a golden glow hung hazily around them, dimming the stars.

The relics!

Rasa carefully crept into the darkness, holding her hands in front of her. The noise below had faded, and she seemed too far from the effects of the masked man to be troubled by his voice. She could see a few blue spirits around her in the night air, and she gradually let Nyx draw closer until they took form, and their voices reached her ears. A young man was staring at her with terror written on his face.

Don't move, he said.

She stopped dead.

Don't move. The voice insisted again. The boy pointed ominously toward the far end of the row of crates, where a deep black shadow seemed to be moving. But she could see the relics. Maybe she could find the one they were after, and they could all leave this place and head home. She crept forward, her bare feet making no sound as she felt her way through the dark. They were filled with a half dozen relics, each one different from the next, but she didn't see anything that she would call a crook. She started moving them around as quietly as possible, her heart racing, until she spotted something on the bottom. It looked like little more than a broken branch, jagged edges on both ends, but it glowed like a relic. Down the shaft were etched the words, 'is not measured by its shadow'.

This has to be it, she thought as she pulled it out of the crate.

Something large shifted on the edge of her vision, and she stuffed the relic in her belt and turned. The shadow at the side of the tower gradually swelled in size, until it filled the space between two pillars, wings outstretched and fiery eyes staring toward Rasa like two menacing slits. At first it just watched her, like it was deciding if she was worth its time.

Run! The panicked voice of the spirit called. *What are you doing? Run!*

"You're not helping," she whispered as she slowly edged backward.

You can't trust it.

"I don't. I'm just hoping it's not hungry."

It's a killer.

She looked at the beast as it watched her, blinking its great eyes, and for a moment everything was shadow, then they opened back up like slits of fire. Maybe they weren't so evil after all, and it was just their riders who forced them to attack.

She kept on skirting the edge away from the beast, but she couldn't get back to the stairs without crossing its path. There were too many crates and barrels scattered in the way. She stepped out one foot into the center of the room, like dipping her toes in water.

"There," she whispered as she locked eyes with the spirit boy. "Easy."

A low growl rumbled from the chimera, and she glanced toward it with alarm. It had its hind legs coiled, and it stared at her with bared teeth.

Run!

Locin had two spit wads stuffed in her ears. It was disgusting, but effective.

"Get up big guy!" She yelled.

Voske was still laying flat on his back, near some shelves. The cultist with the sword was charging her direction, and she narrowed her eyes. "Can you do something to slow him down, Spark?"

Spark didn't answer, but the cultist didn't slow either.

Great.

Locin reached out with her boon and grabbed hold of the cultist's legs, then yanked, toppling him back. The sword in his hand slashed down as he fell and slammed into the floor, cutting through the solid stone like it was water.

"Mire and Nyx," she hissed.

She pushed against him, sending him sliding backward as the sword cut a large gash through the room.

"As much as I'd like to play," she called. "I'm a little busy at the moment." She heard heavy footfalls behind her, and she spun around. "About rotting time."

But to her dismay, it wasn't Voske. The belted cultist was barreling toward her. She turned her power on him and pushed, but he grabbed hold of a pedestal near the center of the room, using it to steady himself. Locin bore down with her boon, pushing until the swordsman came charging again, swinging for her face.

"Nyx it, Voske!"

Locin barely managed to roll out of the way, hitting the ground hard against her side. That would bruise, for sure. She grabbed a loose scroll with her boon and tossed it at Voske as he pushed himself up.

"I'm working on it!" He bellowed as he scrambled to his feet. He had giant pieces of scroll stuffed in his ears, sticking out like whiskers. She would have laughed if she didn't have to dodge another blow that tore through the bookshelf like paper. The two halves stayed for a moment and then collapsed in on each other with a creak.

She rolled on her back and saw the belted oaf barreling toward her, but Voske crashed into him, and they started grappling.

The swordsman was rushing at her again, the monstrous blade raised to strike. She reached out with her boon to catch the sword mid swing, throwing it back over his head, and he snarled. She really wanted to know what this blade was, and how to get one.

Suddenly, Voske and the oaf with the belt pummeled into the side of the sword guy, sending him spiraling to the floor.

It was a pretty even match until the oaf snatched the paper from Voske's ear.

"All brawn, no brains," the cultist mocked.

Voske narrowed his eyes, let out one more guffaw, then punched him in the face before doubling over.

"Nyx it," Locin muttered. "Where is that rotting mask?"

She'd lost track of the man, though his voice still droned somewhere nearby through her muffled hearing. They had to take that guy out. He was single-handedly crippling them.

She turned back just in time to see something flying at her, a heavy chunk of broken shelf. She threw her hands out to knock it away with her boon, but it was too close, and it crashed into her hand with devastating force. She cried out as she locked eyes on the smug swordsman.

"Rotting idiot! Pretty proud of yourself are you?"

His only response was a grin as he rushed toward her again.

She raised her hands to stop him, but her right hand was in excruciating pain. She could barely make her fingers move, and she felt her boon grow weak. It was enough force to make him falter, but not enough to push him back. He drove on, pressing forward against the resistance.

It was useless. She was backing toward the wall behind her now, and the belted brute was on the move too, heading her way. She felt her heart racing as she glanced around. There was nothing but walls and cultists.

But maybe a wall was just what she needed.

Locin pivoted her foot, feeling the grit of the stone under the smooth sole of her sandal, and she smirked. It was time to see what these things could really do.

She took off at a run toward the wall behind her, leaping against the vertical stone, and she kept running, straight up toward the ceiling. She could feel her feet wanting to fall away, but as long as she was moving, the sandals held on. She dashed far above the swordsman's head and rushed across the wall.

"I knew it!" Hikari stared up in wonder. As Locin ran across the wall, flecks of mud cascaded from her sandals, revealing the golden glow of a relic. She pushed off the wall and landed on the high stairs. "I knew you took them!"

As much as he wanted to ask for a turn, their current predicament quickly pulled his focus back. Voske was still down, Rasa was missing, and Weylyn was frozen in some sort of trance.

Thus far he'd been feeling rather useless, standing near the center of the battle, his hands clapped over his ears. He could somewhat wiggle his fingers and make little eddies of light flit about the room, for all the good that did them.

"Hikari!" Locin yelled from on high. "Do something!"

He wiggled his fingers in response. If he reached for his sword he'd be ruined with laughter. Gods, if he tried to itch his nose he'd be ruined with laughter.

Great, now it really is *itching.*

"Weylyn!" Locin yelled. "Help Weylyn!"

He sucked in a breath, not entirely certain how to help, but he ran that way. Mercifully, it was away from the thug with the sword.

He reached the edge of the room in a matter of moments and caught the barest glimpse of torchlight, glowing from behind the outer shelves. *That's right, the torch!* In the chaos he'd forgotten all about it.

He feebly started wiggling his fingers toward the light, not enough to snuff it out, but enough to block it from his eyes.

The loathsome cultist holding the priceless relic had an ugly black blade in his other hand. He seemed frozen as well, staring at Weylyn hungrily. As Hikari approached, the man's eyes darted to him, but he stayed frozen with the torch held high.

"Two for one," he muttered. "Two little bugs in one web."

Hikari came to a stop next to Weylyn and started furiously wiggling his fingers, trying to block the light from reaching her eyes.

The torch man glanced toward the middle of the room with a gleeful smile. "Here they come. The bug squashers."

Hikari could hear footsteps running their way, but the wiggling wasn't working, and another few seconds was going to see them both dead at the hands of these madmen.

He rolled his eyes. He always hated performing in comedies. With one swift motion he stretched out his hands, and took hold of the light, flinging everything he could back into the face of the torch wielder in one brilliant flash.

The man yelled in pain as raucous laughter swelled in the chest of Hikari. He doubled over, but as he did he heard the twang of Weylyn's bow ring out beside him.

Locin fished a dagger out with her left hand, still cradling the right one by her side. The belted man was headed for Hikari and Weylyn now, and she flipped the dagger in the air and grabbed it with her boon, driving it toward the man's back where it stuck like a pin in a cushion, but he didn't flinch.

A shudder rattled the stairs and she looked down to see sword guy slicing his blade through the stone structure.

Gods, he's going to bring down the whole building.

Before she could react she felt something, or *someone*, tugging at her.

"Spark?"

The spirit was back, pulling her attention toward the room above.

"Kinda busy right now!"

She refocused on the belted man as an arrow drove into his gut. A second arrow was already stuck in his shoulder, but he just kept marching forward. What was it going to take to stop this guy?

"You can't stay up there forever!" The swordsman yelled.

"I don't have to, idiot."

He slashed the stairs again, and the tower shook as the steps cracked.

And there was Spark again. Insistent. There was something above them. Locin didn't have time for this. As the swordsman lifted the blade to strike again, she stretched the fingers of her right hand, screaming in pain. She had at least two broken fingers, but she clenched her teeth, and felt the heat of her boon flood her hands as she yanked the sword clear out of the man's grip and held it spinning above his head.

"Ha!" She shouted as he looked mortified. She turned the tip down toward him, and he ran like a frightened child. Suddenly something shifted, like the pressure in the room released, and Locin realized the masked man was silent, but Spark was practically screaming at her now.

She ignored the spirit and fixed her eyes below where Voske was wrestling with the unkillable belted beast. He had three arrows and her dagger stuck in him, and he was currently lifting Voske over his head like a rag doll and tossing him to the side of the room where the wall shivered and cracked at the impact.

"Locin!" Weylyn's voice was heavily muffled, and she couldn't make out the rest.

She yanked the spit wads from her ears. "What?"

Weylyn pointed above. "Rasa!"

So that's what Spark was trying to tell her. She pulled the sword toward her as she started up the stairs.

"Cut down the ceiling!" Weylyn screamed.

Locin froze.

"The ceiling!" She insisted.

Locin spotted the belted man again, roaring like an animal in victory, as he stood alone in the middle of the room. She'd had enough of this guy. She drove the sword into the ceiling above, arcing it in a wide circle. She'd seen it at work, but it was nothing compared to feeling the thick stone melt like mist. The floor above began to crack and slide loose, and the belted man looked up in horrified realization as the weight of the stone pulled free and dropped to the floor below with a thunderous crash.

Voske's head was pounding. Of course it was. It was embedded two inches into solid stone where he'd been tossed into the wall.

He yanked the dry paper from his ears, trying to recollect what had just happened as a cloud of dust filled his vision. He could hear Hikari coughing nearby.

"Everyone alright?"

He got some muffled responses as he pulled himself to his feet and leaned out, looking up through the hole in the ceiling. To his surprise, Rasa was peering down at him, her eyes wide with terror, and her face streaked with blood.

A rumble sounded from the center of the room where the ceiling had fallen. Something was there, a shadowy shape behind the veil of dust.

"Look out!" Rasa called. "Chimera!"

"Mire and Nyx!" Voske tossed a glance toward Weylyn as the dust drifted toward the floor. "Did you know about this?"

She looked at him pointedly. "It was us or Rasa."

Voske rolled his shoulders back, squaring off with the beast as its hideous form came into view. It was black as Nyx, with eyes like furnaces, and coal black horns. And it was angry. It let out a deafening roar that made the whole tower shake and an alarming crack snaked upward from the bottom of the stairs, fracturing the wall like chiseled stone.

"Fine. It's you and me, big guy." Voske brushed the dust off his arms as he walked toward the center of the room.

"It doesn't have to be anyone, idiot!" Locin yelled. "We run!"

Hikari was skirting his way along the wall now toward the stairs. "I'm inclined to agree."

The chimera's eyes darted at the motion, and fire roiled in its throat as its large head turned toward Hikari.

"Hey!" Voske rushed toward it. "I said it's you and me!" He swung a fist upward into the monster's ugly jaw, and it staggered back. As it moved, the floor shifted and creaked, and Voske stumbled to the side. He could see Hikari, pale and frozen, staring wide eyed at the beast.

"Get out of here!"

"This isn't the time for heroics," Weylyn said.

"I'll be right behind you. Just go!"

"Follow me," Locin called, motioning them up the stairs.

Voske closed on the chimera, sizing up his opponent. There was a bunch of rubble scattered across the floor and he snatched a large stone, feeling the coarse grit in his hand.

"Go back to Nyx," he thundered, and hurled the chunk into the chimera's nose.

It snorted and shook its head like a dog, and Voske grabbed another piece, but as he rose to throw the chimera sprang toward him, and one massive tooth clamped down on his shoulder as its talons sank into his ribs. He cried out in pain and slammed the chunk of rock into the creature's head.

Its grip faltered and it tumbled to its side. Voske leapt past and rushed for the stairs. The others were near the top, staring down at him.

"I told you to run!"

Locin waved him up. "Just come on!"

He started up the stairs, but he felt the air behind him crackle with heat, and he threw himself down as flames hit the wall above his head. As soon as the awful inferno died down, he scrambled up the steps. The stone was singed black, and his sandals felt like they were melting as he bounded up.

"Come on!" Locin yelled, sounding urgent.

He could feel the beast closing on him, but there was no turning back now. He leapt through the door as Locin slammed it shut, and a fiery eruption sent flames licking around the edges like a cauldron on a campfire.

Above, the tower was shaking violently as the other champions huddled near the edge with Rasa.

Weylyn looked back at Voske with worry. "There's no way down."

It was a sheer drop to the ground. The side of the tower was bowed and cracked, and the whole thing shuddered as chunks of rock fell and hit the metal plate at the base. It was a dizzying height, and Voske felt his knees quake, but he slapped his hands against his legs and summoned his courage.

"Locin, can you get us down?"

She leaned out over the side. It had to be at least seventy feet down to hard metal below. "Sure." He tried to ignore the hitch in her voice. "No problem."

"Weylyn first."

Weylyn nodded and slipped her bow over her shoulder, then leapt from the tower. For a terrifying moment, she hurtled toward the ground beneath. Locin winced, as she stretched out her hands, catching her halfway down. Weylyn slowed, and tumbled safely to the plate, blue arcs swallowing her form.

Voske looked toward Hikari. "You next."

"That was a bit fast don't you think, darling?"

"Just jump clear of the tower," Locin snapped.

Hikari cleared his throat and paced to the edge, turning to face them. "Well, if I die, just know-"

As he spoke the chimera crashed through the door behind them and the tower lurched. Hikari's foot slipped back, and he tipped over the edge of the tower with a yelp.

"Catch him!" Voske yelled as he turned to face the beast. It was snarling and struggling to wriggle through the doorway and gouts of fire sporadically spewed from its maw, roasting the surrounding stone.

Locin ran to the edge and caught Hikari as he tumbled toward the ground screaming. She cried out in pain, and her hands shook, but Hikari stopped just above the metal plate. Locin relaxed her hands, and he plopped onto the ground.

"Rasa!" Voske yelled. She nodded, running for the side and jumping clear. This time, Locin caught her more quickly, and she was soon on the ground with the others.

Locin turned to Voske. "Your turn, old man."

"And you?"

She smiled, pointing to her sandals. "I'll be fine."

The chimera roared again and Voske glanced its direction just in time to see the side of the tower give way.

There was a horrible moment where the beast surged through, and the stone gave a loud crack, just the sort he would hear at the quarry before a granite block broke loose.

Voske leapt toward Locin, scooping her in his arms and surging for the tower's side as another crack sounded through the stone. Then another. The ground began to collapse under his feet, slanting the whole tower toward the chimera's waiting maw, and Locin cried out, grabbing tightly to Voske.

He leapt over the side and summoned his boon, desperate to keep himself steady as the ground rose to meet them. The strength of Jeza surged through him as he twisted his body, keeping his back to the ground and cradling Locin against his chest. He shut his eyes and waited until he felt the metal plate hammer into his spine like a sledge.

Above, the tower collapsed downward, and the heavy ring of sparks fell, crushing through the lower levels. A cloud of debris exploded into the sky and he twisted onto his side, shielding Locin with his body as chunks of stone and debris showered down on them. At last, the deafening crash settled, and dust filtered lazily through the air. A dark shape winged through the dust, screeching a call as it flew unsteadily into the night.

Voske righted himself, helping Locin to her feet. She looked startled, staring at him with wide eyes.

"Thanks," she managed.

He looked behind him. The other three were across the street, and now that it was safe, they hurried over.

"Gods and Chosen!" Hikari stood with his hands on his head, gaping at the ruined tower. "Is everyone alright?"

Voske stood and stretched out his back. He was covered in blood and dust and every inch of him hurt.

"Could have gone worse," Weylyn said.

"Could have gone worse?" Hikari shouted. "We took down the Gambit of Iyanu!"

Voske grunted. "And worse than that. We didn't get the crook."

"Actually…"

They turned at the voice of Rasa. She reached into her stola and drew out a splintered wooden rod. It didn't look much like a crook, but it glowed with a faint light.

Voske took the relic as she held it out. He smiled. "Well done, kid."

Nearby, the cries and shouts of cultists rose into the night air. They'd be on their way, and fast.

"Let's get back to Sammel's," Voske muttered.

22: Curtailed Ambition

Zengin stared at the cold blade in his hand. It was polished bronze, gleaming like it'd never been used. He tossed it from hand to hand nimbly, one eye on the heavy mahogany door. It opened, and he saw a woman enter, young, too young. Maybe eleven. She had stringy red hair and pale skin. Her eyes gripped him, pleading and pained. The kind of eyes that wanted to die.

Even in the dream, Zengin fought against the false memory. Stolen. Not his. He was raging in his own mind, trapped like a prisoner, trying to claw his eyes out from the inside. But all he could do was watch. All he could ever do was watch.

He set down the dagger and strolled to the girl, grabbing her chin and lifting her face, but her eyes darted away. He spoke with a voice that wasn't his own.

"What's your name?"

She clamped her mouth shut, and he could feel her trembling. He seized her jaw, and squeezed until he forced her mouth open. She cried out.

"What is your name?"

She turned her eyes on him, and he thought he would die. The guilt was too much to bear. He wanted to die. He wanted it to end. But he was a slave to his own mind.

Reach for the dagger, *he thought.* Drive it through your own rotting heart!

"Rasa," she said.

Zengin's eyes bolted open. His neck ached terribly from sleeping sitting up, and he tried to gasp against the dirty gag, now soaked with saliva and blood. He pulled at the bindings on his wrists and it stung where he bled. The agony of the dream still lingered. The intrusive thoughts.

Die. You have to die.

For a moment, it seemed panic would overwhelm him, but he steadied his mind, shut the door on his raging emotions, and calmed himself. He took one slow breath through his nose. Then another. And another. And then he lifted his head coolly and looked around.

Borroka sat at the far end of the rough table, glaring at him with her blade laid bare in front of her. Her eyes were hard as marbles.

"Bad dream?"

Zengin held his head high, matching her cold gaze, refusing to struggle, or even wince against his bonds. She took her sword in her hand and walked slowly toward him. "I was promised that the champions would die. All of them. And no new ones would be chosen."

She stopped and stuck the point of her blade into the table in front of him, letting it dig into the gnarled wood.

Zengin stayed still and stiff. He wouldn't give her the satisfaction of flinching.

"And yet here you are. Meddling snakes, playing at being heroes." She licked her lips. "They came for you. They failed."

That startled Zengin. As far as they knew, he'd gone back to the temple.

She dragged the blade casually across the table, letting it scrape just past his fingers. "But the most interesting part was their attack on the Gambit of Iyanu."

Zengin watched her intently, his heart pounding, and he saw it again in her eyes. That same blood lust he'd felt a thousand times. That bloodlust that was now truly his. Borroka wanted to hurt him, to kill him maybe. Not for any of the reasons she would give. She just wanted to see him bleed.

"I'm going to take that gag out of your mouth. You have one chance to tell me what they were after among my relics. Say anything other than that, and I *will* kill you."

She reached for his gag, and Zengin steadied himself. He had one chance. She drew the dirty cloth from his mouth and he breathed in deeply.

"Which relic did they want?"

"I'll tell you which relic they're after and more. But I want my freedom in exchange."

"Fool."

She raised her blade to strike, but he spoke again, quickly.

"What is it you want? I can offer whatever it is."

"I want the worlds to be rid of you. You're pretentious, just like your rotting gods. They set themselves above us in Sbarga. They exile us to Nyx and make us fight for their scraps in the Midding." She spit on the floor. "I'll see every last shred of them destroyed from Talamh, starting with their champions." She steadied her blade to strike.

"I know how to free Neveri!"

For a moment the blade halted, trembling in her raised hand.

Zengin let the honey of Metnadur into his voice, barely a drop, enough to be effective without her noticing. "Let me live, and I'll tell you about the crook."

She lowered her blade. "The crook?"

"The relic they were after. The way to free him." He eased a little more of his boon into his voice. "With the crook, you won't need anyone else. You'll be free to kill Endring."

She walked away toward the door, but she was tense. Still considering killing him? She wanted to draw blood more than she wanted anything. She glanced back at Zengin. Her eyes were hungry. Greedy.

"I know that look," he said, and then he dared his boon once more. "You don't want to kill just me."

She laughed coldly. "Don't pretend to know me."

Zengin very deliberately looked at Lothe, and she matched his gaze.

"I once cut off a man's ears," Zengin started in a low voice. He swallowed against the memory, glancing back at Borroka as he tried to keep the images flooding his mind at bay. "I remember the blood, and the screams. But most of all, I remember the thrill of it."

"Am I supposed to be intimidated by your little story?" She answered, but her eyes stayed fixed on Lothe, and she glanced at his ears.

Zengin continued. "He couldn't do anything about it. He was completely at my mercy. I just wanted to see what would happen."

She shot a glance toward him. "You? Pretty little thing that you are. You don't look like you've ever held a sword. And I'm supposed to believe *you've* killed a man?"

"Men, women," he swallowed hard. "Children. Killed and worse." He kept his eyes open, refusing to blink for fear the images would overwhelm him. Something inside told him to stop, but he couldn't. He wanted to push her. "You have no idea what I've done."

She believed him. He had no doubt she could see it in him the same way he could see it in her. There was a darkness, one they both tried to hide. He felt sick at the thought. His was forced upon him by a thousand stolen memories. But her? What kind of depravity had she committed to end up here?

Zengin continued. "He screamed. And then he whimpered. And then he was silent. The floor was slick with his blood."

She licked her lips. "Perhaps I misjudged you. You're not what I expected."

He pulled at his boon. "That's right. I'm not. Let me go, and I'll bring you the crook."

She moved close, her sword still in her hand, but she walked like someone in a trance.

"All you have to do is cut the ropes."

She was at the table now, and she held her sword over her head.

"Yes," he said, his words thick with the allure of Metnadur. "Set me free!"

She smirked, and her eyes blinked clear and sharp. He felt terror seize him.

"Maybe *you* misjudged *me*," she said. "You and your rotting gods!"

With one swift blow, she brought her blade crashing down into the table. He felt a sharp, vicious impact, and his eyes darted to his right arm. Her blade had driven clean through his wrist and he stared at the severed hand, trying desperately to pull it back, to move it in any way. But all he managed was to pull his arm back, now free of the rope at his wrist. He screamed as the horror of it overtook him. She grinned at him now, her face spattered with blood, and a dull, throbbing pain overwhelmed him. She used the tip of her blade to shove his hand off onto the floor, and he watched as the gold of his sigil faded to char black.

"Your gods can't save you, Champion."

She turned and marched out of the room, and the door shut with a thud as panic seized him. He pulled his arm and yanked against the other rope, but he couldn't get free, and he felt his head grow light as his blood pooled on the floor.

The gag, he thought. *She didn't gag me.*

He summoned his boon, barely able to hold it against the pain. "Release me!" He yelled, hoping someone was near enough to hear his voice. "Release me!"

He raised his arm, but what else could he do to stop the bleeding? It spurted from the stump and ran down until it dripped off his elbow. His vision began to fluctuate, dark and light and dark again as his body shut down.

"Release me!"

His chin sank down to his chest and his lungs trembled with every breath. He started to open his mouth to yell one more time, but the door of the room suddenly flew open.

He squinted his eyes and glanced upward, seeing a brightly attired figure dash into the room. It was Sammel. In one swift motion Sammel drove a dagger into Lothe's chest. The large man grabbed for the handle in shock, but Sammel quickly jerked it out, and thrust it in again as Lothe let out a pitiful wheeze, then slumped to the floor.

Sammel quickly yanked the dagger free and tucked it into his belt as he turned, spotting Zengin's arm. He just stood there for a moment, taking it all in.

"Help me!" Zengin said weakly.

Sammel looked around the room slowly, then hurried to Zengin's side and sliced into his beggar's shirt, cutting away a thick strip of fabric.

Zengin watched it all in a stupor. Why was Sammel helping him? Hadn't he tried to kill him only two days ago? Maybe this was another dream.

He shook his head, desperate to stay lucid as Sammel tied the fabric tightly around the stump of his arm, drawing it until Zengin groaned in pain.

"Can you walk?" Sammel asked, quickly cutting away the ropes that bound him.

Zengin's head swam. He could feel himself slipping away, and he fought to stay conscious.

"Can you walk?" Sammel insisted. "If you don't, you'll die."

He pushed his remaining hand against the table and struggled to his feet, looping his stump over Sammel's neck.

"This way." He led him toward the door and Zengin focused on his legs, forcing them one step after another.

At the moment he couldn't discern why Sammel was here, and he didn't care, all he could think of was keeping his legs moving, and for the moment that was enough.

23: Highs and Lows

By the time Burz and Illeri reached Sammel's house, Burz' leg had nearly given out. He was tired, frustrated, and wanted nothing more than to be back with his family. He was trying hard to put on a calm face for Illeri, but he was sure she saw through it.

She headed into the larder and managed to find some fresh bread, tea leaves - though neither of them were sure what kind - and a kettle. Burz ate begrudgingly while she warmed the kettle on the hearth, but he had to admit it helped.

"Here." Illeri handed him a painted blue cup with birds on it.

He breathed in deep, and the tea smelled earthy and strange, but it was hot, and he ached, so he drank it. The flavor was deep, and slightly bitter, but it took the edge off his pain more than he expected.

"Thank you."

Illeri smiled kindly and sat next to him. They stayed that way for a while, before the silence became too much for her, and she spoke.

"Do you think he's still alive?"

"I don't know."

"We aren't going to leave him, are we?"

Burz was of no mind to go back for Zengin again, and truthfully, there would likely be too many cultists at this point. He didn't want to admit it, but their failure may have cost them their only chance. "We'll think of something."

She looked less than reassured.

"Zengin's capable," he continued. "And he has the honey tongue. He'll survive."

Illeri poured herself a cup of tea, and took a sip. Her eyes went wide and she set her cup back down on the low table. "Oh."

"What is it?" Burz eyed his cup suspiciously now. It was half empty, and he was feeling a good deal of relief.

"That's not tea."

Burz tipped it warily and then looked back up at her.

"It's fine. Honestly, it might dull the pain."

"It does." He set the cup down all the same.

They sat in silence for what felt like a very long time before Illeri got up and started combing over the contents of Sammel's home. He was a curious sort of man, and Burz wasn't quite sure what to think of him. He had some agenda of his own, that much was clear, but he'd saved them, and for that Burz was grateful.

After a while, Burz had nearly fallen asleep watching the embers in the hearth, but at the sound of the door he bolted upright.

He heard Voske's voice boom from the entry. "Anybody here?"

"Yes!" Illeri called. "Yes, we're here."

Voske came around the corner with Locin and Hikari, ducking into the room.

"You're back," Burz said gruffly. He watched them as if he could find out how it went just by staring. But before anyone else spoke, Weylyn and Rasa came around the corner. "Thank the gods!" He stood. Finally, some good news.

Illeri stepped forward. "Are you okay?"

"We're fine," Weylyn said.

Voske was smiling now. "More than fine!" He held up a rough satchel and pulled out an old scrap of cloth.

As he unfolded it, Burz saw a broken shaft glowing with the light of Sbarga. "Where's the rest of it?"

Voske frowned as he folded the cloth up and shoved it back in the satchel. "Who cares? They can't complete it without this." He leaned out to look behind Burz and Illeri. "Where's Zengin?"

Burz crossed his arms, grinding his jaw back and forth. "We couldn't reach him."

"Fine." Voske remarked. "I guess we'll have to get him." He turned like he would head right back out.

"That's a bad idea," Burz said.

Voske laughed. "You were dead set on rescuing that rotter two hours ago. What changed?"

"We tried," he said sharply. "There were at least two chimera, and many more cultists. I'd wager their numbers have grown now that they know we're after him."

Voske crossed his arms. "So what? We just beat the cultists at the tower, and they were using relics."

Curse his stubborn pride.

Burz squared his shoulders. "We should go back to the temple. Look at you!" Locin was clutching her hand to her chest, Voske and Rasa were streaked with blood, and they all looked exhausted. "We're in no shape for another fight."

"He's right," Weylyn said wearily. "I'm worried about Zengin too, but getting ourselves killed won't help him."

Even Voske had to see it. He hesitated, looking at the tired faces around him. He dropped his shoulders and sighed.

The door to the house opened. Burz tensed, and the others turned toward the hallway. Unnaturally heavy footfalls thumped slowly down the hall, and Sammel rounded the corner with Zengin's body over his shoulders. Both of them were covered in blood.

"Gods and Chosen," Hikari muttered. "Is he…"

"He's alive." Sammel grunted under the strain, and Voske rushed forward to take Zengin in his arms, turning him over.

Sammel locked eyes on Burz as he stretched his back and it cracked. "He needs you."

Burz bit down hard. He wasn't sure he could.

Voske was frozen, staring down at the body in his arms.

"I did what I could," Sammel said. "But he's still in danger."

"What happened?" Illeri asked.

"Mire and Nyx," Voske muttered. He turned to face Burz and lifted Zengin's arm. It ended in a bloody tourniquet where his wrist had been. "Can you even heal this?"

Burz felt a catch in his throat as he heard several gasps and sobs.

Sammel's eyes were still locked intently on Burz. "He won't make it without you."

Sammel was right. He had no choice.

He turned back to the low table and grabbed the blue mug, downing the rest of it. It was cold, and more bitter now, but he felt its relief as he made his way to Zengin and laid his hands on his arm. He called up his boon and felt a vicious pain in his wrist, and a pulsing throb that coursed up through his shoulder. He bore down against it, willing the balm of Uthando until exhaustion took him, and he stumbled back.

Sammel removed the bloody tourniquet to reveal new skin, red and raw, but the wound was closed."

"Chimera?" Locin asked, poking at the raw skin.

Sammel grabbed her hand to stop her. "Borroka."

Illeri looked horrified. "A person did that to him?"

"Borroka is unlike most people. She's sadistic, accustomed to power, and unbothered by blood." He looked warily back down the hallway. "Speaking of which, we left a trail of blood on the way here. The faithful will not be far behind."

"Is everyone ready to leave," Voske asked.

A quick glance around the room said they were exhausted, but eager to go.

Sammel's eyes fell to the satchel at Voske's side. "And what of the Crook? I assume you were able to recover it?"

Voske nodded.

"Good, then follow me." Sammel snatched up a lantern, an old thing with a wick and oil instead of a spark. "I'll get you back to the tunnels safely."

Burz steadied his leg. The herbs had helped, but he wasn't eager for another trek through the damp sewers. Still, he would be home soon, he told himself, and then off to the festivals with his boys, and he could put the crook and this entire ordeal behind him.

It was twenty minutes of sneaking along the dark streets before they reached the tunnel. Mercifully, the clouds had returned, dripping down a light rain and covering the streets in darkness. Even so, Hikari held the light at bay as they crept along, a deeper shadow amid the black.

"Not far," Sammel whispered.

"This isn't familiar," Hikari said. He was starting to feel the strain of his boon, and his fingertips twinged with heat at the effort of holding the light. "Is this the same way we came?"

"No," Sammel said flatly. "It connects to a different route that runs near the Arrtris."

"How can we find our way back then?"

"I'll come with you, but only as far as the river. After that, you can find your own way."

Hikari nodded as they passed through a narrow alley, and in the back door of a home. It was empty, clearly abandoned long before the cultists showed up. They headed down some creaky stairs into the cellar. Hikari gladly released his hold on the light, but it made little difference here in the windowless basement.

He heard the scrape of metal on flint and a shower of sparks momentarily blinded him until the wick of Sammel's lamp caught fire, and a soft orange glow filled the room.

The cellar was musty, full of cobwebs and dirt, and a few crates and broken barrels littered the floors, all empty. Sammel set the lantern down and moved a barrel, revealing a trap door beneath. He pulled it open, and a ladder led down into the sewers. The foul smell of it nearly made Hikari gag.

"Well, a champion must do what a champion must do."

He climbed down first, and Sammel bent over the side and handed him the lantern while he was halfway down. When he reached the bottom, he saw it was much the same as the other sewer tunnel, though drier. He watched as the champions came down, one by one, all looking weary and exhausted. He could relate. He had blisters on his feet by this point, and he couldn't stop thinking about soaking in a long, hot bath.

It was some feat to get Zengin down, lowering his body between Voske and Sammel, as they grumbled about not bringing rope. And to make matters worse, he woke up half way down and nearly flung himself from Voske's arms.

"Calm down!" Voske yelled. "Hold still!"

When they got Zengin to the bottom, he was sullen and miserable, more so even than the rest. Hikari couldn't blame him. He refused to let Voske, or anyone else, carry him any longer, but he finally relented when Sammel offered him a shoulder, and he leaned on the stout man, shambling down the tunnel.

"A little further and you can rest," Sammel said.

Voske boomed back, "We don't need to rest."

Hikari craned his neck to look back down their ranks. Rasa and Weylyn were falling behind, Burz was limping, and Zengin looked ready to pass out again.

Sammel cleared his throat. "You have another hour of walking, to reach the exit. Probably more at this pace."

Voske looked from face to face and finally took a deep breath. "Fine."

"Every good adventure needs rest," Hikari said, trying to sound cheerful as his voice echoed off the sludge-covered walls. "Celebrate your victories, lick your wounds, and tell tales of valor."

No one seemed in the mood to do anything but lick their wounds, and they slid down to the ground with grimaces and groans. They were in a larger intersection of three tunnels running north, south and east. To the West, they heard the murmur of the Arrtris, dull and muffled behind a thick wall of stone.

Hikari set the lantern in the center of the intersection and gratefully sat down beside it, gently playing his fingers through the light, and twisting it upward, like flowers of fire, drifting through the air.

Zengin stared at his arm. He was aware of the others nearby, arguing about how long to rest, but they seemed far away. Water dripped around him, and the sickly smell of rot suffocated him. He leaned back against the side of the tunnel, trying to ignore the thick slime that lined the wall.

Soft red skin covered the stub of his wrist. He held it up, gingerly turning it over in the light. He swore he could feel the tips of his fingers, and he wondered if his hand was still in the shrine of Metnadur, lying on the floor.

He started laughing. He couldn't help it. It somehow felt fitting, after all he'd done. And yet *he* hadn't done any of it. All of this, his whole life, had been done *to* him. And now this had been done to him too. By *her*.

"Zengin?"

He looked up to see Weylyn squatting in front of him.

"You're in shock."

"I assure you, I'm not." He couldn't control the rage dripping in his voice. He hated not being in control, and that only made him more angry. Perhaps, when he met Borroka again, he'd take off both her hands, then her head.

He was aware of the others watching him now, their faces a mix of pity and remorse. All but one. One person watched him with the same detached curiosity he felt battling with his rage. *Sammel*.

He tried to push himself off the ground, but the stump of his wrist slid in the muck, and he landed hard on his elbow. He sat up again and pushed himself off the wall, finally gaining his feet.

Weylyn watched him, but she didn't offer to help. He at least appreciated that. Most of these sops would have tried to lend a sympathetic hand whether their help was wanted or not.

"I'm fine," he said, steadying himself.

Weylyn nodded, and he stumbled his way around the shadows to where Sammel sat, watching him stoically.

Zengin slid down with his back to the wall, and Sammel handed him a clean jar with a cork stopper. It seemed to be filled with water, but when he opened it, it smelled of herbs.

"It's my own blend," Sammel said casually. "It'll take the edge off the pain."

Zengin swirled the contents of the jar. "Bold, considering the last time you mixed a drink for a champion."

Sammel's expression stayed placid. "Do you still believe I want to harm you?"

"No." Zengin gulped down the cold brew, and he did feel some slight relief. He handed the jar back, and Sammel took a swig as well before replacing the cork.

He glanced down at Zengin's wrist, cradled in his lap. "What did it feel like?"

"Agony."

"I've always imagined it would be a sharp pain. Unbearable. Though I wonder how long it would last?"

"I imagine it will last forever." He narrowed his gaze and studied Sammel's countenance. Genuine curiosity was such a rare thing. "Should it shock me that you've imagined this scenario before?"

"I grew up in a village with no healers. One of our farmers had an accident with his plow, and he crushed his leg. The unguilded doctor had to cut it off and seal up the wound. I remember wondering how it might have felt if he were awake."

"He should be glad he wasn't." Zengin wrung his hand around the stub. *So close*, he thought. *So close to death*. He looked up to see Sammel still watching him intently. "Why did you save me?"

"You needed saving."

Zengin narrowed his eyes. "Plenty of people need saving. You don't save them all."

"I might if I knew about it. I suppose it depends on the circumstance."

Zengin tilted his head as he spoke, weighing his next words carefully. "And the circumstances would have to be very unique to incur so much risk."

"It was a calculated risk."

"And what was the reward?"

"Rescuing you."

"Someone you've tried to kill before."

"I suppose the circumstances changed," Sammel said casually. "It was in my best interest to stop you back in Arrajin."

"Your interest, or Endring's?"

Sammel raised an eyebrow. "I'm impressed you figured that out."

"Borroka helped."

"And how much does she know?"

Zengin paused, letting his eyes drift to the others who were huddled around the lantern, taking solace in its light. "She knows he took what she wanted most. She had designs on being a champion."

"I wouldn't say he took it, but he was given it. I suppose it was only a matter of time before she found out." He let out a thoughtful sigh. "Still, this changes things."

Zengin nodded toward the others. "And how much do they know?"

"Only that I'm a friend, and that I helped them get away from Borroka's people."

"She despises Endring. Can I assume he feels the same?"

"He does." Sammel leaned back and pulled something from his pocket, a compass of some sort, though Zengin couldn't fathom how he could read it in the dim light.

"But they both serve Neveri," Zengin pressed.

"He doesn't like to be reminded of that. They both serve the same end, but their means are different. Will you tell the others about Endring?"

Zengin shook his head. So far these buffoons had managed to make everything worse, and even cost him his hand. "No." He looked at the others again, and noted that Locin was watching them intently. "But I imagine they'll find out on their own, eventually."

"You may be right," Sammel said coolly. "It was never a secret that could be kept long."

Weylyn knelt with her hand on the wall. She could feel the pressure change in the air, and the steady rhythm of rushing water beyond the stone. Her senses were heightened, and she pulled on her boon, slamming her eyes shut. A vision flashed in her mind. They were moving on through the tunnels. Voske carried the lantern and the Crook's satchel, leading the way. They were weary, but there was no danger.

Still, she couldn't shake the feeling.

She opened her eyes, and looked up. Dried muck clung to the high curved wall, and somewhere above, Arrajin. She pictured the bridge to the Gods' Mount in her mind, the danger she sensed there. This was different, but similar. She tried again, shutting her eyes and calling up her boon, but she saw nothing but the champions setting out. No danger. No threat.

She sighed in frustration as she let her arm go slack.

"Something wrong?"

She turned to see Burz watching her. He came closer, pressing his own hand to the wall.

"Did you see something?"

Weylyn shook her head. "No peril, just a feeling. I've learned to trust my instincts."

"You've had those a lot longer than your boon."

"They were my boon. My old hunter's boon. It always kept me alert, warned me if predators were near. I could feel them, hear their breath, their heartbeats, tell if they were coming or going."

A sound gurgled in the river, low and creaky. They both looked up at the wall.

"Seems your instincts are still good. There are a lot of creatures living in those murky waters."

"What's the largest?"

Burz shrugged. "Lots of caiman. River wyrms? They can get eight feet or so."

Weylyn shook her head. This felt bigger. Much bigger. "Charybdis?"

Burz laughed. "No. Those stick to the sea."

Voske strolled up. His arms were crossed, and he looked antsy. "Problem?"

Burz shook his head. "I don't think so."

Weylyn leaned into the wall again, her hands sliding along the thick muck and smearing it across the stone. She listened carefully. Something was moving a lot of water.

"No danger right now," she said. "But there's something bigger than a wyrm in that river."

"The river?" Voske repeated. "Right now I'm not so worried about the river. You two ready to go?"

Weylyn nodded reluctantly.

"Good." Voske headed for the lantern. "Alright. Everybody up! Time to get back."

Sammel came striding up to them. "This is where I leave you." He pointed to the tunnel to their left. "This tunnel takes you straight toward the people's quarter."

"You're not coming?" Locin asked suspiciously.

"You can find your way from here. My business in the Sacred Quarter is not complete."

"What business?" Locin pressed.

"Mine."

Zengin made his way over with some effort. "Leave him be. He's helped more than enough."

Voske nodded. "I agree. We owe Sammel a great deal already, best not to rack up anymore debt."

Sammel nodded and then quickly headed back into the darkness behind them, not slowing even a bit as he stepped into the shadows at the end of the lantern.

"Great," Locin pouted. "Now what?"

Burz made his way toward Zengin. "Now we follow the path back home. The sooner we're out of here, the better." He offered Zengin his shoulder, and Zengin begrudgingly leaned on it.

"Home. Yeah." Locin kicked at some grime piled on the ground. "I'll be glad to get out of this rot!"

Weylyn stood as the others moved past and toward the left most tunnel. Perhaps they were right. Whatever had her on edge, they weren't in immediate danger.

24: Shattered Perception

By the time the Champions made it back to the temple, the sun had broken over the horizon and was casting golden light over the pristine stone. Every single one of them must have felt the relief that Voske did as they trudged across the bridge over the Arrtris, then up the gentle slope toward the Gods' Mount.

Messengers ran ahead of them, spreading word of their return, so that when they reached their common room, Aurilis and Gillis were already there. Gillis was biting nervously at his nails, and his shoulders slumped in relief as they entered.

"Thank the gods you're alright!"

But Aurilis was frowning, cold disapproval written on her face. Voske decided to ignore her.

"Came to welcome us back, did you?" Voske forced a smile and squared his shoulders. They were starting to ache, and all he really wanted was a bath, a meal, and a good, long sleep.

"This was foolish," Aurilis said flatly.

Voske's smile faltered. "I call it a victory."

She let her eyes trace their bedraggled appearance. "At least you all came back safely."

"More or less," Zengin grumbled.

Zengin's rough tunic was drenched in blood, and he was cradling the stump of his arm.

Gillis paled. "Ch-champion, is there anything-"

"No." Zengin pushed past the rest of them and headed for his chambers.

An uncomfortable silence engulfed the room as he dug with his left hand for his key, and fumbled with the lock. Gillis made a move like he would go help him three times, but thought better of it each time. Eventually, he managed the lock and sulked into his chambers, shutting the door with a thud.

Aurilis held a hand to her mouth, horrified. "Uthando have mercy."

Voske squared his shoulders, patting the satchel at his side. "We saved lives. If it cost us a hand-"

"A hand!" Aurilis shouted. "You have no idea what you've done! That hand bore the sigil of Metnadur."

Burz stepped forward, glancing sidelong at Voske. "It was a disaster, but Voske isn't wrong. We retrieved a weapon from the cultists. The civilian casualties could have been far greater than one maimed champion."

Her face was livid now, and she struggled to compose herself enough to speak. "You might be the most incompetent champions Talamh has ever seen. Do you not understand where you find yourselves? Many believe the gods have abandoned us, that they killed their own champions."

"Well, that's absurd," Hikari said. "A few rumors-"

"Three major temples have withdrawn support for you. Publicly! The people have lost faith, and many believe you're false champions."

Burz matched her angry tone now. "And just how many civilians would you sacrifice for one Champion's hand? One hundred? One thousand?"

"Thousands!"

The room went silent. She couldn't mean that. She couldn't believe they were worth so much.

"Thousands." Voske chuckled. "Thousands for the hand of one *incompetent* champion?"

Aurilis took an angry step toward him. "You have no idea what you are. You are the chosen of the gods, their face upon Talamh. To the people, you may as well be gods, and if you crumble, everything fails."

The room went silent again. Voske tried to keep his eyes locked on Aurilis in defiance, shoulders back, but he suddenly felt like someone had set two slabs of granite on his shoulders. He bit down against the weight, pulling in a little of his boon, but it did nothing to ease the feeling.

"We went to save lives," he said, "and we did that."

He reached into the satchel to grab the Crook of Bei'ai, but his hand found nothing but air and fabric. He felt his heart skip a beat, and he yanked the pack fully open, staring inside. It was empty. His hands became a white knuckled clench on the sides of the satchel.

He glanced back at Aurilis to see her eyes smoldering. "Well?"

Locin stepped up. "Gods, you big oaf! Just show her the relic." She snatched the satchel away and stared inside. "Mire and Nyx."

"What?" Burz was next to snatch the satchel and stare dejectedly in. "Where is it?"

Voske looked around the group, studying the faces of his fellow champions. Surely one of them wouldn't have taken it. "Sammel," he breathed. "He must have stolen it."

"Surely not," Hikari piped up. "He was an ally."

"Who is this Sammel?" Aurilis asked coldly. "And what, exactly, has he stolen?"

"He helped us," Illeri said. "He saved us, really. He even rescued Zengin. We'd probably be dead without him."

"Dead? So without the help of one passing stranger, eight champions would have died?"

"That's not fair!" Locin said.

"And this relic?" She continued. "This was the dangerous weapon you spoke of?"

"We had it!" Voske insisted. "We couldn't have known he'd betray us. Besides, at least it's out of the cultists' hands."

"Well, let's hope your new friend is less dangerous than them."

"We'll get it back," Voske said flatly.

"No, you won't. You'll get yourselves cleaned up and presentable as Champions. Despite your failures, the people of Erimos are expecting you to put on a bold face. You will swallow your pride and give them what they need." Aurilis stepped back, looked over their bedraggled appearance, and then opened the door. "You're chariot leaves this afternoon."

As she shut the door behind her, silence enveloped them once more. Voske felt like a guildling who'd just been scolded by his master. He hated that feeling, and he thought he was past it cycles ago.

"Well," Hikari said lightly, "I daresay that could have gone better."

"That's it then?" Illeri asked. "We just go to Erimos?"

"Yes," Burz said flatly. "We do our jobs."

Locin stomped off toward the door.

"And where are you going?"

She glanced back without a word, and headed out.

Gillis' voice rose meekly from behind. "Not to rush you, Champions, but we do leave in a few hours. I'll have baths drawn for you all, and if I can assist with any packing you require… in any way…" his voice trailed off as the champions slowly sulked back toward their rooms without so much as a glance his direction, all but Voske and Hikari, who gave him a kind hand on the shoulder on the way by.

"Thank you, darling. You may want to have some food for us after we bathe. It's been a long couple days."

Gillis nodded, seeming grateful to have a job to do, and hurried off to get started.

And Voske found himself alone. He snatched up the empty satchel and slunk toward his room.

The door to Endring's chambers creaked open. It was dark inside, and the window was shut tight. Locin crept in, and shut the door behind herself, locking it quickly.

"Okay, Spark, you were right. He's not here. Nyx it!"

She glanced around, heading toward the other rooms and peeking through the doors. No sign of Endring.

"Rotting old thief. No chance he stashed it here, is there?"

A brush on her left arm told her Spark didn't think so. Of course not. He wouldn't let that relic out of his sight.

"I should have known sooner. The way Sammel was helping us, and the way he talked about the Crook. Gods, Spark! I was so stupid." She made her way over to some drawers and started pulling them open, smudging dirt from her filthy hands across the fine wood. She didn't really expect to find the crook, but she was frustrated at missing him.

"Old coot's probably long gone. Probably flew off to meet Sammel the second he heard we were back."

She opened the last drawer. It was empty. The statue of Neveri, the papers, everything was gone.

"Rot it!"

She slammed the drawer shut, but as she did a small scrap of paper fell free from the corner, a single folded note that had been left behind. She narrowed her eyes and bent down, lifting it up. All that was written on it was a single line.

'A trial to lay them low - The Struggle of Epsis.'

She plopped down on the bed and stared at the words, trying to recall why they sounded so familiar.

"A trial to lay them low," she muttered. "The Struggle of Epsis? Gods, I'm not a scribe."

She folded the note and tucked it into her pocket, then turned her attention to the main room, but something seemed off here too. Other things were missing. As she looked around, she noted most of his clothes were gone, any personal belongings. The furniture was there, the statue of Bei'ai still covered under a cloth, but little else.

She shook her head, taking it all in, and Spark bristled with questions.

"He's leaving, Spark."

Something black caught her eye and she stooped, picking up a feather off the carpet, like a raven's but much bigger.

"He's leaving the temple, and he's not coming back."

Endring stood like a shadow in the center of the sanctum, his hood over his face. The room was silent and empty, but he knew it would be. He had come here often at this hour, when the light of morning warred against the yawning shadows. He'd spent many hours staring up at the face of Bei'ai, and just as many staring down at the cold floor where the truth lay buried beneath a solid slab of stone.

He pulled the gloves from his hands and tossed them aside, kneeling as he caught a glimpse of Neveri's sigil on his palm. He pressed it against the wide crack that ran through the floor. Whatever came after was up to the people. He couldn't force them to listen, but he could speak. He would no longer stand by and let the temple keep the truth from them. They would know of Neveri, and his cruel exile.

He reached in his pocket and felt for the chalk Sammel had given him, little more than a nub. He drew it out and began circling the room in a wide arc. Everywhere he drew, a faint light glowed as he crossed in front of the gods' statues and circled round to the center again. He hesitated, taking one slow breath, then connected the line.

At once, the chalk began to spark and sizzle, and the stone creaked and groaned. The sanctum shook, and he held out his arms to steady himself as he stepped back. He could hear shouts from outside as the stone fissure expanded and cracks spread across the floor like breaking glass. All as one, it shattered and fell away with a tremendous crash.

He peered into the cloud of dust and dark, shifting his eyes to those of a cat. There below, nine statues stood, shrouded in the shadows.

Nine.

How he longed to go down, to bask in their glory. To behold Neveri's likeness. But there was no time. The sanctum was flooding with monks, and Endring turned, throwing up his hands to show his palm. They stopped in their tracks, frozen with shock.

"Tell your Oracles that Neveri's champion walks upon Talamh again!"

He threw his arms to the side with a cracking of bones, and let his robes slip free as they turned to wings. Terror and wonder filled the room as Endring took flight, aiming for the stained glass high above. He crashed through into the morning light, and the sun nearly blinded him. He whirled around to see Arrajin far below, still asleep under the rising sun. But soon they would wake, and Talamh would change. It must.

25: Ancient Mysteries

Burz stood at the bottom of a wide stone staircase. A massive hole had been shattered in the sanctum floor, exposing a deep chamber that had not seen the light of day in untold millenia. At the bottom lay the remnants of the temple floor. The circular slab had shattered, covering the chamber in dust and debris.

"What could have done this?" He muttered.

He knelt on one knee, running a finger through the thick dust. All around them stood shrines to the gods, but they were not like their counterparts that stood in the higher sanctum. In this pit, the shrines were made of darkest obsidian and their barbarous visage was a twisted version of the deities. This Uthando did not mercifully bow, instead he held a flail in his hand, and the cords struck his own back as he cried out in pain. Burz felt his stomach twist in knots as he looked away from the blasphemous statue.

"Who knew this was down here?" Hikari asked.

Burz looked up at those gathered in the dark. All of the champions except Locin and Zengin were present, as were Aurilis, Gillis, a dozen monks and at least four oracles. Judging by their demeanors, none of them knew.

"Well, someone must have." Voske answered. He was standing in front of the shrine of Jeza. Most modern sculptures showed her in a flowing robe holding her sword, Aldaci. Here she was lunging forward, with a battleaxe raised high above her head and her mouth open in a savage roar. Drops of blood gathered on the axe and dripped to her feet, all in incredible detail.

"It's other-worldly," Illeri breathed. She turned in a slow circle and Burz followed her gaze. Strah was curled up on the ground, holding his hands up as though he was being attacked. Desita twirled in a wild motion, her naked body covered only by her long hair and a few wisps of fabric.

Then was the truly damning shrine, the ninth god, shown with the face of a man with beastly horns sprouting from his head. He stood in a patch of briars, and a snake was wrapped around his leg.

"It's an affront," Burz finally said. "These are pagan images."

"I wouldn't say that," Voske answered.

"What else could they be?"

Voske scowled at him. "If Metnadur built the temple, and it's been here unchanged for nearly forever, where did these come from?"

Burz gritted his teeth. There was nothing he could do to gainsay Voske, but for these to be the gods was unthinkable. "This was done by the cult of Neveri," he said, "to debase the gods and make Neveri appear their equal."

"You're out of your head."

Weylyn stood in the center of the room, alert, her eyes fixed above. "I'm more concerned with what was powerful enough to do that."

Aurilis clenched her jaw reluctantly for some time. It was clear that Gillis and the Oracles knew by the way they looked at her. Even a few of the monks knew.

Burz stepped toward her. "Well? Who did this?"

But it was Eprim who answered. "The Oracle of Bei'ai."

"Do not call him that," Aurilis seethed.

"Endring?" Hikari asked. "How in the names of the gods did that mangled old man do this?"

"Most likely a relic of some kind," Eprim said. "But that's not the worst of it."

Aurilis snapped. "Enough, Eprim!"

"They have a right to know. If you won't tell them, I will."

"Tell us what?" Voske demanded.

But it wasn't Eprim who answered this time. Instead a voice called down from the stairs. "Endring is the Champion of Neveri." Zengin made his way down, carefully stepping over debris. He walked toward the statues at the bottom, studying them. "I had to see it for myself."

Burz looked toward the statue of Bei'ai. She was pictured as a young girl, bent over, crying. Beside her, Iyanu stood, holding the sun in her hands.

"Someone explain this." Burz looked back at Zengin.

"Endring can morph into beasts, birds. I'm not sure what the limits are."

Aurilis turned toward him. "How do you know this?"

"Does it matter? You clearly weren't going to tell us."

Burz walked up to Aurilis and looked her in the eye. "Is it true?"

Of course not, he thought. *A false god can't have a champion.*

Aurilis stared at him, stiff-lipped.

"I asked you if it's true."

"Yes." The word came reluctantly, and Burz felt his heart pounding at the revelation. "Nearly two dozen monks saw him turn into a bird and fly out of the sanctum."

"Mire and Nyx!" Voske yelled. "That's it then? The rotting champion of Neveri was right here under our noses." He pointed an accusing finger at Aurilis. "How did you not know about this? He was your Oracle, Nyx it!"

"There were… suspicions."

It was Burz' turn to be angry. "And you didn't think to tell us?"

"Why now," Illeri asked, drawing their attention. She was walking a slow circle around the statue of Neveri, staring up at its vulgar countenance. "That's what I'd like to know. Why did he choose to reveal himself now?"

"And when did he even become the-" Voske wrinkled his nose "-whatever he is now."

"The Champion of Neveri," Weylyn answered. "What's the point in denying what's perfectly obvious?"

Burz grimaced at her words, but he couldn't argue the point. The ability to sprout wings from your back seemed very much godlike, even if it was a heathen god.

"That's it then," Hikari mused. "There are nine gods."

"Correction." Aurilis called out, and they all looked up. She was striding away from the cluster of oracles and her eyes were bunched in an annoyed frown. "There *were* nine gods. Neveri is no longer counted among their number."

Voske folded his arms. "You knew he existed?"

"There's a tribe of Suntarans that worship a fish god named Gogosi, and another on Las that worship a giant tree. The vast majority of these claims have no substance."

"And what about this one?"

She paused, eyeing the statue of Neveri with repugnance. "There have been rumors for as long as I can remember. What this Neveri is or isn't remains to be seen."

"Remains to be seen?" Voske said, aghast. "What remains to be seen? That statue is plain as the nose on your face."

"Not to mention the wings," Hikari pointed out.

Voske wagged a finger toward Hikari. "Exactly."

"Enough!" Burz felt like his head was swimming, like everything in the world had been flipped upside down. "It's heresy. All of it."

"Does it matter at this point?" Weylyn asked.

"Of course it matters."

"I only mean that whether this is a god or some other powerful creature, his cultists hold the Sacred Quarter, and that makes our course clear. Find and capture Endring."

"No." Aurilis' tone was cold and final.

"No?" Voske said.

"Your place is at the festivals. I can promise you we'll do all we can to track down the traitor, but for now, we'll close the sanctum and continue with the tour as planned."

"Close the sanctum?" Illeri asked.

"We'll have to keep the public out of the sanctum for their own safety, not to mention the rumors that are bound to spread about what was found here."

Voske shook his head. "You're just gonna bury this?"

"This isn't the time for this discussion." Aurilis answered. "We must do what we can to restore the faith of the people. Or do you want to see Talamh torn apart?"

"I agree." Burz hated the words as he spoke them. "We can't let the people know until we have answers."

"Precisely." Aurilis smoothed her robes and folded her hands neatly in front. "The best thing you can do for the people is be presented at the Champion's festivals at the appointed times and remind them that the gods have not forsaken them." She looked long and hard from face to face. "Can you do that, Champions?"

A hush fell over the room.

She waited another minute before she turned, and her footfalls echoed up the stairs. Soon the other oracles and monks had followed, and Gillis stood dutifully with his champions, his expression wracked with doubts.

"Gillis," Burz finally said.

"Yes, Champion?"

"Have our things sent to the chariot. We're leaving in less than an hour."

"As you command." He scurried up the stairs, and Voske locked eyes on Burz. He clearly wasn't sold on the idea, but what choice did they have? He grunted his frustration and then headed off to follow the others.

Burz looked one last time at the statues, and most of all at Uthando, the cruel whip against his bare skin, and the lines that scored his obsidian flesh. He raised a hand to his own back, feeling the hills and valleys of scars through the light silk of his chlamys. Part of him wanted this whole accursed chamber to be a lie, constructed by some wicked men a millennia ago. But if it was true, perhaps this Uthando understood him.

He shook the thoughts away and headed up the stairs toward the light of day. For now he would pack, and they would leave on their journey, and he would try to put this place behind him.

Voske was dragging. He'd had no sleep in a day and a half, and while a hot bath and a rather generous meal had refreshed him, he was feeling weary as he headed toward the chariot tether. Most of the other champions were there. A whole team of monks had gone ahead with their luggage, but no one had seen Locin. Gillis walked ahead, and Burz and Hadris strolled beside him with their boys running excitedly toward the tether. Hadris had called them back twice already. Behind, the rest of the champions walked in a rather somber mood, with Zengin last, and sullen. Voske couldn't blame him, and he'd even been feeling a twinge of guilt as they crossed the temple grounds. They might have saved his hand. Considering they lost the crook, maybe it would have been better.

He glanced to the side and saw Burz glaring at him, so he straightened up. There was no room for doubt. He'd made the right call, and there's no way he could have predicted Sammel would steal the rotting crook.

Kyren's voice drew his eyes ahead. "Woah! Look!"

The Chariot tethered on the platform was like nothing Voske had ever seen. The hull was formed like a colossal white dolphin, its snout curved into the front where seven massive pylats fluttered their wings, ready to soar.

Hikari was beaming. "Magnificent!"

"That's for us?" Weylyn asked.

"Of course, darling! The champions of Talamh are setting out on a grand tour. We must go in style!"

Even Illeri seemed enamored with the hulking thing. She moved to the front and took it all in. "Seven pylats! That's the largest chariot I've ever seen."

Voske heard someone running toward them and looked back to see Locin rushing up with a pack over one shoulder and a dingy satchel in her hand. She stopped in front of them all and turned to face them, catching her breath.

"Okay…" she panted. "We gotta talk."

Voske raised an eyebrow. "Where have you been? Do you know what you missed?"

"Sanctum…" She took a deep breath. "Yeah. I saw it."

"And?"

She shrugged. "It was Endring."

"We know that, darling. Did you see the ancient Iyanu? Amazing."

Locin scowled. "Sure. Whatever. Now will you listen or not? I've got something important to say."

Burz turned to Hadris. "Take the boys aboard. I'll join you in a minute."

They all gathered around, and Voske crossed his arms as he nodded to Locin. "Alright. What is it?"

"I went looking for the Crook."

Voske was taken aback. As far as he knew the Crook was back in the Sacred Quarter, probably right back in the rotting hands of the cultists. "Looking where?"

"Endring has it, but I was too late."

"Wait." Hikari held up his hands. "Why does Endring have it? And how? He's clearly been busy here."

"Sammel works for him," Zengin said, and they all looked at him. "At least one of you figured that out. And the crazy one."

Locin scowled. "Ignoring that."

Voske's head was starting to hurt. "Wait. You both knew this, and no one bothered to tell me? How are we supposed to work together if you keep secrets?"

Zengin was glowering at Locin now. "No one ever said we're working together."

Locin sighed. "Look, will you all just listen? Sammel stole the piece of the relic to give it to Endring." She looked pointedly at Voske. "Which I only figured out after we got back, and it was gone. I went to see Endring, but he had cleared out." She fished in the satchel and took out a stained piece of paper. "But this has the location of the other two pieces of the crook."

Weylyn stepped forward. "There are two more?"

She nodded hurriedly. "You saw that thing. It was broken on both ends."

Hikari took the page, scanning it. "But it's nonsense, darling. Just some old poem."

Voske stepped up and snatched the paper, reading it aloud. "In the hands of an old soul, a vice to lay them low, a splintered reed within a red horizon. In the hands of the flourishing, a trial to lay them low, a crown upon a frontier yet unbroken. In the hands of a guide, a sight to lift the spirit, an end to ward away the final fate." He turned it over and stared at the back. Blank. "It doesn't say anything about the relic."

Locin scoffed, taking the paper back and pressing it against her stomach to smooth out the wrinkles. "Of course it doesn't, you big dummy! It's a riddle. I've been thinking about this. It says red horizon and where was the Crook stored in the Sacred Quarter?"

Voske scratched his head. "The Gambit of Iyanu."

"I meant before that."

"The House of Dusk," Burz said.

"Exactly. A splintered piece of the Crook, within a red horizon."

Silence fell, and the champions all looked from one to another and then back to Locin.

"Come on," she stammered. "There's something to this."

"Alright," Voske said, leaning in to glimpse the page again. "Then what's an old soul, or a hand of flourishing, or a trial to lay them low?"

Locin wagged a finger toward him. "The trial is a reference to The Struggle of Epsis."

Voske frowned. "What in Nyx is that?"

"It's a uh…" She blanched.

"A constellation," Illeri chimed in as she pushed forward. "Why do you think that?"

She produced a second piece of paper, this one much smaller than the first. "I found this note in Endring's room."

"By all the gods," Zengin called from behind. "Why are we entertaining the delusions of a mad woman?"

"Alright." Locin stuffed the paper away and threw the satchel over her shoulder, glaring at Zengin. "I've had enough of you. What's your problem with me anyway?"

"I have no problem, but you are crazy, and it's fair to point it out."

"I am not!"

He sighed and then began in a condescendingly slow tone as if explaining something to a child. "Surely I'm not the only one who's noticed. The odd behaviors. The twitching. The laughing. The way you mutter to yourself when you think no one is watching." He wrinkled his nose with a disgusted look.

"Why don't you mind your own business, rotter!" She lunged for him, but Voske reached one massive hand and grabbed the back of her chiton, lifting her slightly off the ground.

Zengin raised an eyebrow. "And prone to violence. Rather like a mad dog."

"Rotting pool of mire! I thought you would all be grateful that I found this, but I guess I gotta find these pieces myself. Worthless, spoiled idiot!" She spat in his direction and then twisted to see Voske. "Let me go, you rotting oaf!"

He set her on the ground, and she smoothed out her chiton before staring at them all with a wounded look.

"Fine. I see how it is."

She stomped off in the direction of the chariot, and Hikari rushed after her.

"Now, hold on, darling! Come back. We don't agree with Zengin."

They disappeared up the long stairs, and Zengin locked his gaze on Voske. "Next time, do keep your dog on a leash, won't you?"

Voske snarled, crossing the distance to Zengin in two great strides. "You speak about a Champion like that again, and it'll be me you have to worry about."

Zengin held his ground, holding up the stump of his arm, wrapped in a golden ornament that held the end of his sleeve in place. "I think you've done quite enough already, Foreman." He shouldered past after the others, and Voske looked back at the remaining champions, all watching him with a mix of emotions.

Burz shook his head. "You're doing a great job leading them."

Voske had half a mind to punch the smug look off Burz face, but the others all just stared at him, so he marched past them toward the chariot.

It was a monstrous thing with five decks, but they'd have to be explored later, for now he just wanted to be alone, and to sleep. He had the monks escort him to his room, but when he got into the bedroom, he found a huge parcel laid out on the bed, and he groaned.

"Of all the rotting things to…"

He moved to pick up the parcel, but it was heavy, and solid, and it piqued his interest. He pulled back the paper uncovering a suit of armor colored in deep crimson and marked with the sword of Jeza. He picked up the helmet and felt the size and weight of it. It was startling how much it reminded him of the illustration of Skard's armor, and he felt a bit of regret. He'd made his stand, and he would wear this armor on all three worlds and be presented as the Champion of Jeza, but he wasn't off to a good start living up to his choice. He dropped the helmet back on the chest piece with a metallic clang, and sat on the edge of the bed with his head in his hands as he felt the chariot lift and his stomach flip.

"Jeza, save us."

26: Through the Cold Dark

Weylyn's hand kept a steady grip on the railing that passed just in front of the wayfarer's field. It was foolish of course, none of the other passengers seemed to be nervous about the flight, and they milled about the deck of the chariot, chatting and laughing and not even bothering to look outside to where the blue skies of Las were quickly fading to black.

The floor stopped vibrating, and Weylyn planted her feet, feeling the solid deck. She took a deep breath, holding it in as the stars came into clearer focus.

The curve of Las curled over the bow of the ship, like a massive sun cresting the horizon of a new world. She felt a flutter in her chest and reminded herself to breathe again.

"Are you alright?" Gillis asked.

She turned to see him approaching, and then let her gaze return to Las. "I never thought I'd regret missing this."

"Apologies, champion. Missing what?"

"This," she motioned to the stars around them. "I had a list of all the things I was giving up by choosing the life of a huntress. Things like a family, a place to call home, traveling off world. But this-" her mind reeled as she let her eyes travel across the endless black around them, "-I'm glad I didn't miss this."

"It changes your perspective," Gillis said. "I remember the first time I travelled the cold dark. It made the worlds feel so big and so small at the same time."

Weylyn felt her stomach flip as the chariot banked, and she sighed. "Do you get used to the motion?"

"They offer a ginger tea on the upper deck. If you'd like, I can bring you a cup."

"Thank you."

He stared at her for an uncomfortable moment before clearing his throat. "Forgive me, champion, does that mean you want a cup or not?"

She shook her head.

"Then, I'll leave you to enjoy the view."

"Actually, there's something else I'd like."

"Of course." He straightened up and put on a dutiful expression.

She thought about asking him to relax, but she didn't think it would do much good. "It's nothing I need, just a question."

"I'll answer to the best of my ability."

She folded her arms, not sure how to broach the subject. "Three days ago on the way into Arrajin, I had a vision. I saw myself by the bridge over the Arrtris. There was a creature. I could feel it in the mist, but I couldn't see it. A predator, I think, and big."

He gulped. "How big?"

"If it's the same thing I felt in the sewers, very." She paused, weighing her words carefully, and trying to recall the details.

"That is certainly different. Was there any more?"

"I was dead."

Gillis' face went pale. "D-dead? Are you sure?"

"I saw my body lying at my feet. Trust me. I was dead."

His eyes widened. "Have you told anyone else?"

"Not yet."

"And did you have a sense of... when this might happen?"

She shook her head. "I'm not sure."

Gillis looked as though he wasn't sure how to respond. "You wouldn't be the first of Strah's champions to see your own demise. It's actually quite common. Perhaps if we could..." he looked around nervously, as if wishing someone else would step in to save him. "The Oracle of Strah might have... some..."

"Don't worry, Gillis." She forced a smile. "I'm only looking for one answer from you right now. Is there a way to relive a vision?"

"You want to see it again?" He looked surprised.

"If I had more to go on..." she let her voice trail off. It was an odd sensation, working to stave off one's own death.

"There is one thing," he said hesitantly. "There's a woman in Vohasi... an apothecary of sorts. She knows how to make vision powder. Champions of Strah have used it in the past to enhance their visions. However… there is a risk."

Weylyn pursed her lips. "Is she trustworthy?"

"I believe so. My predecessor had dealings with her on several occasions."

"Alright. I'll meet with her."

He nodded. "I'll arrange it as soon as we land."

"And Gillis."

"Yes, Champion?"

"I'll take a cup of that tea now."

"Of course, Champion."

Zengin leaned over his arm, cradling it gently. It was difficult to look at, but he forced himself anyway, trying to wrap his mind around the absence of his hand. He was sitting in his lavish quarters on the temple chariot, at a small desk, similar to the type scribes used to complete their work. In front of him lay a piece of parchment and beside it a quill and a pot of ink.

The inventor lamps in the room were all dark but the light of the sun burned through the pale curtains, shining across his desk and setting the motes of dust aglow.

He reached out his left hand and took the quill. It didn't feel natural at all. His fingers bunched up tightly at the end and he lowered it to the page, trying to scribble out whatever meaningless phrase would come to mind.

'Once there lived.'

He stared down at the phrase with scrutiny. The form of the letters was barely legible, the ink was ugly and globbed at the tips.

He let out a frustrated sigh and plunked the quill back into the pot. This was pointless. He was the champion of Metnadur. He never had to lift a finger for the rest of his life if he didn't want to. He could just dictate his words and have them transcribed without any difficulty. Why torment himself?

He turned his fingers over and looked at the tips, they were smudged too.

He pressed them against the page and dragged them downward, leaving three dark streaks across the center.

Pointless.

He grabbed a clean page and started again, with more determination this time.

'Once there lived the son of a nobleman who wanted to become a writer.'

It was even worse than the last. The letters were obnoxiously big and gradually sloped as they traversed the page, like his words were frowning back at him.

A light knock sounded from his door and he glanced toward the sound. He was loath to speak to anyone at the moment, so it surprised him when he found himself standing to his feet.

Maybe he could shoo whoever it was away and have them tell everyone else to leave him alone.

He shuffled to his door and drew it open, fully expecting to see a monk of Uthando waiting on the other side.

"Did Aurilis send you," he began, but then paused when he saw Rasa standing in his doorway.

She had her hands folded in front of her and she looked nervous. Or was that concern?

"Hello," she said, in a quiet tone.

He kept his hand frozen on the doorframe, unsure what to say. Had it been anyone else he could have dismissed them. "What do you want?" he said.

"I don't normally do this," she said quickly. "But I'm sorry for what happened."

He kept the stub of his arm behind the door. There was no reason for him to feel ashamed about it, but he didn't need her gawking. "Who put you up to this? Burz?"

"No, no," she stammered. "It was the spirits' idea."

He took a deep breath and let his eyes wander the hall outside, as though he might spy one of those pesky blue forms peeking through.

"So, I made you this."

She held up a cuff that looked like it might fit over the end of his arm. It was a simple thing, sewn blue linen, and a curious loop was fashioned into the end.

"That's for your quill," she said. "They told me you enjoy writing."

Zengin took the cuff with his good hand and wadded it up in his fist. "Well, they should learn to keep their mouths shut."

She winced. "They're only trying to help."

"I don't need help."

He took a deep breath as her form slumped. She was trying to be kind, that was obvious.

"Of course," she said.

"And I'd rather not have the reminder."

She nodded quickly. "That makes sense."

"Good." He glanced around one last time. "And tell your friends to mind their own business."

With that he pulled back inside and clicked the door closed. She'd looked disappointed. Some part of him thought she might genuinely care, and perhaps he shouldn't have dismissed her so glibly, but he pushed it down. Everyone had an agenda, and she was no different.

He strode back toward his desk, but stopped in front of his wastebasket and threw the cuff into the trash. It was ugly anyway.

That done, he settled in, staring at his inkpot and quill. If he was ever going to write again it would be using his own hand, not some gimmick that a child conjured up.

He reached out and grabbed the quill, then brought it back to the paper, but his hand wouldn't move. In his mind's eye he rushed back to that scene of the little girl with stringy red hair. She had no idea he knew.

He pushed down on the quill, watching as the ink slowly absorbed into the parchment and spread outward in a hideous blot. How was it she still seemed so innocent? Her life had been Nyx, maybe more so than his own. His hand began to tremble as he pressed down on the quill, but he barely noticed the motion. She was a fool, and foolish people only made the world a more dangerous place. If she hadn't gleaned enough common sense to keep her head down, then he wanted no part of her. She was a liability and a-

A sharp snap pulled him from his thoughts as the metal nib of his quill cracked to the side, and sent a dark streak over the edge of the parchment and across the wood of his desk.

He threw the quill to the ground and jerked back from his table. There was an ugly line of black across his words and ink had even spattered onto his clothes.

He swore as he stood to his feet, then marched back toward his bedroom. It had been hard enough to change into his clothes the first time, but this was just more practice. That was what he needed, more practice, more ways to look at what lay ahead rather than to stew about what lay behind. That's why he couldn't accept her gift. It was weakness. He was no one's prey.

Hikari swiftly made his way through the lower corridors of the Tempest. He was on the fourth level of seven, winding his way through the massive chariot, looking nervously over his shoulder for Pirr. Until that morning, he had never met nor heard of Pirr the Playwright, nor was he sure how or why he was on the Tempest, but one thing he was very sure of - Pirr was the worst playwright he'd ever encountered. The man had spent the entire morning hounding Hikari, prattling on about his next great work and how it would change Talamh forever. Hikari had endured drab comedies without a lick of humor, and dark tragedies so laughably bad they may as well have been comedies, and now that he was free of Pirr, he shamelessly intended to hide.

He ducked around a corner and into one of the dining halls, a vast room that smelled like Sbarga, and he could see an elaborate spread laid out in the center of the room for the guests. He leaned into the wall, glancing nervously around until he spotted Illeri. He smiled, fussed over his hair, and then started toward her table, but as he rounded the corner he noticed she was talking with a handsome young man. They were leaning in close, chatting warmly.

Hikari awkwardly tried to turn away, but at the door of the dining hall, he spotted the great round head of Pirr with its thinning gray hair like wispy whiskers. He was searching the dining hall, and he'd be looking toward Hikari next. He quickly pressed in against the wall and sat at an open seat at Illeri's table. She looked up at him with wide eyes.

"Apologies, darling. I need a place to hide for a moment."

Illeri and the man looked out at the room, and Hikari watched as Pirr completed his search and ducked back into the hall. He let out a sigh and sunk back in his chair.

"Who was that?" Illeri asked.

"The worst playwright in all of Talamh. It seems he's got it in his head that only *Hikari of Rel'van* is good enough to play the lead in his masterpieces. I tried explaining to him I'm no longer a player, but so it goes."

He glanced back to see them both watching him uncomfortably. The man especially seemed annoyed. He tried to smile politely, but he had a look in his eyes that said it was going well with Illeri, and he wanted Hikari to go.

"But I won't intrude, darling. You've both been gracious enough. My thanks."

He stood, turning to go, but a strange feeling in his chest stopped him. Instead of leaving the dining hall, he sat at the next table over with his back to them. It was a rather annoying feeling. *Discomfort. Frustration.* He couldn't put his finger on it. He slumped forward and started fidgeting with the place setting.

Slowly, awkwardly, the conversation behind him resumed in quiet tones. Hikari shifted in his seat and strained his ears until he could hear.

"They do," the man said with a light laugh.

Illeri laughed in response. "They can't possibly."

"I'm not kidding. It's about the size of the Star Glass and hideously ugly."

"I can't believe I've never seen it."

"Maybe you will."

Hikari rolled his eyes as he mouthed the words. *Maybe you will.* He knew that tone all too well. The one that made the women weak in the knees.

"I could take you. I've been there a dozen times."

"Gods," she sounded wistful. "I miss it, you know."

"I do. I can't imagine never being in the field again. Being a radiant is more than a guilding. It's..."

"Your whole life," she said.

The romantic tension was so thick, it made Hikari want to gag. Did these two know nothing of subtlety?

"I think..." she began haltingly. "I think it was the only place I ever belonged."

"Certainly you belong as a champion."

She scoffed lightly.

"I think you do," he said.

"Well, so do I!" Hikari snapped.

The table grew quiet again, and he turned his chair around to face them. Illeri looked annoyed.

"Oh, you're still here." The wayfarer said.

"I most certainly am."

Everything in Hikari was screaming at him. *What in the worlds are you doing?* But that feeling in his chest was growing. *Jealousy?* What in the worlds would he have to be jealous about? It couldn't be that. He decided he must be protecting Illeri. That was it.

This swoon-worthy radiant was only after her because she was a champion, and she was too naive to see through his ploy.

Hikari pulled his chair up to their table, and the radiant sank back with a sigh. "There's nothing like being a champion. You not only belong, darling, you're one of few who do!"

The radiant scowled at him, and then turned back to face Illeri. "I think you belong among the stars."

Hikari laughed. "Among the stars. Is that what you're going with?"

"Yes," he said through gritted teeth. "Because it's true."

"A bit cliche though, don't you think? You could have said something like, 'You belong amidst your piers, for only the stars can match your beauty.'"

He smiled, self satisfied, but when he looked back down, the radiant was glaring at him, and Illeri was blushing and looking mortified.

The flustered radiant pushed away from the table.

"You're leaving?" Illeri asked.

"I'm sorry. I'm on rotation soon. But you can come find me on deck?"

She nodded, her shoulders slumping as he marched away.

"Well, he was rather dramatic."

"Hikari!" She turned on him furiously.

"Well, don't yell at me! I was only helping you out. I don't think that radiant had noble intentions."

"Noble intentions? You self-centered, preening-"

"Preening!?"

She sighed, pushing back from the table and placing her hands firmly on its surface. "Everything isn't about you, Hikari."

As she stormed off, he noticed the feeling in his chest swelling again until it was nearly unbearable. Horrible, rotten feeling. He still wasn't quite sure what it was. He was vaguely aware of someone slipping into the chair across from him, and he looked up to see Pirr smiling at him, carrying an armload of manuscripts, and his heart sank.

"Here you are, Champion! I've been looking everywhere for you. It seems we lost track of each other." He plopped the manuscripts down on the table. "Now this is just a few of my best works, but if you'd like to see more afterwards, I would be more than happy to oblige."

Pirr's voice faded to background noise as Hikari looked over his shoulder for any sign of Illeri, but she was long gone. And that's when it hit him. This dreadful feeling in his chest was something else entirely. He couldn't bear the thought of not seeing her or speaking with her. He certainly couldn't bear the thought of her being with someone else. The best word he had for this uncomfortable ache was *longing*.

Voske sat at a tall table, on the topmost deck of the Tempest. *Deck* was really the wrong word for it. It was more of a wide raised platform on top of another raised platform that gave him a broad view over the front of the chariot. Ahead of them, Erimos swelled in size, like an agate ocean filling the cold dark.

He looked absent-mindedly down at his half finished drink, a fruit blend of citrus and coconut. He hated coconut, but the thick cold liquid made up for the flavor, so he didn't complain.

Beside him, Locin sat on a high stool swinging her legs and chattering about something. He wasn't in the mood to talk. He wasn't really in the mood to be awake either, but sleep had been fleeting, so he'd decided to try a different sort of refreshment.

"Gods," Locin said, waving her arm around the chariot. "Being up here makes me sick."

He turned toward her, eyeing the two empty glasses on the table in front of her. "Oh?"

"Yeah. Chariot rides always creep me out a little, but sitting up high makes it worse. I mean, what happens if the wayfarer loses their field?"

Voske looked at the pillars of golden light, rising from the main deck and spreading a canopy across the skybeams. "There are eight of them."

"Well, what if they all have to pee at the same time?"

Yep, he could always count on Locin for enlightening conversation. He motioned to her empty cups. "Sure you're not projecting?"

She crossed her arms and stared at him pointedly. "I'm just saying, I don't like having my life in someone else's hands. I'm the master of my own fate."

"Not today." He smirked.

She gave him a slap on the arm.

Voske looked ahead at Erimos as it drew ever nearer, the red and yellow land punctuated by deep blue oceans. There was a familiar comfort at the thought of returning to those dusty plains and deserts. Erimos still felt like home. He wondered if it always would.

"You're from Erimos, right?"

He smiled wistfully. "I worked in a quarry town in the Northern Expanse."

"So what's it like coming home now that you're a Champion?"

He shrugged. "I hadn't thought about it. but it still feels like home."

"Yeah. That makes sense." She looked at him like she had more to say.

"What is it?" He said. "You have that look."

"What look?"

She knew. He took a deliberate drink, but kept his eyes locked on hers until she shrugged.

"It's nothing. Just a lot going on, you know? Do you believe it all?"

"Neveri?"

She bobbed her head side to side. "Among other things."

"What other things?"

"Things like the gods lying to us. The temple lying to us. Endring lying to us."

"Everyone lying to us?"

She nodded. "Everyone."

A temple attendant bustled past the table, setting another full glass in front of Locin. She snatched it up and took a swallow, then promptly spit it into one of the empty glasses.

"Something wrong?"

"They're cutting my drinks. Like I wouldn't notice," she raised a hand to protest.

"Put your arm down and drink," Voske said. "They're doing you a favor."

"Like Nyx they are."

Voske thunked the bottom of his own glass against the table and stared hard at her. "We're about to make our first impression on a new planet as champions. You want to be blacked out for that?"

"Maybe. It's my rotting choice."

He shook his head. "Doesn't make it a good one."

"Shove it, old man."

He took a deep breath and turned toward her. "Put your hand down."

She stuck her tongue out at him.

"Put it down, or I'll put it down for you."

That at least got her to listen and her arm slowly dropped to her side. "Why do you care?"

"Because I'm your friend, that's why."

She glared at him, but she grabbed her drink and gulped some down. "Happy?"

"Happier than you."

"Whatever."

He was gonna let it slide, but she was still giving him that look. He'd been around enough women to know she had more to say, and she wouldn't let it go until she did. "Alright. Out with it."

She shrugged.

"Something's eating at you, so let's get this over with."

She scoffed. "Oh I don't know, maybe the fact that you all think I'm crazy?"

He raised an eyebrow. "When did we say that?"

"A couple hours ago."

"That was Zengin," he defended. "And if you recall, I stood up for you."

"I remember you lifting me off the ground."

"That was for your own good."

"Sure." She rolled her eyes.

Voske shook his head and turned back to his drink. He was ready for this conversation to be over, but he knew she wasn't.

"It's just, I think I'm right on this one, you know? In fact, I'm sure I'm right."

He glanced her direction and saw her fiddling with that same dumb piece of paper, the one with a single line scribbled across it.

"Let me see that," he said, reaching for it.

She passed it over and he stared at the writing.

"A trial to lay them low, the Struggle of Epsis," he muttered. "Where did you say you found this?"

"In Endring's room," she answered.

He turned the paper over a couple times in his fingers, noting a few black numbers scribbled in the corner. They looked like a date and time, but if it was, that particular moment passed nearly two-thousand years ago.

He fingered the numbers. "And what's this?"

Locin glanced at it. "I don't know. Maybe part of another note that got ripped off."

"Maybe."

He kept on staring at the numbers and thoughtfully sipping his drink, letting his mind wander until he realized he'd reached the bottom of his glass.

"We saw the statues," she pressed, her voice suddenly low. "You honestly don't have questions?"

He was trying not to think of it at all. It felt above his station. A feud between gods was just that. It was no place for a man to stick his nose.

"Nyx it." She leaned in close. "You can't tell me you have no opinion."

"They're gods. I don't think it makes one rotting bit of difference if I have an opinion."

"Fine." She flopped her head on the table, picking at a small imperfection on the edge of the wood. Maybe she was right. Maybe answers were exactly what they needed. The weight of Talamh was on his shoulders now. Maybe he owed it to the worlds to pursue this.

"Alright," he said, bringing a glance from her.

"What?"

"I said alright," he set the scrap of paper back onto the table and pinned it under his finger. "If you're so broken up about this, I'll make you a deal. I'll help you run it down until we hit a dead end. How does that sound?"

She squinted as she straightened back up. "And in return?"

"You stop moping and lighten up."

A smile tugged at the edges of her lips. "Deal."

A shudder passed through the deck of the chariot and they both looked up. The blue hazy sky of Erimos hung just below them now, forming a shell between the planet and the cold dark, and the speed of their descent trembled through the timbers of the deck.

They had arrived.

27: Vohasi

Vohasi was much smaller than Arrajin, despite being one of the largest cities on Erimos. It was known as the City of Progress and flaunted a strange joining of the new and the ancient. Even from a distance it looked like two pieces of a puzzle that didn't quite fit together.

The old city was in the very center, surrounded by an ancient wall that was the same color as the reddish dirt around it. A vast array of buildings were clustered within, starting with the pristine white temple at the very heart, and then working outward to the markets and homes of the socially adept or highly religious. They were made of a patchwork of new materials reinforcing the aged, like the crutches of an ancient man, and all of them were connected by old stairs and alleyways that wound over and around each other in a labyrinthian tangle that could have driven Strah himself mad. Everywhere the symbols of the gods could be seen, and the smoke of incense rose from the nine towers that watched over the surrounding area.

Outside the wall in every direction, the new city spread like a crystal web. Here is where the non-religious guilds were quartered, the miners, masons, guardsmen, potters and a dozen others each had a modest guild hall flying the colors of their gods just above the skyline, but over them all towered the inventor's guild. The sole reason for the city's title, the guild hall was woven of citrine and white stones that turned to dazzling gold in the light of the westering sun. Virtually every major invention of the last five cycles had been birthed within its grandiose halls, and the city reflected just that. The whirr of progress could be felt in the air and the inventor's boon was everywhere, from the cooling fans that showered the streets, to the bizarre presses that transferred ink to paper, to the mammoth windmills that powered the piston bellows of the blacksmiths. It was like walking into another world, a bizarre, crazy, mismatched world.

Locin took ten steps off the chariot at Vohasi before looking down at her pristine white shoes. They were already colored orange by the sand. How did this infernal stuff stain everything so fast? She lifted one and brushed it off with her hand, only managing to smear orange along her fingers which she then brushed along her pink chiton.

"Mire and Nyx," she muttered.

She let her hands hang down by her sides, resolving that she wouldn't touch anything else until she had a chance to get inside and bathe.

"Why didn't we fly into the old city?" she grumbled.

"You've been here before?" asked Gillis.

She looked back toward the chariot. Gillis and the other Champions were just filing down the wooden ramp toward the paved road.

"Once. I flew into old town to meet a… friend."

"Well you weren't a Champion at the time," Gillis answered. "It's tradition for Champions to walk into the old city on their way to the temple."

"Without even a horse?" She looked dismally toward the inner walls. The outer tether rested in the shadow of the inventor's guild, about a half mile from their destination.

"We're lucky it's not farther." Gillis continued. "It used to be until an aged champion collapsed while making the walk."

"Just like Erimos," Locin said. "A city of progress and still stuck in tradition."

"That's a strange tradition," Burz said. "What's the reason for it?"

"It commemorates the journey of Otienu, the ancient Champion of Strah who walked across the desert for eighteen days in order to warn Vohasi of a coming storm."

Locin scoffed at the comment, "Just imagine if he'd had a horse."

"It certainly would have taken less time."

"And we'd have one less dumb tradition to uphold."

She felt a palm slap against her back and she nearly stumbled. She glanced with annoyance to see Voske smiling in a self satisfied manner.

"Listen to Gillis," he said. "The last time a Champion rode in on a horse, the people rioted. I was here for it. All I heard for days afterward was 'a better man than he walked'."

"Yes," Gillis agreed. "That was Carar, the former champion of Strah. The Oracles tried to get him to walk, but he was barely sober enough to stand."

Locin shook her head dismally and set to walking. The sun wasn't getting any cooler.

"If it helps," Gillis offered. "We could arrange for camels to meet us at the inner gates."

"Let's just get this over with," Locin answered. "Then find some shade and a cold drink."

Voske laughed, as he stomped along. "This is fine weather."

She rolled her eyes. "Any place that uses camels doesn't know the meaning of fine weather."

They kept trudging down the narrow path until they reached the main road that led to the temple. Here a large crowd milled among a bevy of tents and merchant carts that lined the sides of the road. Bright colored ribbons had been strung from building to building, crisscrossing their path, and further on, Locin could see the gates to the old city, fluctuating in the heat like a mirage.

"Gods!" She smiled. "All this for me?"

"Us," Hikari corrected.

"Yeah, but I'm the Champion of Iyanu."

"That's true," Gillis said. "You will be the honored Chosen."

"Ha!" She stuck out her tongue at Hikari. "You'll get your turn later, player."

"Well, I'll certainly try not to steal the show, darling, but no promises. I am the leading man, after all."

Locin rolled her eyes and then turned her attention back to the festive decorations. There weren't any drab colors, no worrisome stages where boring speeches might be given, no obnoxious looking religious pools for washing. The strongest smell was that of roasting meat, and the sound was similar to a busy market, ripe with pockets for picking.

She spotted a group of kids throwing rocks at a series of targets, and she summoned the boon of Iyanu. She lifted a rock from the side of the road, then sent it hurtling toward one of the targets, striking it right in the center and sending an explosion of chaff out the back of its frame.

In response a shrill voice rang out. "It's the Champion of Iyanu!"

Her attention jerked toward the voice and she saw a young girl standing in the middle of the road, pointing excitedly. "She's right there! She's here! She's here!"

At her call a whole host of people ran to gawk at the sides of the road and Locin grinned widely, waving to her adoring throng.

No sooner had they started cheering than the gates to the inner city groaned open. From inside a blast of trumpets could be heard, gaining in volume and clarity as the gap slowly widened. As soon as they were wide enough, a mirthful group of women danced out, beating tambourines that sparked with light at every impact. Smoke rolled along the ground under their feet, flowing down the road like water, and they kicked it up as they moved.

Locin stepped a bit quicker and caught up the smoke with her boon, launching it skyward like geysers of steam. The children were squealing with delight, and the applause only grew as the gates drew wider.

Soon she could see a massive metal statue of a feathered serpent. It rested on a rolling platform, its head turned skyward, smoke pouring from its mouth and rolling down its back where bright colored feathers crested from head to tail. A group of gorgeous men stood alongside the platform beating deep leather drums, and from somewhere on the walls, rose petals drifted down to the path below.

"Behold!" A crier bellowed over the commotion. "Locin, Favored Champion of the Goddess Iyanu!"

Locin lifted her arms and the crowd erupted. As she reached the gates the sea of people let out another raucous cheer, and a hundred handsome hands reached out toward her. She cast a look back at Gillis and raised an eyebrow.

He smiled. "You actually thought we'd need camels?"

She put on the crossest face she could muster. "You tricked me."

"I didn't give you all the details. Forgive me, Champion."

She licked her lips and extended her arms, motioning for the strapping young men to raise her onto the platform. She could feel her heart hammering wildly within her chest, and she looked down the road to where the temple of Iyanu stood, draped in bright orange ribbons. The others slowly climbed on behind her, but she didn't pay them any heed. This was her moment, and this was her city, the best rotting city in all of Talamh. She loved Vohasi.

Vohasi's temple of Iyanu was a marvel to behold with a whirring chandelier that sparked with bright light hanging in the center of the sanctum. The back wall was one large mural depicting the goddess Iyanu pulling a pylat from the sun. Rasa let her eyes drift from the mural to the asymmetrical stone that stood in front of it. It was simple, smooth as glass, with no markings or special features. It looked out of place amidst the ornate surroundings, like something from another world.

She walked toward it, her bare feet making no sound at all as she stepped gingerly across the stone floor. She ran her hand along the smooth, gray surface. It seemed to slip under her fingers like the waters of a brook, and yet it was dry and solid.

Rasa looked up and saw Locin watching her with a wrinkled brow.

"What is this?" She asked.

Locin scrunched her nose indignantly. "Haven't you ever been in a temple? Every temple has one."

"We live in a temple," Rasa answered honestly. She glanced back to see Locin coming toward her, and beside her strolled the spirit of a young girl. The same one she'd seen at the Gods' Mount. The light from the spirit seemed to spread out toward Locin, connecting the two of them.

"Okay, fine," Locin quipped. "Our temple doesn't have a choosing stone, but most of them do. Every other one I've been in does."

Rasa smiled. "I thought it might be a choosing stone."

"You weren't taken to the temple for your guilding?"

Rasa looked down and away, feeling a familiar shame wash over her. She wrapped her arms around her waist tightly, and tried to push it from her mind. "No."

"Well," Locin said, "you touch it, and it's supposed to brand you with a guilding." She spat at the base of it before thinking, and then her eyes instantly widened. "Mire," she muttered. She looked around as if speaking to no one, or perhaps the temple itself. "Um, sorry? I come penitent and… something, something."

Rasa chuckled.

"Nyx it! I should have paid more attention."

"Why would you spit at it?"

Locin put a finger to her lips and shushed her while moving closer. "Maybe we keep that between us. It's just habit, you know. I wasn't thinking. Haven't seen one in a while."

"You were unguilded?"

The spirit shook her head and her hair bobbed around her on unseen waves. *She doesn't like it when people say that,* she whispered in a soft voice.

Locin furrowed her brow, her eyebrows drawing an angry black line across her soft brown skin. "I was guilded to the thieves."

"Sorry. I only meant at the choosing stone." Rasa turned, letting her hand rest against the stone. "What happened when you touched it?"

"Nothing," Locin said softly and bitterly. "Stayed there for twenty minutes. They told me it never took that long, but I wouldn't let go. I just knelt there with my hand on that pool of mire, waiting. They had to drag me away kicking and screaming."

"Oh."

Locin sniffled and wiped the end of her sash across her nose. "Whatever. I'm a champion now, so I guess I showed them."

Rasa found herself wondering who *they* were, but her eyes locked on the spirit again who was now watching and smiling.

"Hello," Rasa said, pulling her hand away from the stone.

Locin squinted. "Um, hi?"

I'm glad we finally get to meet. The spirit's voice quavered.

"What's your name?"

Locin looked over her shoulder, now thoroughly confused.

I had a name once, the spirit said. *Locin calls me Spark. It's as good a name as any.*

"Spark." Rasa smiled.

Locin whipped her head back to face Rasa, leaning in. "What in Nyx did you just say?"

The sudden ferocity of the motion sent Rasa stumbling back into the choosing stone, she felt it like a river on her back, cold through the thin fabric of her toga. "I said Sp-Spark. That's your friend's name."

Locin grabbed at Rasa's shoulder, pulling, and she felt her heart start racing. She glanced up to see Locin was smiling.

Spark pressed a hand against Locin's arm, and Locin straightened up as if she felt it.

"Gods! Oh, I'm so sorry, Rasa." She started laughing as she let her go.

Rasa clutched at her chest in an effort to calm her heart and stave off the panic she felt setting in. Locin was a friend. She wasn't going to hurt her.

"You see her? You see Spark?" Locin paused as she studied Rasa's face. "Gods," she said in a gentle tone. "Are you okay? I didn't mean to scare you."

Rasa forced a nod and focused on the kind tone of Locin's voice. "I'm okay."

Spark stepped a little closer. The more distant she was from Locin, the more clear the trailing blue light between them became. Like a loose thread that stretched from one to the other.

Locin gets a bit dramatic sometimes, Spark said. *She means well.*

Rasa smiled. "Thank you, Spark."

Locin let out another quick laugh, drawing some looks from the monks nearby. "Gods, it's true! You really *do* see her."

"Of course. She's always with you. I'm surprised *you* can see Spark."

"I don't." Locin glanced around as if trying to. "Not really. Sometimes I swear I've seen this little flash of blue light. It's so fast, like it's not even there. But it reminds me of the inventor's spark. That's why I call her Spark. Mostly I just *feel* her."

Rasa locked her eyes on Spark. "You're connected somehow."

I'm not sure why, Spark said. *We've been like this a long time.*

Locin gave a light giggle that rumbled into a roaring laugh, drawing the attention of the others again and frowns from a few.

"Sorry," she called, unnecessarily loudly. "Gods, sorry." She turned glad eyes back on Rasa. "Sometimes I thought I was mad. Too much time alone, you know, feeling like someone was always there. But if you see Spark, well, Nyx that! I'm sane as a dog at a table!"

Rasa chuckled. She couldn't help herself. Locin's joyful relief seemed contagious.

"Thieves call on spirits," Locin whispered. "Nothing like you, but we can use them to trick people, or for a distraction. That's the thieves' boon. It's like knocking on the veil of Nyx, and they answer. I used my boon a lot, but eventually I started feeling like the same spirit kept turning up to help me. It would do the same things, knock back in the same way, you know. Like when an old friend comes to visit, and you know who it is just by the way they rap their knuckles against the door, how hard, and how long, and how many knocks and stuff. It was like that. Then I started seeing it out of the corner of my eye, just a spark, but when I'd look it'd be gone, and I'd think I imagined the whole thing."

"Spark," Rasa said with a smile. "It's a good name."

I think so too, Spark said. *I had been in Nyx so long when we met that I'd forgotten my name. But I like Spark.*

"Spark and me are always together now, even after I lost my thief's boon."

Rasa held a hand toward the blue thread between Locin and Spark, but her fingers just passed through it. "Whatever this is that holds you together must be too strong to break even though you lost your boon."

"Then I guess we're stuck together to the end!"

Spark laughed, and it sounded like glass bells.

"Gods!" Locin said. "You really see her?"

"Do you want me to tell you about her?"

Locin's face suddenly went serious. "No! Yes? Gods! I don't know. It's just, we've been together like this so long. It'd be weird to change things."

It's okay, Spark said softly. *Maybe when she's ready.*

Rasa nodded to the spirit. "Okay. When you're ready."

"Sure, just give me some time, you know. I gotta get used to this whole thing. It's weird that someone else can see her… and talk to her." She scowled. "No telling my secrets, Spark!"

Spark was grinning. *I know plenty.*

Rasa smiled. She noticed Voske was making his way over, with his eyes fixed on them.

"Locin," he called.

"Yeah?"

"We need to talk."

She shrugged. "Fine." And then turning back to Rasa, she added, "Listen, maybe just keep Spark between us for now? I don't know. I feel like it'd be weird if everyone knew."

Spark sighed. *She'd lose an advantage. Always thinking like a thief.*

"Okay," Rasa said. "I won't tell them."

Locin thanked her and then headed after Voske toward the door of the temple.

Spark lingered for a moment as the thread between them stretched away, growing faint and thin. *I'm glad we met, Rasa.*

"Me too."

Spark frowned. *I should go. I don't like to stay too far from Locin.*

"Okay."

We'll speak again. Soon!

"I'd like that."

Spark nodded and rushed after Locin, into the outer halls of the temple.

Endring sat at a modest table on a balcony overlooking the main road through Vohasi. He wore a deep red tunic and white trousers, stained orange by the desert sand, and a white cloak was pulled low over his face.

His presence here was not without peril. Certainly the entourage from the temple would recognize him, but they'd be foolish to expect him here, which gave him at least a modicum of safety. He crossed his foot over his leg and swirled the drink in his hand, looking over the throng of festival goers that steadily poured into the city. They were mostly attired in white to ward off the sun, and orange to honor Iyanu. They cooled themselves with hand fans and pouches of water from the deep wells under the city.

He looked back to see a familiar, brightly attired patron pushing through the interior of the restaurant toward the open air balcony. If Sammel's garish garb would go unnoticed anywhere, it was here. He bustled onto the overhang and plopped into a seat opposite Endring.

"Erimos is quite stifling away from the coast." He pulled at the front of his shirt, ruffling it back and forth.

Endring pushed a second glass of the cactus wine across the table. "I'm glad you made it safely."

Sammel nodded and scooped up the glass, taking a long draught. His expression soured. "Quite bitter."

"I imagine their wines weren't always so bad." Endring let his eyes wander to the outskirts of the city and the dusty land beyond. "This whole area used to be green and fertile."

"That's difficult to imagine."

"I've read descriptions in the oldest records, fields of low, green tea trees, or sugarcane twice as tall as a man. Can you imagine it? The endless rains of summer, and the changing season of a long, dry winter." He breathed out a sigh. "I pity these people. They have no idea what Talamh was. What Talamh should be."

"I should like to see fields like that," Sammel mused.

"In time, I hope you will." He smiled as he watched Sammel down the rest of the bitter wine. He was glad to have a friend here. "You were delayed. Is it good news or bad?"

Sammel raised a hand and tilted it side to side. "A bit of both. You managed to draw Borroka's ire. She's moved on from attacking the temple and seeks your head instead."

Endring took a deep breath. It wasn't exactly comforting to know Borroka wanted to kill him, but at least he knew. "That does seem both good and bad."

"That was the good news."

Endring raised an eyebrow. "Oh?"

"She's also learned of the Crook."

Endring felt his heart skip a beat, and he stared back at the crowd while not really looking at anything. "How much does she know?"

"She's figured out it's in three pieces, that you have one of them, and that she doesn't need you in order to free him."

"So everything."

Sammel tilted his hand again. "She doesn't know where the other two pieces are."

"Neither do we."

They sat in silence watching a group of monks struggle to shift a massive bronze harp into place atop a small stage while a few women walked the street hanging orange ribbons from the rooftops. The shouts of merchants were already beginning to sound, and from the nearest stall the smell of desert bisque made Endring's stomach growl.

"So much," Sammel remarked, "just to celebrate the one chosen."

Endring could feel his eyes on him, but he ignored it.

"Borroka will be hunting the other pieces in earnest." Sammel continued. "She has contacts on Erimos, and Suntara too, more than a few, access to scholars, access to mystics-"

"What would you have me do?" Endring asked.

"All I mean is the resources of the temple could guarantee we find these first."

Endring narrowed his eyes and finally looked back toward Sammel. "No."

"You said she seemed sympathetic to our cause."

"No, Sammel."

"As a champion she'd be above scrutiny."

"Then why don't you talk to yours?"

Sammel shook his head. "I'm not certain Zengin trusts me, despite saving his life."

"Why not?"

"He didn't know about the theft of the Crook at that point, for one."

Endring shook his head. "I already left Locin a clue to occupy her. If she starts running it down, we'll be able to tell."

"And if she doesn't?" Sammel folded his hands on the table, tapping his thumbs together. "Knowing the other pieces are on Erimos and Suntara is not enough. We *need* her, Endring. Or at least we need the temple."

Endring sighed and raised his drink once more, sloshing the bitter liquid. It was hard to swallow.

28: The Star Glass

Voske and Locin between them knew exactly one person who knew anything about stars, and after the Sacred Quarter she wasn't exactly on the friendliest terms. So it was rather surprising when Illeri's face lit up at the prospect of helping solve their mystery, and the first words out of her mouth were, "I know just the place."

An hour later the three of them stood in one of the most incredible structures Voske had ever seen, and he found himself wondering how, in all his trips to Vohasi, he had never made the time to see it.

The Star Glass.

The whole room was filled with curved panels that connected in a large sphere, like standing in the middle of a glass globe. The panels themselves were made of Onyx stretched so thin you could see through them, a marvel of the architects guild, and all along the panels, lights flickered like stars.

"This is cool," Locin said with a casual flip of her head. Her expression held more wonder than she'd probably admit as she strolled along the narrow path that led from the door to the suspended platform in the center of the room.

"Just wait," Illeri answered. "It gets better."

She was standing in the center of the platform in front of a podium with several drawers, a crank, and a series of levers. She pulled one of the levers and the lights in the room went dark, as flickering starlights on the panels burst like diamonds through the black.

Voske carefully walked out on the thin metal walkway toward the center. All around them were stars, above, below, everywhere, and the cold draft through the room made him shiver.

"The date on Locin's page was the sixth Riving of Harvest," Illeri said, "in the year 406."

She spun the crank to the side, and suddenly the lights started whirling around until the entire room felt like it was spinning. Voske gripped the railing, his legs growing wobbly at the sensation.

Illeri kept talking nonchalantly. "That would make it Fallow in Northern Erimos, and the Struggle of Epsis would be high in the sky." She stopped cranking and the lights mercifully stopped spinning. "Right there."

Illeri was pointing to a cluster of stars that looked more like a blob of clay than a picture in the heavens, and Voske scrunched up his face, trying to make sense of them as he joined the women in the center.

"You can see Epsis' spear," Illeri said, tracing down a line of bright stars. "It pierces into the great serpent, coiled around his feet."

"Yeah," Voske said. "I kinda see that."

"And how does that help us?" Locin asked.

"That depends on what we see," Illeri answered. "The time on the note shows the beginning of the seventh watch." She adjusted the crank again, almost imperceptibly this time, and the stars shifted slightly to the right, then she drew one of the levers up and just the barest amount of bluish light began to glow across the canvas of stars, until, for a moment, Voske felt like he was outside watching the moon rise over Govere.

"Gods," Locin muttered from beside him.

"What," he whispered back.

"Just… gods."

He nodded in silent agreement.

"There." Illeri stepped back from the podium, studying the starfield.

Voske squinted, but he couldn't see anything but stars. "There what?"

"This is the exact moment on the note. The atmosphere, everything. Now we just have to hear what they have to say."

Voske leaned toward Locin. "Who's they," he hissed.

Illeri's eyes went wide, and she glanced at them sheepishly. "The stars."

Locin cleared her throat. "Do they, uh, speak up often?"

"I just meant, if we study them, they might tell us what we're looking for."

Voske leaned to the side, and then tilted back the other way, staring at the dots of light until his head started to hurt. It still looked like a blob to him, but the more he looked at it, the more he thought the bottom three stars made a *v* shape, like the point of an arrow. "Is it pointing to something?"

Locin leaned her head over to see from his point of view. "Pointing to what?"

He shrugged. "The crook?"

She glanced at him like you would a particularly stupid child. "Please stop. You're embarrassing me."

"You have a better idea?"

"Yeah. Don't be stupid."

"Actually," Illeri strolled over to them, "he might be right."

"I am?"

"He is?"

She bit her lip, studying the constellation. "Well, not exactly, but stars can point to a place."

Voske passed Locin a wry smile. "And what place is that?"

"The place where the constellation is at its zenith, on this date, at this time."

"Okay. How do we find that?"

"I can look it up."

"How long will that take?"

"I'm not sure." She slid open a drawer and started leafing through parchments. "But everything I need should be here."

Voske nodded. It felt like this could take a while, so he set his eyes on a metal bench near the door.

Hikari strolled through the wayfarer's guild of Vohasi with an easy air. He had a guildling on each arm, both young and pretty, and absolutely swooning over him. They peppered him with questions and ate up every response, leaning close as they guided him through the guild hall. At last they stopped at an elaborate door painted all round with stars.

"Here it is!" The brunette smiled sweetly as she pulled him toward it. "The Star Glass!"

She pushed the door open, and he felt himself pulled forward into the room.

"Magnificent!" He pulled free and took in the breadth of the room. The onyx panels stretched away on every side, as though he was adrift in the cold dark, and star lights glittered like pearls.

He looked back to see the girls giddy with the moment, and just behind them Voske sat on a low bench rolling his eyes.

Hikari cleared his throat. "As I was saying… You have my utmost thanks for leading me here. How shall I ever repay your kindness?"

Naturally, they were both falling all over themselves to stay, offering any more help he might need. He thanked them again, and assured them if he needed more help he would personally come find them. They said their longing goodbyes, then said them again, and finally, begrudgingly, made their way out the door.

Hikari stood up straight, smiling graciously until the door clicked shut, then his arms deflated at his sides, and he cast Voske a sidelong glance.

"Friends of yours?" Voske smirked.

Hikari ran a hand through his hair, smiling glibly. "New acquaintances."

"How come I never get those kinds of *acquaintances*?"

"Your intimidating physique, darling. It scares them off."

Voske harrumphed.

Hikari walked a couple paces into the room. "So this is a Star Glass?"

"Apparently."

"Breathtaking!" He glanced back at Voske. "And what are you doing here?"

"I was going to ask you the same thing."

"Looking for you, of course. I was told I'd find you here."

Voske walked to Hikari's side. "Nothing interesting back at the temple?"

"Are you kidding? I could have picked from a thousand spectacular events, but I chose you, my friend."

"So, more lectures?"

Hikari smiled. "Mostly. Hadris was doing some sewing. I could have joined her, I suppose."

Voske laughed.

"Should be much less dull once the festival kicks off," he continued. "Apparently sundown is going to be spectacular."

"I'm sure it will."

Hikari frowned. "You three are going to be there, surely?"

"Hopefully. We'll see how long this takes."

"And what *is* this, exactly?" He let his eyes drift back to the room. Illeri and Locin were in the center, pouring over some parchments.

"Just running down a hunch"

"Very well," Hikari pouted. "Keep your secrets. It's still more exciting than a lecture."

"Or sewing."

Voske chuckled, though Hikari barely heard it. He was watching Illeri now, running a finger along a piece of parchment as she read. There was something about her. Hikari couldn't quite put his finger on it. He'd had no shortage of beautiful women throwing themselves at him for most of his career. But Illeri had something he hadn't seen in the others. It intrigued him.

"And there are beautiful women," Voske commented.

"They are quite lovely," he said in a dreamy voice.

Voske grinned. "I was talking about those two you came in with."

"Ah, yes of course." Hikari nodded quickly. "They were lovely too."

Voske was staring at him with a knowing look.

He crossed his arms. "I only meant, these two are lovely as well." He uncrossed his arms, suddenly very aware of how he was standing.

"You're not fooling me, player. I've had that look on my face enough times to know it. So which one is it?"

"Whatever do you mean?" He could feel his voice going squeaky, and quickly recovered. "Which what?"

"It's Locin, isn't it?" Voske smiled, self satisfied.

In love with Locin? Well, he could certainly play the part. He straightened up, and glanced back at Illeri. "Well, why not? She's a fine woman. And those freckles are simply adorable."

"Sure, she's pretty. And loud. And snarky. And I'm not sure she likes you."

Illeri brushed some stray hair over her shoulder, intently focused on her work. "I... don't know how she feels."

"Well," Voske pressed, "go ask her."

He looked wide-eyed at Voske. "Just like that?"

"Yeah. Why not?"

Hikari scuffed his foot against the metal grating, and he tensed as an unexpectedly loud clang rang through the room. "She looks… busy. I don't want to bother her."

"Wait." Voske stared him down. "You're scared?"

"I'm not scared, darling. Just perhaps a bit… hesitant?"

Voske laughed, drawing a look from the two girls that made Hikari want to climb in a hole and hide.

"How in Nyx is that?" Voske continued. "You're Hikari, player of Suntara. You must have had your fair share of women." He looked Hikari over, head to toe. "More than your fair share, I'd wager."

"You would think so, now wouldn't you."

Voske stared blankly for a moment until Hikari's comment registered, then his eyes went wide.

"No?"

Hikari shook his head.

"But surely there were women."

"Women who were interested. All the time, of course. I have it all, you know. Fame, fortune, dashing good looks." He put on a charming smile. "Who wouldn't be interested?"

Voske smirked. "Locin, maybe."

"Locin? Right, Locin!" Hikari cleared his throat.

Voske shifted for a moment, as though letting it all sink in. Hikari could almost see his carefully crafted persona crumbling in Voske's mind moment by moment.

"So you never…" Voske looked back at him with an almost pained expression. "I mean, not one woman?"

Hikari sighed.

"I've seen you flirt with every woman in the temple. I mean you and that Desitan monk with the large-" he glanced at Hikari and must have seen the horrified look on his face "…eyes… I thought you two, for sure."

"I'm a player, darling. I know how to play the part." He sighed again. The truth was out. Why hide it? Voske wasn't the first one to learn he wasn't all he seemed, and he'd hardly be the last. "Truthfully, I've never even kissed a girl. Not off stage, at least." He let his eyes drift back to Illeri. "Not because I liked her."

Things got uncomfortably quiet, and he looked back to see Voske smirking.

"Yes, let's mock Hikari."

"I'm not mocking." He chuckled. "Okay. I'm mocking a little."

Hikari dropped his shoulders and stared down at his feet. It was hopeless.

Voske clapped a hand on Hikari's shoulder. "I could talk to Locin."

To Hikari's absolute horror, Locin answered.

"Talk to Locin about what?" She was watching them with a furrowed brow, standing in front of him with Illeri beside her.

Hikari laughed nervously. "It's nothing, darling. Just some tips on thieving."

"Sure," Voske said unconvincingly. "Thieving."

Hikari glanced at Illeri who was holding a parchment and practically beaming. "Do you have something there?"

"It's in the desert," she said with near breathless excitement. "Not far from here."

Hikari smiled broadly. He couldn't help it. "What's in the desert?"

Locin nodded to Hikari, her eyes on Voske. "He in on this now too?"

Voske shrugged. "Why not?"

"What?" Hikari hated being left out. "What are we talking about?"

"Locin's clue," Voske said. "The second crook piece."

"Truly? And you've found it?"

"More or less," Illeri motioned to the levers in the center of the room. "I'll show you."

They followed her to the center of the platform, where she pushed one of the levers. Above them one of the stars swelled in size, as though they were moving toward it. Hikari could see why the stars so enamored her. It was incredible, as though he was soaring through the cold dark.

"It turns out the date and time you found was the exact moment of the Second Solstice in 406, the very moment when Erimos is as close as it ever comes to The Struggle of Epsis." She pulled back on the lever and the star above them stopped growing, now nearly as large as a man. Hikari could see great spouts of golden fire erupting from the surface like a geyser. "That's Galnathor," she said. "The eye of the great serpent, the brightest star in the constellation, and its zenith would be directly over a specific location in the desert."

Voske glanced at Locin. "You have any idea what she's saying?"

Locin smirked. "Sounds like she's saying we've got a map."

29: The Festival of Iyanu

The back alleys of the ancient city of Vohasi wound over and around each other. Everywhere they went little stairways led down into darkness, and Weylyn's sense of direction was only kept by the rainbow glow of lamps glimmering against the Eastern sky. In the distance the drums of the festival could be heard, and squeals of children echoed from outside the city walls.

"This way." Gillis said.

She looked forward to where the orange light of his inventor's lamp glared against the orange sand walls.

"I don't think it's much farther."

Weylyn pulled her cloak a bit tighter and kept close on his heels. She could hear the two burly monks of Jeza behind her, grunting as they slid down the narrow path, then up a craggy set of stairs, to an unassuming sand brick home.

"The Apothecary of Vohasi," Gillis whispered. "She's a recluse as I understand it, and…"

Weylyn noted Gillis' white knuckles, clenched around the base of his lamp. "And?"

"Forgive me, Champion. She's known to be rather disparaging of those chosen by the gods. Perhaps if she didn't know who you were…"

Weylyn nodded toward the door. and Gillis slowly turned, rapping his knuckles softly against the filthy wood.

For a minute there was no reply, and Weylyn cleared her throat. "You're certain she's here?"

"I hear she never leaves."

"Not even for the festival?"

As though in response the door cracked open and a light plume of smoke flowed outward. It smelled of tobacco and dill.

"What," croaked the voice of an old woman.

Weylyn squinted into the dark. The apothecary was cloaked in dingy green. The fabric drooped from the top of her head and across her shoulders, spilling down her frame until it piled on the floor by her feet.

"Thesa?" Gillis asked.

The old woman raised a long reed pipe below the hood, and moments later a billow of smoke poured out. "What do you want?"

Gillis straightened up, doing a pitiful job at looking important. "We have need of your services."

"Truly," The crone's head raised, and Weylyn saw the barest glisten of her eye in the lamplight. "I ran out of mugwort yesterday."

Gillis coughed and quickly shook his head. "We're here for something else. May we come in?"

Thesa leaned forward, her gaze slowly sweeping across the monks of Jeza before she withdrew into the home. To Weylyn's surprise her scratchy voice called out. "Close the door behind you. No sense letting in a draft."

Gillis motioned the guards to wait outside, and he and Weylyn followed her in.

The front room was set up like a shop, but far less luxurious than the shops in Arrajin. Two of the walls were covered in sealed pottery jars. They were stored on shelves that ran from the floor to the ceiling, and each was labeled with black letters scrawled in a barely legible hand. In the middle of each wall a sconce held a single bright candle that cast heavy shadows across the floor and rippled through the cloying smoke.

Thesa shuffled to the corner and sat down in a large brown chair, finally pulling back her hood. Her eyes were wide and sunken. She had a large mole that protruded from her right cheek and faint whiskers traced her lips. Slowly she lifted the reed pipe back to her mouth and clenched it between her teeth, letting her clouded eyes drift from Weylyn to Gillis and back again.

"Now then," she said. "Why would a Champion visit my little shop?"

"No one said anything about a Champion," Gillis answered.

Thesa looked at him with disdain. "And I suppose those guards were for you? Don't play stupid with me, boy."

"We're paying customers," Gillis answered. "That's all that matters."

"I have little need of coin."

"And if you help us now, you'll never want for it again."

"Bah," Thesa waved a gnarled hand, and leaned back in her chair. "Keep your coin, lackey."

Gillis' brow furrowed. "I don't need to remind you of the power the temple holds."

"Is that a threat? And what, pray tell, would you threaten me with? Death?" She hacked out a cough at the word, and her lungs rattled at the effort.

Gillis was doing his best impression of looking angry, but Weylyn reached out a hand and laid it on his shoulder. She stepped past the young man and held up her palm, revealing the shining sigil of Strah.

Thesa's eyes flashed cold, and she slowly lowered her pipe. "Strah," she mused. "Must be here for vision powder."

"Can you make it?" Weylyn asked.

"I can. Vision powder like you'll not find anywhere else, but what assurances do I have if it goes wrong?"

"What do you mean?"

"Vision powder is known to have certain… side-effects. Most of the time it's harmless - bad headaches, not much more - but every so often things turn out much worse."

Weylyn felt a tightening in her throat. "How so?"

Her pale lips stretched in a sneer. "You may go so deep you drown."

Her words hung in the air like the strike of a gavel.

Thesa slowly raised the reed pipe back to her mouth and drew the smoke deep into her lungs. "Such is the price of knowledge."

Weylyn slowly straightened up, weighing the warning carefully in her mind. "So be it."

The hint of a smile cracked Thesa's lips. "What is it that has you so spooked I wonder. A vision of destruction? Death of a loved one?"

"It's a personal matter," Weylyn answered.

"Your own death then."

"That's enough," Gillis snapped.

Weylyn held out a hand to calm him. "Yes."

"And shall I pass along my condolences? Tell you how sorrowful I am that one of the illustrious Champions will die?"

"I don't expect you will," Weylyn answered, "And I don't care if you do."

Thesa's eyes narrowed, and she studied Weylyn for a minute before she suddenly stood to her feet. "Wait here."

She wandered from the room, and an ominous quiet settled in her place.

"I can have the powder tested," Gillis whispered. "Make sure it's pure."

"That's alright, Gillis. I'll test it myself."

"But, Champion-"

Weylyn shook her head. "I'll test it myself."

The young man looked pained by her reply, but he did finally nod his assent.

Moments later Thesa emerged back into the room carrying a leather pouch tied at the top with a bit of string.

"Scatter it into a fire," she said, extending the pouch toward Weylyn. "Breathe the smoke, a deep breath, and hold it in."

Weylyn took the pouch with an uncertain hand. It felt heavy, as though it was filled with sand. She nodded slowly to the old woman. "And your payment?"

"Consider it a gift," Thesa said. "But I'll add one favor. Don't tell anyone you came to my store. Not everyone looks fondly upon the Champions, or upon the gods. I don't need people learning I gave you what you wanted."

"And why did you?" Weylyn asked.

"Who's to say I did?" She flashed a toothy smile. "Farewell, Champion."

Burz and Zengin followed the Archon of Vohasi across the roof of his palace. He was a small, thin man whose luxurious robes swallowed him up, like a child playing at being Archon. His palace, on the other hand, seemed to stand up to every inch of its lavish grandeur. It was set back from the festival road, and tall enough to dominate every structure but the inventor's guild. The sandstone roof had been transformed into a sanctuary of lush vines and flowering trees, far removed from the dry heat of the streets below. The gentle thrum of pumps could be heard as they drew water from the deep wells and misted it through the air, until the whole place felt like the jungles of Las.

Burz raised his hand and tickled the leaves of a rosewood tree as they passed beneath. A cool drop of water splashed refreshingly against his arm. He was both galled by the extravagant landscape, and comforted by the familiarity.

"I can't tell you how honored we are, Champions," the archon said in a nasally voice. "The last time Vohasi was chosen as a festival seat was two hundred years ago." He looked back at them with a shaky smile. "Of course, when we heard the temple in Heshron withdrew their support, we were happy to accommodate. They may be the seat of Iyanu's worship, but the sparks of the inventors are the beat of her heart."

He led them down a small walkway lined with trumpet vines before emerging into a spacious area at the front of the roof where a polished oak table and chairs had been placed. Below, a thousand different lights lined the festival road, each pointing toward the sky and glimmering a different color through the hazy atmosphere over the crowds. Apparently they were meant to dine in full view of the people.

"I had planned to introduce the Champions all at once." The little man looked warily from Burz to Zengin. "Do you know when the others will be arriving?"

Burz glanced around uneasily. It was just like them to not show up. "Perhaps they-"

"They aren't coming," Zengin interrupted.

"Oh." The Archon blanched as the thought settled. No doubt it was some grave insult to him and his city. "That's… that's very unfortunate."

"It isn't personal," Burz assured him. "They aren't the most… reliable."

"Of course," he said, unconvinced. He seemed distracted now, glancing down at the crowds below.

Zengin sighed loudly. "What are you not telling us?"

Burz felt the weight of Zengin's voice, something more than a commanding tone, and he tensed. But it was effective. The archon quickly started tripping over his words to respond.

"Ou-Our city has been troubled of late. Lots of talk of the gods abandoning the people. I-I fear if the champion of Iyanu isn't present for her own festival, things could turn very sour."

Burz raised an eyebrow. "Dangerous?"

The archon shook his head. "N-no. They're not that brave, these malcontents, but they are loud, outspoken really." He squirmed under Burz' gaze.

Zengin laughed, and the Archon stared at him with terror. "*Malcontents*. You mean you?" He held up the stub of his arm on display. "You doubt we're really *chosen of the gods*, do you?"

"Yes." The man squealed. "N-no… I… only meant… there are rumors…"

"Go!"

The vitriol in Zengin's voice would have sent the man running on its own, but the honey was still there too, lending weight to every word. Even Burz felt it pressing him to leave as he watched the sniveling Archon scurry back through the trees.

"That was unnecessary."

They strolled to the edge of the roof, staring down at the street below. The noise of the festival was just far enough from their high perch to be subdued, but it was vibrant and full of life. The skies above Vohasi had transformed from a black canvas of stars to a vibrant tapestry of color. Lining the streets, a raucous display of inventions billowed and sparked and whirred and coughed smoke into the air that made a hazy backdrop for the columns of light. The people down there were coarse, and stained, and loud, but Burz longed to be with them.

"Taking the high ground is never unnecessary," Zengin said, glancing over at Burz.

"High ground?" Burz scoffed. "You talk as if it's a battle."

"Of course it is. Every conversation, every interaction, every relationship."

"That's a depressing way to view life."

"Everyone has an agenda, soldier. They fight for their point of view, and you defend, parry, riposte. If you enter a conversation without knowing its warfare, you get slaughtered."

It was so outlandish, Burz thought Zengin might be kidding, but the more he studied his expression the more he was convinced he was deadly earnest. "You're right. I *was* a soldier, and we learned to defend others, not just ourselves. There's value in laying down your pride and giving preference to someone else."

"Humility is a fine trait," Zengin sneered. "The problem comes when you're the only one who has it."

"Humility is a virtue, even if you stand alone in it."

"It's no wonder Uthando chose you. A god with a penchant for self-flagellation would see some merit in your particular brand of weakness."

Burz ground his teeth. "Perhaps you should hold your tongue until you've healed."

"Didn't you heal me?"

"It's dangerous to speak out of the bitterness of a fresh wound."

"And here I thought the Champion of Uthando could heal all ills."

"We know each other," Burz said in a low voice. "We don't have to speak to each other - we certainly don't have to be friends - but we don't have to be enemies either. We can just ignore one another."

"I know *you*," he corrected. "I very much doubt you know me."

Burz scoffed. "Son of a corrupt Archon. Grew up with everything he ever wanted. Broke all the rules, and everyone looked the other way. Concerned with no one but yourself. It's no wonder you don't understand Uthando's mercy." He turned to face Zengin, and the throb in his leg was more noticeable than it should have been. "Did you have designs on supplanting your father? Is that why Metnadur chose you?"

A cruel, cold smile spread over Zengin's lips as he kept his steady gaze on the festival. "You know me so well."

"I came for you!" Burz snapped. "I came to Metnadur's shrine to save you. The others wouldn't help. I was the only one willing to show you mercy, the only one willing to give you a chance."

Zengin's face stayed placid, but the fingernails of his left hand dug into the low wall, scraping along the sandstone.

"Whatever grace you had here, it's spent. No champion wants anything to do with you."

Burz was satisfied. He'd said his peace, and he turned his back, letting his eyes drift over the oak table, spread with pristine white linens and a decadent feast. He wasn't hungry. In fact he was miserable. All he wanted was to be with Hadris and the boys, and for a moment he regretted telling them to go enjoy the festival. But wasn't that his duty? He would be here, honoring the temple, doing the right thing, and freeing his family to enjoy their night.

Still, he missed them.

"Isn't that your family?" Zengin said, his tone almost sinister.

Burz wanted to ignore him, but he turned with a sense of dread and followed Zengin's pointing finger down to the street below. He saw Hadris first, laughing and talking. Even from here he could tell she was beaming under the lights of the festival. Kyren and Orin were there too, ecstatic as they rushed around. They were happy. So he should be happy, but as he watched, he spotted Locin talking with Hadris. Rasa was there too, and Hikari and Illeri. Orin went running toward the last figure, who towered over the others, and leapt into his arms as the massive man tossed him up into the sky and caught him safely. It was Burz' turn to dig his nails into the sandstone.

"Voske," he seethed.

Illeri and Hikari lagged behind the others, strolling through the endless diversions and novelties of the festival that clamored for their attention. There were so many lights and colors and squeaky, buzzing noises it almost overwhelmed her, but not half so much as Hikari did.

"…and the lights! Ah, but they weren't half so wondrous as this, of course."

He was chatty - more so than usual - and he'd spent the last hour rambling about festivals, parties, and a particularly lively city he once visited in the heart of Suntara. Every few minutes he'd stop and look at her with an expectant gaze as if he was waiting for something, but she couldn't fathom what.

And there he was, doing it again. She wondered how long he'd been quiet and staring at her, and how long she'd been scowling.

"Sorry."

He smiled charmingly. Why did he also have to do that? It made her head feel fuzzy and her cheeks warm.

"I lost you somewhere, didn't I?"

She tried to nod, to say something, but she just stood there staring at him blankly. She didn't know what to do with Hikari. Sure, he was charming, and handsome, and he often knew the right thing to say, at least on the surface. But deep down, it was exactly the *wrong* thing to say, because it wasn't real. How could she believe he might be interested in her when everything he did felt fake?

"No matter. You're back now," he pressed on. He was looking at her in a way that made her uncomfortable. The way his gaze lingered.

She looked down, and he flicked his fingers, pulling at the strands of light, bringing a few shining pearls together and looping them around her neck until they glowed like tiny stars. She could see the soft light reflected on his skin, and she blushed.

She glanced up at a laugh from Voske, and realized they were falling pretty far behind. "We should catch up."

He sighed. "Oh."

Everything she said seemed to be wrong too, and she suddenly couldn't fathom why Hikari was back here trying to entertain her. Normally he'd be in the front with Voske and Locin, up to their usual antics. Did she just look lonely? Miserable? She glanced at him as they hurried along. "I'm okay, Hikari."

"Hm?"

"I'm fine. You don't have to entertain me."

"Oh, certainly, darling." He looked disappointed. "Is my company disagreeable?"

"Well, no." *Sometimes.*

"Good!" He said cheerfully. "Then I'll stay."

She sighed. "But why?"

"Why?"

She sighed. Again. "Why?"

He tapped his fingers idly on his chin as he considered his answer. "I suppose I want to apologize."

"For what?"

"My intrusion this afternoon on the Tempest. It was most egregious."

She frowned. "Most people just say, 'I'm sorry.'"

"Ah, right." He clapped his hands behind his back and glanced her way. "I'm sorry."

She nodded.

"So all's forgiven?"

She shrugged.

"Gods and Chosen! How much penance do you need?"

"Me?" She snapped. "None."

"Meaning I'm forgiven," he said, his voice growing tense, "or I'll never be forgiven no matter what I do?"

"So that's it? You're just trying to buy my forgiveness?"

He sighed, exasperated. But he was finally starting to seem real. Not the perfectly crafted *Hikari of Rel'van*. Just Hikari. "What do you want?"

"I want you to stop!" She turned sharply to face him, and he matched her.

"Stop what?"

"This!" She threw her arms wide, motioning to everything and nothing.

"The festival? Of the two of us, I'd think you'd have the easier time of that, darling."

She latched onto the last words. They sounded almost snarky, and it made her smile. They felt like the only genuine words he'd spoken for the last hour.

He huffed as he put his hands on his hips, and they stood there, both tense and quiet. It still may have been preferable to his endless prattle.

After a few moments, he glanced up, looking around the festival, and then, as if he spotted something of particular interest, he rushed off.

Illeri stared for a moment, looking awkwardly around. She couldn't see the others now, and she decided to hurry ahead. Maybe she drove Hikari away at last.

Good.

Or was it? She found herself glancing back over her shoulder as she caught the others. They were staring at some contraption that billowed smoke into the air as it spun wool into thread. The longer she stood there staring at it, the more she felt uneasy. She hadn't meant to be harsh. She decided to go back and apologize, if she could find him. She turned, but to her surprise, Hikari was just rushing up behind her, carrying a glass sculpture shaped like a pyramid. He stopped in front of her, and his easy smile was back.

"Here."

He handed her the sculpture, and she turned it over in her hands. It was solid glass, and heavy for its size.

"A gift."

"What is it?"

He smiled, as he reached up and pulled light down from the sky above, directing it into the glass. The light passed through and split into a rainbow that spilled out across their feet and spread across the hazy ground.

"It's called a prism stone," he said. "I've seen them before. I think… They're beautiful."

She looked up to find him staring at her again in that uncomfortable way, but it didn't feel quite so uncomfortable this time.

"Thank you."

Voske's voice interrupted them, booming over her shoulder. "There you two are. We thought we lost you."

Hikari straightened his toga and plastered on a perfect smile. "Not lost at all, darling. Simply enjoying the sights!" The light fell away and the rainbow faded. The moment was past, and he was Hikari the player again.

Illeri sighed as she fell in line with the others, but she clutched the prism stone close as she strolled on down the street.

The colors of Vohasi were more wonderful than Rasa could have imagined. They shimmered through the starry-eyed expanse like a sky bound sea, and the spirits dove through the collage, swirling around the pillars of light.

She preferred to keep her focus above, with the spirits. Below, the crowd pressed in, and dark eyes seemed to watch her from every face, leering. Still, she was safe, she reminded herself. She was with the Champions. She *was* a champion, and no one would dare touch her now.

She glanced around at her own group and allowed herself a smile. Spark had asked her to come, and the others seemed genuinely glad when she asked if she could join. Mostly they were being led around by Burz' boys who would dash madly from one station to the next, oohing and ahhing at one contraption or another.

Behind them, Voske and Locin strode alongside Hadris, and behind them, Hikari and Illeri.

Voske had instructed the escorting monks of Jeza to give them some space and to keep a low profile. Thankfully, the crowd hadn't recognized them, and why should they? They were dressed comfortably, but not lavishly, and no one would expect the Champions to be mingling with the crowd.

"Look at this one!" Kyren exclaimed.

He was standing in front of a small keg that slowly spun in a circle. A sign above it read 'Veil-fire nectar'.

"You've a good eye, young man," called the vendor. "Two marks will buy you a vision beyond the Veil of Nyx."

Kyren stared at him, wide-eyed. "Really?"

Voske paced up behind Kyren and clapped a hand on the boy's shoulder. "Really?"

"That it will, sir," the vendor replied. "Just one sip and a glance through the looking glass will give you sight into the realm of the spirits, to see what dark deeds are being performed in the realm of the dead this very night."

Rasa glanced to where the spirits were playing in the lights. *This should be interesting*, she thought.

"Please," Kyren immediately yowled. "I want to try."

"Me too," voiced Orin.

Hadris eyed the man dubiously. "I don't know."

"I assure you, madam, it's perfectly safe."

She still looked skeptical, and seemed like she was about to say no, when Hikari swooped in with a dashing smile, and pointed her towards the next booth. "Forgive me, darling, but weren't you just saying you wanted a gift for Burz? There's a row of vendors just here! I've been to Vohasi before, I'll have you know, and let me just say that these inventors excel at making the finest of gifts. Shall we?"

He offered her an arm and waited as charmingly as Rasa had ever seen anyone wait.

Hadris nodded reluctantly. "Alright. As long as you're careful?" She gave a pointed look at Voske who grinned in response.

"I'm always careful."

Once Hadris and Hikari had gone, Voske's smile broadened as he looked at the boys first, then the vendor.

"Three, if you will." He quickly produced six marks from his pocket as Locin edged to his side.

"You know this guy is full of mire, right?"

Voske shrugged. "Who's to say?" As he answered he took a cup of the 'nectar' then swirled it once before downing it in one gulp.

"Smells like grape juice," Locin said.

Rasa held back a chuckle as she wandered forward and peeked around Voske, watching the looking glass. It was a couple inches shorter than Voske and just as broad, rimmed by silver filigree. She leaned into her boon, calling on Nyx, but all she could see was her reflection peeking back at her, and the same blue spirits swirling in the sky as before.

"Wow," Kyren exclaimed, apparently seeing something different in the glass. "Look at them!"

Orin actually looked a bit nervous at what he saw, and Voske laughed heartily. "I'll be a raw-boon. So that's Nyx!"

Locin scoffed, but by this point Orin looked a little terrified, burying his head in Voske's arm.

"Oh, fine!" Locin snatched out a couple marks. "Give me some of that."

"I'd like some too," Rasa added.

"And me," said Illeri.

In another moment, the three women were sipping nectar, and all staring at the looking glass. Slowly Rasa saw an image start to take shape. There was *something* there, an odd contortion of a shape, or a tear where a person had once been. It almost made more sense if Rasa looked at it sideways, like there was a pattern that swirled overtop her reflection.

"What do you see?" She whispered to Illeri.

Illeri's face was frozen with dread. She blinked back tears as she spoke. "Nothing. Just clouds."

Rasa glanced toward the top of the reflection. Behind them a myriad of colors painted the night sky, and in the distance the pop of fireworks showered down over the city. She squinted, staring at the spirits that ducked and danced about the display. Her eyes followed one spirit in particular, it rose into the air in a whimsical back and forth pattern, like it was a young girl skipping toward the stars, until it suddenly scurried back down, as though frightened to go any higher. Above, a golden spirit swam through the sky, twisting and roiling like a thundercloud.

"I saw a d-dragon," said Orin in a shaky voice.

"I see it too!" Kyren exclaimed.

Rasa pulled her eyes from the golden spirit and squinted toward the form in the mirror. It wasn't a dragon, but she wasn't sure exactly what it was. It moved in an agitated pattern, like an angry giant pacing the halls of Nyx.

"It's beautiful," Illeri commented.

Locin just laughed in response. "I see a cerberus with three skulls for heads."

"Gods and Chosen," Voske agreed, "I see that too."

Rasa squinted. For a second she thought she saw the cerberus, but the more she leaned into her boon the more she could tell it wasn't there, yet the golden spirit remained, more vivid than ever. She felt her stomach tighten.

A hand brushed her arm, and she started. Spark was beside her, her eyes fixed on the golden spirit and her hand reaching for Rasa. Her touch was almost solid, and Rasa pressed deeper into Nyx until she felt Spark's fingers as solid as her own. Spark stared wide eyed for a moment.

Rasa?

She slipped her hand into Rasa's, and they both turned their eyes on the golden spirit above.

Locin laughed, and it startled Rasa. She let her boon fade a little, and Spark's hand slipped away as she looked back down.

"You've all been had. That juice was laced with braze oil."

"Braze oil?"

"Sure." She spat. "Fortune tellers use it to dupe poor saps who don't know any better. The stuff just shows you what you want to see. Look, now I see a horse riding a dog."

They were all silent, and for just a moment Rasa saw the ridiculous sight, front and center in the looking glass, a horse riding on a dog. Even Orin dared to look again.

Kyren started giggling wildly. "And the dog is riding a chicken!"

That got them all laughing, and Rasa pulled back from her boon, eager to escape the ominous sight of the golden spirit and join their mirth.

"This is a total sham," Locin said.

"Bah," Voske was laughing heartily and tousled Kyren's hair. "Still worth the two marks. How often do you get to see a horse riding a dog riding a chicken?"

Kyren started giggling again, and Rasa felt her tension ease. It was hard not to smile. She glanced once more toward the sky. The golden spirit was still there, but at least it had faded to a hazy cloud.

You saw it too. She started as Spark spoke.

Rasa ran her hand up her arm, feeling a sudden chill. "What is it?"

I don't know.

"Braze oil," Locin answered. "Didn't you hear me?"

Rasa's eyes snapped back to the front. "Right. Of course."

"Is everything alright?" Illeri asked.

"Yes."

Voske called back to them. "You three coming?"

She looked to where Voske and the boys were already moving, Kyren inexorably tugging toward the next stall.

"Yes," she answered.

She wandered after them, trying to refocus on the celebration, but she couldn't quite elude the disquiet that pursued her down the street, like a predator just out of sight.

30: Badlands and Portents

The festival lights still soared over the heart of Vohasi as night wore on, but further out, they had begun to relinquish their hold until the edges of the city sat under an onyx sky that faded into a silver horizon.

Weylyn watched the desert from her perch on a high balcony of Iyanu's temple. A dry, smoky mist was rolling across the city, and a haze hung in the air, unable to reach her here. She'd missed the festival, but she didn't mind. The thought of so many people sounded exhausting, and she much preferred the quiet cool that the night wind carried.

She clutched the pouch of vision powder, and at her feet sat an iron brazier, waiting only for a spark. Yet she hesitated, content to feel the cool a while longer.

The old crone's words still hung in her ear.

You'll drown.

She could almost feel the weight of the waves crushing her. But in her other ear lurked a similar voice.

Swift death from the mist.

She squeezed the pouch. Had her vision been a surety? Maybe there was a detail she'd missed, or a glimpse further into the future.

So deep was she in her own thoughts that the sound of the door behind her barely registered in the back of her mind. She turned to see Rasa, standing nervously in the opening.

"Rasa," she said, and she quickly tucked the pouch into the fold of her toga.

"Sorry. I didn't know you were here."

"It's alright. I'm glad for the company."

The young woman tiptoed onto the balcony and skirted around the brazier.

"I'm surprised you're awake," Weylyn said.

"I couldn't sleep."

"Neither could I. How was the festival?"

"It was a little overwhelming," she said brightly.

"Too many people?"

Rasa shook her head. "Not like that. In a good way. It was fun. Locin gave me a perfume that smells like elderberries. She didn't even know how much I like elderberries."

Weylyn smiled. "I'm glad you enjoyed it."

"I wish you had been there."

Rasa leaned out over the balcony as silence engulfed them. She seemed a bit different tonight, like the shadows weren't clinging so close. Her eyes were a bit brighter, and her smile felt more ready.

"Did you see any of it?" She asked.

Weylyn shook her head. "Only from up here."

"Why?"

"I had a lot on my mind."

Weylyn's eyes wandered to the brazier, still dormant in the middle of the floor. She reached in the folds of her toga and drew out the vision powder, holding up the pouch.

"What is that?"

"Vision powder." She hesitated. She didn't want to drag Rasa into this, but she'd rather not be alone. "It can induce visions, and make them clearer."

"You're trying to see something?" She held out a hand, and Weylyn gave her the pouch, watching as she carefully undid the string and peered inside. The warm smell of herbs drifted into the still, night air. "Why?"

Weylyn brushed the question aside. "There are risks in using it."

Rasa, who still had her nose very close to the pouch, pulled back with widening eyes.

"It won't hurt you. You have to burn it."

"Oh." She glanced at the brazier. "That's why you're up here?"

"It's quiet up here. Peaceful."

Rasa nodded her understanding. "I like high places too." She handed the powder back to Weylyn. "How dangerous is it?"

"I'm not sure, but I was hoping you could help me."

She brightened at the prospect. "How?"

"Watch over me."

"Why? What will happen?"

Weylyn swallowed against a lump that was forming in her throat. "I don't know."

"Then why do it at all?"

Weylyn squatted by the brazier, staring in at the cold kindling. She blinked, and tried to grasp at the memory of her vision, but it drifted away like smoke in the wind. *There was* something *in the mist*, she recalled. Something that loomed in her memory. Something that could threaten all of Arrajin.

"I have no choice," she said.

She struck the flint, and the sparks caught, sending tiny curls of smoke upward around her hair.

"Okay." Rasa sat down across from Weylyn, and nodded with a determined look.

Weylyn opened the pouch. Her senses were overwhelmed with the aroma of thyme and bay, and something bitter that turned her stomach.

"How long will it take?" Rasa asked.

"Not long, I hope."

Weylyn poured the herbs over the burgeoning flames. The powder cascaded across the heat then quickly blackened and started smoking. She steeled her will and closed her eyes, breathing deeply of the fiery fragrance. Dizziness began to overtake her, and she felt as if her body was tumbling forward even though she was sitting still. She felt her eyes burning, and she opened them.

She was outside of Arrajin, staring down at the same stone bridge she had seen before. Rain pelted the stones with a constant slapping sound. It was familiar. The same stone covered in muck, the same river rushing by below.

A thunderous roar rolled over her as a tidal wave deluged the bridge. In the mist, she could see a writhing form that coiled and lunged. It had a massive snake-like head and kicked up a wall of mist into the afternoon sky.

She looked down, expecting to see her broken body at her feet like before. But it wasn't her. It was Rasa. Her eyes were frozen in everlasting pain and her stomach had been ripped open. Her red hair floated around her head in the flood of water.

"Rasa!" She heard herself scream.

"WEYLYN!"

The terrified screech of Rasa pulled at Weylyn's mind, and suddenly the vision was gone. She was back on the balcony, flat on her back and gasping for breath.

Rasa knelt over her, shaking her vigorously.

She blinked through the haze of her mind and her arms trembled as she slowly remembered the vision powder.

"Are you alright," Rasa asked.

Weylyn nodded mechanically, but stayed focused on Rasa, her eyes slowly traveling from the young woman's face to her stomach and back again. She looked perfectly healthy.

"You fell backward." Her voice still held an edge of panic. "You weren't breathing."

Weylyn sat up. Her chest felt tight, and her breath shallow. "How long was I out?"

"Five minutes."

"It felt like no time at all."

"What did you see?" Rasa asked.

Weylyn shook her head and her eyes traveled once more to Rasa's stomach. "I'm not sure."

"What do you mean?"

"Something…" her voice trailed off and she looked back at the fire, still barely smoldering under the heap of dust. "Different," she finally said. "Something different."

The festival kept on at a fever pitch for the rest of the evening as the barrels of wine ran low and the merchants started cutting it with water to preserve what was left. The fireworks still popped overhead, though less frequent, and there was hardly even a slowing down of the excited energy. The Champions, however, had slowed down, and Kyren had even nodded off, nearly falling asleep on his feet the way only children can. Hadris and Rasa had taken the boys back to the temple hours ago, leaving the others to attend to the pressing business on Voske's mind.

He found himself surprisingly awake as he picked his way across the festival grounds, dodging around litter and pockets of people who didn't recognize him in the dark. In one hand he held three tankards of cool water, sweetened with honey, and with his other he munched on a sweet tart that tasted somewhere between an orange and a coconut.

He brushed through a curtain at the far side of the festival grounds, into a pure white tent that glowed with light. Inside, Hikari, Illeri and Locin were seated around a map with pins stuck in it. Voske recognized it immediately as a map of Erimos, and he set the drinks down with a thunk against the palmwood table.

"Here," he said, motioning to the beverages.

"Voske, you spoil us," Hikari said as he snatched up one of the drinks. He tipped it up and drank greedily.

Locin took a thoughtful swig and sloshed it around her mouth. "Where's yours?"

"Drank it on the way back," he answered, then slid the third to Illeri, who hadn't even acknowledged his entrance.

She was leaning over the map, staring at the two pins near the very center, one in Vohasi, and the other in the middle of the Varrin Badlands.

Voske pointed his pinky at the pins while he took another bite of the tart. "What's that?"

"She thinks that's where the map leads," Locin answered.

"She's sure?"

"Very," Illeri finally answered. "But this map," she tapped on the table, "is useless."

Voske pulled up his chair and leaned over, looking down at the pinned locations. "How so?"

"There's no topography, no roads, nothing."

Voske eyed the spot again. "That's about right."

She peeled her eyes away from the map, and stared at him, bemused.

He set his finger down in the middle of the badlands. "Nobody ever goes there. A few stubborn souls, a couple quarries, a couple cactus, you won't find much else."

"Well, why aren't those on the map?"

He shrugged. "Some places are too small to mention. It's not like they can include everything." He glanced back at the pin. It wasn't all that far from Govere, and for a moment his thoughts drifted to Klief and Rix. How would the quarry be getting along without him?

Hikari was leaning out over the map as well, and he tapped his finger on the city of Bravesh on the opposite side of the badlands. "I thought so," he mused.

"Thought what?" Voske asked.

"Bravesh," Hikari answered. "It's the second stop on the festival route. We'll be flying right over the badlands. We can just stop on the way."

"You can't *just stop* on a chariot," Illeri answered. "There has to be a tether, unless you want your chariot to sink into the sand."

Hikari folded his arms. "Not even for five minutes?"

"Will it take just five minutes?"

Hikari clamped his mouth shut and looked back at the map. "Perhaps not."

Voske nodded along as he took another bite. He could almost taste Lorhk's cactus syrup, sweet and thick. "There's another way," he muttered.

They all turned toward him and he took a moment, enjoying the suspense. "Pylat's aren't the only way to cross the badlands. How many of you have heard of a sand skiff?"

"No," Hikari said wide eyed.

"Sounds like a bird," Locin added.

"More like a boat," Voske answered. "A land ship. We used to use them to haul slabs of granite from the quarry."

"Back in the good old days," Hikari joked.

"That's right, all of five minutes ago. Anyway, we can ride out across the flats and take all the time we want to poke around. Skiffs won't sink."

"And how fast are these things?" Illeri asked. "We're due in Bravesh tomorrow afternoon."

Voske licked his lips and sat back from the table. "Then we best leave tonight."

"Is that safe?"

"Safe enough," Voske answered. "I've ridden across that desert a thousand times."

The others exchanged tired glances, until Locin finally clapped her hands against the table. "Nyx, what's the worst that could happen? I'm willing to go snoop around."

Illeri nodded her assent as well. "We might not get another chance," she said. "We should tell the others."

Hikari coughed loudly. "Best to let them rest, darling. Don't worry. I'll make sure I leave them all a note explaining our detour and that we'll meet them in Bravesh."

"Will that sit well with Aurilis?"

Voske grunted and tapped on the map. "Of course not. That's why we're not asking."

"Definitely," Locin agreed. "Just don't tell them everything in this note of yours."

Hikari gave her a puzzled look. "Meaning?"

"Meaning I trust the temple about as far as I can throw them."

"Just say we're going sight-seeing in the Varrin," Voske said.

Hikari looked at him blankly. "Do people do that?"

"God's no! That's a terrible idea."

Hikari bobbed his head thoughtfully. "Well, that does sound like something you'd do."

"See, I knew you'd come around, smoothy," Voske winked. "Leave the arrangements to me. Just find a couple waterskins."

"Done," Locin said. "When do we leave?"

"Within the hour," Voske answered. "If everything goes according to plan, we'll be in Bravesh before the temple pylat arrives."

A dry fog of hazy colored smoke clung to Vohasi, obscuring the stars. Late night celebrants had turned into early morning stragglers, and the smell of stale beer lingered over the exhibits. Weylyn ambled through the fading crowd like a specter, her mind carefully picking apart every possible scenario. Was the vision powder faulty? Could her boon ever make a mistake? But in the end she couldn't shake the image of Rasa dead on the bridge.

She reached in her pocket and pulled out a crumpled note. She'd received it as soon as they reached the Vohasi temple. It simply read, 'Completed survey of the Arrtris. Found nothing. Eprim.' She sighed as she stuffed it back in her pocket. She hadn't imagined the beast she sensed in the sewers. Part of her mind wanted to believe there was nothing to worry about, but she knew too well how animals worked. They weren't static. They moved and migrated and hunted. Whatever it was, it'd be back.

Once she reached the edges of town, the smoky haze was clearer. She could breathe easier here and see out past the edge of town into the rolling dunes of the Varrin. Part of her wanted to run off into the desert, a new world to conquer. She felt the itch to explore, and she wondered if that would ever be her life again.

It will, she thought.

"Weylyn?"

She turned at the voice to see Hikari trotting down the road toward her. He had a large water skin slung over his shoulder and wore a crisp blue chiton. It was more water than he'd need marching around the festival, and she raised an eyebrow as she stared at it.

"Going somewhere?"

"Oh this? Well, you know, darling, adventure awaits." He was trying to look serious, but she could tell he was bursting at the seams to talk about it - whatever *it* was.

"Adventure?" She grinned, feeling that old rush of anticipation, the very same she used to feel before picking a random direction and heading out someplace she'd never been.

His eyes lit. "Oh, very well. I suppose telling you won't hurt. Come on then. Just ahead."

She fell in behind him, following him to the far end of an adjoining street where she saw Voske, Locin and Illeri. They were busily moving a few bags onto a peculiar contraption. It looked nearly like a boat with a large white sail, but it sat idle atop the sand

"Weylyn!" Illeri called.

Weylyn waved to them and swung onto the platform, staring from face to face in confusion. "I thought you'd all be asleep by now."

Hikari scrambled up the ramp behind her, drawing a frown from Voske.

"What part of 'don't tell anyone' did you miss, smoothy?"

He shrugged sheepishly. "It's Weylyn! She's not going to stop us."

"From what?" She asked.

"We're going on a trip," Locin said.

Voske rolled his eyes as he set down the large pack he was carrying and walked to a small lever that looked nearly like a rudder at the back of the sand ship.

"A trip?"

"Uh huh."

"Are you coming too?" Illeri asked.

Weylyn squinted out at the desert. She could feel the more prudent side of her saying this was a foolish idea. They were scheduled to leave for the festival of Strah in several hours, and she'd be sorely missed if she was late, but the wide expanse of the Varrin stretched out before her, beckoning. "Where are you going?"

"Into the badlands," Voske said.

"On an adventure, darling!"

"We'll still be in Bravesh on time," Illeri added from behind her. "Just a different way of getting there."

Weylyn looked back toward the temple. She could see the upper spire, jutting above the fog. All that awaited her there was more agonizing about her vision, something she'd much rather avoid.

Voske was wrapping a length of rope around a peculiar post in the center of the sand ship and looking at her expectantly.

"Alright," she said.

Voske let out a hearty laugh. "That's it? No word about where we're going or why?"

She smiled. "'Adventure' was good enough for me."

"And that's why we like you." Voske set his hands on his lower back and stretched. "Alright, everyone ready?"

"Aye!" Hikari sauntered to Weylyn's side and looped his arm through hers. "An extra set of eyes could only help in our glorious quest!"

"And what is *our* quest?"

Voske yanked the rope and a deep whir began vibrating through the deck. Weylyn felt Hikari leaning on her for balance as the ship gently rose, hovering just a couple feet above the desert ground.

"Don't worry, darling. We'll fill you in on the way."

Stars glittered in the dark sky above the desert. The night was cool and pleasant, and Locin leaned out over the rail of the skiff, watching the moonlight dance across the dunes. The sun would be up in another hour or so, and hopefully they would be to the relic by then.

She kicked at loose sand on the deck, sending it between the slats of the rail where it quickly vanished behind them like a wisp of smoke. She just wanted to get this over with. Normally she'd enjoy the thrill of heading out on a heist, but not today. She felt antsy, though she wasn't sure why.

Spark pulled her attention toward the back of the skiff. Voske stood at the rudder, steering. He was smiling as Illeri stood beside him with her eyes on the stars. Hikari lounged nearby, laughing lightly. Even Weylyn looked happy, perched by the rail. Locin couldn't quite hear them over the noise of the skiff, but they seemed to be having fun.

Spark was tugging her their direction, but she resisted.

"Leave me alone."

Spark insisted. She was always like that, trying to force Locin toward people.

"It's not my thing. Gods, Spark! You know this. I'm a loner."

The shiver in her left arm told her Spark wasn't buying it.

Illeri pointed up and to the right, and Voske slowly turned the rudder. Locin felt the skiff drift, and she steadied herself against the rail.

The four of them did look happy, which just made Locin angry. She turned her attention back to the sand. It didn't matter what she wanted. She'd learned her lesson the hard way. She wouldn't get close to anyone ever again.

"Hey!" Voske's voice yelled over the ambient noise. "Locin!"

She glanced back to see him waving her over. "What?"

"Come join us!"

She shrugged.

"You've been alone up there all night."

She rolled her eyes, but she pushed herself off the rail and straightened her toga as she sauntered back toward them, whispering under her breath to Spark, "I'm not going because you want me to."

As she approached, the others all grew silent, and she nodded awkwardly. "So, I'm here."

"You looked pretty serious over there," Hikari offered with a casual smile. He had some bright light from the two full moons coalesced around his fingertips, pulling it this way and that in a formless blob. "Lost in your thoughts?"

Weylyn smiled. "She wasn't thinking. She was talking."

Locin shot a glance at the old huntress.

"I saw your mouth moving."

Locin shrugged off the old feeling that she was crazy as her mind searched for Spark's presence.

Rasa saw her. She's real.

"Talking to the stars perhaps?" Hikari pulled at the light with his boon, and for a second it seemed to waver with a red hue. "I dare say, we must be better company than that."

Illeri cast a sidelong glance toward him. "The stars are better company than you'd think."

"No doubt," he said sheepishly. "I only meant that we can talk back."

"I was talking to the smartest person on the skiff, obviously." Locin smirked. "Me."

She felt a sharp pinch from Spark and winced, hoping no one would notice.

Voske laughed. "Sure, kid. Sure."

"Smarter than you, for sure, old man."

"Easy now."

Locin nodded to Hikari. "What in Nyx are you doing?"

"I have a theory, darling. I'm trying to test it."

She shrugged, and then sat down against the rail facing them. She could feel Spark's grating happiness. She really did like these oafs. *Too* much.

Silence started to engulf them, but Hikari quickly leaned back with an easy sigh and pointed toward the desert. "We're getting close, or so says Illeri. It's astounding how Voske can navigate out here. Every dune and cactus looks the same to me."

"I've been through these dunes more times than I can count, making runs to Vohasi and Bravesh with blocks. Let me tell you, I wouldn't want to make this trip on foot. Nothing but endless desert."

"The quarry is here in the desert?" Illeri asked. "You actually lived out here?"

"Seriously?" Locin straightened up. "And you aren't even gonna show us your place?"

Voske brushed them off with a wave. "Nothing to see. Just sand and rocks."

"Were you born here?" Illeri pressed. "Oh, veer left. See that star? Try to keep it ahead of us."

Voske gently shifted the rudder. "Born on Erimos?"

"Here, in this desert."

"Nah, just came here for my guilding. The quarry needed labor, and I was a laborer."

Hikari nodded. "Well, to my understanding, there are labor guilds all over Erimos. Did you grow up nearby?"

Voske was scowling now, keeping his eyes dead set on the sand. "Near enough. What about you, pretty boy? Grew up in the fanciest city on Suntara, I suspect."

Hikari laughed. "Darling, I grew up everywhere. My father traveled with the theater troops. We went where they did."

Illeri glanced up at him. "He was a player too?"

"Well, not like *me* to be sure." He turned sharply, pointing out in the desert. "So how close are we?"

"I just told you," said Voske. "It'll be another half an hour, maybe less."

"Bet you had a fancy estate, huh?" Locin asked. "Little baby Hikari, crawling on some white sand beach."

Hikari smiled. "Well, of course, darling. All the best players are born on Suntara. Desita smiles on the sapphire world!" He coughed lightly, and then looked around until his eyes rested on Weylyn. "Weylyn, darling?"

"Me? I've already told you. Born in the Shinoam."

"Ah. Yes."

Awkward silence started to engulf them again, and this time Hikari seemed content to let it, standing and walking a little ways away to the railing, but he kept pulling at the light in his hand, and it seemed to have a pale blue tint now.

The silence was fine by Locin. Or it would have been, if it had lasted. But it was Illeri who broke it this time.

"I grew up in Harmund, near the Valley of Iyanu."

Hikari turned around. "Truly? I've never heard of Harmund, but the Valley is magnificent! Red rocks towering on either side of the gorge. I once played a show in Tena'bai."

Illeri looked down with a frown.

"Sure," Locin said. "Tena'bai might be nice, but you ever been *in* the gorge? It's a pool of mire."

Illeri coughed lightly, and her cheeks flushed. "Harmund is in the gorge."

Locin shrugged. "Oh."

"It's okay. Locin's not wrong. The gorge is full of poor towns. We had a lot of unguilded down there. A lot of the people down there call it Bai'Vaden."

Hikari's expression was softer now, and more somber. "Valley of Lost Souls?"

Illeri nodded. "I used to run away at night, sneak out my window. There was this mesa right outside of town, pretty small, but right in the middle of the gorge. I could look up between the ridges, like black walls, and see the stars. It always looked better up there."

"I used to run away too," Locin said. "Then one day, I didn't go back." She kicked at the railing. "Rotting, worthless life any way. Bet my parents didn't even miss me."

"I'm sure they did," Weylyn said solemnly.

Locin scowled. "They didn't want me around."

"Even if that's true," she said with a pained expression. "I can't imagine they didn't feel your absence."

Locin brushed her off and nodded back to Illeri. "What about your parents?"

Illeri shrugged. "I never knew my father. My mother… let's just say Harmund has a lot of vices you can fall into."

"I'm sorry to hear that," Hikari said with a mournful glance. "Is she still in Harmund?"

"She passed the Veil a long time ago. It was a mercy, I think. She didn't have an easy life."

Locin shifted, turning away. She didn't want to hear about this, or think about it. It made her think about her own family, and that rotting ache she felt. But she was good at stuffing it down.

"I'm so sorry," she heard Hikari speaking softly. "Truly I am."

Silence fell again, and this time they all seemed content to let it lie. That is until Hikari jumped to his feet and yelled.

"Aha!"

Locin started. "Gods! What was that for?"

"Look!" He said excitedly, pointing to the back of the chariot. He still held his right hand up, but she didn't see the moonlight anymore. "Just there!"

Locin glanced to see a flock of hyppogryphs soaring beside the chariot, their feathers glowing in the bright moonlight. "So what? I've seen gryphs before."

"Ah, but not like this you haven't! I made them."

Voske laughed. "Sure you did, player."

"I most certainly did." He glanced around as though looking for a way to convince them, and then his eyes rested on Weylyn with a sparkle. "Care to assist, darling?"

"Okay."

"Try and shoot one."

A slow smile spread over her lips as she pulled an arrow out of her quiver and strung her bow. She pulled it taught, and nodded to Hikari.

"Ready!"

The arrow flew toward one of the gryphs, but in an instant they all scattered, disappearing and reappearing around the chariot.

Hikari was grinning. "Again?"

Weylyn grabbed another arrow, and fired as the gryphs bolted to the front of the skiff.

"Once more?" She asked.

Hikari nodded again.

The pluck of Weylyn's bow sounded, and the gryphs appeared to the side of the skiff where an arrow immediately soared through the lead gryph's eye.

"You cheated!" Hikari cried. "You can't use your boon."

Weylyn smiled smugly as she put her bow away. "You are."

"Well to be sure, but that's different."

"Neat trick," Voske said with a laugh.

"How did you do that?" Illeri asked awestruck.

Hikari was beaming now. "I've been thinking of my old boon. I could create illusions, shapes and shadows and the like. I figured if I could do that, I should be able to do it with light. It was a simple matter of learning how to separate out the colors." He nodded to Illeri. "The prism stone gave me the idea." He twisted his hands again, and a fluffy rabbit hopped across the middle of the skiff.

"It has a shadow," Weylyn said. "How is that possible?"

"Ah! I'm rather proud of that little detail." His voice was starting to sound a bit strained. "That's where I pulled the light from to make the illusion. Clever, don't you think?"

He let the illusion vanish once more, and shook out his fingers, blowing on them. The tips looked a bit red. "I think that's all for now."

Voske laughed. "Not bad, smoothy. Not bad."

Locin glanced up again. The sand ahead was giving way to something else, dark shapes that rose over the dunes.

"What's that?" She asked.

"Hm." Voske fixed his eyes on the horizon. "Not rocks. Lines are too clean. And look at those angles!"

As they sped closer, she noticed more and more of the shapes rising high into the murky predawn sky.

"I've never been to this part of the desert," he continued. "I'd remember this."

Weylyn returned to her perch, watching the desert intently. "They're buildings."

"Buildings? No city this big would be off the map," Voske replied. "Little towns, watering holes, a quarry or two, sure. But this?"

He was right. As they sped nearer, it became clear that the sprawling structures could have rivaled Vohasi in size and scope. But they were in ruins, half buried in sand.

"Mire and Nyx!" Locin exclaimed. "A whole rotting city out here hiding in the desert?"

Voske shrugged. "Not a city anyone's lived in for a long time. Look at these arches! This thing must've been beautiful in its day."

"And what day was that?" Hikari mused. "It looks like it's been buried for ages."

The skiff was just nearing what must have been the entrance to the city once. Half an arch stuck out above them, black against the night sky. It looked like it had been broken more than worn down by time.

"We're close," Illeri said. She looked pointedly at Voske. "Very close."

"Meaning the relic is in this city? It's huge. How do we even start looking?"

Locin stared out at half buried homes with arched windows shaped in smooth sandstone. If only Endring had given her more to go on. But they were here now. There was nothing they could do but search.

31: From Dawn into Dark

The sun had barely breached the horizon as Burz climbed on the deck of the champions' chariot. In the heart of Vohasi, the last stragglers of smoke and light drifted lazily into the sky, and the sounds of the festival had dwindled in the quiet of early morning.

Burz carried Orin in his arms, still asleep, and Kyren was nestled against Hadris, his head on her shoulder. They had been asleep by the time Burz got back to the temple late in the night, and he took no pleasure in waking them for the early departure.

Orin stirred in his arms. "Where are we?" He muttered.

Burz glanced at Hadris. She smiled. He tensed. He was sure she saw it, and he had tried not to, but his frustration from last nights' festival was still fresh.

"Just sleep." He set Orin down on a soft bench near the side of the chariot's deck. "We'll be in Bravesh in a couple hours."

Orin yawned sleepily, and curled up in a comfortable position as Hadris laid Kyren beside him.

The others were coming up the deck now, at least the two that had shown up. Zengin and Rasa. Burz huffed loudly. Somehow, this had to be Voske's influence.

"Are you alright?" Hadris slipped her hand in his.

He nodded stiffly.

"No you're not. What happened last night?"

Burz shrugged. "You tell me."

Her tone was starting to change now, taking on a defensive edge already. "I *thought* we had a good time at the festival."

"Good."

She pulled her hand free, scowling. "You didn't?"

"It was perfect. I spent the night being paraded around the city's elites with the bitter son of an Archon."

Zengin stood on the far side of the deck, looking out over the tether. He held his head high, as always, so he could look down on everyone else.

"I'm sorry," she said a bit softer. "I was hoping you'd come down to the festival. Some of the others did."

Burz scoffed.

"What?"

"They brushed off their responsibility, so I should too?"

She matched his tone fully now. "Yes, every once in a while. What is wrong with you today?"

"I saw you." He turned to face her. "I saw you and the boys last night, down at the festival."

Hadris looked wounded. "You *told* us to go. If you had wanted, I would have gladly stayed with you. You know that!"

He sighed. "It's not that. I'm glad you had fun."

"You don't seem to be."

"It was the others. They're like children. They do whatever they feel like with no concept of duty."

"Some of them *are* children. They'll grow into being champions."

Burz scoffed again. It wasn't Rasa or Locin he was angry with. "Voske is no child."

It was Hadris' turn to scoff. "Is that what this is about?"

"The others look up to him. If he showed even a little decorum, they'd follow his lead."

"Are you angry because he's leading them, or because you're not?"

He glanced at her as if it was a ridiculous notion.

"Did it ever occur to you that perhaps you could learn something from Voske?"

"He's an idiot. What's worse, he's an idiot who thinks he's always right."

"Maybe sometimes he is."

"And here I thought you would support your husband."

She turned away and huffed angrily. "Gods have mercy! I wish Uthando had never chosen you."

That one stung. Burz felt the impact like a blow to his chest, and it knocked the words out of him. Did she really prefer the broken, guildless cripple? Was he *worse* than that now?

After a few moments she looked over, and sighed as some of the tension drained out. "I only meant that I feel like I'm losing you, Burz. I like you better as a husband and a father than a champion."

"Well, I'm a champion. You can hate that, but you can't change it."

"I'm not saying I want to." She rested a gentle hand on his forearm.

This was his chance. This was the new life he'd prayed for. But he never imagined a miracle to feel so… painful. "Hadris-"

"High Oracle!" Gillis was running up the ramp to the chariot now, sweaty and out of breath, and waving a piece of parchment in the air. "High Oracle!"

Burz pulled away from Hadris' grip and walked to meet him. He stopped near the other champions, and Aurilis made her way over with a worried expression.

"Well?" She snapped. "Have you found them?"

"I'm sorry… Oracle," Gillis panted. "Found… this."

He handed her the parchment, and then bent over with his hands on his knees.

As Aurilis read, her face grew more and more angry. When she was through, she glanced up at the others.

"They're gone. They've taken a sand skiff out into the Varrin Wastes."

No one knew quite what to make of that, but Burz felt that same anger bubbling over again.

"That's it then," he snapped. "Voske can't even be bothered to show up at all anymore."

"They said they'd… meet us in Bravesh," Gillis said.

"What's in the Varrin Wastes?" Rasa asked.

Aurilis frowned. "Nothing."

The path through the buried city turned out to be an easy one. Many of the buildings were fully buried below the dunes, and only the tallest towers jutted upward like the arms of a drowning man. They were made of cut stones, orange like the sand around them, and smoothed by the Erimos winds. One tower leaned heavily to one side, domed by a green-shingled roof. Weathered chains hung down from the highest window, and Illeri reached up, jingling the links as they passed underneath. They were cold to the touch for now, but they wouldn't stay that way for long. Already the rays of morning could be seen glowing across the sand, and the stars had all but vanished from view.

"How long has this been here?" Weylyn asked.

"Not sure," Voske answered. "That stone work's about two hundred years old though."

Hikari passed him an inquisitive look. "How would you know?"

Voske pointed toward one of the towers. "See the lintel above the window? That vertical stone pattern hasn't been used in a hundred years and the stone tracery hasn't been used for at least two hundred. Everyone started using metal. I'm not sure anyone alive even remembers how to bend stone that delicate."

Illeri followed his fingers to an impressive tower that must have been the upper apartments of a beautiful gallery. The window was filled with delicate stone work that spiraled up and outward from the center, though all the surrounding glass had long since shattered free.

"No one?" Hikari asked.

"Nope," Voske answered. "It's one of those weird things. If skills aren't used they can get lost to time."

"But how do *you* know that?" Locin asked.

Voske glanced her direction. "What?"

"I mean, you were a stone cutter. How in Nyx would you know about that?"

"He was a stone cutter," Hikari offered. "It's not that far removed."

Locin propped her hands on her hips. "Yeah it is. That's like saying a vintner and a drunk are the same."

Voske raised an eyebrow. "Am I the vintner or the drunk in this example?"

"Which one do you think?"

Illeri tried to ignore them and turned her eyes back to the city, scanning their surroundings for anything that looked out of place. With the loss of the stars they were very much on their own with regard to finding the piece, and in the back of her mind she could feel time quickly slipping away. Bravesh was still hours beyond them.

"Illeri," Voske called. "Which way?"

"I'm not sure," she answered. "Let's try to get to the center."

"Any particular reason?"

"If this place really is two hundred years old, then it was likely built around a temple. And if a relic was stored here-"

"That's where it'd be," Voske finished. "I knew there was a reason we brought her along."

"Cause she's smart," Locin answered. "See, if she said the thing about the stone, I'd believe it."

Voske frowned back at Locin. "I know a few things."

"Of course you do," Hikari answered. "Illeri just knows more."

Voske's frown only deepened in response, and Illeri leaned harder on the railing, eager to stay out of it.

"You know what," Voske snapped. "Ask us a question then. Anything you like, we'll see who knows what."

Hikari rocked onto his toes and back again. "Alright. I've got something. A man goes for a walk in the middle of a rainstorm. He's got no hat, no hood, and nothing to keep the rain off, but by the end of his walk, not a single hair on his head is wet, why?"

Voske chewed over the question and stamped his foot against the deck for a minute before Hikari spoke again.

"Give up?"

"Of course not," Voske barked. "I'll get it."

Weylyn raised a hand, but Hikari shook his head. "Sorry, darling. Just these two. I'll ask you the next one."

She frowned and turned her eyes back toward the city.

"Illeri?"

"He's bald," she answered.

Hikari clapped his hands together. "See, I knew she'd get it!" His smile lingered on her a bit longer. "She's brilliant, you know."

She felt her cheeks flush, and she looked away.

"Bah! If I wasn't having to steer I'd have gotten it."

"Of course you would, darling. Of course you would."

"Fine," Voske retorted. "Try this then. A man went to a store and bought a-"

"Ahead!" Weylyn's voice called.

"What?"

She was pointing out over the city center, and her voice was strained. "What could have caused this?"

They followed her gaze ahead to where the temple should have been. There were bits and pieces of the structure still left, a tattered wall of ancient brick, a spire with a chunk torn out of the base, and a broken veranda that used to be the second floor of a sanctum. Most of the city thus far had looked abandoned, but the temple looked torn asunder.

"Mire and Nyx." Voske waved his hand over the control mechanism, bringing the spinning shunts to a grinding halt.

"By the gods," Hikari said.

Voske leapt down off the skiff. "Come on."

Weylyn leapt off deftly, landing easily in the sand and stalking forward toward the ruined temple.

Hikari jumped down and offered Locin a hand, then Illeri. She took his hand, and her stomach fluttered as she climbed down. He lingered there for a moment, and she glanced up to see him smiling.

"Gods!" Voske called. "What in Nyx is that smell?"

Illeri pulled her hand away as she felt herself blush, and she quickly marched forward into the sand.

"Rotting mire, that's what!" Locin pulled her toga over her mouth and nose.

"I'd say something's living here," Weylyn said coolly.

The smell hit Illeri as she caught up. The fetid stench of something rotten was drifting on the desert wind, and it seemed to be coming from the temple.

Voske called back to Hikari. "Grab the water."

"Right you are." He grabbed the large waterskin and slung it over his shoulder, marching after the others.

"Living?" Locin asked warily. "As in…?"

"I don't know," Weylyn said. "But I know a nest when I see one."

Voske glanced around side to side. "Nest?"

"Inside." Weylyn tapped the sigil on her palm, the coiled snake of Strah.

"Right. Didn't see what it was though?"

She shook her head.

Voske reached the edge of the rubble and tossed a couple broken chunks aside, then dusted off his hands. "Alright then, any ideas of where this thing would be?"

"Temples aren't all that different," Locin said. She motioned them toward the back where a large section of wall had collapsed. "If they're going to store a relic, they put it one of two places. On display, or in the vault."

"Are you sure, darling? The smell seems to be getting worse this way."

Voske grunted. "Of course it does."

Locin picked her way around the rubble until she found what she was looking for. "Here. Wanna help me out, big guy?"

There was a chunk of debris twice as big as Voske, but he lifted it easily and set it aside revealing a tunnel that led down into dark. A fresh wave of the noisome smell blasted Illeri, like the scent of feces and death all rolled into one. It turned her stomach, and she threw her arm over her nose, but Weylyn just squatted by the hole and peered in as if she couldn't smell it.

"That's the way," she said.

"Well," Voske said, hands on hips, "care to give us some light?"

"For you, darling, anything." Hikari quickly gathered the threads of light until he held a bright orb above his palm that lit the way down. They could clearly see the sand strewn floor, nearly two stories below the cracked stairwell. He cleared his throat. "I vote our next adventure is somewhere that doesn't smell like a latrine."

Voske clapped him on the shoulder as he entered the tunnel. "Come on, smoothy. And watch your step."

Tired. That's what Burz felt as he slipped out of his chambers. So far the glamorous life of a champion looked a lot like what he knew of the Tajerim bureaucrats, and he hated it. He strolled past the rows of doors, eager to be out of the housing level and under the free sky above. He paused for only a moment as he passed the High Oracle's chamber. He heard her angry voice, muffled through the door. She wasn't the only one angry.

Burz headed up on deck. He carried his whetstone with him and a simple bowl he'd taken from the kitchen, a rough wooden thing. It felt far better in his hands than the gaudy gold ones he was getting used to. This was an honest man's bowl. He carried it across the Tempest's deck to the chariot's well. It ran straight down through every floor, and held their supply of water. He filled it and set it on the edge as he looked out over the radiant field and the Varrin wastes below. Somewhere out there Voske was off shirking his responsibilities again. Maybe it shouldn't have bothered him so much, but that's not how men behaved, and it rankled him. Everything about the big, obnoxious man rankled him.

He drew his sword and laid it down on the lip of the well, dunking the whetstone in the bowl to soak it, and then he started, focusing keenly on the task at hand. He carefully drew the stone along the blade, and the sharp zing of the bronze grating along the stone comforted him. He'd missed these rituals, and he felt like Burz the soldier again.

A shuffling noise from the stairs caught his attention, and he saw Gillis emerging from below deck. His cheeks looked flushed, and he was pacing back and forth in tight little circles, oblivious to everything but his stewing, so much so that he nearly ran straight into Burz.

"Gillis."

He jolted at his name, and his eyes darted around until he spotted him.

"Champion," he squeaked out the word, "how may I assist you?"

Burz raised an eyebrow. "Have you ever used a whetstone?"

Gillis looked mortified. He stammered for a bit and then said weakly, "Perhaps I can fetch a Jeza monk?"

"Gillis. I don't need help. Just relax." Burz turned back to his work, flipping the blade and starting on the other side, focused on keeping the bevel even.

"Right. F-forgive me, Champion. I am not… I'm not myself." And then he just stayed there, stamping his feet like a nervous foal, and muttering under his breath.

Burz set aside the stone and took a cloth from his side, wiping the blade. Once it was dry, he carefully slipped it in its scabbard and gave Gillis his full attention.

"Aurilis sounded angry."

He nodded.

"What about?"

"N-nothing. Nothing important, at least. Nothing you need be concerned with."

He clenched his jaw. "It's not hard to guess."

Gillis' shoulders sagged. "It's not?"

"No. And every bit of her ire is deserved."

"It is?" He squeaked. The poor man looked as if he would faint. "Per-perhaps I should tell her…"

"Tell her what?"

"To find my replacement now."

"Replacement?" Burz stared at him, slightly taken aback. "Why would you want that?"

"I don't!" He said earnestly. "The High Oracle thinks… She doesn't believe I'm qualified to be your liaison."

"Why not?"

Gillis looked at him, stunned. "Why not? I have failed utterly, haven't I? Most of the Champions disappeared under my watch, and the others…"

He glanced around the deck, and Burz followed suit. Rasa was hunched near the front looking terrified, and Zengin sulked near the aft radiants, looking more dour than usual. Burz grimaced. All of it was Voske's doing.

Gillis sighed. "You're miserable too."

"That has nothing to do with you."

"It's…" he began questioningly, but then shook his head with resolve. "Of course it does, Champion. It's my job to see to your needs, to ensure the Champions are happy."

"You can't make anyone happy. You can provide them comfort, distractions," he said, "but those things don't make people happy."

"At this point I'd settle for mild contentment."

Burz smirked. "You aren't responsible for other's choices."

He paused, pondering his words. "I don't think the High Oracle sees it that way. She told me if anything like this happens again, she will…" he cleared his throat, "…reassign me."

Burz frowned. "She should take into account that Voske doesn't listen to anyone, not even her."

"She knows that well enough." He opened his mouth like he had more to say, and then shut it again.

"What is it?"

"Are you familiar with the temple's history, champion?"

"Sure."

"The rebellion of Turik?"

The name tickled some distant memory of his guild days. "Marched on the temple?"

Gillis nodded and then started reciting like a guildling on testing day. "It was the Fallow of 1312 when the champion Turik led the monks of Jeza against the temple. They attacked the Gods' Mount and seized control of the inner sanctum."

"The rebellion was quelled after half a cycle or so, wasn't it?"

"Yes, but many lives were lost. Talamh was shaken. And the rebellion only ended with the death of Turik and the choosing of a new champion."

"And what? Aurilis thinks Voske is gonna lead a rebellion?"

Gillis looked at him nervously, as if hoping for some reassurance.

"Voske is an idiot. He's headstrong, and a troublemaker, but an organized rebellion? He couldn't lead a pig to slop."

"Either way, the blame for any chaos he might cause is falling squarely on me."

"It should fall squarely on him."

Gillis looked alarmed by the idea. "But he's a Champion."

"And?"

Gillis swallowed hard. "It's alright. I'll do better." He had his head held up straight, but his shoulders still slumped, like they carried the weight of Talamah.

Do better? The only one who needed to do better was that overgrown man-child.

A call from the wayfarers pulled their attention to the front. Bravesh was clearly visible now as they dropped the radiant field, and the desert heat fell over the Tempest. It was a lush, vibrant city ringed by a deep blue circle of water. Clean white buildings and green vegetation spotted the landscape, an oasis amidst the rolling dunes of the Varrin. At its center stood the library of Strah, a massive stone building with marble columns and two wide doors. Before the doors towered a fountain in the god's image. He was crafted of solid bronze, holding a tome the size of a man in his outstretched hand, and water fell from the tome, splashing down his arm and across his feet. As Burz watched, a geyser erupted on the far side of Bravesh, feeding the ring of water and misting the city.

"Bravesh," Gillis said softly. "It's breathtaking."

The pylat dropped toward the tether, and into the dull roar of the crowd that rose to meet them, and Burz felt frustration swallowing him up.

32: The Trial of Epsis

Weylyn peered through the slick, oily corridor of the reliquary. It had been utterly destroyed. The sandstone bricks were covered in a goopy tar-like substance that stuck to the walls and pooled on the floor, sucking at the soles of her boots.

There were signs this was once a venerated place, the smeared remnant of a painting or the broken head of an idol. They were scattered pell-mell around the forgotten ruin.

"What in Nyx happened here?" Voske asked.

Weylyn knelt to the floor, running her finger tips through the sludge. It smelled of musk.

"An opposing city state?" Hikari speculated. "Perhaps someone who opposed the temple?"

"The cult," Voske growled.

Weylyn carefully stood and edged down the path, keeping her eyes trained on the darkness ahead. Several side passages broke away, disappearing into parts unknown. One of them appeared man-made, square corners, polished stones, but most were rounded in shape, scored by massive grooves that ran from floor to ceiling.

"Gods," Locin said. "Are you even listening to yourself?"

"What?"

"You think the cult attacked a temple in the middle of the desert in a city nobody's heard of? Yeah Voske, that makes sense."

"I'm not saying it makes sense, just this rotting mire makes me think cult."

Weylyn narrowed her eyes. Along the left wall lay a pile of scales as big as dinner plates. They were midnight black and dry to the touch and the pile stretched deeper into the tunnel by at least thirty feet. She snatched one from the pile and the sound clattered off the walls with a scratchy echo. It was hard as a stone, unbending in her hands.

A sharp inhale pulled her attention back to the group. Locin was rubbing a hand along her spine and looking nervous. "Son of a serpent."

The rest turned to look at her and Voske folded his arms. "What's wrong?"

"We're not alone in here."

As she spoke a sound echoed from somewhere in the dark. It wasn't a footstep, more of a scuffing noise, as though someone's body was being dragged through the burrow ahead of them.

"Did anyone else hear that?" Illeri asked, shrinking toward the entrance.

"It's an animal," Weylyn answered.

They all looked at her sharply.

"Something large. Scaled. Something that can dig."

"Gods!" Hikari said. "Are you trying to scare us, darling?"

"It's working," Illeri whispered.

Hikari shone his light further into the tunnels. They were dripping wet. "I mean. What are the odds the Crook is even here anymore?"

Weylyn stared back down the tunnel and called on her boon, feeling the burning in her eyes. She blinked away reality, and her vision filled with the inside of the burrow. She was standing further in, at a dead end, and in front of her lay two relics, a mirror, and the head of a staff. They glowed with the light of Sbarga, and nestled around them were five eggs, each the size of a man's head. The floor here was covered in sludge. It ran thick along the walls and dripped from the ceiling, coating the white shells. And behind her she could feel a presence slithering in the dark.

"It's here," she said as the vision retreated.

Hikari cleared his throat and pulled at the strap of the water skin. "Well, at least we don't have to guess about it."

"Any idea where?" Voske asked, striding forward to Weylyn's side.

Hikari pointed the light toward each passage as she glanced around the interior. Most of the recent tunnels were lightly used, jutting away from the main path, but one near the far end was coated black.

"This way." She waved their party forward and heard them shuffling nervously behind her. "Keep your voices low," she hissed, "and the more light the better, it can probably smell us in the dark."

"Maybe we should notify the temple," Illeri whispered from the back.

"And let them take the credit?" Voske grumbled. "Like Nyx."

"It's alright, darling. Just stay close to me."

"Quiet," Weylyn snapped.

She crouched as they reached the sodden tunnel. Here the rank odor of musk clogged the air until Weylyn raised the neck of her tunic, covering her nose against the scent.

"*This* tunnel?" Hikari questioned.

"Yes."

"By Desita, these were new shoes."

Locin moved up to Weylyn's side, her wide pupils staring into the darkened passage. She was holding out a hand in front of her and groping the air. "There's something back there," she hissed. "Gods, it feels like a stone."

"Might it just be stone?" Illeri asked.

"Then it wouldn't be breathing."

Weylyn picked up a loose piece of rubble from the floor and tossed it into the darkness, listening to the soft squish as it lodged in the sludge ahead. "How far ahead?" She asked.

"I'm not sure."

"Fine. Come on." She looked back over her shoulder at the others. They were standing at the ready, Hikari's light blooming above his hand, and behind them loomed a shadow. It was taller than a man, with scales of onyx and dark feathers spreading from its neck. The tip of its tail spread out like a caudal fin and its forked tongue flicked hungrily toward the light.

"Look out!" Weylyn yelled, and she quickly swung her bow toward the creature, loosing an arrow toward its serpentine eye.

It reared back, and the arrow plinked harmlessly off its scales.

"God's and Chosen!"

The others quickly spun around and Hikari's light barely caught the body of the beast, gliding along the slippery floor without a sound. Weylyn stared hard at the scally back. There was a chink in it's armor, a wound, not much larger than the hilt of a knife barely a yard behind its head.

"Kissandin, watch over us," Illeri whimpered.

Voske ran after it, but it had disappeared into a side passage with frightening speed. "What in Nyx was that thing?"

"We should leave," Illeri stammered.

"When we're so close?"

"We can come back later."

Voske whirled around, his eyes pinched tight. "It ran away, you saw that. It's just as scared as you are."

Hikari lifted a trembling finger. "I'm, uh, not so sure of that, darling."

"Weylyn? What do you think?"

Weylyn called up her boon, but all that greeted her eyes was the same vision as last time. Two relics, waiting at the bottom of the burrow. "Keep a keen eye," she said, then stepped into the dark.

The deeper tunnel sloped down at a shallow angle, and her feet slipped as she crept through the muck. Hikari's light was just as bright here, but somehow it seemed lessened by the black walls of the tunnel, until it felt as though they were creeping through the cold dark with only the light of a single star pulsing from their midst.

They pressed deeper, turning one last corner before they finally saw another glow, the gentle gold of a relic deep within the bowels.

"There it is," Voske called, far louder than Weylyn approved. "Come on!"

They eased their way toward the light, slipping their way through until they reached a dead end, just as Weylyn had seen, but there was no other presence here now.

"Found your rotting nest, Weylyn," Locin whispered, staring down at the relics.

"Let's be glad they're not hatched," Hikari mused.

"I don't know, maybe the babies are cute."

"Well, if you want a pet, go ahead and grab one, but don't ask me to sit it for you."

Weylyn picked up the head of the Crook, a simple wooden curve that came to a sharp break, and upon it were inscribed the words 'The darkness of night'.

Hikari leaned down, peering into the mirror. "I wonder why they were left behind?"

"Just hurry," Illeri said

Weylyn quickly stuffed both relics into her satchel then took her bow back off her shoulder. "Out we go."

She moved for the exit but stopped at a loud cracking sound from behind them. They all wheeled to see Voske standing over the eggs with a rock. The shells had been smashed open and yolk was spilling onto the ground.

"Voske," Locin snapped. "What in Nyx?"

He tossed the stone to the floor and strode back toward the front of the group. "Ready."

"Gods, no. Are you *trying* to make them mad?"

"They're animals, and dangerous ones."

"Yeah, that's kinda my point, idiot."

He stepped back toward her with a sour expression. "We're champions. We don't leave problems for other people."

Locin slapped her open palm against her forehead. "Gods, it's like talking to a monkey sometimes. We're in the middle of a desert!"

"And?"

"And we're kinda the only people around for a hundred miles!"

"Shhh," Weylyn scowled at both of them.

She crouched again and started for the exit as they sullenly fell in line, but she was even more on edge. Walking up through the sludge was considerably harder than going down, and she had to return her bow to her back, going down on her hands and knees and clawing her way to make any progress.

Behind, she could hear the others, cursing the ground as it slipped under their feet. Their hands sank into the sludge, and their legs burned until they reached the top of the incline, where the air grew just barely fresher.

Weylyn tugged her shirt down from over her nose, choking in a mouthful of putrid air as she propped her hands on her knees. "Remind me," she called back. "Not to come along next time."

Voske laughed aloud. "And miss all the fun?"

"Some of us are too old for this."

"Some?" He scowled playfully. "You're including me in this?"

"Fine. One of us."

Locin finally scrambled to the top, followed quickly by Hikari and Illeri, and Weylyn breathed a sigh of relief. "Let's hurry."

Ahead of them, the deep slope exited back into the main corridor and Weylyn could see the crumbled remains of the reliquary wall. She started striding forward, but her feet suddenly shifted beneath her, and she felt herself dragged back.

She snatched the bow from her back and spun around, seeing Locin with her arms raised. The young woman's eyes were wide with alarm, and she pointed toward the exit, where a heavy slithering sound could be heard.

"Gods and Chosen," Hikari breathed.

Just in front of them, blocking the way out, a feathered serpent rose. Its feathers spread out to either side, filling the passage, and its tongue flicked toward Weylyn in ominous quiet.

Illeri screamed and the sound of scuffling feet sounded behind, but Weylyn kept her eyes straight ahead, studying the serpent's movement. Its body was slowly coiling as it watched and waited.

"Is there another way out?" Hikari yelled.

"No," Locin answered.

"Marvelous."

"Then we go forward," Voske growled. He strode to Weylyn's side and pounded his fist into his open palm.

"Through that?"

"Through that."

"Voske," Weylyn snapped. "Be careful."

He bore down on the monster, his fists ready, and it jolted toward him. For being so big it was frighteningly fast. Its maw snapped like a thunderbolt, but he caught hold of its teeth, holding the dripping fangs only inches from his skin.

Weylyn raised her bow to fire, but the snake pulled back, recoiling and staring at him with that same deadly expression.

"See if you can run past!" He yelled.

Weylyn ducked a bit closer, searching the length of the serpent's body, but there was no sign of the chink she'd seen earlier.

"We're hardly going to leave you behind, darling."

"To be fair, I would," Locin said. "I can't get by."

Voske glanced over his shoulder with a scowl as the snake struck again. He barely caught it this time, and his muscles rippled as he forced its mouth open. "Can't you boon it out of the way?"

"Boon it?" Locin chided. "That's what we're calling it?"

"Just *do something!*"

Weylyn kept staring until she was sure. The chink in it's scales wasn't there. This wasn't the same serpent.

A sudden cry pierced the tunnel behind and the light went dark.

Hikari.

She wheeled around as the sound of a mad scramble filled the tunnel, and she felt a spray of liquid slosh across her feet.

"Hikari!" Illeri screamed, but the sound came from everywhere at once, mingled with the thrashing of the great serpent and Hikari's own voice, crying for help.

Weylyn dashed backward, following the tumult and reached into her pack, seizing hold of the mirror and pulling it out. It wasn't much light, but in the encompassing dark of the burrow it lit up the walls and reflected off the onyx scales, just ahead of her.

"Weylyn!" Hikari yelled as he saw the light. He was being dragged backward, through the muck, helpless against the power of the beast.

Please. Weylyn thought. *Please give me a target.*

She threw the mirror and watched as the light spiraled down the tunnel, landing just beside the great serpent's body, and the glow glinted off the flaw in its armor.

"Weylyn!"

She charged forward and slid through the ooze, gliding along the slick as she drew her bow taut. She passed just under the eyes of the great serpent and fired.

The arrow drove deep into the chink in its scales, and it quickly squirmed back, letting Hikari tumble to the ground.

"Come on!" She yelled, snatching him up to his feet. "Run!"

He gathered the meager light from the relic and shone it forth, revealing the others waiting in the passage ahead. The second serpent lay at Voske's feet, its neck had been crushed, and its body was lifeless.

"Come on!" Voske yelled, waving them ahead. "Are you alright?"

"Lovely," Hikari called back, but there was an obvious tremor in his voice. "Let's make our exit, shall we?"

They charged back the way they'd come, rushing out into the main corridor and back through the reliquary, finally bursting into the blinding light of the outside where they risked pausing to breathe.

Weylyn glanced back to where Hikari stood. His arm was bleeding from a nasty scrape and his side was soaking wet, but he was alive.

Voske walked closer and set a hand on his shoulder. He laughed. "Now that's what I call a win!"

Hikari nodded shakily.

Weylyn slowly let her gaze wander the group. They were red-faced, panting, and smeared with grime.

"Come on then," Voske said. "Outside's not getting any cooler."

"About that," Hikari answered. He pulled the water skin from his back and let it fall to the ground. It hit the sand with a weak flop, completely empty.

"Wonderful," Locin whined. "I was about to ask you for that."

"How far away is Bravesh?" Weylyn asked.

"Another five hours," Illeri answered, and her voice still sounded weak. "In the heat of the day, that's not going to be fun."

"Do we just stay here then?"

Locin wrinkled her nose. "In this mire?"

"No," Voske answered. "We're leaving, but not for Bravesh."

Hikari raised an eyebrow. "Somewhere else you have in mind?"

Voske grinned. "I told you before. I know a place near here."

"The quarry?" Hikari said in a dubious tone.

"Not just the quarry. The best rotting watering hole in the Varrin."

33: The Story Circle

The library of Strah was a marvel of Talamh. It rose three stories, the walls lined with rich palm wood, and endless shelves packed with more tomes than Zengin had ever seen in one place. The center of the room had been cleared, leaving a wide open marble floor that glistened in the light of the sun as it showered through the glass ceiling. All around the edges of the room an ornate polished rail fenced in the second and third floors where more books and scrolls were on display. Golden lights hung down from above like suspended pylats, shimmering as the sun drifted toward the horizon, and the sky grew deep blue overhead. On the first floor, hundreds mingled, and Zengin had no doubt thousands more were gathered outside in the streets where the people celebrated the Chosen of their gods. Nearby, dozens of well dressed congregants were filing onto the second floor balcony from two sets of golden stairs.

"It's starting, I think." Rasa said. "They said sunset."

Burz sighed. "And no sign of the others. Again." He dropped his hands to his hips in frustration. "Voske I expect this from, but Weylyn?"

Rasa leaned out over the rail, watching the people below. They were sorting themselves into groups of fifteen to twenty, standing in circles facing one another. "What are they doing?"

The last thing Zengin wanted was to dredge up old memories. Zengin the boy, standing in a circle with the other guildlings of Strah as they told stories of home and family. And then poor little Zengin telling his lies.

"Story circles." He practically spit out the words like bile.

"What are story circles?"

Torture.

"It's a long standing tradition of the followers of Strah," he said. "To share your history, you must be truthful and demonstrate who you really are."

The voice of Aurilis broke in. "Which is exactly what you're going to do." Gillis stood at her elbow, and behind them on the widest part of the balcony a circle was forming with the stuffiest of the guests. *Their* circle. "We are short five Champions, including Strah's, and it's imperative that you are well received here."

"And why is that?" Burz was snippier than usual. Zengin hadn't missed his fight with Hadris on the chariot ride. Even a dullard could have picked up on it.

"Because, Champion, you are losing the support of temples and guilds. I don't need to remind you how serious that is. Gillis has informed the people that the others were detained and may join us later. The official presentation of the Champion of Strah and the festival proper will begin in a couple of hours once the star of Strah appears." She pointed to the domed glass ceiling that filled most of the center of the room. "Gods willing, Strah's Chosen will be here by then."

Aurilis led the champions to the wide balcony. Burz took a spot by the back wall, his back to the shelves of books, and the guests started closing in around him. To the untrained eye it might look like polite nobles lining up, but Zengin saw it for what it was. Scheming serpents jostling for the positions closest to Champions. Zengin held off, to the dismay of many sycophants that watched him greedily. He entered the circle last, forcing a beady-eyed Bureaucrat to move so he could stand beside Burz. He knew how to play the game. Rasa was crammed by the railing across from Zengin looking like a mouse in a trap.

A stuffy man in a gold trimmed toga and pompous headdress came forward with an insincere smile, but Zengin didn't miss the mortified look he was hiding in his eyes. Zengin didn't know where Weylyn was, or why, but he was glad she was gone, and he got to watch them squirm.

The man in the headdress held a simple brass goblet aloft. "Ordinarily, the Champion of Strah would choose the first storyteller." He cleared his throat nervously, and then started glancing around the circle, as if deciding what to do. His eyes happened to land on a large man whose toga was tucked around his enormous gut. He had a tuft of curly gray hair that sat frazzled atop his head, and the moment his eyes met him in passing, he gave a shout and rushed forward.

"You think that I should begin?" He snatched the goblet as the man glared at him, and the other guests huffed. "What an honor!"

The man in the headdress begrudgingly held his hands up and addressed the crowd, plastering another smile on his face. "Let us share our histories with truth and sincerity! May Strah favor our stories!"

He slunk back to his spot in the circle, and the other man lifted the goblet. He opened his mouth to drink, but suddenly a voice interrupted and he looked perturbed as he searched for the source. It was Burz.

"What is the significance of the goblet?"

The group started to murmur until they noticed it was the Champion of Uthando who spoke.

The man with the ridiculous headdress stepped forward again with a polite smile. "Apologies, Champion. We should have explained our tradition. This goblet is a relic."

Burz was frowning. "I could tell as much."

"Of course. More specifically, it is the goblet of Jeza. Anyone who drinks the wine from this goblet must tell the truth."

"That seems a powerful tool. Is it always kept in Bravesh?"

The group was clearly antsy, but no one would accuse a champion of delaying the festivities, so they bit down their pride, and the man in the headdress answered again.

"It's kept in a vault and pulled out for festivals such as this."

Burz scoffed. "That's a trivial use for a sacred relic."

The man's smile wavered. "Perhaps. And yet, some might say a celebration of the gods themselves and their divinely chosen champions, is the most important use of such a relic. Don't you agree?"

Burz grunted a reply.

The man looked flabbergasted as he stared around the circle for a moment before turning back to the fat man. "Continue then!"

The fat man looked slightly annoyed at his prestigious moment being interrupted, but he gladly placed the goblet to his lips and took a sip. And then he began.

"I am Feridas of house Vrie, most esteemed leader of the Jeweler's Guild of Erimos proper."

Zengin clenched a fist. If he knew one thing, it was that people who introduced themselves as *most esteemed* were the lowest kind of scum Talamh had to offer.

A woman flicked at her toga, sending the hanging gems that encircled her skirt clattering against one another. "Tell me true, Feridas, where were you born?"

"I was born in Anra'Dor, where I spent my youth in the pursuit of much pleasure and very little knowledge."

Giggles erupted from the group, and one man raised a hand as he spoke. "Tell me true, Feridas, what was your favorite pleasure of them all?"

Feridas' lips curled in a wicked smile. "Leoma. Beautiful as a delicate spring flower. Though, there was nothing delicate about her in bed." He chuckled as the other participants feigned shock between smiles and giggles.

He blathered on from there for another few minutes about his guilding, and how he became a powerful and wealthy jeweler, and eventually guild leader. Every so often he would be interrupted with a question, many of which delved more into his less than reputable pursuits. Zengin found the whole thing distasteful in the most familiar way.

"Alright, Feridas!" The man in the headdress called at last. "Perhaps it's time for another to tell their story?"

This went on for a few more rounds, each story teller growing more brash and boorish. Zengin was used to this, but he could sense the revulsion building in Burz. He smirked, guessing how long before Burz put an end to the vulgar display.

"Chosen of Bei'ai!" Called the woman holding the goblet now, a spindly hag with cold eyes and a colder smile.

Rasa looked most out of place of all, pressed against the rail and wringing her hands nervously. Her already pale skin blanched as the woman strolled through the middle of the circle.

"Perhaps it is time to hear from a Champion? Would you like that?"

The group gave a cheer as the woman held the goblet in front of Rasa. She looked up with terror written on her face, and suddenly Zengin's humor soured. This was no longer a game. It was deliberate, conniving. They could see Rasa's discomfort plain as day. It didn't surprise him that this vile woman sought to extort secrets from a champion. It had been a long time since any noble truly feared or respected the gods and their chosen.

Rasa hesitantly took the goblet and sipped. "I'm, uh, Rasa."

A wicked looking woman beside her leaned over with a tone meant to be motherly, but it made Zengin's skin crawl. "Tell us your position, dear."

"Champion of Bei'ai. I was born on Erimos."

"Tell us true!" Shouted a skinny man across the way. "How old are you, dear Champion? You can't be but a cycle!"

"Fourteen years," she said nervously.

Gasps went up with a smattering of laughter and a 'so very young!'

"Tell us true, what was your guilding?"

"I had no guilding. I was never taken to be guilded."

The nobles talked amongst themselves now as they studied her curiously.

Zengin tensed. He knew enough of her history to know where this was headed. This whole display was making him sick, and he felt an overwhelming desire to be anywhere else.

"Tell us true, then. What did you do before becoming a Champion?"

"Tell me true!" Zengin yelled as he stepped out into the circle. He strolled to Rasa and took the goblet from her as the crowd grew silent and stared at him. "Is it a child you wish to manipulate? Do you fear a true challenge?" He held the brass goblet aloft and studied it in the light before tipping it to his lips and drinking. The wine was sweet, and he felt it rush to his head like a cold wind.

"Champion," gasped the little man in the headdress as he scurried forward. "This is quite outside of tradition."

Zengin stared down at the man with dark eyes. "And I know how much you love your traditions. You see, I am Zengin, Champion of Metnadur. I grew up the son of an Archon in Tajerim. I am all too familiar with your games and your politics." He held up his left hand with the goblet, walking the circle. "Have you no questions? Surely you must want to know something."

Those gathered looked from one to another. He had taken the reins, and they clearly didn't like it.

"Nothing?" He stopped in front of a pompous man with a golden laurel on his bald head. "You! What would you ask a Champion?"

The man scowled. "Tell me true, are you a true champion?"

Zengin sneered. "I was chosen of Metnadur, called and marked with the sigil of my god."

"Tell me true," called another trembling voice, "where is your sigil now?"

"Rotting on a floor of stone, red with my blood."

The circle grew uncomfortably quiet, and the man with the headdress stepped forward again. "Perhaps we've heard enough stories for this evening."

"Have you heard enough already?" Zengin asked. "Fine. Then perhaps I'll ask you questions instead."

A nervous murmur spread through the crowd.

"Champion-"

"Tell me true!" Zengin said. "Did you honestly believe I wouldn't see through this farce? Did you think you could push and press the chosen of the gods, to deceive and manipulate? That is what you're best at."

It was Aurilis' turn to object. "You've made your point, Champion!"

"Have I? My lips have tasted the wine of this relic. I can speak no lies, so hear me true! I have lived among people like you my whole life. I have seen the true depths of your depravity. You sit in your golden palaces above the rest, better than. And yet there are none in Talamh so vile, so bloodied and vulgar as you!"

"Enough!" Yelled the man in the headdress, forgetting himself for a moment. "How dare you insult us?"

"Insult?" Zengin countered. "But I can speak nothing but truth. So when I tell you of the Archon of Del'pha who strangled the life from a guild master who refused to work around the tariffs for him, or of the Master of the Groundskeepers guild of Arrajin who bought slaves by the dozens-"

"Zengin!" Aurilis snapped.

He raised his voice so it carried to the whole room, and the story circles below grew quiet. "Or what of the noble in my own home of Tajerim who raped his servant and drove a knife through the heart of his child to hide the affair! Tell me true, are you any different than they?"

Silence answered him. As he expected. Their faces were a wash with rage that masked their shame. Zengin tipped the brass goblet and poured the wine out on the marble floor, letting the empty cup drop with a clang. "This charade is over."

He caught sight of Rasa as he turned to march out of the circle. In a sea of confused and horrified faces, she alone looked grateful. He had a thousand thoughts rush to his mind, playing across his face in a parade of emotion. Grief. Sorrow. Shame. She saw them all, and some recognition lit in her eyes. She met him with her own shame before dropping her gaze to the floor.

Aurilis was already striding toward Zengin to meet him, but he had nothing to say. He held a hand to silence her and walked past. He was done.

34: Lorhk's

The late afternoon sun baked Voske's skin as he wrangled his hair together, tying it with a bit of string. Nothing felt more familiar than stepping off a sand skiff to the sight of stone homes and simple shops clustered together across the rocky ground of Govere. The whole town was home to less than five hundred souls, and nearly a third of them were quarry men.

At the center of town, an arched stone shrine stood in the open air with a towering statue of Jeza in all her glory. At her feet stood a well, and all around it, the bulk of the buildings spread out like the spokes of a wagon wheel. Off toward the north was Lorhk's, and further on Voske's old house, and eventually the quarry.

"This is it?" Locin said with a disappointed tone.

"I'd say she's more than she seems, but she's not."

"It's simple." Weylyn was smiling. "I like it."

Voske smiled as he strolled forward under the shade of the well's gazebo and pulled the bucket up with ease, taking a deep drink. He held it out for Illeri.

Illeri had her eyes on the sky where the sun was sliding toward the western horizon. "We should hurry. We might still make it in time for some of the festival." She carefully dipped a cupped hand in the bucket and took a gulp, then Weylyn drank heartily.

"Come on!" Locin said. "You can't bring us all the way here and not show us the sights. Who cares if we're a little late."

Hikari took the bucket next and lifted it to his lips. "Well to be fair, we still need a new waterskin, not to mention a meal. I suppose if we see a bit of the town along the way, it wouldn't hurt." He passed the bucket to Locin, and she drank greedily.

"There's only one thing you need to see in Govere." Voske folded his arms and gave them the most serious look he could muster. "Lorhk's."

"Lorhk's?"

He smiled. "Lorhk's."

They took a minute to wash up in the well water, and then headed out. On the outskirts of Govere, past the well and the shops and the clustered homes, Lorhk's straddled the edge of the desert. It was little more than four pillars with one wall and a rickety wooden roof that sprawled over the desert sand. The ground inside was packed hard as stone from the constant flow of patrons, and five tables were scattered around, each a different shape and size. Along the wall was a long counter where Lorhk stood wiping a spill with an old gray cloth.

"Lorhk's?" Hikari asked with an intrigued smile.

Voske nodded. "Best place for a bite to eat and a draught of ale on all Erimos."

Locin smiled as she strolled inside, a hand on her hip. "I like it!"

"It's magnificent, darling. It reminds me of stories I've heard of places like this. I half expect some assassin to be lurking in the corner or something."

Locin slapped his arm. "This is Voske's home! It's not seedy. It's *quaint*. Trust me, I know seedy."

"I only meant it's got a certain quality about it, like something from an adventure story."

Voske laughed, a laugh like he hadn't laughed since he left Erimos. He felt comfortable. He felt home.

"What's this?" yelled the rumbling voice of Lorkh. "I know that laugh. Gods and Chosen!" He left the counter and made his way over, slapping Voske on the arm. Lorhk was nearly the same height as Voske, but flabby and scruffy, donning a dingy stained tunic that may have once been white. He had one eye that always trailed off to the right. "If it isn't the mighty Voske, step foot back in my little watering hole! Never thought we'd see the likes of you 'round here again. Too high and mighty for us little folk."

Voske squared his shoulders and smiled wryly. "I'll always make time for the little folk."

Lorhk turned toward the farthest corner of the tavern and called, "Klief, Rix, look who the gods dragged in!"

"More friends of yours?" Weylyn asked.

The two men came over with smiles and surprise written on their faces.

"Mire and Nyx!" Rix shook his head.

Klief held out a hand and grabbed Voske's arm. "This is something. I'd wager it's the first time a Champion's ever set foot in Govere, huh?"

"That's a safe bet." Voske was sure no previous Champion even knew Govere existed.

"What have you brought us?" Rix asked, eyeing the others as Locin stepped out and smiled broadly.

"My fellow champions," Voske said with mock sternness. "So mind your manners, boys!"

"Men," Rix corrected, winking at Locin.

She smiled playfully at him, and then turned her eyes to the bar.

Lorhk gasped loudly. "Champions? Here? When word spreads… Well, I don't know what I'll do. I won't be able to keep up anymore. You've doomed me, Voske!"

Voske laughed. "You'll have to hire some help. And maybe you can finally afford some walls!"

"Well, is this a watering hole or not?" Weylyn said as she strolled toward the bar. "How about some drinks?"

"And food," Illeri added quickly. "We're in a hurry to get to Bravesh."

"Right," Klief said with a wry smile. "Some big to do about a festival there for some fancy folk."

"It starts tonight," Illeri continued. "We told the others we'd meet them there."

"Others?" Rix asked.

"Other champions."

"Mighty Skard! Of course there's others. All eight at the festivals? Why didn't we go to these blasted things, Klief?"

"Eh." He waved a hand dismissively. "We aren't fancy enough for festivals, Rix. Best we stay in the desert where we belong."

Voske laughed. "Woulda said the same about me not long ago. Maybe Champions aren't as fancy as you think. Mire! You got five of 'em here."

"Five!" Lorhk was still reeling.

"So rushing off then?" Klief pointed to their small table in the corner where a deck of cards and a few coins were scattered about. "Shame you can't stay for a hand or two, for old times' sake."

"Well, we gotta eat and get some water before taking the skiff to Bravesh. I suppose a quick game or two while Lorhk's getting us set." He looked back at the others, and Weylyn nodded. "If the Champion of Strah says it's okay, who are we to argue?"

Rix just stared wide-eyed at Weylyn and shook his head.

Hikari was beaming at the news. "Excellent! I tell you, it's just like an adventure story!"

Kleif, Rix and Voske set to work pushing two of the small tables together as Lorhk headed back behind the counter.

"I could do with a little wine," Illeri said timidly, drawing a smirk from Lorhk.

Rix laughed. "Sorry, lass. Lorkh here don't do wines. Meads and liquor, sure, but nothing fancy or fruity. Just good, earthy stuff."

"Give 'em your special," Klief yelled.

"Water for me," Voske called.

At once Lorhk grabbed five large mugs as easily as if it'd been one and retrieved a wooden pitcher from behind him on a shelf. He filled four of the cups mostly full from the pitcher, a sandy gold liquid. Lorkh retrieved a decanter of a deep brown liquor that smelled like almond when he pulled the stopper, splashing a healthy dose in each mug. The last mug he filled with cold, clear water, and slid to Voske.

Voske lifted it gladly, and drank as Hikari took one of the meads.

"Honey mead," Hikari mused, staring down at the mug. "And the dark liquor?" He glanced hopefully at Lorkh.

"Strong," came the gruff reply. "Very strong."

Voske lifted his cup and glanced down the line at the others. "Drink up, friends! You won't find better anywhere on Erimos."

"Noticed you're not touching it," Hikari said, warily.

Voske pointed at the cards on the table. "Gotta stay sharp."

Locin was already halfway through her drink by the time she sauntered to the table.

Hikari wandered over to Rix who sat shuffling, and he pointed at the cards. "The artwork on these is quite unique."

The scrawny man looked up, taking in Hikari's appearance, no hair on his chin, chest, or legs.

"I've a bit of a collection."

Rix laughed overly loud. "What's this, Voske? You brought us a smoothy? This in't no place for one o' you. Might get dirty."

Hikari simply grinned as Voske shot a fist out, hitting Rix in the arm. The yelp from Rix told him it might have been harder than intended, but he didn't regret it.

"Watch your tongue!" Klief snapped. "That there's a Champion."

"Aye, and a smoothy."

"It's fine, darling. I assure you, I've been called worse."

Hikari headed for a seat by Illeri, but Voske stepped between them and steered him toward a seat by Locin. He wasn't gonna let him be a coward forever.

"You sit here." Voske winked, as he shoved Hikari down on the seat, and Locin stared up at him questioningly.

"You're getting weirder, old man."

Klief was studying Hikari now, a glint of recognition in his eye. "You're not just a Champion. You're Hikari. I saw you a half year back in Irys. *Skard and the Dreylyn Wars*?"

Hikari gave a dramatic bow with one arm.

"What are you on about?" Rix said disdainfully.

"He's famous."

"'Course he is. He's a Champion!"

"Before that! Anyone's seen a play in their life knows him."

"Well, I never seen a play." Rix spat on the ground. "So who's in for cards?"

"Me," Locin called.

"I'll play." Weylyn slid into the chair beside Illeri. Her bow never left her back, and she sat forward on her seat as if she might need to get up and sprint away in a moment. Voske wondered if she ever fully relaxed.

"Oh, I'll watch," Illeri quickly added, staring down at her still full mug.

"Game's Monk's Folly," Kleif said as he gathered the cards. "Familiar with it?"

Locin and Weylyn nodded, but Hikari shook his head.

"It's Gryph's Nest," Voske said, "only nines are the full card instead of gryphs."

"Ah, simple enough."

"Since when do you play smoothy games?" Rix asked with a narrow gaze.

"He hasn't always lived on Erimos you know," Kleif chided.

Voske felt a sudden uneasiness at the words as all the others glanced at him.

"You cutting the line?" Rix asked, eyes widening a bit.

"Hadn't he ever told you?"

"He didn't tell us either," Locin said.

"Where else did you live?" Rix pressed. "I thought you was guilded straight way to the Erimos laborer's. You work someplace else?"

The table got suddenly quiet, and Voske frowned, kicking himself for ever letting that slip to Kleif.

"Leave him be," Klief said. "Don't matter if he wasn't born here. He's one of us."

Voske clenched his fist, hoping no one would notice Klief's second slip. But they did. Of course.

"Voske *was* born on Erimos." Illeri said.

Klief looked up wide-eyed as he realized his mistake. "Did I say he wasn't?"

"You did." Rix scowled.

Voske shrugged. "I've lived here so long, it sure feels like it."

Illeri was frowning deeply. "You told us on the skiff you were born on Erimos."

Voske gulped down some water, and then met her gaze. "I let you believe that. That's not the same thing as saying it."

"A lie of omission then," Hikari said.

Rix shuffled the cards. "Where *was* you born? Las?"

"Erimos is my home, always will be."

"That don't answer my question," Rix mumbled as he dealt the cards.

Voske grabbed Locin's hand as she went to pick her cards up. "No cheating!"

She shot back a wry smile.

"It's common to leave the place you're born," Weylyn said.

"Gods, I did!" Locin was busy sorting her cards now. "I left as fast as I could."

"Common to lie about it too?" Rix grumbled.

Hikari had the first play. He slipped a four onto the pile. "I left home to join the player's guild on Suntara. I have no regrets."

Illeri shot a glance at Hikari. "I thought you were born on Suntara."

Hikari coughed. "Did I say that?"

Voske lifted his cards to cover his face, grateful he wasn't the one in trouble anymore.

Hikari quickly recovered, donning his easy smile again. "Well, darling, it's hard to keep track of all the places I've been."

Locin laughed. "Was anybody telling the truth on the skiff?"

Illeri looked perturbed. "I was." She stared down into her still full mug, swirling the contents.

"It's quite strong," Hikari said. "You don't have to-"

In a brazen moment of defiance that impressed Voske, she lifted the mug and gulped half of it down in one go. She came up spluttering like a drowning dog at the end.

Kleif laughed. "Gods and Chosen! She'll be feeling that tomorrow."

Rix slammed down a seven as he glared toward Voske. "Born on Las?"

Voske set his face like stone as he looked over his own cards.

"Had to be Las," Rix pressed, unwilling to let it go even in his relatively sober state. "No way you were ever a smoothy."

"Sorry for my friend's lack of manners," Kleif said as he glanced at Hikari. "He's never been out of Govere, as far as I know, but he sure doesn't like Suntarans."

"I've been outta Govere plenty. I've even been on Suntara once. Snooty know-it-alls think they're better than the rest of us."

Klief smacked Rix hard on the arm before turning to apologize to Hikari again.

"Well," he said with a sheepish glance toward Illeri, "we just established I'm not really Suntaran, so I suppose it doesn't apply to me."

Rix slammed his cards down on the table. "I'll play when Voske answers, not before."

"Gods!" Voske yelled in frustration. "Does it make a difference if I was born on Suntara? It's not my home now. Nothing left for me there." He shot an angry glance at Kleif. "Last time I tell you secrets."

Rix started with a laugh that grew louder and sounded almost like a wail at the end. "Our Voske, baby smooth and dainty, loafing in the sun? Hard picture to conjure, that!"

“Eh,” Kleif said with a sidelong spit on the dirt floor. “He's still Voske. Finest foreman we ever had. Don't make a lick of difference to me where he was born.”

“Look, I left that life behind me when I joined the Laborer’s Guild.” Voske caught sight of Locin for a moment, tapping a finger methodically. She paused and then smiled, nodding as if to herself. “Gods, you're already cheating, aren't you?”

She looked up at him, wounded eyes at odds with the wry smile at the corners of her mouth. “Voske! I’m a respectable Champion, and a lady no less.”

“And a dirty cheater,” he muttered. He stroked his beard as he picked up his own cards.

Rix threw a card half heartedly on the stack. “Suntara,” he muttered. “What kind of labor do they even have on Suntara? No quarries there, right?”

“None I’m aware of,” Hikari said.

“There’s labor everywhere,” Kleif said coolly, picking up his mug and drinking deep.

“He said he moved to Erimos when he became a laborer,” Weylyn said flatly. They all looked toward her, and she shrugged. “He just said it.”

Voske felt his heart sink.

“What?” Rix asked.

“He said he left that life behind when he became a laborer. I assumed he meant the life he had on Suntara.”

“Gods.” Locin laughed.

Kleif frowned. “You told me you were two cycles when you left Suntara. If you weren’t a laborer, what did you do for all those years?”

“I worked.”

“Doing what though?”

Voske shrugged. “Working with stone. Making buildings.”

“But you weren’t a laborer.”

Voske was completely exasperated by now. He had lived nearly sixteen years on Erimos without anyone knowing about his former life.

“Wait.” Illeri looked up at him as if she’d solved a puzzle. He’d seen that look before, and he’d never seen her solve one wrong. “You were an architect?”

He sighed.

"How do you figure?" Hikari asked.

"He just said he made buildings. And the lintels."

"Yes!" Locin yelled. "The lintels! I knew he shouldn't know that!"

Voske shrugged. "So what? I was an architect." It felt almost painful to say the word, like dragging up every hard memory from that life and staring at it.

"Mire and Nyx!" Kleif let out a low whistle.

"That's a prestigious position," Hikari said. "I knew a couple architects on Suntara. Talk about wealth!"

"Architect?" Rix said, raising an eyebrow. "That's not even the Laborer's Guild."

Kleif leaned in close, catching Voske's eye. "How in the world do you go from one of the most prestigious jobs on Suntara to a quarry foreman in the armpit of Erimos?"

"You weren't a laborer?" Rix said in a wounded tone.

"No," Voske mouthed the word dryly, not able or willing to give any more explanation at the moment. "It was a long time ago, another life. And now, I'm a Champion."

They were all looking at him like he was a stranger, Klief, Rix, even Lorhk, like they didn't even know him. Maybe this wasn't home anymore either. He wasn't an architect. He wasn't a quarryman. He was a Champion, or so he'd been told.

"People don't just change their guilding," Weylyn said in an even tone. "Did you lose it?"

"Can the gods do that?" Hikari asked with wide eyes. "Can they take your guilding and reguild you?"

"They're the gods," Voske mused, as if they were discussing someone other than himself. "I imagine they can do whatever they rotting want."

"Hm," Kleif grunted, lifting his mug for another long draught. "Any reason you never told us about this?"

Voske shrugged. "It never came up."

"A smoothy," Rix said. "Not just a smoothy, a fancy one with lots of money."

"So you lied?" Illeri was scowling deeply.

"Is everyone gonna be mad at me? Look, I'm sorry I didn't tell you I was from Suntara. Mire and Nyx!"

"You both lied." Illeri glanced toward Hikari.

Hikari ran a hand through his hair as he laughed nervously. "Ah, yes. I did grow up on Suntara, at the player's guild. So it wasn't fully a lie."

"Oof," Kleif grimaced. "Not the best answer, friend."

Hikari looked like he was scrambling for another when Lorhk strolled over with five steaming plates of Govere's finest - roast hyppogryph and a dressed salad. Plain, hearty food. The smell of it brought a rush of fond memories over Voske's mind.

Hikari leapt from his seat and grabbed a plate, handing it to Locin. "Excellent timing, darling. Excellent timing."

Illeri was looking flushed now as she sloshed her mug around a bit. Hikari set the plate in front of her and she sniffed the meat. "I haven't had gryph in years."

"Gryph?" Hikari's eyes went wide. "This is hyppogryph?"

Lorhk nodded proudly. "The finest."

Voske poked at the tender meat. He didn't have much of an appetite.

"Maybe we should just head to Bravesh." Illeri sighed.

"Hey!" Locin said around a mouthful of food. "I'm starving, besides, we're in the middle of a game!" She set down her fork and pulled out her coin purse, jingling it. "So, whose turn was it?"

35: Truth Be Told

Burz stared out the tall arched window of the library of Strah at the streets below. The mood inside had turned dour since the story circles had ended, but outside revelers ate and drank and raised cheers to Strah and his chosen. He'd lost track of Hadris and the boys somewhere in the endless hours of small talk, and that was fine by him. He'd been too harsh on her, obviously, but he wanted to cool his head for a while before apologizing. For now, he found himself hiding in a quiet corner between rows of books on solid wood shelves.

He turned back to face the library, and was surprised to see Zengin a row over, idly running a finger along rows of spines. He made his way over, and Zengin acknowledged his presence with a nod.

"I suppose I don't have to tell you how stupid your little show was."

Zengin smirked. "Are you here to thank me?"

"For putting a stop to their games, yes. Not for the rest of it."

"I've noticed you don't have much stomach for this." Everything Zengin said sounded condescending, whether he meant it to or not.

"For what?"

"You slip away faster than the rest. If I had to guess, you aren't one for the politics or the revelry. So what do you do for fun?"

"What do you do for fun?"

"Nothing." Zengin pulled a book from the shelf and flipped it open.

"Not a single thing?"

"I lost the capacity for fun a long time ago."

Burz leaned against the shelf, crossing his arms. This conversation was going nowhere. He wondered if he could even trust anything Zengin said. "Whatever I feel about your behavior, all those things you said were true. They had to be. You drank from the goblet."

Zengin closed the book with a thud. "I've seen more evil than anyone ever should."

"I'm sorry."

"I'm not." His tone was cold.

Burz sighed. "You aren't the only person who's seen wicked men."

"You mean your regiment?"

Burz instantly regretted bringing it up.

"They weren't wicked," Zengin droned on, "just ordinary. Men follow orders because they trust."

"You don't."

"Because I'm not stupid."

"You were stupid enough to get your hand chopped off."

Zengin met his gaze with pure vitriol. It burned in his eyes, and dripped off the edges of his sneer. "Did you know she cut off my hand because you tried to save me? If only *you* hadn't been so stupid."

Burz wondered if that was true. Did he cause this?

Zengin carefully set the book back on the shelf, clumsily maneuvering it in its space with one hand. It was painful to watch and not help. "Did you learn, I wonder?" He looked back up at Burz. "Or are you just as naive as you were before?"

"Learn what?"

"That in his heart, every man is wicked. It's not about finding the good people or learning who to trust. There are no good people."

"I don't believe that."

"Like I said, you're stupid."

Burz pushed off the shelf as Zengin reached for another volume. "There's not one person? Not a single soul you've ever thought was good? Someone who doesn't deserve your ire?"

"Rasa."

For a brief moment, Zengin seemed startled by his own answer, and somewhere in Burz peripheral, a thought stirred. Zengin was still under the effects of the goblet.

"You can't lie, can you?"

"No," Zengin said flatly. "Not for another couple of hours, I suspect."

"Hm." Burz studied him, but he gave nothing, holding his placid stare. "So you'll answer anything I ask truthfully?"

"I suppose I could simply not answer. But, yes. I'm not exactly a closed book."

"But you keep secrets?"

"Of course I do."

Zengin moved closer, and something in his stare set Burz on edge. He felt every muscle tense, ready for danger.

"We can play this game if you wish, Burz. But I'm not sure a man of your temperament is cut out for it."

Burz held his ground. "Where were you guilded?"

"To the Oracles of Strah."

Burz nodded.

Zengin let a grin curl across his lips. "Is that all you've got?"

"Have you ever killed a man?"

"More than one. I would have told you that without the goblet."

"Did you enjoy it?"

His grin faded. "Which time? You'll have to be more specific."

Burz felt like a coiled spring, every sense he had sending up alarm bells. "What are you hiding? What's behind all the cloak and dagger and the tempered exterior? Who are you, *really*?"

His face was stern and his eyes were empty voids, like staring into the cold dark. "A monster."

"Would you kill again?"

"I intend to."

He brushed past Burz to walk away, but Burz grabbed his arm.

"One more. Would you turn on us, on the Champions? Would you hurt any of us?"

For a moment, it looked as if he would simply walk away, but as he pulled his arm free, he breathed out his answer.

"Absolutely."

Night had long since fallen over the desert. A cool breeze filled Lorhk's as the warm fire light of lanterns gave the place a homey glow. Hikari sipped on his mead, just starting on a second mug. Locin had a substantial pile of coins in front of her, but it didn't seem to be affecting Rix and Klief as they clinked their mugs, splashing some mead over the dirt ground. They were singing a song he didn't know, and even Voske joined in off key with his booming baritone. Weylyn even seemed relaxed, something he hadn't been sure was possible. Up until now, he'd always seen her alert, like she was always looking for something that wasn't there. Illeri was leaning into the table with her head on her arms, three empty mugs in front of her, and her eyes bleary from the stiff drink.

"Thass a good song," she said.

Locin laughed. "Gods! Were you listening to the same racket I was?"

"Reminded me of the snowy gryphs' mating call," Weylyn teased. "Awful screeching. Used to keep me up at night."

Illeri tried to pull her head up and look serious, but it fell back on her arms as she slurred out her answer. "They did their bess!"

Locin tapped on the table as she looked over her cards. "Your move, Hikari."

"Right you are, darling." He shifted a couple cards around in his hand. Lion's high wasn't a great draw. Normally he could bluff his way through, but Locin was unstoppable. Still, folding felt silly when he didn't care how much he lost, so he sent a coin flying into the middle and dropped a seven on the stack.

"You know," Illeri said, "I been watchin' this… thingy… for what's many hours now, and I still don't get it."

Locin smirked. "They don't seem to either."

Voske harumphed. "You're cheating. I just can't figure out how. Shoulda learned my lesson about playing cards with you."

"You should have." Weylyn smirked at him.

Locin and Hikari laughed, as Voske's face soured.

"Cheated then too."

"Did you play much on Suntara?" Rix asked with an edge in his voice.

"Who has time for cards when you're loafing in the sun all day?"

"I'm out." Rix dropped his cards on the table. "Rot it all, Klief. When was the last time I lost this much in a single night?"

Klief chuckled as he sipped on his mug. "At least your money's going to a Champion, and a pretty one, no less."

Locin leaned over her cards with a wry smile. "I won't go easy on you just because you're flirting with me."

It was just Hikari, Locin, and Voske left now.

"Your move then," Voske said, eyes locked on Locin.

She met his gaze with a steady smirk and dropped a nine on the pile. "Full."

"Mire and Nyx!" He boomed. "No way you do that now unless you know."

"Know what? Wait, do you have a gryph, Voske? I guess I know what your play is then."

"Final," Voske said, slapping down his gryph. Locin let her mouth curl in a full smile, her eyes fixed on him.

It was Hikari's move, but Locin just leaned in toward Voske. "There it is. Guess I'm winning this one too."

"Hey! I'm still in this game, darling." Hikari said, leaning back with his cards close to his chest as he glanced between Voske and Locin.

"Not with lions high," Locin said without thinking, and then at once she turned to him with wide eyes.

"I'll be…" Kleif smiled.

"Out," she said, dropping her cards face down in front of her.

"I knew you were cheating," Voske said with a grin.

Rix looked angry, but he bit his lip, a tinge of respect in his eyes. Or was it fear? "Just got swindled outta a week's pay by a Champion. Nyx it."

"I wasn't gonna keep the money. Gods!" Locin pushed the stack toward the center and the coins rolled around the table with a clatter. "Not like I need it."

"How?" Klief asked with a smirk. "I've seen cheaters before, but never like you. How'd you do that?"

Illeri reached for the pile and grabbed a single coin, a simple copper thing. She set it up on its side and flicked it, sending it spinning back in the pile. "Momma used to play. Hours an' hours an' hours. Drinkin' too. And worse."

"Bet she didn't cheat," Voske said, slamming his cards down.

"More like she got cheated. Monks use' t' come through town. They said they were monks. They'd play at the tavern, take everyone's coin and sell Desita's Bliss. Momma never had the money, but she'd get it somehow. I'd find her in the morning, passed ou' on the kitchen floor."

Klief frowned. "Eh. My old man was the same."

"Never met my old man." Illeri shook her head. It bobbed like a dinghy in a storm on her arms. "Momma told me he was one o' me… Wayfare. Wayfare-er. Thass it. He'd come through on a big chariot, pylat big as a house. Flew over the gorge and blotted the sun righ' out. Said he wass a good man. Wass gonna come back for us."

Weylyn looked at Illeri sympathetically. "That doesn't sound so bad."

She waved a hand dismissively. "All lies. Prolly just some low life… maybe one of thoss monks. But I believed it."

Hikari reached across the table and touched her arm. "That's why you became a wayfarer?"

She pulled away and looked up in horror at all the people watching her.

"You okay?" Locin asked.

She scrambled to her feet. "I need some air."

She stumbled toward the exit, past the glow of the lanterns, and into the shadowy street.

Rix lifted his mug and motioned after her. "She ends up in the desert, she'll get lost real fast."

Hikari and Weylyn both stood, but Hikari held up a hand.

"I've got this, darling." He rushed out after her without waiting for an answer.

The sky was a sea of stars as he hurried along the hard packed road that meandered toward the town. The cool of night had settled, and he shivered in his light toga, rubbing at his arms. Illeri was a little ways from the road, heading for the shrine that shimmered like a beacon, the pale stone of Jeza's form almost glittering in the moonlight. He picked up his pace until he caught up to her.

"Wait a moment, Illeri. You shouldn't run off alone."

She rolled her eyes at him. "I've charted the col' dark. I think I can find my way around…" she threw up a few random fingers as if counting, "…*ten* shacks in the desert."

"Ah, yes. But have you ever charted anything while drunk?"

She picked up her pace as if to shake him, but he matched her as they drew closer to the towering shrine.

"I'm nah drunk," she stammered. She stopped and turned toward him waving a finger in his face. "I can drink. I juss don't. This? This wass nothing."

"Of course, darling."

Her eyes fixed on her own hands as she swayed slightly from side to side. "My hands feel funny."

"That would be the liquor on which you are certainly *not* drunk."

He held a hand out, touching her arm to steady her. She tried to turn away, but lost her footing and stumbled into him, catching herself with a hand against his chest. He shuddered at the touch. Her hand was warm and soft, and he wanted her to stay, but she pulled back, and brushed his hand off her arm.

"It wassin bad," she said. "Well, bad at first, burned like… fire." She grimaced. "But o-ther than that, not bad."

"We'll see how you feel tomorrow," he said softly. His eyes lingered on her hand. "I don't envy you that."

For a moment she seemed to have forgotten she was mad at him, but she quickly remembered, and she frowned deeply. "Champions are spose a' be better. Better than lies. You lied. You're… you're… a liar." She threw her hands up in frustration. "You made *me* lie! We said we'd be a' the feas' , and now-" She looked at the deepening night above and sighed.

"Well, what is acting but a lie?" He said weakly. "Perhaps I've simply become accustomed to the habit."

"You think I'm stupid."

"Of course not! You're one of the most brilliant people I know. Didn't I prove that with the riddle?"

"You mean with stars… and books… and… stuff."

"Right!"

She huffed angrily at him and turned toward the shrine, making her way in through one of the arches.

Inside, the moonlight rippled off the stone as a soft wind blew through the hardy shrubs.

"You think I'm stupid wi' people," she said. "You think you can lie, and I won' know, 'cause I'm stupid."

"Not at all," he answered. He suddenly felt a little trapped, and he wished he'd let Weylyn come after her. "I'm not sure what to say here, darling."

She sighed, sitting down on the lip of the well. "I just wanna be in Brav-esh."

He sighed as he sat beside her. "I don't know why it bothers you so much. Truly. Everyone exaggerates, tells half truths. It's life."

"Nah everyone. I told you abou' my family."

"I admire that," he said softly. "You speak your mind, share your soul. That's hard for most people."

She stood and started for the far side of the shrine.

"Wait! Where are you going?"

"The skiff," she snapped.

"Alright," he said sharply, "now hold on!" And then, without taking any time to think it over, he started. "I grew up on Erimos. We were poor. My father... well... he was unguilded."

She turned to face him. "You lied! Again! You said he was a player."

"Well, now, I didn't say that. I said he traveled all over with the players."

She rolled her eyes and turned away.

He started again, and this time he let his guard down. His tone was soft and open. "They're called strikers."

She stopped, and he walked around in front of her, catching her eye.

"Theaters hire them to clean up before and after shows. They make very little money, and they're looked down on by most of the guilded, but it was work, and I think my father truly enjoyed it."

"Why would you lie about that? Do you hate Erimos so much?" She took on an affected tone as she threw an arm over her head dramatically. "Suntara is sooo prestigious! Why not be from *there* instead?"

That wasn't it. He didn't hate Erimos. He didn't hate his family. He loved it here. But he could still hear the voices of his guild mates on Suntara, the way they teased him about his ragged clothes, his guildless father, even his accent. It was just easier to pretend.

Hikari cleared his throat, choosing his words carefully. "I didn't mean any offense. I'm very fond of Erimos."

She shrugged. "I don' care. You can hate it, for all I care. Iss a lot of rough, empty land."

"Then why in the name of Desita are you upset?"

She started laughing. "You don' get it? You don' see that just maybe I'm upset *that you lied*?" She stepped closer, locking her eyes on him fiercely. "You're *always* pretending. Hikari, the great player of Suntara!"

"I'm not always pretending."

He looked away from her and out at the desert, deciding whether she was too drunk to leave out here alone, wanting to be anywhere but here. Who was she to say these things to him, anyway? She didn't know anything about him.

"But why me?" He asked desperately. "Why not take all this out on Voske? He lied as much as I did!"

"Thass different."

He was exasperated at this point, and he threw his arms up over his head. "How?"

She matched his tone, shouting into the dark, empty streets. "'Cause *you're* different! 'Cause I like you!"

An awkward silence slowly settled in, swallowing them both up. Hikari felt a mix of emotions as she stood there, drunk, staring at him as the moonlight shimmered on her skin. She was beautiful, and frustrating, and he had no idea what to say.

She sighed. "I wanna like you, anyway. You look so nice, and you always smell so nice… But I don' even know you. You're just… playing a part."

"I… had no idea."

She rolled her eyes. "Sure."

"Truly! I mean it."

"Don't let it go to your head. Every girl *likes* you, Hikari. I'm not special."

She turned and started walking past him, but he quickly ran to catch up.

"But I don't like every girl."

She scoffed. "You like enough of 'em."

He sighed.

"You know, I saw you so many times."

"What?"

"Plays," she said. "I saw your plays los' of times. *King Ovare, The Lay of Time, Dance of Night*… los' more."

"You did?" He tried to keep from smiling.

She nodded, biting at her lip. "I love plays. Every time we landed in a port with a… wass it called… theater, I would go. And you can't go to theaters without seeing Hikari."

"Well, that much is true."

For a moment she let her eyes wander back to the stars overhead, and she was distant again.

"Illeri?"

She stopped walking and looked back down at him. His heart was pounding. Why not throw caution to the wind? Why not tell her the truth? He'd never loved a woman. He'd never been with a woman. He wasn't who she thought. And maybe it was just a trick of the moonlight, or the sleepy look in her deep, brown eyes, or the way her hair cascaded around her collar bone, but maybe, just maybe, he was falling in love with her.

"Illeri. I-"

She suddenly lurched forward with a horrible retching sound and emptied the contents of her stomach onto the hard packed sand at his feet.

He sighed.

"I don' feel so good."

"Yes, well, that would be the three Lorhk's specials." He stepped around the vomit and offered her his arm. "I think we best get you back to Lorhk's, darling. Perhaps he has the antidote."

"An'idote?"

He smiled. "Strong coffee and something to eat."

She nodded, slipping her arm in his, and they turned back toward the tavern.

Just another festival, Zengin thought as he strolled the streets of Bravesh. The moons had risen, and with it the level of unsavory revelry. Sure, the streets were littered with the usual celebrants, the fireworks of a few Desitan monks, and the laughter of the raucous youth. But the youngest were long since in bed, the respectable back in their homes, and he was too accustomed to the darkness to not see clearly. The bloodshot, drunken eyes, the women flaunting themselves like dogs in heat, and the lascivious men who watched them - this was the real face of Talamh, and all in the name of the god of prudence.

He wouldn't sleep in a place like this. He knew what went on in places like this. Instead he had donned his commoner's garb and wandered the midnight streets, observing the smiling frauds, tricksters, and charlatans. But if he hadn't been out on the streets, he would have missed the man who crept through the crowd with purpose, taking no part in the celebration. He was obscured under a dark cloak, but the orange whip at his side was unmistakable.

He had tracked Sammel through Bravesh and across the deep blue circle of water that held back the desert. Now he was standing at the top of a dune with his back to the city, watching. Zengin wasn't sure what to expect. He stood at the water's edge for a moment, but Sammel never turned or even flinched. He dipped a hand in the cool water, letting the drops slip off his fingers and splash back down.

"Are you coming up?" Sammel asked flatly.

"It depends. Are you here to kill me?"

Sammel threw back his hood and looked down at Zengin with a curious expression. "I was going to ask the same."

Zengin shook the water off his hand and scaled the dune. Beyond, moonlight shimmered on the sand like waves in a dry ocean.

Sammel kept one eye on the desert and one on Zengin. Deep rings scored the bottoms of his eyes, and his face bore the stubble of many days.

"You're more clever than I thought," Zengin said. "I never saw you near the crook."

"It was obvious you would figure out it was me." He looked at Zengin pointedly. "I don't have it on me."

"Of course not. It's safe with your champion, I'm sure. But why are you here, in Bravesh?"

"I'm watching for the others."

"Hm." *The Varrin Wastes,* he thought. *Of course.* "The second piece."

"I wasn't sure if you knew." There was something else in Sammel's countenance, something behind the weariness. But what?

"I suspected," Zengin lied. He should have known. He felt angry he hadn't seen it, but he shook off the feeling. It wouldn't happen again. "And you intend to steal this one as well?"

"If I get the chance."

Doubt. That was what he saw in Sammel's eyes. Did he doubt he could steal this piece, or was it something more?

"But why?" Zengin asked, though he had already guessed the answer.

Sammel raised an eyebrow. "Where is your honey tongue today?"

"I don't need it."

"Then you already know why."

Zengin straightened up. He slipped his hand under the folds of his toga, clumsily - useless left hand. But it was all he had, and it gripped the hilt of his dagger.

"If Endring wanted to stop the cultists, he would have left the crook piece with us. The only obvious answer is that he wants to assemble the relic and use it himself. That's why you're here."

Sammel's own hand was under his cloak, no doubt gripping the whip.

"And where is Endring? Did he send you alone to do his dirty work, or is he watching?"

"He's nearby." Sammel cast a furtive glance toward the sky. It was barely more than a tick, but Zengin caught it.

"And how is the Champion of Neveri these days?"

"Driven."

Driven. It was an interesting choice of words. "So are you, by the look of it."

Sammel rolled his neck. "I do what I must."

"Don't we all?"

Sammel let his eyes stray back out to the desert. "Do you plan to turn me in?"

"No."

"Then you'll let me go?"

Zengin narrowed his eyes. "What happens if Endring gets all three pieces?"

This time Sammel wasn't so forthcoming.

"I can force you to tell me."

"I know," Sammel said calmly.

Zengin took a breath, keeping his hand ready on his dagger, but he knew killing Sammel would accomplish nothing.

But I want to watch him bleed.

"So, will you?" Sammel asked.

"What?"

"Will you force me?"

The honey of Metnadur was right there, begging to spill over into his words, but he swallowed. "No."

Sammel raised an eyebrow. "Why not?"

There it was again. *Doubt.* "Because you're not sure."

"I am quite sure what would happen if Endring had all three pieces."

Zengin shook his head. "You're not sure you want him too."

He looked as if he were pondering this. His hand slipped back out of his cloak and away from his whip, and Zengin relaxed, withdrawing his hand as well.

"It's not a weapon in the way you may think," Sammel said slowly. "Perhaps it would have been more accurate to call it a *tool*, but I suspect that description wouldn't have spurred the champions to action."

"What does it do?"

"It's the key to releasing Neveri from Nyx."

Zengin thought through the revelation. It was clear now. They needed to free their god from his prison, and the crook is how they would do it. "And you're not sure summoning the spirit of a vengeful god is such a good idea?"

Sammel took a beleaguered breath and glanced back toward the night sky. "He believes it will make the world right again."

"And what do you believe?"

Sammel shook his head. "I believe in him."

Zengin's thoughts drifted to Borroka. If her cruel malice was any reflection of her god, Sbarga would be better off without him. "The champion is supposed to exemplify the will of a god upon Talamh."

Sammel looked at him quizzically. "So it's said."

Zengin licked his lips. If this doubt could be nurtured just a little more, it might compromise Sammel. "When I was captive," he said deliberately. "Borroka said she was meant to be champion. She expected to be."

Sammel nodded, letting the idea sink in.

"Perhaps she speaks the truth, and Endring was made champion simply because he was there."

This thought seemed to resonate with Sammel, and his doubt flashed to the surface for a moment.

Zengin pressed. "If Borroka is the will of Neveri…"

"I don't know," he mused cautiously.

"And yet you continue to pursue his release."

"I don't."

Zengin narrowed his eyes. "But Endring does, and you are ever loyal. Tell me, what debt do you owe him?"

Sammel rocked on his feet. "The debt of years. We've worked side by side for over two cycles."

"And in all that time you never bothered to think if you were wrong?"

"No."

"Do you now?"

Sammel pursed his lips, his eyes dutifully scanning the desert. "If I do, it's only because he's changed. I think he's so focused now, he can't see anything else."

Zengin lifted his chin. "And you content yourself to watch him dig his own grave. Why?"

"I wouldn't just watch him dig it," he said flatly. "I would bury myself beside him."

"You're insane." No more insane than he himself, he supposed.

Zengin stayed another few minutes, watching the unchanging landscape before he turned to clamber back down the sandy dune.

"I'll see you again, Zengin," Sammel called after him.

He was sure he would. For tonight, he would let him wait, and watch. He'd have a much harder time stealing the second relic, and that was not Zengin's concern. He had planted a seed, and if anyone could talk sense into Endring now, it was Sammel.

36: Heroes Aren't Made From the Cautious

By the time the last five champions made it to Bravesh, the morning light was just beginning to crest the horizon. Voske stood at the rudder of the skiff, carefully guiding the craft to the edge of the pylat tether. Weylyn stood beside him, looking like she'd had a full night's sleep as she stared keenly ahead toward the city, even though none of them had slept since before the festival in Vohasi.

"Aurilis isn't happy," she said with a sidelong glance at Voske.

"Is she ever?"

The edge of her mouth curled in a smirk. "Apparently we 'disgraced the city'."

Hikari and Locin were sitting silently nearby. They were bleary eyed and stiff, but they were still better off than Illeri who was passed out on the rattling deck.

Voske slowed their approach when he spotted the temple's massive chariot. Servants were carrying gifts up the ramp, and a group of dignitaries stood at the bottom, dressed in outlandish attire and talking with Aurilis.

"Looks like a party," Voske muttered.

"Wow," Locin answered. "Makes me glad we missed it."

"What, you don't like wearing circus clothes?"

"I like the shoes. I'll skip the rest."

Voske glanced her direction. "I've never seen you wear anything but sandals."

"You don't know everything about me."

"Voske." Weylyn's voice pulled his eyes back to the front.

A line of Jeza monks were moving into their path, spears raised. Their commander was yelling something unintelligible over the noise of the shunts, and Voske waved a hand over the spark, bringing the whirring blades to a grinding halt.

"What's that?" he yelled to the commander.

"I said that's close enough," the lithe man replied. "State your purpose here."

Voske could feel the power of his title going to his head, and he strode toward the bow with a grin. "I'm the Champion of Jeza," he called back. "With me are the Champions of Iyanu, Desita, Kisandin, and Strah. As to our purpose, that's none of yours."

The Commander looked skeptical of his claim at best. Voske looked down at his grit-laden toga. He might not have believed him either.

"Voske," shouted a voice, and he glanced back at the dignitaries. From their midst Burz was striding forward alongside Aurilis and Zengin. They were dressed just as elaborately as the rest of the crowd.

"Burz!" he yelled back with a smile, waving intentionally with his right hand as he winked at the commander.

Immediately the monks fell back to either side, nearly tripping over themselves to make way for the champions.

He felt someone stumble to the rail beside him and he turned to see Illeri, squinting at the crowd. "Why is everything so bright?"

Voske laughed. He hopped over the bow and landed in the sand, feeling the familiar squish under his feet. "Do you need help down?"

As he spoke Illeri plopped to the ground beside him, in a cloud of dust.

He grabbed her and raised her up as the others scrambled down the ramp to join them.

"That… was a bad idea," Illeri mumbled as she rubbed her hand along the small of her back.

"No kidding."

"Are you alright," Burz asked as he neared.

"Right as rain," Hikari answered.

"I was talking to Illeri."

"Fine." She managed a pained smile, as though that would prove her point.

Burz frowned as he looked from face to face, and Voske followed his gaze. The five of them were dirty, smelly, and in a word, rumpled.

"What in the worlds happened?" Burz asked.

"We decided to act. It's not as though anyone else was doing anything."

"Act how?"

Voske flashed a triumphant grin and motioned to Weylyn. She pulled out the crook and handed it to Voske. It was hard to see the glow of the gods in the bright outdoor light, but Burz' eyes still widened in recognition.

"What were you thinking?" snapped Aurilis. "Do you know what a disaster this has been?"

Voske's smile faltered as he turned her direction. Apparently she wasn't aware that this was a win for them. "It's the Crook of Bei'ai," he tried, though he was fairly sure she already knew what it was.

"It's a trinket, best left in the care of the temple, and one for which missing a once-in-a-lifetime festival to honor the gods was not worth."

Voske scowled. "It's a weapon, and very much worth retrieving. But I would have missed your stuffy festival for a sandwich."

Aurilis was turning red by this point. "It was a disgrace on this city."

Zengin scoffed. "That festival was a disgrace on this city."

"High Oracle," Hikari trilled. "You must know there was no harm meant." In a swift motion, he snatched the crook from Voske, and climbed back on the deck of the skiff.

"Hey!"

Hikari let his voice rise so the crowd could hear him. "We embarked upon a quest in the name of the gods, to bring a sacred relic back into the fold!" He held the crook aloft, pulling some of the light away until the faint orange glow was noticeable. "I tell you, people of Bravesh, that it was no easy feat! A battle for the ages against foes most deadly!"

Voske had to give it to him. He knew how to play the audience. He leapt gracefully around the skiff, sure to hold the crook up in his wounded arm with the blood soaked bandage. And despite it all, he seemed less dirty and smelly, and just plain more heroic than the rest of them. Voske smiled.

"Bodies as long as the mighty Tempest, heads bigger than a man! They had manes of feathers that ran down their scaly backs, black as a crow's! Their fangs were like knives of polished ivory, sharp and deadly!"

He threw his left arm up, swirling it around as the sky seemed to churn in response. The light twirled around and came together until, in the midst of a dark cloud, two massive forms took shape. The two serpents slithered across the sky in tandem, just like the ones they'd fought, but much larger. Their fangs were longer, dripping venom, and hideous wings sprouted from their backs. Even their eyes glowed an ominous red. The crowd gasped as the serpents shot out forked tongues and lunged toward them.

"The beasts nearly finished us, but our mighty Voske, Champion of the great lady Jeza, crushed one of the great feathered serpents into powder with nothing but his bare fists!"

One of the illusions exploded into a massive golden shower, and Hikari leapt to the end of the skiff and grabbed Weylyn's right wrist, holding her hand up in victory so that her sigil burned brightly. More brightly than it should. Voske was sure he was adding some extra light.

"The second beast had me, gripped in its fangs. Certain death was all that awaited! But Weylyn, Chosen of Strah came to my aid. Chosen for her prudence, and her prowess as a huntress of Shinoam, her arrow struck true!"

The second serpent exploded in a vibrant shower of sparks, and the crowd thundered their applause, with many a cheer for Strah and his Chosen. Hikari waited patiently as the noise grew quiet, then he let Weylyn's arm go and bounced back to the center of the skiff. "My injury is but a nuisance compared to the vast drubbing these mighty Champions bestowed upon those beasts. And now, they shall never again trouble the Varrin Wastes or take what is ours!" He held the crook head aloft as he bowed dramatically.

The crowd exploded in a final roar, and Hikari's face beamed as he climbed back down and handed the relic to Voske. He clapped Hikari on the shoulder and yelled. "Well done!" Although his voice was swallowed up in the tumult.

Locin smacked Hikari on the arm, and he stared at her.

"Hey!"

"You didn't mention me!"

"Sorry, darling. Next time I'll tell them you *booned* the beast."

As the screaming crowd died down, Voske turned to smile smugly at Aurilis, and found her arms crossed and her expression unchanged.

"A snake?" She pointed at Hikari's bloodied arm. "That's what happened to you?"

"Big snake," Illeri managed, holding her head and looking unsteady.

"And what happened to you?"

"Different snake," Voske said quickly.

"Mead," Illeri added. "Lots of mead."

Burz shook his head. "Mead. Of course."

"You were out drinking?" Aurilis asked.

Voske folded his arms now, glowering at the pretentious woman. "Call it a celebration."

"Impressive you were able to find any," Zengin quipped. "The desert being what it is."

He wasn't helping.

Voske took a deep breath and held out the piece of the Crook. "Look. We had a job to do. We did it. Plain and simple."

"It wasn't your job." Aurilis was still scowling as she took the piece from his hand. "Might I suggest, *Champion*, that next time you have a simple errand to run you engage with the temple first. There are tens of thousands of Jeza monks, but there are only eight of you."

"Of course," Voske muttered. "And partying is more important than actually doing the work, apparently."

She looked like she had more to say, but the crowds were pressing in now, and Gillis rested a hand on Aurilis' arm. "Hikari may have saved face, High Oracle, but he may have also stirred them into a frenzy."

The Jeza monks were pushing back against the crowd as another cry rose, first from a few, then it began to spread until the whole of Bravesh cried out.

"Praise the gods! Praise their chosen!"

But Aurilis had her eyes fixed on the fancy dressed nobles. They stood dourly by the chariot ramp. Hikari had done nothing to smooth things over with them. But who cared? The people loved him. The people loved *them*.

After their long excursion, Hikari was eager to wash away his weariness, not to mention the smell. He quickly made his way to the lowest deck of the Tempest where the bathhouse waited. He'd seen other baths on other chariots, but this one blew them all away. The wooden walls were barely visible behind lush blooming flowers. The floor and the pool itself were woven of marble, and steam filled his senses with the fragrance of jasmine and bergamot. He sat on the edge of the bath dressed in a clean himation, his legs dipped in the hot water, soaking out the aches of their adventure in the desert. He leaned forward dipping a finger in and swirling some jasmine petals in a little whirlpool.

"They said I would find you here."

He looked up at Burz' voice to see him cautiously walking through the steamy room.

"Well, one must always look their best." He leaned back, casually kicking his feet through the water. "I hear we missed quite the party."

Burz harrumphed.

"Well, even if the festivities fell flat, I do regret not seeing the archive. I hear it was fabulous."

Burz motioned to his freshly bandaged arm. "It looks like you saw some exciting things of your own. A feathered serpent?" He added skeptically.

"All true, darling, every word of it."

"Big as a chariot?"

Hikari smiled. "Perhaps a bit embellished."

"And the wings?"

"Definitely embellished. Ah, but the crowd did love it!"

Burz shook his head, and then reached for Hikari's bandaged arm. "Let me see."

"Truly, I'm fine, Burz. Save your strength for the real injuries."

"As far as I know, you're the only one on board who's injured."

He grabbed Hikari's arm firmly and pulled the bandage off. A red line ran along his arm from his elbow nearly to his shoulder. It wasn't a deep wound, but it stung as Burz peeled the cloth away, and Hikari grimaced.

"Hold still."

Hikari had the sensation that his arm was being dipped in the bath at his feet, like the steaming water was soothing away the pain. Every ache faded as the feeling moved from his elbow up to his shoulder. The stinging subsided, and he watched in amazement as the wound closed and disappeared entirely.

As Burz let go, Hikari held his arm up, stretching it out. "Gods and Chosen! Seeing that never gets old."

"It was foolhardy to go into the wastes alone."

"Perhaps, darling, but heroes aren't made from the cautious."

"Neither are they made from the dead." He stood again, sighing as if he were tired.

"Forgive my bluntness, Burz, but you're looking a bit worn. Perhaps a dip in the bath might serve you well. It reminds me of the bathhouses of Leo'Na on Suntara. The Uthandan monks who tend them claim they have healing properties."

Burz nodded, although he seemed distracted.

"Was there more on your mind?"

"The fight with the serpent."

"Jealous you missed it? It was an intense battle, to be sure-" he swung his arms in a mock fighting motion "-always but a hair's breadth from certain death! but in the end, we were victorious."

Hikari gave a bow and came up smiling, but he noticed Burz was frowning deeply, and his smile fell away.

"If you're worried about missing it, darling, don't. I'm sure we'll face many more epic endeavors in our years as Champions - may they be many."

Burz shook his head. "You could have been killed, and you make light of it?"

"Ah, but isn't that a risk Champions take? I for one don't intend to shy away from danger."

"You're a player, Hikari. You can't act your way through battles."

"I'm a champion," he said, a little wounded. He pulled his legs from the water and stood as the water dripped from him and echoed off the cold marble. "I did alright for myself."

"And that sword of yours, did you even draw it?"

"There wasn't the need. I had my boon, and-"

"And blinding your enemies won't always work. You'll need real skill to stay alive."

"I'm not incapable."

Burz sighed. "I didn't mean to say you were. But you're determined to be in harm's way, that much is clear, so…" He had his arms crossed now, looking Hikari over head to toe. At last his assessment was complete, and he nodded. "Alright. I'll do it."

"Do what, exactly?"

"Teach you to fight."

Hikari felt excitement creeping up. "Really? With a sword?"

"Yes."

Hikari gave a shout that echoed through the room.

"If you insist on putting yourself in danger, I'm not going to leave you unprepared, but it won't be easy."

He nodded eagerly.

"It takes discipline and hard work."

"Darling, I was a player. Do you know the discipline and hard work *that* took?"

"Good. We'll start when we land in Kerata."

Hikari was so excited he started for his quarters at once.

Burz called after him. "Where are you going?"

"To get my sword!"

"I'm not training you yet."

"I know, I know. I want to practice wearing it!" He turned and gave a dutiful salute to Burz. "From now on, I shall be prepared at all times and in all seasons!"

Burz laughed as Hikari turned away, but he spun back once more and pointed to the steaming bath.

"I mean it, darling. Take a dip. It'll do you a world of good."

He ducked out the door, and then peered back in, watching as Burz knelt, dipping an arm in the warm water. After a moment, he stood and pulled off his toga, easing himself into the water, and Hikari rushed out into the corridor, eager to get back to his room. Next time he faced a mythic creature, he'd be more than ready.

37: Kerata

Rasa leaned out over the rail of the Chariot until she felt the slight tingle of the radiant field against her forehead. Below, Erimos sped by, wild land that had begun to shift from the sandy desert and rocks of the wilderness to a low sweeping grassland cut through with blue rivers that shimmered in the sun's light. Tufts of plants and sparse trees sprawled across the rolling land, and wild herds of pegasus could be seen rushing along the ground, leaping to flight and soaring through the blue sky.

The sun was barely above the horizon. The golden rays and the glow of the radiant field made her feel like they were sailing on sunlight. It wouldn't be long now before they arrived at another temple in another city. Something about all this travel reminded Rasa too much of her old life. She rubbed at her arms, letting her gaze focus back on the land below where she could just make out a pride of lions milling restlessly near a watering hole.

Some voices drew her attention and she saw Zengin making his way out on the deck, being greeted by a few monks. He caught her gaze and made his way over as she dropped her eyes back to the lions, quickly fading from view as the Tempest flew past.

"Are we the only two up on deck?" Zengin asked.

Rasa nodded, pushing her hair behind her ear. "I guess so."

He leaned into the radiant field, taking in the sights below. "I find Erimos to be rather drab, don't you? The same endless, dry brown."

"I like it."

"Hm."

For a moment they both stared out in silence, but Rasa paid little heed to the landscape now. Her thoughts drifted back to the festival the night before. Zengin knew her past. He seemed like the kind of person who just knew those things. He'd known so many other secrets, and she wasn't sure how or why, but he *knew*.

"Thank you," she said softly.

He gave her a quizzical look. "So far I've interrupted your peace and insulted Erimos. Which of those things are you thanking me for?"

She shook her head, and strands of red scattered across her face. "I didn't mean that."

He stared at her, waiting for her to continue. It made her uncomfortable, and she looked back at the land below where they were passing over a thin stream. She tried to inch away without him noticing.

"I meant for the festival. You stopped that awful story circle."

"Ah. Burz thanked me for that as well."

She risked a glance toward him again. "Why *did* you stop it?"

This time it was Zengin who averted his eyes, something she had never seen him do. "It's an awful tradition, rather dull really. I couldn't bear another moment of the drudgery."

"It felt an awful lot like you were doing it to help me," she said.

"Did it?" He poked a finger idly at the radiant field, looking anywhere but at her.

She was used to that. It seemed men either looked at her, or looked anywhere else. This was preferable, but the embarrassment on Zengin's face was so familiar, almost personal. But she was sure she would have remembered him. Their faces still haunted her nightmares. All of them.

"So… you know?" She gulped, and her throat was suddenly very dry. "I mean, about me?"

"If you mean do I know what you were before, then yes, I do. I have no intention of telling the others."

"I haven't told anyone here." She reached out to the radiant field and pressed her palm against it. It resisted her with a warm push, and her fingers tingled. "But, *how* do you know?"

He cleared his throat. "If I tell you, it will likely make you even more uncomfortable."

She'd been uncomfortable for most of her life, and she wasn't eager to be again, or to have this conversation, but she stirred up her courage and nodded reluctantly. "Okay. Tell me."

He sighed, as if he'd been hoping she wouldn't press the matter. "Are you familiar with the order of Strah?"

She knew so little about the world. She felt embarrassed as she tried to muster an answer. "They're scribes, aren't they? They write the books we saw in the library?"

"And their boon?"

"I don't really know. It has something to do with gathering stories?"

He held up his right arm, stretching it out in the sunlight, and she tried not to look at it. It felt rude to do so.

"If the monks of Strah touch someone while using their boon, they'll live whatever memory that person is thinking about. It's more than just seeing it. You're there. It's unbelievably real. You see what they saw. You…" his voice faltered, and he pulled his arm back, cradling it by his chest. "You do what they did."

"Oh." She felt her cheeks flush, and she wrapped her arms around her chest as revelation sunk in. She wanted to crawl into a hole and hide. "That boon sounds awful."

He laughed, but it wasn't harsh or cruel. "Most people don't think so. They're fascinated by the idea. But I suppose you and I are alike in that way."

"What way?"

"We've seen the true face of humanity, and we've no desire to delve into anyone's mind."

It was true, she'd seen her share of evil. But she still wanted to believe it wasn't true, at least not of everyone. "Maybe not all people are like that."

"I'm surprised you've any optimism left. I certainly don't."

She wrinkled her brow. "You had this boon?"

"I did."

"I thought you were unguilded?"

"Everyone did. When my father realized I had been guilded to the scribes, he paid a small fortune to hide the truth. I was kept at home and forced to wear gloves like an unguilded."

"Why would he do that?"

"Why?" He turned to face her. "Because that was the most powerful advantage any Archon could hope for. A few well placed remarks to trigger a memory, a subtle touch from me, and he had all the information he needed to obliterate his rivals and secure his empire. Most people wouldn't understand how a father could do that to his own son, but they don't understand what power does to men."

"I understand." *It isn't just power,* she thought, *but poverty too.*

"I see." He turned his eyes back to the sunlit land. "I've lived the memories of the most wicked men and women in Tajerim. Every depraved indulgence. Every vengeful act. Nothing men do can surprise me anymore."

"I'm… sorry."

He glanced back at her with a look of surprise. "*You're* sorry?"

She bit her lip, not sure how to respond.

"I just told you what I know, what I *lived*, and you're sorry." He shook his head.

"I'm sorry you lived like that." She stared at her feet, her cheeks hot with shame, but how could she not acknowledge his pain too? "No one should have to go through that. Especially a kid."

"How do you do that?" He asked.

"Do what?"

"Care for others. You've seen the same depravity I have, and yet you seem to think people are worth caring for. I assure you, I am not."

She turned her eyes back out. The sun was rising higher now, and clear blue sky surrounded their chariot. They were flying over a town, a sprawling mass of stone houses nestled on either side of a river.

"You don't just know what I was," she said softly. "You *saw* what I was."

She risked a glance, and the answer played out on his face.

"I recognized you when I first saw you, from the memory of a Suntaran noble." He glanced at her. "I imagine this is difficult for you."

She felt all the old emotions bubbling up inside her. Shame. Anger. Grief. It wasn't him. He didn't do it. Still the emotions flooded her, and she felt sick.

"I shouldn't have told you."

She shook her head. "You didn't do it. I don't blame you."

"I'll leave you alone."

She heard his footsteps moving away, and she was grateful. She slammed her eyes shut. *Don't cry*, she told herself. They would be in Kerata soon, and she didn't want the others to see her like that.

She forced her eyes open and wiped at the tears that pooled in the corners. Below, the grasslands rolled on. The chariot was following a road now, simple dirt that ran across the plains. She could see a few groups of people walking or on horseback, no doubt heading into Kerata for the festival. They looked small from her vantage point on the chariot. She made her way to the front, climbing on the low wall and looking out at the horizon. Just past the golden wings of the pylats, she could see Kerata, a sprawling city with mud homes and stone towers, and at its center rose the great arena, a circle of stone capped with the flags of the city and the banners of Jeza and Uthando. Another city. Another festival.

Kerata wasn't much to look at. It rested in a sprawling plain tufted with patches of long grass and spreading trees that grew from a spindly trunk to a leafy mushroom-like cap. The homes were quaint, formed of woven mud that made it look as if they had grown up out of the dirt. But there were two things that stood out from the rolling grass and dull brown homes.

The first was the arena. It was breathtaking in both size and intricacy. Its walls were made of quartz, glimmering a milky white with veins of red and copper. Around the base, massive Pegasus sculpted of pure white marble looked as though they were rising out of the ground, lifting the arena toward Sbarga. If she'd stopped there, Locin would have guessed the arena had eaten up all the wealth of the city, explaining the mud homes and simple dirt roads. But then there was the second thing that stood out. The Archon's palace.

If the arena had cost a fortune, the Archon's palace had cost two. The walls were paneled with gold, the tiles pure marble inlaid with gold. The chandeliers were gold, and the filigreed paintings and mirrors. She'd even been offered wine in a golden goblet, which she'd quickly guzzled and slipped the goblet in her satchel. It was hard not to jingle when she walked by this point.

She was grinning, and so was Spark. It felt like the old days. That is, it would have felt like the old days if she'd been invited in and escorted around to see all the valuables in the old days. This was easy. No more tricks or schemes. They were basically begging her to take their stuff.

"You look happy," Rasa whispered. "So does Spark."

Locin's smile faded.

They were strolling down a long hallway now, somewhere on the third floor of the palace. The place was a maze, and she'd paid less attention to where they were going than she would have in the old days. She didn't need an escape route anymore.

"She won't tell me why," Rasa continued. "But she says she's glad to see you happy."

"Whatever." She pushed her way forward, away from Rasa. This wasn't anything like the old days. Back then it was just her and Spark.

Gods, I miss those days, she thought. Being a champion had its perks, but she felt restless, like it was time for a change. She'd been ordered around by the temple long enough, and she wanted to be free again.

As she reached the front of the group, she heard the Archon chattering about the south wing. Apparently that was where they were.

"The very best," he said in a jovial voice, "spare no expense, that's what I told them. No soul is going to find us skimping - not in my home!"

They stepped through the opulent archway at the end of the hall to a wide parlor. It had benches and a fire pit in the center, and the bulk of the south wall was an open window down to the city. Locin strolled over and looked out on Kerata. The arena filled most of the view, perfectly centered on the window.

"I'll leave you to rest," the Archon said. "You'll want to bring your appetites tonight. The southern courtyard has fountains that flow with mead."

Then he laughed and marched out, heading back down the hall. A contingent of the monks went with him, but more stayed than usual. They were red clad Jeza monks, and they seemed alert, stationing themselves around the room. Sixteen of them, to be precise. Each pair seemed keenly focused on a particular champion.

"Rot it," she muttered, and she felt Spark lean in curiously. She nodded to the pair of monks very specifically *not* looking at her. "I know when I'm a prisoner. Should have gotten out while I could."

"So," Voske clapped his hands together and started rubbing them, "I'm off to the arena. Who's coming?"

Gillis stepped into the arched door and held up a finger. "Perhaps we can discuss the itinerary first, Champion."

"What are you talking about, Gillis?"

"I knew you would want to see the arena, of course, so I've made arrangements for anyone who would like to go. But after that, we will come back here for the feast."

"Here?" Voske crossed his arms over his chest. "Why don't we just go to the arena and then see-"

"Apologies, Champion." It was cute watching Gillis try to be stern. "I must insist. We have a tight schedule to keep, but I've given you two hours at the arena, during which time anyone who desires may sign up for the tournament."

Hikari raised an eyebrow. "What tournament?"

"Tomorrow," Gillis said. "You'll all be in attendance, of course. A private booth has been set aside, but it's also tradition to allow the Champion of Jeza to compete, should he desire to do so."

"Huh." Voske replied. "What kind of tournament?"

"Hand to hand combat. Boons are forbidden. This is a test of strength to honor the goddess."

Voske smiled. "Maybe this festival won't be so bad."

Motion in the hall caught Locin's eye as they continued talking. There was someone out there, someone trying not to be seen.

Spark sent a shiver up her back.

"Yeah, I know." She edged around the room to try and get a better view. It was a kid, maybe ten. He had dirty clothes and worn gloves on his hands, but she saw something gold glinting from his pocket. His mouth moved like he was whispering, and she heard a noise nearby, by the far wall. Someone was whispering her name.

She smiled. Everyone else in the room had heard it too, and they were looking that direction, distracted in the way only a spirit could distract someone.

She sidled closer, heading for the door, but before she got to the boy, a Jeza monk spotted him and charged over, grabbing him by the arm. Locin rushed forward, waving the monk away.

"Hey… Tig…," she said weakly. "Where ya been?" And then to the guard, "Old friend. We go way…" she looked at the young kid, "…back." She grabbed him and started pulling him back down the hall.

"Hey-" he started, but she slapped a hand over his mouth.

"Listen, kid, I'm trying to save you here. Just shut up and walk with me, and I'll even let you keep those trinkets you got." She pointed to his pocket, and he shoved a gold box further in. His pocket jingled, and she smiled. "Pretty stupid coming here. The guild send you?"

"Are you Locin?"

She stopped walking and looked at him. Her two monks were following, but they were trying not to be seen, which left them out of ear shot. "What'd you say?"

"I was s'posed to find Locin." He screwed up his face and looked at her sideways. "I guess that's you."

"Who sent you?"

The boy reached in his pocket, gold jingling around as the Jeza monks listened with suspicion. Finally, he retrieved what he was after, and he pulled out a crumpled note, smiling proudly.

"I can't read," he said. "So I don't know what it says, but a man told me to give it to you. He gave me a shiny coin, but I woulda come just for the gold." He grinned widely. He was missing a few teeth.

Locin took the paper and nodded. "Well, I got the note. I'm assuming he promised you another coin when you got back, so scurry off."

The little thief ran off down the corridor jingling like a maraca, and Locin turned her back on the monks, blocking their view. She slowly unrolled the note, and read: 'Cobbler Sallu in Kerata. Nightfall. A frontier yet unbroken.'

"Endring," she muttered, and Spark pulled at her. "It's not like I trust him either, but…"

Spark tugged at her again.

"It's not like I'm gonna stick around here forever."

"Locin!" Voske was coming down the hall now with Hikari, Burz, and a handful of monks. "You coming? We're heading to the arena."

Hikari patted the sword at his side. "Time for my first lesson. I could use your endearing encouragement."

"Nah."

"So what," Voske asked, "you gonna just mope around this place?"

"I don't know." She stuffed the note in her pocket. "I don't know what I'm gonna do."

Burz had never seen a sight to rival the arena of Kerata. He stood in the center, staring at the ascending rows of seats that climbed into the sky like mountain steppes. It nearly made him dizzy. Around the upper rim were engraved in large letters the motto of the warrior's guild: No justice without mercy. No mercy without justice. And above waved the red and copper banners of Jeza and Uthando against the clear blue Erimos sky.

"By the gods!" Hikari's voice pulled his eyes back down. He was wielding a wooden practice sword, his own gaudy sapphire one hanging at his side, and his opponent had him leaping about like a frog after a fly.

Burz laughed. "It's not all defense, Hikari. You've got to strike!"

Burz smiled proudly as he watched Orin swing his own wooden sword toward Hikari, swinging high and low as he leapt from foot to foot.

"He's quite good."

"Of course he is! I trained him."

That seemed to embolden Orin and he rushed forward, but Hikari spun around and gave him a whack on his backside with the flat of his blade.

"Ha! A point for me, darling."

"Alright, alright," Burz said. "Not bad, but you both need to work on your form." He lifted his own wooden sword and turned it over in his hand. He hadn't held one of these since he was twelve, and it brought a smile to his lips. He twirled it easily around in his grip before holding it at the ready. "Who's got what it takes to take me on?"

"Me!" Orin leapt up eagerly, licking his lips as he looked down at his feet and shuffled them into position.

Burz pointed to his left foot. "Back a bit. It's about balance, remember. Practice until your feet move on their own, then you can focus on your opponent more easily."

Hikari shifted his own feet around, matching Orin's stance perfectly.

"Not bad, player." Burz said.

"I know how to follow a cue, darling."

"Remember, spacing is everything." Burz bent his knees and bobbed up and down, keeping his feet steady. "Be aware of yourself, your opponent, and the space between."

"More a dance than a fight," Hikari said cheerily. "At least that's what we were told."

Burz smiled. "You can dance on stage, but in the real world, the man you're facing doesn't want to dance. He wants to run you through, and if you give him the chance, he will."

Burz nodded to Orin first. The boy smiled and then carefully stepped forward, striking a few blows, reluctant at first. Soon, he was swinging with all his might, and Burz batted aside the blows with pride.

"Not bad," boomed the voice of Voske. He was strolling over with his hands across his chest and a couple Jeza monks marching warily nearby, matching his steps, and trying to look as if they weren't. "You got a good arm, kid."

Orin was beaming. "I'm gonna be a soldier, just like my Ada!"

Voske shot a side-long glance at Burz. "That so?"

"He hopes," Burz said, biting down his frustration. He should at least pretend to get along with Voske.

Voske bent down, hands on his knees, and smiled at Orin. "If I were a god, I'd pick you."

"Really?" He squealed. "My choosing is tomorrow!"

"Is it now? Want me to put in a good word for you with Jeza?"

Orin was ecstatic by now, thanking the big oaf and rushing around in circles.

Burz was furious. "Don't you have somewhere else to be?"

Voske scowled. "And miss this? Two legendary fighters sparring? And look, Hikari's here too!" He winked at Orin.

Hikari smirked. "Burz is an excellent teacher I'll have you know. Come on then, Burz. Shall we demonstrate?"

Burz locked his eyes on Voske for a moment and then turned to Hikari, feeling the wooden hilt in his grip, judging the space between them.

"Step to the side, Orin."

"Ha!" Hikari grinned. "Let the fight begin!"

Burz stepped forward and thrust his sword toward Hikari's chest. He knew Hikari wouldn't be close to ready for it, but it didn't matter. Voske was watching.

Hikari brought his own sword up and batted the blow away, but he was woefully off balance and Burz twisted his blade back around and tucked it under Hikari's chin.

Hikari flashed a sheepish smile.

"You forgot your feet."

"Right you are, darling!"

They reset. Hikari charged this time. Burz let him come at him a couple times, easily stepping out of the way before he blocked a blow with his blade, and swatted Hikari on the back with the flat of it.

Voske laughed. "Gonna let him beat you like that, player?"

Hikari shook his head. "If he wasn't so fast, it wouldn't be a problem."

"I'm not fast," Burz answered. "I know what I'm doing. Try to block me and counter attack this time. You don't have to overpower me, just deflect the blow away from your body."

Hikari seemed nervous now, choosing to simply stand his ground and bat away Burz' attacks.

"You have to threaten me."

"Right you are!" Hikari bobbed to the side, dodging a blow, and then twirled around and held his sword aloft. "Prepare to die, you scoundrel!"

Burz stopped dead and stared at him in disbelief.

Voske was guffawing now.

"Threaten me *with the sword*."

Hikari chuckled lightly. "Ah, of course."

As they reset again, Burz glanced at Orin. He was standing by Voske with his hands on his hips and a proud smile. He was *proud*. Proud to have the champion of Jeza as a friend, but not proud to have the champion of Uthando as a father?

"Again?" Hikari asked tentatively.

Burz nodded. "Your turn."

This time when Hikari rushed him, he easily side stepped, throwing his strong leg out and tripping Hikari. The poor man went tumbling into the dirt, and in the blink of an eye, Burz was on top of him, wooden sword at his throat. It wasn't a contest.

Hikari dropped his own sword in the dust and held his hands up defensively. His hair was disheveled and his toga dusted brown.

"Point taken, darling. I'll mind the feet."

Voske scoffed. "So you took down a helpless player. Proud of yourself?"

Burz tensed, turning his back to Voske. Why defend himself against a moron?

"Helpless?" Hikari scrambled to his feet. "I'll have you know, I've won more than a few fights in my day."

"Yeah, but how many of them were scripted?" Voske asked.

"Never underestimate the power of a quick wit and a sharp tongue."

Voske laughed. "I'll take a sharp axe over a sharp tongue any day."

It was Burz' turn to laugh.

"Something funny about that?"

He turned back to face Voske. Orin was still at his side, staring between the two men. "What's funny is you boasting about your skills with an axe when you've never even seen a battle."

Voske held his ground, crossing his arms over his chest. "I've fought plenty, soldier. I've never needed anything but my fists."

Burz stepped closer. "You have no idea what it is to be a warrior."

"No idea? Really?" He bellowed. "Gods! Someone should let Jeza know she put the wrong man in charge of her army."

A few of the nearby Jeza warriors laughed.

"It takes more than a mark on your hand to be a leader."

Voske stepped closer. "It takes more than a bum leg and a past to make you a soldier."

"And yet here we are!" Hikari ran forward, resting a hand on Orin's shoulder. "All happily chosen by the gods. Who can argue with that, right?"

"I signed up." Voske nodded to a table on the far end of the arena. "I'll prove my worth in the tournament. Are you willing to prove yours, or are you a coward?"

Burz tossed the toy sword in the dirt and set his eyes on the table. He wasn't about to let Voske keep talking down to him. He was a fool. The only advantage he had was his boon. In the tournament, they'd be on even ground.

He stormed up to the table where a warrior sat writing names, and he held up his right palm. The man gasped as he saw Uthando's sigil, and he stared at Burz, slack jawed.

"Burz, Champion of Uthando."

"T-two?" The man stammered. "Never in all the worlds have *two* champions competed."

Hoarse whispers gushed from those gathered near the table, and spread across the tournament grounds like wildfire. Burz turned around to see every eye trained on him, and in the center of the arena, Voske, glowering.

38: Cobbler Sallu

The feast of Kerata was less like a festival and more like a gang of ruffians swearing, drinking, and howling at the moon. The rules were a bit looser here, as were the manners. Mead flowed from three different fountains, and unwashed tankards got passed around in circles. Sure, there were a few stuffy holdouts to the revelry, but the Archon wasn't one of them. He walked the feast yard clad in scale mail and bellowing greetings to a thousand old friends.

Basically, everything was just the way Locin liked it, messy, fun, and laid back, but it was hard to appreciate it at the moment. Jeza monks were scattered around the feast with a keen eye for the champions, and Locin was starting to feel like a dog in a pen. On top of that, Endring's note was heavy in her pocket. She still hadn't decided if she even wanted to meet with him. It wasn't like she owed the old man anything.

"Look at Aurilis."

Voske's voice pulled her from her musing. He stood alongside her, currently chuckling and motioning with his mug of juice.

The High Oracle was standing in the corner of the celebration, holding her toga close and watching the revelry like a wet nurse might watch a teething toddler, worried she's going to get bit.

"Yeah," Locin smirked and sloshed her drink.

"Gods, were the other feasts like this?"

"I wouldn't count on it." Locin took a long swig, feeling the burning in her throat.

"Leave it to Jeza," Voske said proudly. "No one throws a party like we do."

"Here, here."

Their mugs clanked with a hollow ring and Locin quickly guzzled another gulp. Nearby a group of warriors started singing some terrible off-key tune, but it was jolly enough.

Voske started humming along, splashing juice as he waved his mug back and forth.

Locin scowled. "What's gotten into you?"

"What?"

"You're… happy."

"I'm always happy!"

She shrugged, turning to look around the courtyard. She felt antsy. It made his happiness grating.

"Guess I am happier than usual. You gotta admit, it's a good feast, and a tournament tomorrow."

"Oh, right. You're just excited about fighting Burz."

"I didn't say that."

"And taking out some frustration on his face?" She smirked.

Voske held two fingers close together. "Maybe a little."

Locin scoffed and turned back to her drink. She could feel the tipsy liquid starting to sway her back and forth, and suddenly the singing didn't actually sound *that* bad.

"You're going to watch, right?" He asked.

"Sure. I'll watch sweaty men beat each other senseless for a few hours."

"Good, good. That way you can see me win."

"No boons. Right?"

"What, you think I can't win without it?"

She let her eyes travel up his hulking form. Sometimes she actually forgot just how intimidating he was. "Nah, you got this."

He grinned. "You bet your life I do."

He leaned back with a glint in his eye, as though he was appraising her.

"What?"

He shrugged. "Just thinking. Imagine if we hadn't all gotten chosen at the same time, if it was just me and the old champions."

"Want to be rid of me that bad?"

He laughed. "Just the opposite. You're growing on me, kid. It'd be pretty dismal without you around."

Alarm bells were sounding in her brain. She suddenly wanted to be anywhere but here, and she dropped her hand in her pocket, feeling the crumpled note. "We gotta get you drunk, old man. You sound way too sober."

He waved her off and lifted his mug. "To friendship."

She stared at it, telling her arm to raise her own, but it didn't budge.

A shiver ran up her right arm. Spark wanted her to join the toast.

Mercifully, Hikari's voice interrupted. "Gods, where have you two been?"

He was scuffing their direction with a streak of mud running down the side of his yellow toga, though he didn't look the worse for wear. Of course he was smiling in spite of it. She wasn't certain he did anything else.

"We've been standing here the whole time," Voske said.

"Ah yes, standing in this little out of the way corner. How bizarre that I couldn't find you."

Locin nodded to the nearby fountain. "Staying close to the good stuff."

"Darling, there's more to life than just drinking." He gave her his best charming smile. "There's dancing, for one."

Voske coughed loudly at the word and sauntered backward, looking at the two of them with a dumb smile. "Well, that's my cue to leave"

He winked at Hikari before spinning on his heel and strolling into the crowd, singing along with the jaunty tune that just wouldn't die.

Locin raised an eyebrow. "Well?"

Hikari laughed lightly. "My fault, I'm afraid. Voske may be under the mistaken impression that I find you attractive."

She kicked him in the shin.

"Ouch! What was that for?"

She scowled. "I *am* attractive."

"To be sure." He looked her over, rubbing his ankle. "I meant more affection rather than simple desire."

"Simple?"

He smiled casually. "There's no end to women with perfect breasts and hair like silk, curves that can make a man weak in the knees."

She smiled. "Do you like my silky hair, Hikari?" She shook her wild curls, and they bounced around like a lion's mane.

"You know what I mean." But his eyes darted away now. And was he… blushing?

"Hikari? Are you in love?"

"Not with you, darling, despite what Voske may think."

She laughed. "Well, what gave him that idea?"

"Ah, well you see…"

"The great Hikari at a loss for words." She grew more serious now, handing him her mug. "You *are* in love."

"My thanks." He took the mug and drank deeply.

"Spit it out, player. Who is she?"

"Like I said, there's no end to beautiful women. Gods know I've seen my fair share of them."

"Yeah, yeah."

He sighed. "I want something more, something deep and… real."

"Nobody gets that."

A man walked by, and Locin reached up and grabbed one of his two full mugs, sloshing some mead on herself. He started to turn angrily, but she kicked out her hip and winked, and he simply smiled as he raised his second mug to her and stumbled off into the crowd.

"I don't believe it," Hikari said. "I've seen it before, two people in love, sharing the deepest parts of their soul."

"How deep is your soul, exactly?"

He sighed. "Not half so deep as hers, I'm afraid. Therein lies my problem. What if I'm not enough for her?"

"What?" She slapped his arm. "Worlds famous player *and* a champion? If that's not enough for her, she better find a way into Sbarga."

"She's just…" his voice sounded distant and dreamy. "She's like an ocean, and I'm afraid if I dive in, I may drown."

"Just 'cause you say it all poetic, doesn't make it mean anything."

"What do you think?"

She looked at Hikari questioningly. "What?"

"What do you think I should do? You're a woman, certainly you have some advice."

"Yeah. I'm a woman, not an ocean. If she's here, she's probably half drunk. Put on the charm, take her to your room… I assume I don't have to explain the rest?"

He scowled at her. "I'm not interested in that."

She looked at him skeptically.

"Well, not that I'm not interested, per say. But I want more. I think I do, at least."

He was staring through the crowd now. It was subtle, but he was leaning a little to see something, or *someone*. Locin leaned over and matched his gaze. On the other side of the mead fountain, she saw Illeri.

"Gods and Chosen!" She laughed. "Are you cutting the line?"

"What?" He looked at her defensively.

"Illeri? It's Illeri?"

He rubbed the back of his neck idly. "Well I… it's just that…" He slumped forward. "Yes."

"And you're too scared to tell her?"

"I did start to, but things didn't go as planned. We haven't really spoken since then."

"Just go talk to her, Hikari."

"What if she says no?"

"No to what?"

"Me."

"Has anyone ever said no to you?"

He shrugged. "I suppose not, but she's different."

"Look, at some point you gotta take a chance on somebody, right?"

A tingle up her right arm reminded her that Spark was very much still listening. Locin frowned and rubbed at the spot, getting rid of the feeling. She was suddenly feeling antsy again. The crowd felt too close, and the high walls felt like a prison. She let her hand drift to Endring's note.

"By the gods, you may be right!"

"Great," she said half listening, letting her eyes scan the high walls around the palace until she spotted the gate. There were a handful of guards, nothing she couldn't handle. "Go dance with her."

"Right!" Hikari gulped and then bobbed forward on his feet. And then he slumped back, resigned. "But perhaps later, after some more mead."

"Whatever."

Hikari cleared his throat and glanced at her sheepishly. "One last thing, darling. Might we keep this between us?"

"Yeah. What about Voske though?"

"Ah, yes." He chuckled nervously. "I suppose I'll simply have to tell him it didn't work out between us. Your fault, of course."

"What? But Hikari, my love!" She pursed her lips and stood up on her tiptoes, making smooching noises at him.

He laughed as she settled back down.

"I dumped you, player. That's my story."

Hikari tousled her curls. "You're a good friend, Locin."

The night air closed in around her, and suddenly the corner seemed very much exposed. "Yeah," she managed. "I gotta go. Don't wait too long, or she'll dance off with one of these big, hairy men."

He nodded to her with a half smile.

She didn't wait for a further reply, but instead strode away into the crowd. She didn't want to leave, but she couldn't stay here. She could feel Spark brushing her arm, trying to pull her back.

"It's fine Spark," she hissed. "I just gotta get some air."

She set her sights on the outer gates where the city stood in the orange light of the setting sun. Nightfall would be arriving soon, and she knew just the place to help clear her head.

The feast was wonderful and terrible. Lots of laughter filled the air, and the people toasted and cracked wise. Even the spirits seemed to be having a great time. It was as if they were all old friends, even if they'd only just met. On the other hand there were a *lot* of very large men, ham fisted warriors that jostled and swore. Rasa was certain most of them were good people, but that was the problem. She was just as certain they weren't *all* good people.

For most of the feast she'd tried to stay out of the way. She'd talked to Weylyn a bit, and a few spirits, but aside from that she'd kept to herself, sitting atop a low inner wall and dangling her bare feet over the edge. No one seemed to mind.

Currently she sat eating a crisp slice of honeydew and watching Locin and Spark. Locin was edging toward the outer wall, talking to thin air, and Spark kept tapping her in different ways, either brushing her shoulder or her cheek or even stomping on her foot. It was comical to watch.

Finally, Locin pointed toward the gate and Spark's shoulders drooped. The spirit floated to the sentries posted just inside the walls and whispered in one of their ears.

The man started looking around until Spark moved quickly to the wall and started slapping it hard. There was no way it could make a sound, but somehow it got the sentries' attention. The one motioned to his fellow, and they both walked toward the sound as Spark moved further away, still slapping.

Locin, meanwhile, quickly reached the gate and slipped outside. She was smooth.

Rasa bit her lip and quickly stood to her feet, her curiosity piqued. She hurried along the top of the wall to where it joined the outer and jumped, easily swinging up and over, then dropping to the stony road outside. She winced at the impact, then turned and sprinted, her bare feet padding lightly across the even paving.

In a few minutes, she caught up to Locin and Spark. It wasn't hard to pick out the tell-tale blue line that connected them. She kept a short distance behind, ducking around strangers as they wound their way toward the heart of the city.

"Young miss," called a deep voice from across the street.

She looked toward it to see a man flagging her down.

"Young miss, can I ask you a question?"

Her heart leapt into her throat and she ducked her head, scurrying down the road and trying very hard not to fall over her feet. The protection of the temple suddenly felt very far away.

"Young miss? Can you hear me?"

She ducked around a corner and huddled against the wall, her breathing shallow. Her eyes darted up to a windowed building across the street. She could probably climb to get away. She shut her eyes, suddenly feeling foolish. She was safe. It was only a question, nothing more.

She pressed her back into the wall behind her and let Nyx close in until the voices around her seemed to dim, and she felt cold fingers touch her arm. Her eyes fluttered open to see the spirit of a young boy watching her with bewilderment. He was standing in the middle of the street with a hand in the pocket of his ragged shorts.

Are you alright?

Rasa nodded and eased away from the wall. "I am. I was just… It was a memory."

Are you lost?

"No," she wrung her hands and glanced down the street. She couldn't see Locin anymore. "You didn't happen to see a young woman connected to a spirit pass this way, did you?"

Sure. I saw 'em. Went in the cobbler's shop, just ahead on the left.

Rasa frowned. It wasn't as though Locin needed shoes.

I wouldn't follow her though.

"Why not?"

She didn't look very happy.

Rasa felt her throat catch. Still, it was Locin. They were friends. "Thanks."

Sure thing.

She could see the sign for the cobbler shop from where she stood, like a big brown boot jutting out over the walkway. "I'll be careful."

In a flash the boy was gone. No doubt retreated to some other corner of Nyx.

Rasa pushed past her trepidation and paced toward the shop. There were bright, warm lights glowing through the oval windows, and the smell of old leather and olive oil drifted outward. She hunched low as she neared until she heard Locin's voice, murmuring from inside.

She slowly padded to just below the window and peeked over the edge. Inside she could see Locin and another man who looked suspiciously like Sammel. They were seated in two cushioned chairs with their backs to her while a cobbler held a thick sandal up to Sammel's foot. Behind them, Spark was pacing the room, muttering to herself in words that Rasa couldn't quite make out.

"There we are." The cobbler said as he finished strapping the sandal in place. It was clearly far too big, but he placed his hands along the sides, sliding them down the length of the shoe. As he did the leather gradually tightened, shrinking until it followed the curve of Sammel's foot perfectly. "How's that?"

Sammel held up his foot and glanced at Locin. "What do you think?"

Locin passed him a withering glance.

"I think the straps are too thick," he said, deftly unstrapping it. "I require something that breathes a bit more."

"Ah," the cobbler answered. "I have just the thing." He snatched up the shoe and scurried from the room, leaving the other three, for the moment, alone.

"I swear," Locin hissed. "If you sent me that note just to try on shoes, I'll boon you across this room."

Sammel cleared his throat. "You'll *boon* me?"

"Yes. Now out with it. Whatever you have to say."

Instead of hurrying, Sammel seemed to relax all the more, folding his hands behind his head and leaning on the high backed chair with an air of leisure. "We want you to steal the second piece of the Crook."

Rasa took a sharp breath, and immediately crouched lower.

Both Locin and Spark were leaning away now, like Sammel was a venomous snake. "Excuse me?"

"You look surprised."

"Of course I'm rotting surprised."

"I don't see why. You have figured out we want them, haven't you?"

"Thought you might when you nabbed the first one. Seems pretty obvious now."

He nodded.

Locin's foot was twitching with agitation. "Then why not steal it yourself?"

As though on queue the back door of the shop flew open and the cobbler bustled in carrying a new sandal, this one already the right size. He knelt in front of Sammel, holding it up proudly.

"Much better." Sammel said as he slipped the sandal over his foot. "Can it be dyed?"

"Of course," the cobbler answered. "White, black, brown."

"Sky blue?"

The old man scratched his head at the request. "I suppose."

"And do you have any with straps that rise up the calf?"

The man looked aghast. "You might have said that in the first place."

"Apologies."

The cobbler slunk back out of the room, and Locin leaned toward Sammel. "You know, if you wanted privacy, there's better places."

"I wanted a new pair of shoes. And you still owe me an answer."

"You first," Locin said.

Sammel cleared his throat. "Pinching an item in the middle of a dark sewer is not the same as robbing a palace."

"I know a local kid who might think different."

"He has a thief's boon, is not currently wanted-"

"And he can't fly through windows." Locin interrupted.

"It's not that simple," Sammel said. "Now. I've answered your question. How about you answer mine?"

Locin paused as though deep in thought and Rasa leaned into the sill, straining to hear.

"Where *is* Endring?"

"Not far from here."

"Then why didn't he ask me himself?"

"He couldn't risk it."

Locin sighed, shaking her head. "You gotta give me something more here. I want some answers before I agree to anything."

Sammel nodded.

"What is the crook? Like, exactly what does it do?"

A sudden motion caught Rasa's eye. Spark was staring at her, mouth agape.

Her heart caught in her throat as she stared at the spirit, pleadingly. Spark seemed as startled as she was, and for a moment she just watched Rasa, but her eyes darted to Locin. Rasa knew she could alert her. Maybe she couldn't *tell* her Rasa had overheard, but she could certainly draw her attention to the window.

Rasa dropped down, her heart hammering. She rolled to her side and sprinted back out to the road, then away through the crowd, praying Spark hadn't given her away.

Voske sat in a row of seats in the archon's palace, shifting uncomfortably. The seats were comfortable enough, the air inside was cool, and the company wasn't disagreeable, but he still felt out of place.

Following the feast, the champions had all been invited to a spectacle, a play called *To Nyx and Back*. The seats were arranged in a circle with the champions together on one side and the other guests ringing the perimeter.

The play wasn't half bad, sharp-witted, just the sort of thing Voske might have enjoyed twenty years ago. Had he ever been to a play as a laborer? He couldn't recall a time.

"There's only one question then," the lead player's voice rang out. "What manner of death shall it be?"

"The one where I die in bed," said the sniveling sidekick. "At the old age of a hundred and five."

"You would die an ailing man, on your back?"

"Yes. A long, long, long time from now."

Voske's eyes wandered across the circle to where a group of young teenagers lounged. They were the children of the elite. Self-assured, care-free, they drank the archon's wine and laughed at inside jokes, barely paying attention to the production.

Was he really like that at their age? Pampered and prideful, capable of nothing that disagreed with his indulgences? He shook his head.

"And when the shadow of Nyx looms over Talamh and blackens the sky?"

As the player spoke he twirled his finger, summoning an illusory storm cloud that swirled ominously over the scene.

"Then I'll take a nap in the shade."

A few laughs rang through the theater.

Sounds like Burz.

Voske looked to his side to comment to Locin, but her seat was empty. He glanced to the other side where Hikari sat quietly mouthing the lines of the lead role. He looked way too engrossed in the production to appreciate the jab.

Voske slumped back in his seat. The wealthy youth were slipping out now, a couple bottles of wine in hand. They'd lost interest in the play, and were off to make their own fun. He was about to look away again, when he saw Rasa slip through the closing doors. She was wringing her hands and looked rather out of sorts.

He watched as Weylyn spotted her and headed over. Soon they were ducking back out to the lobby.

Voske stood, motioning for Hikari to let him by.

"Antsy, darling?"

"I'll be back," he whispered, then ducked out of the circle and around the outside.

As he neared the door, a terrified looking pair of Jeza monks stepped in his way. The first spoke in a trembling tone.

"Forgive me, Champion. We have orders to-"

"Gotta pee," he said flatly.

The monks exchanged a nervous glance.

Voske was getting tired of this already. Would Aurilis watch his every move for the next fifty years? Mercifully, she didn't look like she had that long left to live.

Voske grabbed the hem of his toga like he was about to lift it. "Move out of my way, or get me a goblet."

The monks went wide-eyed and slowly shifted out of the way.

He pushed his way through the door and spotted Weylyn and Rasa sitting on a plush bench near the entrance. One of the monks had followed him, but he paid him no heed as he headed over. Weylyn had her lips pursed thoughtfully, and Rasa's cheeks were flushed, and her breathing heavy as if she'd run here.

"Everything alright?" He asked.

Rasa gave Weylyn a wary look, and the old woman nodded to her.

"Voske needs to hear this."

"I followed Locin into town," she began. "During the feast. I know we weren't supposed to leave, but I saw her slip out, and I was curious."

"So you broke the temple's rule?" He smiled. "That'll earn you points in my book."

"She met Sammel there."

Voske tensed. *What in the world would that old thief be doing here?* "You're sure?"

Rasa nodded. "It was him. She went to meet him at the cobbler."

"What in Nyx for?"

Rasa bit her lip, hesitant to continue.

"Apparently he asked her to steal the crook piece," Weylyn said.

"Didn't he already do that?"

"The second one," Rasa said. "The one you brought back from the desert."

Voske's eyes narrowed, feeling his ire rise. "Why would Locin do that? Why in Nyx would they even ask her?" But some part of him deflated. She was a friend, and he trusted her, but hadn't she kept her distance? She was a thief, after all.

"She knew to meet him," Weylyn said flatly. "She had to know he'd be there."

Voske swallowed hard. He didn't want to grasp what she was implying, but it was plain as the nose on her face. Locin was in contact with Sammel. Maybe even Endring.

"If she did betray us," Weylyn pressed, "it was some time ago. Maybe Endring gave her all those papers."

"Bah." Voske waved her off, pacing back and forth, but he knew she was right. She'd been talking with them at least since Arrajin. Which meant before they even knew what Endring was. Had Locin known?

"What do we do?" Rasa asked. "Do we warn Aurilis?"

"No." He told himself he had a good reason for his answer, but those rotting monks were watching him from across the room. If Aurilis didn't trust him, he wasn't inclined to trust her either.

"Are you sure?" Weylyn asked.

"I'm sure." He stared at the double door where he could hear the muffled voice of the lead actor, and a rumble of conjured thunder. He'd go back in and watch the show. Tomorrow, he'd fight in the tournament, and nothing would happen to the relic. It couldn't.

"It's Locin."

39: The Tournament Begins

Burz woke before the sun. He always did, even during the days he couldn't walk when he would lay in bed watching the sunrise.

He sat up as a warm breeze rippled the curtains, carrying a fresh, earthy scent. His leg was stiff from sleeping on it, and he pulled it to the side and stood up, catching sight of his face in the mirror. It looked drawn, and the crow's feet at the corners of his eyes more pronounced. He looked old. He shrugged it off and headed for a basin and pitcher, both opulent pearl, and he splashed his face and chest. The mornings had been his favorite time, before his family was awake, before he was a father, or a husband. He was just a man.

He moved to his dresser and slipped on a simple chiton, something light and easy to move in, and then he headed to the window to watch the sun as it broke over the horizon and colored the plains in gold. He used to cherish this time, time to pray and sit alone in the stillness, but today he just felt anxious.

"Jeza," he muttered. "Watch over my sons. Uthando, keep their feet from slipping. Help me live with the same fire you felt, when you gifted the holy shrines, giving of your own divinity, so that we might know you. Help me live as your chosen."

He paused, losing his train of thought. Being a champion didn't feel much like the blessing he had hoped for, and as much as he tried to control his thoughts, there seemed to be no safe place to land. Every aspect of his life seemed to be in upheaval.

He heard Hadris moving around behind him, and he turned to see her slipping on a delicate pink toga. She sat down at the mirror and began combing her hair and pinning it in place.

"Good morning."

She nodded to him sleepily.

"You were quiet last night at the feast."

She shrugged.

He started to turn back to the window.

"That's it?"

Burz dropped his shoulders and turned to face her. "I don't want to fight."

"Neither do I," she said, her voice terse.

"Then just tell me what it is. What did I do now?"

She cocked her head and stared at him dumbfounded.

"Am I supposed to know?"

"Orin's choosing is today."

"Of course, but not until sundown."

She sighed sharply. "You knew Orin's choosing was today, and yet you signed up for this ridiculous tournament."

"I'll be done long before sundown."

"He was so excited to spend the whole day with you, Burz. His *last* day with you."

Burz slumped down in his chair. "It's not like we'll never see him again. Whatever his calling, we'll find a guild hall close to us. Arrajin has hundreds of different guilds, and we can visit him as often as you like."

"It's his choosing day. He wants to spend it with his Ada, and instead you'll be in that arena trying to prove something to yourself that everyone else already knows."

He turned his eyes back out the window, but the golden grass was green again, and the world had lost its magic.

"You don't have to prove anything," she continued. "Uthando chose you. That means you're worthy to be a champion."

"Not everyone sees it that way."

"So what?" She stormed off, but there was nowhere to go, so she started angrily pacing beside the door. "What are you hoping for here? You beat Voske and everyone sees you're better? What if he beats you? Then you get to feel unworthy for the rest of your life?"

"I get to feel like I tried!" He said. "I get to feel like I'm not a useless cripple."

"You honestly think you're useless? So, what, I'm watching my husband die for nothing?"

He shrugged off the comment. "I'm not dying. Far from it, in fact."

"Really?" She strolled over and brushed at the wrinkles on his face. "Can't you see yourself, Burz? You didn't look like this before we left Tajerim."

"No. I looked like a cripple who laid in bed while his wife waited on him hand and foot."

She drew back her hand. "Was that so bad?"

"Yes."

He saw in her face how much he'd wounded her, but it was the truth.

She turned away, sniffling as she started slamming dresser drawers, looking for gods knew what.

"You know I'm grateful. I wouldn't have made it if you hadn't…" he sighed, running his hands across his head. "But it's my job to take care of you and the boys, to do something useful for the worlds. I'm no good to anyone if I can't do that."

She slammed one last drawer shut and then turned to face him. "You're good to me. You always were. And to the boys. I'm not ready to lose you because of your own stupid pride."

He just dropped his arms to his sides and stared at her. What else could he do?

Hadris headed for the door. "Sundown. Don't forget."

She stormed off again, all the way out the door this time, leaving Burz alone by his window, watching the rolling plains. He hadn't really enjoyed mornings in months. He wondered if he still just got up early as a ritual, like a habit he couldn't break.

He pulled himself from the chair and headed out. Maybe he could clear his head at the arena. At the very least, he could fight, which sounded even better.

As the sun rose over Kerata, the tournament finally began in earnest. From all corners of Talamh patrons and archons and fisticuff enthusiasts gathered together in order to take in the spectacle. The outside of the arena was overflowing with drinks and humanity as the merchants hocked their wares to the sweaty crowd.

Inside, Locin sat with the hood of her cloak pulled low as she slouched in her seat further up the stands. It wasn't that she was afraid to rejoin the champions, but she was enjoying her current level of freedom. If she went back, she'd have to dodge Aurilis' red-robed guard dogs to get away again. She'd spent the night drinking at a local tavern, then laying out under the stars, dreaming about all the other places she could go. Not that Kerata was a bad place, but it was a big realm out there. A *very* big realm, and she'd never done well if she wasn't free to roam it.

Her eyes drifted to the champion's private box, only thirty yards below and off to the side. She could see Hikari and Gillis standing at the edge, talking excitedly while the others sat behind, patiently waiting for the fights to begin.

She felt a prick from Spark, and she rolled her eyes.

"What? You miss those buffoons?"

She felt Spark's 'yes' as a pinch in her right shoulder.

"Well, I don't."

Spark tugged at her harder. She was concerned.

Locin leaned back and sipped her drink. "Relax. We'll go back. Eventually."

She settled into her chair and folded her arms, listening as the murmur of the mob swelled with anticipation. A crier was taking the stand just above the dirt of the arena. He looked pleased by the response.

"Fair people of Talamh! Welcome to the festival of combat!"

The horde cheered wildly, and Locin pulled her hood over her ears. It was the kind of roar that shook the ground and thumped inside her chest, and it made her feel alive.

"To the honor of Jeza!" The crier called.

"To the honor of Jeza!" Echoed the crowd.

Soldiers in full garb pushed two massive doors open at opposite ends of the arena, and the first combatants entered to thunderous applause.

Spark pulled at Locin, and she brushed it off.

"First few matches'll be dull," she said sulkily as the noise died down.

The man next to her looked over oddly. "Ya think?"

I wasn't talking to you, she thought.

"Yeah. Anybody who's somebody gets straight through to the top of the bracket. Including the Champions."

The man's eyes lit. "I heard there are two!"

Locin smirked. "That's right. One of them is ten feet tall, and the other has four arms."

The man's eyes went wide, and then he snickered. "You're messing with me. How would you know anyway?"

"Oh, I know 'em personally."

The man laughed. "Sure, and I just ate breakfast with Kissandin."

Locin's mood was beginning to sour, and she eyed the champion's box.

Spark tugged at her as if to say, 'you could be in there with them'.

She waved a hand around as if she could shoo a spirit. "Rot off," she whispered, careful this time to not be heard by the man.

A shiver ran up her spine suddenly, a different kind of feeling. Spark was telling her to be alert. A flutter of wings startled her as a solid black raven perched by her shoulder. She leapt up and threw her arms at it on instinct. The rotting thing took flight, landing a couple feet away on the low stair wall, and it cawed.

What do you want? She thought. She watched the way it cocked its head, staring at her with human intelligence.

"Go away." She wasn't in the mood for another rendezvous.

She turned to sit back down, but the blasted thing dove at her, ripping at her hair with sharp talons. She felt one scrape her neck, and she held a hand over the scratch.

"Son of a serpent!"

The man beside her stared angrily her direction.

"Not you," she said sourly. "The rotting bird."

But when she looked up, it was gone again.

The man looked at her like she was crazy, and then turned his attention back to the fight below. The crowd cheered and groaned with each blow, but she barely noticed.

He has to be somewhere.

She scanned the arena until she saw it again, an unusually large raven perched above a storeroom. It caught her eye, and then dove in through a high window.

Her curiosity had gotten the best of her now. Of course, he knew it would. And she had a score to settle. She rubbed the scratch on her neck as she pushed her way through the crowd. They were everywhere, crammed in seats, clogging the stairs. She could hardly move, but she fought her way around to the back of the storeroom where a locked door greeted her. In a moment, she had booned it open, and she slipped inside, locking it behind her.

The room had a low row of windows that scattered dusty light on a sliver of the floor. In the corners were stacks of shields and a few pieces of worn armor, and someone leaned on the opposite wall, clad in a dark robe.

"What in Nyx do you think you're doing?"

"I needed your attention."

"I should return the favor."

Endring strolled closer, keeping his form out of the light. "It was hardly a scratch."

She sighed, kicking at some dusty armor on the floor. "I haven't decided yet. Gods! You only gave me a few hours."

"That's not why I'm here. Something's changed."

"What, a bunch of fowlers came to the festival?"

"Borroka's on her way."

All her frustration at the interruption suddenly vanished. "What?"

"Borroka is on her way here, now."

"Uh… and what am I supposed to do about that exactly?"

"Steal the crook," he said hoarsely. "Before she can."

Locin laughed. "Gods. You expect me to fall for that?"

"I thought you understood our cause," he said sharply.

"Yeah. Sammel told me about your crazy plan to pull Neveri out of Nyx."

"When we talked in Arrajin, you seemed eager to help. Has your conviction waned?"

"This isn't about that. It's about you lying to me. I took too long deciding, so now Borroka is magically on her way and I have no choice but to do what you want, and to do it now. Nice try, you old rotter."

He stepped close, grabbing her arm in an iron grip. His hand felt too strong for a man, and his fingers were rough and leathery. "I am not playing games. Borroka *is* coming, with an army."

Locin jerked free, but she felt a shudder. Spark was pulling her attention outside, somewhere distant. Could it be possible he was telling the truth?

"Is there an army coming?" She whispered.

"Yes."

'Yes'.

Her heart started pounding in her chest. *An army, here? And he thinks I can do anything about it.*

"I don't know how long we have," he said. "The crook is in the Archon's palace. I suspect you know better than I exactly where."

She shook her head. "Aurilis has it locked up tight. Voske never should have handed it over to the old shrike, if you ask me."

"Find it."

She heard the familiar sound of cracking bones and fluttering feathers, and she glanced up to see the dark robes falling to the ground as a shape disappeared out the window. She smacked the flat of her palm on the door.

"Rot it, Spark. What are we gonna do now?"

Voske felt the prize fighter's punch batter his side like a hammer blow. He gritted his teeth at the pain, but he kept his feet under him. If there were two things you could learn in a quarry, it was how to never quit, and how to take a hit. Another blow assailed his ribs, and he grabbed for the fighter's arm, but the man was too fast. The cheers of the crowd pulsed through the air and the fighter wiped a sheen of sweat from his forehead.

"You're cheating," he spat. "You've your boon to thank."

Voske laughed a bellowing sort of laugh. He could feel the boon of Jeza, eager to flood his veins, but he kept it in check. "You think I need it to fight you?"

"I'd bet my last mark. No one's that strong, to not even flinch."

Voske spit to the floor of the arena. "And if I told you I hadn't so much as tickled the boon of Jeza, what would you say?"

"I'd say, prove it."

The man charged Voske again and drove a kick into his thigh. He had the legs of a horse and Voske winced at the powerful strike, but he wasn't going to show it, especially not now.

"See," the fighter exclaimed. "No one takes that without showing."

"Another strike for Barruk!" The announcer cried. "He's giving the champion all he can handle!"

"Apparently I do," Voske retorted, and he readied himself again. There was no way he could block Barruk, the man was just too fast, but maybe he could trade.

Barruk sneered and moved closer again, sending a fist squarely toward Voske's head. Voske leaned into the blow and counter punched, straight to the gut. At the same moment Barruk's fist battered into Voske's jaw, Voske's own blow folded the warrior in half. Barruk staggered backward, gasping and wide-eyed, and Voske rushed after him. He grabbed both sides of his head, and brought his own noggin crashing down with a meager thunk that did little justice to the impact. Barruk sank backward into the sand, then lay, looking up at Voske like his world was spinning as a trumpet sounded his defeat.

"Behold!" the announcer cried. "The Champion of Jeza stands victorious!"

The crowd erupted as Voske shook his fists in the air, basking in the moment. He wiped blood from the corners of his mouth as he looked back down at the man.

"Cheater!" Barruk yelled. "You tapped into your boon and you know it!"

Voske smirked down at the young man. "Is that so? Then maybe you'd like to see what the goddess's boon is really like."

As he spoke he summoned the strength of Jeza and sent a foot hurtling into the sand. The ground below trembled and the people yelled in alarm, as the quake rattled the walls.

Barruk's mouth hung open in amazement and the cheers of the crowd grew all the louder.

Voske smiled and held out a hand to the warrior. "Come on then." He grabbed his wrist and helped him up. "If it helps, I'll be feeling it all tomorrow. That was a Nyx of a kick."

Barruk still looked astonished, and only replied by crossing his arms over his chest and bowing.

Voske clapped him on the back as the announcer continued bellowing what an awesome display it was, then the two combatants parted ways, each heading back toward the sides of the arena.

By the time Voske reached the staging room, he was already starting to feel the ache, but it didn't really worsen his mood. He was sure Burz was taking just as much of a beating in his matches, and that would be the only fight he really cared about.

He strode through the door with his mind on nothing but a glass of water and a window seat for the fights, but he paused when he heard Weylyn's voice.

"Voske."

He looked to see the other champions, save for Burz and Locin. They were standing in a tight-knit circle and looking oddly serious.

"I thought you were all in the stands," he said, more confused than anything. "Did no one watch the fight?"

"This is important." Weylyn's voice carried a serious tone.

"What happened?"

"Locin."

Without another word Weylyn stepped to the side revealing Locin in their midst. She looked at Voske with bewilderment.

"Hey. You wanna tell me what's going on?"

He stalked closer, coming within arm's reach, and looked her over. "What's going on is a tournament. Where have you been?"

"Around. Talking to my people in the city."

Voske frowned. "Your people?"

"Yeah, you know, thieves."

"We know… A little too well actually."

"What's that supposed to mean?"

Voske reached a hand to his forehead, gently massaging his brow. "What do you want, Locin?"

She frowned. "What I wanted was to come join you all, but now I'm thinking maybe that was a mistake."

"And that was it? You just wanted to join us?"

"Yes!" She hesitated and glanced away at the corners of the room. "And no."

"She came here to see you," Hikari volunteered. "Rasa saw her coming, so the rest of us got curious and-"

"Fine," Voske cut him off, then turned back to Locin. "What is it?"

"It's Borroka," Locin blurted. "She's on her way here."

Voske frowned. He certainly hadn't forgotten the shrike from the Sacred Quarter. "She's on Erimos?" he asked incredulously.

"Yes, and she's got an army."

He shook his head in disbelief. "What, she just left Arrajin? Came out for the fights?"

"I don't know."

"Why would she do that?"

"I don't know anymore than that."

"Oh, I'm sure you don't."

Locin scrunched up her brow. "What in Nyx does that mean?"

"It means you're not as crafty as you think you are, that's what." Voske pointed toward Rasa. "Rasa saw you with Sammel."

Locin's eyes widened and she took a step back, spinning to look for Rasa, who was busily hiding behind the others. "What?"

"That's right," Voske growled. "She heard you scheming to steal the crook."

"That's a load of mire!"

"Then where were you last night? Hmm?"

"I needed some air."

"Sure you did."

"I did! The temple's on us like a monkey on scrap. I felt like I was gonna lose my mind, so I headed out, cleared my head. That's all!"

Voske folded his arms. "And you just happened to meet Sammel?"

"I saw him, but I never agreed to help him. I'm on your side."

"But I heard you," Rasa piped up from the back. "I heard you talking about stealing the crook."

"Stay out of this, shrike."

Voske grabbed Locin's arm. "Leave her out of this. It's between me and you."

She jerked away, glaring at him, then turned and looked at the others. Every face was a mixture of suspicion and disappointment.

"You gotta believe me," she urged. "They're coming."

Hikari reached out and set a hand on her shoulder but she instinctively pulled back.

"Surely you can see where we're coming from," he soothed. "They would be mad to attack here."

The venom crept back into Locin's voice. "She's as rotting mad as they come. You saw what she did in Arrajin."

Voske glanced at Zengin. There was an unsettling glint in his eye that made Voske's hair stand on end.

"Precisely when," Zengin asked, "did Sammel say Borroka would arrive?"

"Today. I'm not sure when."

Voske felt like his head was swimming. "And you trusted him? He's the enemy!"

"Oh yeah, Voske. That's why he warned us about an attack. That makes total sense."

"What attack?" Voske growled. "I don't see any attack."

"It could be a ruse," Illeri mused. "A diversion so he can access the crook."

Voske pointed at Illeri. "Thank you. Exactly. It could be anything, and you're just leading us up the garden path."

Locin's arms were stiff at her sides now and she stared from face to face around the group. "So that's how it is? I risk my neck to save you all, and what, just get yelled at for it?"

"Don't give me that," Voske snarled. "For all we know you're working with Endring right now."

Her arms shook as she answered. "Fine," she spat. "But don't blame me when an army shows up and starts torching the place."

"I'll take my chances."

She glared at him a moment longer, then stormed past, slamming the door on her way out.

Hikari took a deep breath and started to move after her, but Voske caught his arm. "Don't."

He looked back at Voske with uncertainty. "She's still a champion."

"She's not thinking clear. Give her some time to get her head on straight."

"So we just let her go?"

"That's exactly what we do."

Voske strode back to the windows and stared out to where another fight was just starting.

"And if she's telling the truth?"

He stayed focused on the match, wishing with every fiber of his being that he could be fighting

"Voske," Hikari insisted. "What if she's telling the truth?"

"Liar's lie," he answered, looking back at the group. Most of them looked uneasy. "Endring's a liar, Sammel's a liar, Locin's a liar. If she's thrown in her lot with them, then fine, but that doesn't mean I'll believe a word any of them say."

"Keep an eye out," Weylyn added. "Just in case."

Voske grunted and turned back to the fight, watching as the opponents laid into one another, and his hands gripped the stone of the sill, gradually crushing it to rubble.

40: The Final Round

Locin brushed through the crowd that was streaming toward the arena. The final match was coming soon, and word had spread that for the first time in the history of the festival, two Champions would be sparring.

A fat man stumbled into her, his sweaty arm slapping into her shoulder.

"Rot off!"

She shoved back, though she could hardly move his blubbery form.

He glared at her. "What's your problem?"

His companion leaned over to see her, a scrawny kid with a face full of freckles. "You rot off!"

She had half a mind to show them her sigil, put them in their place, but a score of Jeza monks stood around the plaza, and she didn't need that kind of attention. The crowd swiftly carried them off on its current toward the arena. All she wanted was to be anywhere else.

Eventually, she squirmed her way through the crowd to where the last stragglers meandered. Beyond, the whole city sat like a ghost town, empty windows and quiet shops with signs indicating they were closed. Everyone was at the fight.

She could sense Spark, but she'd been quiet since they'd left the others nearly an hour ago. That was fine by Locin. She wasn't in a talking mood. Still, she was glad to have Spark near.

She spotted a pub on a corner with arched windows wide open, begging any air that was willing to gift it with a breeze. She made her way past the obvious closed sign and peered inside. The window might keep most men out, and maybe some really fat women, but she could fit just fine.

"Idiots."

She wriggled through and headed for the bar. And there was Spark with a prick on her arm.

"I didn't ask you."

She spotted a bottle of green liquor that looked interesting, and she hopped the counter, standing on the back bar to reach it.

Spark did not approve.

"Like I said," she said, hopping down. "I didn't ask you."

She clenched the cork with her teeth and pulled it free, lifting the liquor to her lips. It burned down her throat, but the cool minty flavor and the boon used to imbue it made her feel oddly cool.

"Gods! Some kind of local drink? I gotta get a few bottles before we leave."

A deep voice broke in. "We call it Tarc."

She started as she saw a man coming down the steps. His hair was white as snow, whiter in fact than his dingy toga, and his face had more crevices and ravines than the Haribesh Valley.

"Gods, you scared me!"

"I scared you?" He made it to the bottom of the steps and turned to see the door still bolted shut. "How'd you get in?"

She pointed to the window and then took another gulp.

"Ah."

Locin reached into her coin purse and took out more than enough for the whole bottle, dropping it on the counter. The barkeep's eyes followed her palm closely, but she gave up nothing.

"I'm surprised you aren't at the arena," he said.

"Neither are you."

"I'm heading that way. You don't seem to be."

"Let's just say I've had all I can stomach of Champions for a while."

"I see."

She lifted the bottle and let the light from the window catch the milky pale green. "By the way, *Tarc* is a horrible name."

He smiled. "It's short for Tarcboraket, the man who first created it."

"He has a horrible name too."

"Well, he's been dead almost a hundred years, so I doubt he cares anymore."

Locin felt Spark tugging at her, but she wasn't going back to the arena. She wanted to be away from the others for a while.

The man strolled toward the bar and leaned over, grabbing a glass and setting it in front of her. "Mind if I join you?"

She tipped the bottle and filled his glass.

The man lifted it and drank deeply. "So, what did they do?"

"Who?" Locin took another swig. She could feel her head starting to buzz.

"The Champions."

"Oh. They just think they're better than everyone else, you know? I don't like that."

"Some people are better than others."

She scowled at the man. "Not those idiots."

Spark pinched her arm, and she bit the inside of her cheek so she wouldn't react.

"*Some people*," Locin began pointedly, "might think I should give them another chance. You know, be the bigger man."

His eyes wandered her frame, and he smirked. She was anything but *big* and *man*. "And you don't want to do that?" He pushed his glass forward and she topped it off again.

"They had their rotting chance. More than I should have given 'em."

"They must've really slighted you, huh?"

She rolled her eyes. "Obviously." And then she gulped down another swig. "I thought I learned this lesson already, you know? You gotta look out for yourself. Nobody else."

"That's highly cynical for someone so young."

Locin scoffed. "Once you've been through enough mire, you aren't young anymore. Age doesn't matter."

He nodded and downed the liquor in his glass.

"I have this philosophy, see? You gotta be the first one to leave. Nobody ever stays forever, and it hurts a lot less to be the one to go."

Spark was tugging furiously now, but Locin gulped down some more of the liquid. Soon Spark would fade away like all the rest of her troubles.

"What if you're wrong?"

She looked at the man sharply. "What?"

"What if one day someone stays?"

She laughed. "You've only had two shots, barkeep. You're already drunk."

"Maybe." He stood with some effort. "I'm going to the fight. You have to leave now."

She held the bottle up. "I'm taking this."

"You paid for it."

Locin shuffled her way back out, staring for a moment after the old man to where the arena towered over the city. The sounds of the crowd shook the very ground as anticipation swelled in the air. Maybe the gods themselves would come down to watch such an event.

And Spark was still there. Relentless. She tugged with all her strength toward the arena, but Locin wouldn't budge.

"For the last time, no! I tried to warn them. It's not my problem anymore."

Locin kicked at the dirt as she sulked away from the arena. She felt Spark pulling further away as she stayed behind, and soon she was gone, and Locin was alone.

Rasa sat on the edge of the Champion's box, her legs dangling through the slats of the stone railing. Below, the brown dirt floor of the arena was empty. The excitement of the crowd had been building more and more as the time drew near for the final fight. The announcer appeared on his balcony and held up his hands. A cry erupted from the crowd that shook the very stones of the arena, and Rasa gripped the rail above her as some loose dirt bounced off the edge and scattered in a little cloud over the rows below.

She let her eyes wander up the impressive height of the arena. She'd never seen anything so big. Tens of thousands of spectators were crammed in on all sides. Behind her, Hikari and Illeri were on their feet, staring out over the arena. Zengin had disappeared some time ago, and Weylyn was pacing nervously. Plates had been set out on stone tables covered with fancy cloth, every kind of delicacy Kerata had to offer, but no one had touched any of it. The mood was tense and anxious.

"Gods and chosen," Hikari marveled as the roaring crowd fell again to the dull murmur of a thousand conversations. "Desita herself could hardly have conjured such a show."

"I don't know," Illeri said, trying to keep her focus on the arena, but she kept glancing nervously around. "Maybe it's not for everyone."

"You mean you aren't enjoying this? Two men punching each other until one falls down?" Hikari smirked playfully. "What's not to like, darling?"

Rasa noticed the way Illeri nodded without looking at Hikari, the way his cheeks tinged with color as he quickly looked away too.

"Well," he continued, weakly. "Voske and Burz should be fun to watch. Two champions sparring for the title of 'Greatest Warrior in all Talamh'. I, for one, am excited to see this!"

Rasa.

A familiar voice called to her from beyond the veil. She had been blocking out Nyx most of the afternoon without even realizing it, but there was an urgency in the voice. She slowly let her boon creep in, feeling herself drift toward the abyss. It was like placing a hand on the veil, but less tangible. She saw spirits gathered around the arena, as excited for the fight as the living.

Rasa.

She turned to see Spark kneeling beside her. She looked worried. Rasa gave a glance toward the others, who were still talking. They seemed a little more distant now as Nyx grew close. She felt nervous. Was Spark angry with her for turning on Locin?

I need your help.

"Me?" She was a bit startled, but relieved that they seemed to be okay.

I tried to get Locin to come, but she's so stubborn.

"I'll help if I can."

Locin was telling the truth, Rasa, and the others wouldn't listen. Borroka is coming.

Rasa tensed. "But Sammel…?"

Spark nodded. *I know. But she really didn't agree to help them. She was just…* She bit her lip like she had more to say, but thought better of it. *But it doesn't matter now. You're all in danger, the whole city.*

"I… I don't know what to do."

You can tell the others, maybe the temple? There are lots of warriors here.

Rasa held a hand out instinctively toward Spark, letting it rest on the ground near the spirit. "Spark, is she working with Endring?"

She bit her lip. *Sort of.*

"But you say we can trust her?"

Yes. She doesn't want Borroka to get this relic. And she certainly doesn't want anyone getting hurt.

Rasa nodded. "I'll do what I can."

Suddenly Spark tensed. *Hurry. I think they're close.*

Rasa could feel it now. The spirits all around the arena seemed to be shifting as a commotion spread. *Something* was coming.

Rasa jumped to her feet so swiftly that the other three stopped their chit chat and looked at her.

"Locin was telling the truth!"

Weylyn stopped her pacing. "What?"

"Locin was telling the truth about Borroka. Her army is coming."

Hikari took a step forward. "Where? Here? To Kerata? How could you possibly know that?"

Rasa glanced at Spark who stood tense.

"The spirits," Rasa said. "They sense it. They think it's close."

Weylyn turned for the door. "I'll tell Aurilis. You all stay here." She ducked outside without hesitation.

"Gods," Hikari ran a hand over his mouth. "We've got to do something. We've got to fight!" He leaned out over the railing and looked up at the sky. "They'll come from above, no doubt. Chimera, chariots, maybe both. If only we could see them coming."

Rasa leaned out, pointing to the high flags that flew around the upper rim of the arena. "I can get up there."

Hikari looked at her with wide eyes. "Are you certain, darling? That's an awful long way up."

She nodded her resolve.

"Very well. We'll go after Weylyn, see if we can't stop this blasted army."

He glanced at Illeri, who was terribly pale, her hands behind her gripping the rail so tight her knuckles were white.

"Better yet, Weylyn is already headed to get help. Perhaps I will try to get to Voske and Burz before the fight starts. Can you stay here, Illeri? Keep an out for us?"

She looked insulted, but she merely nodded.

"Perfect. Then off we go." He smiled nervously at Rasa. "Time to be heroes."

Rasa followed Hikari out, but he soon disappeared toward the barracks as she started for the exit. The crowd was packed, and more still tried to fight their way in, all eager to see the final round. Rasa pushed her way to the doors, but she got jostled by a large man and fell against the doorframe, trapped by the press of humanity. She couldn't get through, and she couldn't get back. The crowd hardly seemed to notice, shouting and cheering as she felt panic seizing her.

"Spark!"

Spark looked around, frantic, pushing against the people that blocked her path.

Move!

Spark kept shoving at the crowd as Rasa pulled Nyx close, but it was no use. The spirit's hands pressed and pushed against the people, but she couldn't move them.

A small crowd of spirits was gathering now, looking on curiously. Rasa looked at them, pleading.

"Help me. Please!"

Another spirit took up the cause, helping Spark shove against the man that had Rasa pinned, and then another, and another. Soon a dozen spirits were pushing in tandem, and the man stumbled, leaving just enough space for Rasa to inch forward. Several more spirits rallied at their progress, and a path emerged as the air around Rasa grew cold and thick with spirits. She pressed forward, outside and away from the crushing crowd.

"Th-thank you," she said, as the spirits circled round her.

She edged toward the outer wall. It rose nearly straight up into the sky, rows of windows and arches punctuated with ledges and statues of the mightiest warriors of the past. Before her, the wing of a pegasus soared thirty feet above. It was a dizzying height to the top, and she second guessed herself as she stared at the flags and the crisp, blue sky.

You can do this. Spark said, and the other spirits smiled and nodded. *We're with you.*

Rasa turned back to the arena wall as she felt a surge of spirits at her back, and she gripped the lip of the wing and began to climb.

Burz stood in front of the fighter's door to the arena. He pressed his sandals into the hard packed dirt at his feet, feeling the grit of the ground. His leg had been aching more with each match, but he fought back the pain. He could manage it. His blood was pumping and he could feel the thrill of battle, not unlike what he'd felt as a soldier. Whatever happened, he would give it his all. He finally had a chance to put Voske in his place, and he planned to take it.

Outside he heard the muffled voice of the crier announcing the match as the stillness of anticipation filled the air.

"And now, fair people of Talamh, I give you, Burz, Chosen of Uthando!"

Burz pushed open the door to the roar of the crowd. He let his eyes scan the arena, packed beyond comprehension. People were crammed between the seats and up to the fence that surrounded the fighting area, they were seated on the high walls and standing everywhere there was space. The cheers were nearly deafening. As they quieted, the crier pointed to the far end of the arena.

"And Voske, Chosen of Jeza!"

The roar intensified again, even louder than before, the ground shook under their applause as Voske threw open the heavy doors. Burz was sure the titan had grown a foot. He stretched out his arms and roared back at the crowd as they both strode to the center, closing until they stood only a few feet apart. Voske looked angry.

"Voske," Burz said, careful to not let his own emotion show.

"Burz," Voske answered, and he stamped the ground like a bull before it charges.

Burz planted his feet and lifted his chin, quieting his doubts. *Fight. Bleed. Die.* The rather unhelpful mantra of his old guild hall echoed in his mind as the crier called out over the din.

"Jeza, give you strength!"

Voske rolled his shoulders. "She already did," he growled.

A trumpet sounded to start the match, and Voske immediately sped toward Burz. His size and strength were terrifying, but Burz kept his wits as he dodged out of the way, taking a glancing slap on his shoulder.

Voske turned sharply to face him. "Running already?"

He planted his feet. He'd fought bigger opponents before. He needed to use Voske's momentum, and arrogance, against him.

Voske rushed again, heaving a punch toward his face. Burz grabbed his arm and spun around, sending Voske barreling out the other side and giving him a swift kick for his trouble.

Voske hit the ground and quickly rolled with his momentum. He was on his feet again almost immediately and looking even angrier as the roar of the crowd assaulted the air.

"What's wrong Voske," Burz yelled over the din. "Can't keep your feet today?"

Voske sneered and stomped closer, "I'll keep one in your teeth."

"Big words. Let's see you back them up."

Voske moved in again, this time a bit less brazenly. Burz managed to dodge a couple of blows at first, but they kept coming, swing after swing. Voske pressed him toward the edge of the arena until he was out of space. Finally, a jab went wide and Burz slapped the arm away, then sent a haymaker into Voske's jaw that made his knuckles ache.

For a moment he felt his spirits soar. He actually had a chance of winning this fight, but his enthusiasm was short-lived.

Voske turned back to face him and bent his neck to the side with an unsettling *pop*. "Was that it?" He growled.

He grabbed Burz' throat with one hand and heaved him to the side, sending him spiraling into the dust.

Burz quickly rolled to his feet, but Voske was on him already, raining down another flurry of blows. There was no way he could sustain this.

Burz yelled and threw his fist up, catching Voske mid swing so their knuckles jarred together. Pain ripped upward through his arm, but he ignored the sensation and quickly grabbed hold of Voske's wrist, then pulled the big man off his feet, flipping him to the floor of the arena amidst a cloud of dust.

For a second Voske was disoriented, and Burz had a moment to catch his breath. He turned to look toward the crier, but it was clear that the fight wasn't over, and the trumpet didn't sound.

"We both know how this ends," Voske said, standing to his feet and brushing at the dust on his arms. "I'll give you this one chance to quit."

Burz spat at the comment. "You always win, don't you? That's what makes you such a rotten leader."

Voske smirked. "Because I should be a loser like you?"

"Because when you finally do lose, it's going to be worse than you can imagine, and you're going to take everyone around down with you."

Voske wrinkled his nose. "At least I'll take you down first." He charged again and this time he was too fast.

Burz was blown from his feet. His battered arms slammed into the ground, and he tumbled across the arena, landing in a heap staring up at the sky. That's when he saw a figure on top of the outer wall, silhouetted beside the sun.

They whistled and waved, jumping up and down perilously close to the edge.

Rasa?

He heard the thudding footsteps of Voske closing in and he quickly put up a defensive arm.

"Stop!" Burz yelled. "Voske, stop!"

Voske paid him no heed and kept closing until a roar echoed off the walls of the arena. It wasn't the crowd this time. It sounded like rolling thunder. And then another roar.

Voske halted. "Is that Rasa?"

The roars reverberated again, and in another moment a cry of alarm went up from outside the arena.

"What is this?" Burz breathed, his mind scrambling.

"By the gods," Voske muttered. "She was telling the truth."

"Who was?"

Before Voske could answer, a large Chimera flew into view overhead, then another, and fire streaked the sky.

41: The Battle of Kerata

The palace of Kerata was an impregnable fortress. Its gilded halls were a testament to the plunder of ages past, and its walls and ballista would be daunting to even the greatest armies of the age. But then, those armies didn't have chimera.

Endring stood still in the shade of the inner yard, his ears tuned finer than any man. He heard every sound around him: the earth shaking crowd at the arena, the slow drip of a dry mead fountain, and somewhere in the distance above, the deep, rhythmic *woosh* of chimera wings.

He glanced at Sammel. He was leaning forward, also listening, though Endring doubted he could hear anything but the wind.

"She's close."

Sammel laid a hand on his whip, flipping open the leather buckle that held it. He let the long coil unwind, and as the end hit the dust, it sent the tiniest ripple of air out in all directions, a sound only Endring heard.

Above, even Sammel must have heard the sounds of chimera now, swooping toward the city. The cries from the arena had shifted from excitement to horror. A column of fire streaked the sky, a show of force to terrify the people. Endring felt his heart racing, and his boon ready. He leaned out from the shade and studied the sky above, a perfect clear blue.

"You know," Sammel said. "We don't have to stand with them."

"No," Endring said. "We don't. But better the crook stay with Aurilis than with Borroka."

"Aren't they all our enemies now?"

Endring smiled wearily. "Some more than others."

At once eight chimera flew into view, circling the palace. At their head, a solid black chimera, larger than the rest, lifted its massive head and let loose a roar that announced Borroka's arrival. She was riding on its back, her dark sword already extended over the palace, as though claiming it for her own.

They swooped low and landed in the courtyard. Borroka was sitting proudly on the great black beast, but she sneered as she saw Endring and Sammel.

"Look here. It's our exalted champion." She hopped down. The other cultists dismounted, two from each chimera. The beasts snorted, keeping their eyes on Borroka, as though waiting for her signal to attack. "Have you come to fight me?"

"Only if I must," Endring said. He could smell sulfur on the chimera's breath.

Sammel gave the barest flick of his whip and a blast of air rushed around their feet.

"I see you brought your lap dog," she scoffed.

"And I see you brought your cats."

She stroked the black chimera's fur under its chin, and then she nodded to her men. "Get the relic at all costs."

As one, the men charged the palace entrance. Endring let his boon take over, contorting his form. He felt his teeth sharpen into fangs, and coarse hair sprouted from his body. His hands became paws, and his fingers sharp claws. He could feel his new found strength as his muscles tightened to strike.

Sammel struck a blast from his whip, and five men were blown backward. Three charged Endring, but he leapt to the side, avoiding them. He wanted Borroka.

He galloped toward her on all fours, but a spray of chimera fire shot across his path. They were hopelessly outnumbered.

"I can't keep them out!" Sammel yelled, and another shockwave tore through the air. By Endring's count, nearly all of Borroka's men had made it inside. He had to pray there was some small garrison that was not at the festival.

He ducked another gout of fire and charged Borroka. But she twisted aside and dragged her blade across his back. He winced at the pain as fire separated them again.

"Is this it, *Champion*?" She taunted. "When I heard you had received Neveri's boon, I could hardly believe it. *You*. Worthless pet of Bei'ai." She spit toward him as the fire between them died down.

"You profane the name of Neveri," Endring growled. "He would never have chosen you."

Her gaze darkened in response. "Then let's just find out."

Endring surged forward again. One last bound and he'd reach her throat. He could nearly feel his teeth tearing into her flesh.

He lunged, but the great black chimera dove between them. It bared its teeth and heat rolled off its tongue like an open oven.

Endring barreled into its side, and groped with his claws, tearing at its haunches. A blast from Sammel knocked its back legs from under it, and Endring leapt onto its back, sinking his fangs deep into its neck. It roared with anger as flames shot from its mouth. It took off, spinning violently through the air, but Endring dug further in, tearing at its flesh. Beside him, mighty wings droned in his ears, blocking out all other sounds as they rose higher and higher over the city, then tipped, flailing through the sky. Endring started to lose his grip.

He dug his claws into its neck, and with one last surge of power, lengthened them like daggers, twisting them around until the creature's blood painted the sky. One last gurgle sounded from the beast, and then they were crashing full speed toward the ground. Endring retracted his claws and pushed his body free. One large wing slapped him as the creature fell past, and he spun in the air. He called on his boon and cried out as wings burst from his back, catching the wind. The stress of the wild motion nearly tore his wings apart, and he shouted in pain. The chimera crashed into the ground below, but he steadied himself, soaring upward. The black beast was a tangle of flesh and bone, splayed across a rooftop.

He turned for the palace. He could see Sammel standing alone in the courtyard. Three chimera prowled around him, gradually closing in. The closest one opened its maw, and Endring could see ripples of heat pouring from its mouth.

He called on his boon again, and his skin hardened to wyvern scales. He thundered to the ground, wrapping Sammel in his wings just as the fire let loose, scorching his back like a searing iron. The scales of his back fused under the tremendous heat, and he ducked to the ground with Sammel, huddling together in the inferno.

The flames bore down on them, until a pained roar rang out and, for a moment, the heat relented.

Endring uncurled his wings and stared behind him.

The fire-breather had an arrow straight through his eye and all around them the sky shifted and cracked, as a pack of immense dire wolves stepped out of the light, hackles up and baring their teeth at the chimera.

"Need a hand, darling?" yelled a voice, and Endring felt a rush of hope. They still had a fighting chance.

Zengin smelled blood. The palace halls were quiet and still, but it wasn't a peaceful stillness. The chill of Nyx hung in the air. He rounded a corner, following distant voices, and he nearly stepped on the body of a soldier. Blood pooled from a gash across his chest, spilling over his lifeless form. Zengin stepped over him, carefully making his way down the hall, keeping his sandals clean. Blood was a pain to wash out.

The next corridor held two bodies, both soldiers. They'd been unprepared, and Borroka's men had shown no mercy. That wasn't surprising. She was ruthless. She would attract only the most depraved and vile to her cause.

He drew his dagger, clenching the hilt. He could hear harried voices ahead, muffled through a door. He leaned in. There were at least three of them. Four. And they were coming toward him. He pressed himself into an alcove between two pillars just as the door flew open. Four men came through in single file. The man in the front carried a tattered cloth wrapped around something - undoubtedly the crook piece.

"The others are probably back already," the first man said.

The second man answered in a gruff voice, "Don't matter. Orders were get the relic. They'll wait."

Zengin was sure no more were coming, and he stepped out, grabbing the last man. He was the smallest of the four, a match for Zengin in height, but a scrawny thing. He let out a yelp as Zengin pressed the dagger to his neck.

The others turned, and the man with the gruff voice reached to the top of his head and drew a silvered mask down over his face. He motioned to the man that held the relic. "Go. We got this."

Immediately Zengin felt a surge of laughter welling in his chest, but he stuffed it down, he wasn't one to laugh at anything.

The man with the crook rushed away, and the masked man slowly drew his sword from his hip.

Zengin focused on him. "Tell me where Borroka is, and you'll live."

The gruff man sneered. "Why would I do that?"

"I'll kill your friend." He pressed the point of the dagger to demonstrate his point.

"No!" The man sniveled. "P-please!"

"He's not my friend."

"Darv!" The smaller man pleaded.

Zengin leaned close to his ear, drawing on his boon as he spoke so low that only the small man could hear him. "You want to live?"

The man tried to nod, nearly slicing his own throat on the dagger's razor sharp edge.

Zengin pointed his dagger at the third man who stood ready and tense by the wall. "Kill him, then give me your sword, and you will live. I swear."

A shudder passed through the man's body and his hand drifted to the sword at his side.

"Do it now!"

Zengin released his hold, stuffing the dagger back in its sheath, but the honey of Metnadur had done its work. The man whipped his sword from his belt and rushed his friend. He ran the blade straight through the man's heart, and drew it back out, handing it to Zengin before the gruff man could process what was happening. As it sunk in, rage filled his voice.

"You killed Brock! You rotting traitor!"

The sniveling man fell to his knees as Zengin drew near the gruff man, sword at the ready. "Where is Borroka?"

The gruff man glared at him from behind the mask. "That wasn't funny."

The words were laced with raucous humor, but Zengin tamped it down as he studied the mask. "Is that a relic of Metnadur?"

"Laugh, rotting gods above. Laugh, you fool!"

Again a wave of humor hit him, but Zengin's face remained placid. "Maybe *you* should laugh first. That might help."

The man let out a nervous chuckle, but it was enough for a foothold.

"More."

The laugh sounded again, just a little louder.

"With feeling!"

From somewhere deep within a guffaw shook the man's chest, then a second, then he doubled over, cackling like a lunatic. He held his sides, wheezing to breathe, until Zengin's sword thrust into his neck, cleaving through his spine.

His laughter ended in a gurgling wail and he slumped to the ground, his blood filling the mask of Metnadur.

Zengin took the clean sword from the man's hand as he lay in the throes of death.

The sword was razor sharp, and decently crafted. He suspected a smith or two must be in their ranks.

"Fine work." He turned it over in his hand as he approached the sniveling man who now knelt on all four. "I suspect it could cut clean through bone."

"Y-you swore. Y-you'll let me l-live!"

"And I'm a man of my word."

Zengin towered over the man, catching his gaze. "I want you to tell Borroka something for me."

He nodded furiously. "A-anything!"

"Tell her Zengin, Champion of Metnadur, will not rest until she's dead."

He lifted the blade and in one clean strike, severed the man's right hand at the wrist. He tumbled forward, screaming out in pain as Zengin stepped over him. His toga was streaked red with blood. He let the sword slip from his hand. It clattered against the stone and he stared at it, watching the droplets of crimson, as they pooled on the white marble.

"Out of the way!" Voske yelled as he charged toward the palace, but the normal deference to the champions didn't seem to be in effect.

People ran to and fro, screaming and yelling as the roars of chimera split the sky. For all the good it did. They weren't really getting to safety, and they were keeping Voske from that shrike of a cultist.

He called up his boon and tried again, his voice rumbling out around him. "I said, OUT OF THE WAY!"

The very ground seemed to shake under his voice. It scared the people more than the chimera, at least for the moment. They split before him, scurrying out of his way, and he motioned Burz to follow him through the gap.

A few of the beasts were strafing the city, raining blasts of fire seemingly at random and sowing chaos. The majority, however, were at the Archon's palace. From here he could see flashes of feathers and fire, circling the gold domed roof.

"I don't see the others!" Burz yelled.

"They'll be there," Voske called back.

"How do you know?

"Because Sammel said she was coming for the crook. They all heard it, same as me." And then he muttered, "If only I'd rotting believed it."

"Sammel!?"

Voske grunted. He didn't have time to explain it now. They were nearly to the palace. He charged around the side and toward the front gates as a wave of fire singed overhead. He fell to the ground, Burz beside him.

"I hate these things," he said, arms over his head.

"Seven of them," Burz said sharply.

"Men or beasts?"

"Beasts. Lots of men too."

Voske poked his head up as the fire subsided. He could see several chimeras clawing and fighting with a horrifying beast. It looked half lion and half hyena and it ducked deftly in and out of the fray, scratching and biting. Alongside it a pack of monstrous wolves appeared from thin air, then disappeared just as fast, throwing the already chaotic scene into further uproar.

A blast of air exploded outward from somewhere near the palace wall. Voske searched for the source and saw Sammel pinned there. Hikari was with him, and Weylyn, sending arrows sailing into a chimera that reared in front of them.

A man darted out of the temple. His eyes were darkened by the sunken rings of the cult, and he was holding a tattered cloth that faintly radiated the light of Sbarga. He spotted Voske, and took off at a full run.

"That's the Crook," Burz barked.

"I know, I know." Voske sprang from the stairwell and charged along the side of the palace. The strange beast was biting into the neck of a chimera now, and blood gushed out around its jowls. It twisted and wrenched upward, but its claws slipped free, and it tumbled to the ground. The beast's legs were splayed out to its side and a golden glow radiated from its paw, marking a strange sigil Voske had never seen before. Revelation sunk in as he watched.

Endring? Mire and Nyx!

Voske turned his focus back on the cultist with the crook. He was nearly to a chimera now, as it swooped down low.

"No you don't!"

He barreled forward with all his strength as his boon turned his legs to iron, but it wasn't enough. The rotting cultist leapt atop the beast, and it soared to safety.

"Rot it!"

"Voske!" Hikari yelled. They were still pinned down near the temple, and a few cultists were closing in.

Voske barreled into the fray, slamming his weight into one of the chimeras, sending it tumbling into its fellows. The beast righted itself, but immediately took an arrow through the chest as the light of the portico shifted again, A blinding whirlwind enveloped the enemy force until they staggered back, trying to escape the dazzling radiance.

A horn blasted over the din. A battle cry. Voske readied himself for more, but the cultists fell back, piling onto their mounts and fleeing skyward. He looked up to see a woman with a horn to her lips, signaling their retreat. Anger swelled. He'd just gotten to the battle, and it was already over?

"The Crook!" He yelled, but there was no way he could reach them.

One last arrow struck the wing of a chimera as they retreated, eliciting an angry howl but little else.

"Aaaaahhhh!" Voske was stomping around the remains of the battle now, red-faced and fuming.

Two chimeras and a handful of cultists had fallen amidst a spattering of blood and feathers. Voske found one of the chimeras still barely breathing and he pounced on it, snapping its neck, and then he slowly resigned himself, letting the strength of Jeza drain out of his body.

"Rotting mire!"

It was only then that he remembered the strange beast that had been sparring with their enemies, and he looked around until he spotted Endring. The old man stood shakily nearby. His legs and chest were bloodied, and gore dripped down from fingernails that had been claws only moments ago.

Burz quickly ran to one of the fallen cultists and took the man's weapon, pointing at Endring's chest.

"You," Burz growled. "What are you doing here?"

Endring turned his head to the side and hocked a glob of blood onto the ground. Voske's stomach turned as he realized it likely wasn't his.

"I'm here for the same reason as you," he said firmly, "to stop Borroka."

"And why would you do that?"

Sammel had edged forward now, behind Burz, his whip coiled in his hand, but before he could do anything, Weylyn had an arrow nocked and pointed at his chest.

"I wouldn't," she said coolly.

Endring sighed. "What will it take for you to believe we are not enemies?"

"You did steal the crook piece from us, darling." Hikari nodded to Sammel. "He did, anyway."

"And you believe it would have been better off with Aurilis?"

"Perhaps." Hikari's voice sounded weak.

"Your piece is now in the hands of the faithful. I still have mine."

"For now," Voske said, moving closer. He studied the old oracle. He looked very different than he had back at the temple, and there was no denying the sigil or his boon.

"We have to turn him over to the temple," Burz said.

"Do we?"

Burz looked at Voske, surprised. "Are you mad?"

"Maybe," Voske bit the inside of his cheek. "Sammel did save us. They tried to warn us about this attack, too, and risked their lives to stop it."

"And asked Locin to steal the crook," Hikari countered.

Voske shrugged. Sure they did, but maybe they had good reason. Either way, they seemed a more helpful ally than they were a dangerous enemy. At least for now.

Another horn sounded. Pegs were flying in from the barracks with Jeza monks astride them, and more rushed toward them on the ground.

Voske shook his head. "Great. The cavalry."

Endring took another deep breath and his expression pained. "I'm too old for this," he said. "If you believe I'm your enemy, then kill me, otherwise let me go."

Burz readied his arm, but his muscles stayed rigid. "You're forgetting the third option. We could hold you until we know the truth."

"And turn them over to that shrike of a High Oracle?" Voske asked. "They've helped us more than she has, for sure."

Endring looked up at the sky where the pegs were closing in, a few already swooping down to land. He started walking backwards away from Burz.

"Stop," he snapped. "Not another step."

But Endring kept moving away, edging toward Sammel. "I pray when we meet again, we may fight side by side for the sake of Talamh."

"We'll see," Voske said.

Burz' arm was trembling now, but he didn't react. He simply let Endring go. He reached Sammel, and they watched with horror as he transformed. His bones seemed to break and remake themselves as wings sprouted from his back and he took on a bestial appearance, almost like a miniature chimera. Jeza monks were landing now, rushing forward, but Voske called for them to halt as Sammel climbed on Endring's back, and they took flight. No doubt Aurilis would hear of this, and all the better. She needed to know that no matter how many restrictions she imposed, he was a champion, and she didn't control him.

42: Chosen

Locin sat on the palace roof overlooking the courtyard. She was dangling a near empty bottle from her fingers, watching the dredges of pale green liquor slosh up and down the sides. Below, Aurilis had been pacing for the last fifteen minutes with Voske, Burz, Gillis, and a handful of monks as her audience. She would shout, and then Voske would shout. And then they would all get quiet and pace around.

"Locin?" She turned to see Hikari making his way up. "I thought that was you. What are you doing up here?"

She raised the bottle so fast to show him that the liquid sloshed violently, sending a little spray out onto her hand. "Drinking."

"Gods. What a day, huh?" He sat beside her, looking dreadfully uncomfortable. "Listen, darling, I wanted to apologize. You tried to warn us, and we didn't believe you."

"It wasn't you. It was Voske." She fixed her eyes on Voske. He had his arms crossed, staring down Aurilis now as she yelled some more. "Rotting oaf." She shook her bottle at him. "It's between me and him."

"Any of us could have stood up for you. I certainly should have. Perhaps things could have gone differently."

"Yeah, well. You didn't, and now that shrike Barroka has the relic."

"Well, not all of it."

She shrugged. What did that matter?

"We're leaving tomorrow morning, apparently. No end to the tournament or anything. Tragic, really. I suppose it could have been worse, but we don't seem to be off to a great start as Champions."

"Nyx it, Hikari! Can't you see I want to be alone?"

He looked wounded, and she felt bad.

"Look, I'm sorry."

"It's alright, darling." He stood brushing at his toga. "I understand. I just want you to know I'm sorry. The way Endring helped fight Borroka-"

"What?" She looked up at him sharply. "What did you say?"

"I only meant, I may have misjudged him a bit. Maybe we all did. He and Sammel really tried to stop her."

"They were here?"

"Of course, darling. You should have seen him. He was like a… well a beast of some kind. I didn't even realize it was him at first."

She stumbled to her feet, and Hikari grabbed her arm to steady her.

"Careful, darling. You seem a bit past tipsy."

"Where is he? Did the temple take him?"

"Ah, there's the thing. More than likely the reason for Aurilis' ire, I'm afraid. After the battle, Voske let him go."

She looked back down. Aurilis was gone now, and Voske was leaning against the wall looking angry, his fists clenched and his muscles tight.

"He did?"

"Oh, yes. There didn't seem any point in holding him after he risked his life to save the relic. Besides, there's no love between Voske and the temple. I'm not sure Burz was too keen-"

Locin gave Hikari a light shove as she stumbled past. She'd heard enough. She wasn't sure what to make of it, and she was still angry. None of this would have happened if they'd listened.

"Where are you going, darling?"

"To pack. We're leaving soon, right?"

"So I've been told."

"Great." She was ready to get off this planet anyway.

Burz sat on the ground beside a man who was writhing in pain, his left side severely burned. This would be his second, and he already passed up three that seemed too far gone to save.

He placed his hands on the man's shoulder, feeling the singed flesh, barely letting his palms touch the skin, and yet the man cried out in anguish.

"Hold still."

He was feeling weak, and tired. The tournament had battered his body already. How was he supposed to push himself any further? Yet he called up his boon, the warmth of it filling his palms. He could feel burning across his left side, and he bit down under the pain. He kept going until he saw the man's skin turn from black to red. It wasn't perfect, but it was enough that the other healers could take over with their balms and salves. He would live, and Burz couldn't afford to give too much to any one person. There were too many to heal as it was.

The man nodded his thanks through haggard breaths, and Burz pushed himself up off the ground. His leg buckled, and he felt himself impact the dirt road. In a moment, two monks were there to help him up. One was Gillis. He waved them both off, and struggled to his feet, leaning heavily on his good leg.

"Do you have more in you, Champion?"

No, he thought. *Not a single one.*

"Of course, Gillis."

"Two more," he said softly. "A-at most. I don't think you should push beyond that."

Burz nodded and they started scouring the street. They were just outside the arena, where the wounded were being brought. It was amazing how much damage a dozen chimera could do.

Above, the sun was low, and already the sky was tinged red. He straightened his shoulders, hobbling down the road, looking over the men and women gathered there. Most had mild injuries, and the Uthando monks were already tending to them. He spotted a couple of bodies, already gone, charred and unrecognizable.

Crying caught his attention, and he turned to see a young girl, maybe half a cycle. She looked to be about Kyren's age. She had scrapes on her arms and legs, no doubt from falling while running from the beasts. She sat on her mother's lap, clutching a ragged looking stuffed dragon.

"Burz!"

He heard someone calling, and he turned to see Hadris and the boys running down the road. His heart leapt with relief. *They're safe. Thank Uthando, they're safe!*

"Ada!" Kyren ran up to him and grabbed him so solidly that he nearly fell backwards, but he steadied himself as pain shot through his leg, making sure to stay upright. Soon Orin and Hadris were there too, all knotted up in an embrace.

"You're okay," Hadris said, the same relief in her voice. "Thank the gods!"

"I'm fine. Just helping here. There's much to be done, and-"

"Burz." She pulled back and nodded down to Orin.

"I know," he said quietly. The sun was dipping low. He had been watching it anxiously for the last hour. "But I'm not done here."

She pursed her lips.

"I'm sorry. These people need me."

She sighed, pulling the boys away.

"Maybe tomorrow-"

"No."

He looked at the boys, and then back at her. He made it a point to never argue in front of them, but this one couldn't wait. He spoke softly, keeping his tone calm. "What do you expect me to do?"

"Nothing." She sighed. "I'll take him."

"Hadris-"

But Gillis' voice called to him, breaking his train of thought. "Champion! Over here!"

He was a little ways down the road, pointing to someone. *One or two more.*

"If you'll just wait," he pleaded with Hadris. "I won't be much longer, and-"

"Sundown. It's their tradition."

"Ada?" Orin said. "Are you coming with us to the temple?"

He knelt, knowing how hard it was going to be to get back up. "I'm sorry, these people, they need my help."

"I understand. You're a champion."

Burz smiled, tousling the boy's hair. "That's right. I wish I could be there, Orin, but your Ama will take you-" he looked up to see Hadris resigned, but she nodded "-and when I get home, you are going to tell me all about it."

"Yes, Ada!"

"Come on," Hadris said, managing as cheery a voice as she could. "Let's hurry to the temple, and let your Ada work."

He watched for a moment while they ran out of view, and then he gritted his teeth and stood, marching toward Gillis.

The departure for Suntara didn't happen as soon as Voske hoped, which led to an excessive amount of time to mull over what had happened. It was misery. All he wanted to do was wash his hands of this whole rotting place, to go back to Arrajin and crack some cultist skulls, or go back to Lorhk's and down an entire barrel of cactus mead, or at least to Suntara and grab that last piece of the crook. Right now that was the only option that felt within reach, so that's what he focused on. What he *had* to focus on.

"What in Nyx is this about?" Locin's voice fell flat in the dull air of the wine cellar.

It was a ridiculous place for Champions to have to meet, but Aurilis had her lackeys everywhere else. At least here they could talk in private, and even now he kept his voice down.

He looked around the circle. Locin, Hikari, Weylyn, Zengin, Illeri, Rasa. Everyone but Burz.

"Voske?" Locin pressed.

"This is about taking things into our own hands," he said. "Who else is tired of the temple interfering?"

He looked around the circle, but was mostly met with blank expressions.

"Go on." Weylyn said.

"The way I see it, we got the first piece of the crook, then Sammel nicked it for Endring. Maybe that's on us, but *they* shoulda known Endring wasn't on the level. Then we got the second piece and *they* took it for safekeeping, and what happened? Gone. Just like the first."

Locin was scowling deeply, and Voske nodded her direction. "You were right about that one, kid. I should have listened."

She toed the ground but didn't reply. Her eyes looked bleary.

"We get one more chance on Suntara," he continued. "We grab the third piece, and we keep it ourselves. No more temple. No more Aurilis. No one from outside this room."

Illeri raised her hand, just barely. "Do we know where it is?"

"We'll figure it out."

"Of course you will," Zengin scoffed. "The same way you figured out the first two."

"We found them fine."

"No. Endring did. Who gave you the location of the first relic? And who told you about the Trial of Epsis?"

Voske scrunched up his brow. He really hated whenever Zengin talked.

Hikari cleared his throat. "Can we not contact Endring?"

Everyone stared at him, and he smiled sheepishly. "I mean, if he's the best way to find it, then it stands to reason we need his help."

"Isn't he on the wrong side?" Illeri asked.

"He's on Neveri's side," Locin said.

"Which is wrong, isn't it?"

They all took a moment, mulling over the notion. Certainly Borroka was evil, but Endring?

"We don't have to trust him," Voske said. "We use him to get the final piece, and make sure to not lose it this time."

"Use him and ditch him," Locin commented. "Sounds about right."

"And where would we put it?" Weylyn asked. "You can't just carry it around every second of every day."

"If that's what I have to do," Voske growled. "I'll rotting do it. I'm not gonna lose again. I don't care if I have to tie it around my neck. It's staying with me."

They fell silent, and Voske looked back at Locin. She was staring at the corners of the room, anywhere but at him. "Locin, do you have a way to contact Endring?"

She shrugged. "Maybe."

"Good. Set up a meeting."

She finally looked at him, alarmed. "With you?"

"Yes, with me."

"He's not gonna like that."

"Too bad."

She muttered something under her breath, but he couldn't quite tell what.

"That settles it," he said, clapping his hands together. "Locin and I will get all the information we can, then we'll grab the crook. Anyone that wants can come along." He smirked. "Aurilis can get as mad about it as she rotting well pleases. We're the chosen of the gods, and we'll do as we see fit. Who's with me?"

One by one they slowly acquiesced, and Voske's chest swelled. Things were finally going to go right. They had to this time.

By the time Burz made his way back to the Archon's palace, the sun had long since set. He was dirty, and tired, and every muscle ached. His leg hurt so much it was stiff. All he wanted was sleep, but he forced himself to swing by the baths and quickly clean the dirt and blood. The city seemed to have settled into an uneasy slumber, though the palace itself was filled with monks and warriors as though it was day. They made their way around silently, like walking shadows, and he counted himself among them. He passed noiselessly through the lavish corridors to the north wing and into his chambers. The parlor was dark, and he could see the door to the boys' room was shut, but a flickering glow shone from his bedroom. Hadris always preferred candles to the stark light of the inventor's lamps.

He pushed the door open silently, and shut it behind. She was kneeling by his dresser with a trunk open, packing away their things. She'd laid out a fresh traveling chlamys for him for the next day. She barely glanced over her shoulder as he entered, but it was enough for him to see her face. She was still angry. It felt unfair. It's not as if he'd been off at the tavern or celebrating with friends. He was working, healing people. He had half a mind to fall into the bed without saying a word, but he sat down on the bed behind her and sighed.

"We're leaving early," she said wearily. "The monks will be by for our things at dawn."

He nodded, running a hand over his head against a faint scratch of stubble. How would he even find time to shave?

"How did it go?" He asked.

She instantly tensed, harshly wadding up a toga and shoving it in the trunk.

"Hadris?"

But she just kept on packing.

"Come on!" He said, too weary to keep an even tone. "This isn't fair. I was helping people."

"You're always helping people. You'll go on helping them 'til you die."

"Is that it? Are you angry I missed his choosing, or do you still just resent me being chosen?"

"I've never resented that," she said, though her tone stayed harsh and angry.

"Fine. I'm too tired to fight about this tonight. Just tell me about his choosing."

She evidently finished with his drawers and moved on to packing some things from a nearby shelf.

"Are you punishing me?" He stood and made his way over to her, grabbing her arm to stop her as she reached for some trinket. "Hadris!"

She spun to face him, and he could tell she'd been crying.

"Just tell me where he was chosen."

"He wasn't."

Her words barreled into him, and he let her arm go, stumbling back.

Unguilded? How could he be unguilded?

Hadris turned back to her work. She had nothing more to say. What could she say?

He was suddenly alert, despite the utter exhaustion wracking his mind and body. He backed out of the room and into the parlor where he stood breathing sharply, staring through the dark toward the boys' door.

Unguilded, and I wasn't there.

He pounded a fist into the soft couch. How could he have not been there?

His thoughts suddenly flew to Orin, and he headed to the door, easing it open. As his eyes adjusted, he could see the two boys on either side of the room, asleep in their beds, their things packed in trunks. It was still and silent, and he slipped in and headed for Orin's bed, moving a stool beside it. He sat there for some time, unsure what to do, or even what to feel. He felt pain, and he wondered if Orin did too. He lifted a hand and brushed Orin's face. He stirred a little, rolling on his back, and Burz could see the stains of tears down his cheeks. He suddenly looked so small and lonely. He took his son's hand in his own, and his emotions welled to the surface. He had failed. He'd failed as a champion, as a husband, as a father. He rested his head on the edge of the bed and squeezed Orin's hand tightly as he wiped tears from the corners of his eyes. There was no answer, nothing he could do to fix this, but he wouldn't let Orin be alone, not again, so he stayed there on that stool, resting his head on the bed until his exhaustion took over, and he fell asleep.

43: Visions of Nyx

Spark walked along a vague corridor, like a shop through a filmy window. She didn't feel the wooden planks of the deck under her bare feet. There was no smell, no movement of air or brush of skin as a young man moved by. She felt herself being drawn down the corridor, the thin blue trail in front of her pulling her back to Locin. Everything was muffled voices in a sea of blurred colors. She wasn't fully in Nyx. She hadn't been in a long time. But she was farther from Talamh here, away from Locin.

But every step closer to Locin brought Talamh into clearer focus. She could make out the wall next to her now, smooth wood painted in a vibrant green and trimmed with gold. She reached out to touch it, but her hand passed through. The low murmur of the spirits in Nyx was fading now, and another sound came into focus. Locin. She was speaking quietly, barely above a whisper, and Spark couldn't make out the words. The voice came from somewhere ahead, and she was being compelled toward it. She stopped in front of a door, now clear and sharp, the same smooth wood as the rest of the chariot, and she passed through.

Suddenly the pull lessened. Locin sat on a plush couch in a room that was not hers. It looked like some noble's chambers, decked out lavishly. But it was no noble. Just a masquerade.

The man sat on the couch beside Locin dressed in a fine chlamys of silk with a hood draped across his head. It was pulled back enough for gray curls to peek out above his forehead, and she recognized Sammel's heavy, square face.

"Makes no difference to me," Locin said. "Rotting morons should believe me this time though. I think they learned that lesson."

"Good," Sammel said. "And Voske?"

She shrugged. "He's coming around. Don't think he'll ever really trust Endring, but if it gets him the crook piece, he'll be willing to take the help."

Sammel nodded, and a flutter caught Spark's attention. She looked to the side where a flamboyant parrot was spreading its wings.

"Why's he staying like that?" Locin wrinkled her nose. "Can't he just…"

Spark took a step closer, and Locin looked up. She could sense her presence now, though she didn't smile, not even a hint of one.

"He's being cautious," Sammel said, and then he leaned closer to Locin and whispered. Spark leaned in to hear him as well. "And I suspect he likes it."

"Oh?"

"If I had his boon, I'm not sure I'd bother being a man anymore."

Locin chuckled. "Gods, not me. I like being a woman."

She leaned back and crossed her legs, but Spark was sure she shot a wary glance her direction.

Sammel stood. "It's settled then. You tell Voske, and he'll be there."

"Sure." Locin stood, reaching into a silver bowl and grabbing a handful of berries. She popped one in her mouth. "Hopefully he'll be a person, or it'll be a weird conversation."

In response, the parrot flew across the room, narrowly darting over Locin's head. She threw a hand up instinctively, and then scowled as she headed for the door.

"Fine. I'm going."

She passed right through Spark, and for a moment she felt almost solid. Locin shivered, and then headed back out to the hall.

Spark followed her.

Locin.

Locin stopped. "What do you want?"

Spark held out a hand as if to pull on Locin's arm. Her hand still passed through, but it was different, like pressing your fingers through water. Or she thought that's what it must be like. It had been ages since she pressed her fingers through water. The feeling slipped away as Locin pulled her arm free.

"Wasn't sure I'd see you again."

Of course you were. Spark let her eyes drift to the blue light that ran between them, pulsing back and forth. *I wouldn't leave you, Locin.*

Locin started walking again, sauntering down the hall. "So what? You went and warned them? Still didn't help. I told you they don't listen."

Do you really blame them? You're planning to run away. No one knew that. Only Locin and Spark. And Spark hated it. *They aren't like the others. They really care about you. I wish you would see that.*

"Maybe it's for the best. Makes it easier."

Spark sighed.

Locin softened her tone. "I know you like them. But I told you not to get too close. We can't trust anyone, Spark. Gods! You of all people should know that."

They came to the stairs and headed up to the deck. The chariot was alone in a sea of stars. The cold dark reminded Spark so much of Nyx.

Locin headed to the rail and leaned over, poking at the radiant field. "Gonna tell them about this too?"

Does it matter?

"Well, it won't matter. I'm telling Voske anyway."

You could tell him everything. You could try trusting him.

She frowned. "It was pretty stupid, you know, you leaving like that."

You didn't give me a choice.

"Luckily, I was just fine." She tried to sound flippant, but her face looked pained. Spark was her only close friend, the only one, maybe, who really knew Locin.

Oh, Locin. I wish I could help you more. She touched Locin's cheek.

Locin trembled. "Just… Don't leave me again, okay? It's lonely when you're gone."

Okay. Spark leaned beside her, looking in Locin's eyes, aching for Locin to see her, to fully hear her. If only she could really talk to her.

Locin stared her direction, glancing around as if she longed to see Spark too. "We just gotta get through these festivals. After that, who knows? I'm a Champion, Nyx it! We can go off on our own. Just you and me, like it's always been."

Like it's always been. She sighed. She wanted that, just her and Locin, but it made her sad too. Locin needed more.

"One more thing," she said, turning her eyes back to the stars. "I know you talk to Rasa. Nyx it, Spark, if you tell her any of this, I'll hate you forever! If I leave, or help Endring, or whatever, it's my business. Got it?"

Spark frowned.

Locin turned, her eyes searching again. "Rot it, it's not their business, Spark. Promise me you won't say anything!"

Spark reached out to Locin's right hand, letting her fingers press through. *I won't say anything.*

"Good." Locin smiled. "We'll be back on Suntara soon. That's where we met."

I remember.

"Who knows? Maybe it really will be like the old days."

It will never be like the old days, Locin. You're a champion now.

But part of Spark wished it could. Back when things were simple, and fun.

Weylyn sat in the back of a posh theater in the lower decks of the Tempest. It was small, room for a hundred people, a green room with green curtains, and gold lights that glittered with the inventor's spark as they cast their glow at the stage. A young woman was on stage, wearing a simple toga and moving about through a conjured forest. The room was nearly full. In the front, rows of seats lined the area by the stage, but back here pairs of plush green seats sat with a table nestled between each. Gillis sat on the other side of her table.

Weylyn had never been one for stage shows, or much of the other entertainment found in the many towns and cities of Talamh. She preferred to be outdoors, but in the cold dark, that wasn't much of an option.

Gillis laughed beside her. Evidently she'd missed a humerus line. He glanced up and saw her looking at him, and he mustered a polite smile.

"Are you enjoying the show, Champion?"

"It's fine."

"I see. If you'd like them to perform a different play, I can speak with the director."

Weylyn stared at him dumbfounded.

"They usually have a list of several options prepared."

Weylyn glanced around the room at the other people that now laughed in concert as a young man appeared tangled in some conjured vines, comically flailing his arms.

"They would switch the play in the middle?"

"Of course. I believe Champion Nyris was somewhat picky. It was rare a troop didn't have to change plays at least two or three times. Don't worry, they come prepared when they know Champions will be on board."

Weylyn sighed, slumping down in her seat.

Gillis started to stand. "I'll get the list so you can-"

"By the gods, Gillis, sit down! The show is fine."

He sat dutifully, his back stiff as he awkwardly pretended to watch the show for a while, but his eyes kept darting to Weylyn.

"Is there something else I can get you?" He pressed.

Weylyn smiled lightly. "This is Aurilis' doing, isn't it? She's scared you into an uproar."

Gillis slumped back in his chair, looking defeated.

"Relax, Gillis. I'm not unhappy. Just a bit troubled."

His face squirmed around with a question, his mouth opening and closing several times before he spoke again. "Is it your vision perhaps?"

She turned to face him, and he held a hand up apologetically.

"I don't mean to pry, Champion. It's just, you did use the vision powder? I wasn't sure if…" he fizzled.

"I did."

"And… Did it bring clarity?"

"Absolutely not."

He leaned back, relaxing a bit as he mused on this information. Sporadic claps rose from the audience. When the applause died down, he looked back at her.

"I don't understand. I've never read of a case when vision powder didn't show more detail. Perhaps it was inferior quality?"

"It showed me a little more," Weylyn clarified. "But it also showed me something different."

Gillis sat up straight. "A new vision?"

"It was the same, but the details changed."

He was fascinated now, and he had completely forgotten his usual stiff decorum. He leaned in with wide eyes. "How so? Did you still witness your… well, your demise?"

"All the details leading to that moment were the same, but this time it wasn't me."

"Truly? But it was exactly the same other than the person? No detail different?"

"I got a better glimpse of the creature this time. Some sort of scaly monster. Sea serpent or the like."

"In the Arrtris? Gods and chosen. The temple should look into this at once!"

"They have."

He looked at her, startled.

"I felt its presence in the tunnels under Arrajin. After that, I asked Eprim to look into it, but the monks found nothing in the water."

"Incredible." His voice was distant as he mulled all the information. "But if you saw it, we must assume the creature will be back."

"But when?" She leaned back and stared toward the stage again, though she paid no attention to the play. "I don't have a single doubt that it was the same moment. So what do you think it means?"

Gillis tapped his fingers thoughtfully on the plush arms of the chair. "It would be rare with vision powder, but yes, I suppose it's possible."

"What is?"

He bobbed his head side to side. "Well, visions of Strah are often a warning. They *can* be changed. Perhaps what you saw is another possible outcome?"

"Another outcome?"

"Different might be the way to say it. What if there's a path you take in which you die, and a path in which you don't?" He smiled with excitement. "Two possible futures. That must be it. Bless the gods! So you simply need to find out how to choose the right future, and you'll live!"

"And if I live, the other vision comes to pass?"

"It's happened before. I read a story of Yekar, the third champion of Strah. He claims to have seen two visions, one where the city of Helrosh was flooded and one where it burned."

"Those are not great options."

"No. But they discovered the dam was weakened and could break. Yekar ordered it not be repaired."

"And the city flooded?"

Gillis squirmed. "Well, technically there was a fire at the forges. It burned a quarter of the city before the dam broke and put out the fire. But I suppose it would have burned the whole city otherwise."

"You aren't helping, Gillis."

He suddenly remembered himself, stiffening up as he jolted like he'd taken a blow to the chest. "Apologies, Champion."

"Oh, relax. Aurilis isn't here judging you. It's just me, and I happen to like you."

A proud smile played out across his face.

A rolling mist billowed through the room as howling wolves echoed from the stage. Gillis still had one eye on Weylyn.

"Perhaps we can find a way," he said at last.

"A way to what?"

"To prevent your death, Champion. To choose the other vision. I should be glad to-"

"I wouldn't do that for all the worlds, Gillis."

"What? Why not?"

"If I did, the other person would die?"

He slumped in his chair. "Most likely."

The players' voices were sounding out around them, but Weylyn didn't pay them any heed. She couldn't shake the feeling of her own mortality. She'd always been aware of how fragile life was. She'd nearly died more than once. But this felt different. She was safe here, surrounded by guards and comfort, empowered by the divine essence of a god himself, and yet she never felt so mortal.

"May I ask, Champion, who was the other person?"

Weylyn felt her chest tighten as she forced out the name. "Rasa."

Behind them, there was a quick intake of breath, and a scuffling sound.

Weylyn turned to see Rasa stumbling toward the back wall. They locked eyes as Weylyn stood, and then Rasa was gone, scurrying out of the theater.

Gillis stood sharply. "I'll send the monks to find her."

Weylyn held a hand up to stop him. "If Rasa doesn't want to be found, she won't be."

"What do we do then?"

"I'll speak with her when I can."

Gillis nodded.

Weylyn imagined neither one of them felt much like taking in a show now, but after a minute or so they both sunk back into their seats, each staring blindly in the direction of the stage, lost in their own miserable thoughts.

"Gillis."

"Yes, Champion?"

"Don't tell the others. I'm not ready for them to know. At best they would worry, at worst they would make some foolish attempts to change things and may make them worse."

"It could be a long way off," he ventured. "Perhaps far in the future?"

Weylyn conjured the image in her mind. That was easy. Keeping it out of her mind was the difficult part. She could see clearly Rasa's lifeless body, her hair, her face, all just as it looked now. Young.

So *very* young.

"Perhaps," she said with a half smile.

44: The Sapphire World

Suntara had well and truly earned its title, the sapphire world. Most of it was rolling blue ocean, spotted with islands and archipelagos that held some of the most decadent cities and lavish beaches in all the realm. Hikari couldn't remember a time when the sight of it hadn't filled him with the warmth of home. He'd traveled plenty, but Suntara was the hub of the arts. This is where he learned his craft, where he spent most of his time. Coming back always felt like moving downstage. This was the main plot, the important part. But as he looked down at the deep blue waters, it felt different this time.

He could see the smooth white beaches ahead, and beyond, the dazzling spires and colorful mosaics of Avi'Suron, but it felt a bit emptier than usual, like heading downstage only to find the audience gone.

He sighed, strolling along the deck of the Tempest, aware of the hum of chatter from the many guests piled on deck to watch their arrival. He felt alone, which was something he'd rarely felt in his life, and he decided to seek out some of the other champions.

He spotted Rasa first, squished in beside the strut of the skybeam, and trying to stay out of the way. She had her back to him, staring over the ocean far below, but her fiery hair was hard to miss.

Hikari straightened out his toga and put on a casual air as he strolled up to her. "Lovely, isn't it?"

She started, and for a moment he thought she'd topple over the edge into the radiant field.

"I'm sorry, darling. I didn't mean to scare you."

She shook her head, and wiped at her cheeks. Her eyes were red, as if she'd been crying. "It's okay."

"Whatever is the matter, Rasa? If someone has upset you, I will…" he trailed off as she shook her head. "Alright. Nothing like that then."

He settled in beside her, and they both stared out over the waters as Avi'Suron swelled to fill the horizon.

"You know, I've been feeling rather odd myself. Perhaps it was the attack. Things just don't feel the way they used to."

She frowned, her eyes steady on the sea.

"Have you ever been to Suntara before?"

"Yes." She sniffled.

"You know, it used to be my favorite place. I mean, who doesn't love the sand and the surf, the glistening sun on the murals and stained glass."

He glanced over, but she seemed distant. "Was it a boy?"

Rasa made a face at him. "What?"

"Ah, Nevermind then." He breathed a sigh of relief.

Rasa slumped forward into the rail, her cheek brushing the golden field. "Hikari."

"Yes, darling?"

"What's the happiest memory you have?"

The question caught him off guard. He thought of the day he was guilded as a player, the day he was chosen as a champion. A dozen happy memories of the stage jumped to the forefront of his mind. And then he thought of home.

"I was seven. It was my birthday. Gods, that was ages ago."

She perked up, leaning back to see his face. Of all the captivated audiences he'd had in his life, this one felt special.

He smiled and cleared his throat. "I slept late. A habit, I'm ashamed to say, of which I am still rather accustomed. My mother had cooked me my favorite breakfast. My father traveled with the players a lot. He was… an instrumental part of the troupe. He was supposed to be away on my birthday."

The memory felt strange as he dredged it up. He almost never talked about his life on Erimos. He was Hikari of Rel'van, and whatever he'd been before that he'd put very far behind him. But it felt good to dip back into those days.

"Did your father come home?"

"Hm?"

Rasa was watching him with a hand on her chin. "Your father. I'm guessing he was home."

"Smart, girl. Yes, he was home, but let me tell it, darling. It's more dramatic that way."

"Sure."

"He had these boots he would always wear. They were old and worn, caked with the history of his whole life, I think. He was away so much, and I was rarely able to go with him. Whenever I saw those boots by the door, tucked in on the left, just under the pegs that held our coats, I always knew he was home."

She smiled. "His boots were there."

"Would you rather tell this story?"

She chuckled.

"Well then." He smiled. "As soon as I saw those boots, I knew somehow he'd come home for my birthday. I was much older when I found out he'd passed up a job to be there. I have no doubt that set my parents back for a while. And in spite of it, my mother had prepared a veritable feast for breakfast! That night I went to a play with my father. Mind you, I'd seen plays before, but usually from the outside, or on my father's shoulders in the back of the room. This time," he held up a finger emphatically, "this time we were seated. I've no idea how he managed tickets. Most likely a friend gifted them to him. He had a few, you know, players and playwrights. Oh, but it was magical! I spent the next year getting every copy of every play I could find in our local library and memorizing the lines of every part. And it paid off, don't you know."

"Plays," she muttered, her voice caught between happy and melancholy. "Plays make you happy."

"Yes! Well, no."

She looked up at him curiously.

"I suppose it wasn't the play."

"Why do you say that?"

"Because I don't even remember which play it was."

"What do you remember?"

"The boots." He glanced out at the fast approaching city. She sniffled, and he frowned. "I've upset you?"

She shook her head, but she couldn't talk as she was clearly holding back tears.

"It's alright, darling. You have a family now. You know that right?"

She nodded as her lips trembled.

"Come on then. Come on." He pulled her close, and she cried into his toga as he watched the pylat dip toward the sandy beach. "Chin up, Rasa. Everything will be alright."

The Tempest landed at a tether platform just outside of Avi'Suron, and within twenty minutes Voske stood on the shore, staring out at white-capped waves that rolled into the beach with the soothing voice of the ocean. He breathed deeply, taking in the salty air, thick with the fragrance of hibiscus. It was almost enough to make him forget the last couple weeks, to transport him back to his youth when he was carefree, playing in the surf with his brother.

The beaches here were different from the sand of Erimos. That was coarse and brown. This was nearly white, and almost as soft and fine as dust. White canopies lined the beach, curtained for privacy, but open to the ocean, a place for them to change into their festival garb. Apparently they were going to head into town in full costume. Servants swarmed Voske, fretting over fits and accoutrements, makeups and perfumes. It was humiliating, and yet he couldn't deny there was some part of him that missed this life.

His own garment was a crimson Himation, open chested, and beside it rested a mask, half crimson, half gold, split down the middle by the sword Aldalci. He couldn't even imagine the ribbing he'd receive if Klief and Rix could see him.

"Lovely. Absolutely dashing," exclaimed Hikari, dragging Voske from his thoughts.

The other male champions were in the same enclosure, with the women separated by only a hanging sheet. It wasn't very private, but this was Suntara after all.

Hikari was fawning over his bright yellow himation that dipped into orange. It was blanketed by red feathers dipped in gold, and two servants were aligning a pair of phoenix wings that seemed to sprout from his back. His hair was styled in a fiery red crest, glowing orange at the tips. His bare chest and arms glistened with oil.

"Feeling good, smoothy?"

Several oil-chested servants stopped and glowered at him, and he cringed. He wasn't on Erimos anymore.

"Quite."

At least Hikari was in a good mood. Burz was slumped in a seat at the back of the canopy, tapping his thumbs and staring at nothing. His copper garment lay beside him, untouched. Zengin had at least gotten changed; a gaudy silver toga with golden tassels and peacock feathers, and a mask of precious jewels that hid his eyes from sight.

Voske gradually pulled his traveler's chlamys up and over his head, feeling a weary ache in his arms. He set it aside and frowned at the crimson himation. "How long do we have to keep these on," he said as he gathered up the cushiony material in his calloused hands.

"All night," came Locin's voice from behind him. "Unless you want to run around naked."

He turned around to find her looking in from the ocean side. "I'm changing here. Do you mind?"

"Nothing I haven't seen before."

She wore an orange peplos with yellow gauzy fabric that rolled down her hip on one side, and she held her mask loose in her hand. It was the shape of a pylat, but pink in the center, fading to orange as it neared the wingtips. She looked taller, and her eyes were orange. Lines of orange and pink ran down her arms like sun rays.

Locin squinted at Burz. "What's taking you all so long?"

"We on some kind of schedule?" Voske asked.

"You know Gillis. Everything's on a schedule."

Voske pulled the himation over his waist then wrapped it over his shoulder. He was just happy he still remembered how to fold one of these things.

He caught sight of himself in a mirror. His muscles suddenly looked more defined and his eyes flickered with fire. He turned, flexing his arm. "How long do we have?"

"About this long."

As she spoke three men closed in around him. A couple went to his back, affixing a short post behind his wrapped shoulder by a crimson leather strap. It jutted a couple feet above his head, and its white and crimson banner fluttered in the sea breeze.

The third servant approached him with a bottle of oil in one hand and a razor in the other. Voske looked at him skeptically.

"For the festival tonight," the man said in a quite serious tone, and he nodded the razor toward Voske's chest.

It took a moment for Voske to fathom his meaning, but when he did he felt a deep horror. "What in Nyx are you suggesting," he hollered. "Keep your dainty, slack-boon, smoothy hands to yourself! My gods man, some of us have a shred of self-respect."

Hikari moved to intercept and guided the man away, making sure to explain that Voske was indeed a barbarian which suited Voske just fine.

"Nice going," Locin said, as she made her way under the canopy.

He shook his head. "I don't understand it. Is anyone on Erimos that pushy? I think not."

She shrugged. "Different opinions." She sidled past one of the smooth chested servants and ran a hand across his oiled chest. "I kind of like it."

"First off," Voske retorted. "I didn't need to know that. Second, if I wanted to go shaving my chest, or my beard, or anything else, that's my business."

"What else were you thinking about shaving?"

He rolled his eyes. "I thought you weren't talking to me anymore."

She shrugged, and leaned toward him, poking at the pole strapped to his back. "I'll talk. Maybe *you'll* listen this time?"

"Am I ever gonna live it down?"

She shrugged. "Maybe, with enough groveling."

He turned away from the mirror now, giving her his full attention. "So? You really here just to gawk at me?"

"I mean, there's a lot to gawk at, but no. I heard from our mutual acquaintance."

"Already?" Voske looked around suspiciously. "We just landed."

"He's resourceful."

"And fast enough to keep up with a chariot?"

She ignored the question. "He says he'll meet with you."

"When?" Voske asked.

"Tonight. At the festival," Locin tapped the mask in Voske's hand. "He'll be wearing one of these."

"Just like that?"

"Too easy for you?"

Maybe.

Maybe it was just his own doubt, or how easily Locin was able to contact Endring, but he was suddenly unsure about this whole thing. Still, he wasn't one to second guess himself.

"Fine. But how will we find him?"

"We'll find him. Trust me."

Voske poked his head around the canopy's edge to where Gillis was waiting by a row of carriages, and beyond him the city of Avi'Suron. Voske knew it by reputation as a city of beauty and indulgence, just the type of place to host a masked ball. It twinkled in the distance. Its white towers were capped with domes of gold, and yellow banners fluttered in the sea breeze. Everything about the vista was idyllic, and yet Voske couldn't shake the foreboding that still grasped at his chest.

45: Masquerade

Avi'suron's temple of Desita was every bit a match for the city. Its high white arches rose like tree branches, intertwining under a golden dome. The temple was airy, with limited walls and high windows that let in the sea breeze, and at its center was a grand, round room flanked with statues of the most beautiful creatures Illeri had ever seen. They looked like women, but their skin was like bark, and their hair vibrant flowers that trailed down their backs and pooled at their feet. Every guest wore some lavish outfit, and every face was masked.

It felt like a dream. Illeri looked down at her own garment, turquoise silk that tightened at her waist and fell in billows. At the bottom, teal waves crested up to her knees where white caps almost seemed to splash when she moved. Large waves crested off her shoulders like pauldrons, and a mask covered her face.

She was standing with Weylyn and Hadris, who wore similarly extravagant costumes, though both women were quiet and somber. It seemed a strange mood for such a party, surrounded by the fireworks of Desitan monks, and the raucous music and laughter. Still, she was grateful. It was as if they had their own little haven of quiet among the party-goers.

The wide open round floor was covered with dancers in bright and beautiful colors that swirled around like flower petals drifting in a breeze. Dancing was something Illeri had never learned, and she'd turned away a dozen costumed men with gleaming chests before people stopped asking.

Between songs, the petals flitted out of the center, and she caught sight of three figures watching the floor from directly across the room. Hikari stood in the center, easily recognizable in his fiery himation. On either side of him stood Burz and Gillis, looking as somber as Hadris and Weylyn. For a moment, Hikari seemed to be looking directly at her, though it was hard to tell through his mask, and she quickly looked down at her feet, choking on air.

"Are you alright?" Weylyn asked.

Illeri managed to nod as she kept coughing.

Gods, she thought. *I threw up on him. On Hikari!*

She didn't have the nerve to face him after that. Most of the night was a blur, but as far as she could recollect, he kindly came to rescue her from the desert, and she thanked him by throwing up. And maybe yelling at him? It was all still so fuzzy. She shook her head.

"I'm so sorry," Hadris said with a sigh. "I know I'm not the best company tonight."

"It's alright," Illeri said softly. "I'm not in much of a partying mood."

"Me neither." Weylyn leaned out around Illeri and glanced at Hadris. "I heard about your boy. I can't imagine what that was like."

Hadris nodded gratefully, and Illeri wondered what had happened, but thought better of asking.

After a few more somber moments, Hadris laughed softly. "We're quite a group, huh? I almost feel bad for the people of Avi'Suron.

"How so?" Illeri asked.

"I haven't seen a single champion set foot on the dance floor. They probably were hoping for some joyous celebration of the gods and their chosen. And they got us."

Illeri chuckled, and then subtly pointed toward the three men across the way. "They look as miserable as we do."

Hadris sighed. "Burz' mood may be my fault, at least in part. We've been fighting."

"I'm sorry."

She waved Illeri off. "We'll be fine. Married people fight. It's not the first time, and I'm sure it won't be the last, but... I guess I never realized how hard being the wife of a champion would be."

Or being a champion, Illeri thought.

"Well," Weylyn said. "I suppose Gillis may be rather somber on my account, at least in part. I shared a rather... unpleasant vision with him."

Illeri looked at her curiously. "Anything we should know about?"

But she shook her head. "No. It's nothing concerning you or the temple. We're safe here."

Illeri nodded, though it did little to assuage her worry.

"Hikari looks down too," Hadris said, and then both women looked at Illeri.

She flushed, and she was thankful for the mask. "That's not my fault. I don't think…" she sighed. "Maybe it is?"

Weylyn laughed. "No one's blaming you. We've all been through a lot. I think we all have a right to be a little morose."

The other two nodded their agreement, and then fell into another somber silence.

Near the edges of the room, Illeri spotted Rasa. She was wearing a dark costume that was purple near her waist, but faded into the black of the veil as it spread out. It had long draping sleeves studded with pale blue gems. She moved around the edge of the room like a shadow, and Illeri saw her stoop and pick something up off the ground. It was a flowered mask, no doubt abandoned in the revelry. As she swapped it out for own black mask, she was smiling.

At least one of us is happy.

Few things made Hikari feel more at home than a masquerade. He'd been to more than a few in his days as a player. Even one in Avi'Suron after a production of *Seldir at Yvonth*. He'd met Veshri that night, the last champion of Desita. And now *he* was here as her Champion. He held up his hand and looked at the golden sigil. It burned brighter than the golden feather tips of his outfit, shimmering in the dim room.

Parties were what he was made for, making the rounds, sipping fine wine, flirting with beautiful women. But he didn't feel much like doing any of that. Instead, he'd spent most of the night standing on the sidelines with Burz and Gillis. He didn't have the stomach for it anymore, and no one had asked, perhaps put off by the proverbial black cloud that was hanging over the three of them.

He caught sight of Illeri as the dancers drifted across the dance floor. She was wearing a turquoise peplos that draped her curves in a satisfying way that nearly made Hikari blush. Her mask was an aqua color with gold strands that swirled back and mingled with her brown hair, pinned up in spirals. She was stunning, but she looked miserable. It was a shame, really.

A servant came around with a golden tray, and Hikari took a crystal goblet, sipping the wine. It was sweet, and fragrant, and it reminded him of fresh picked strawberries.

"This is quite delicious."

Gillis nodded absent-mindedly. "It's made in small batches on the island of Peloch."

Hikari raised an eyebrow. "How do you know that?"

"Before you arrived, I was given several selections to choose from, and I decided this would suit five of you best."

Hikari smiled. "Well, my interest is piqued."

After a moment, Gillis realized Hikari was looking at him expectantly. "Champion?"

"Which five?" He said cheerily. "And how *do* you know that?"

"It's my job to know your preferences," he said, fully attentive now. "You, Burz-" he nodded toward him "-Locin, Illeri, and Weylyn."

Hikari held the goblet toward Burz. He hesitated, but then sighed and took it, drinking some. "That is excellent."

"And the others?" Hikari asked, enjoying the diversion. "Zengin prefers brandy, and neither Rasa nor Voske drink."

"Truly astounding."

Burz took another sip, and Hikari realized he wasn't getting his wine back. He turned his attention back to Gillis.

"I don't think any of us fully understand how much it is you do, Gillis."

"I simply do my job, Champion."

Burz raised his near-empty glass. "Well, you do a fine job of it."

Hikari sighed. He scanned the room, spotting Locin and Voske. They were seated at a table, no doubt anxiously waiting for Endring.

"You know, I've been to dozens of parties like this. Normally, I love them. All the beauty, the dancing, the food - by Desita, is there anything better? And yet, here I am at the biggest celebration of our lives, and I find myself disinterested. What's wrong with me, Gillis?"

He glanced over to see Gillis rigid and nodding, a dutiful steward.

"Do you consider us friends, Gillis?"

Panic washed his expression. "Friends, Champion?"

"Yes. Friends."

"That's not… traditional."

Hikari laughed. "Nothing about this is traditional, darling. Eight new Champions, and a new liaison all at once? I assume that's never happened."

"The most was three Champions at once after the battle of Dai'kera."

Burz chuckled. "You're a walking archive."

"It's part of my job to know the history of the Champions."

"It's more than that, though," Hikari guessed. "Isn't it?"

Gillis looked sheepish.

"I know that look, darling, that fire in your eyes. It's passion. But is it for history in general, I wonder, or just Champions?"

He cleared his throat. "I suppose I have always been fascinated by Champions. I wanted to be one since… well since long before I was guilded as a judge."

"That's not uncommon." Hikari mused. "I've reenacted many a champion's epic deeds on the stage. I always wondered what it would be like to live such a tale." He glanced at Burz who had finished the wine by now, a point that made Hikari frown. "What about you? Any infatuation with our predecessors?"

Burz looked utterly depressed as he shook his head. "No. I always wanted to be a soldier. I…" he shifted uncomfortably. "I used to dream of being chosen to the warrior's guild."

Hikari looked above Burz's head, as though he might actually spot a raincloud forming. "Well, quite a trio we are."

A few more minutes passed, and Gillis got squirmy. "I should…" he looked around the room, forcing himself to focus. "I should see to the others."

Hikari lightly touched his shoulder to keep him from scurrying off. "Relax. Voske and Locin don't want to be interrupted, and we can see the rest from here. Besides, aren't there swarms of servants making the rounds? They've checked on Burz and I five times in the last hour."

Gillis frowned. "I told them every ten minutes."

Hikari laughed. "Gillis!"

It was clear he was trying very hard to relax, which only seemed to make him more tense.

Another servant came by, and Hikari grabbed three goblets this time, handing his companions each one. Burz wasted no time downing his wine, but Gillis stared at his uncomfortably.

Hikari lifted his goblet toward Gillis. "Well, I think it's time we became friends, don't you?"

"If you prefer, Champion."

"Wonderful! First, you can start by calling me Hikari."

Gillis' eyes went wide.

"Second, drink the wine. Actually, let's do that one first. It may help with the second."

Gillis took a tiny sip.

"You know, Burz has already downed two."

"It'll be three in another eight minutes," he said gruffly.

Gillis tipped the goblet, sipping a bit more.

Hikari frowned at him.

"No?" He asked awkwardly.

"No." Hikari cleared his throat with great ceremony and tipped his goblet, gulping down half of it. He hated to do it, missing out on so much of the body and flavor, but he would do what it took. When he was done, he smiled and held a hand out to Gillis.

Gillis dutifully nodded and tipped his goblet, gulping down the wine.

"Perfect, now, relax! Enjoy yourself. Let's see," Hikari started scanning the room. There had to be something they could do.

He spotted Illeri again, her arms over her chest rubbing at the golden bangles on each arm. He frowned. She looked even more out of place than Gillis. For a brief moment their eyes met, but she quickly looked away, staring at the floor below like it was the most interesting thing in the worlds.

"Let me ask you, Gillis. What do you think of Illeri?"

"She looks miserable. I should go-"

"Gillis!"

The young man snapped to attention. "Champi- yes, Hikari?"

"Relaxing, remember?"

He nodded.

"Besides, I asked what you thought of *her*, not her current frame of mind."

"Right. Sorry."

"I imagine there's nothing you could do to make her happy."

Gillis deflated. "I know."

Burz was glaring toward the three women, his eyes fixed on Hadris. "She's a woman," he said. "Nothing really makes them happy."

"And what is going on between you two, darling?"

Burz looked up sharply. "Nothing."

"Sure."

Gillis looked timidly at Burz. "It's not uncommon for champions to have marital problems."

Burz glowered at him. "I said we're fine."

"Apologies, Champion. I meant no offense."

Burz stewed for a moment, and then relented. "It's harder than we thought it'd be."

Gillis nodded knowingly. "Very few champions ever have families, or even marry."

Hikari slumped as he looked back at Illeri.

"Not to imply it doesn't happen," he quickly added. "Perhaps you and Illeri…" he trailed off as Hikari looked at him nervously. "Apologies, Ch-Hikari. I didn't mean to… I know it's not my… um…"

"It's not your fault, Gillis," Burz said. "He's been pining over her all evening."

Hikari rubbed the back of his neck, feeling more than a bit foolish. "Well, darlings, I had no idea I was so transparent."

They fell into an awkward silence again. Perhaps a *brooding* silence. It hung over them like a tangible presence, dampening the festive mood.

"It's worth it," Burz said at last.

"What's that, darling?"

"All of it. Marriage, children. It hurts like Nyx, but I wouldn't trade it for all of Sbarga."

A servant came by, and Burz grabbed two more goblets, gulping down half of one in a single draught.

Hikari thought about grabbing another glass himself, but he had no taste for it. He could see clouds gathering over the seas through high arched windows, and he realized, for the first time in his life, he wanted to *leave* a party. He looked hesitantly from Burz to Gillis, and then handed Gillis his empty goblet.

"I think I'll get some air."

The festival of Desita was a glorious dance of lights and colors and sounds. The monks of Desita had gone overboard with a fireworks display that set the dark clouds ablaze, and the performers of Avi'suron played the most hauntingly beautiful music. The kind that picked you up and carried you off to a place where life was just as hard but somehow more beautiful and hope filled. The food was decadent, the people were vibrant, and the masks were fascinating.

Rasa had started the evening with an expensive looking black mask that looked more like a shroud. It wasn't ugly. In fact, it was beautiful in its macabre way, but when she'd found a bright flowered mask on the ground, she'd surreptitiously swapped to the happier color. Later on, she'd found a discarded mask that looked like a white dove, and then another that made her think of a cat. A bright, happy pink cat. She kept each one. After all, if they were lost, then she might help reunite them with their proper owners.

She had made her way around the room a dozen times, staying out of the way, passing by men and women who laughed and joked like old friends, strangers who danced, hidden by their masks like ships passing in the night, and passionate lovers discreetly tucked in dark corners. It all made her uncomfortable, but it also made her ache.

She came across a familiar face now, watching her from under a silver mask trimmed with vibrant peacock feathers that fanned out around him like a lion's mane.

"Hello, Zengin."

He slowly turned his gaze away and back toward the center of the room, where the dancers were gathering for another song. She leaned out and looked at his arm. It was encased in a golden cuff that covered his wrist. She'd never seen him wear the one she made him, but that was okay.

"What happened to your mask?" He asked.

Rasa pulled her collection out and showed him. "I liked this one better. It's happy." She squared her shoulders. "I'm Happy Rasa."

"And the black one?"

She slipped the bright pink mask off and placed her own back on. "Champion Rasa."

"Perhaps you should find the others all happy masks." He glanced down at her. "I've been watching them. They're all rather dour tonight."

"And what about you? Do you need a mask?"

"I always wear mine," he said, tapping his head near his ear.

"Oh."

He went back to his watching, and she thought about making the rounds again, but her feet were growing tired, and she was glad to rest.

"Do you ever…" she bit her lip as she glanced up at him. "Do you ever wish the masks were real?"

"What do you mean?"

"Like they could change you, maybe?" She recalled the merriment she'd heard from the other guests. "When I hear them being happy, laughing, it makes me feel…" she wasn't quite sure how to put it into words.

"Heavy."

"Yes. Exactly. Heavy."

"And how do you know they don't feel heavy too?"

She wasn't sure, really. But when she heard them laugh it sounded light, like a gust of cool air on a still, hot day. "They don't seem heavy."

"Then they're stupid." He looked down at her. "Only stupid people are happy."

Rasa'd had enough solemnity for the moment. She slipped her black mask off, and placed the flowered one on her face.

"And who is this?" He played along.

"Hidden Rasa."

They stood there for a moment as the song ended and the colorful dancers slipped away to ringing laughter. And she felt it again. *Heavy.*

"Is it ever *too* heavy?" She asked.

"All the time."

"And…" she caught sight of Weylyn across the room watching the dancers saunter away. "And what do you do about it?"

"You ignore it."

She sighed. That wasn't helpful at all.

"We're not mindless beasts," he continued. "You can *choose* to feel or not."

"I used to shut my eyes," she started, her voice trembling. "I'd pretend I was far away, with my family."

"Do you have a family?"

She shook her head. "They sold me when I was a baby. But I pretended I did. A happy one that loved me."

"You have masks too," he said, pointing to her head. "You don't need the gaudy ones."

"Maybe." She ran a finger along the painted flowers. They felt almost real as the petals rose from the mask. "But I like them."

"And what's that?" He pointed to the white mask in her hand.

She brushed her thumb along the feathery edge. "Pure Rasa."

"Hm."

"Is there a Pure Zengin?"

"I don't think there ever was."

"I think everybody's born pure, but some people just lose their way."

He didn't reply, and she sighed, looking for Weylyn again, catching glimpses of her through the dancers that were rollicking back through the center to a happy tune.

Her life, or mine.

It all felt unbelievably heavy at the moment. She would never ask Weylyn to make that trade, but Weylyn had insisted she would. It didn't make any sense. Weylyn was skillful, wise, *pure.* The word stuck in Rasa's mind, something she could never be.

She looked down at the dove mask. She'd insist, that's what she'd do. She'd insist Weylyn let her go. It was the only choice that made any sense. She would face her death like a champion. *Brave Rasa.* And maybe, in the Midding, she'd be free. Free from the heaviness.

She called up her boon, and Nyx closed in like a cold wind. Blue spirits twirled around the dancers like their shadows.

"Do you think…" She started weakly. "Do you think it's different on the other side of the veil?"

"I've always hoped."

She sensed in his tone the same ache to be free.

"Life is a rather wearying affair," he said.

She nodded. It was for the best then. And on the other side, all the scars would be gone. She let her hand brush the white mask once more, the most beautiful in her collection. Gold rimmed the eyes, and plush white down covered the edges. She pulled the flowered mask off, and slipped the white one over her eyes. Maybe in the Midding she could be reborn.

Pure Rasa.

Locin sat on a table next to trays of food, carefully watching the party-goers, not that she'd be able to pick Endring out of the masked crowd, but that wouldn't stop her from trying.

Voske was beside her, gnawing a large chunk of meat down to the bone. A pile of bones was starting to build up on the table beside him.

"Gods! How much are you gonna eat?"

He glared at her as he dropped another bone on the pile.

"You need to relax."

"I'll relax when this is over," he growled. "If he sets us up-"

"He won't. Nyx it, keep your voice down."

Voske sighed and wiped his wrist along his mouth. "So, where is he?"

"Close. I'm sure."

"You think." He reached up a hand, running it along the pole that extended from his shoulder. "I wish we weren't so obvious."

"Just relax. Tension draws attention."

"So do ridiculous outfits."

She shook her head. "Not when *everyone* has them on. It's not about going unseen, it's about blending in."

Voske huffed and grabbed another piece of meat. "Easy for you to say. You're short."

"I could be taller than you and still do it. You just gotta remember three rules. Tension draws attention, laughter draws attention, and kissing makes people look away."

He chewed a thoughtful bite. "Is that so?"

"Yeah, so if we're too obvious you can kiss Endring."

He choked and slapped a hand against his chest, gagging until a piece of meat flew out of his mouth onto the floor. "I didn't need that image," he wheezed.

"You're welcome."

She felt a bristle up her spine as Spark pulled her attention behind to a corner of the room. She turned and scanned the faces there, a sea of masks.

Spark insisted he was there.

A glint of gold caught Locin's eye and she spotted a man standing by a pillar dressed in black and gold. His mask was rather plain, but it covered the whole of his face, wrapping around the side of his head and forming raven's wings that stuck out the back.

Locin hopped off the table and straightened out her peplos. "Let's go."

Voske stiffened. "He's here?"

"This way."

Locin sauntered through the crowd, Voske being about as graceful as a rhinoceros as he marched along behind her.

First, she stopped at a counter attended by monks of Desita and smiled. "Some wine for the Champion of Jeza?"

"Juice," Voske corrected.

She turned and frowned. "You need to relax."

"Juice," he insisted.

"Whatever." She snatched the drink and handed it to him. "Just don't spew it on me."

They made their way to the corner, where Endring moved quietly to meet them. He reached out and grabbed her hand, folding it in his like they were old friends.

"You spotted me."

"It wasn't hard. Don't worry. I only meant it wasn't hard for me." She glanced into the corner where a half-moon sofa curved along the outer edge of the grand room. "Here?"

"After you." Endring gestured them forward, and Locin slipped past then watched painfully as Voske backed toward the sofa, never letting his eyes off Endring until he was seated.

"He's not going to stab you in the back," she hissed.

"So says you."

Endring settled into his seat and leaned forward, studying Voske with a cautious expression.

Voske matched him move for move and for a moment it felt like no one was going to say anything.

"Hey," Locin elbowed him in the side. "Tension draws attention."

"Fine," Voske relented. "Locin tells me you can point us to the Crook."

Endring's gaze narrowed. "I have an idea of where to look."

"Then why agree to meet us?"

Endring steepled his fingers, but didn't bother to answer. "You'll recall the third verse of *Morning Light*. In the hands of a guide, a sight to lift the spirit, an end to ward away the final fate."

"Something like that," Voske agreed.

"Exactly that," Endring snipped. "Words are of vital importance."

"Fine. What you said, but we already had that information."

"Yes." Endring leaned back and crossed his legs, watching Voske carefully.

"Then why not give us the rest?"

"Because I'm not convinced you're the type of man to be trusted."

Voske started cracking his knuckles. "That goes both ways."

"As the only one here who is not posturing," Locin hissed. "Can I just say we should get this over with? Endring, can you get the Crook by yourself?"

Endring slowly shook his head.

"Alright, then out with it."

"I need some assurances first."

Voske tilted his head back, staring at Endring coldly. "Like what?"

"I want the Crook. That should be obvious to you by now. I can give you the clue, but when you find it, you have to give me the piece."

Voske scoffed. "Why in Nyx would I do that?"

"Because I can store it away, somewhere Borroka will never find it. The temple has already proven unreliable in this regard."

Voske shook his head. "You already have one piece. Just keep that one."

"Not good enough."

"It'll have to be." Voske leaned forward. "Here's the thing, you're going to give us the clue because we've already proved we're so rotting good at recovering these things. You'll give it to us because it splits Borroka's attention between you and me. And you'll give it to us because having a chance to steal it is better than never finding it at all."

Locin stared at Voske, impressed. For being such an oaf, he still managed to surprise her.

Endring's jaw was hard set and he studied Voske, unflinching.

"Tell me," Voske said. "Why did you try to stop Borroka?"

Endring's voice softened. "Because as hard as this might be to accept, I very much care about Talamh, and the temple, and Borroka would see it all burn."

Voske leaned in closer. "But you're so different. That's why you're trying to piece together a weapon."

"Not a weapon."

Voske leaned back, ever so slightly. "Then what is it?"

Endring took a deep breath. "It's the key to righting the worlds, Voske. It's the key to unlocking the Veil of Nyx, and letting a soul return to Talamh."

"Neveri," Voske muttered.

"Surely you've seen the way the worlds are out of balance. A beautiful facade over a broken order. Hmm? No more seasons. No more change. We're a stagnant and dying people. Plants and animals suffer, one out of nine children go unguilded, entire cities are lost! The temple presides over a broken realm and this key, *this crook*, will bring the realm back into order."

Voske leaned all the way back, staring at Endring like he'd seen a ghost, but Locin just leaned in. There was something about Endring's passion that made him like a flame, and she was the moth.

"Voske," she hissed, glancing his way. "We can't stay here long."

Voske folded his arms over his chest. "Give us the clue."

Endring nodded slowly, looking from Voske to her then back again. "Very well. It's not much, but it's all I've learned. The guide is Kisandin."

Voske scowled. "That's it?"

"That's it."

He shook his head and looked back out toward the party. "I'll have to tell the others, put our heads together."

Endring nodded. "As you say, you've all been very good at recovering these things. I'm confident you'll succeed."

"Right." Voske motioned to Locin then stood, meandering back toward the party.

She rose to follow him but stopped at a touch from Endring. "Locin."

She looked back at him with a nervous glance.

"There is one last item I'd like to discuss."

She looked toward Voske. He was waiting for her in the center of the floor, and Spark was relentlessly tugging her that direction. For a split second her heart was hammering, but she stuffed the feeling down and turned to face Endring. It couldn't hurt to talk. "What do you want?"

"I have one more favor to ask," he said.

46: Unmasked

The festival dragged long into the dark hours of the morning before the champions were finally able to escape the crowd. They stole away behind the temple, retreating down a long stretch of beach that ran to the horizon in either direction. The dull, gray light of the stars barely pierced the low hanging clouds, and the moon was hidden from sight. The sand was scattered with shoes and masks and other bits of costume, until all that was left was them.

The small fire Weylyn had built flickered in the sea breeze, casting long shadows, and the eight champions stood around it, lost in thought.

Voske had told them the true nature of the crook, to rescue a god from Nyx. It felt impossible, but at the same time it was the only thing that made sense.

And yet all Burz could think of was his family. Here he was, faced with the fate of three realms, and every time he thought of Neveri, all he saw was the broken face of Orin lying in his bed with tear-stained cheeks.

"The guide is Kisandin." Hikari muttered, drawing Burz back to the present. "That's all he said?"

"That's all," Voske confirmed.

Burz listened in silence. He wasn't happy when he found out Voske had been talking to Endring, but he wasn't angry either. It was hard to stay very mad for very long when your life was busy falling off a cliff.

"Can you solve it, Illeri?"

"It's not much to work with."

"Why leave all the pressure on her shoulders?" Hikari defended. "The rest of us can pool our knowledge, come up with something."

"Sure," Locin said. "But my marks are on Illeri."

Burz looked at Voske. It seemed as though the large man had become the de facto leader of their group. It was disconcerting, but Burz was too tired to object, at least for the moment.

"Voske."

Voske looked at him, but he was missing his usual smug confidence. Maybe he was tired too.

"When we find this thing," Burz said. "What do you plan to do with it?"

"Keep it. The temple's proved unreliable."

Burz, to his amazement, found himself nodding. He couldn't remember ever agreeing with Voske.

"Unreliable," Locin spat, kicking at the sand underfoot. "More like rotting liars. They hid the truth from everybody."

Illeri leaned out to look at Locin "I don't think Aurilis knew about-"

"Who knows what that shrike knew? She's lied to us, believe me. And somebody knew about Neveri. Some other High Oracle back who knows when. You don't lose a whole rotting god and not know."

Burz scrunched up his brow. Maybe it was all the drinks, but he found himself nodding along with Locin too. Gods, he needed a hot tea.

"The temple follows the gods," Weylyn said. "They don't kill the gods."

"I'm not saying they did," Locin said. "But they knew about it, and they chose to let that piece of information be lost to time."

"Who *can* kill a god?" Hikari asked. "Presumably only the other gods, yes?"

"I suppose," said Illeri, "but why?"

"Maybe he broke a law?"

"Are there laws in Sbarga?"

"No." Zengin said flatly. "The gods are a law unto themselves. It wouldn't have been anything he did that was worthy of banishment. It would have been what he was."

"They're all full of mire then," Locin said. "He can't change what he is."

"Or," Illeri raised a finger. "Maybe he's the only one that didn't. Think about the statues in the old sanctum. That Jeza looked bloody and terrifying, but normally she's pictured as composed and just. All the gods were like that."

"Primal." Zengin said.

"Neveri's literally the god of change," Locin snapped. "Are you saying the god of change is the only one that can't?"

Illeri shrugged. "It's just a theory."

"A dumb theory."

Not dumb. Burz thought. *Just circling the truth.*

"Simmer down," Voske barked. "Being at each other's throats isn't gonna help."

"The point remains." Zengin said. "When the gods banished him to Nyx, they had a reason. Undoubtedly a good one."

"Yeah, right," Locin retorted. "They're idiots, all of them."

"So says the seventeen year-old girl about a being older than Talamh."

"Shut up, pelican boy."

"They're obviously wiser than us," Hikari said, keeping his voice incredibly level. "But does that mean they never make mistakes?"

Locin kicked a bit of sand into the fire, making it crackle with protest.

"They do." Weylyn answered, "They're still learning, same as us. They just have an awfully large head start."

"That's a Nyx of a mistake." Locin mused. She was staring sulkily into the fire, like her thoughts were somewhere else.

"Was it?" Burz asked.

"Huh?"

"A mistake. You think banishing Neveri was a mistake?"

"Of course. Look at the rotting state of the worlds. Of course it was a mistake."

They all paused to consider her words. It was hard to imagine what the consequences of a ninth god would be. Destabilizing, surely, but then change always was.

"Just think about it," Locin said. "Talamh doesn't change. Everything is just *stagnant*." The words almost didn't sound like her own. "And what about the unguilded? They're overlooked because there's no god to choose them."

Immediately, Burz saw Orin's face again, staring back from the flames, and he felt his heart hammering. Could it be true?

"I mean, that doesn't sound so bad," Hikari agreed.

Zengin started laughing in a cold, scornful way as he looked around the circle.

"You got something to say, pelican boy?"

"You're all actually considering this, aren't you?"

Illeri shrugged. "They're just saying maybe something was lost when Neveri was banished."

"Something worth getting back," Locin muttered.

Zengin's eyes stopped on Burz. "Even you? After all your dogmatic talk of heresy."

Burz felt like his mind was at war with itself. Everything from his past wanted to agree. The gods were righteous. They didn't make mistakes. But the vision of his son kept his tongue rooted to the roof of his mouth. Finally, he managed to work it loose, but even then he only shook his head. "I don't know."

Zengin stared around the circle one last time, a look of disgust written on his face. "You're idiots. All of you."

Without another word he spun and trudged away, back toward the temple.

They watched him leave, but no one made a move to stop him.

At length, Voske spoke again. "We can debate this later. For now, let's focus on finding the relic. Anyone got any ideas?"

Most of the eyes turned to Illeri, but she slowly shook her head. "Not yet."

"Then think. Endring and the cult are both looking for this thing, and we need to get there first." He looked around the circle. "Rasa, can the spirits help?"

Rasa, who had so far been very reserved, looked up with alarm. "Oh. I uh… They haven't said anything."

"Did you ask?"

"Not yet."

"Well, talk to them. We need all the help we can get."

She nodded feebly.

"Now, does anyone have any other ideas? Anyone?" Voske looked around the group, but no one really looked back.

Finally, Weylyn turned and walked away from the fire.

"Weylyn?" Voske called. "Are you quitting?"

"Just getting some air."

"I think I will too." Illeri said, as though she now had permission. "I need to clear my head."

Next Rasa slunk away, then Locin, then Hikari, until only Voske and Burz remained, standing on opposite sides of the fire.

Voske's fists were tightly wound as though he was still fighting, but he had no one to fight. His lips moved in silent frustration. Frustration with the gods perhaps?

Burz shook his head, gods knew he could relate to that, but unlike Voske, he didn't have any fight left. He felt hollow, as though his heart had been left behind in Kerata.

At length, even Voske wandered off. Burz was tired, halfway to drunk, and miserable. He was confident they didn't need him to solve this riddle, and even more confident that he needed sleep. His body was far from healed after Kerata, and his mind yearned for the thoughtless still of slumber. So he slunk back toward the temple, torn whether to pray for their success to gods he was no longer sure he knew or understood. So he stayed silent, slinking home like a shadow.

Weylyn strolled down the sandy beach, listening to the surf. The stars overhead were hidden behind black clouds, and a few crabs scuttled along the water's edge, dancing just outside the waves and snapping up flotsam that washed ashore. Nature, it seemed, was not at all bothered by the tribulations of people, and the serenity soon began to overtake her, as though each breaking wave was scrubbing the corridors of her mind.

She kept walking until she heard footsteps behind her. The petite footsteps of a teenage girl. She glanced back, and her suspicions were confirmed.

"Rasa."

Rasa wrung her hands together and tottered closer. "Hi."

Weylyn took a deep breath. "I suppose it's time we talk."

The young girl nodded, and for a while they strolled down the beach in silence, listening to the water roll up and down the sand.

"I heard you talking to Gillis," Rasa said at last.

"I know." This wasn't a conversation she'd been looking forward to, but it had been inevitable.

"I was just wondering…" she began, and then she took a deep breath and squared her shoulders. "How do I die?"

Weylyn raised an eyebrow, impressed with her courage. "You mean, how do *I* die?"

"But…" Rasa shifted uncomfortably as they walked. "It was me. You saw me when you used that powder."

"I saw *me* in Arrajin, when I first had the vision."

"That's… is that normal?"

Weylyn chuckled. "I don't know. I haven't been the champion of Strah for very long."

"Right."

She glanced over as they walked. Rasa had taken off her mask, and her dark garb trailed around her tiny form, contrasted by her pale skin and fiery hair. She looked almost like a ghost, making barely a noise as her bare feet sank into the sand.

"If you think it will help, I can tell you about the vision."

She looked grateful, nodding with determination.

"Alright. Both visions were basically the same," she began. "It's raining on a bridge." She shut her eyes, hearing the heavy drops slap against the stone. "I can hear a roaring sound, an animal maybe, but like nothing I've ever heard before."

"A Chimera?" Rasa asked.

Weylyn shook her head. "More like… a leviathan, if those were real." She heard it echo through her mind, saw herself standing on that bridge as the stones at her feet trembled. "It shakes the ground."

She opened her eyes to see Rasa looking terrified. Weylyn reached a hand out, giving her a light squeeze on the arm. "That only means it can't sneak up on us."

Rasa tried to smile, but it didn't seem to help much.

"I know it was in Arrajin." She continued. "I recognized the bridge. The first time, I saw myself…" She glanced back at the girl. "Nevermind what I looked like. I was dead. We'll leave it at that."

"And the second vision?"

"I saw you."

"And… you're sure we were dead?"

The vision of Rasa's broken body, gutted and splayed across the cobblestone played through her mind, and she quickly shut it down, feeling an unbelievable grief start to well. "Yes."

Rasa took a deep breath and turned her eyes back to the front. They were nearing a stone jetty that curled out into the waves. The top looked craggy, but passable, and they scrabbled up the side together, then began to walk out over deeper water. There was a light sea spray from the waves as they folded against the rocks, but the farther out they walked, the lower the waves became, until they were meager swells, like the bobbing ripples of a massive lake. The festival lights grew distant, and it became more and more difficult to see until the dark water began to blend with the stones underfoot.

Rasa stopped. There was a gentle lapping in front of them now, signaling the tip of the jetty. The ocean was practically placid out this far, which almost made the water seem more dangerous, and Weylyn instinctively reached for her back, only to be reminded that her bow had been left behind on the chariot.

"It's beautiful," Rasa said, kneeling by the water's edge.

Weylyn relaxed. "The ocean?"

"Yes."

"You know, I had never touched one until we arrived on Suntara."

"Never?" Rasa looked up, surprised.

"I was born and raised in the Shinoam. I never left until Strah called me."

"Not me." Her voice sounded sad. "I went everywhere. But I was born on Suntara." She dipped a hand in the black water.

"Rasa."

She looked up at Weylyn.

"I won't let you die."

"I heard you say that to Gillis. I… I think you should know what I was… before."

Weylyn furrowed her brow. There was a somber tone in Rasa's voice that she didn't like. "Before you were chosen?"

"Yes."

"I've guessed some, child," she said softly. "You don't need to tell me."

"But… I'm broken."

"We're all broken. You don't live in the worlds and not get broken, Rasa."

"More broken?" She ventured. And then she sighed. "They used to keep me in this room. The ceilings were so high, and there were these hooks for flower pots. They never had flowers, but the hooks were still there. I used to think if I could get some rope…"

"Why are you telling me this?"

She looked up and nodded as if resolving something inside herself. "Because it should be me, Weylyn. My life is-"

"I'll have none of that!" Weylyn grabbed Rasa's hands. "If you're trying to tell me your life isn't worth saving, you can stop now."

"But-"

She lifted a hand to Rasa's cheek, slick with tears. "I won't hear of it again. Do you understand me?"

Rasa nodded. "But… why?"

She tipped her chin up to look eye to eye. "Because you are not broken, Rasa. You are going to live a long and happy life, and someday when you're old and gray, you're going to tell your grandkids about me." She smiled warmly. "Everyone deserves that, a chance at a good life. Maybe more than one chance." She swallowed a lump in her throat. "I felt that way once when I was young too." She could feel all the memories trying to bubble up, and she was surprised how much it still hurt after all these years. "I went out in the woods, and I sharpened my hunting knife. I thought it was the only thing that would take the pain away. I thought I was too broken to keep living."

"You did?"

"Yes."

"Why? What made you so broken?"

"I lost something very dear to me, and I didn't think I could live without it." She knelt beside Rasa, and pulled down her toga to reveal an ugly scar at the top of her breast. "I got this far. I would have done it, I think, but there was this woman… She was like a mother to me, really. She had been looking for me, and by Uthando's mercy, she found me just when I needed her."

"She stopped you?"

Weylyn nodded. "She showed me my life was still worth living. And I can say, forty years later, I'm so glad she did. I've had a good life, Rasa. And you will too."

She pulled Rasa into an embrace, and the young girl melted in her arms, sobbing.

"Weylyn," she said, muffled.

"Yes, dear?"

"Thank you."

Locin was in the water up to her knees and the edge of her toga dipped into the waves. The ocean stretched out in front of her, farther than the eye could see. Maybe there was an island out there, she wondered, a place you could sail to where no one could find you.

The thought was ridiculous, but it wasn't the first time she'd had it. The island could be a place to escape from the expectations of everyone, a place she'd never let anyone down, and no one could hurt her in return. What might that be like? A simple place with coconuts, lots of coconuts, and maybe a pet monkey who could do all the cooking and cleaning and find the food in the first place. And maybe she'd take a ship's worth of chocolate with her. How long did chocolate last anyway?

She spit into the water and her thoughts turned dreary. When she was a thief, she could hide if she wanted, just go find a forsaken corner of a forgotten city and hole up a while. Now that she was a champion, she wasn't so sure that was possible. It was like carrying a heavy stone on your shoulders. At the start, it doesn't feel so bad, until you figure out you can never put it down. Ever. You're just stuck with it. That's what she was. Stuck.

"Out here alone?"

Voske's voice pulled her from her thoughts. She could feel him behind her, but she didn't turn around.

"I was."

"Right. Not so much anymore, I s'pose."

A large wave rushed in and she leaned into it, letting the water slap into her thighs and drench even further up her garment.

"Little late for a swim," he said. "You going for a dip?"

She thought about turning to face him, but resisted the temptation. "Weren't you working on the puzzle thing?"

"Bah. Illeri's on it. I figure she'll crack it eventually. Besides, I don't imagine you're out here to ponder any riddles."

"I did my part. Now it's up to the thinkers."

"Don't do much thinking yourself?"

"I'm more of a doer. Same as you."

"Hey, I think about stuff."

She glanced over her shoulder. The big guy had his hands folded in front and wore the most mild mannered expression she'd ever seen on his face.

"You got family around here?" He asked.

She wrinkled her nose. "Why would you ask that?"

"I don't know. You're from Suntara."

"So are you. You got family around here?"

He frowned. "I got a brother. Haven't spoken in years, and I'm not lookin' to change that." He nodded to her. "Your turn."

The memory flashed in her mind, plain as day. An estate on the beach with a wide porch and columns that curved up like cresting pillars of water splashing against the underside of the roof. And between each pillar hung an inventor's lamp, lit up like green stars in the black night.

"Nope," she said. "Just me."

"Surely you have parents somewhere. I don't imagine you just sprang up out of a rock."

"Sure. Everybody's got parents. That don't make 'em family."

"Why not?"

She turned back to the water and dipped her hands in the cool waves. "Why isn't your brother family?"

"He didn't approve of my choices," he said flatly. "He cut me out, not the other way round. And yours?"

"Do you know what it's like to not be guilded? Gods. Talk about a humiliation." *That was it,* she thought. *That was the first time I imagined that island.* "I ran off. My parents were talking to the monks, lookin' like I just stabbed their hopes and dreams through the heart. So I ran away. Went down to the beach on the edge of town."

"Did they come looking for you?"

She laughed. "Gods, no. I wouldn't have been that hard to find."

"Well," Voske moved up beside her, letting the water slap his legs. "What'd you do?"

Locin shrugged. "Kicked the sand. Cursed the gods. Smashed every shell I could find. Then I dove in. I swam out as far as I could, which wasn't very far. Swallowed half a wave getting washed back to shore. I thought maybe..." she felt her throat close up. *I thought I could swim away, find my own island where no one could ever find me.* "I decided there was nothing else I could do. And I was hungry, so I went home."

"Well, weren't they happy to see you?"

"I don't know," she said. "Never went in. You see, we had these lanterns all over the property, green sparks that lit up the place. We turned 'em out every night at the same time. My Ada was like that." She bit her lip. "We had one lantern out at the front gate, old, wiry thing, but brighter than the rest. Sometimes when my brothers and sisters were out late or coming home to visit, he'd say, 'Not this one, Locin.' I'd ask him why not, and he'd go on about leaving one lantern for 'em so they could always find their way back."

"Ah," Voske said. "And that night?"

"Not a single, rotting lantern." She smacked her hand into the waves. "I figured I wasn't welcome anymore, so I left. Never saw any of 'em again."

They stood there for a while, the waves lapping at their knees, the stars overhead, Locin thinking about her island, and at last Voske broke the silence.

"Thanks."

She looked at him warily. "For what?"

"Telling me. Couldn't o' been easy."

"Whatever." She stiffened. "Not like I rotting care."

"Locin-"

"Hey, I need some air." She spun to face him.

"We're outside. How much more air can you get?"

"I don't know. I'm gonna go find out though."

Before he could answer, she ran off down the beach. For the barest moment she felt an urge to go back and join him, but she didn't feel like it tonight. Back there was where the baggage beckoned, waiting to tie her down with responsibility and heartache, but out here she was free… and cold… and alone.

Hikari dug his toes into the cool sand of evening, feeling the gentle lap of the ocean curling around his feet. His dry sandals dangled limply from his hand and slapped together in a pleasant cadence, in keeping with his leisurely pace.

Illeri had broken away from the group and was sitting by herself on the dark shores, her form barely visible in the waning firelight. She didn't look up as he approached and instead doodled in the sand with a piece of driftwood, every so often erasing the image and starting again.

He sucked in a breath and tapped his free hand against his thigh. He didn't want to interrupt her, but if he didn't talk to her soon he was going to lose his nerve altogether. He knelt down close by and stared at her drawing. It was a rather large looking animal with four hoofed feet and a long snout.

"Pretty horse."

She looked up with alarm, and the stick fell out of her hand, but she calmed down once she saw it was him. "It's a cow."

"Ah," he looked at it again. "Really?"

"See the ears? Horse ears don't stick out to the side like that."

"I thought those were spots on its head."

She pointed the stick just above them. "Then you thought it didn't have ears at all?"

"No, I just assumed you hadn't drawn them yet."

They fell into horrible silence and Hikari glanced back the way he'd come. Maybe talking now was a bad idea.

"Drawing helps me think."

"You do it often?"

"I used to. Not with a stick though."

He summoned his courage and sat down cross-legged beside her, then motioned for the stick. "May I?"

She handed over the wood without a word and Hikari looked at the wide blank canvas before him. What was he going to draw? He'd never been any good at this.

He jabbed the end into the sand and started dragging it around, trying to form a crab. "I'm not sure this helps me," he said. "I'm just focused on the picture now."

"That's the point."

"Hmm?"

"If you focus on something other than the problem then you can get surprised by a solution."

Hikari narrowed his eyes, which only made the already dark night even darker. "I'm not certain I follow."

"Think about when you've been struck by inspiration," she said. "What were you doing? Were you racking your brain trying to come up with an idea, or were you doing something mundane?"

"This isn't mundane," he argued. "I'm focused on the picture."

"On the palm bush?"

He dropped the stick into the sand with a sigh. "It's supposed to be a crab."

"Oh?" She cocked her head to the side. "I think I can see that."

He looked down at his drawing, and a light chuckle escaped his lips. It really did look like a palm bush.

"I just keep thinking about that verse," she said. "The message of it, the meter of it. Is there something in the words themselves? Maybe if we mix it around and put them back together in a different order, you know, that sort of thing."

Hikari died a little inside. This wasn't what he'd wanted to talk to her about at all. "Guide hands in the lift spirit," he croaked, "final ward to end the sight fate."

"Yep. Still nothing." She flopped back in the sand.

Hikari looked down on her reclining form with a mixed sense of longing and trepidation. "Going for the full body drawing this time," he quipped.

She smiled. "I'm trying to distract myself again."

He lay back next to her and tucked his hands under his head, mostly just staying focused on his own breathing, and trying not to stare at her. The sky overhead was just as ominous and dark as it had been all night, like it was an overbearing chaperone, threatening to rain if they got an inch out of line.

"And what a distraction it is," he commented. "Nothing like a sheet of dull gray to wow the senses."

She laughed. "I'm trying to envision the stars behind it."

Hikari squinted at the inky black and imagined a bunch of polka dots scattered around the canopy. "I'm imagining a mighty cow constellation, directly above us."

She shook her head. "The closest to that would be the Ox, and it should be right over there." She pointed out over the water and close to the horizon.

He raised an eyebrow. "You're sure?"

"Positive."

"You actually know where these things are?"

She gave him a worried glance. "Is that weird?"

"I mean a little bit, sure, but I suppose sailors know that sort of thing."

"True."

"But then sailors are always on the same planet and in the same general area."

She squirmed under the observation, but Hikari was smiling.

"Alright, now I'm imaging a big blue star. The brightest in the sky."

"That would be Ravthere. This time of night it should be right about there."

She abruptly sat up as the sound of the ocean crashed back in, and at once every light he had gathered vanished into thin air, but she didn't seem to notice.

"What's *it*?" He stammered.

"The final fate. It's a shipwreck."

"The riddle? That's what we're talking about?"

"Yes," she said excitedly.

Hikari's head was spinning, and he tried to push down his misgivings. How had she still been thinking about the riddle?

"I assumed if Kisandin was the guide, it was referencing the stars again," she continued. "The Eye of Kisandin watches the cold dark."

"Right. And?"

"Kisandin also watches the seas!" She quickly stood to her feet and brushed the sand from her toga. "We should tell the others."

He weakly raised himself up to a sitting position. "What? Now?"

"Of course!" She grabbed hold of his hand.

Immediately he felt his heartbeat quicken. Her skin was so soft, and the last thing he wanted to do was to trudge back down the beach to the others.

"Come on." She urged, tugging on him to get up. "I'm telling you, I'm right about this."

He nodded and looked longingly back down the beach one last time. "I believe you," he said, and he scrambled to his feet and grabbed up his sandals once more. "Back to the others then."

47: In the Hands of the Guide

The sun was still lazily swimming along the horizon as Burz made his way down the boardwalk through Avi'Suron. He'd been more than a little surprised when Voske woke him, and he'd quickly dressed and said goodbye to a begrudging Hadris before slipping out. He regretted all the wine as he squinted against the growing light. They were headed away from the temple now, an almost chilly sea breeze rushing across from the shore where the gulls were crying over the surf.

"I take it you solved it?" he asked.

Voske nodded. "Illeri did."

"Figures." He watched Voske tensely. "And why come tell me?"

Voske scoffed. "You're still a champion, whatever I might think of you."

Burz bit down a rebuttal, and they continued on past smooth white buildings. The street vendors were out setting up their wares, and he could hear the calls of men working down by the docks.

"Does Aurilis know?"

Voske glared at him.

"Right. So we've got another chariot?"

"No chariot," Voske said. "There's no tether where we're going."

"And where is that?"

He looked around warily. "Don't feel comfortable saying."

"Gods and chosen." Burz sighed. "You'll come get me, but you don't trust me enough to tell me where we're going?"

"You might not be the only one listening," he growled.

"Fine. Can you tell me anything about it?"

Voske gritted his teeth, answering in a whisper. "It's a lighthouse. Apparently that's the clue."

A lighthouse didn't seem like a lot to go on. Burz was kicking himself for leaving. Maybe if he'd been there when they made the discovery, it would make more sense. And he was kicking himself for the wine. He rubbed his head as he groaned.

"No tether, so how do we get there?"

"Chartered a boat."

He mulled this information over. "We'd need to find a captain we could trust, and-"

Voske suddenly turned on him with an angry expression. "*I* already chartered a boat. I took care of it while you slept, soldier."

It was too early for Voske's nonsense. He crossed his arms over his chest and stood his ground. "You done?"

"I don't like you," Voske said tersely. "But you're one of us, and you've every right to come along. Just don't forget who's in charge."

Burz laughed. "You?"

"That's right." He spun back on his heels and they kept on in silence, though Burz dropped back a bit, following at a distance until he could see the pier. The other champions were already gathered - all but Zengin - and a dozen Jeza monks were there too, standing between them and the boat with Gillis at their head.

"Mire and Nyx!" Voske swore. "How did he find out?" He glanced at Burz.

"Considering I didn't know until you banged on my door this morning…"

Voske grunted, but he couldn't argue with the logic of it.

They marched down to the pier, and Voske strolled right up to Gillis, who seemed to shrink at his approach.

"Ch-champion, I must insist-"

"Like Nyx," Voske said. "Champions insist. *You* step aside."

Gillis swallowed hard, but didn't budge.

"I don't want to *make* you move, Gillis."

"I certainly don't want that either, Champion, but I have my orders."

Hikari stepped forward. "Gillis, darling, I thought we were friends?"

"I… would very much like to be, but Aurilis-"

"Rotting, old oracle!"

Burz stepped forward, briefly considering putting a hand on Voske's arm, but he thought better of it. His head ached, and he was sure a blow from Voske's fist wasn't likely to change that.

"Listen, Gillis, this is important."

The young man opened his mouth to speak, but then shut it. He looked uncertain.

"Do you trust us?"

"I want to, Champion."

Burz held his hands out in a conciliatory motion. "You have the judge's boon. Ask us anything. We'll tell you the truth."

Gillis thought this over, and then nodded slowly. "Where are you going?"

"See!" Voske boomed. "I can't tell him that!"

"To get the third crook piece," Burz tried.

"Mire and Nyx!"

"Why?" Gillis asked.

"To protect it," Burz said. "To keep it out of the hands of the cultists."

"And Endring?"

Burz glanced at Voske and then back at Gillis. "Yes. We aren't working with him, and we don't trust him."

Gillis nodded, satisfied so far.

"See, darling? Nothing to fret over."

"That's not exactly true," Gillis said mournfully.

Burz sighed. "If he lets us pass, he'll be forced out of the temple."

"What?" Hikari stared at Gillis, and he nodded.

"Like Nyx," Voske said. "That shrike can't do that. Not while I'm champion."

"I'm afraid she can," Hikari said. "*She* is in charge of the temple, including all of the monks. We are not."

Burz frowned. "We still need to pass."

"Gods, man!" Hikari said. "Do you know what you're asking him?"

"I do. But it's no less than any of us risk."

Gillis met his gaze at that, and there was a glint in his eye. "That's true. You risk your very lives for Talamh. How can I not risk something as simple as my position?"

"Gillis!" Hikari stepped toward him, but he held a hand up to stop him.

"It's alright… Hikari. It's what a friend would do." Hikari shook his head, and Gillis turned to face the monks. "Step aside, and let the champions board."

They dutifully filed down along the pier as the champions headed up the gangplank. Voske slapped Gillis gratefully on the shoulder as he headed up, and Burz went last, stopping to speak to him.

"You're a good man, Gillis."

He nodded. "I hope I'm doing the right thing, Champion."

Me too, he thought. *Me too.*

The trip across the White Sea was somber, hours baking under the sun with everyone milling about restlessly. Maybe they were all anxious, or they could feel the shift in the winds, but no one seemed in the mood to talk, which suited Locin just fine.

By the time they neared their destination, the sun was starting to droop toward the western horizon. The boat creaked like an old woman's bones as the seafarers bent the wind to their will, throwing it hard against the sails. Ahead, they could see the town, an ancient looking thing that was probably once beautiful, full of smooth stone buildings and red roofs, but green moss climbed the walls, and the stone was aged and stained with the long years. Over it all towered the lighthouse, formed in the likeness of Kisandin with his hands outstretched over the city below like its titan guardian.

Locin leaned out over the side of the gunwale, squinting against the bright sun as the ship rose and fell over a swell, sending a spray of cool sea water across her skin. Spark was pouting beside her, relentlessly sending shivers up her spine and pulling her to look this way or that.

I'm not changing my mind, she thought, not daring to speak with such tight quarters.

Rasa was nearly at her feet, sitting on the deck dangling her legs through the rail and staring at the turquoise sea. Hikari stood beside her looking miserable, and a little green.

They hit another swell and he grimaced. "Merciful gods. Would that I never have to ride in one of these again."

"I like ships," Rasa said softly. "They feel alive."

Locin looked at her questioningly.

Rasa nodded to the water below. "The way the ship moves. It's not smooth like a chariot. It rises and falls, like the ocean is breathing." She glanced back up at them. "I'm scared of the water though."

"Not me." Locin leaned out, gazing at the depths below. They were passing over an ominous sight now, sitting on the shallow floor of the ocean. Buildings. Rows and rows of homes, and winding, empty streets like rivers on the bottom of the sea. The homes were thick with sea slime and yet still easily recognizable with the same smooth stone and red roofs.

"Gods! What happened?"

Hikari sighed. "Tragedy. Nearly two-thirds of the city was lost, almost seventy years ago. They had a tether before that," he added mournfully.

They passed over top of a temple, its spindly spires reaching up dangerously close to the ship's hull, like skeletal fingers trying to climb their way out of the depths.

The seafarers whistled sharply as they gathered the wind and slowed the ship, turning it toward the docks, and Locin glanced nervously up at the crow's nest where a large albatross was perched, still watching her. He'd been there since they left port, and mercifully no one else seemed to have noticed.

A sharp pinch from Spark pulled her eyes back down, and she felt herself being tugged from behind.

Nyx it! She thought, but the pull was relentless, so she turned.

Voske stood by the captain looking serious and big. He was pointing out over the bay toward the lighthouse.

Locin slipped away, tucking herself as far into the corner as she could.

"Forget it, Spark," she said, barely a whisper.

But Spark pulled even harder. Toward Voske.

"You like him so much, you can stay."

Spark pinched her so hard she had to bite down on the inside of her cheek to keep from yelping.

"Rot it!" She glanced up again to where the albatross perched, staring ahead now at the lighthouse. "I know you don't like it. You've made that clear since last night, but Endring's right. We need to get this piece."

A knot formed in her stomach.

"Yes, *we*, Spark."

We. The word echoed in her mind. At least for a while. When it no longer suited her, she'd leave Endring too, go off on her own or with someone else. *Never get too close. Never stay too long.* That had served her well, and being a Champion wasn't going to change it.

Spark was like a dog playing tug of war now, incessant, rhythmic yanks.

One last piece. One last time, and she could leave this life behind. She'd be a Champion wherever she went, but this way she'd be free of Aurilis and the temple looking over her shoulder at every turn. And she'd be free of…

She gave into Spark's tugging and turned toward Voske. A pang of guilt shuddered through her.

He'll turn on you too, she thought. *They always do. Everyone abandons you, so you better jump ship first.*

The ship was rolling toward the pier now, and Voske came strolling over. "You alright, kid?"

She rolled her eyes. "Don't call me kid."

He smirked. "You know that's just gonna make me do it more."

His tone was kind, and it made her angry. She couldn't afford to doubt now.

"Whatever," she said. "Let's just get this rotting relic and get home."

"My thoughts exactly." He winked at her and then strolled toward the side of the ship.

The anchor dropped, the gangplank was placed, and Locin let her eyes drift up to the lighthouse. It was so much bigger up close, towering over them and casting a black swath of shadow across the bay. A flutter caught her eye as the albatross took off from its perch, and flew toward the lighthouse. She felt as if Kissandin himself stood watching her, ominous and monstrously large. She shivered as she stepped down the gangplank and set foot on the docks. For the first time, the pull from Spark was gone. She was there, but she was quiet, merely being dragged along by Locin.

"We'll be okay," Locin whispered to the air. "We always are."

48: The Final Fate

Inside, the lighthouse of Kissandin was just as imposing as the outside. The walls were imprinted by barnacles and reefs of coral, as though the monolith had been dredged up from the heart of the ocean.

Single floors contained entire museums, or galleries of artwork, honoring the gods, and ancient spirits wandered the exhibits, as though trying to remember some piece of their past lives.

Rasa brushed her hand along a painting set on the wall of the eighth level. She was keeping count as she spiraled up. Since no one knew exactly where the relic was, the champions spread out, disagreeing on how best to look for it. A few had scurried up to the top, but some trailed behind, searching more thoroughly. Rasa had tried to stay with the group until the last of it had splintered here on the eighth floor, leaving her alone in this gallery.

She kept telling herself to keep looking, but she found herself distracted by the breathtaking art. The painting in front of her depicted Kissandin, an old man with white hair and bulging muscles. The gods were always depicted like that, shapely, strong. She wondered if it were true. Kisandin was draped in a pure white toga, waist deep in the ocean as waves crashed all around. She brushed her fingers across the cresting waves, feeling the coarse bumps of the painter's strokes.

Rasa?

She jolted at the intrusion, and turned to see Spark behind her. She looked troubled.

"Spark? Is everything alright?"

Spark pinched her mouth tightly. She was staring past Rasa at the painting.

Rasa followed her gaze to the canvas. "Do they look like this?" She asked softly. "I mean, have you seen a god?"

Spark moved closer and reached toward the painting, blue wispy fingers hovering close. *I've never seen Kissandin. I saw Bei'ai once. She was beautiful.*

Rasa watched Spark out of the corner of her eye. "What did she look like?"

Spark bit her lip as she conjured the memory. *She had skin like alabaster, and her eyes were kind. More than kind, really. Warm. Like sunshine.*

"You've been to the Midding?"

No. Bei'ai comes to Nyx from time to time, to look after the lost souls there.

"Right."

Rasa turned her attention back to the painting, until she felt the cold brush of Spark's skin on her arm. It was still a strange sensation.

"Are you sure you're alright?"

Spark pursed her lips tightly. *I keep my promises. At least, I try to.*

Rasa nodded, but truthfully she didn't understand at all.

Sometimes you make a promise, and you think it'll be okay, but something... changes. Is it okay to break those promises, do you think?

"I suppose it might be. I don't really know."

Spark sighed. *She would never forgive me.*

"Locin? Did you make Locin a promise?"

She nodded.

"And what changed? Is she in trouble?"

I don't know. She could be.

Rasa reached out without thinking, and she felt the girl's hand lock with her own. It was so close to solid. "Tell me, Spark! I want to help Locin."

She's afraid. She always runs away when she's afraid. Spark looked up at her meaningfully. *But I can't...*

"Afraid? Of what?"

Getting too close. I told her she could have a home here. I tried to make her see that. But she's so stubborn!

"A home where? The temple?"

Spark nodded.

"Is she leaving?"

Another nod.

"When?"

Spark looked upward, as though she was staring through the ceiling above toward the upper levels.

"Spark?"

Spark bit her lip. There was more that she didn't want to say.

"What is it? You have to tell me."

I promised her I wouldn't.

"Then help me guess!"

Spark nodded emphatically, scrunching her face like she was thinking.

"Is she leaving right now?"

Soon. As soon as…

Rasa felt a sinking feeling in the pit of her stomach. "…as soon as we find the crook?"

Spark gave the barest hint of a nod.

"Why would she want to go?"

That's not the right question.

"Oh," Rasa said dejectedly. "What is the right question?"

All that got was a dumb look in response.

"Right. You can't tell me. But it has something to do with her leaving?"

Yes.

"Is she leaving when we get back to the boat?"

Spark gave a tense shake of her head.

"Sooner?"

She nodded. *But… she's not leaving alone.*

Rasa furrowed her brow. "She's leaving with another champion?"

That didn't seem right. Rasa couldn't imagine any of the others leaving, and yet Spark's face lit up and she bobbed her head side to side as if Rasa was close.

"A champion…" she tried to follow Spark's nonverbal cues "…but not a champion?" And then it struck her. "Endring?"

Spark nodded wildly.

"But why would she… Spark, is she stealing the crook and giving it to Endring?"

She didn't even have to wait for Spark's reply. She could already feel it was true. She opened herself to her boon and felt it rushing in like never before. She could sense Nyx, swallowing her up. She steeled herself and let it come. She was suddenly aware of spirits all around the lighthouse. She could hear their chatter forming clearer words, loss, longing, curiosity. She could see the strand that connected Spark to Locin, an opaque cord rising through the ceiling above, and somewhere above them, an ominous presence rose from the belly of Nyx, drawing the attention of many.

She felt fear grip her and she started to pull away, but Spark grabbed her wrist. She felt fully solid now. Rasa opened her eyes and saw the desperation in her face.

Please.

She nodded and looked around at the spirits. They were all taking notice now, drifting toward the top of the tower.

"Where is Locin?"

As if in answer, Rasa *felt* the spirits keenly. She had no other word for it. It was as if her body was moving up through the tower with them, and yet she stayed still, anchored to the floor on the eighth level. She felt dizzy as the sense of motion overtook her, and for the barest moment she saw a tear form from thin air. On the other side she could see Locin. She was standing at the top of the tower with her back to Rasa, she held a metal bar, and she was staring at two great gems.

Locin?

Rasa started, and the tear suddenly collapsed, leaving only a wide-eyed Spark where it had been.

"Did you-"

I saw it too.

Rasa caught her breath. Her mind was reeling from questions she didn't have time to ask.

"I need to find Voske. He'll know what to do."

Voske stared at the staggering amount of stairs behind him. His legs had started to feel it two floors ago, and he realized he had called up his boon unintentionally. Warmth flooded his body, and the strain in his thighs was gone. He was alone now, wandering floor to floor and looking hopelessly at endless rooms full of useless trinkets. Not a relic in sight, and if there were, this place would be much better guarded. He hated to admit it, but he was wishing he'd stayed with Illeri. She had a knack for solving these kinds of things.

He rounded another set of steps and took a look at the room he found himself in. He had to be near the top. Rows of books filled an alcove with a few plush chairs, and some tables and plants were scattered around the room.

"What'd they run out of ideas?" He muttered.

Still, under the clutter, the seamless walls rose onward in a gentle slope. He couldn't help but marvel at the architect's design and skill, wielding his boon like a sculptor with clay, forming something this massive and intricate. He wondered if it had been a whole team of architects.

He had just settled on plopping down in one of the inviting velvet chairs to catch his breath when he heard scrambling footsteps coming up the stairs behind him - the soft slap of bare feet. Rasa emerged and looked around in a quick circle until her eyes rested on him.

"Voske!" She was winded, and her legs shook from the exertion of running up so many flights. "You're here."

"Did you find something? Do you know where the crook is?"

Rasa pointed up breathlessly to the last few flights of steps, and Voske moved to dash up them, but she held a hand out to stop him.

"There's more."

Voske sighed. "There always is."

"Locin…" Rasa took another haggard breath and looked at nothing beside her as if it were something. "She's planning to take it."

"The crook?"

Rasa nodded. "She's planning to take it to Endring."

It felt like a blast of air had knocked the breath from him. But it wasn't true. It couldn't be. He pushed back the gnawing feeling inside that it *was*.

"She wouldn't."

Rasa shook her head, and he could tell by her eyes she believed it. "I'm sorry, Voske. I know you two-"

"Mire and Nyx! She's a lot of things, Rasa, but she isn't a traitor."

Rasa glanced at the nothing beside her again.

"What? Your spirits tell you this? You ever think they might be lying?"

"Not just any spirit. Spark."

Voske shrugged. "Is that supposed to mean something to me? Spark?"

"She's… Locin's spirit," she tried.

Voske stared at her blankly. None of this was making any sense.

"Haven't you wondered how Locin always seems to know things?"

Sure, she knew things she shouldn't. Couldn't. The way she cheated at cards. The way she always had the upper hand.

"So what?" He said, crossing his arms over his chest. "She's a thief. She's sneaky."

"Spark was her spirit. She helped her when she had her thief's boon."

That growing sense of the inevitable clawed at the back of his awareness. "She lost that boon," he said weakly. But it made sense. It explained so much. "She doesn't have that power anymore."

Rasa pointed into the space above them as if trying to show Voske something he couldn't possibly see. "They're connected. The bond didn't break when she lost her boon. I don't understand why, but I can see it, as clear as the sky."

Voske grunted, started to speak, and then grunted again. He had no answer, and he couldn't hold back the clawing truth much longer.

"She's at the top," Rasa insisted. "You can ask her yourself."

"Fine." He started up the stairs.

Rasa was wrong - she had to be - and this was how to prove it.

He felt the strength of Jeza rush through him as he ran up the stairs, taking them three at a time, clearing the last few floors until he came out in a wide room. The walls were lined with ancient silver mirrors, and the center held a strange inventor's device that sat still and lifeless, a series of glass and mirrors and gears that were motionless within. Two great gems, clear as glass and tinted green, looked out over the sea. A door sat open on one side of the room leading out to a balcony. He could see straight across Kisandin's shoulder and down his massive stone arm where gulls perched.

Burz stood by the wall with the gems, his arms outstretched. Illeri was there. And Locin. She had a metal bar resting casually on her shoulder.

"Locin." Voske's voice boomed out and filled the room, and all eyes turned on him.

"Thank the gods!" She said as if nothing at all were wrong, and he felt silly for believing otherwise. But still…

Locin pointed to Burz. "Tell this oaf to move, will you? Or I gotta make him."

"What's going on?"

"The crook," Illeri said softly, but her voice wavered. "I think it's in the eye."

"What?"

"He's the guide," she said swiftly. "Ravthere guides the chariots, better known as the eye of Kissandin. It's said that its sister star, Devthere lights up the realm of Nyx and guides lost souls to the Midding."

Voske was thoroughly confused now, and he waved his arms frantically at Illeri. "What is your point?"

Burz sighed. "Kisandin guides us with his eyes. Illeri *thinks* calling him the guide in the clue means the crook is *in* one of the eyes."

"Okay." Voske shrugged, but he still kept a wary eye on Locin. "So what's the problem?"

Burz scoffed. "You're asking me to sit by and let them destroy a priceless monument on a whim. All I'm asking for is some more time to-"

"Ugh!" Locin threw her arms up in frustration, and Voske kept his eyes on the metal bar.

Rasa scrambled up behind him, and it felt like the truth itself was closing in from behind, but he fought it back.

She's not a traitor.

"Just tell this moron to move, Voske. We gotta do this!"

"What's the rush?" He asked cautiously.

Locin turned to face him, and for a brief instant he saw it on her face. *Guilt*. She *was* in a hurry. She *was* a traitor.

"Mire and Nyx," he muttered.

She must have seen the truth finally grab hold of him, because she tightened her grip on the bar.

He remembered trapping a rabbit once as a boy. He had herded it into a corner, and the moment it knew it was trapped, it turned and looked at him. He never forgot that look. He saw it in Locin's eyes now.

"Why?" He asked, unable to hide the sting of betrayal in his voice.

She sighed. "Gods. Whatever you've got in your head, big guy-"

"Why?" He yelled. He could feel his boon surging through his shoulders and winding his biceps like a spring.

But she seemed to have no answer.

"Burz. Don't you let her near those eyes."

Illeri sighed, strolling away toward the far wall in defeat. But Locin's face streaked with panic.

"You don't have to do this, Locin."

Her eyes darted behind Voske to Rasa. "Rotting, useless spirit! I hope you stay lost in Nyx forever, you-"

Voske took a step forward, and she backed up, but Burz was just behind her. He looked at Voske with confusion.

"What's going on?"

"Nothing!" Locin's voice screeched in desperation. "Voske's lost his rotting mind!"

He bent his knee to make a run for her, but at once she threw her arms up and pulled them forward, sending Burz' body flying away from the wall and slamming into Voske. He stumbled back on the stairs and narrowly avoided sending Rasa tumbling back down a few flights.

The sound of glass shattering echoed through the room. Voske pushed Burz off and scrambled to his feet. More glass broke.

"Locin!"

She was reaching into the base of the second eye, and he saw her pull out a bundle of cloth. She locked eyes for only a second, and she dashed for the door out onto the balcony. He was after her instantly, while the others were still reeling, trying to understand what was happening.

Locin was running full speed along the great statue's shoulder and outstretched arm. She was fast, but he leaped in bounds across the stone, barely mindful of his footing. She reached Kisandin's hand, and she turned. Voske was right behind her now.

"What's your plan, kid? Jump?"

"It's not personal." Her voice was strained.

"Like Nyx!"

"Gods, Voske! You know me. You've always known this is who I am."

"It's not who you have to be. Don't pretend you have no choice."

"I'm the stray. You don't like me, you feel *pity* for me. You took me in, tried to give me a home, but some part of you knew I'd bite your hand one day."

"That's not true."

"Of course it is, Voske. I am who I am, who I've always been. A rotting thief."

She glanced down over the edge beside her, and Voske took the opportunity to leap at her, knocking her to the ground. He held her there, pinned against the stone, the sea lapping at the shore dizzyingly far below. She was helpless. Her terrified eyes reflected his own fist, pulled back, ready to strike, enough strength to shatter her bones.

"I couldn't stay!" She squealed as she scratched at the arm that pinned her.

He shook his head. *It's Locin.*

"Rot it, Voske!"

His body burned with Jeza's strength so intensely that it ached. But it was Locin. She was a child, and one that reminded him so much of himself as a kid. Selfish, prideful, foolish. He couldn't hurt her. He could never hurt her.

He loosed his grip and moved off her small body, standing over her. "You have to come back with us. You know that right?"

She nodded feebly.

"I don't know what happens after that."

"Thank you," she barely mouthed the words.

He just stared at her. She was trembling, just like that rabbit. "This changes things. But I'll never hurt you, Locin."

She propped herself up on one elbow, her voice shaky. "Please believe me. It's not personal."

He furrowed his brow, but before he could formulate a thought, she suddenly rolled to the side and over the edge, her body disappearing into the blue sky. He jolted forward, throwing his arm out, reaching desperately for her as emotions swirled up through his chest, but his hand grabbed air.

A sound pierced the sky around him, wings driving hard against wind, and heat brushed his face as he rolled away on his back, staring up at the blue sky. A chimera swooped into view with smoke billowing from its bared teeth. Locin sat on its back, clinging to its mane. As it soared past, Voske spotted a golden sigil burned in its right paw.

Endring.

He sprang to his feet and roared as rage overtook him. He felt the spring in his arm let loose, and his fist pounded into the hand of Kisandin, breaking a large chunk off two of his fingers that fell in a cloud of dust on the grassy shore below.

It was over. They had lost again.

49: Quiet

The trip back to Avi'suron was Nyx. The squall that tossed the ship about on the White Sea, the battered state of Burz' mind, the look on Gillis' face when they disembarked. It was all Nyx.

Voske and the others had disappeared as soon as they got back, hiding gods knew where. Most of them slunk back to their chambers at the Desitan temple to change, maybe pack for the next festival. But Hadris was there. And Orin. And it was the last place in Talamh Burz wanted to be.

So he walked around the temple in a haze until he was found by some monks and escorted to see Aurilis. He wondered if this misfortune had befallen him simply because she couldn't find the rest. Maybe facing Hadris would have been better than facing Aurilis after all.

No.

Aurilis he could stare down without a care in the worlds. He didn't love her. He didn't even like her. Hadris would have been a whole different matter.

His clothes were still damp from the rain as the monks led him into the temple chamber that Aurilis had been assigned. The ornate desk was covered in parchments and books, and it looked as if she hadn't slowed down on her duties one bit while traveling with them. The High Oracle herself was pacing the room with a calloused expression, like a guard arresting a vandal for the fifth time. Just as expected, but no less destructive.

"Gillis sent word of your failure."

Burz frowned. "It was hardly mine."

"Were you not there?"

"I only meant Voske-"

She gave an exaggerated huff at the name. "I wouldn't have thought you the sort of man to pass blame."

She was right, which made it sting all the more. Wasn't he the same honorable man he used to be? Loyal guard of Tajerim?

"I was there. I couldn't have stopped them from going, but perhaps I should have tried."

She nodded approvingly. "Did you wonder why I called for only you?"

"I assumed you couldn't find the others."

She laughed. "I know exactly where Voske is sulking. But he's not a man of reason. I'd get further talking to a training dummy."

Burz smiled inside, but he kept his expression stiff.

She stopped her pacing and turned to face him. "Was Locin the only one?"

"I assume so. No one else left with her or seemed to have any idea what she was planning."

"Vohasi will be in revolution over this," she said. "I received word that three more temples on Las declared you false champions, and the city of Kai'jin has set up a shrine to that abomination Neveri. I don't think you appreciate just how tenuous your circumstances are."

Burz was tense, tired, and aching. The temple had done nothing but pile pressure upon pressure on his shoulders since the moment he'd arrived at the Gods' Mount, and he was starting to buckle.

"You've been playing at being champions this entire time, running off on quests to gods know where and doing gods know what while the rest of the realm goes up in flames!"

"And what have you done?" Burz snapped. "The temple failed to get any of the pieces of the relic. You failed to defend the Sacred Quarter. You even failed to protect the last eight champions. You want to talk about failures, then I suggest you start admitting your own."

For a moment she stared him down with wrath burning in her eyes, but then she simply started pacing again. Maybe she had no defense.

"The champions are out of control. It's weakened you and the temple."

"Voske won't be your puppet," Burz said, and then to his own surprise he added, "and neither will I."

She glanced at him sharply. "This isn't an age for heroes, Burz. It's an age of civilization. Champions are no longer called to fight wars and conquer realms. The sacrifice they have to make for their people is to put on their fine clothes and parade themselves around festivals and feasts."

That life sounded like anything but a sacrifice. It sounded easy, and safe. They'd gotten into trouble every time they'd ventured off that path, and it was costing Burz more than the rest. He wondered how many years he'd already lost off his life.

"Can you do that?" Aurilis pressed. "Can you convince the others of that?"

Was that really why Uthando called him? To sit at dinner parties and make small talk with Archons? He rubbed at the sigil on his palm.

"No."

"What?"

"No," he repeated. "I can't convince them that's best. I can't even convince myself that's best."

"Gods and Chosen." She flew back into her restless pacing. "The best thing, the *only* thing, for you to do is to represent the gods in all their dignity and civility. To restore the faith of the people."

"The people," he muttered, "or the archons?"

"Is there a difference?"

"Yes." He lifted his chin and took a deep breath. "We need to go back to Arrajin."

"Absolutely not! There're still four more festivals."

"Then postpone them. Or cancel them. I don't care which."

She lifted her chin. "Have you heard nothing I've said? Do you intend to turn every city-state in Talamh against you? These are our sacred traditions."

"Talamh is past dinner parties!" He stepped toward her, and she stopped her pacing again. "Rubbing elbows with the wealthy temple donors isn't going to save you. You can dress us up and parade us around like fools, and you will lose temple after temple and city after city. Do you know why?"

"Why?"

"Because the temple is stagnant. You can't adapt. Talamh is changing whether we like it or not. Neveri is here to stay, at least the idea of him. He has a champion walking on Talamh, for gods' sake!

The people know they've been lied to. They sacked an entire quarter of Arrajin while the temple couldn't protect them. They don't need symbols. They need heroes!"

She scoffed, but her eyes belied her. He was getting through, at least in some small part.

"Endring is heading to the Veil," he said.

"I assumed as much. But he will never step foot on the Gods' Mount!"

"He'll find a way, mark my words."

"And you think you can stop him?" She asked.

"I think *we* can stop him. The temple has failed just as much as we have, but if we go back to Arrajin together, and stand against him…"

His voice trailed off. He saw Orin again in his mind. Would the image of his broken son haunt him for the rest of his life? Did he even want to stop Endring?

Aurilis sighed. "I can't have Voske running roughshod over the worlds. He'll destroy everything."

"I agree. But you and I, together, we can stop Endring and unify for the sake of Talamh. Working together is the one thing we haven't tried."

"And Voske? He'd never agree to work with the temple."

"Then we leave him out." *Why not? The big oaf will just make a mess of things again.*

Aurilis frowned. "Alright. We'll return to Arrajin. You'll get your chance to play champion, but we work together."

Burz nodded, but she wasn't done.

"*You*," she said emphatically. "I'm done working with Jeza's chosen, and you should be too. He's one antic away from being banished from the temple."

"Just him?"

"Yes. The way I see it, it's been Voske dragging the rest of them into his nonsense. I don't think anyone else should suffer for his mistakes."

Some part of that appealed to Burz. Voske gone from his life forever? But it also made him angry. Who was Aurilis to banish a champion?

"Well?" She pressed.

He shook his head. In the end, he had to do what was best for Talamh, even if it meant siding with Aurilis. She wasn't wrong.

Voske had been responsible for every bad decision that had brought them here, as far as he could tell. If the stubborn oaf had listened to him even once, things might have gone very differently.

"Alright," he said. "You and me."

The mood among the champions had gone from bad to worse. It was one thing to lose a relic during the chaos of a battle, it was quite another to have someone you thought a friend steal it right out from under your nose.

Upon arrival back in Avi'suron Hikari had quickly bathed and changed into a dry chlamys, but he hadn't bothered to shave, or perfume, or even eat. It was enough to wash away the damp of the rain, and he wasn't in the mood to care about much else.

He sat idly in the guest wing of the temple, watching the waves crash on the shore outside and trying to think about anything but Locin. Illeri was there, as were Weylyn and Rasa. The three of them sat around a table on the far end of the room that had a conspicuously empty fourth chair. He could join, but he didn't want to do that either. Today was, for lack of a better word, rotten. The kind of day he wanted to sweep into a dust bin and throw into a swift river, never to be seen or recalled again.

He sagged a bit further into his chair, only bothering to look up when the echo of an opening door sounded through the hall. Gillis strode out past the three women who all watched him like they might watch a man doomed to exile. They looked like they wanted to say something, but had no words. Hikari had none either, but he wasn't about to let Gillis leave without a word from someone, so he flagged him down, inviting him to sit in the chair across from him. Gillis mildly joined, sinking into the plush green fabric that somewhat dwarfed his youthful physique. Hikari smiled at him somberly.

"I'm guessing you've spoken to Aurilis," Hikari started, not wanting to pry too hard into the poor man's business.

"Yes," came the mild mannered reply.

"Hence the long face, no doubt."

Gillis stared out the window, drowning his thoughts in the same waves Hikari had been watching. "She's removed me from the position of liaison."

Hikari nodded his understanding, wishing to the gods he had something helpful to say. "What will you do?"

Gillis shrugged. "It's a little late for me to join a judge's guild. I have a sister who works at a fruit farm near Arrajin. I figure they might need some help."

"Unguilded labor?"

Gillis ran a hand through his hair. "Like I said. It's a little late to try to become a judge again."

Hikari shook his head. Misery, that's all this trip had become. Pure misery.

"You'll be assigned a new liaison," Gillis added, his voice quavering. "One that won't be so inadequate."

"Are those your words, or Aurilis'?"

"Does it really matter?"

"Of course it matters, darling! Nevermind what Aurilis says. Nevermind what anyone says. You can't be pushed around by other's opinions of you." He felt like a hypocrite, but he knew the sentiment was true, even if he hadn't abided by it in his own life.

Gillis kept his hands in his lap, wringing them together.

"For what it's worth, I'm sorry. I think we were all so caught up in our own story that we didn't stop to consider the larger ramifications."

"I hardly think my employ counts."

Hikari shrugged. "Maybe in the grand scheme of things none of this will count, but it matters to you, and that means it should have mattered more to me."

Gillis forced a smile, but his eyes darted to the door. "For what it's worth, thank you for your friendship, Hikari."

Hikari nodded. He was grateful for the sentiment, but at the moment all that did was make it sting more.

"If it's all the same," Gillis said, standing wearily. "I think I'll head back to my quarters."

Hikari stood with him and placed a hand on his arm. "I will see you again, yes?"

"I'm flying back with the Tempest."

"So that's a yes?"

"Yes."

Hikari pulled the young man into a hug and gave him a clap on the back. It wasn't helpful, it probably wasn't even welcome, but he wasn't sure what else he could do. "You know. If you've a mind to stay, I could use a scribe, someone to write speeches for me and the like."

Gillis pulled back and that same weariness still clung to him. "That's alright. I think I need some time. Just to get away and clear my head."

"Well, if you need anything…"

"I know." Gillis nodded, then paced out of the wing, walking briskly away from the Champions and leaving Hikari alone once again, still staring out at that gods forsaken ocean of beautiful turquoise waves.

The rest of the afternoon was quiet. Everyone was quiet. They were quiet when Burz told them they were heading to Arrajin. Quiet as the monks carted their belongings to the Tempest. Quiet as they strolled up the gangway to the departing cheers and cries of Avi'Suron. The cheers were for someone else. A mythical idea that the people held that wasn't true now. Maybe it never had been.

Mercifully, it was soon engulfed by the quiet, and the champions all shuffled below deck save for Voske. He stood topside, staring out across that wide turquoise ocean and imagining he could see all the way to the distant shore where the lighthouse of Kisandin loomed. He stood quiet, unmoving, unspeaking, unblinking. And inside he raged.

There was a profound stillness that swallowed chariots. The great silent flapping of the pylat wings, and the smooth gliding of the vessel, engulfed in the blackness.

Rasa felt it even here in her chambers. She needed to sleep. She was so tired. But something about the stillness made the nightmares worse.

She lay on her side, curled up on a pile of covers in the corner of the room, staring at the plush bed stripped down to the chunky feather mattress. She could sense the spirits on the edge of her mind, and she called on her boon, letting Nyx rush in around her. At first she saw them like blue sparks that took shape until they had faces and features. She let her soul tip further into the dark of Nyx, until they started to have substance. They passed by her in waves, and she felt the brush of their skin, and the soft tickle of their clothes against her arms and face until she was adrift in an ocean of people.

A hand grabbed her shoulder, and she gasped for breath, pulling back until only one spirit remained.

"Spark?"

You seem restless. Are you okay?

Rasa sat up and stared at her, grateful for the company. "I thought you would be…" she traced the blue line that stretched off into the distance. It was faint, like a fading mist.

Spark frowned. *She doesn't want me around. She's angry that I… I betrayed her.*

Rasa grabbed Spark's hand and squeezed lightly. "You tried to save her."

She doesn't see it that way.

"Maybe someday she will."

Spark laughed. *Locin? I doubt it.* She nestled down on the blankets beside Rasa. *Can I stay with you for a while? You know, until she…*

"She'll forgive you." Rasa tried to smile reassuringly, but she didn't feel it. She had no idea what the future would hold. That was Weylyn's domain.

Maybe. She let her fingers play through the faint blue line. *I'm not sure I can ever be free of her. Not really. This will always be here, pulling me toward her soul.*

"Do you want to be free?" Rasa asked.

Spark sighed. *I don't know.*

"She's a very lonely person. I don't think…" Rasa bit her lip. She wasn't sure Locin could live without Spark. But that was too much pressure for any person, or spirit.

She's only lonely because she's so afraid. She's afraid people will hurt her, or reject her. She looked at Rasa. *You've been hurt a lot. How do you trust people?*

She shrugged. "I don't, not at first. I have to make a choice, you know. I have to remind myself that there are good people." She felt suddenly indescribably sad as she thought of Weylyn. "Most people just take. They use you and hurt you and move on. But sometimes you meet someone who puts you before themself. It changes everything."

Maybe that's what Locin needs. She needs a friend like that.

Rasa reached out and took Spark's hand. "I think she has one."

Spark tried to smile, but it quickly faltered. *It doesn't seem to be enough.*

"Maybe someday it will be."

They nestled down by the wall, hand in hand as the black of Nyx wrapped itself around them. Rasa wasn't sure she could sleep, but she was glad to have someone beside her through the long dark watches of the night.

50: Alone

Halfway between Suntara and Las a small, innocuous chariot was born through the cold dark by a single pylat. It was a cargo vessel for those who wanted things moved quiet and quick. The guide had been paid enough marks to charter a chariot twice this size, and the cargo was nothing but three passengers and their personal effects, the easiest job imaginable.

If only he'd known how badly the temple wanted them found, maybe he would have thought twice about taking the job, but he didn't ask any questions. That's why they hired him.

The chariot smelled of mildew and the floor gritted below Locin's sandals. Even during her thief days this would have been a flying pile of scrap, but it was all the more highlighted by her experience aboard the Tempest. Did this have in-flight performances? No. Male and female servants? No. All the food you could eat any time you asked? They did have a crate of lemons, and that wasn't nothing.

Most of all they had silence. Lots and lots of silence. Currently Locin was sitting in a storage room, squirming uncomfortably in the ominous quiet.

"Spark," She hissed into the empty air. "Spark?"

It had been nearly a day since she'd last felt the spirit's presence, and she was starting to hate the quiet. Maybe she had run with Spark for too long, grown too dependent, but it felt like this latest complication had pulled the floor from under her feet, and she needed someone to catch hold of.

"Stop being such a baby," she muttered. "I know you can hear me."

She strained to feel Spark, but all she felt was absence. It was unnerving. A panicked thought erupted in her mind that said she'd pushed away the one person she couldn't lose.

"Spark," she hissed again, but all she heard was the thump, thump, thump of bare feet somewhere outside the storeroom.

She snatched a lemon out of the crate beside her and tossed it in the air, then caught it again. "Fine," she said, settling against the wall. "Be that way."

She lifted the lemon to her nose and wrinkled at the scent. The smell alone made her lips pucker.

There was a light knock at the door, and Endring slid inside. Somehow, the old man seemed creepier every time she saw him. The way he crouched when he walked and constantly sniffed the air, like he was becoming more animal than human.

"There you are," he said. "You might not want to eat that. It's very sour."

She raised an eyebrow and flopped the lemon back into the crate. "Tell me something I don't know."

He nodded methodically and seemed to appraise her. "Is there a reason you're sitting in the dark?"

"I was trying to get some rest."

"They have cots, you know."

"The cots full of lice you mean? No thank you."

Endring gradually let the door swing closed behind him. "And here I thought you were talking to Spark."

Locin stiffened. It was bad enough Rasa knew her secret. She couldn't afford anyone else finding out.

"Well?" He pressed, and she was grateful she could no longer see him in the dark.

"What in Nyx are you on about?" She tried weakly.

"Did you know that wolves have excellent hearing?" he said. "You might be whispering, but you're hardly silent."

"Well butt out," she chided. "It's none of your business."

Endring took a step closer and lowered his voice. "We're in this together now, Locin. You, me, Sammel. Which means your well-being is very much my business."

Locin thought for a moment about booning him in the face with a lemon. She'd just gotten out from under the constant, smothering care of the temple, and she wasn't looking for another mother.

"Who's Spark?" he asked again.

"An old friend," she said. "At least she *used* to be my friend."

"And where is she?"

"Dead."

Endring looked mechanically around the room, and Locin felt a smug satisfaction. *Can't hear and smell* everything, *now can you?*

"I see," he said.

"And good riddance," she added, then she sat down on a rickety stool and put her hands on her knees. "Why are you really down here? Unless you came just to eavesdrop."

"I could have done that from the deck."

She scoffed.

"I thought it was time we discussed what's next."

"You want *my* input?"

"You misunderstand. I want to explain our course of action so that it doesn't take you by surprise."

She folded her arms. "Nothing could surprise me these days."

"Very well." She saw him shift in the dark. He looked like a deeper shadow in the corner of the room, and she wondered if this really was better. "Once we reach Las, we're going to rendezvous with Borroka. She'll be expecting us."

Locin felt her jaw go slack, and she quickly clamped it shut. "You rotting pool of mire! You were working with that shrike the whole time?"

"Hardly. I despise her, likely more than you do. But she has a piece of the crook, and we need it."

"So steal it! It worked with the other two."

"Those were easier. I think the risk would be too high, especially since she'll hand it over with no objection."

"Why in Nyx would she do that?" A disquiet was falling on Locin, and she started to think she'd gotten in deeper than she wanted. *Gods, Spark! I need you!*

"Because she and I want the same thing. Neveri freed."

"But she's rotting mad!"

"It's worse than that," he said coldly. "She's wicked. But our goals align, for the moment."

Locin frowned. "Somebody just has to pull Neveri out of Nyx, right? Isn't she just as likely to kill us and take the crook herself?"

"The thought did cross my mind."

Locin shook her head. "And you're going to just walk into her camp? You're an idiot."

"If it took my death to right the realm, I'd gladly pay that price."

"Not me! You can leave me outta this one."

"Relax," he said. "I'm not looking to make you a martyr. I do have a plan, you know."

That wasn't all that reassuring. She slumped down and crossed her arms

"Don't you want to hear it?"

"Your brilliant plan? Oh, sure. Let's hear how we're *not* going to all die."

"Borroka doesn't know how to use the crook. She needs me."

"You hope."

"I'm also Neveri's champion. That doesn't mean much to her, but it means something to many of the cultists. She can't turn on me without risking losing her army."

"Fine. She needs *you*. What does that do for me?"

"You and Sammel's safety are part of the deal, obviously."

Locin tapped a skeptical foot against the floorboards. "You're putting a lot of trust in a shrike who's mad as a dog in the mud. You know that, right?"

"If I must, I must." He shifted toward the door, but didn't open it. "The third piece, you have it on you?"

Locin's arms tightened. "Maybe."

"You can keep it," Endring said. "I just want to see it."

She hesitantly pulled it from her belt, and handed it over. It was a simple stick of wood. Straight cut, with no blade on the end or decoration other than the faint golden glow and the end of a phrase that read 'but by its light'.

He lifted it toward his face, and the relic's glow illuminated his features, making deep shadows in the crags of his gnarled skin. His eyes gleamed in a way that deepened the unsettling feeling brooding over her, and she instinctively reached out with her mind to try and feel Spark.

Rot it!

Suddenly her thoughts flashed to Voske. She *missed* him. She told herself it's just because Spark was gone, and she was feeling out of sorts. The feelings would pass, and she would adjust.

"We're so close now," he said in an eerie tone.

Locin held out a hand and wiggled her fingers. "Alright, you saw it. Now give it back."

Endring nodded and gently let the piece roll back into her hand. "Get some rest if you can," he said. "We're still a few hours out from Las."

Locin nodded and watched until he left, then tucked the Crook back into her belt and folded her arms overtop. She situated herself on the hard stool with her back against the equally hard wall, but it was clear she wouldn't get any sleep. She tried shutting her eyes, but every time she did, she felt terribly alone, so she contented herself to stare around the dark closet, waiting for the time to pass.

51: Gods and Chosen

Weylyn crouched below the golden curve of the wayfarer's field at the bow of the Tempest. The golden pylats were spread out just beyond the field, their double wings beating in time as they moved through the stormy skies over Las. It was a striking contrast, brilliant gold framed against the swirling black clouds.

She watched the creatures carefully. The turbulent winds seemed to have no effect as their wings gently rose and fell, gliding on the lightning that arced from cloud to cloud.

She heard the guide's voice yell something from behind, and the Tempest turned, gently aligning with the darkest part of the storm. Moments later, sheets of rain pelted the radiant field. The drops hit the light and erupted into a puff of steam, creating a tail like a comet that hung in the sky behind them. She took a deep breath, remembering the cool scent of rain, and wishing she could smell it through the field.

They flew headlong into a giant stack of clouds, fearsome enough to concern a hunter in the field, but the wayfarers didn't hesitate. There was a brief moment when the clouds brightened, and the golden glow of the pylat swelled as the chariot shot out the other side of the storm stack. The sky peeled back into a beautiful cobalt blue, and she could see the crystal sea far below them, foaming against the shoreline as they traced the coast southward.

"Five minutes to Arrajin," the guide called from behind her, and the chariot turned inland, gliding along the final leg of their journey.

They kept on the same course until she could see the brown ribbon of the Arrtris peaking through the jungle canopy. It flowed against them, making its way to the coast, and as her eyes traced its course upstream she could see the glint of white stone, striking against the treeline, like a patch of new cloth on an old garment.

Arrajin was just as they had left it. The city crawled on below as their chariot swooped closer. Smoke rose from the Sacred Quarter where the cultists still huddled around fires in makeshift camps. There would be no fanfare here, no swarm of pilgrims to see the Champions. No one knew they were coming.

She shifted to the side and gripped the rail, leaning out toward the radiant field to get a clearer view of the city.

She called on her boon until the sight of Strah filled her vision, and the city shifted below. Instead of pristine white stone, the temple was charred black. The spire of Jeza had been ripped out of the ground and driven down into the river like a fisherman's spear, and the overflowing water had flooded half the city. A trail of destruction was cut from the temple straight to the city center, and the buildings had been reduced to heaps of rubble. Chimeras swirled through the sky, streaking fire and smoke down, and over it all there was a presence, some wild thing. It roared, and she covered her ears. The city shook and the sky seemed to split. For the barest moment she caught a glimpse of a form, monstrous, brooding over the city, taller than the trees, higher than the peaks of the spires.

"Chains to landing position!"

The sharp rattle of the chains brought her back, and she gasped for breath. Her mind was reeling at what she had seen. Ordinarily she preferred time. Time to mull over the vision, to solve the when and how, but something in her told her they didn't have time.

Morning gave way to a harsh afternoon, the sun beating down mercilessly on the temple training ground. Voske was sweaty, bare chested in a pair of trousers and sturdy boots, his muscles aching with the strain of hard work. It reminded him of the quarry.

He opened and closed his fists. They were dirty, bruised knuckles. He was starting to feel it even through his boon. He'd been at this for hours, taking out his frustration on the wooden dummies that now lay in crumpled piles of splintered wood and scattered hay.

He'd moved on to the Skard stone now, the towering pillar of solid rock that sat in the center of the courtyard.

He took another swing, striking the stone as hard as he could. His knuckle bones were like iron, refusing to crack at the impact. No one else was trying to train anymore. The few scattered Jeza warriors who were near all clung to the outside of the training yard, watching as Voske landed another blow.

Someone cleared their throat intentionally behind him, and Voske lowered his arms.

"What?"

Eprim answered him. "I heard you were back."

Voske glanced back as he pushed the sweat from his eyes. Eprim was surveying his broken training ground and ruined dummies with a mix of frustration and amusement.

Voske wasn't in a talking mood. "What do you want?"

"New equipment, apparently. Are you going to wreck this place every time you get upset?"

"I'm not upset." He took two more quick strikes at the Skard stone. "I'm training."

"I can see that." Eprim stepped over some splintered wood as he continued taking in the full scope of the destruction. "Maybe next time you can go straight for the Skard stone? It would save me a lot of trouble."

"Is that why you're here? Come to goad me into an apology?"

"I'd hardly think of it. But I am Jeza's Oracle. One of my jobs is to assist her champion."

"You're gonna break some stuff too?" He stretched out his muscles, and he could feel his body trying to relax, but he wasn't done, so he drove another flurry of blows into the fist-sized dent in the smooth stone.

"Not at the moment. I came to check on you."

Voske laughed. "Not your idea, I'm guessing."

Eprim smirked. "I said, 'give him space, and he'll work it out on his own.'"

"Smart man." Another volley of punches. "So who sent you? Aurilis? She seems awfully worried with what I do."

Eprim kept his face placid.

Not Aurilis, Voske thought. *She doesn't care about* how *I'm doing, just* what.

"Apparently you've been through a lot, and people are… concerned."

"People." He scoffed, but then it hit him. *Burz.* "Rotting, useless, one-legged soldier. What'd he ask you to do?"

"To… *talk* to you." He said it like he enjoyed the thought as much as Voske.

"We both know that's not happening."

Eprim sighed. "Still, I can't imagine it was easy, being betrayed."

He felt his whole body tense instantly.

Rot it! Why do I care so much?

He lifted his arms, clenching his bloodied fists, and he started again, but the stone wouldn't budge.

"It wasn't your fault."

Voske roared as he drove his fist into the rock. Several Jeza monks ducked further out of sight on the edges of the courtyard, but Eprim held his ground, cool and calm.

"You two were close?" Eprim asked.

"She was a rotting thief. I shoulda seen this coming."

"She may have been a thief, but she was also a friend."

Voske turned his attention back to the stone in front of him and started again. He wouldn't stop until… he wasn't sure. He just wanted to keep hitting things.

"What'd Burz say? He concerned my feelings are hurt?"

"He's concerned your judgment is compromised."

Now Voske was really angry, he threw his head back and laughed. "That rotting pool of mire!"

But Eprim didn't relent. "Burz isn't the only one concerned. If Endring moves against the temple, she'll likely be with him. Are you prepared for that, Champion? Are you prepared to fight her?"

Voske wanted it to stop. Eprim, Burz, Aurilis. He couldn't even think with everyone breathing down his neck. And Locin. *Rotting Locin!*

He reached for his boon like never before, letting the fire of it coarse through his body until he thought it would kill him, and he turned back to the stone, pain spreading from his shoulders down through his chest like he was burning from the inside out. Then the pain started to dull as the strength of Jeza flooded him, and he threw his fists over and over and over against the stone until the ground shook at his feet and his bones nearly cracked. Then he roared as he summoned every bit of his strength into one final blow, driving his fist into the dent.

A thunderous crack filled the air and the whole temple seemed to shift as a line spread from his fist up and down the thick slab, cracking it straight through.

"Gods and Chosen." Awe and terror filled Eprim's voice.

As stillness settled, Voske felt his boon drain out of his arms at last, and a weariness like he had never known overtook him. He slumped down, sitting in the coarse sand, staring up at the cracked pillar.

"Tell Burz and all the others that I'll fight *anyone* who makes themself my enemy. You got it?"

Eprim nodded, and hurried out of the training ground, followed by the last remaining monks. No doubt they were scurrying off to tell what they'd seen. Voske didn't care. His body was spent, and he fell back against the hot sand, staring up at the bright sky. And he smiled.

The Sacred Quarter had become a dump. Refuse littered the streets and the picturesque images of the gods had been defaced and smeared with gods knew what. It smelled worse than the sewers, and Endring tried to dull the animalistic sense of smell he'd started becoming accustomed too. Anyone that hadn't fled the quarter had been forced into slavery, and they walked the streets in red robes, kicked and mistreated by their cultist conquerors.

There was no way this was the same city Endring remembered, the pinnacle of worship to something more profound than themselves, a place men came to be inspired to a higher ideal and to pay homage to the mighty deeds of their ancestors. It made him nauseous, and angry. Still, Borroka had something he needed.

He, Sammel, and Locin followed their cultist guide up a narrow flight of stairs to a rooftop that had a good vantage point over the rest of the quarter, and in the distance he could see the Gods' Mount, still glimmering in all its glory. He paused at the sight. When Neveri was released these wrongs would finally be righted, and Borroka would be exposed as the bloodmonger she was.

He looked to his right to see Borroka, swaggering their direction. "I didn't think you'd have the gall to show up." She had a new Chimera by her side and a familiar fire burning in her eyes.

"Borroka."

"*Champion*," she sneered with derision, and then she glanced at Locin. "I see you've taken to your own kind."

Locin scowled. "Remind me why I can't kill her."

"Peace," Endring said sharply.

Borroka laughed. "She's feisty, I'll give her that."

"You're here to deal with me," he snapped.

"Then why even bring your lap dogs?" She motioned to Locin and Sammel. "Don't you trust me?"

"I trust you stand to lose more by turning on me than you're willing to part with." He motioned to the cultist guards standing around the edges of the roof.

That seemed to dampen her mood a bit, and she frowned at him.

Endring pulled his crook piece out from his robes and held it up. He motioned for Locin to do the same, and she reluctantly pulled the other piece out and showed it to Borroka.

"I heard," she said disinterestedly, but she couldn't hide the glint in her eye. "All three in one place." She reached into a pouch at her side and pulled out the final piece. They seemed to pulse in each other's presence.

She sneered, and then nodded to her men. "Kill them."

Immediately Sammel snatched his whip from his belt, and Locin pushed her hands out, hurling two cultists across the roof.

"Enough of this!" Endring yelled. He quickly sprang forward and claws sprouted from his fingers. He let his form twist and change as pain momentarily shot through him. The pain was nothing compared to the thrill as his biceps grew and fur sprouted from his chest until he was more beast than man. "Tell your men to stand down," he said in a guttural growl.

"Why would I do that?" She asked.

"Because I am Neveri's champion!" He pointed to her men. They were having a standoff of their own now. Some looked ready to charge at Endring, but the others stood in the way, defending him.

Anger flashed across Borroka's face.

"Besides," Endring continued, "I know how to use the crook. You don't."

She ordered her men to stand down, though it obviously pained her to do so, and they stood for a moment facing each other.

He let his primal form fall away as he sank back to a mere man. "It seems you have no choice. We must work together for the good of Talamh."

"For Neveri," she countered. "To Nyx with Talamh."

"Even if you have the assembled crook, you still have to know how to use it. How to draw the right spirit out of Nyx. I'm more familiar with the Veil than any one of your men. I can pull Neveri back into Talamh."

Borroka's eyes tightened. "It's a shepherd's crook. How hard could it be?"

Endring didn't flinch. "If you want to risk fighting your way all the way into the Veil of Bei'ai only to fail, then suit yourself. I wash my hands of it. But if you're smart you'll give the top piece to me."

She didn't soften, but she also didn't order her men to attack again. "You expect me to just hand it over?"

"Everything I've done, I've done for Neveri." Endring took a step closer as he spoke. "The only question that remains now is, do you trust me?"

"No," she answered.

He felt his heart sink. Perhaps Locin had been right, it would have been better to try to steal it.

"That's why I'm coming with you," she said.

"What?"

"You heard me." she answered. "I'm coming with you, and we'll pull Neveri from the ashes, together."

"You think they'll let you walk in the temple after what you've done?"

She stepped closer to him. "You think they'll let you walk in after what *you've* done?"

"The plan was never to *walk* in," he said casually. Sneaking in himself felt possible, but bringing Borroka along…

"Me too," said Locin. "I'm not giving my piece up to either of you lunatics. We all go, or none of us do."

"Just like that?" Endring demanded.

Locin scowled at him. "Yeah. Like that."

"And how do you propose the three of us get in?"

She shrugged. "Best think of a plan, bird man."

Endring's mind was scrambling. He could see it on Borroka's face. If he didn't have a plan now, she'd more than likely kill them and storm the temple, hoping she could figure the crook out. And she would, eventually.

"Fine," he said at length. And then he looked at Borroka. "But we'll need your cats."

Rasa stared at the murky Veil in front of her. It was with her all the time now, the door to Nyx. She could feel the cold of it pressing around her every time her boon crept in, sending a chill through her back and shoulders that spread in icy tendrils down her arms and legs. But here the Veil was real. She could see it. Touch it.

She pressed her hand to the skin of it, and her fingers sunk in, spirits dancing at the motion. This was who she was now, a lost soul. That's who she had always been, really. For a brief moment she wondered what was even tethering her to Talamh. What kept her from just drifting away into the abyss? She had the sensation that she was falling forward, the whole world going sideways as she reached her mind past the clamoring spirits and felt for the depths of Nyx.

Rasa.

The voice of Spark brought her back, and she gasped a breath as she pulled her hand away from the Veil.

Spark was behind her, glossy eyes watching with curiosity. "Spark?"

There's something important you have to see.

"What is it?"

She glanced over her shoulder nervously. *Just come with me.*

Rasa was tired. She wanted nothing more than to rest after their long weeks of travel, but she took in a breath and pushed back against the weariness. "Of course."

They walked together out of the Veil and into the hall of trees. Rasa couldn't help but stare at Iyanu's, lovely dark branches with fragrant red blossoms. They crossed the hall quickly, but Spark stopped at the door of the sanctum. She was smiling brightly, and it made Rasa smile too.

"What's going on, Spark?"

I want you to meet someone. Just, don't be afraid.

"Why would I be..."

A light caught Rasa's eye, like a faint golden flicker seeping out under the sanctum door. She let Nyx rush around her, and the light grew brighter. The golden spirit. Her heart started to pound, and she would have instinctively pulled away, but Spark grabbed her wrist and tugged her forward.

It's safe. It's not what you think.

Rasa furtively pushed the door open, staring inside. In the center of the room a massive golden spirit hung in the air.

It's alright. Spark said. *It's* her.

Rasa squinted at the golden form and cautiously let the realm of Nyx draw closer. A host of blue spirits hovered nearby, peeking out from the shrines of the gods, all staring toward the golden form with rapture.

Slowly, the golden spirit came into sharper focus. She was breathtaking, bathed in gold with skin that glowed like lightning and eyes that glowed like a hearth. Luscious black hair cascaded across her ivory shoulders, and her gloved hands beckoned Rasa closer.

"Bei'ai," Rasa breathed.

Her own champion's toga suddenly felt woefully inadequate, and she brushed futilely at her stringy, red hair. She reached her fingers down to her hip, giving it a swift pinch. Sure enough, a flash of pain said she wasn't dreaming.

Rasa, Bei'ai said with a voice like a cold breeze.

"I... I... Yes?"

We don't have much time. My brother is coming.

"Neveri."

Yes. He's coming to take his revenge.

"On who?"

Bei'ai frowned, but it wasn't angry, just worried. *On us.* Her eyes drifted to the orbs the statues held. *He intends to sever us from this realm.*

Rasa followed her gaze. "The tethers."

Tethers. That's an interesting name. They are mara, that which binds. The brittle link of a mooring chain.

"They bind you to Talamh?"

The goddess shook her head. *They bind Talamh to us.* She strolled to her own statue, staring up at the golden sphere she held near her heart. *Only a god is strong enough to break them. Neveri can't reach us in Sbarga, but he can cut us off from Talamh.*

"But that would mean..."

No more boons, no more Champions, no more temple. Neveri would be the sole god of this realm.

Rasa felt a shudder rush down into her stomach. "That sounds horrible."

It would set Talamh adrift on a path not even Strah has foreseen. We would be forever separated - Talamh would go its own way.

Rasa felt a panicked whisper echo through the room, and she glanced at the spirits, each had a fraught expression, eyes wide with horror. "And the dead?"

Forever trapped in Nyx, unable to cross the Veil.

Rasa felt Spark's cold hand grab her arm as the spirit tucked in close. "What can I do?"

Take these tethers. Hide them. Keep them away from Neveri at all costs.

"But he's still in Nyx."

As though in response a shout rose from outside, a cry of alarm, too muddled to distinguish the words, but crystal clear in its purpose.

Pray that he stays that way.

Rasa's eyes widened. Normally she'd pray to Bei'ai.

"They won't let Endring in," she stammered. "No one would do that." She looked nervously toward the front doors of the sanctum. She could see Jeza monks rushing past, swords drawn.

You may not have much time.

Rasa quickly climbed the statue of Bei'ai, lifting the orb from her cupped hands. She had an idea where to hide them, a place even Neveri might never think to look.

52: Reunion

Burz stood on the edge of the tether platform. A small chariot was boarding, a single pylat, slated to head straight for Tajerim. Overhead, clouds gathered downriver.

"It looks like you'll be flying straight through a storm." He looked at Hadris. She was standing there with the boys, her face as cloudy as the sky. "I know you hate flying through storms."

"We'll be fine," she said softly. "I don't understand why you're sending us away."

"I'm not gonna put you in danger."

She sighed. "There's no way Aurilis will let those cultists on the Gods' Mount."

"It doesn't matter. My gut says you go, so you go." She used to trust his instincts implicitly, but now she just stared at him with a questioning glance. "I'll come get you as soon as this is over. Maybe we'll stay in Tajerim for a month." He pressed a hand to her cheek. "Forget all this champion nonsense."

But she just shook her head. Did she not want that? Or did she not believe he would?

He turned his attention to the boys now. Kyren threw himself against Burz' legs, and he scooped him into his arms. "Be good for your Ama."

He nodded, and Burz set him down, reaching for Orin, but he pulled away. He looked sullen as he glared at Burz, and it stung, but he kept a rigid smile on his face and his eyes fixed on Orin.

"I love you both, and I'll be there as soon as I can."

He felt Hadris grab his arm as Orin turned and marched toward the chariot.

"Give him time," she said softly.

Calls from the temple drew his attention, and he turned to see something dark flying over the city, black specks approaching fast.

"Is that what I think it is?" She asked.

Burz nodded. "Endring. Now, go!"

Hadris nodded and hurried up the gangplank. Burz watched the chariot rise into the sky, turning over the Arrtris.

He looked back at the city. The cultists were getting closer now. He could make out the form of the beasts and their riders, silhouetted against the sky. On the temple grounds, the Jeza monks were assembling in front of the portico. He hurried to the front where he found Aurilis and Eprim.

"Burz," she said. "Is your family safely away?"

He nodded.

"Good. Uthando willing, it will be for nothing. Shall we?"

Burz waved an arm for them to pass then fell in beside, heading a little ways into the field to wait.

Eprim sighed, glancing at Aurilis. "I still wish you'd let me do this alone. If they move against you-"

"Oh, let him try," she said sharply. "I've been High Oracle for thirty-seven years. I'm not about to back down to one rogue Oracle and his flying lions." She glanced at Burz. "Besides, I'm confident it won't come to blows."

A commotion in the ranks behind them drew Burz' attention. Someone was forcing their way through. Several someone's. Voske emerged with Hikari and Weylyn. He motioned the other two to stay at the front, and he started jogging out toward them. He was wearing the red armor Atrius had made him, in the same style as Skard's. Burz shook his head at the sheer audacity. After all his failures, he thought *this* was a good idea?

Aurilis groaned. "Whatever he says, *he* is not to negotiate with Endring. In fact, it would be best if he didn't speak at all."

"Good luck with that."

Voske jogged alongside the three of them. "Gonna start without me?"

"Yes," Aurilis said sharply.

"Like Nyx."

She glanced at Burz for support, and he shrugged. He wasn't much inclined to back up Voske or Aurilis. He'd had enough of both of them.

He let his eyes drift back up to the swarm. They were crossing the river now, and the roar of a chimera rang out over the temple grounds. He let his hand drift to the hilt of his sword and said a silent prayer for mercy.

Wind whipped at Locin's hair from her perch atop the mighty Chimera. She clung to its feathers, leaning in against it, her senses filled with the stench of it, and her heart racing from the dizzying drop below as they soared over Arrajin toward the god's Mount. She could feel Sammel behind her, and she felt grateful for his arms and legs that pressed against her and gave her some sense of safety.

Below, she caught sight of the Gods' Mount and its eight spires across the Arrtris, and suddenly she was thinking about them again. She muttered a curse. No matter how much she tried to shove the thoughts down, they were barreling toward the temple. She didn't know if the other Champions were there, and she hoped to the gods they weren't, but either way it drew her thoughts to them. She'd only done what she had to do.

It wasn't personal.

Then why did it feel so personal?

She suddenly felt painfully alone. All she wanted was the familiar sense of Spark's presence. Where in Nyx had she gone?

The beast banked and she instinctively grabbed hold of Sammel's leg.

"It won't drop you."

She pulled her hand back. "It better not."

She could see the Gods' Mount now, a wide circle of perfect green. Inside, lines of red clad warriors were scrambling to the rooftops and around the edge of the temple. Apparently they'd been spotted.

"How do we know they won't just attack us," she called over the wind.

"Aurilis might be dead-set against us, but Endring trusts her."

"Good for Endring."

She took a deep breath and looked to their side. Two dozen chimera carried a host of cultists with Endring and Borroka in the lead.

Locin swallowed hard. This wasn't what she wanted. She wanted to get rid of the stench of being unguilded, to prove that she was worthy. She wanted to spite Aurilis and the temple. But she didn't want war. Gods willing, it wouldn't come to that.

"Gods, they got a lot of monks down there," she said, leaning closer to Sammel.

"Yes," he said flatly.

She found something in his even tone comforting. "You're not worried?"

"Why would I be worried?"

"You really think Aurilis is going to let us walk in there and free Neveri without a fight?"

"Endring has a plan. I'm confident it will work. You'd be surprised what people will do to save lives."

"Rotting Nyx! That's your plan? Just hope she'll give in so the chimeras don't eat everybody?"

He glanced back at her, and there wasn't a shred of fear in his expression. "She cares about her people. Attachments can cause men to compromise their beliefs."

"And what if they want a fight?"

"Then we give them a fight."

"Rotting gods above."

She felt the Chimera turn toward the ground, and her stomach flipped as she leaned in, gripping its feathered sides. The chimeras swooped low, landing on the outer edge of the verdant hill. Locin quickly slid to the ground. Her legs felt wobbly after the ride, but she hurried to join the others. The cultists marshaled alongside their chimeras, leering toward the lines of red. Already the Jeza monks were within arrow's reach.

Locin stood beside Endring. Borroka sneered at her from Endring's other side, and something about her smug expression made Locin uneasy about this whole thing. She'd give anything to knock the smirk off her stupid mouth.

"Stay ready," Endring said, "but keep your men in line." He looked from Borroka to Locin as he drew out his piece of the crook. "It's time."

Borroka lifted her own piece and handed it to Endring without the slightest hesitation. He set it into his, twisting until they snapped together then set his cold animal eyes on Locin.

"Your turn."

Suddenly her head raced with doubts and her heart was pounding. Something in her screamed this was a bad idea, but she couldn't back out. She was in. She never took a job she didn't finish, and she always got more than her cut. She drew out her crook piece. It shimmered a faint gold as she pulled it free of the cloth and handed it over, watching as Endring twisted it in place. She swore she felt a shift in the air as it locked tight, and golden light pulsed from the completed relic.

Across the field, Aurilis stood alongside Eprim, Burz, and Voske.

"Come on," Endring said.

"Me?"

"I need you in the front with me."

Locin felt her stomach twist. "Wait, what? Seriously?"

"You could help us end this without bloodshed."

"Like Nyx I can! I just double-crossed these people, and you think seeing me will put them in a friendly mood? You're a rotting idiot!"

Endring stepped toward her with such serious intent that she stepped back. "You want the same thing as I do. No death." He eased back a little and softened his tone. "Trust me."

She glanced back at Borroka, the hunger in her eyes. Endring was her best chance. She believed him when he said he didn't want anyone to die.

"Fine."

Endring turned and led Locin, Sammel, and Borroka toward Aurilis as the cultists and their beasts held their ground behind them. All along the portico, archers stood with bows aimed at the four of them. It felt like wading into a wasps' nest.

Voske watched her with a pained expression. "That's close enough!"

It looked like he was ready to tear off across the field and take on the cultists himself, but a touch from Eprim on his arm steadied him.

It was Aurilis who spoke next. "What do you hope to accomplish here, Endring?"

"You know that answer already." There was a low growl in his voice as he spoke.

"Do you honestly think I'll let you step foot in this temple?"

"I do."

"Like Nyx!" Voske roared. "You'll get to the Veil over my dead body."

"Gladly," Borroka said, but Endring held out a hand to stop her.

"I believe it's in everyone's best interest for you to let us pass. Once Neveri is free, we'll leave in peace."

Aurilis laughed. "I actually think you believe that, Endring. But whatever this Neveri is, I'm not convinced he'll go as peacefully as you say."

"Do you not trust me? I've spoken with him countless times. I know his mind!"

"Trust you?" She snapped. "You've betrayed the temple! You've betrayed me!"

Voske locked eyes on Locin, and she dropped her gaze again in shame.

"You left me no choice," Endring answered. "It was you who hid the truth. Did I not speak to you of Neveri for years? And yet you refused to see what was right in front of your face!"

Voske and Burz gave Aurilis a wary glance.

Is this his plan? Locin thought. *Turn the champions against her?* It felt shaky at best.

"We've seen the truth," Burz said. "But what's past is past. It's not worth the risk of tearing Talamh apart."

"Talamh is already tearing itself apart! Can't you see it? Change is coming back into the worlds, whether you like it or not. If we resist it, it will destroy us."

"You say change," Aurilis countered, "but what you mean is chaos. All this will bring is death, destruction, and war. Is that what you want? War?"

"I don't want war," he said, his voice filled with fire. "I want restoration. I want to see the unguilded restored! I want to see deserts bloom! Without change, things stagnate and die. Is that what you want? A barren realm?"

"My answer is final," she said sternly. "You will not pass without a war."

He sighed. "We were friends once. Does that mean nothing?"

"Not enough."

Locin felt her heart sink. It seemed Borroka would get her way.

Endring turned to face Voske now. "Then I'll give you one chance, Champion. Will you let us pass?"

"He has no authority to make that decision!" Aurilis yelled, her voice cracking with anger.

But Locin saw the faces of Jeza's warriors. Many looked skeptically at Aurilis. Perhaps enough were loyal to Voske. Perhaps they could avoid bloodshed.

Locin stepped forward, just a few feet from Voske, placing herself between he and Endring. "Mire and Nyx! It's me, Voske!"

His jaw tightened. "Yeah. It's you."

"Rot it, old man! I get it. You hate me. Whatever. But if you don't let us pass, it's gonna be bad. Borroka's crazy, and you know it."

"Makes me wonder why you joined up with her."

"I didn't, you rotting oaf. Think for once! We're here to save the whole rotting realm. You know Neveri's real! He's a god!"

"God or not," Burz said, stepping forward. "We can't let you pass."

Locin looked intently at Voske, pleading. "Come on, old man!"

He stared at her, his eyes cold as glass and gave his answer in a tone of finality. "No!"

Endring moved closer. Locin could feel him right behind her now.

"Why?" Voske said softly. "Why did you do it?"

She shrugged as she felt Endring grab her arm. "Hey! I'm on your side, dummy!"

Endring held the crook up in front of Voske. "Do you know what this does?"

"Yeah. You use it to pull Neveri out of Nyx." His eyes were glittering, and she hoped he wasn't fool enough to lunge for it.

"Not just Neveri. It can pull any soul out of Nyx, did you know that? I'll make you a deal, Voske. If you order the monks to let me pass, I'll pull a soul out of Nyx for you before I free Neveri."

Voske laughed. "Rot in Nyx!"

A familiar presence prickled the edges of Locin's senses, and she gave up struggling. Could it be?

"Perhaps I will," Endring said, as he handed the crook to Sammel. "I deserve it for all I've done. But my offer stands. A soul for a soul."

She was sure now. She felt a shiver up her spine that set the hair on the back of her neck on end, and a smile tugged at her lips.

"Spark?"

She felt a sharp pain as a blade drove into her back. Her breath caught, and she felt a desperation set in. Everything felt cold, and Voske was yelling. She looked at Endring. His eyes looked deeply troubled as he pulled the dagger free, and she watched her own blood dripping out on the soft grass. In that single moment, she felt panic, then pain, then nothing. Everything seemed distant now, the shouts of the armies, the warmth of the sun, the feel of the soft grass beneath her feet. It all faded away, and she heard a comforting voice.

Locin?

"Spark?"

53: The Crook of Bei'ai

Voske watched in horror as Locin's body slumped to the ground, a pool of crimson flooding out around her. Rage was overtaking him, and he could feel reason slipping away. He roared in anger as he lunged for Endring, but Sammel's whip cracked in front of him and knocked him back into the grass. By the time he was on his feet again, Sammel, Borroka, and Endring were surrounded by chimera, and a blast of heat scorched between the two armies as a warning. He felt someone grabbing him, and turned to see the monks of Jeza closing ranks around him. Weylyn rushed up to his side, her bow drawn and aimed at Endring.

"Do it!" He roared. "Kill that rotting monster!"

"No!" Aurilis shouted. She marched out in front, holding up her arms. "He wants this. He wants to justify a war."

"He killed her!" He seethed as he turned to face Aurilis.

"Another Champion will be chosen. It's just a matter of time."

Voske's boon surged through his arms, and he threw the monks off him in one motion as he stomped forward. "You rotting old shrike! She's not just some champion. She was Locin!"

Aurilis turned on him sharply. "She betrayed you. She turned on us all."

Voske cried out in rage, but before he could dart through the ranks to kill Endring, he heard Aurilis yell to the monks. They surrounded him, grabbing at him, trying to stop him. He tossed them aside easily, but more piled on.

"Voske!" Burz yelled, leaping in front of him. "Enough! You'll get us all killed!"

So many voices were shouting. A Chimera let out a howling roar, and the cultists clamored across the field.

"Voske," Endring called.

He steadied himself and glowered at the old man.

Endring held the crook up. "Her body will fade quickly, and it will be too late to put her soul back inside. If you want her back, you must decide now!"

"I'll kill you for this!" Voske yelled.

"If you do that, she dies too. Take me to the Veil. I swear to you I will pull her soul from Nyx and restore her to you."

Voske's mind was racing. Could he trust Endring? There had to be a way to get Locin back and still stop them from pulling Neveri free. He was strong enough. He could do it.

"You have little time." Endring stared down at the crumpled body of Locin, her blood soaking the ground. "Her body will be too far gone, and another will be chosen."

"You godless pool of mire!" Voske spat.

"You can save her, Voske," he continued. "Choose now!"

"We will not!" Aurilis shouted. "One life is a small price to pay to keep you from the Veil."

Aurilis' voice was strong and sure, but Voske could feel the monks shifting around him. They were less certain. If he wanted this, they might listen.

"We'll take you to the Veil." Voske was shocked to hear his own words.

"We will not!" Aurilis commanded.

The monks were even more conflicted now and several of them stared at him keenly.

Voske shouted, ignoring the High Oracle. "If you try to deceive us, I will end your life."

"You have my word," Endring yelled.

"Enough of this!" Aurilis cried. "Warriors of Jeza, take the Champions back to the temple. This is over!"

Again the monks hesitated. Certainly they were used to listening to Aurilis, but could they defy the will of their Champion?

"Listen to me," Voske cried. "You will step aside and let us take them to the Veil." He looked to his side where Burz stood, his uncertain gaze mirroring the monks. "She'll need a healer."

Burz slowly nodded, and Voske strode out toward Endring. The tremors of chaos in the temple ranks swelled. Several monks moved to intercept Voske, but others surrounded him, giving him a clear path.

He pressed forward to Locin and scooped her lifeless body into his arms, slick with blood. He sneered at Endring, but then nodded and turned back to face the warriors of Jeza.

"I am the Champion of Jeza, Chosen of the goddess. I carry her boon. I command her warriors! Step aside and let us pass!"

At once the monks began to move, slowly at first, hesitantly, but soon they had cleared a path straight to the doors of the temple.

Without hesitation, Voske strode forward into the midst of their ranks.

"Voske!" Aurilis cried. "Don't do this! Releasing such an evil for the sake of one Champion is folly. You must see that!"

"She's not just one Champion," he snarled.

He looked down at Locin. She looked like a little rag doll in his giant arms, her body limp and her eyes staring lifeless.

Many of the soldiers gripped their weapons and sneered as they passed, a few looked like they would step forward, but at one look from Voske they backed away.

It was only Weylyn who dared step in his path.

"Move," Voske snarled.

But Weylyn held her ground, holding an arm out to stop him. "Listen to me, Voske. I've seen what comes of this."

"I didn't ask for your input."

She spoke low for his hearing alone, and her voice was urgent. "I saw a vision of the temple in ruins, Voske, the city burning. If you do this, it will destroy Arrajin."

His voice was a low growl. "Move or I will move you."

She pointed toward the city. "How many will die for this one life? Is that worth it, Voske?"

He hesitated. "Your visions are warnings. They can be changed."

"It's not worth the risk! She made her choice."

"And I'm making mine." He pushed Weylyn aside and kept on.

Everything seemed distant as he climbed the great stone steps and wound his way through the sanctum and into the hall of trees. He heard a sigh from Burz, and he looked up to see the tree of Iyanu. Its petals were falling in droves, swirling down as the color faded out of them. They crunched under his feet and he looked down to see Locin's blood splashing against the dead brown petals.

"Wait," Endring said as he stopped. "Just me, Sammel, and Voske."

Burz clenched a fist. "If I don't heal her-"

"So heal her." There was a sharp authority in Endring's voice. He wouldn't change his mind.

Voske walked to Burz and held Locin's lifeless body out.

Burz shook his head, his voice near a whisper. "You need me, Voske. You can't let them free Neveri. No matter what." He gave an intentional nod to Locin's body.

Voske scowled. "You think I don't know that? If you heal her, you'll be too weak to help me anyway."

Burz sighed. They both knew that was true.

"Fine," he said reluctantly. He laid his hands on her broken body, and Voske watched as the wound in her chest closed up and the blood stopped flowing.

Burz stumbled from the exertion. "I'll wait here."

As Voske turned to go, he felt Burz grip his arm.

"Don't let them win, Voske. Even if it means you can't save her."

He nodded. But he *would* save her. He had to.

"I don't know how much time we have." Endring stood by the door to the Veil. "Before we enter, we must come to an arrangement."

"Arrangements have been made," Voske growled. "Open the door."

"Loose ones yes, but not-"

"Open the rotting door!" Voske yelled.

Endring looked back at the burly man, drawing himself up to his full height. A solid six inches shorter than Voske. "You might intimidate others, Champion, but I have no time for your blustering, and neither does Locin. I will pull her soul out first, then Neveri. Then, you let us leave. You must give me your word!"

"And you'll take my word?"

"You're the Champion of justice, aren't you? I believe you'll keep an oath."

"Fine," he snarled. "Let's go."

"Gods and Chosen," Burz muttered.

Endring glanced at Burz and then nodded to Voske, opening the door and leading the way down into the Veil.

Voske made his way down the dark stairwell into the eerie expanse. The normal blue spirits were gone, and the whole of the veil was filled with a golden light, like the sun had finally risen in Nyx.

"What in Jeza's name is that?" Although he feared he already knew the answer.

"Neveri."

Voske knelt down beside the statue of Bei'ai, laying Locin's body just a few feet back from the Veil.

Endring paced to the edge and held the crook up above his head, plunging it through the Veil like he was driving a spear into the heart of a beast. He held it there for a moment, muttering something below Voske's hearing. As his voice rose and fell, ripples formed in the Veil echoing out from the staff and pulsing through Nyx.

Within moments a small blue light appeared, miniscule against the warm yellow field. It settled into the middle of the crook until the whole thing glowed blue, and Endring slowly drew it back out, swinging it toward Locin's vacant body. He placed the top of the crook against her lips, and the spirit trembled as it flooded into her body.

She coughed violently.

Voske desperately longed to rush to her side, but he turned his attention back to Endring who had plunged the crook back through the Veil and was muttering again, louder this time. The room was growing cold as the golden light gathered in the crook.

Voske lunged toward the old man, but a crack of Sammel's whip blew him back onto the stone floor. He started to push himself up, and a tremble ran through him as he saw his fingertips so close to the Veil he could almost feel the cold pull of it. He lurched upright and called his boon, feeling the rush of warmth flood his muscles.

Endring's voice grew strained now as he seemed to be struggling to contain the power of the golden spirit.

Voske lunged forward again, ready this time. As Sammel snapped the whip, Voske dug his feet into the ground until the stone cracked. The force of the shockwave hit him, but he pushed back against it, grabbing the whip as it coiled around his arm. He held it, the glowing strands hot in his hand, and he yanked with all his might, throwing Sammel to the floor. He set his eyes back on Endring, charging toward him as he drew the crook back through the

Veil, the golden spirit tearing through the black. The air in the room was sucked into the crook as the spirit passed through with the sound like a crack of thunder. The crook flew from Endring's grasp, and he stumbled back as the spirit took form, rising over them, half man, half beast.

"Neveri!" Endring called.

A shockwave exploded from Nyx as if all the air it had sucked in were released in a mighty blast, and Voske was knocked off his feet as the thunderous roar of Neveri filled the room, shaking the temple.

"No!" Voske yelled. He leapt to his feet, summoning every bit of his boon as he sprang toward the monstrous form of the god. It was equal parts man and beast, some abomination like he'd never seen. He could feel the pulsing strength of the creature as he grappled with it. It felt familiar, like the rush of his own divine boon.

But he was no match. Neveri grabbed Voske with one great hand that crushed his chest. He felt the boon of Jeza swelling in him, keeping his ribs from shattering as the monstrous grip tightened.

"You thought to fight a god?" Neveri's bestial mouth twisted in a sneer as his other hand wrenched Voske's arm until he could see the golden sigil burning brightly in his palm. He laughed. "Jeza. I should have known." His eyes were filled with contempt.

Voske gasped for air as he held the crushing grip at bay. The world was starting to fade, and the sound of his heart pounding in his head started to drown out all else. Suddenly the grip released as he was thrown with unbelievable force into the solid stone wall. He felt his body crack as the rocks around him gave way and he toppled to the floor. His boon faltered, and the world went black.

54: Neveri

Locin hurt. She'd never hurt like this before. She felt like every bone in her body had been broken. Someone was in front of her, and she strained to see as she blinked her eyes open. It was a young girl. She wore a simple toga, and long hair hung about her shoulders like it was bobbing in water. She was frowning at her. But something about her was off. Was she even real?

Locin? She spoke.

"Spark?"

Suddenly the figure faded into a ghostly outline, hollow against a background of ominous black.

Am I dead? Locin thought.

She reached a hand up to her face, feeling her own skin. It was cold, but as her fingers lingered, her cheek began to warm, and an annoying prickly sensation began flowing out through her body.

She struggled to lift her head, and immediately the world began spinning.

Where am I?

There were three statues just behind her of some goddess. Or was it one statue? And why was everything so dark?

Then she heard a voice. She thought it was a voice. It reminded her of Spark. *You need to hurry, Locin.*

From somewhere above her she could hear a deep impactful sound, like when someone slams a door at the end of a long hall. Only deeper. The room she was in trembled in response, and she threw up, spewing the contents of her stomach across the sacred floor of…

Where am I again?

She looked around warily and the three goddesses slowly merged into one. The world slowed its spinning, and she spotted another form. Someone was lying on the floor in front of a huge depression in the wall. A bunch of crushed stone had fallen down over them, and they weren't moving.

She crawled closer on hands and knees. She would have used her feet, but the annoying prickles hadn't reached that far down yet.

Then she heard that Spark-ish voice again. It was like the usual shiver down her spine, only in her ears, and it formed words. *He's alive.*

"Hey," she hissed, but the sound was overpowered by the booming that thundered from above.

She reached the figure. It was a man, and he was big. *Very* big. She leaned over his side and sucked in a breath. It was Voske.

"Hey," she said, patting her hand rapidly against his cheek. "Hey, you alright?"

His crimson armor was wet with blood, and she held her face closer, listening for breath or a heart beat. Anything.

"Hey!" She tried again, this time she shook his shoulders.

As she did, a memory rankled at the back of her mind. What was it now? This might not be a good idea?

"Voske!" She yelled, and immediately the memory surged to the surface.

Rot.

She had stabbed him in the back.

She placed a hand on her own back. Wait, that wasn't it. *She* had been stabbed in the back? Yes? Both?

A groan from Voske sent her scrambling backward. She stared at him in total silence until he shifted. He pushed his weight off the floor and sat up, looking about as disoriented as she felt.

"What in…" his voice trailed off when he saw her. "Locin?"

She wasn't sure if she was supposed to be afraid or relieved, so she just lifted a hand and mildly wiggled her fingers.

In response, the loudest boom yet resonated from above, and more debris clattered out of the hole behind Voske.

He gradually stood to his feet with a wince and brushed the dirt from his clothes. "They're fighting outside."

Locin looked up, still waiting as the trickle of memories returned. "This… this is the Veil of Nyx. Isn't it?"

He gave her a meaningful look. "Yes."

600

Endring. The Crook. Neveri. It was all coming back. "Did he do it?"

He stared back at her, and his face gave her the answer.

Endring pulled a god out of Nyx.

"Then why are they fighting?"

Voske rolled his neck back and forth and tried to hide the clear grimace that accompanied the motion. "My guess? That god of yours isn't as benevolent as you thought."

"God of *mine*?" She objected. "I never wanted *him*, I just…" Her voice trailed off. She wasn't really sure what she wanted anymore.

"Come on," Voske said with as much fire as a matchstick. "We need to get up there and help."

"You're hurt."

"No kidding."

"But how… How do you know I'm on your side?"

"I think you don't want people to die. I'm counting on it."

She nodded.

"Now come on."

She walked after him up the stairs and out of Nyx. There was something frustrating about his response and about her own feelings. She didn't feel resentful, or sorrowful, or even fearful. She only felt… dull.

She felt a shiver up her spine, and Spark tickled her ear with words again. *Be careful above. Neveri is tearing everything apart.*

But it couldn't be Spark. Spark didn't speak. At least not to Locin.

Still, she looked around and saw a ghostly outline walking the steps beside her.

"Spark?" She whispered.

The figure's head turned, but she couldn't see a face, more just an outline of where a face should have been. *Locin.*

Locin shook her head in amazement. She thought she should say something more, but it all felt like a dream, and she couldn't come up with anything to say.

"Ready?" Voske called back to her.

Locin looked back to the front where the door to the Veil had been ripped open. There was a choking dust clogging the air, and from here the crashing thunder above sounded like the lightning was very close at hand.

"Yeah." She answered.

Voske started jogging and Locin tucked in behind him as the ghostly figure rushed ahead.

She reached the top and gagged on the dust. The roof had been ripped off the hall of trees, and the sanctum beyond had been cracked open like an egg. For a moment her eyes locked on Iyanu's tree. A branch had been snapped off in Neveri's fury. All around the trunk dead brown leaves piled up as green buds opened and blossomed red in its boughs.

There were screams coming from somewhere close by, and a thunderous crash pulled her eyes west toward the barracks. She felt her heart jump into her throat. Was this Neveri? He was taller than the buildings, brooding over the city like a storm. His legs were like an ox, eleven horns sprouted from his head, and six wings from his back. He roared like a tidal wave and brought his fist down on the inner wall. It might as well have been a sand castle.

You need to run. Now! Spark said.

"Voske!" She yelled. "We need to run. Now!"

She glanced his direction to see his mouth agape. He just stood there, frozen in place.

"Voske!"

His fists were clenching and unclenching. "Yeah," he answered. "You're right." He looked back toward the sanctum. "There have to be others. Let's get them out! This way!"

He took off at a run, and Locin hesitated. She glanced back at Neveri. With three steps he could be on her, and what were the odds he'd spare her life? She thought about dashing off on her own. She wasn't welcome anymore, so why stay with them? But she felt terrified, and she didn't want to be alone.

She looked back the way Voske had gone and started running, back toward the broken halves of the sanctum. She didn't have time to worry about anything else right now. She just had to live.

Zengin stood atop the temple crier's platform, gripping his dagger and staring at the destruction. The sanctum was cracked in half, the portico strewn with rubble, and the mighty statues of the champions held the remaining roof up futilely. Fires dotted the Gods' Mount, and a swath of destruction was cut across the temple grounds toward Arrajin. Over it all, the monstrous form of Neveri seethed. He was unmatchable, fierce, but his vengeance was more like lightning than a storm. It was focused. He cracked the images of the gods and shattered their depictions. He ripped open rooftops and cleansed the walls with fire. He wasn't the destroyer of the Gods' Mount - he was the owner, exterminating the pests inside.

The other champions were running to and fro, evacuating children and the elderly to the tether. Anyone fit enough was directed across the river. They fled into Arrajin, and the bridge was clogged by a stream of humanity, all desperate to escape Neveri's wrath.

Is this what you wanted? Zengin thought. *You fools and your bleeding hearts.*

When Neveri had emerged, any thought of battle was abandoned. The Jeza monks had broken ranks, and the cult had ridden across the Gods' Mount, looting the barracks, the houses of healing, the vaults of the temple itself. He knew Borroka was somewhere inside, knew she was reveling in the slaughter. He curled his lips in a snarl. To come so close and still be out of reach…

"Zengin!"

Burz was running across the field with a group of young guildling monks. They wore the cobalt blue of Strah, and their arms were full of as many weathered scrolls as they could carry. They looked terrified, but also mystified, like they couldn't comprehend what was happening.

"Take them to the chariot!"

He scowled at Burz. "Take them yourself."

"I have to go back for more!"

Zengin stared at the temple. A few forms still ran toward the tether from within the clouds of dust and ash, but the chimeras were starting to circle, raining fire on the refugees.

"Zengin! Now!"

He looked back with a sneer. "No one else is leaving alive. Have you looked at the city?"

Burz followed Zengin's finger to where black smoke curled up from the People's Quarter, just beyond the Arrtris.

Burz' arms fell limp at his sides and he took a halting step toward Arrajin. "The cult?"

"The Sacred Quarter attacked as soon as Neveri broke free."

"Nyx."

"Burz!" Boomed a voice. They turned to see Voske charging across the temple grounds with a group of pilgrims.

"Get them across the river," Burz called. "Chariots are running out of space."

"Brilliant," Zengin said drably. "The city will fall within hours, but yes, let's send them there."

Burz shrugged. "It's face the cultists, or face that." He pointed to Neveri.

Zengin looked back at the hulking deity. He hated when someone else made a good point.

He tucked his dagger into its sheath and climbed down as Voske stopped. The pilgrims kept running to safety, and as they cleared, Zengin spotted Locin in their midst. She huddled sheepishly behind Voske, staying a short distance away.

"What is she doing here?" Burz growled.

"Back off," Voske said, putting himself between them.

"First, you trade the whole of Arrajin for her, and now you bring her along as if nothing happened?"

"The city?" Locin said softly. "What's he talking about, Voske?"

"Nothing. Don't worry about it, kid."

Burz laughed. "Sure. Don't worry about it, so he doesn't have to face his own mistake."

Voske clenched his fists.

Zengin didn't have time for this. He waved for the guildlings to follow and strode down the path toward the tether. Behind, he could hear Neveri's footsteps growing louder, and he looked back, seeing the ominous form stomping their direction. He quickened his pace, and the children followed suit, to the sound of heavy breathing and scratching paper.

They reached the tether in short order. Hikari and Illeri were already there, as was Weylyn, standing sentry with her bow drawn and her eyes trained on the temple. She let an arrow loose, taking down a cultist half a field away, for what good it did.

Zengin guided the guildlings to the ramp and gritted his teeth as a few young voices cried out their thanks.

"Zengin!" Weylyn called. "Is that the last group?"

He looked back out to see Voske and Burz approaching fast with Locin right behind. "Yes."

"Where's Rasa?"

"I haven't seen her."

The old woman's face went white. "She never arrived."

He followed her gaze back toward the temple and felt a twinge of worry. He didn't want Rasa to die.

Neveri was near the front of the sanctum, where the last survivors were fleeing the fires in the temple. He crushed them beneath his feet, and they scattered in horror, but where else could they go? They were the last, a huddled group of refugees fighting down the hill toward the tether, but there was no way they would make it.

Weylyn hopped down and started running toward the temple, but Voske intercepted her and started dragging her back. "You'll get killed, woman!"

"Let me go!" She yelled. "She's in there! Let me go!"

Zengin just kept his eyes steady on the carnage atop the Mount. Voske was right. There was nothing anyone could do about it now.

A roar sounded across the temple grounds, and fire streamed down from the gaping maw of a dark chimera, setting a line of the field on fire. Above, dark gray clouds hovered low over the treetops. Rasa said a silent prayer for rain as her eyes darted to the Arrtris and Arrajin beyond. Fires dotted the city, and they were spreading. And over it all loomed the bestial form of Neveri. She had to get out. She'd done her part, stashing the orbs away somewhere safe, or at least she hoped it would be safe.

The ground trembled under her feet, like all of Las was groaning under the weight of this god. Cries were sounding, and she saw desperate stragglers rushing across the green fields toward the safety of the tether. Somewhere above, a chariot was rising into the darkened sky, but she could see the smooth white hull of the Tempest down the hill. There was still a chariot, a chance of escape.

She rushed across the field, running as fast as she could, the grass soft under her feet. She reached for her boon and felt it crash in, the abyss of Nyx at her back, and the ominous flames of the chimeras ahead. She watched a woman stumble in front of her, screaming in terror as she scrambled to her feet, and all around the field blue spirits watched with a passive curiosity that chilled her, perhaps there to welcome any new souls to Nyx. She wondered if they would welcome her soon.

She felt her chest start to hurt. She couldn't remember the last time she'd run like this. She wasn't much of a runner. She never had been. She was falling behind the stragglers ahead, but she had to keep going, to hope that the chariot didn't leave before she got there. They would wait for her. They wouldn't leave her. At least she was sure Weylyn would wait for her.

The ground quaked, and she turned to see Neveri. He let out a hungry cry as he crossed the field in two great leaps, grabbing one of the monks from the group ahead of her. Terrified screams rose as the rest scattered, still running. Neveri broke the man's body with a flick of his wrist and tossed him back to the ground just a few feet in front of Rasa.

I have to get to the Tempest.

She saw the ghostly face of a young spirit watching her, but her eyes were less passive. She looked concerned, but helpless to do anything.

"Help!" Rasa cried. "Help me!"

Neveri was laughing now, and the sound of it rang in her ears like a violent rumble. She glanced at the long stretch of green between her and the chariot at the bottom of the hill.

The tether. I need to get to the tether!

She squeezed her eyes shut. For the first time Nyx felt safer than Talamh. She found some comfort in the cold stillness of it at her back, and she let her boon rush over her. The spirits swirled around her, a thousand voices all speaking at once as she felt the brush of their cold skin. She felt as if she were stumbling into the dark, and her hands flew out in front of her. She expected to feel the cold skin of the Veil, but she felt something else. A warm body.

Rasa opened her eyes. She had run straight into a bedraggled looking monk. Several more stood in front of her, clambering to get passage on the last chariot that sat at the tether.

She swallowed her boon, stuffing it back down as Nyx faded. The curious spirits disappeared, and she found herself at the tether, chaos all around her. She could see Aurilis on the deck of the Tempest, shouting down as monks streamed up the ramps.

She looked back. Had she run that fast? The green field stretched behind her, and a ways up the hill she saw the same stragglers who had been ahead of her. Neveri stamped around, snuffing the life out of them. If she'd still been there, she'd be dead.

But how had she crossed the whole field in an instant? It was impossible.

She recognized the booming voice of Voske. "We did all we could!"

She turned to see him nearby, and she pushed her way through the crowd to where he stood. Illeri was there, and Hikari. She saw Burz and Weylyn, and Zengin. And as she burst into the small clearing, she came face to face with Locin.

She looked worn. Her toga was soaked through with blood, and she had her arms wrapped close around her body. She was huddled behind Voske, as if she were hiding from the others.

Their eyes met, and Rasa smiled. "Locin!"

Locin glanced up. Her eyes were narrow. Was she sad? Angry?

Maybe both.

Weylyn came running through and grabbed Rasa by the shoulders. "Thank the gods!"

"I'm okay," she managed, pulling her eyes from Locin.

"We should go," Voske said. "We're all here. I think we've saved as many as we can."

Burz nodded, but he turned toward a pylon beside the tether and climbed up. "Just another minute. Let me see if any more are coming."

A roar sounded from nearby and Weylyn tightened her grip on Rasa. "We may not have a minute."

55: The Beast at the Bridge

Burz stared out from the top of the tether pylon. The temple was cut through from the Veil to the portico, a ruined mess of stone that was charred black. The temple grounds were littered with the fallen and red with blood. Even the last few Jeza monks were retreating over the bridge into Arrajin. The city was ablaze with cultist fire, and Burz snuffed bitterly at the scent of ash on the wind. He should never have doubted. This was no god. This was some abomination that had crawled from the bowels of Nyx to tear the worlds apart.

A violent tremble pulled his eyes to Neveri. He was shaking Jeza's Spire in his monstrous hands. In a terrifying display of strength, he wrenched it from the ground, sending a tremor through the Gods' Mount that nearly made Burz lose his footing. He watched with horror as Neveri threw the spire like a spear toward the Arrtris, driving it into the river beside the bridge and the retreating monks. He went down on his knees as the pylon shook violently, and the Arrtris swelled its banks, rushing over the bridge and washing several monks into the river.

As the shaking stopped, Voske shouted from below, "Mire and Nyx! What was that?"

"We gotta go!" Burz shouted.

The Arrtris was churning around the spire now, starting to back up and spill into Arrajin. He hopped off the pylon and rushed over to the other Champions. A large black thunderhead had moved in from the coast and he could see lightning flashing in the distance.

"Are there any more coming?" Weylyn asked.

Burz shook his head sullenly. "No."

The last of the civilians and monks were streaming up the gangway to the deck of the Tempest. The champions hurried to the bottom of the ramp, but they hadn't even set foot on it when a squad of Jeza monks stepped into their path, swords drawn.

"Out of the way!" Voske bellowed, but they didn't move.

Aurilis stood at the top of the gangway. Her High Oracle's robe was torn, and she trembled as she stared back toward the temple. When her gaze finally fell to the Champions, her eyes were filled with rage.

"I warned you, Voske! One last chance. And you chose to bring this destruction down on all of Talamh!"

"You want to blame me for this?"

"All of you!" Her eyes were hard like stones.

Burz took a step forward. "Take the others!" He yelled. "Voske and I will stay!"

She sneered at the idea. "No. You were all a mistake."

Burz looked frantically toward the city, the fires were spreading like a blanket, covering the roadways. "You can't leave them. Will their deaths be justice?"

"Yes," she said sharply. She looked at Locin cowering behind Voske, and her voice became colder. "Tell me, Voske, was her life worth all this?"

For once there was no snarky reply, no cocky grin. Locin's expression was hollow, and she stared blindly at the old woman. "I'll stay too," she said flatly.

"Like Nyx!" Voske shouted.

But Aurilis just stared at them, unflinching.

"We'll die!" Illeri pleaded.

"And eight new Champions will be called. If only the gods would spare us any more of you!"

At a raise of her hand the tether lines were cut, and Burz felt a gust of air shove him back as the pylats started flapping their wings.

"Stop!" Voske yelled. He still looked tense, but he didn't try to stop them. Did he believe they deserved this? Did he see how much they'd failed?

Burz stepped backward, fading behind the others. Somewhere east his family was waiting for him in Tajerim.

"Maybe," he muttered, "we deserve our fate."

"You don't mean that," Hikari said.

"Maybe I do."

Everything he held sacred was burning around him, and what had he done to stop it? He could have refused to heal Locin's body. He could have fought Voske. He stood by and watched the worlds end without so much as a word of protest. How long, he thought, until the fires they'd unleashed reached Tajerim? How long until his family paid for his mistakes?

"Rotting shrike!" Voske's voice sounded weak. He must have seen it too. They did deserve this.

The Tempest rose quickly above them and turned east, heading directly away from the temple.

"Focus," Weylyn yelled. "We need to go!"

"Where?"

"Away from here!"

A shout from behind made Burz instantly tense. The cultists from the Gods' Mount were descending toward the tether. He whirled back to the bridge over the Arrtris. The river was roaring over the banks and lapping at the boardwalk in the Trade Quarter. It would quell the fires, but the flood was rising steadily. It still seemed a better option than staying on the Gods' Mount.

"We can cross into the city," Burz said.

"The city is under siege!" Hikari protested, panic in his voice.

But the cultists and their chimera were closing in. "We'll be cooked alive if we stay!"

"There's another way!" Illeri called. They stared at her and she pointed frantically to the bridge. "I might have a way to get us out, if we can get to the Trade Quarter."

Voske gave a frustrated cry and then turned toward Arrajin. "Fine. Let's move!"

Weylyn ran. The other champions were ahead of her, the cultists behind. She could hear their jeering in the distance. It was doubtful they knew they were champions, or they would have pursued them with more intent. But it was clear they had won, and they mocked the last of the fleeing survivors.

Her lungs were already aching, and she sneezed at the cloud of dust and ash that draped the Mount like a blanket. She pulled the edge of her toga over her mouth as they passed through a vicious cloud of black smoke.

"Don't stop now!" Voske yelled from the front. "Come on!"

Arrajin was thick with ash. The fires on the south side were sending black clouds drifting north, and it was hard to tell where the smoke began and the fires ended.

"Gods!" Hikari yelled. "The river!"

The water burgeoned just below the trusses, and the cresting flood splashed over the top of the bank.

Downstream, the tower of Jeza stuck up out of the middle of the river, the waters piling up and frothing around it as the river roared like a wounded beast. The bridge was slick with water but clear for the moment. She was sure they could make it across.

"Don't stop." Voske panted. "Just a little farther!"

Weylyn kept sprinting all the way to the edge of the bridge. No sooner had they reached it than the banks gave way upstream and a thousand gallons of muddy water rushed toward them. They all scrambled onto the bridge as it shifted and groaned under the pressure.

"No going back now," Burz said.

Neveri was still roaring over the temple, stamping the life out of whatever resistance was left. The cultists had given up their pursuit, content to let the Arrtris have them.

Weylyn kept her eyes on the river, outpacing the others as they made their way across the slick stone. The water was churning uncertainly, doubling back on itself and swirling around as a thousand little whirlpools came and went every second. She frowned. There was something else about the water. It didn't just swirl. It seethed. A torrent of bubbles surfaced at the center, and just below the waves she could see a shadow as big as a tree, but it was moving against the current.

Just as Weylyn reached the Trade Quarter, a swell hit the bridge, sweeping the champions off their feet. For a sickening moment, she thought it might take some of them into the Arrtris, but they managed to hang on. Rasa, who had fallen a bit behind, fell hard into the rail. She almost went over - she *should* have gone over - but some invisible force pulled her back, holding her on the bridge. Weylyn felt her breath rush back, and she sighed, relieved as the girl stumbled to her feet.

A sudden drop of water flecked against Weylyn's neck, then another, then a third. Fat, pelting drops. It wasn't from the river. It was rain. She looked up as a rumble of thunder rolled through the sky. A rush of recognition swept over her like a tidal wave.

This was it. The bridge. The rain. The beast.

Her eyes darted back to the river where the shadow loomed. A guttural roar erupted as something broke the surface, sending a white spray across the bridge.

"Rasa!" She screamed. "Run!"

Rasa's eyes widened as Weylyn charged her direction, pushing her way past the other champions. Rasa was running as fast as she could, but the bridge was shaking violently, and the timbers began to crack under the strain as several heads lurched out over her. It towered thirty feet above, and from each scaly mouth hissed a forked tongue. The monster leered down at Rasa with hideous rage, the kind that only men are supposed to feel. Rasa screamed as Weylyn charged into her side, knocking her to the ground.

Weylyn felt the impact like a distant memory, or something out of a dream. It wasn't pain. More like a savage puncture. It froze her in place and she looked down. Mighty jaws had clamped around her torso, and a bloody incisor was puncturing where her chest should have been. For an instant she remembered standing on the jetty looking out over the dark ocean, and she smiled at Rasa.

"Run," she mouthed weakly. "Live."

Everything grew strangely still, as if she were fading into black. It was as if time froze, and the only sound she heard was the beating of her own heart. But that quickly stopped. The pain disappeared, and she saw a young girl standing beside Rasa. She glowed blue as she stared wide eyed at Weylyn.

She was vaguely aware of Voske barreling through, slamming into the beast. He grabbed Rasa and dashed for Arrajin as the hydra tossed Weylyn's body to the shore. Strangely, she didn't go with it. She was alone in a dark place, watching through a dirty window as the champions huddled on the boardwalk. An explosion of light sent the beast shuddering back long enough for Voske to scoop up Weylyn's body. Her arms flopped limply in his grip, and she looked down at her arms. They were at her sides where she stood on the bridge. They were glowing blue, and she felt terribly cold. Suddenly a cold hand slid into her own, and she looked up at the young girl.

The girl smiled faintly. *I'm Spark.*

Weylyn.

56: Ashes

Big drops of rain slapped on the stone roads as the Champions ran through the trade quarter. Illeri's lungs burned as she tried to keep her bearings. She was soaked through. The rain was a welcome cool against her skin, but it did nothing to stop the ache in her legs or her heart pounding in her head.

The whole quarter was a tangle of rubble and great stone buildings. The streets were mostly empty now, but they could hear frantic cries in the distance, and every so often a chimera screeched overhead. The battle was over. They weren't streaming down fire or fighting anymore. They were taking a victory lap. Wild whoops sounded from the cultists on their backs as they swooped over the ruins of Arrajin.

Lightening cracked the sky, and Illeri pointed toward the corner of the agora, toward the shabby facade of Yzod's shop. His sign hung loose on one chain, and the corner of his store was blackened by fire.

"Here! This way!"

They rushed to the shop, and Illeri thanked the gods as the door opened. She could see lamp light from the back room. They piled inside to the sad melody of the music box, and the room filled with the pants and heaves of the tired champions.

All but Voske.

He looked like he hadn't been running at all, his breath steady and his face stone. He carried Weylyn's lifeless body in his arms, and Illeri looked swiftly away.

Yzod dashed in from the back of the shop holding a large metal pipe over his head and trying to look as menacing as possible.

"Gods and Chosen," he lowered the pipe as he spotted Illeri. "You scared me."

"Yzod." She was still panting from the long run.

"What in Nyx are you doing here?" He eyed the others warily. "Didn't the temple evacuate?"

She shook her head. "We…"

"We didn't make it," Hikari said, strolling stiffly forward. His hair and toga were soaked, but he still managed a smile, as he held up his palm and the sigil of Desita glowed gold. "Hikari, Champion of Desita. And these are my fellow Champions."

Yzod's eyes fell on Weylyn, and he said flatly, "Is she dead?"

Illeri heard a gasping sob from Rasa. "Yes. She died to help us get away. Please, Yzod! The Phoenix…"

His mouth twisted in a frown. "It hasn't been tested properly."

"What's the Phoenix?" Burz asked.

"A chariot," Illeri said. "Please, Yzod. We need to get out of Arrajin. They'll be looking for us."

Hikari's eyes went wide. "He has a chariot?"

"How else did you think he would get us out?"

"Gods if I know. A boat or something? Do we even have a wayfarer?"

Yzod spoke again, but his expression was unreadable. "We don't need one."

"So you'll take us?" Illeri asked.

"Why do I get the feeling you're bringing trouble with you?"

"We probably are," Burz said honestly. "But we *do* need your help. Passage out of the city. That's all we ask."

"She's never flown more than a couple of tests. I don't want to risk going far."

"Tajerim," Burz said sharply. "We need to get to Tajerim."

Voske grunted. His arms and legs dripped with Weylyn's blood, but he refused to set her down. "We won't be safe there for long, but it's a start."

Illeri clasped her hands tightly, and held them in front of Yzod. "We wouldn't be asking if there was another way. The chariots have all gone, and the temple…"

"What?" His eyes were sharp. "What happened?"

"The temple fell to the cult."

"And that beast we saw? What was that thing?"

Voske grunted. "They claim it's a god."

Yzod's eyes widened, and he stared from face to face. "Is it?"

"It's a rotting monster." Voske looked down at the body in his arms and his shoulders sank. Illeri watched as the last bit of his will drained out of his face, and she suddenly felt dizzy with fear. If Voske thought it was hopeless, what chance did they have?

"Please," she stammered. "Please help."

Yzod gave her a pointed look. "This is why I prefer to work alone." He looked them over again. Weary, broken, covered in dirt and blood, and Weylyn…

"Fire and Nyx. You're telling me the temple is really gone?"

"Yes."

"That fast?"

Burz shook his head. "No one's ever seen power like that. He could tear the whole city apart if he wanted."

"And what about the city?" Yzod chided. "You're just abandoning it?"

Shame and doubt played across their faces. It seemed no one had a good answer.

Zengin strolled forward. He looked less troubled than the rest, and something in his eyes looked off. "The city's as good as gone. Now, will you help us or not?"

Yzod glanced over his shoulder toward the back room of his workshop. "Fine," he said. "Follow me."

They all quickly filed into where the Phoenix stood. Yzod already had the pylat outside, held by a makeshift tether just beyond the large sliding doors. He had been leaving.

Another roar from the victorious chimera rattled the shop and Yzod quickened his pace. "Help me get the tow cables, we've got to get her outside."

"No need," Voske answered.

He gingerly passed Weylyn's body to Burz, then bent low, putting his shoulder against the chariot.

Yzod looked at him incredulously. "You really think you're gonna just-"

The chariot groaned loudly, cutting him off, then began slowly sliding forward along its track.

Yzod shook his head in disbelief. "Nevermind then," he stammered.

Within a minute Voske had the chariot fully outside, and Yzod tossed a set of chains to Illeri. "You all get aboard," he shouted. "We'll get her hooked up!"

The others piled onto the deck as Illeri and Yzod settled the chains into the great metal rings that secured the pylat to the chariot.

"Thank you," she breathed.

Yzod met her gaze, his eyes looking doubtful, but he nodded. "Who am I to refuse aid to the Champions?"

She gave a weak smile, but she couldn't help but wonder how long that sentiment would last. Aurilis blamed them for all of this. How long until all of Talamh did the same?

"Alright." Yzod settled the last link in place and strode back to the chariot. Once they were both aboard, he brushed the sphere at the center, and the inventor's spark whirred to life, humming out that familiar note that hung in the air as rays of green light criss-crossed the skybeams, shielding them from the pelting rain.

Lightning flashed over the city, and a peal of thunder shook the ground.

"Thank the gods for the storm," Yzod called over the rumbling sound. "The clouds will cover us."

He took one chain and motioned to Illeri to grab the other. They pulled back, and the pylat fluttered in protest, then took flight, gently rising into the air as the Phoenix rocked beneath it.

A little chirp pulled Illeri's attention to the small wyvern on the rail, and she felt the barest hint of a smile crack her lips. Ryshi was cheerfully tottering along the frame, oblivious to their desperate circumstance.

"Gods and Chosen."

Voske's voice pulled her gaze back to the front to where the whole of Arrajin spread out before them. The spire of Jeza stuck up like a jagged spear from the Arrtris. The rain had put out the fires, but ugly black smoke still curled from the ruined hulk of the city, and water flooded the streets. At least a dozen chimera whirled over the ruin, like dark specks circling their prey.

Illeri had grown up with the idea that Champions were heroes. She didn't belong with them. She wasn't a hero. But maybe none of them were? Maybe champions were just people after all.

The Phoenix stayed in the clouds for a while, surrounded by lightning that crackled through the thunderhead. Yzod was charting the course to Tajerim by a compass mounted on the sphere in the center of the deck. He told them it'd be less than twenty minutes, but it felt like an eternity.

Up until now, Voske had felt the steady burn of Jeza's strength coursing through his body, his muscles hard as granite, and his lungs unwavering. But as he stood watching the storm rage beyond the radiant field, his boon drained away.

Every part of him ached, his muscles weak and spent. He hated this part. He tried to roll his shoulders back, and they screamed in pain. His boon had kept him alive as he crashed through solid stone, but it was gone now, and he felt every bit of his encounter with Neveri.

His clothes and hair were soaked through, and the air inside the pale green field felt stifling. His mind was starting to clear, starting to bring questions and doubts to him that he didn't want to face.

This is all my fault.

He clenched his fists and pushed down against the rail. The bones in his arms shot pain through his body like they would split, and he slumped forward.

"Are you alright?" Hikari asked, strolling closer.

"Fine."

The rotting chariot was too cramped. Seven Champions and the wild eyed inventor all crowded around the deck and the sphere that whirred with its strange green spark. He wanted to be alone, but the only empty space on the deck was at the back. By Weylyn.

"I think we're all feeling it, darling," Hikari droned.

Voske pushed away without a word and marched to the back. Burz had laid Weylyn on her back and crossed her arms over her chest. Her silver braid was matted against her neck, caked with her blood. Her skin was icy white, and her eyes shut fast. He felt the lack of her. This? This was just a husk. Weylyn was gone, off in Nyx, or gods willing the Midding. A place he was sure he'd never see.

"Rot it, Weylyn. It should have been me."

He let his hulking frame slump to the deck, his knees hit the wooden planks so hard that it jarred through his body. He leaned forward, supporting his weight with one fist.

"You tried to warn me. But gods, I'm so stubborn. I thought we could have it all. Get her back. Stop that…"

What? God? Monster?

He tightened his jaw against the rage. "It should have been me."

The soft voice of Locin broke in behind him. "Voske?"

He straightened up, wincing against the pain in his back. He couldn't find any words, so he stayed still, waiting for her to get it over with.

She walked up and stood beside him, her eyes glossy with tears as she looked over Weylyn's broken body. "She traded her life for Rasa's. Why? Why would she do that?"

"Because that's what champions do." He gave her a sharp look. "They're selfless."

She sniffed as tears splashed on her cheeks. Her toga was still red with the blood of her own death, and for a moment a thought flashed across his mind.

Why Locin? They'd been able to pull her soul back from Nyx, after all the rotting mire she'd done. She hardly deserved it. And Weylyn was gone forever. It felt unfair.

She stifled her tears and started again. "I wanted to say-"

"It's probably best if you go."

She turned toward him, her expression pained. "What?"

He stood, gritting his teeth. It was hard to see Locin as anything but a kid, drenched like a stray in a rainstorm, dirty and bloodied. And she was just a rotting kid. "When we get to Tajerim, you should go."

"Just like that?"

He gave her a hard look. "We didn't betray you, Locin. Did you expect to walk right back in and be one of us again?"

She laughed coldly. "What I expected? Gods, I don't know! I didn't expect to die and have my rotting soul ripped back out of Nyx. Do you know what that's like?"

He stared at her. Her eyes were cold black marbles.

"You should have left me dead."

"I'm starting to agree."

A black cloud passed her face. He couldn't take it back, and he wouldn't try. He hated he'd said it out loud, but he meant it. Weylyn told him to leave Locin dead. She'd asked him how many lives was he trading for hers?

He looked down at Weylyn's corpse.

Too many.

Locin brushed the tears off her face, smearing dirt and blood. "I wasn't gonna stay any way. I knew I wasn't wanted."

"I *wanted* you to tell me the truth." He leaned closer and her cold marble eyes stared up at him. "But you couldn't be bothered to do that. You made your choices. If you don't like them, blame yourself."

She steeled her face. "You don't know what it's like, being unguilded. It's like the gods just kick you in the teeth, then everybody else joins in. You're dirt! You're worse than dirt!" Her voice cracked as she spoke and she quieted down. "Endring wanted to fix that, make things like they used to be before the rotting gods changed everything."

"Yeah? And how did that work out for him?"

"At least we did something. What did you do besides fail at everything?"

He clenched his jaw as he felt his boon trying to creep back in. He was weak and tired, and sure he couldn't have mustered much even if he wanted to. He stuffed it back down and turned away from her.

"As soon as we land, you're gone. I have nothing left to say to you."

She slunk back to the crowded front of the deck, and Voske set his gaze on the treetops as they cleared the storm at last. He could see Tajerim now, and the glittering sea. He took a deep breath, trying to shake her words. He had failed. At everything.

57: Shattered

Endring stood in the door of the inner sanctum staring at the wreckage of Neveri's return. The roof was split down the middle, and the stained glass ceiling had shattered across the marble floor, spilling into the ancient sanctum below. The statues of the gods had been destroyed. Uthando's head was lying in the corner, Desita had been broken in half, and Jeza was torn limb from limb. Even below, the gods were defaced by the cultists, all except Neveri.

Endring made his way through the room, the shards of glass crunching like brittle bones at each step. He stopped near the top of the stairs to the lower sanctum, and picked up a large piece that hadn't fully shattered. It shimmered as it caught the light, a depiction of Metnadur as he raised this temple from the ground, an everlasting monument to the gods. Endring turned the piece over, and it sliced his finger. He flinched, as it slipped from his grasp, shattering into a hundred tiny slivers that spilled down the stairs into the darkness below. He held his finger up and stared at the tiny red drop that rolled down the inside of his knuckle.

"Are you alright?"

Endring looked back to see Sammel carefully entering the sanctum. He squatted down and studied Uthando's head on the floor, staring into the stony eyes as if he might see a spark of life inside.

"I am," Endring said, but it didn't sound convincing, even to him.

Sammel slowly stood and looked at Endring. "It's bad," he said with an uncertain quaver that Endring had never heard from him before.

Endring felt the hair on the back of his neck stand on end, and he looked out through the broken doors. The fires of Arrajin had been drowned by the rain, and a dense column of steam now rose from the city and curled in the upper winds.

"He was… angry. I've felt only a fraction of the scorn he's endured, and yet if I had it in my power, who's to say what I would do?" His eyes caught a glimpse of a young monk of Jeza, lying mangled on the Gods' Mount, and he quickly looked away.

"You would never have done this," Sammel said matter-of-factly.

"Where has he gone?"

"He's taking counsel with Borroka."

Endring looked sharply at Sammel. "And he didn't call for me?"

"You're worried she was right."

Endring shook his head mournfully. "He's not the Neveri I know. Sammel, I…" He called to mind the countless conversations they'd had in the depths of Nyx. "He spoke about change, and balance, and hope for the lost. He was sad, certainly, and angry perhaps. Broken-hearted at the rejection of his siblings. But he was lost, and forgotten, just like us." He leaned toward the central pit, gazing at the dark statues of the gods.

"Is that what he was," Sammel asked, his voice growing more sure, "or what you wanted him to be?"

"Both," Endring said with a bitter smile, "I wanted him to restore that which was lost. To restore fairness…" his voice faded with the last word. It sounded so trivial now. Was this what fairness looked like?

Sammel looked around them at the ruined sanctum. "I don't think that's what you wanted."

Maybe Sammel was right. Endring wasn't sure what he wanted anymore. "Oh?"

"I think you wanted the lowly lifted up, not the lofty brought down."

"And what of you, Sammel?" Endring answered. "What did you want out of all this?"

"To see what could be, I suppose."

Endring snorted in reply. Maybe that was his blindness. He had envisioned a better world so often that he couldn't see the truth of it. There would always be suffering, always death, and the only way to make it *fair* was for all to suffer together.

"The real question is," Sammel continued. "Where do you think he'll stop?"

Endring raised an eyebrow. "Stop what?"

"Destroying the images of the gods. In a real sense, the worlds were crafted in their image, and the people. Nearly everything in Talamh is a reflection of Sbarga."

Endring stared once more at the statues. They hadn't been simply knocked over, they had been torn asunder with terrible malice. "I don't know," he answered in a trembling voice. "But I fear how far he'll go."

The streets of Tajerim were just as Burz remembered. Dirty alleys and tight winding streets of brown stone running between rows of tall buildings with sharply angled roofs. It felt strange to be here again. To be home.

He could feel the nagging ache in his leg, the weariness. He felt on the verge of breaking down as he led the way through the streets. Yzod had left them at the tether. Locin had leapt off the chariot before it reached the ground and slunk into the city alone. He couldn't say he was sad to see her go. The rest followed him in a bloodied and beaten parade, Voske in the rear with Weylyn in his arms. They drew more than a few looks, but they weren't the only battered refugees he saw meandering through Tajerim. People scurried out of their way at the sight of them, especially Voske, towering over the others, his crimson armor stained a deeper red.

And Weylyn in his arms.

He pulled his eyes away. It stung to see her like that, pale and lifeless. A reminder of how utterly they'd failed. Despite it all, the ache, the defeat, he pressed on, desperate to find rest, desperate for the warmth of Hadris and the boys, desperate to be back home. He'd never imagined that was something he would feel about Tajerim, but now it felt like the only thing keeping him moving. They were getting closer, out of the dense winding streets to the more open edges of the city where farms and fields mingled with low buildings that spread out. The homes here were old and musty, but he loved the space.

"Is it much farther?" Illeri asked softly.

"We're close."

"Thank you, for letting us all come with you. I don't know anyone in Tajerim."

Burz glanced back over his shoulder at the others - at Voske. He didn't want them anywhere near his home, but they were all in shock, and they needed someplace safe. He knew it was right. He hated his constant need to do what was right.

"Of course," he said, letting his gaze drift back to Illeri. She looked dazed as she followed along the stone street.

"What will we do?" She asked.

"I don't know. Let's just get somewhere safe, and we can figure it out."

"I'm sorry." She turned to meet his gaze. "I know this is just as hard for you."

He nodded as he rounded another corner onto a familiar street. The last thing he wanted to do was comfort someone else. His world had just been shattered. *The* worlds had just been shattered. Not just for him, but for all of them. For everyone.

"It's not the first time I've lost everything." He looked back at her. "It's hard. There will be days you won't even want to get out of bed. But you find a way. You keep getting up. You keep moving forward."

"Until what?"

"Until you're out the other side. You always come out the other side eventually." He sighed. He'd had to do it before, and the thought of doing it again wearied him until his bones hurt. "You just have to find something to hold on to, Illeri."

"What do you hold on to?"

Burz glanced up. In front of them, a humble stone home rose with a little yard beside it. It was old, but well cared for, with a bright blue door he had painted himself. Hadris hated the color when he brought it home. He felt a smile curl his lips as he remembered arguing about it until she caved, on the condition he would repaint it if she still hated it. He could see her face smiling as they stood in the street staring at it. 'It's a happy color', she'd said, 'and our home is happy, so it fits'.

Hikari strolled up beside him. "Is this it? It's rather charming."

The way he said *charming* made Burz wince, but he wouldn't let anything spoil this moment. He pointed to the side yard. "There's a creek around the back. You can wash up." He nodded to Voske. "Set her in the side yard. I have plenty of wood stocked."

Voske nodded solemnly and headed around the side, the others following in their little macabre parade.

And Burz headed straight for the door. He held his hand against the bright blue paint, brushing the smooth surface of the wood. Before he could reach for the knob, the door opened from inside. Hadris stood with gleaming eyes, an expression of deep relief as she gave a little gasp. They threw their arms around each other, and suddenly the aches felt distant. He held her, and he realized how much he never wanted to let her go again. He didn't want to be a Champion, a hero, a soldier. He just wanted to be here.

The exaltation of Weylyn should have been a grand occasion at the temple with the worlds watching. She was a champion. But more than that, she was a hero. And yet, instead of a burning pyre at the top of Strah's spire, her body was laid hastily on scrap wood beside Burz' house. Her urn would not be carried with reverence down into the spire's vault. There would be no celebration of her life, no flight of the Phoenix.

The champions stood around the pyre in strained silence. Hikari had spoken a few words, but Rasa couldn't remember any of them. All she knew was that they were beautiful, and they made her cry. She could hear a few murmurs every so often. A shared look or an indignant scowl would soon follow. She was determined to ignore all of it. They were here for Weylyn.

So they waited and watched. The crickets stopped chirping, and the stars scattered themselves across the cold dark. The lights of the city started to fade, and the moon sank below the trees, and still they waited and watched as the quiet tension grew.

Rasa kept her hands in front of her. She clutched a small wooden box that Burz had found for a burial urn. It was a simple box with a picture of an eagle carved crudely on the top. It may have seemed an insult to other champions, but Rasa thought it would be just perfect for Weylyn.

She tried to stay focused on the happy memories she'd made with her. They had only known each other briefly, but in that time, she'd become the closest thing Rasa knew to a mother. Was this what it felt like to lose a mother? She told herself it was childish to compare her loss to someone with a lifetime of memories, but the ache in her heart told her it was no different. It was like losing your mother at the beginning, before you've had the chance to get to know her. It felt unfair. She clutched the box tighter, and she let Nyx swallow her up, the familiar chill of it spreading through her. Blue spirits were sparse here, but a few swirled around the pyre or wandered the edges of the yard like passing shadows.

"Weylyn?" She whispered, but it was no use.

She'd tried several times, but she wasn't there. That was a good thing, she told herself. It meant she was in the Midding, in her place of honor. And who deserved it more?

Still… she ached to see her.

Zengin stepped up beside her, staring into the flames. He was frowning deeply.

"Are you alright?" he asked.

She felt her emotions dangerously close to the surface and decided it would be safer to nod.

"Good."

They fell silent, and Rasa wasn't sure if she should say something else. "I… I think this is what she would have wanted. For her exaltation I mean, something small with just friends there to see her off."

"You're probably right."

They fell silent again and Rasa heard Voske sigh and stamp his feet somewhere behind. She looked back, and her spirit sank even lower. Everyone looked restless. They all stood far apart, as though no one wanted to be close to anyone else. Rasa frowned. This isn't what Weylyn would have wanted at all.

As though taking Rasa turning around as a sign that the exaltation was over, Voske started to wander off toward the gate to the front of the house, but as soon as he put a hand on the latch, Burz spoke, and his voice was terse.

"Where are you going?"

"What do you care?"

"Running off?" Burz strolled toward him. "Sounds about right."

The big man turned to face Burz now, scowling down at him.

"You made a mess, and now I'm left to clean it up?"

"You rotting pool of mire!" Voske spat. "You're gonna take the high ground now? Perfect soldier Burz, huh?"

Rasa swallowed hard. She didn't know what to say to stop it, and when she tried to speak, a lump in her throat choked out the words.

"Weylyn didn't deserve this," Burz pressed. "She was a real champion. She knew when to sacrifice a life for the good of others."

"Yeah?" Voske's voice rose as the tension in the air became stifling. "That why you healed Locin's body? If you were so eager to let her die, you sure as Nyx could have."

Burz stepped closer. "All I've done for weeks is clean up your messes. Who was it healing the wounded every time Voske the whirlwind was done storming through a city? Who was appeasing the people at *every* festival while you ran off doing gods know what?"

Voske laughed. "That's right. The Archons' little lap dog. You licked their boots while *I* tried to save Talamh."

"Tried and failed," Burz snapped. "Talamh would have been better off without your help. You leave a trail of destruction as wide as the Arrtris everywhere you step!"

"We're going to have it out here then?" Voske yelled. "Is that what you want?"

"Wait," Rasa croaked, but neither man could hear her over their own ego.

"What I want?" Snapped Burz. "You started this, the same way you always do. Voske the Unbreakable, the man who can do no wrong."

"You're a piece of work, Burz. So what if I got some things wrong? At least I wasn't cowering under Aurilis' skirt!"

"You got *everything* wrong, Voske. Everything you touch turns to mire, just look at her." He pointed to Weylyn as he spoke, and Voske went red in the face.

"So I'm to blame for her death?"

"Of course!"

"Not Locin. Not Endring. Just me?"

"You were the one who chose your lying pet thief over the whole rotting worlds! *You.* And wasn't it Weylyn who tried to stop you?"

"Shut your rotting mouth, now," Voske growled, but he wasn't shouting anymore.

His voice had taken on a deep, guttural tone that made Rasa's stomach twist into knots. She took a step back.

"I heard what she said," Burz hammered. "'Don't do this. People will die.' But, of course, Voske, the glorious champion of justice, couldn't be bothered to listen."

"You're a waste of breath, Burz."

"And now look. People died. Hundreds of people. Soon it will be thousands, and all because you wouldn't listen."

"AAAAHHHHHH!" Voske hurled a punch toward Burz' head.

Burz ducked backward, and Rasa heard a scream. Hadris and Burz' sons were standing close to their home, watching in horror.

Burz punched Voske in the gut, but the giant of a man didn't seem to feel it. He swung hard at Burz, catching him in the chin. Rasa wanted to look away, but it was all happening so fast, a flurry of blows as the two men went at each other. Burz threw a punch at Voske one last time, and the big man smashed his head into Burz'. He crumpled to the ground, and Voske landed a kick that sent him sliding across the dirt.

Nearly against her will, Rasa ran forward between the two men and held her hands up toward Voske.

"Wait," she pleaded. "Not this, Voske. Please don't do this."

Her heart was drumming frantically in her ears, but Voske hesitated. His eyes moved from Burz to her, and his arms hung limp by his sides. He turned away, pacing near the gate, and then he headed for his red armor, piled by the fence. He grabbed it and flung it out into the yard in front of Burz.

"We're done!" And then he was gone, through the gate and out into the city.

Something in his words rang out like a death toll. They were done. The Champions were done. It was over. She could feel it, and she could tell from the looks on their faces, the others did too. There was nothing left for them here, together.

That was wrong too. They needed to stay together. Rasa could sense that, but she didn't know how to put it into words, so she watched helplessly as the others scattered. First Zengin, pulling his hood over his face and slipping away like a shadow. Soon Illeri and Hikari were gone too. She wondered if she should go, but it wasn't over. Exaltations lasted until sunrise, and Weylyn deserved that much, so she went back to her silent vigil.

Hadris had sent the boys inside, and she brought out some water and fussed over Burz as he stood sulking. Eventually, Hadris disappeared too.

The wood was gone now, and the bones were nothing but ash. Rasa expected Burz to leave as well, but he didn't. He came quietly over and helped her scrape some of the ashes into the box.

Neither of them spoke for a long while. The cold stars started to fade one by one, and a crack of pale light broke the horizon.

"You're welcome to stay here," Burz said.

Rasa looked up from the ashes. "With you?"

He nodded. "We'll put a few blankets down in the common room. As long as you need."

She nodded gratefully.

"Are you tired?"

"I should be." She looked up at the sky. The clinging night held on ominously above, and it was eerily quiet. "I think I'll stay up a while though."

He patted her on the arm. "Take all the time you need. We'll leave the bedding down when you're ready."

She nodded gratefully and watched him until he walked inside, then she sank to the ground and huddled close to the last fading embers.

"I'll miss you," she whispered.

She wrapped her arms around her knees and sat until the pale light at the horizon exploded into golden dawn. The song birds broke out in music, and a light breeze began to blow in from the coast, as though the world wasn't aware of her sorrow.

Rasa stood shakily to her feet and turned to go inside, but as she did, she heard a sharp cry from the east. She looked back to see a phoenix. It swooped over the treeline just as the first rays of sunlight pierced the sky. It flew through the fading smoke from the pyre and began winging a fast circle, drawing the smoke after it until its red wings were ablaze. Rasa watched it soar higher and higher until it disappeared from view and the spiral of smoke was swept away by the wind.

58: Free

Locin sat at a dirty table in a grimy tavern. Tajerim was like any other city. She'd never been here before, but she knew where to find liquor and a place to lay low. And anything else she wanted. It hadn't taken her long to steal a pair of leather boots, some trousers, and a silk tunic that was a bit too big. She had it tied up at her waist. She was Locin the thief again.

Dim lantern light sparsely revealed her surroundings, and she was sure that was for the best - grimy walls and a lingering smell of smoke and must. The tables and chairs were worn down and scratched, and the glasses had a film that never cleared even when they were washed. Places like this had been all too common to her not long ago, a far cry from the immaculate luxury of the temple.

Rotting temple, she thought.

She was sure that if it wasn't for the temple, she never would have died. They could have let Endring pass. They got what they deserved.

But even as the thoughts drifted in and looked for a place to settle, she felt an emptiness overtake her. The temple was going to be destroyed no matter what. That had always been Neveri's plan. And the truth was, she wasn't mad at the temple. She was mad at Voske.

She wasn't fully sure how she had been brought back. She'd guessed it involved the crook, and she was sure it involved Voske. They'd all looked at her like she was some rotting monster. Maybe she was. Nothing felt right since she'd come back.

But Voske had made his feelings clear.

She reached for the bottle in front of her only to find it was empty. She tipped it up, staring down into the dingy brown glass before tipping it the other way and letting it roll into the other two bottles. They clinked noisily and she turned to see the tavern master wiping a table. He was moving the dirt around more than cleaning it.

"More!"

He glared at her and continued wiping.

"I want more!"

"No."

She grabbed the rag from his hand with her boon and pulled it over to herself, letting it spin in the air above her table.

He came over to snatch it, but she grabbed it with her left hand and stared him down.

"Are you planning to pay now?" He asked angrily.

"Nope." She held her Champion's sigil in his face.

"That may have gotten you the first three, but no more. The temple's done, and I have a business to run."

"Defying a Champion of the gods? Mire and Nyx!" She spit on the floor, which only made him angrier.

"This isn't a house of mercy, and you aren't anybody's Champion. Now get out, or I'll call for the guard."

He snatched his rag out of her hand and marched back to his table without so much as another glance. She told herself it didn't matter. She was above him. And she was leaving anyway.

She got up and strolled toward the door, spotting an expensive bottle of liquor behind the counter. She grabbed it with her boon, and it flew softly into her hand as she pushed the door open and stumbled out into the street.

Everything outside was hazy from the drink and a heavy fog that had rolled in off the sea. All she could see was the rough bricks at her feet and the dotted lights of lanterns shining through the mist. A chill had settled in, and she wished she had a cloak with her as she hunched down and headed out into the night. The liquor would keep her warm, she decided as she pulled the cork stopper out with her teeth and spit it into the road. She lifted the bottle to her lips and let the hot liquid burn down her throat and flush her cheeks.

Footsteps sounded behind her, but the street was quiet otherwise. They put her on edge, but even more so when she realized they were following her from the tavern.

"I'm not giving it back," she called, thinking he must have seen her take the bottle.

But the footsteps persisted.

"Rot off! I won't come back here. Ever. Okay?"

She quickened her pace and ducked around a corner where she had a view of the bright moon over the sea, and the statue of Kisandin that lorded over the port. After a few paces in her new direction, she heard the footfalls again. Her agitation was turning to panic.

"I said rot-" she spun around to see nothing behind her in the fading fog but an empty brick street. But she *knew* someone was standing there, right behind her. As she strained her eyes against the parting mist, she saw a blue haze of light by the street lamp, and she sighed.

"Spark."

I didn't mean to scare you.

It wasn't audible, but it was clear, like a memory being dredged up in the back of her mind.

The bottle slipped from her hand and shattered against bricks as she stared, dumbfounded.

"What in Nyx is going on?"

You heard me at the veil.

"Sure, but I thought I was crazy. Besides, I still had one foot in Nyx." A horrifying thought came to her. Maybe she still did?

Where are you going?

"Rot if I know. Nobody wants me around, so I left." She scowled. "That's your fault, huh? Couldn't keep a secret."

The blue haze was taking form. The young girl she'd seen as she gasped back to life. But she didn't want to see her. She shoved the feeling of nearness away and stared at her feet as Spark faded back to a murky haze.

I wanted to help you.

"By selling me out?"

Any way that I could. I don't want to argue about this again.

Locin perked her head up. "Again?"

I just wanted to say I'm sorry I wasn't there. Maybe I could have seen it coming.

Locin felt a rush of emotion, not the least of which was a wild terror. She was losing her mind, breaking apart. She threw her hands over her ears. "You're not real. I can't really hear you." She squinted her eyes harder, trying to shut it all out.

It's me, Locin. You're not mad.

Locin's eyes shot open. "Prove it!"

She watched the blue haze move around beside her and she felt the familiar pinch on her arm that told her Spark was annoyed.

And suddenly it was all very real. She felt tears start rolling down her cheeks. "You're real."

A flash of a memory filled her mind, the young girl with soft billowing hair that she'd seen as they pulled her soul from Nyx. But it was clearer in her mind. The girl was smiling at her, and she threw her slender arms around Locin. She felt... happy.

She fixed her eyes on the haze that was Spark. "I saw you in Nyx."

Did you?

"Don't you remember?"

Spark was silent.

"I remember. You must!"

Still the haze bobbed silently in the mist.

Locin started to pull nearer to Spark, to let her face form features, but she felt that same emptiness clawing at the back of her mind, that same feeling like Nyx would swallow her up.

"Spark? Spark!" Panic tinged her voice.

I'm here, Locin. I think you could see me if you wanted.

Locin shook her head, laughing madly. It was too much. "I can't do this." She stumbled back away from Spark and then took off at a run down the street, the salty wet air slapping her in the face as the mist parted in front of her and swallowed her up again from behind. She had no idea where she was going, or even why. She felt hollow, and she wanted to outrun that feeling. She felt her foot slip against the damp stone beneath her, and she toppled forward into the street, feeling the hot scrape of stone against her arm as she caught herself.

"Nyx it!"

The whole realm was against her. She turned her arm over and saw a red scrape along her forearm. It stung as she touched it. She could just make out the form of a young girl bathed in blue light bending to touch the scrape, and she yanked her arm away.

Are you okay?

She couldn't outrun her, and truthfully it wasn't her she wanted to outrun. It was Nyx. But as she cradled her arm, the fresh wound anchored her. It seemed to remind her that she was very much alive.

"I was with you?" Locin said. "I was in Nyx and not the Midding?"

Maybe you just hadn't made it there yet?

Locin shook her head. "They don't want me there. It's okay. I don't want to be there anyway. It's dumb."

It is dumb. I like it in Nyx. It's not so bad.

"Yeah. It's not so bad." But she could feel that emptiness closing in again, and she pressed her hand against the burning scrape. She was alive. She was alive…?

"I don't know where I'm going. It'll probably be like the old days, just getting stuff where I can, not getting caught."

That's okay. I liked the old days.

But every time Spark spoke, she felt like she was being pulled back to Nyx. There was that emptiness again, and the sting of her wound faded a little.

"You can't come, Spark."

She didn't answer, but Locin could feel that it wounded her.

"I need to be alone." Her heart felt like it was being torn out as she said it. If she sent Spark away, maybe she could find life again. Maybe Nyx would go away too.

But she would truly be alone.

When we were in Nyx-

"No." That was the last thing she wanted to hear about. She raised her voice. "Go, Spark."

But she could still feel her presence, see her blue shape looming in the mist.

"Just rotting go!"

And slowly Spark pulled away. Locin could sense her grief, and it mingled with her own. But she needed to clear her head. To think. She couldn't do that with Nyx hounding her steps. As Spark's presence faded, she turned toward the docks, gulping down salty air, curling her toes in her boots. She was alive.

She pressed hard on the fresh scrape until she cried out from the pain. She was alive.

She was Locin the thief again. Alone and unwanted, just the little girl that stumbled away from that rotting choosing stone. Unchosen. Unloved. But she'd survive, like she always had.

The streets of Tajerim were crowded. Sailors, merchants, pilgrims, all were common sights in the inns and on the many ships that crowded the waterway. Refugees though, were new. The already crowded streets had become absolutely choked with them in the hours since Neveri had been released. Already the temple of the gods had been ransacked and a priest murdered. Rumors were everywhere that the faithful of Neveri were planning an attack on the city, and who knew if those were true?

Zengin ducked through the crowd, his head up and eyes alert. If only those morons had listened to him and left that relic in the lighthouse where it belonged. Instead, they'd doomed the worlds, and worst of all him. Here he was back in Tajerim of all places. Though he didn't intend to stay long. He'd be gone in a day or two, hopefully without trouble. He wasn't oblivious to the glances he'd been receiving from a few of the guards, no doubt his father's loyal lackeys.

He ducked away from the main thoroughfare and wound his way down a back alley to a seedy traveler's hostel. The rooms here were separated by thin excuses for walls, and the beds were little more than ratty scraps thrown down on the hardwood floors, but it was secluded, and he cared little for amenities. He wouldn't sleep tonight, anyway. He made his way quickly up to his room, ignoring the hapless refugees who were no doubt paying to sleep in the hallway.

When he reached the door he paused, staring down at the light that escaped the crack in the bottom. A shadow moved slowly back and forth across it, a sure sign of someone pacing within. His gaze tightened, and he became suddenly aware of the long knife, strapped to his thigh. How had the old pool of mire already found him? Did he slip up here while he was paying at the desk, or did he know his son that well, and had paid the man more to ensure he was given this room?

Either way, Zengin pushed through the door. The Archon of Tajerim was inside wearing his typical resplendent tasseled toga, pure white, like he was a spotless virgin. His graying hair was cut neatly above thin eyebrows and brown eyes, Zengin's eyes, and in his hands he clutched a book covered in green velvet.

"Zengin," he said as their eyes met. "Son."

Zengin felt the word twist into him like a dagger. "What do you want?" he replied, keeping his voice measured. "I see you have your ledger."

"Yes, yes. A reminder of better times." His father beckoned him into the room as though he was inviting him into his own home.

Zengin slid inside the door and brought it to with a click behind him. "Were you watching the tether?"

"Well," his father confessed, "after the first chariots started arriving, I assumed the champions would be close. I was surprised to not see you on the Tempest." He paused and watched, but Zengin would give him nothing, so he simply shrugged and moved on. "My men tracked you to that poor man's house. It's a shame Uthando would pick one such as that. At least Metnadur has better sense."

"I know you didn't come here for the small talk."

His father squinted and walked to the rough-hewn table in the corner of the room. He scraped a chair outward and sat down. "Sit, won't you?"

Zengin followed him to the table and noiselessly slid in his chair. He could still feel the sheath of his knife, itching at the sweat on his skin.

"Times are changing. Certainly you know that better than most."

Zengin watched him placidly.

"A god? A real god out of the depths of Nyx! And you saw him?"

"A monster," he seethed. "Death loosed on the worlds."

A wicked grin spread across the Archon's face. "Death is not always a bad thing, my boy. With the temple fallen, there's power to be grabbed."

Any power there was, Neveri held firmly. Zengin rested his elbow on the table, letting his fingers play along his lips. He could feel his hatred of this man tightening his chest, and he focused on keeping his breathing even. "And how is that?"

"Destabilization always reeks of opportunity. All *we* have to do is land on the right side. Have I taught you nothing?"

"You've taught me plenty."

"That's right. I raised you to have a nose for opportunity. If we play our cards right, we can make more money than men have ever imagined. And more than that, power! We can demand the fealty of the surrounding city-states. Who knows? Tajerim could become the new holy city, first to welcome Talamh's true god."

The idea of calling that abomination a *true god* sent a fiery rage through Zengin's mind, and he clenched his jaw tightly as his fingers pulled the dagger from its sheath without a sound.

"Think of it, Zengin! You and I united behind Neveri, welcoming him into our city. A Champion, choosing to stand with him."

His father locked eyes with him now and they stared at each other. For a brief moment, Zengin could see just as much loathing in his father as he felt.

"Can you imagine what we could accomplish? With the silver-tongue of Metnadur instead of that pitiful scribe's boon. We could truly bend the worlds to our will."

Zengin straightened up in his chair. He could smell the burning of vardingrass through the window. The manager of the hostel had slipped outside for a smoke. "Do you know when I was chosen?" Zengin asked.

His father tilted his head. "I didn't even know you'd been named Champion until I heard it fourth hand from a cabin-boy on a merchant vessel. But then, you already know that."

"It was right after Chancellor Finch died."

His father trembled at the name and looked out the window. "Bloody awful mess. And a shame too. Finch was an invaluable asset." His father paused and gave him a pointed look. "What are you getting at?"

"There are many types of ambition, father."

The older man stiffened. "Are you saying that was your doing?" He laughed. "My boy, you've never hurt a soul!"

"And if I had? Would that ambition meet with your approval?"

He spat. "That's not ambition. That's folly! We lost a hundred-thousand marks when he died."

A long blast resounded from the water-front marking the morning watch. They would only sound twice more.

Zengin slowly leaned across the table. "And still you're blind to it," he sneered. "Let me spell it out for you. There's more than ambition for money, and more than ambition for power."

"And what other kind of ambition is there?"

Another blast, so loud it rattled the decrepit walls.

"Revenge," Zengin answered. "Ambition for revenge."

His father's eyes widened in realization just as the third blast sounded. The old man choked out a scream, but it was cut short by the blade at his throat. A gush of foul air poured from his neck instead, then a gush of blood, as his head fell back against the chair.

Zengin carefully wiped his blade clean across the shoulder of his father's once pristine white toga. It was incredible how many times he'd fantasized about this moment.

He slowly tucked the knife back against his hip as the room grew cold, and he turned to the door. He grabbed the handle but paused one last time to look back. His father's ledger still lay on the table, somehow clean of spatter. He quickly walked back and snatched it up.

"Here's to better times," he muttered.

He stared down at the book. His father was the last tie he'd had to Tajerim. He should have been free of the wretched city now, but he felt something odd. A kind of emptiness. He thought of Weylyn's body burning on the pyre, and the look in Rasa's eyes when he spoke with her. And he was angry. This was supposed to be it. He was supposed to be free.

He slammed the ledger on the table, staring at the useless stump of his right arm. He was damaged, just like Rasa. Just like all of them. Useless, damaged champions. And then he thought of Borroka. That was it! He wasn't free. He still had one more person on whom he would get revenge. He would need some information, but he always knew where to get that. He picked up the ledger and tucked it in his toga before slipping out, locking the door behind him.

Cold water swirled around Burz' feet. He wore a comfortable pair of trousers, the ones he'd always worn working around the house. The rough spun cloth was coarse and familiar against his legs as he bent over the cool stream. He cupped his hands and leaned out, pouring the cool water over his head. It was mid morning, and the sun was creeping up over the jungle. A brief rain shower had left Tajerim sticky and warm. He dipped his hands back in the stream and let the cool water spill down his tired arms. Hikari had made some wild claims about the healing waters of the bathhouses, but there was no water in the worlds more healing than his own cold creek.

A soft intake of breath sounded behind him, and he turned to see Rasa staring at his bare back. He started to reach for his tunic, but he pulled his hand back and dropped his head. He was painfully aware of the tangled mass of scars that covered his back as she made her way to the creek.

He looked her over. She wore a simple toga, too big, but wrapped and pinned around her to fit well enough. And she carried a pack on her back. And Weylyn's bow and quiver.

"You're leaving?"

She bit her lip. "I'm glad you asked me to stay, but…"

He nodded as he grabbed a towel off the grass and wiped the water from his face. "It's not home. I understand. Where will you go?"

"I don't know." Her eyes strayed to his back as he dried it, and she dropped her gaze.

The scars covered most of his back and his shoulders, and they ran down his arms in cruel lines. He'd always worked hard to hide them as best he could, even in the elaborate outfits the temple had put him in.

"I was a soldier for a long time," he said as he tossed the towel back on the grass. "Eventually I became a captain. I had thirty men under my command."

She glanced up at him, curious. He wasn't exactly sure why he was telling her any of this. It just felt right.

"One day we were ordered to raid a house and arrest some people. We were told they were dangerous criminals." He laughed. At the time, he trusted his orders, but it all felt so absurd now.

"That's funny?"

"Not at all. I was just thinking of the other times we'd done it. We were told, and we believed it. How foolish I was." He sighed. "After an arrest, we would drag them to the stocks and lock them up. Every time. Without question."

He eased back, sitting on the soft grass, and she sat beside him.

"We found several people in the house that day, men and women. We took them out to the square. I remember this one man. He was so old he could barely keep up. He stumbled, and I put out my hands to catch him. He felt…" he looked down at his own hands as he tried to remember what it had felt like "… frail."

He stopped and dropped his head. He could still see the man's face so clearly, old and wrinkled with a scraggly gray beard. But his eyes were what he remembered most. They were a deep brown, and they were pleading with him.

Rasa's tender voice called him back. "So what did you do?"

He took a deep breath. His body was tense, like it didn't want him to go on, to dredge up the past again. But why not? It was there anyway, lurking in the shadows of every waking thought.

"When we got to the stocks, we were ordered to beat the prisoners," he confessed. "I commanded my men to stay where they were. I wasn't stupid. I had seen the corruption of our Archon and the guilds of Tajerim, people being arrested for making an enemy of the wrong person. It was unjust. It was an affront to Jeza and Uthando." He stopped and locked eyes with her. "Have you ever seen the warrior's guild emblem?"

She shook her head.

"The sprig of yarrow that represents Uthando is wrapped around the sword of Jeza." He tried poorly to demonstrate with his hands. "Uthando restrains Jeza's anger, and she cuts through the excess of his mercy." He looked at her young face as she sat fixed on his words. "No mercy without justice. No justice without mercy."

"Did your men listen to you?"

"At first. But we were ordered again, this time with the threat of punishment if we failed to act. My men started to move, and the prisoners cried out. I couldn't just stand there, so I stepped between them. I was told if I did not move, I would share their fate."

"And you stood there anyway. You let them beat you." She raised a hand, tracing a raised scar that ran from his elbow to his shoulder with her finger.

He felt anger trying to rise, the same rage and frustration he had felt for so long, but after all he'd been through, it seemed so petty and unimportant. He felt something different now. Grief.

"I have scars too," she said softly. "Mine are on the inside though. It wouldn't do to have me marked up on the outside." He saw tears glint on her cheeks.

He sighed, and it was like something left him with that breath. "It's been over a season, but sometimes I wake up and I can still feel the strike of the whip."

"It's been almost two years for me. I still can't sleep most nights."

He sighed, slipping his tunic over his head. "You get distant, but you never get away."

She gulped a breath and something in her voice sounded hopeful. "Maybe."

"Where will you go, Rasa? Do you have any family?"

She shook her head. "I was raised by..."

"I'm sorry."

"I don't think about it all the time now. I did at first, when I got away. I always thought he was coming to take me back. I'd dream that a lot. Now I can forget most of the time."

He nodded. "Me too. I've tried to shove it all down. Keep it out of my mind. But now I'm back here. In Tajerim."

"You push it all away, down inside somewhere," she said. "But then something reminds you. A sound. A word. The smell of orange blossoms and tea." She dipped a finger in the creek and swirled it around. "And it all comes back up like yesterday's dinner, and you realize it was there the whole time."

She looked up at him again and something was different. There was a light in her eyes he was sure hadn't been there before.

"But maybe it doesn't have to," she said. "What if you let it go? What if you really, truly forgive them, and you don't have to stuff it back down?"

"Do you think it would work?"

She smiled faintly as she brushed her cheeks dry. "I always felt worthless, like I didn't have any purpose. I was damaged. A lost soul."

He nodded his understanding. What good was a soldier who was banned from fighting for his people? He'd been broken and lost too.

"Weylyn told me something before…" she stifled a sob. "She saw a vision of what happened on the bridge."

"What?" Burz couldn't believe what she was saying. Had Weylyn known she was going to die and not told them?

"She saw the vision twice. One time, she died. The other time…" she let tears rush down her cheeks as she looked up at him. "It was me, Burz. I was supposed to die on that bridge."

He pulled her in and held her to his chest as she sobbed. "Gods, Rasa. I'm so sorry. You shouldn't have to carry the weight of that."

She shook her head. "It's not a weight. I mean, I miss her. I wish I could've taken her place, but… she chose me, Burz. She gave her life. For *me*."

Rasa pushed free, and Burz handed her the towel. She nodded gratefully and wiped her face.

"I feel like I have a second chance to live, like I was reborn on that bridge. I know it sounds silly, but I've never been loved before. But Weylyn…"

"She was the best of us," he said.

"She loved me enough to die for me. And I don't want to live in the past anymore. I want to let it all go and be like she was."

He laughed as he cupped her chin in his rough hand. "Maybe she wasn't the only one who was the best of us."

She smiled gratefully, and then stood as he pulled his hand back, brushing the grass from her toga and shouldering her pack.

"Say goodbye to Hadris and the boys for me?"

He nodded.

"One more thing, Burz."

"Yes?"

"What happened to that old man at the stocks? Did you set him free?"

He felt the memory surge back up, the man's face lying on the ground as both of them were beaten. Burz had been beaten nearly to death, but that man, he was so old and frail. He had reached out and grabbed the man's hand as the life drained from him, and the last look in his eyes was gratitude. At the time, it felt stupid. He watched this man killed as his stand had done nothing. Why would anyone be grateful for that? But in this moment, he saw it differently. That man didn't die alone. He died knowing someone was fighting for him.

"He was freed," he said.

She smiled. He watched her head through the side yard until she disappeared through the low wood gate. He felt the memory of that man's face lingering in his mind, and the betrayal of his men. He felt it all, anger, fear, grief. He wanted to shove it down again. But what if Rasa was right? What if he could let it go?

He let it all bubble up, and he slammed a fist into the damp earth as tears rolled down his cheeks. He grieved the man. He grieved his friendships and his guilding. And then he splashed his face one last time with clean water. He had work to do. But as he stood, he felt different somehow too. Lighter. Free.

59: Tethers

Illeri stood alongside Yzod, staring at the Phoenix. The sun was high over their heads, and Illeri was hot and tired and hungry. Ryshi must have felt the same as he cooed pitifully at her feet. She bent down, offering him her hand, and he shot up her arm onto her shoulder.

"Fire and Nyx!" Yzod moaned. "They're charging me twenty marks a day just to tether her here."

It was strange. Yesterday she'd had all the wealth and power of three worlds at her back, and now…?

"Maybe there's some goodwill left for a champion?" She tried. "I can ask around and-"

"Bah. Don't bother. I wouldn't be able to live with myself if the cultists got you on my account."

He glanced at her gloved hands. She'd traded a gold pin from her hair for them off a refugee. She was regretting it a bit now. She should have held out for something of more value.

"Best keep those on, and keep your head down." He gave her a wary look. "You sure about this?"

"About what?"

"Staying with me and Ryshi. You don't owe us a thing."

She nodded firmly. "I want to stay. I can't exactly be a wayfarer again, but this…" she touched the hull of the Phoenix fondly. "It's the closest I'll ever get."

Someone cleared their throat behind, and Illeri smelled…

"Pie?" She turned to see Hikari smiling sheepishly and holding out a whole tray of meat pies, and her stomach gurgled loudly.

"Ah yes," Hikari said. "The baker was just bringing them out on my way by. Turns out, she was a huge fan. Can you blame her?"

Illeri felt a surge of emotion in her. She was happy to see him, but it was more than that. She would have been devastated if she never saw him again. But that was silly, and she swallowed it down. "Why are you here, Hikari?"

He looked like she'd taken the wind out of his sails. "Am I not welcome?"

"I didn't mean that," she said, blushing. "I just thought… well, I thought you'd be long gone by now."

He set the pies down and looked over the Phoenix, running an idle hand along it. "Truth be told, I was on my way out, darling. I found a chariot heading for Suntara. I suppose I figured I'd have some status left there. But…" he glanced up at her, and she felt her heart flutter. "Well, I suppose I couldn't bring myself to leave."

"Good," Yzod said, stepping between them and picking up a pie. "We could use some help with the Phoenix."

Hikari and Illeri both looked away, and she turned her back so neither of the men would see how red her face was.

"We need to find a place to hide her," Yzod continued, throwing a chunk of meat to Ryshi. "Somewhere it won't be seen, and I won't be charged for tethering it."

Hikari clapped his hands together. "Right you are, darling. Right you are!"

Endring stared around the large domed room, its octagonal walls, and the eight sided table he knew so well. The Oracles had met here more times than he could count, dull meetings that droned on. But now its pristine walls were covered in rough graffiti, and the eight alcoves that once held the banners of the gods now sported crude banners in a deep green that bore the beastly symbol of Neveri. The same symbol emblazoned on his right palm. He brushed his fingers over it, the gold light swirling beneath the blackened face that met him there, half man, half beast.

He sat uncomfortably in his old chair, the seat of Bei'ai's Oracle, and found himself wondering about the other oracles. Had they gotten out? He hoped so. Neveri's wrath had taken the warriors of Jeza by surprise, let alone the scribes, the dancers, the servants. These were all simple people trying to live their lives, and far too many had been cut short.

Across from him, Borroka sat straight backed, sneering with bared teeth. "You wear that mark poorly." She nodded at his right palm, and he realized he was still idly rubbing it. "Does it still suit you, Oracle?"

Endring dropped his hands to his lap. "You gloat? Wasn't this a victory for us both? For all Talamh?" But even as the words left his lips, he knew it wasn't true. A twinge of regret shot through him and nearly caught his breath.

"A victory for our god."

The doors burst open, and a few guards made their way in, followed by Neveri. He'd settled on a more human appearance now, but taller than any man Endring had ever seen. He had broad shoulders and a mess of dark hair that ran halfway down his back in wild waves. His face was smooth and handsome, but his yellow eyes were beastly.

He looked over the two of them, his sneer not unlike Borroka's, and his eyes settled finally on Endring. Was it contempt in his eyes?

Endring dropped his gaze to the table, praying under his breath to Bei'ai for mercy.

"The city is ours," Neveri's voice rolled over them like thunder, carrying a wave of fear with it. "Tell me of the faithful?"

Borroka began, "More join our numbers every day. We've spread them throughout the city to deal with any dissension."

"Good. Every symbol and icon of my siblings is to be torn down."

Endring looked up sharply, and Neveri's eyes locked with his. He felt his heart pounding. "You mean to tear down our history? Those are some of the most sacred-"

"Sacred?" Neveri spat the word. "False allegiance to gods who neutered the world. The past is dead and gone. There is only me now."

"And the restoration of balance? The guilding?"

Neveri straightened to his full height, his eyes fierce.

Endring looked away, his body quaking under the glance.

"We spoke of this, didn't we?"

"O-Often," he stammered.

"Of peace and restoration of balance. But tell me, my Champion, do they deserve it? Those who tore Talamh apart, who created the unguilded?"

Endring heard footsteps as Neveri rounded the table, and a firm hand grabbed his chin, fingers cold as ice and sharp as talons. He turned Endring's face up, dragging a finger from his free hand along the marred flesh.

"They have, all of them, turned their backs."

Endring trembled as he spoke dryly, "Not Bei'ai."

Neveri clenched his jaw, but he let Endring go and kept walking around the table as Endring slid gratefully back into his chair.

"True. My beloved twin sister. She alone gave me refuge. Did you know the others planned to destroy me? To wipe me from existence so I would not taint their perfect realm?" He placed his hands on the table and leaned over it like an executioner's axe. "But Bei'ai gave me a place to hide, to live among her lost ones in Nyx."

"But even she turned on you," Borroka said smugly. "She should rot with the rest of them."

He covered the distance to her in a moment and had her in the air by her throat, her feet dangling.

"Watch your tongue! She is still a god, still your better!"

He let her go and she slumped down into her seat, clutching her throat.

Neveri returned to his place at the table and leaned against it for a moment as if lost in thought.

Endring sat silent, breathless, waiting for him to speak, and yet dreading it.

"And the mara?" he said slowly, his voice dripping with threat. "Have you found them?"

"No," Borroka choked. "They weren't in the sanctum."

"The Mara?" Endring managed in a mere whisper. "The divine orbs are missing?"

"I have my men scouring the grounds," Borroka placated. "We'll find them."

Neveri gripped the edge of the table, his fingers dragging through it like iron and leaving gouges through its polished surface.

"What do we need them for?" Endring asked.

Neveri's voice came out like the low growl of a chimera. "To be free of them all. Of Sbarga, and Nyx, and my brothers and sisters. To break the chains they've used to bind this realm."

Endring felt pain rip through his chest. "You mean to sever us from the gods?"

Neveri raised his chin. "Yes."

"But that won't restore us," Endring exclaimed, his voice trembling. "It will only worsen the divide."

"Then let them taste the bitter wine they've forced the worlds to drink."

Endring shook his head. One out of nine unguilded would become eight. The oppressed would become the oppressors, and he would be the Champion of *this?*

He stared at Borroka. Her eyes were gleaming. This is what she wanted. To be above the rest, to make them suffer at her feet. He saw her brutality mirrored in Neveri, and he felt sick. She had been right all along.

"Rally the faithful," Neveri growled. "But above all bring me the mara. Soon all the worlds will worship one name, pray to one god, and the two of you shall sit beside me, one at my right hand, and the other at my left."

Endring held back the nausea that accosted him, swallowing down bile that crept up his throat. This wasn't what he wanted. This wasn't what he'd been promised. This was madness.

The streets of Tajerim seemed strange to Rasa. She had spent a good amount of time on Erimos, living on her own in sprawling towns with packed dirt roads and low stone buildings. But here wooden houses and shops towered over narrow brick streets. She started to feel lost as she meandered around corner after corner. She passed a few people making their way along the streets, always careful to stay away from them, but it was hard with such narrow paths. She needed a clearer view.

She spotted a low eave on the side of a shop. She steadied her pack and grabbed hold, pulling herself up as another group of people made their way toward her. She laid flat against the roof, waiting for them to pass, and then she kept climbing, higher and higher until she reached the top where a smooth stone chimney shot up overhead. She stood looking out at the city, a sea of roofs and chimneys with winding streets that all meandered toward the docks. She could see a statue of Kisandin near the port, and several ships bobbing on the water.

"That's better." She said as she took it all in.

If she could get the lay of the city, she'd feel more comfortable walking around. But to what end? Was this home now, or would she leave the city and head somewhere else?

She sat down on the edge of the roof, feeling alone. She slipped the pack off her back, setting Weylyn's bow and quiver aside as if they were made of glass. She couldn't bear the thought of scratching them. It occurred to her that she had never really owned anything, never had any sentimental attachments. Everything before wasn't hers, and when she became a Champion, nothing felt like hers. Showy clothes that were chosen for her, trinkets and wealth given to her. But it felt like they were given to someone else. A Champion. Not some ragged, broken girl.

She brushed a hand along the smooth wood of the bow. Even this wasn't hers. But maybe it was now. The other Champions were the closest thing Weylyn had to family, and Rasa wouldn't part with that now for anything. For the first time she had something in her life that meant something, because she had someone who meant something.

She pulled her pack open, stuffed with little more than some bread and hard cheese and an extra toga. But nestled inside was the wooden box, latched tight, that held Weylyn's ashes. She pulled it out, clutching the warm wood in her hands, and she hugged it close to her chest as tears dropped down to the roof.

"I wish you were here. I don't really know what to do now. You always knew what to do."

She brushed her hand across her face. "I've been alone my whole life - even when people were around - but it never bothered me. I don't want to be alone anymore. Gods, why does it bother me so much now? I should be used to it."

She heard a familiar voice intrude. *I hope you never get used to being alone again.*

"Weylyn!"

She turned to see her blue form smiling, and she stood up, setting the box down beside her. Before she had even realized what she'd done, she rushed at Weylyn, her boon swelling around her, and she fell into an embrace, weeping into her shoulder as Weylyn held her. They were alone, the black night of Nyx swallowing them up as they held each other. Weylyn was cold to the touch, different, but no less comforting.

You're not alone, Rasa.

"Weylyn," she blubbered. "I missed you."

It's alright.

She felt her boon wearing on her, and realized how much effort it was taking to be able to touch Weylyn, effort she didn't have to give right now. She held on a little longer, her body weak from lack of sleep and grief, and then she pulled away and let Talamh drift back in.

"How are you here?" Rasa asked. "Shouldn't you be in the Midding?"

Weylyn waved off her question. *The Midding was boring. Now, tell me what's happened?* Weylyn's eyes scanned the city below, the port and the ocean beyond. *Why are you here by yourself? Where are the others?*

Rasa sat down again, suddenly spent.

Take your time. Weylyn said.

"The others are gone."

Where?

She shrugged. "Home, I guess. They don't want to be Champions anymore."

Weylyn simply nodded as she took it all in.

"I didn't really have a home to go to, so I'm just here."

They left you alone?

She shook her head. "Burz wanted me to stay with him and his family, but it wasn't home."

Rasa looked up at Weylyn to see her looking out over the city. She looked distant.

"Are you okay, Weylyn?"

She fixed her eyes back on Rasa and smirked. *That's a strange thing to ask a dead person.*

Rasa smiled for a moment. "You look sad."

She shook her head. *Thoughtful, maybe, wishing I had done more. But not sad.* She reached toward Rasa, and she let her boon rush in for a moment as Weylyn tucked some stray hair behind her ear. *I have no regrets.*

"I'm glad you're here now."

Me too. Have you slept lately?

She shook her head, feeling exhaustion pressing all around her. So much had happened, she hadn't even thought to sleep, and she was afraid of the nightmares.

Do you have a place to sleep?

Rasa shrugged. "Here? It wouldn't be the first time I've slept on a roof."

I suppose it's not unlike sleeping in a tree. I've done that plenty. Get some rest. I'll watch over you.

"Won't you get tired?"

She smiled warmly. *I don't think the dead can be tired.*

Rasa laughed, and as her grief broke she felt every bit of the weariness of the last couple days. She tottered back to where the wide chimney was nestled by the flat top. She set her pack as a pillow and curled her back against the warm chimney stones as Weylyn sat down facing her. Watching over her. And she fell into a restful sleep, the first one she remembered having in a long time without nightmares.

When Rasa woke, the moon was up, and she was glad for the heat from the chimney. She was aware of voices nearby, a tense conversation in whispers. She sat up and glanced around for the source. And then she remembered Weylyn. She let her boon slip in, and Nyx pressed around her until she saw Weylyn standing nearby with another spirit, talking quietly. Weylyn was frowning deeply. She looked at the other spirit.

"Spark?"

Both women turned her direction, and Weylyn came close and knelt beside her. *Did we wake you?*

Rasa shook her head. "I don't think so."

Spark was watching them, looking troubled.

Did you sleep well? Weylyn asked.

"Yes. What's going on?"

Spark came closer, wringing her hands. *I came to find you.* She gave a nervous glance toward Weylyn. *I didn't know what else to do.*

"Is Locin okay?"

Spark's smile faded. *We haven't really been together since she left.*

"Why not? Are you two okay?"

It's not important right now. I've been speaking with some of the spirits. They say Neveri is searching the temple.

Weylyn tensed. *I told you, Spark, drop it. That's not Rasa's burden to bear.*

"For the tethers?" Rasa stood. "He can't find them."

Weylyn was frowning deeply. *Spark told me about what you did, hiding those. It was brave of you, but you already did your part.*

"Is he close to finding them, Spark?"

She drew her mouth in a tight, worried line, hesitating as she glanced at Weylyn again. *It's only a matter of time.* She turned to address Weylyn. *If there were anyone else, I would go to them.*

Rasa reached for her pack, cinching it up and slipping it on her shoulders. "Then I'll go back. I can get the tethers and take them out of the temple, find someplace safer."

Don't try this alone. You should tell the others, Weylyn said. *If anyone can convince them to help, it's you.*

Rasa shook her head. "They're all gone, Weylyn. There's no one but me."

You can not go in there alone! Weylyn looked at her with a terrified expression.

"Someone has to." Rasa did her best to straighten up and look like a champion, though she was feeling anything but. "We can't just give up."

Listen to me. I admire your bravery, but you need the others.

"I know," she said exasperated, her own fear magnified by Weylyn's. "But I don't have anyone to help me. They made their choices, Weylyn. I can't change that. You taught me to not be afraid, to do what's right. I'm going! But-" she looked at her pleadingly "-will you come with me?"

Weylyn heaved a sigh, her expression tense.

"If you don't want to-"

Of course I'll go with you, Rasa. I'm just still trying to think of a way to talk you out of it.

Rasa smiled with relief. "Well, you can't. So that's that."

I'll come too, Spark said. *But how will you get into Arrajin? The Pylat tether is crawling with cultists.*

"Then we'll take a boat. I'll stowaway. I've done it before."

Weylyn shook her head. *A boat it is then.*

Rasa let Nyx crash in around her, nearly swallowing her up as she rushed the two women, pulling them into an embrace. "Thank you."

She felt Weylyn's hand cradle her head. *I told you, Rasa, you won't be alone anymore. Ever.*

60: A Homestead, a Stowaway, and a Swath of Destruction

Burz crouched low, ready for anything his enemies could throw at him. He had his eyes keenly on the tree line, where the ambush would come from. Waiting. Watching. A rustle of leaves drew his attention, and he heard a barbaric call as Kyren and Orin came rushing from the trees, sticks in hand.

Burz matched their ferocity, charging at the younger boy. Burz took one whack from a stick, and then he scooped the boy up on his shoulders and started running.

He put an intimidating growl in his voice as he yelled. "Ha! I've caught your leader!" He could hear Orin yelling as he chased after him, Kyren giggling over his shoulder. He slowed down enough to feel the impact of Orin's stick, then he whirled around and swooped his free arm down, pulling Orin up to his chest as the boy yelled and dropped it. Soon they were all in the grass near the tree line, wrestling around until Burz groaned dramatically and gave up the fight.

Hadris called to them from the side of the house. Breakfast was ready. She stood in a simple toga of soft white, her hair twisted up as it often was on hot days.

In this moment he felt light. Happy. Some of the weariness of the previous weeks seemed to fall away from his shoulders. He stared for a minute, trying to drink it all in as the boys yanked him to his feet. The way Hadris' skin glistened in the sunlight, the sound of the boys' laughter, their home standing like it always had, quiet and content, far from the bustle of the temple.

"Alright," he said as the boys yanked his arms. "I'm up. I'm up!"

They made their way back up to the house, and Hadris sent the boys in to clean up. She was smiling, her lips a soft pink. He grabbed her and kissed her, feeling a rush through his body.

"I've been away too long."

Hadris was still smiling, but he knew her well enough to see the sadness in her eyes. He didn't care. Whatever it was, it could wait. He went to pull her in for another kiss, but she stopped him with a hand to his chest, and he dropped his head with a sigh.

"We should talk."

"Now?"

She steeled her expression. Hadris was nothing if not stubborn.

"Fine."

"I heard some news this morning at the market. Word is spreading about the temple and Nev-"

"Anything but this. Please."

She frowned. "You and I both know you can't just stay here. I want you to. Gods, I want you to. But-"

"But what?" He whispered. "But maybe we could restart? Maybe I could plant a garden this year, okra, arugula, maybe a big lime tree in the corner?"

He saw the same ache in her eyes that he felt in his heart. The dream of a life that could never be.

"Talamh needs its Champions."

Burz laughed harshly, running a hand over his head. "Talamh's Champions caused this."

"The world would have broken either way. Maybe it would have looked different, taken longer, I don't know." She sighed. "I talked to Gaelver."

"He was at market?"

She nodded. "He just came downriver. Cultists have been traveling out of Arrajin, sneaking into Tajerim. He thinks it's only a matter of time before they-"

The boys came spinning back around the corner.

"Come on!" Orin yelled. "I'm starving!"

"Me too," Burz said with a sidelong glance at Hadris. He wasn't having this conversation. Not now. "Let's eat."

The boys cheered and headed in, and Burz went to follow, but Hadris caught his arm, staring him down.

"Fine," he relented. "Just give me a few days, and I'll think of a plan."

"Burz, we might not have days."

"At least give me one day."

She held him fast, frowning. "So you can talk yourself out of it? You should start right away. Besides," she slipped her arms around his waist, "you can do your planning here. It's safe, out of the way."

"We could run?" But he knew he couldn't. He felt it. He would do the right thing again, no matter the cost.

"Where?" She said sadly. "If you don't stop him, where could we run?"

He wondered how long he'd have to keep giving. Until he was spent? Until there was nothing left? Why had Uthando called him, made this his burden to bear?

"Okay," he said at last. "I'll head out after breakfast, see if I can find Voske."

"Voske?" She looked surprised. No wonder. He'd made his feelings about the man clear.

Burz shook his head, but his mind wouldn't let go of the idea. "I can't do this without him."

She nodded as the boys yelled impatiently.

He drew her in for one last kiss, and his body ached for more. He didn't want to leave this again. He almost couldn't bear the thought of it. But she was right. Soon Tajerim wouldn't be safe. Soon nowhere in all the worlds would be safe, unless they stopped Neveri.

Rasa. Wake up.

The scent of river water filled Rasa's nostrils, and she became suddenly aware of the sound of oars, thunking against the side of the boat.

She'd stowed away on a merchant vessel, heading back toward Arrajin. It wasn't difficult. Only the most profiteering souls wanted to risk such a trip, and a skeleton crew manned the packed barge.

Her eyes peeked open letting in a sliver of light. "What time is it," she muttered.

Almost midday. Weylyn answered.

Her eyes fluttered open completely, revealing a bright patch of sky glinting through the small gap in the crates above her.

"Midday!" Rasa said with alarm. "We were supposed to arrive before dawn."

We were delayed. But that's not the problem.

Rasa eased upward and peeked over the boxes, taking in the outside world. The sailors were working the oars, steadily guiding the barge with a nudge here or a paddle there. The buildings of Arrajin rose up on either side of the boat, flooded and vacant, and they floated down the submerged path, gradually making their way toward the displaced tower of Jeza that sprouted from the water like a sea stack.

We passed the ports of Arrajin five minutes ago, Weylyn said.

"I thought we were stopping in Arrajin."

Spark showed herself now, sitting on top of the crates and staring toward the captain's cabin. *We were supposed to. The quartermaster must have lied.*

"Why would he do that?"

They could be smugglers.

"Smugglers?" Rasa said uneasily. She'd had some experience with smugglers in the past, none of it pleasant.

Spark shrugged. *Not sure why else they'd lie.*

They emerged from the edge of Arrajin into the upriver jungle. The low-lying land here had been thick with underbrush, but water off the Arrtris hadn't yet dried and it looked more like a dirty marsh. They followed the line of sludge until the right bank turned to a rocky shore on the far side of the God's Mount.

A call went up from the sailors and they steered to starboard, making for a small pier that jutted out over the sludge.

Rasa rose to her tip-toes and looked over the crates. There were a dozen cultists standing along the pier. The one in front looked to be in charge, and he picked at his teeth with a cruel dagger.

"Remember," the boat captain called to his crew. "Keep your eyes sharp and blades sharper. No offloading until we count the coin. Paolus doesn't want to take any chances with this lot."

A few minutes later the boat thunked against the pier and the sailors hastily tied it off.

Rasa sucked in a breath and shrank down behind the crates.

They're running supplies to the cultists. Spark said in disbelief.

Weylyn immediately crouched beside Rasa. *How well can you swim?*

"Swim? I don't know how to swim!"

Then grab your bow, Spark shouted.

Rasa quickly grabbed the bow off her shoulder and fumbled to snatch an arrow from the quiver, holding it to the string with trembling fingers.

Weylyn stared down at the bow then back at her with a deep frown.

I count fourteen on the dock, Spark called down, *and six sailors on the barge.*

"Twenty?" Rasa said with alarm. "How many arrows do I have?"

Weylyn placed a hand on her arm, and she felt her hair raise where her hand rested. *Put the bow away,* she soothed. *You're not fighting today.*

Rasa felt her heart pound as she realized what Weylyn meant. She'd been a captive for the first twelve years of her life, and the idea of being a captive again made her sick.

She looked down at the arrow and then back up to Weylyn. "I can't! I can't get taken. I don't want that again. Gods! Please not again."

Spark turned around and peered down from the crates above. *You have another idea?*

Rasa took an unsteady breath and looked down at the sharpened arrow in her hand. She doubted she could kill even one of the cultists, but if she fought them, then at least she might die. That would be better.

It won't be the same as last time, Weylyn said.

Rasa could hear the voice of the captain, close at hand, they'd be unloading in a matter of minutes. She clutched the arrow to her chest and looked upward. "What if it is?"

It won't be.

"How do you know?"

Weylyn grabbed her cheek, firmly but gently. *Because I'm with you.*

Rasa let the arrow fall from her hand and reached out for Weylyn, wrapping her arms around her, feeling a comforting warmth and the cold touch of a spirit all at once. They stayed, locked in an embrace until a sharp grating sounded from just beside Rasa.

She looked up to see an astonished sailor and a cultist standing side by side. The cultist pointed a finger at her. "Who's this?"

"I-I have no idea," stammered the sailor and he quickly drew a bronze sword from his hip. "Who in Nyx are you?"

Rasa felt her throat catch, but the arms of Weylyn steadied her, and she found her voice. "A stowaway," she answered.

"You picked the wrong barge, sweetheart," he waved his sword at her bow. "Drop it."

She let the bow fall to the deck.

"Now climb out of there. Easy does it. There, good. Have I seen you somewhere before?"

Rasa kept her hand in a tight fist and shook her head.

"You was trying to get to Arrajin weren't ya," he spat to the deck. "Rotten luck for you."

She nodded.

"Ah well. I've stowed away before. How in Nyx did you even fit in there?"

"She's flexible," the cultist said. He was leering at Rasa in a way that made her uncomfortable.

"Just run along out of here," the sailor said. "Go on."

Rasa glanced back at the crates. "Can I keep my bow?"

"I'll fetch it for ya," the sailor said before hopping over.

Rasa looked at Weylyn and Spark with wide eyes. They were both nodding enthusiastically.

"Here it is," the sailor said, handing her bow back to her. "You know, I can't help but think I've seen you somewhere before."

She shook her head, feeling a sudden optimism. "I don't think so."

The sailor furrowed his brow, then shrugged and waved for her to follow. "This way then."

He led her back toward the gangplank and the eyes of all twenty men followed her to the edge of the pier. She was almost free.

She felt her sandal make contact with the solid wood pier when a loud voice rang out.

"Wait!"

She turned to see the cultist leader approaching. He still had his long dagger, but now she could see that his teeth looked sharper than they should have been.

He walked until he was within arms reach and stopped, looking her over. "You're a rotting champion!"

Rasa, run!

She jerked away, but he already had hold of her arm with a vice-like grip. She spun her free hand around to scratch him, but he caught that wrist too and held her palm up, revealing the golden sigil of Bei'ai.

"Looks like you boys were carrying more than you knew!" He yelled.

Weylyn rushed forward, driving against the man with all her strength, pushing and striking him, but the man didn't seem to feel it. Rasa tried to jerk away but he bore down cruelly until she winced in pain.

"Lord Neveri'll be happy when he sees this."

Spark rushed forward now, helping Weylyn beat against the cultist, but he didn't waver. It wasn't enough. Rasa pulled on her boon until Nyx threatened to swallow her up.

"Help!" She screamed, but there was no one to help. Soon even Weylyn and Spark had stopped, staring at each other with worry.

The men laughed cruelly. "There's no one to help you, lass."

"We'll sell her to you," called the captain of the barge. "Twenty-thousand."

"Ha! I like your pluck floater, but you missed your chance."

"Here me out," the captain yelled back. "There's twenty men here. That's a thousand for each of us. You get the praise for returning a champion and pocket a few marks for your trouble. Every man here profits!"

There was a cheer at the prospect.

Rasa felt light-headed. She couldn't be sold again. She stared at Weylyn who still seemed to be desperately trying to think of a way out.

"No," Rasa squeaked. "Gods, no. Please!" Her knees gave out and she buckled to the ground. Her breath came and went in short pants.

The men laughed derisively. They weren't the type to have mercy.

She felt cold hands grab hold of her shoulders and she opened her eyes to see Weylyn crouched in front of her. *Hold on.* Weylyn said. *It's not over, Rasa. I'm here!*

Rasa nodded, desperate to retain control of her faculties.

"Sixty-thousand it is!" The cultist leader called back. "Any prize so worthy as a champion is worth at least that and the followers of Neveri pay their debts."

The other men were smiling wickedly.

"Done!" came the reply.

"Come on then, shrike." He jerked Rasa to her feet. "You'll be seeing a god soon. Hope you're ready!"

The cultist dragged her up a back path to the Gods' Mount, one that entered into the storehouses under the Oracles' wing. He carried her bow and quiver in one hand, and both her wrists wrapped in his other.

At first she pulled against his grasp, but before long she relented and began to walk in step, the way she had been taught. She could feel her old patterns at the edge of her thoughts, trying to convince her to comply. Resisting someone so much stronger wasn't virtuous, it was foolish, better to just comply and survive.

Rasa.

She looked at Weylyn and felt a surge of fight pump through her again. Weylyn wouldn't give up.

We'll find a way. You won't be here long.

"I know," she answered, though she didn't feel it. "I'm not giving up. Not this time."

"Shut it," the cultist snarled, and he jerked her nearly off her feet.

They kept walking until they reached the upper tier of the Oracles' wing. Here the massive dining hall of the Gods' Mount had been transformed into a makeshift throne room, and a throne of granite and grey-green velvet sat at the far end. Upon the throne was seated a man who appeared to be in his twenties. He looked nearly human, with his long black hair and piercing yellow eyes.

"My god," the cultist said as he entered. "My men and I have acquired a champion of the old ones! We agreed to pay her captors handsomely for this prize to the amount of-"

"Take whatever amount they want," Neveri answered. He leaned forward, studying her carefully from across the room, and somehow Rasa felt he could see her perfectly.

The cultist hesitated. "They've asked for a hundred thousand marks."

"Then take twice that," Neveri snapped. "And tell them it's a downpayment for the next champion they capture."

The cultist practically shook with vile excitement. "Y-Yes. Thank you!"

He rushed back out of the throne room, and Neveri stood smoothly to his feet, and she realized how monstrously tall he was. He crossed toward her. "Which of my *siblings-*" he said contemptuously "-do you serve?"

Rasa held up her palm, revealing the moon and stars of Bei'ai, and Neveri paused as though struck by the sight. "Everyone out of the room," he commanded.

His attendants quickly bowed their heads as they retreated into the hall.

Neveri licked his lips, pacing closer. "And did my sister send you here?"

Rasa shook her head.

Don't tell him anything. Spark cautioned. She walked to Neveri and paced a circle around him as though appraising him. *He's not that frightening in this form.*

"That's a shame," Neveri continued. "I thought perhaps she had begun to truly care for me." He stopped in front of her, and she could smell his breath, stale and putrid. "Of all my siblings, she was always my favorite. My dear, sweet twin. We played together, grew old together. And yet they turned on me. Even my sweet Bei'ai."

He grabbed Rasa's chin, pinching so tight that it ached, then jerked her head upward, staring down into her eyes. "Of course," he said. "I eventually came to realize it wasn't her fault. She couldn't stand in the way of our older siblings any more than I could, so she did the next best thing. She preserved my spirit in Nyx."

He let go of her chin and turned away. "How foolish of me to believe that she'd go as far as to aid my revenge. I suppose she is still as guilty as the others."

Rasa rubbed a pained hand across her chin. "I understand."

Neveri laughed, a deep, horrible laugh. "A mortal says they understand. What hubris!"

As though he knows nothing of hubris, Weylin said. *He's the one trying to shatter the realms.*

Neveri's eye twitched, and he turned back toward Rasa. "I wonder. How much has my sister been working against me? Has she told you of my plans?"

Rasa shook her head.

Don't say a word, Spark hissed. *He can't prove you know anything.*

"All I want is what's mine," he mused. "I want to see the worlds put back together with nine gods instead of eight. Would you deny me this?"

He's lying. Spark insisted. *He wants the orbs, just like Bei'ai said!*

Neveri suddenly whirled to the side and stared straight at Spark. "So, she is working against me."

Spark's eyes grew wide with panic.

He sneered at the spirit. "I didn't spend two thousand years in Nyx for nothing." Then he looked back at Rasa, and his fingers slowly sprouted outward, taking the form of sickle-like claws. "And now, you'll tell me everything else."

Burz stood in front of a worn down tavern. It hadn't been hard to track Voske. He'd left a swathe of destruction across every tavern and watering hole on the port side of Tajerim. Every place was the same - a hulking beast of a man came in drunk, left drunker, and smashed the place to bits.

The current tavern keeper was cowering around the corner of the building, staring helplessly at the closed front door as the sounds of crashing and roaring sporadically flooded the street.

"What about the guard?" Burz asked with a raised eyebrow.

"Yep," the trembling barkeep said. "Wend and Forz came by."

"Well?"

He pointed a shaky finger at the smashed front window. "Wend came out there, and Forz ran out the door."

Burz sighed.

The tavernkeep looked up at him hopefully.

"Don't suppose you want to come with me?"

The man's eyes went wide, and he shook his head vehemently.

Burz composed himself and started to head around the corner, but the barkeep grabbed his arm.

"Uh, try to save the white cups if it isn't too late." He looked sheepishly at Burz. "Wife's mother gave them to me. She comes by to check now and again."

Burz rolled his eyes and yanked his arm free.

He strolled to the front, and jolted as something smacked the door from inside and shattered. He took a deep breath and plunged in.

Drunk was an understatement. Voske was mindless, wild. He let out a loud roar as he lifted one of the two remaining bar stools and tossed it into the wall where it splintered into pieces. The place was destroyed, just like the last two taverns Burz had seen.

Voske lifted the last stool and turned toward the door. He stopped with the stool over his head as he spotted Burz. Slowly, recognition seemed to dawn on him, and his brow furrowed.

He dropped the stool to the floor. "You!" He growled.

He started toward Burz with a terrifying ferocity, but Burz ducked to the side, dancing easily out of his drunken grasp.

"Hold still, you rotting pool of mire!"

"Voske! It's me, Burz."

"I know who you are, you stupid-"

He tripped as he tried to spin to catch Burz, and he fell flat on his face. He stayed there, blood gushing from his nose where he had hit the hard floor.

Burz took his chance. He dove in close and called his boon, drawing out the effects of the alcohol as Voske tried to push himself off the floor. It seemed to be working, and Voske sighed, clutching his head.

"Better?" Burz asked, jumping back to safety as Voske sat up and leaned his back on the battered bar.

Voske groaned.

"Now can I deal with that?" Burz pointed to his bloodied face.

"Yeah."

He moved in close and used his boon again, healing up his nose, and taking the edge off the headache he must have had.

"A little more?" Voske asked, squinting.

Burz shook his head. "I think I'll leave some. Consider it a lesson." He sat down on the floor beside Voske.

"They call you to get me?"

"I came looking."

Voske looked at him incredulously. "Why in Nyx would you do that?"

"I've been asking myself the same thing."

Voske groaned as he leaned his head back and shut his eyes. "Haven't done that in a long time."

"Smashed multiple taverns to bits?"

Voske managed a weak laugh. "Gotten drunk. But yeah, I did some damage back then. Probably nothing this impressive."

"Champions don't do anything small."

Voske pushed himself to his feet with some great effort. "I guess not." He started shambling toward the door, but stopped as Burz spoke.

"We have to go back, Voske."

The big man's shoulders dropped. "Why in Nyx would we do that?"

"You know why."

He turned back to face Burz, and his gaze was angry. "I caused this, Burz! I'm the last person to fix it."

Burz stood to face him, folding his arms over his chest. "Is that really how you feel?"

"Do you know why I was a laborer? I was an architect, Burz, and a rotting good one! I had everything. And then one of my buildings collapsed." He heaved a sigh. "Do you know what it's like? Facing a grieving mother who just lost two sons? And the worst part was she didn't get justice." He held up the golden sigil of Jeza. "I'd been drinking. I was always drinking back then. But the court didn't care. All they cared about was how much money they got from the architect's guild." He stared at his palm for a while, drifting into his thoughts.

"So?"

"So I got justice for her. I begged Jeza to take my guilding away. I held my hand on that rotting stone for nine hours."

"Did she take it?"

"She changed it. I guess her idea of justice was sending me to Erimos to labor in a quarry."

"And was it justice?"

He shrugged. "Maybe not. I loved that quarry."

Burz laughed. He couldn't help it. "You wanted to be punished?"

Voske glared at him. "I deserved it."

"Did it occur to you that justice would have been you staying an architect, carrying the weight of your failure so you never let it happen again? You didn't want justice. You wanted to run."

Voske advanced on him instantly, standing face to face as he glowered down at Burz. "I'm no coward!"

Burz held his ground. "I didn't say you were. But maybe it's time to fix what you broke instead of running from it."

"I can't!" He bellowed, and for a moment Burz thought he was about to unleash a second round on the tavern, but his shoulders slumped, and he let the fire drain out of him as he dropped his gaze. "I can't."

"Maybe not. But maybe we can."

Voske looked up at him questioningly.

"I was so blinded by my own pride, I couldn't see it before," he admitted. "But together, we can win, Voske. We can stop Neveri. We can save Talamh."

"What are you saying, Burz?"

Burz held out a hand. "If you lead us, I'll follow you."

Voske's eyes went wide, but there was a hint of hope in them. "Just like that?"

"Just like that."

"And you have a plan to beat Neveri?"

Burz cleared his throat. "Still working on that one." He gestured with his hand again. "But if I can learn to fight alongside your stubborn butt, how hard could it be?"

Slowly Voske lifted his hand, and they locked forearms tightly. "Back to Arrajin?"

Burz clapped him on the arm and turned for the door.

"Are you sure you can't ease this headache a bit more though?"

"It's good for you. A lesson learned."

"And the taverns?"

"Three that I know of."

They stepped outside and the little barkeep looked relieved. He ran past as soon as Voske was clear of the door and rushed in. They heard the sounds of his wailing as they walked away, and Voske cringed.

"I'm going to need to pay for all this, aren't I?"

61: Captive

"Bless me Champion, chosen of Neveri. Bless my heart to not grow cold to the fight, and my feet to not stumble on the shifting path."

Endring looked down at the ruddy youth who knelt before him. His eyes were ringed with dark warpaint, his arms were tattooed with the fangs of a snake, and a blood-stained machete hung from his waist.

Endring reached out a gruff hand. He grabbed the youth's chin and raised his eyes to his own.

"I bless you," he said. "I bless you to lift up the downtrodden, and to go wash that muck off your face."

The youth's eyes widened. "But these are the eyes of Neveri. We rise from darkness."

"Of course you do," Endring answered. "But you don't bring the darkness with you. Now, wash!"

The youth looked at the rough hewn door behind him, a door tucked into the bowels of the temple. "Who will guard the prisoner?"

Endring squinted. So it was true, they had captured a champion. "I wish to speak to the prisoner. They won't escape before you return. Go get something to eat and refresh yourself."

The man bowed again. "The champion of Neveri is most gracious."

Endring huffed and shooed him away, then eased through into the poorly lit room. He quickly shifted his eyes to those of a cat and the darkness lit up. There were only three cells in the temple prison, if you could even call it a prison. Really, it was just a storage basement filled with boxes and trinkets and a few training weapons. The cells were typically used for monks who got too rowdy or drunk, and they were furnished with nothing more than a wooden table, and two buckets, one for water, one for waste, and it was best to not confuse the two.

"Hello," he hissed, gently sliding past a row of boxes. "Is anyone there?"

He heard a stirring from the far cell and walked to the wooden door, putting his eyes to the tiny window at the top.

He could see Rasa curled up within. She was stripped naked, and bloody gouges ran down her arms and legs. Her arms were wrapped around her knees and she shook violently from the cold. She was softly murmuring, as though she was talking to someone else, though he couldn't see anyone else in the room.

"Bei'ai," Endring choked. "Have mercy."

He quickly slipped the cloak from his back and pushed it through the door. It hit the ground with a light flop.

She looked up at the sound. Her eyes looked swollen. "Endring."

"Yes," he answered. "Are you alright?"

"We're alright."

He craned his neck, straining to see the corners of the room. "Who else is in there?"

Rasa edged forward and grabbed the cloak, then draped it over her shoulders. No doubt she was still freezing.

"How long have you been here?"

"A day."

"One day," Endring mused. She looked beyond wretched. If this was the aftermath of one day, he couldn't imagine what one week would look like. "Who did this to you?"

"Neveri."

Endring sickened at the name. His mouth went dry, and for a moment he didn't say anything at all.

"I'm sorry," he finally stammered. "Why?"

She walked closer and stared up at him, as though trying to make up her mind. "No," she said aloud. "I don't think it's a trick."

Endring squinted. Either she was going mad, or she was speaking with a spirit.

"Do you know what he wants," she asked, though she wasn't looking at him.

Endring shook his head vigorously. "No. From torturing you? No. God's no. This is… This is sadistic."

She nodded and it became apparent that she was barely able to stand.

"Has he said anything?" Endring inquired. "Asked anything of you?"

She cocked her head to the side. "I know," she said, still talking to the walls. "He's our only chance."

"Who is?"

"He wants the god's tethers. From the sanctum."

Endring shook his head in confusion. "The orbs? How could you possibly…"

"Bei'ai told me."

"Bei'ai told you," Endring muttered, still wondering if she was half mad. "Of course she did. Why wouldn't the goddess intervene?"

"You don't believe me?"

"Why not stop Neveri from coming out? Why not stop the champions from being murdered? Why now?"

Rasa convulsed and fell forward into the door, then slowly slid down to the ground, out of sight.

"Rasa!" Endring yelled. He slapped a hand against the thick wood. "Are you alright?"

"I'm here," came the weak reply.

Endring lowered his head into the door and stood in silence, then slowly sank downward and propped his back against it. He blinked back tears of rage. Neveri had gone too far. The destruction of the temple was unwarranted, the devastation of the city was egregious, but this? This was depraved.

He laughed, the eerie reverberating laugh of a madman.

"Endring?"

Endring, yes, that was the name, the name that would be forever accursed, the man who had destroyed the realm out of his best intentions. He slapped his hand across his face, then he slapped it again. He sprouted claws from his fingers, ready to tear apart the unmarked side of his face.

"Endring." Her voice was so weak.

"Yes?"

"You should take your cloak back."

He heard her scuffling within and he shook his head, though she couldn't see it. "No."

"If he finds me with it, he'll know it was you."

"Rot *him*." Endring growled. "I don't care what he thinks."

The scuffing stopped and for a moment everything went quiet. Endring hung his head low and twiddled his thumbs. How had it come to this?

"You can't help me if he knows," she said softly. He heard a faint scrape, and the cloak fell back through the slats. He picked it up. It was wet with her blood. For a moment, rage seethed, and he let his fingers slip into talons that tore at the bloody fabric. He took a breath, and his fingers were fingers again.

"Do you know where the orbs are," he finally asked.

"Don't ask me to tell you."

Endring shook his head. "But you haven't told him?"

"No."

"And how long do you think you can hold out?"

"As long as I need to. I'm not alone."

Endring raised an eyebrow. "Who's with you?"

"Weylyn."

"The Champion of Strah?"

"She was."

Endring finally understood her meaning and he felt his mouth go dry. That was more blood upon his own head. "Tell her I'm sorry."

"She heard you."

He nodded and stared back toward the door, he wondered when that plucky young guard was going to return, and slowly an idea began to take root in his mind. "I can't let you go," he whispered.

"I understand."

"He would kill us both, and you're hardly in condition to run." He felt his will coming to grips with the idea now, and he lowered his voice. "Tell me truthfully, Rasa. How long can you hold out?"

There was no answer for a moment, then a simple, "I can."

"Good," he answered, and he stood to his feet and dusted the dirt from his toga. "I will return for you. Do you understand me? I will return within days to secure your freedom."

There was still no answer, but he was confident she'd heard him.

"Very well then."

"Find Burz," came the sudden reply.

He leaned back in toward the door. "What was that?"

"Find Burz. He's in Tajerim."

Endring took a deep breath. He couldn't imagine Burz being glad to see him.

"He can help," Rasa insisted.

Endring placed his hand on the door one last time, as though she might feel the heat of his palm. "Very well," he said. "I'll find him, and we'll set you free together."

With that he turned and strode from the room, and in the back of his mind the gears began churning. If anyone had the power to stand against a god, it would be the champions, but it would take more than just he and Burz. It would take all of them.

Lower Tajerim was a dirty place full of grimy dockworkers, unguilded laborers, and smelly fish markets. Its rough brick streets ran past rows and rows of tightly packed homes and shops. But Upper Tajerim was a whole different world. Sprawling estates and guild halls sat on smooth stone courtyards with vibrant trees and flowering gardens in earthy beds. Upper Tajerim was where you came to steal.

Locin peeked around a corner, eyeing the miner's guild hall, an elaborate stone building with a glass domed awning set with glittering gems. She strolled closer, looking down the street like she was looking for someone or something. Then she lifted a gloved hand and pulled on her boon. She fixed her gaze on a gem out of the corner of her eye and tugged very lightly. It wiggled in its setting.

She smiled. She could do this. She would come back after dark and strip every last one of them from their glass prison. That should be just the kind of antic to draw the thieves' guild's attention.

There was one here. Every city as big as Tajerim had a thieves' guild. She'd never been here before, but she'd heard about a heist or two they'd pulled off. Truth be told, she wasn't sure why she wanted to find them. She wasn't planning on sticking around that long, and she could do just fine on her own. Turned out her new boon was pretty handy for her old life.

But she was lonely, and the thieves were the closest thing to family she had. She missed Spark terribly. Sending her away hadn't even helped. She still felt Nyx hounding her everywhere she went -

as she fell asleep overwhelmed by the sensation of being swallowed by the cold dark, or when a cool mist blew and she swore she saw a blue haze lingering in its wispy tendrils.

She turned her attention back to the gems, trying to calculate the worth of them all, as she casually strolled down the street. She felt a disapproving pinch.

"Shut it, Spark." And then it hit her. "Spark!"

She felt it again, the black of Nyx, but it was going to be there no matter what she did. She turned toward Spark and let the dark envelop her as she saw the girl take shape. It was a strange sensation. Locin stood in the middle of Upper Tajerim on a late afternoon, and yet she felt a chill and the press of another realm against her skin.

I know you wanted me to go, Spark said. *But I wouldn't bother you if I didn't have a good reason.*

It was a great relief to have Spark back, but she couldn't show it. She wasn't sure why, but she just couldn't, so she simply shrugged. "Whatever. I'm glad you're here."

Spark smiled. *Me too.*

"Okay, so you see that miner's guild? Gaudy, I know, but hear me out-"

Locin. Her tone was serious.

Locin frowned. "Gods, Spark. Why can't we just have fun? Why is everything always serious?"

It's Rasa.

"What's Rasa?"

Rasa is in trouble. I came here to ask for help.

Something like guilt grabbed hold of her, twisting her stomach uncomfortably. "And here I thought you came for me."

I am glad to see you, Locin. Really.

She wasn't in the mood for this. She was free, and she intended to stay that way. "I'm not a Champion anymore, Spark. If I could rub this rotting mark off my hand, I'd do it!"

She needs help, Locin.

"Then go find someone to help her." She started down the street, but Spark walked along beside her, keeping pace. "I don't care!"

Yes you do. I know you better than anyone, Locin. You miss them.

"I don't!"

You've run from everyone your whole life. And for what? So you can be miserable and alone? They were kind to you, much kinder than anyone else ever was.

"I liked you better when I couldn't hear you," Locin muttered.

They were your family, and you betrayed them.

Locin picked up a rock from the street and threw it as hard as she could at the blue form of Spark. "Shut up!"

The stone clattered against the wall of a shop and fell to the ground. As it stopped, silence fell and the only thing Locin heard was her own haggard breathing.

After a moment, Spark started again, but her voice was different now, harder. *Rasa is in trouble. Neveri has her. She would give her life to save you. If you don't care about that, you don't deserve a family.*

Locin watched as she disappeared back into Nyx. She could feel Spark slipping away again until her presence was nowhere to be found.

"You're wrong!" She yelled to the empty space where Spark had been. "Rotting, worthless spirit! Wrong!"

She picked up another rock and threw it as hard as she could at the shop wall. Then she felt her anger start slipping away, just like Spark had, leaving behind the empty dread of Nyx. It ate at her from inside as she glanced around the street. A few random passersby were staring at her like she was mad, winding their way to the far side of the street. Who cared what they thought? Who cared what anyone thought? She didn't need a family, and she never had.

62: Rally

If there was one virtue that Voske had always known he lacked, it was patience. Didn't have a complete plan in place? Wing it. Didn't find a festival to your liking? Leave. Didn't have enough men for the job? Do it yourself.

So when Burz told him the retaking of the temple was 'going to take months', it didn't sit too well with him.

The two men were huddled around the table in Burz' home looking over maps of the three worlds and any other soldiery documents Burz had managed to scrounge up. Most of the marks on the maps were foreign to Voske, and it didn't help that he had a head splitting hangover from the night before.

He pressed a damp towel against his forehead and gritted his teeth as Burz motioned to the city states around Arrajin and prattled on about the commanders stationed at each one.

"Vorashe is cautious," Burz said, tapping on a city named Rausk. "He doesn't like to commit to any plan that has what he calls a 'propensity for failure'. He's smart though. If we play our cards right he may come around."

Voske pushed the wet rag down harder. "How many troops?"

"Rausk has a garrison of two-thousand. How many would he let us use?" Burz waved a hand side-to-side. "Debatable."

"So let me get this straight," Voske said, moving his finger around the map, "so far you've said these are 'debatable', 'unlikely', and what was this one again? 'Too pitiful to make a difference'?"

Burz leaned back from the table and folded his hands behind his head. "I'm trying to be realistic."

"We're the champions," Voske protested.

"And five days ago that meant something, but word of Neveri is spreading like wild-fire. No commander is going to happily send his men into a death trap."

Voske took a deep breath and stared back at the miserable little maps and charts. This was why he'd become a quarryman, less talking and more doing.

"What about here in Tajerim?" He finally asked.

Burz gave him a wary glance. "Not an option."

"Why not?"

Before Burz could answer, a rap on the door interrupted their strategy session, and he headed to answer. Voske leaned back in his chair and started drumming his fingers on the table as he poured over the map.

"What about uh… Parlend," he called back over his shoulder.

He looked back to see Burz, frozen in the doorframe. "Burz?"

He slid his chair away from the table with a grating screech, and sauntered to the open door. Endring was there, standing alongside Sammel. There were dark rings under Endring's eyes and both men were breathing hard.

Voske felt his blood boil.

"Voske," Endring said as they locked eyes.

He quickly stepped to Burz' side and bared his teeth. "Endring."

"We didn't come here for trouble," Endring said.

Voske exchanged a glance with Burz, who looked just as confused as he was.

"Why *did* you come here?" Burz asked.

"For your help."

Voske's jaw tightened. "Our help? Like we helped you in the Sacred Quarter? Or maybe this is more like the lighthouse? Or, I don't know, how we all worked together at the temple?" He reached out a burly hand and seized Endring by the neck, then hoisted him off the ground.

He looked frightened, but he didn't resist the motion. "Voske," he wheezed. "I know you're angry."

Voske laughed in response. "This? This is mercy, Endring. Be grateful you weren't here last night."

Sammel uncoiled his whip but stopped at a motion from Endring.

"You might want your friend to help," Voske snarled. "You're not going to last long otherwise."

Endring tried to speak, but he was barely able to gasp for air. Sammel was tense, but held perfectly still.

"Let's hear him out," Burz said.

"You've got to be kidding me!"

"I'm not saying you have to let him go," Burz said. "Just let him speak. He wouldn't have come here if he wasn't desperate."

Voske frowned at the comment. Burz wasn't wrong, but it was painful to admit it. He let up the pressure on Endring's neck ever so slightly.

"I'm not here for me," Endring wheezed.

"Then tell us what you *are* here for."

"Rasa."

"She's not here."

"I know," Endring panted. "She's at the Gods' Mount."

Voske released his grip, and Endring fell to his knees, gasping for air. "What did you say?"

"I said, Rasa is at the Gods' Mount."

"Why would she be there?" he stammered.

"She was trying to stop Neveri."

"*Our* Rasa?"

Endring nodded.

"You're full of mire." He looked up at Burz, but his eyes looked clouded by the news. "Burz," he called. "Tell me you're not buying this."

Burz cocked his head to the side and shrugged. "She did seem different when she left."

"Different how?"

"More confident. Resigned maybe."

"Nonsense," Voske shook his head in disbelief. "This is just another setup. That's all this is."

"Then how did I get these?"

Endring reached to his back and handed Voske a wrapped bundle. He pulled it open to see Weylyn's bow, quiver, and pack. It was unmistakable.

"She's been captured," Endring said.

Voske felt sick as he handed the bow over to Burz.

Burz looked up sharply. "Is she well?"

"No," Endring answered. "Neveri hasn't been kind."

Voske felt a surge of anger. "If that godless pool of mire so much as touches her…"

"I'm afraid it's too late for that," Endring said. "But it's not too late for her."

"Where is she being held," Burz asked, looking up from the bow.

"In a cell below the temple."

"We'll need some assurances," Burz said.

"And you're right to insist."

"We need to know everything. Where they have guards stationed, where Neveri eats, where he sleeps, times, armaments, everything you can tell us."

"Done."

The four men all looked at one another, as though no one was sure what their next step should be.

"One more thing," Endring said. "We'll need all the help we can get. Where are the other champions?"

Voske felt a twinge of guilt. It was probably his fault that they scattered.

"Close by," Burz answered. "I don't know that anyone has left Tajerim yet."

Sammel raised a finger. "The Champion of Bei'ai left."

"Fine," Burz agreed. "Rasa, but hopefully no one else."

"And where are they?" Endring asked.

Voske nodded. "I'll round them up. How hard can they be to find?"

"All of them?" Burz asked dubiously.

He didn't need to say 'Locin'. They exchanged a glance that said it all. Burz didn't trust her. He didn't want her around. But something in his glance told Voske he'd defer to him.

"All of them," he said, and he swallowed hard.

Burz nodded.

"I can help," Sammel said. "I have some understanding of the Champion of Metnadur. I believe I can find him."

"Fine," Voske said, and then he looked at Burz. "And what will you be doing?"

"Getting us an army."

"Tajerim? I thought you said they weren't an option."

He shrugged. "We're desperate."

"Fine. Let's get this done. Rasa's counting on us."

Burz nodded, and Voske wasted no time heading for the door. Of all the champions to find, he had a good idea that Illeri would still be with the Phoenix. And how hard could it be to find a chariot?

Hikari held light in letters along the hull of the Phoenix, feeling his boon heating his fingertips. He watched Illeri as she traced each letter with care with a simple paint brush until the word 'Phoenix' was emblazoned across the chariot.

She pursed her lips. "Is it crooked? I think it's a little crooked."

"Nonsense, darling!" Hikari took a step back and his sandal sank in a patch of slimy mud. He sighed as an oink drew his attention to the pig watching him. "Remind Yzod that I was willing to negotiate the marks to stay at the tether."

Yzod leaned out over the chariot's deck, taking in the fresh paint. "This is more discreet."

"And more smelly." Hikari pouted.

"It's not forever," Illeri assured him. "Just until we can find a shop, someplace permanent."

They fell into an awkward silence as all three exchanged glances. Up until now, Hikari thought he'd been alone in his feelings of discomfort. But apparently they shared his concerns. They couldn't stay here. Neveri already had a growing foothold in Tajerim. Where could they go beyond this new god's reach?

The pig beside him snorted, and Hikari looked at it, flustered. "Well, permanent is a relative word. Perhaps we can find another city? Suntara maybe? It is quite lovely."

"So was Arrajin," Yzod murmured.

The words stung, but he wasn't wrong. The most storied city in the whole of Talamh, and it had fallen under their watch. Hikari tried to push the sobering thoughts away. There was nothing they could do about it now.

"I hope most of the people got out," Illeri said.

"Plenty did," Yzod answered. "Just walk down the street. Tajerim is stuffed to the gills."

"I know, but how many got left behind?"

Hikari thought about plugging his fingers in his ears, but that sounded rude at best, instead he stared at the Phoenix and tried to distract himself. The little chariot was endearing enough, but it lacked the impression that the temple chariots left, just a common thing really. Unremarkable.

He could hear Illeri and Yzod still commiserating and he hunched his shoulders, as though it would help block out the sound. Wings, that's what it needed.

"Wings," he said aloud, bringing their conversation to a halt.

"What?"

"It needs wings. Something in gold perhaps?"

"Like an actual phoenix?"

"Why not?" He smiled abashedly. "Wings could help."

Illeri frowned. "We need to keep things practical."

"Why's that, exactly?" He folded his arms, looking hurt. "When everyone's down and out, that's exactly when you need to be impractical, larger than life."

"What for? So you can impress everybody?"

"No, darling. You misunderstand. Wings are more than just a status symbol. Wings are freedom. They're like a well tailored toga. You don't look good to draw everyone's eyes to you. You look good to elevate everyone else."

"That doesn't make any sense."

He smiled. "Just trust me. Wings, that's what we need."

Illeri sighed. "We need a safe place."

"No place is safe with Neveri on the loose," Yzod said. "We need someone to stop that monster."

"Then let's stop him," A gruff voice said.

Hikari looked at the pig for a second, bewildered, until he noticed Voske strolling up. "Voske!" He smiled widely.

Voske wrinkled his nose as he stepped past a couple sow's wallowing in a mud puddle. "Something wrong with the tether?"

"Well, this was considerably cheaper, darling. Meaning free."

Yzod nodded. "And they've been feeding us for free. Have you ever had fresh bacon?"

The pig grunted one last time and waddled toward the sows.

Voske smiled. "Well, if you lot are so content, I don't suppose you'll be interested in what I have to say."

Illeri straightened up, inadvertently wiping some paint across her cheek. "What is it?"

"We're going back," his voice grew solemn. "Rasa's in trouble."

"In Arrajin?"

He nodded. "We're going to get her, and to knock that rotting god off his throne."

Hikari felt a surge within him and he glanced at Illeri and Yzod. He could see the same eagerness in their eyes. Running was no way to live.

"So," Voske said. "You in?"

They all exchanged a glance, but there was no hesitation in any of them.

"I'd like another hour," Yzod said. "We have a couple things to finish here."

Voske nodded. "You'll have that and more. We're still rounding up the others."

Hikari felt joy bubbling up inside. "Others?" He couldn't contain a smile.

"That's right. We're going back. All of us."

Burz stood in front of the warrior's guild of Tajerim. It was a square building made of plain, gray stone. A wide portico extended out in front, held up by thick round pillars, and from the top, red and copper banners flew the colors of their gods. He stared at those banners as the wind pulled and twisted them, finally spreading them out again in all their majesty. This place had been home to him for most of his life. He grew up here in the guild barracks, he trained in the dusty courtyard, and he served in the cobbled streets.

He let a hand drift unconsciously to his shoulder, to a raised scar that ran down his back, and he wondered if this was the right call. These men were loyal to the corrupt Archon, despising what was right in favor of what they were commanded. Could he even trust them? Did he even have a choice?

He set his jaw and headed in. He was greeted by the entrance hall, a high vaulted room filled with the history of the guild. He knew it well, from the old suits of armor and the weapons hanging with honor to the trophies and medals the guild had earned. And on the back wall, prominently displayed, the seals of their gods - Jeza and Uthando. But it wasn't as he remembered. The large seal of Jeza hung there alone in polished brass, and beside it an empty circle of stone wall, darker than the area around it. Burz threw back his hood as he made his way over, letting his palm rest on the smooth, cold stone where Uthando's sigil had been.

"What have they done?"

He heard footsteps coming down the hall, and he turned to see two soldiers in full armor coming out from a side passage. They started as they saw him, and his eyes locked on one that he recognized.

"Jepa."

A flash of memory overtook him and he could see Jepa's face, grimacing as he lifted his hand to strike.

Jepa's eyes were wide. "C-Captain?"

"Who is he?" The other soldier asked. He was young, Suntaran by the look of him. Likely a recent transfer.

Burz held his right palm up for the boy to see the golden sigil of Uthando.

His eyes went wide, and his face grew pale. "Gods and Chosen! A champion?"

Burz pointed to the empty space on the wall where Uthando's sigil should have been. "When did he do this?"

Jepa shook his head. "I'm not sure you should be here. Just because you're a champion-"

"When?"

He sighed. "Right after we heard you were chosen."

Burz tensed, but he tried not to show it. "Where is he?"

"It won't do any good."

He took a few quick steps toward him, and Jepa stepped back, his hand falling to the hilt of his sword.

"I'm not angry. I don't care about revenge. You know me better than that. At least I thought you did."

"Then why are you here?"

"Because I need help."

Jepa stood dumbfounded. "From him?"

Burz looked at the two men. Despite their leadership, they were soldiers. They were capable. And with any luck, they felt some obligation to the gods. "From all of you."

The new recruit cleared his throat. "I'll meet you in the courtyard, Jepa." He scurried off down the hall.

"The courtyard?" Burz asked.

Jepa nodded. "He called us all out for a meeting."

"Well, let's go then. We don't want to be late."

Jepa stared defiantly for a moment, but he knew it was pointless. Burz knew his way to the courtyard as well as the next soldier. He reluctantly started down the passageway, looking crestfallen. "Is it as bad as they say?" He asked in a hushed tone. "The temple is gone, and the gods have abandoned us?"

"Look at your palm," Burz said. And he did. The warrior's seal was seared against his skin, the sword and the yarrow. "Does it look like they've abandoned us?"

"But the temple fell. And the Champions-" he looked at Burz hesitantly. "I only mean, it doesn't look good from the outside."

"Do they all feel like you?" Burz nodded toward the door to the courtyard ahead. "The men. Are they loyal to the eight or the politicians?"

Jepa shrugged. "What do you want me to say, Captain? It's Tajerim."

"So it is."

"If it helps," he added. "We're all pretty fed up with the politics. They've been getting worse, especially since you…" His voice fizzled into a despondent mutter.

Burz paused with his hand on the door. There was a heavy air of regret about the soldier, one that Burz had often fantasized about.

"It's past."

"I just thought you should know, I didn't want to do it."

Burz clenched his hand around the handle tightly.

"None of us did. We just… we felt like we didn't have a choice."

Burz nodded tensely. "It's in the past, Jepa."

"Still, for what it's worth… I'm sorry."

He bit down the brief flash of anger that tried to swell in him. He had let it go. He wanted to tell Jepa he forgave him, that everything was well, but he only managed a curt nod before pushing the door open and heading into the courtyard.

Every soldier of Tajerim who wasn't out on patrol was there, filling out the large, dusty meeting ground. Some wore their soldier's garb, while others were dressed in light togas or tunics. He recognized far too many of them. His eyes locked on a young boy around Orin's age, wearing some simple padded armor and a small tabard with the colors of Tajerim. A practice sword swung from his side and he looked about with wide eyes and a nervous smile.

Burz pulled his eyes away from the boy and toward the center of the courtyard. His old guild master, Farad was there, standing in a large circle of sand and surrounded by his soldiers.

"It's chaos," Farad exclaimed, stamping his foot on the storied ground. "And your job is to quell that chaos. We're upping our patrols, rounding up dissidents. Terrik has the new rotation posted."

As Burz stared at the man's weathered face and white hair, he realized he'd balled his fists for a fight. Could he really do this?

"What about the Archon?" Asked one of the soldiers. "Are the rumors true?"

Farad frowned. "Yes."

A murmur went through the room, and Burz leaned over to Jepa. "What happened to the Archon?"

Jepa's face twisted like he didn't want to speak, but he sighed and said, "Murdered."

"For now the council of elders has assumed control," the old man continued vehemently. "But they stand with the Archon's wishes. Tajerim *will* extend peace and friendship to this new god."

Burz sucked in a breath. Just how rotten had the soul of Tajerim become?

"After what he did to Arrajin?" Shouted a shaky voice.

Farad turned toward the young soldier with fiery eyes. "Neveri is a god! He is coming to Tajerim, and soon. Would you have our city burn before his wrath?"

The soldiers grew quiet, muttering among themselves, but Burz could sense the discontent. More politics. More corruption. A vengeful god crawling out of Nyx and they were expected to just follow along without question?

"We will round up any and all opposition. The ones who are fleeing can go, but the ones stirring up trouble-"

"Enough!" Burz began pushing his way through the crowd as Farad searched angrily for the source of the interruption. Most of the soldiers gasped and whispered with recognition as Burz made his way forward.

Farad's eyes finally landed on him as he stepped into the center of the yard, and his mouth twisted into a malicious sneer. "You? What are you doing here?"

Burz held up his hand to reveal his sigil. The newer soldiers gasped as one at the recognition that a champion was in their midst.

Farad glowered. "So I heard. But you are no longer a soldier of Tajerim, and are no longer welcome here!"

"Neither is my god, it would seem." Burz quickly turned to face the men, refusing to let his leg so much as wobble as he stood beside their leader. "And how long until you strike Jeza's seal from your wall?"

"Those gods turned their backs on us!" Farad countered. "Their temple has fallen."

"Their champions stand!"

Another murmur ran through the soldiers.

Burz turned his attention to the men now. "Tell me, will you turn your backs on your gods?"

"No," Jepa yelled in response. "We serve the gods!"

"Good," Burz answered. "Because the champions of the gods call for your aid!"

Silence answered his cry, and Farad laughed derisively. "Your gods have abandoned you, Burz. Just as they abandoned you when you were a soldier. The old ways are over."

Burz turned on Farad fiercely. "The old ways of mercy?"

"Mercy is for women. We are soldiers!"

"You are fools!" Burz turned his back to Farad, walking the slow circle and making eye contact with as many of the soldiers as he could. They were troubled, unsure. He needed to tip them over the edge. "I've seen your new god. Black as night, with horns of bone rising like spikes from his arms and legs. He's larger than the towers of Tajerim! I watched him rip apart the temple, and pull the spire of Jeza out of the ground. He devastated Arrajin, drowned the city. Do you think he won't do the same here? He'll tear Tajerim apart until your buildings crumble and your bodies drown in the sea!"

"Arrajin defied him!" Farad yelled. "We won't make the same mistake."

"So you cower in fear?"

Farad stepped toward him, furious. "Never! A wise man knows when a battle is futile. A living, breathing god walks the worlds again. It's folly to resist!"

Burz turned his back on Farad again, locking eyes with the soldiers. "Perhaps it is. Maybe it's a fight we can't win. Would you sell your souls, then? Serve this monster to protect your own lives? Tell me," he said, and he could see the uncertainty in their eyes, "do you live only for your comfort and safety, or is there something more, some ideal you aspire to? Truth? Justice? Mercy? Would you lay down your lives to protect Talamh?"

The men slowly leaned in. There was no more shuffling, no more murmuring, just an inscrutable silence that hung over the gathering.

"We will keep our lives, *and* protect Tajerim!" Farad howled. "We will serve as the sword of Neveri!"

"And which weapon is more honorable, a sword or a shield? And which warrior is more valiant, the man who attacks and can fall back, or the man who stands before his home with nowhere to run? When you come to that place, and I pray you never find yourselves there, all you can do-"

"You left this order a disgrace! And now you really expect to come back and pollute our minds with your weakness?" He stared at Burz with a haughty gaze. "Men, throw this so-called Champion into the stocks. He can await judgment from the new god of Tajerim."

Burz straightened up, prepared to be led away, but none of the soldiers moved. They all stared at him expectantly.

"That was a command!" Farad screeched. "Now!"

Jepa stepped forward and locked eyes on Burz. "All you can do is what, Captain?"

Burz took a deep breath feeling pride well in him. They were still honorable men. "When you've done all you can to protect the people you love, all you can do is offer your body as a shield. The Champion of Jeza and I are marshaling an army. I won't pretend that we have good odds of beating Neveri, but we're going nonetheless. We will fight and die as men of Talamh, and I beseech every one of you to fight with us, bleed with us, die with us, and uphold your sacred honor."

Silence again reigned until Jepa walked into the center, and stood face-to-face with Burz. He extended his arm and they locked wrists.

"No justice without mercy," Jepa said.

Burz smiled. "No mercy without justice."

Jepa turned and drew his sword from its sheath, raising it high over the gathering. "Fight!" He yelled.

"Bleed!" came the unified cry.

"Die!"

Burz drew his sword alongside a hundred other blades, all pointed to the sky, as the cry rose over the barracks.

"Fight, bleed, die! Fight, bleed, die!"

The men slowly paced into the center, crowding around Burz until their swords became a phalanx, and still shouting the anthem in one voice.

"Fight, bleed, die! Fight, bleed, die!"

"For Talamh!" Burz roared, and the anthem dissolved into a wild cheer that sent tremors through the ground. Tremors that, Burz thought, must be felt all the way to the Gods' Mount, to the throne of Neveri himself, for the men of Tajerim were coming.

Zengin was good. Sammel had tracked over a dozen people down in cities Tajerim's size. It had never taken long, but he'd been hunting Zengin for almost three hours and hadn't even found his first clue. He was strolling through a crowd of refugees that clogged the streets, and he wondered how much worse it would get before Tajerim burst at the seams like an overstuffed tunic.

The sun was drifting lazily toward the horizon, and sweat beaded his brow and trickled down his neck behind his ears. It didn't bother him much anymore, but he took note of it, nonetheless. He had his eyes on the crowd, scanning faces. He'd given two dozen marks to clameyes and urchins thus far, and gotten nothing but bad leads, but he was far from ready to give up. He ducked around a corner into a relatively quiet street near the temple of Kissandin. The temple was defaced, the statue of Kisandin draped with animal furs and smeared with paint. Most of the refugees were staying near the docks and the tether, begging for passage out of the region, maybe off Las all together, but it was clear Neveri's influence was spreading. Soon, no world would be free of him. Just as he wanted. Zengin had been right to fuel Sammel's doubts.

Movement from behind caught Sammel's eye, and he reached for his whip, but it was snatched away before he could get a grip on it. A man in a black cloak and hood stood with it uncoiled, ready to strike.

"Stop!"

The honey of Metnadur hit Sammel like a wall, locking his muscles in place.

"Hmm," he said, feeling the strain of his resistance. "I've been looking for you, Zengin."

"Oh? Borroka send you for my other hand?"

"I don't follow her, nor Neveri."

Zengin scoffed. "And Endring?"

"He's broken from them both as well."

"If only you'd listened to me sooner. If only any of you had." Zengin took the whip and tossed it gently to Sammel.

Sammel grabbed it and started coiling it again. "I heard about your father. My condolences."

"Save them for someone else," Zengin said coldly. "I assure you, no one in this city mourns him."

He carefully set the whip back in its place at his hip, but he still felt Zengin's words holding him. "Let me go."

"Fine." The honey broke, and his muscles relaxed. "Perhaps you can help me," Zengin mused.

"What do you want?" Sammel asked.

Zengin pulled his hood back and studied him. "I assume you still know a decent amount about Neveri and Borroka and their plans."

"We've already told all of that to Burz."

This seemed to catch Zengin off guard, though he barely showed it. "Did you? And why was Burz asking?"

"We needed help."

Zengin scoffed. "So you released an angry three-thousand year old god from Nyx, and it's not working out how you'd hoped?"

"No."

"What baffles me is how any of you believed it would."

"Endring wanted to believe," Sammel said. "Hope is a powerful drug, even when it's false."

"And what about you, Sammel? Why did you believe? Was it all truly some ridiculous sense of loyalty?"

"I suppose I wanted to believe too."

Zengin stared at Sammel with glassy eyes but he didn't look sorrowful, only distant. "And what does Endring want now?"

"To stop Neveri."

Zengin stared at him placidly.

Sammel tried again. "I'm sure you've realized the peril your city is in. When Neveri moves on from Arrajin, this is the first place he'll come."

"Good riddance."

"You don't care for this place?"

"Most definitely not," Zengin said. "You can send Endring my condolences. He's lost more than I have in the last week."

"We could still use your help," Sammel said.

"And I could use yours. Where is Borroka?"

The honey of Metnadur slammed into Sammel's mind again, wrenching the truth from him, but he didn't resist. "With Neveri, on the Gods' Mount."

"Does she plan to leave?"

"Not as far as I know. If you want to strike her, you'll have to do it there." Sammel's hand drifted to the whip on its own as Zengin's boon held his mind in an iron grip. "And what about us? Will you help us?"

"Help you? After all this?"

Sammel shook his head. "Rasa wasn't responsible for any of this."

In an instant, the hold of Zengin's boon broke again. Was it real concern Sammel saw in Zengin's eyes for a passing moment?

"She's being held by Neveri," Sammel continued. "She's in great danger."

But Zengin quickly recovered. "I don't see how that's my problem."

"Maybe I misjudged."

"Maybe you did. I suppose the illustrious champions are mounting a rescue of some sort?"

"Something like that."

He laughed. "Idiots."

Sammel stayed tense as he shifted to face Zengin more fully, but Zengin merely gave him a sidelong glance. "He's torturing her for information," he said, "or perhaps for sport. If he's left to have his way, she won't survive the week, especially if he gives her over to Borroka."

Zengin's face twisted into an angry sneer that made Sammel take a step back.

"Tell Endring I'll help," Zengin said, "but only on one condition."

"Name it."

"I kill Borroka."

Locin hunched over a rough wooden box, emptying the contents of her stomach for the third time. She shifted, and her foot bumped an empty bottle that rolled a little ways across the cobbled street, clinking loudly.

"Rotting liquor."

She felt her stomach wrench again, and she retched into the box.

It was night, pitch black, and she had stumbled into some gods forsaken corner of Tajerim where the alleys smelled like rotting fish. Or maybe that was just the vomit. Either way, she was alone. Even Spark hadn't come back, and the stillness seemed to be closing in on her like the mist.

She repositioned, trying to get comfortable with her back against a rough stone wall. She was angry, at everyone, at no one, at herself. She threw her head back and smacked it against the stone.

"Rot it!"

The darkness seemed darker. Were there clouds overhead, or was it Nyx hovering over her soul, claiming ownership? Either way it sent a shiver up her spine, and she pulled her knees up to her chest. A million scenarios played out in her mind. What if she hadn't helped Endring? What if she'd never become a champion at all? What if she'd gone home after her choosing and never become a thief?

But what was the point of those thoughts? What was the point of anything anymore? She would be alone forever, not dead, not quite alive.

A light in the mist caught her attention, and at first she thought it might be Spark. It was little more than a flicker, or a glow in the pale mist.

"Spark?" She whispered hoarsely. "Spark? Is that you?"

She felt no reply, but the light was coming closer. It was green, like the glow of the old lantern outside her childhood home, swinging back and forth as it drew nearer. She tried to burrow into the wall with her back. Whatever it was, it couldn't be good.

"Back off!" She yelled. "I got a weapon."

The lantern stopped for a second, swaying in an arc like the person was looking for the sound of her voice. Maybe just some stranger wandering home late. Good riddance then. She suddenly hated that rotting green light. She just wanted it to leave. But to her dismay, it started coming toward her again, faster now.

"Didn't you hear me?"

"Locin?"

A form stepped through the mist, towering over her. It was Voske, and he carried a single inventor's lantern in one hand. He hunched down in front of her, staring at her as he held up the lantern.

"You look like Nyx," he said.

She felt a wild ache explode inside. She wanted to *hug* him.

"What do you want?" She said, wiping at the dried vomit that clung to the corners of her mouth.

He smiled at her, and to her surprise it was a warm smile. "I've been all over Tajerim looking for you, kid. You're not easy to find."

She stared at him. She had no words, just a bubbling hope fighting for space in her mind. *Why? Why would he come looking for me?*

Voske stood, and held out a hand for her. She just stared at it blankly for a minute.

"You didn't think I'd leave without you, did ya?"

Her hope won out, and she stretched out her hand, cold and clammy. He grabbed her arm gently, his own hand warm, and he lifted her to her feet.

"Voske…"

He shrugged. "There's nothing to say, as far as I'm concerned. You're family, Locin. Always gonna be, whether you like it or not."

Her eyes started leaking - *rotting eyes* - and she threw herself against him, wrapping her arms around his waist so her fingers barely touched.

He laughed, throwing an arm around her. "Come on then. We're heading home."

63: Fight. Bleed. Die.

Five hours later, Voske stood with his arms crossed looking out from the deck of the Phoenix as Yzod and Illeri tightened the chains. The pylat knew a journey was coming, and it flapped its wings restlessly as the early sun drew long shadows over the field. Zengin was there, brooding, and Hikari and Locin were talking idly, like the old days. Only it felt nothing like the old days. Hikari had lost a bit of his youthful boyishness, and Locin looked worn and world weary. Nearby, Endring stood with his cloak over his face, talking with Sammel. They were allies now, which was hard to wrap his mind around, but they were strong, and he felt he'd be glad for their help before the end.

"This time," Voske muttered.

They were all together again, and they were gonna do it right. This time would be different. This time they would win.

Still, nagging doubts pulled at him, and he dropped his head as he leaned into the chariot's rail. He'd failed over and over again. As long as he'd been with Burz and Endring planning, he'd been able to keep his doubts at bay, but now it felt real, and he was alone. What if he couldn't do it? What if he wasn't the champion he hoped?

He clenched his jaw, angry at his own mind, until a sharp whistle drew his attention. It was Endring, and he was looking straight at Voske and pointing to the sky above. Voske looked up, and a wave of relief washed over him as he saw several dozen pegasus winging their way toward them. Each one carried a soldier bearing the mark of Tajerim in the center of their chest, and at their head, Burz rode a dappled stallion that sped through the sky like a bird of prey.

Voske smiled as they settled to the ground, filling the field with the eager stamping of hooves. It was starting to look like a proper army, and though he was loath to admit it, he was glad Burz was back. He watched as the old stone skin dismounted and led the pegasus up to the side of the chariot. He looked tired too, and a lot older. His face was grim, but Voske could see a fire in his eyes.

Burz led his stallion right up to the edge of the chariot, and Voske vaulted over the rail to meet him. "How many?"

"Sixty of Tajerim's finest."

"Good." Voske looked over the men again. They had some of that same fire. "Good."

The painted peg held its head up, spreading its wings idly.

"He looks ready for battle," Voske said, nodding toward the beast.

Burz smiled, patting the stallion on the neck. "His name's Sauri. He was my old war peg when I was Captain of the guard. Finest and fastest." He glanced around at the Phoenix and the other champions, all watching the new arrivals.

Hikari had already made his way over and was marching along in front of some of the soldiers with a nearly comical gait, his estimation of a soldier's march, no doubt.

"How are they?" Burz asked.

"Ready."

"And you?" He glanced back at Voske, who did his best to hide the doubt in his eyes. "Ready?"

He nodded firmly.

Burz looked him over head to toe. "Almost."

"What do you mean almost? I'm as ready for this as I've ever been!"

Burz stepped back by Sauri's flank and untied a heavy parcel that was resting there, lifting it and carrying it to Voske. He laid it in his arms, and Voske felt the weight of it.

"What's this?"

"It's yours."

Voske untied the rough rope and pulled back the dingy burlap to reveal the red armor Atrius had made for him, still stained with the blood of his friends. For a moment, he wavered. It was a reminder that he had failed. He'd loosed this evil on Talamh. He'd let Weylyn die. He'd even stormed off and let Rasa face that monstrosity alone. He felt that old instinct creeping up. He couldn't fix this, and he should stop trying before he made it worse.

"I've been a soldier a long time," Burz said. "The best fighters aren't the ones who stroll into battle and get the easy win. Those soldiers get cocky, and eventually they get killed."

Voske looked up at him. He was standing with his arms crossed and a stern look on his face that he could only describe as determination. Burz was in this, win or lose.

"The best fighters are the ones who go down over and over and over, but you know no matter how many times they fall, they're getting back on their feet and fighting again. They get humbled, but they get stronger. Those fighters? Those are the ones I want by my side. They pick battles because they're worth fighting, not just because they know they can win. They have a fire forged in Nyx, stronger than iron. They might fail a thousand times, but in the end, they win because they persevere." He held a hand up toward Voske, and he smiled. "My troop has a creed. Fight. Bleed. Die. It means we don't give up, even if it means our death. We die heroes."

Voske grabbed his forearm as a fire swelled in his chest. "We die champions!"

Rasa stared through a haze, the only sound the slow drip of blood against cold stone. *Her* blood. She tried to move her arms, but they were stretched out to her sides and bound in place, and she could smell the stench of Neveri's breath clouding the air of the prison. Her heart broke as she realized he was still here, and she felt a dry sob welling in her throat.

Her breathing was labored and painful, and she was certain her ribs were cracked. Maybe all of them. Her skin was a mess of cuts and burns, all from the claws and breath of Neveri, and the moments without his presence were becoming less and less.

He stepped into view. Deep crimson flecks covered his face and chest, and coagulated under his claws. How did she have any blood left? "Do you know what my sister was before she became the goddess of lost souls?"

Rasa gasped for air. She wasn't sure she could answer if she wanted to.

Don't listen to him. He's a liar.

Neveri sneered at Weylyn's voice. "Hardly. You did see the… what do you call it? Ah yes, the *old* sanctum. I call it the true one. The original, crafted by Metnadur himself before they became ashamed of who they were. Before they buried it, and me."

Rasa remembered the old sanctum's Bei'ai. She looked so sad, a little girl sobbing. The memory hit Rasa in the chest, and she felt tears squeezing out of the corners of her eyes.

"Sorrow. Grief. Emptiness. She became the goddess of lost souls after, once she made Nyx and it started filling up."

"And… What about you?" She managed in gasps.

He laughed. "I've always been what I am. The god of animus! Of change. My siblings became ashamed of what they were. They tried to change themselves. But me? I didn't change. Ironic, don't you think? But how could I? My whole nature was already change, growth, disorder. They thought it was chaos. They wanted me to be tame, like them." He spit on the floor.

Rasa felt her eyelids growing heavy. She wanted to drift off into the dark again, but instead she let her boon cover her, and Nyx grew close.

Weylyn leaned into her field of vision. *Rasa? Stay with me! You can beat him, just listen to my voice.*

She focused on the feeling of Weylyn, but it was hard to feel anything in her weakened state.

"Your friend is optimistic." Neveri let a claw scrape her cheek, and the fresh sting overpowered the other pains for a moment. "Let's try this again shall we? Where are the orbs?"

Rasa stayed silent and his claw bore down harder, ripping into her cheek until she screamed. "You have a clear way out of this," he crooned. "You've lasted long enough, more than enough for your friends. They all abandoned you. You don't owe them anything more."

Rasa felt his words trying to take root and she shut them out. "It's not… their fault," she whispered. "They don't know I'm here."

Neveri laughed cruelly. "Of course they do. Do you think I'm so naive that I can't keep track of my own champion?"

Rasa felt a tinge of panic. Endring had gone, she was sure. Then why hadn't the Champion's come? It felt like she'd been here for weeks, but time was blending together, and the only voice that kept her sane was Weylyn's.

Don't listen to him. He's trying to confuse you.

"Of course, it's in their self-interest to stay away," Neveri mused. "If they came back, I would kill them, and their deaths would be much swifter than yours."

Rasa felt a stirring within her. A swift death, that was something she could hope for. If Neveri killed her, then she'd never give up the tethers, and she could pass the veil and be with Weylyn.

"You're a hypocrite," Rasa managed.

Neveri stopped dragging his claw, and his eyes narrowed. "Am I?"

"You claim you love your sister, but you torture her champion."

Neveri raised his chin. "You're a prop in a play of gods, easily broken and easily replaced."

"I'm the chosen of Bei'ai," she answered.

"Which means you're the most lost soul of all. My sister always had an affinity for *broken* things."

Rasa managed a weak smile. "That's right." She felt a warmth on her hand and glanced to her side. Weylyn was there, holding her hand in a tight grip, and she felt a strength welling up in her chest. "I was broken. I was lost. But I'm found again now, and I won't ever give you what you want, so you may as well kill me!"

He hesitated, as though noting the change, then saw Weylyn out of the corner of his eye. "Enough," he yelled aloud and swung his fist through Weylyn's form, but all he found was empty air. "Let go of her. I swear I'll peel the skin from her flesh!"

Rasa tightened her grip on Weylyn's cold hand. "You can't break me." She said. "The most you can do is kill me, and even then I'll be against you."

Neveri's countenance darkened, and he turned back toward her with a wicked glare. "So be it."

He extended his claws and slashed through her side. She cried out as the pain overwhelmed her, and she held tightly to Weylyn.

64: Rescue

In the skies over Arrajin a cloud appeared, a peculiar thing, small yet frightfully dark, like the worlds' tiniest thunderhead. It breezed along above the canopy, dropping no rain, casting no shadow, and moving faster than the wind. At its core a bevy of shapes flew, drawing steadily closer to the Gods' Mount, a tangle of feathers and hooves, flying in tight formation and at their center, a single chariot shrouded by darkness.

Hikari stood at the front of the Phoenix, holding his arms out to his sides and keeping his hands raised as he pushed on the light. A bead of sweat trickled down to his eyelash, and he blinked it away, keeping his focus.

Round about the Phoenix the pegasus flew in formation, each just a shadowy figure obscured by the murky aura.

"How long can you keep this up," Voske asked from behind him.

Hikari threw a look over his shoulder. "You know me, darling. The show must go on."

"You need something to sit down on?"

Hikari could feel the strain of the light, pressing against his arms, and he nodded.

"Just hang tight," Voske answered.

"Thirty seconds to landing," Yzod yelled from the chains. "Let's hope the wingers slow with us or we'll be scraping feathers off the skybeam for weeks."

Illeri walked to the second set of chains and gathered them up, waiting for Yzod's signal.

"Alright," Yzod commanded. "Landing position!"

They both yanked back, and the chariot lurched forward, setting Hikari off balance.

He quickly caught himself and forced his hands out again, despite the protestation of every fiber in his arms.

"Here," Voske said, thunking a chair down behind him. "Sit."

"Thank you," Hikari answered, quickly lowering into the hard wood frame. "No pillow?"

Voske smirked, "Spoken like a true smoothy."

Hikari winced at the pain in his arms. "Yes, well, some of us just like to be pampered."

"I can tell."

Endring walked up beside him and placed his hand on the wooden back of his chair. He was staring intently at the looming spires of the Gods' Mount, little more than darker shadows jutting into the black sky.

Voske whacked Endring on the shoulder. "Once we're inside, how long do you think we'll have?"

"That depends on when the faithful spot us. Borroka can have a hundred chimera in the air within minutes."

"A hundred chimera against sixty pegs. Do we like those odds?"

Hikari could hear Endring grinding his teeth at the prospect. "Let's hope the men of Tajerim know how to ride."

"Prepare for landing! We're coming down hard!"

Hikari pushed back against the chair as the Phoenix jolted to the ground.

The wooden frame creaked at the impact, and Yzod jerked back hard on his chain. "Easy, girl,"

"Alright, Champion," Voske muttered, pinching Hikari on the shoulder. "We could use some cover."

Hikari stared forward, trying to make out the form of the temple through the haze. "Endring," he said through gritted teeth. "How far?"

Endring paced forward, studying the skyline of the God's Mount. "Fifty yards," he judged. "Straight ahead."

Hikari nodded, and a shower of sweat cascaded from his brow, then he pushed his arms forward, shoving against the boundary of light and forcing it further out, until the wall of the temple was drowned in darkness. It felt like holding his hands against a hot oven and his arms shook at the effort.

Voske took a knee beside him. "Do you have it?"

"Don't talk," Hikari answered through gritted teeth. "Just run."

"Follow me!" Endring yelled, sprinting for the exit.

Voske, Locin and Zengin fell in behind him, leaping quickly from the chariot and charging across the temple grounds toward the demolished eastern wall.

Hikari's arms started to spasm with pain, but he kept pushing, forcing the darkness even farther until blisters broke out along his fingers.

"Gods… Gah! Why… does… this… have to hurt so much?" He shut his eyes and focused until a soft touch gripped his arm.

He opened them to see Illeri kneeling beside him. "You can do this," she said. "I believe in you."

He gave her a pained nod and shut his eyes again, but this time he focused on the feeling of her cool touch, soft against his skin.

Breathe in. Breathe out. Breathe in. Breathe out.

"They're at the door!" Yzod yelled.

The burning sensation came back with scorching ferocity and his arms gave out. The field around them collapsed and the light of day rushed across the Phoenix and the pegasus army, now naked before the eyes of the Gods' Mount.

Hikari sank into the chair, barely registering the broken state of the temple. His head flopped backward, and his eyes traced the skyline where the forms of chimera could already be seen, soaring over the rooftops like a swarm of locusts coming to devour them.

This was it. This was what had become of the temple. Chunks were missing from the solid stone walls as though a catapult had battered them to pieces, the massive paving stones had cracked like pottery, and the side entrance was reduced to little more than a pile of rubble.

Voske stared aghast at the destruction.

"Nyx it, Voske!" Locin was straining her boon to lift a pillar that was blocking the entrance. It shuddered, barely lifting off the grass. "Help me already!"

"Right." Voske worked his shoulder under the edge of the pillar as Locin started lifting it again. He could feel the crushing weight of it, but his boon warmed to the challenge, and he easily tossed it aside, sending it crashing to the ground in a cloud of dust.

"Well, that was subtle," Zengin said as the ground stopped shaking. "I suppose they know we're here now."

"They already knew." Endring pointed to the sky where a flood of chimeras poured over the temple. Several had heard the sound, and were rapidly flying their way.

"Come on," Voske quickly ducked through the crushed doorway. At least the passage beyond looked relatively clear.

Endring squeezed through behind him. "She's on the lower levels. Through the quartermaster's office and into the cellars. This way."

"Wait!" Locin stopped and they turned to face her. She seemed to be listening. Her expression changed as she stood there until she looked upset.

"What is it?" Voske asked.

Locin pulled her arms tight around her stomach. Voske couldn't remember ever seeing her so disquieted. "We have to hurry. We have to get Rasa to Burz."

"Burz is flying around on a pegasus," Endring answered. "And hurrying will just get us caught."

She looked hard at Voske. "She doesn't have long."

Voske felt anger bubbling inside, and he turned it on Endring. "Rot it! Get us there quickly."

Endring looked skeptically toward Locin. "Raising an alarm will not save Rasa."

"Neither will standing around. Let's move!"

They hurried around the corner. The back halls had been cleared of debris, but ruined in every other way. The tapestries, the busts, the artistic triumphs of a thousand masters had taken a mere six days to destroy. How was he supposed to fix any of this?

"Neveri has been torturing her," Locin continued.

"You know a lot of things you shouldn't," Zengin said. "Care to tell us how?"

"Nope."

Zengin looked at her skeptically, and then he and Endring headed on down the corridor.

Voske hung back, glancing at Locin. "Is it… Spark?"

She looked up at him with a mortified expression.

Voske looked around warily. He'd always been a little creeped out by the idea of spirits watching him. "Is *Spark* here now?"

"Rasa told you." She sighed. "Of course."

"You trust this spirit?"

Locin looked to her left and then nodded solidly. "With my life."

Voske nodded, although the idea of it was still disconcerting. "She can hear me?"

"And see you," Locin smirked, reading his discomfort.

"Right. Spark… is Endring telling the truth?"

Locin listened for a moment. "As far as she can tell. Rasa's where he said she is."

Voske frowned and glanced forward, watching as Endring and Zengin disappeared down another passage. "He better be."

They caught up to the others and redoubled their pace, half running down the hall until Endring suddenly raised his arm, motioning for them to stop. "Quiet," he whispered. "Patrol." He edged forward, listening intently at the corner. "I'll speak with them. They may still trust me."

Voske started to protest, but the old man was around the corner before he could utter a word. He leaned into the wall, listening.

"There's a battle outside," Endring said in a commanding voice. "You men get to the stables."

"Champion," came the suspicious reply. "We heard you'd run off."

"Then clearly you heard wrong."

"This whole wing is supposed to be off limits. Lord Neveri's orders."

"Not to me," Endring said.

"How did you even get in here?"

"This isn't working," Voske whispered. He locked eyes with Locin. "How many?"

"Three."

"That's easy."

"Armed," she added.

They could still hear Endring arguing with the cultists around the corner. It sounded like it would be over soon.

"Okay," Voske said. "When I give the signal-"

A commotion erupted, the sounds of men in pain, and Voske hurried out of hiding just in time to see two of them scurrying off down the passage. The third lay dead with deep slashes across his throat, and Endring stood with one hand full of sharp claws.

Voske rushed past Endring, and the other two lost their footing, both falling to the floor at the same time. They grabbed for their swords, but the blades were stuck fast in their sheaths.

Voske wrapped an arm around each man's neck, dragging them back toward their dead friend while they kicked and struggled until they slumped unconscious at his feet.

"Someone likely heard that," Zengin said.

Endring's hand changed back to its natural form with a sound like cracking knuckles, and he motioned them to follow. "We're close."

They pushed through a dimly lit office of stone, then down a dark hallway. One final guard was quickly subdued by Zengin, and they strode into a storage room with three heavy oak doors against the far wall.

The farthest door had iron slats across it, and Voske could see Rasa inside, laid out on a table with blood pooled across the floor. Her eyes were shut and her skin unbelievably pale.

"Mire and Nyx!"

He yanked at the door, and it wouldn't open, so he grabbed the bars and summoned his boon, ripping the entire door clean out of the wall and tossing it into a pile of crates. He made his way in, but he froze, staring at her body. He was suddenly terrified she was dead.

"She's alive," Locin said, though her voice sounded queasy. "But she needs help fast."

Voske rushed forward, emboldened by the revelation, and lifted her body in his arms. She was light as a feather. He felt grief trying to take hold as he stared at her, wondering how many of his friends he would have to carry like this.

Endring quickly threw his cloak over and began wrapping it around her spindly form. Voske fought down the instinct to pull her away. Instead he watched closely as Endring worked and awkwardly assisted as the old man tucked the garment around her with trembling hands. There were tears glinting from the corners of his weathered eyes.

Moments later he clasped it at the front. It was laughably big on her, but it looked warm.

"Thank you," Voske growled.

Endring nodded and gently slid the back of his hand across her cheek. "She's very young."

They heard the sound of footsteps and yelling out in the passage, and Endring stiffened. "We need her to talk."

Voske squinted at him. "What?"

"Ask her about the gods' orbs."

"The what?"

"Shut up," Locin snapped. "We need to get her to Burz."

Endring frowned. "This might be our only chance. We're here now."

Voske didn't know what Endring was on about and he didn't care to. "We're leaving." He stared down at Rasa's bloodied face. He wouldn't watch another one die. He couldn't. "We get her to Burz."

65: Escape

Zengin was tense, his hand on his dagger under his cloak. They were deep in the heart of the temple, a place crawling with cultists, and he listened to the sounds of footsteps nearby as they headed away from Rasa's cell.

"Just a bit farther," Endring urged. He was in the lead, pacing noiselessly down the ruined hallway. "We'll take the stairs up just before the Oracles' wing, then double back to the exit."

Rasa groaned, and Voske held her closer. "Hurry."

Her eyes had fluttered open now and she was smiling weakly. "You came."

"Yes," Voske said. "And we're getting you out."

"No." She clutched at his shirt before her arm fell limp. "We can't go. Not without the tethers."

Endring rushed back to her side. "Tell us where they are!"

Her eyes fluttered shut as her head rolled back on Voske's arm.

Endring reached out to grab her. "Rasa? Rasa!"

Voske pulled her away and glared at Endring. "Enough!"

Zengin stepped back, listening intently but not to Voske. He couldn't hear the cultist voices any longer, and it set him on edge.

"You don't understand," Endring chided. "If we lose those orbs, we lose everything."

"You picked a Nyx of a time to bring this up."

"You wouldn't have believed me earlier."

"That a fact?"

"Quiet!" Locin snapped.

They all looked at her. She was looking nervously down the hall. "They're coming this way. A lot of them."

Voske glanced back at Endring. "Is there another way out?"

"Not a safer one."

"Alright." Voske quickly strode to Zengin and held Rasa's body out.

His eyes went wide. "What?"

"I need my strength to get us out of here. You can use your boon without your hands."

Zengin stared at her limp, bloodied body. The part of him that reveled at the sight of blood felt somehow perverse at the sight of her broken form, and it made him sick. "I…"

"Locin can't carry her, and I need the beast." He nodded toward Endring.

Zengin straightened up. It was clear Voske wasn't asking. He held his arms out, and Voske gently laid Rasa's body across them. She was lighter than he expected.

Voske turned to Endring. "I need you up front with me. Preferably looking a bit more intimidating."

Endring made his way forward and threw his robe off, leaving him bare chested. His muscles bulged outward and hair sprouted from his feral hands until his upper body resembled a wolf with sharp fangs and long claws.

Voske nodded approvingly. "Locin. Toss stuff at them, and don't hit us."

"You're no fun."

He turned his attention toward the passage and the two of them stood ready as Neveri's forces rounded the corner. There were more than a dozen, all lightly armored and armed.

"The plan is to get out," Voske said. "No unnecessary detours."

Zengin and Locin fell in behind them as they started down the passage. Voske gave a loud roar that startled the cultists, and they froze as he and Endring barreled into their ranks.

A noise from behind caught Zengin's attention, and he turned to see two guards rounding the corner.

"Stay back!" He yelled.

Immediately they froze, and seconds later they were blown from their feet as Locin sent them careening into the far wall. She used her boon to grab a door from the side of the hall and ripped it from its hinges, wedging it into a narrow arch behind them.

The cultists were quickly back on their feet, and they charged the door, but despite their best efforts, they couldn't move it.

"Come on!" She yelled, and she sprinted ahead.

Zengin clutched Rasa a bit tighter and started running again. The fighting ahead had moved around the corner. Three cultists lay dead on the stone floor, and as he passed, he noticed two of them were mauled by animal teeth. He licked his lips as he made his way to the next passage, following the sounds of the battle and struggling to keep up.

At least the trail of blood and destruction was easy to follow. He passed a few more bodies, and he could hear the others ahead. A passage opened on his left and right. The one to the right would lead him out of the temple. But he stopped as he looked left. He heard voices, the gruff voice of a woman - a voice he recognized. He crept down the left passage and peered around the corner cautiously. Borroka stood with her back to him, giving orders to several cultists. They nodded and turned, running out of sight and leaving her alone.

Zengin felt rage flooding his senses. He glanced down at the stub of his arm that peeked from under Rasa's leg. He wanted to kill her. He wanted it to be slow and bloody. He could almost smell her blood.

He knelt to set Rasa's body down, when her eyes fluttered open.

"Voske?" She said weakly.

"Shh," he replied. "It's me, Zengin."

He felt anxious. *Set her down*, he thought. *You'll miss your chance.*

He started to let Rasa slide to the floor, but she grabbed at him.

"Don't leave me!" She said desperately.

And suddenly he felt something he couldn't remember feeling in a very long time. Was it compassion? He didn't want to leave her. He didn't want her to be alone.

"I'll be right back," he said, frozen with her still clinging in his arms.

Her weak grip slipped away and her eyes shut. He stared down at her face, slick with blood, and her breath was so slight, he wondered if she were still breathing at all. He felt the war inside him, his need for vengeance, and his concern for Rasa. He couldn't let her die. All the rest of them, but not her. *Not her.*

Before he could talk himself out of it, he scooped her body back in his arms and glanced one last time at Borroka before turning and hurrying for the exit. As he burst out into the light of the temple grounds, Voske rushed to his side.

"Gods and Chosen!" Voske said. "I thought we lost you!"

Zengin nodded weakly.

"What happened to you?" Locin asked. "You were right behind me!"

"I got separated," he said. "We're fine."

"We'll be fine if the Phoenix hurries back," Endring said, his eyes on the sky. "Stay close to the wall!"

Zengin peered out to where two lines of cultists were flowing out of the temple, blocking their escape to either side.

He quickly looked to the skies. Several Chimera were circling nearby, and they could see the pegs fighting above. But no chariot yet. They tucked tighter along the wall, and it felt very much like a noose was closing around their neck.

"Come on," Voske seethed. "Where in Nyx are they?"

Illeri nearly lost her footing as the Phoenix banked hard to the left. She grabbed hold of the rail, feeling a bit nauseous as another blast of fire nearly singed them. She could feel the heat of it off to their right. They'd been dodging the same chimera for the last five minutes, and the pegs were too busy to notice.

Hikari grabbed at the light around the chimera, pulling it into a blinding ray that he shot into the creature's eyes. It roared as it veered off for a moment, but it was quickly on their tail again, and Hikari's hands were too blistered and sore to hold the light for long.

"He's got a friend!" Yzod yelled as he pulled the pylat's chains. They banked again, but more gently this time.

"No matter!" Hikari yelled. "We'll best two as easily as we've bested one!"

"This was easy?" Illeri called, her eyes wide.

"Sure, darling. Like a walk on the beach."

"I've tried walking on sand," Yzod replied. "That's not easy. Blasted stuff swallows your feet and makes it impossible!"

Hikari sighed. "Come on troops, I'm trying to keep up morale here!"

Illeri peered down over the railing toward the temple. They'd spotted the others about a minute ago, but they needed an opening to land. She could still see them pressed against the side of the temple. Foot soldiers were spilling out all over, and it was only a matter of time.

"Come on then!" Hikari yelled, making fists in the air toward the new chimera and its rider. "Show us what you've got, beast! Ow!" He winced in pain as he unclenched his blistered hands. "Got any other tricks up your sleeve, Yzod?"

"We could run through the wingers. Try to lose them?"

"And take out half our army?" Hikari's eyes went wide.

"What have you got left?" He asked, staring at Hikari.

He steeled his expression. "What do you need?"

"If you can signal the pegs somehow, make them split. We fly through the middle and blind the chimera. Give our boys a break and lose our tail. We just need them all distracted long enough to land."

"Ah! Now that sounds like a plan I'd come up with."

"Great minds, eh?"

Hikari laughed a bit too loud. "Illeri, darling?"

She looked at him nervously. "Y-yes?"

"It might go better if you can help us out." He pointed toward the chimeras ahead. They had flanked the flyers of Tajerim and had them split. "Those chimeras on the left, can you freeze them while we deal with the main force?"

She felt like her heart would leap into her throat. "I don't know."

Hikari made his way over and rested the back of his hand on her cheek, smiling at her. "You're a Champion, darling. I have faith."

"I'll try."

"Excellent!" He nodded to Yzod. "Ready?"

Yzod jerked the chains to the left and they banked hard, then back again, angling for the center of the fray. "Hold on!"

Hikari steadied himself and threw as much light as he could toward the pegs. They split around it, and the oncoming chimera scattered and faltered as they ran headlong into the blinding radiance.

"Now, Illeri!" He cried, and then he yelled out in pain as the Phoenix went driving through the middle of the fight.

Illeri locked her eyes on the chimera to the left, eight in total. She felt her heart racing and her hands shaking as she tried to steady herself. "You can do this," she hissed, focusing on the chimera. She felt her boon filling her senses, like the warmth of the radiant field. It stretched out from her fear, coiling around the chimeras and slowly grinding them to a halt until they hung in the air, completely frozen in time.

"I did it!" She shouted, her fear turning to elation. "Hikari, I did it!"

She glanced back to see him wincing in pain as his hands were curled in front of him. Despite that, he smiled.

"I knew you could, darling."

She turned back to focus on her boon as Hikari yelled to Yzod.

"I'm spent, Captain. It's up to you and the lady now."

The Phoenix wound its way through the pegs and rose over the oncoming chimera. Illeri could see the men of Tajerim regrouping below and charging on with a fresh wind. They cried out their thanks as they rushed at their enemies.

But the victory was short lived. A wild roar erupted from the temple, deep and rolling like thunder. It echoed across the Gods' Mount, and the ground shook as a monstrously large beast rose from the hillock, towering over the temple and bathing it in shadow.

"Neveri!" Came the cry from the pegs.

Illeri felt her knees grow weak. Her focus disappeared, and she felt her boon slip away. The flanking chimeras came back at full speed, crashing into the side of the battle.

Yzod banked the Phoenix back toward the temple, narrowly avoiding a swipe from Neveri's talons as he ducked low toward the ground.

"We're running?" Hikari asked, staring back at the fighting behind them.

"We're finishing the mission."

"You're going to land without the pegs?" Illeri felt sick. "We won't survive."

"We have to try, or none of us will survive."

She leaned back over the railing. She could see the others again, still holding by the temple, but Neveri's forces had closed in around them.

"Hurry then," she called. "They don't have much time."

Wind rushed by Burz as he leaned in low over Sauri's neck. Neveri had come out of nowhere, and the pegasus balked and whinnied, sensing the danger. "Steady," Burz called, patting his hand against Sauri's neck. "Steady!"

Chimeras and pegasus alike scattered out of the dread god's path as he thundered across the field.

"On me!" Burz cried. "Regroup on me!"

A few riders started flying toward him, but most had fled to the opposite side, creating an easy path for Neveri straight to the Phoenix. Burz could see the chariot now, flying low toward the temple.

"Uthando, save them," he muttered.

A dozen pegs were at his side, and their riders stared slack-jawed at the beast. Only Sammel looked resolute, and Burz shouted his direction.

"Can that whip slow him down?"

"I doubt it."

The Phoenix was turning toward the far side of the temple now, but they'd never reach the ground in time.

"Distraction it is," Burz called. "Aim for his eyes!"

He kicked his heels into Sauri's flanks, and the dozen riders surged forward around him. The sky began darkening with Hikari's boon, and the light coalesced at Neveri's eyes, shining into the god's vision. He paused for only a moment to shield his eyes, but it was enough. Sauri flew like a messenger of Sbarga, straight toward his mark, and Burz raised his sword, feeling it cleave the wind above him. "For Talamh," he thundered. Neveri roared in anger and surged past the light, straight into Burz's blade.

The sword stabbed into the god's eye and wrenched from Burz' grasp. Sauri quickly pivoted away, swinging around for another pass, but the sight that greeted Burz wasn't one of victory. The riders who had been moments behind him had been devastated. Arms sprouted from all over Neveri's body, snatching and grasping like the spawn of Nyx. A dozen eyes blossomed from his face, replacing the one he had lost, and they all stared at Burz with hatred.

"Fall back!" Burz cried, but only Sammel broke away, cracking shockwaves behind him to repel the grasping hands of the god.

Men and pegasus alike were crushed in his deadly hands. Their bodies made sickening popping sounds, and gore drizzled to the ground through Neveri's fingers.

Burz felt his stomach convulse. "Retreat!" He screamed, and he waved away the Tajerim forces on the far side. "Get back! Get away from him!"

The pegasus scattered to the winds as Neveri locked eyes on the Phoenix. They were nearing the temple doors, and the monster's hackles rose as he lunged forward again.

"Sauri," Burz whispered in the pegasus' ear. "I'm glad you're with me." He slapped his heels into Sauri's flank one last time, but another shot past him, already flying full speed. It was Jepa.

"Jepa!" Burz yelled. "I said retreat!"

Jepa looked over his shoulder with a repentant smile. "Sorry, Captain," he yelled. "You never listened either."

A dozen arms seized upward as he reached Neveri, but Jepa leapt from his saddle, diving through the air as his peg was ripped apart. He drove his sword into Neveri's chest, but was quickly peeled away by two mighty hands and his body was twisted in two.

"Jepa!"

Neveri threw the young man's corpse to the ground in disgust, then his eyes slowly rose to Burz again. "Is this all you have to offer?"

Burz' hands trembled under his gaze, but he felt something welling deep inside. He would resist, to death if need be. "All we are is opposed to you!" He yelled. "You will have no portion in Talamh. Not now. Not ever! Talamh is her people, and her people reject you!"

Neveri gently waved his hands, and the army of chimera flew back into view taking up positions around their god.

"Wrong," Neveri sneered. "*You* rejected the one true god of Talamh. You are alone." He threw his arm forward. "Fly, soldiers of Neveri! Kill all those who would oppose me, for this is Sbarga's day of reckoning, and it begins with the death of the champions!"

Burz yanked back on Sauri's reins and swung around. There was no more time to be bought.

"Fly!" he yelled. "Fly now!"

Those who remained surged again, but this time away from the temple, beating their way through the sky in a panicked retreat, and Burz could only hope that the time they'd bought was enough.

Endring stood alongside the champions of Talamh. He could taste the blood of Neveri's faithful, still wet along his tongue, and the sharpened senses of the wolf clouded his mind. He could smell the charred air from the battle overhead, and hear the quickly closing footsteps of a hundred pursuers. His adrenaline still flooded his veins, urging him to continue the hunt, but his human reason kept the instinct in check.

Distant screams echoed from above and he turned his nose skyward. The pegasus army flew pell-mell away from a looming specter. It was Neveri.

Slowly, the hair on his back burrowed back into his skin and his eyes returned to the clarity of a man's. He could still taste the blood of men, but now it turned his stomach, and he spat it out.

"Endring," Voske said from beside him. "You might want a fighting form, if you know what I mean."

"I know." He answered. The faithful had them totally surrounded in a wide perimeter, their swords were drawn and they slowly stalked inward, like a pack of wolves watching for a weakness.

He reached a trembling hand to his lips, wiping away the bloody spittle. If he was going to die, he wanted to die as a man.

"Can you see Burz?" Zengin asked.

Endring looked back at Rasa. "How is she?"

"Fading."

"There!" Voske pointed to the Phoenix. It was flying low, just coming around from the far side of the Gods' Mount, and a dozen chimera were in close pursuit. "Come on," he said. "We'll meet them halfway!"

"We're surrounded," Locin said.

"Then at least get away from the walls. Now move!"

They started running down the slope, waving frantically as the Phoenix approached.

All around them the faithful quickened their pace, tightening the net, swords and bows drawn.

"Champions," boomed the voice of Neveri. "Fleeing so quickly?"

As he spoke his eyes wandered to the Phoenix. It was rushing past him at speeds no flyer could hope to match.

Neveri's many legs cracked and morphed, transforming to a thousand thundering hooves. He charged after the chariot with frightening speed as the sharpened horns of a bull pierced out from his head. "Fight me!" He challenged. "Won't even one of you call upon the power of your gods? Surely they have not left you defenseless."

The Phoenix suddenly lurched forward under Yzod's pylat, swinging wildly like an unhinged pendulum, then it slammed into the ground with the alarming sound of splintering wood. It skipped like a stone across the temple grounds, then impacted again, and a third time, tearing up the verdant ground with great gouges of soil.

The champions came to a stop as the rattling contraption barreled toward them, knocking aside a dozen faithful like kindling, then grinding to a halt just a hand's breadth from Voske's nose.

"Come on!" An unseen Yzod yelled. "Get on!"

A yell went up from the cultists behind, and they loosed a volley of arrows. Endring quickly ran to Rasa and hardened his back till his skin gleamed like a turtle's shell, but he never felt the impact.

He looked up with amazement to see every arrow stuck in midair. Quickly they spun around and banded together like one massive javelin. It was Locin. She held up a hand, as though she gripped the mighty shaft, and turned it to face Neveri.

Neveri slowed his approach and smiled with contempt. "Well done, Champion. Now throw it. Slay me where I stand."

She hurled the javelin forward, straight toward Neveri's face, then, in a clever motion, flicked a broken board from the Phoenix up behind the mass.

Neveri laughed and batted the javelin aside. "You pitiful-"

That was as far as he got before the jagged beam drove into his neck.

His words were choked short, and he looked startled by the blow. Even the faithful stopped their advance, staring toward their god with alarm.

"Locin!" Voske yelled. "That's our cue. We're leaving!"

She ignored him and walked slowly toward Neveri, pulling the beam out and stabbing it upward again.

But this time the tip glanced off his skin like it had struck a bone of iron. He snatched the splinter from the air and drove it deep into the ground. "That," he seethed. "Was your last mistake."

He charged again, his hooves churning the ground.

Still Locin plied her boon, jerking her hands upward, but the beam wouldn't budge from where Neveri had driven it.

"Locin!" Voske yelled again. "Gah!"

He rushed forward and grabbed her up.

"Voske," she snapped, "you idiot, why didn't you run?"

"I had to save your hide!"

Endring ducked after them, swinging up the Phoenix's ladder as a chorus of arrows pounded into the deck.

"Hang on!" Yzod yelled, and he loosed the chains, letting the pylat shoot upward.

They all sank to the deck at the sudden motion and Hikari yelled over the wind. "A bit much isn't it!"

As though in response the claws of Neveri swiped down across the Phoenix, narrowly missing Hikari's leg, and ripping the side railing away.

"Never mind!" Hikari yelled again.

A few seconds later, Yzod tightened the chains, and Endring gained his feet. He could see the remains of the pegasus army trailing off to their side. He sharpened his eyes. The pursuing chimera were falling behind, but the men looked bloodied and weary.

He picked out Sammel and Burz from their number and steadied himself with a deep breath. Maybe this hadn't all been for nothing.

The voice of Neveri cut through the air once more, though now it was distant, like an unseen waterfall in the jungle. "There is no place you can go!" He yelled. "Talamh is mine. There is no more place for champions, because there is only one true god!"

He turned around and for a moment the group all looked each other over. They were all dirty, sweaty, and spent.

"You all look terrible," Hikari jabbed. "Except you of course Rasa. You look lovely as always. Is she awake?"

Rasa opened her mouth in response, but no one could hear what she said.

"We need to get her to Burz." Voske said. "We can't wait until Tajerim."

"She's not the only one in need of help." Yzod added.

He was pulling the chains back and forth, and seemed to be putting up quite the struggle just to keep flying in a straight line. "No way the Phoenix can make the flight. Not like this."

"And where would we land?" Zengin asked.

"There's only one place I'm aware of." Yzod said. "At least Ryshi will be glad to be home."

66: Interlude

Burz kept Sauri at a steady pace just behind the Phoenix. It hadn't taken the expected course toward Tajerim and instead had turned Southward, passing over the city of Arrajin toward the Trade Quarter. Fortunately, the forces of Neveri hadn't pursued them farther than the Arrtris. The lumbering chimeras had descended back to the Gods' Mount and even Neveri had diminished from the horizon, leaving only the light trails of smoke as evidence of their battle.

Below, the city looked worse than he remembered. Sections of the river bank were entirely washed out while other areas were charred black and there was a clear path of destruction carved from the Sacred Quarter all the way to the Pilgrim's Bridge.

People scurried from home to home, scarcely daring to look up, and pointing slack-jawed when they did. One young woman started screaming and waving as though they might come down to rescue her. Burz shut his eyes for a moment. They couldn't save these people. They'd barely saved Rasa.

When he opened his eyes again, he saw the Phoenix gently descend, angling for the large field behind Yzod's old workshop. The pegasus riders began circling, eager to set down, and he felt a sense of relief. As the rush of the battle left him, his body began to ache. His muscles protested every move, and his head felt light. He wanted nothing more than to land and find the softest bed available.

Sauri seemed to share the sentiment and landed heavily among the troop of sweaty pegs and soldiers. A dozen of them looked injured or scorched, and Burz felt his hopes for rest sink. He was the healer. He had to do this.

"Burz!" Voske yelled.

Before he'd even swung out of the saddle, Voske was rushing toward him with Rasa in his arms. She looked dead, and she was covered in blood.

Burz felt his heart sink lower.

Hikari ran up beside Voske, the rest of them close behind. "She needs you, Burz. Quickly."

He nodded as he climbed down from Sauri and took her body from Voske. She was clammy to the touch.

He knelt to the ground in the midst of the throng and felt Uthando's mercy flowing out through his arms. He could feel dozens of piercing cuts like knives across his body as the echo of her pain transferred to him. He felt his lungs spasm. His ribcage felt like it was being crushed, but he kept pouring into her, exchanging her pain for his comfort until the world began to fade around him. But slowly her color returned, and her shallow breath became stronger.

"It's done," he said weakly, and he laid her down on the grass. He spotted Hikari now, standing with his hands curled, covered in blisters and scorched red. His heart sank, but he tried to stand, wobbling until his leg gave out, and he fell to his knees.

"Hikari," he waved him forward.

"Not yet, darling. After that, I think you need to rest. I can wait."

He nodded gratefully.

"Weylyn?" Rasa's eyes fluttered open, and she caught sight of Voske towering over her. "Voske!"

She looked around until she spotted Burz, leaning back on the grass, utterly spent. For a moment she seemed disoriented, and then she smiled as tears started rolling down her cheeks.

"You came! You all came."

She threw her arms around Burz' neck, and he nearly fell back. But he smiled gratefully at her touch.

"Thank you," she whispered. "Weylyn said you saved me."

As she pulled from the embrace, Burz looked at her quizzically. "Weylyn?"

Rasa nodded. "She was with me the whole time," then she looked over Burz' shoulder, and he got the impression she was no longer looking at the living. "She's the reason I survived. Well, all of you really. Thank you."

"Well, we weren't about to leave you in danger." Hikari said.

She looked back and grabbed hold of his hand which brought about a cry of pain.

"Oh! Sorry, sorry. Are you alright?"

"I'll live," he answered with a grimace. "Just in need of some aloe."

Rasa stood to her feet and started hugging the people around her, and for a moment Burz didn't feel like they were in a ruined city, teetering under the threat of an angry god.

"And Locin. Where is Locin?" Rasa asked.

Locin edged forward through the crowd and instantly a familiar tension hung in the air, but Rasa didn't seem to notice. She threw her arms around the older girl, much to Locin's stiff surprise.

"This is from me and Spark."

"Umm. Yeah. Good to see you too."

"And where is Voske?"

The big man stepped front and center and Rasa gave him a hug that was barely above his waist. He gently returned her embrace until she pulled him down and whispered something in his ear.

Burz watched as Voske's countenance went from endeared to gravely serious, and he nodded.

"Alright," he called as he straightened up. "We need watchmen posted at the perimeter, get your assignments from Burz, and stay ready, we're not sure how long Yzod needs to repair the Phoenix."

After he had addressed the men, he stepped to where Burz was just struggling to get off the ground.

"Once you've given them orders we need to talk."

"About what?"

"Orders first, talk later."

Burz squinted. "Why do I get the feeling I'm not going to like this?"

"Because you've got good instincts. See you in ten minutes."

Voske trudged away, and Burz squared his shoulders, doing his best to shrug off the ache in his body. He had a feeling it would be a long time before he could rest.

Twenty minutes later Voske was pacing the floor of Yzod's shop. He was stuck somewhere between the pumping adrenaline of the battle and the overwhelming reality that was settling in and dragging his thoughts down. Sure, Neveri wouldn't be expecting them back so soon, but it was madness to go. They were outnumbered, there was a hydra standing between them and the temple, and none of that mattered if they couldn't find a way to deal with Neveri.

He heard a soft knock against the wall and saw Burz just trudging up the short step into the shop.

"How are your men?" Voske asked.

"Battered and bruised. We lost fourteen in the battle."

"Fourteen," Voske repeated. "Nearly a quarter?"

"We got lucky. It could have been much worse."

Voske nodded, then folded and unfolded his arms. This didn't make what he had to say any easier.

"What was it you wanted to speak about?"

There really wasn't a good way to say it, so he just dove in. "We need to go back."

Burz gave a tired nod. "With enough rest and the surrounding city state's support, we should be able to make another attempt in… why are you shaking your head?"

"It has to be quicker than that."

Burz raised an eyebrow. "How much quicker?"

"Today."

Burz laughed. It wasn't a derisive laugh, but it made Voske annoyed all the same.

"What's so funny about that?"

"I'm not sure how much you saw of the battle, but I just watched a god crush a dozen men and pegs like they were grapes."

"You think the men would refuse?"

"I think their courage is on a knife's edge just to stay in Arrajin."

Voske walked to Yzod's counter, placed his hands flat on the top, and stared down at the shape of his fingers. "Neveri's close to finding the orbs."

"The orbs?"

"The orbs, the tethers, whatever you want to call them. Rasa says she hid them."

Burz squinted. "I'm not sure what we're talking about."

"The rotting orbs…" Voske's voice faded out, and he shook his head, pushing his knuckles into the countertop. It was hard enough to convince himself going back was a good idea, let alone convincing Burz. "You know, the shiny ones from the sanctum."

"You're talking about the mara?" Burz said slowly.

"Whatever they're called."

"And?"

"And if Neveri gets his hands on them… well, he'll shatter the realms, or maybe burn them to ash." Voske let out an exasperated sigh. This all felt like too much for him to understand. "Rasa says it'll be bad if he gets them."

"And you're taking her word for it?"

"I made the mistake of not listening before."

Burz nodded thoughtfully.

"She says it's now or never."

"She's a child. I'm not sure she understands what she's asking."

"Maybe, but Endring agrees."

"And you're trusting him now?"

"What choice do we have?"

Burz shook his head. "It's madness."

"So what? You want to sit back and watch while the worlds burn?"

Voske felt frustration building in him, muscles tensing in anger as he stared across at Burz' cold expression. He wasn't about to back down now, and the longer Burz stayed silent, the more restless and stubborn he became.

The noise outside faded, and the air inside thickened.

Finally, Burz sighed. "I'm not against you, Voske."

It was disarming. Voske was in the middle of planning his argument, ready to fight against Burz' rotting practicality. Instead, he simply shook his head, letting the tension drain out of his muscles.

"You might want to be on this one," he said.

Burz smirked. "I didn't exactly say I was with you, either. This might be impossible."

Voske let a wry smile curl his lips. "Isn't that our domain? The impossible?"

"And if no one will go?" Burz asked. "You'd go alone, wouldn't you?"

"That's not my first choice."

Burz leaned in. "You're insane. Have I ever mentioned that before?"

"Once or twice."

They fell silent, and Burz stepped away from the counter then started pacing back and forth through the room, as though trying to bring himself to grips with the idea.

"Burz," Voske finally said. "How many pegs can you put in the air?"

"Forty-two," he answered. "Forty-four at the most, and that's putting wounded animals back in the sky."

"Forty-four it is," Voske said. "We only get one shot at this."

Burz slowly nodded, then put his hands on his hips. "Two hours," he said.

Voske raised an eyebrow. "Is that how long Yzod needs?"

"That's how long I need. There's no way the cultists destroyed the entire garrison of the city on their way through. I'm going to find them."

Voske nodded, and felt a familiar strength returning to his arms. "Good," he answered.

"And Voske."

"Yeah?"

"If we're going to rejoin the battle, we'll need proper weapons this time."

Voske nodded thoughtfully. "Agreed."

67: Hope

The battle was over. They were safe. At least *safer*. Neveri had let them escape over the river, and why shouldn't he? They were no match for him. He had no incentive to come after them now. And still Illeri's hands wouldn't stop shaking.

She fumbled with the wooden cabinet in front of her, but the more she tried to steady her hands, the more they shook. She felt someone behind her, and Hikari rested his arm against hers, drawing her eyes.

He smiled softly. "We're alright, darling."

She nodded, and resumed her fumbling, but she felt him wrap an arm around her, careful not to use his hand, and he pulled her in. For a moment she turned her attention from the cabinet and pressed against him with her head on his shoulder.

"We're safe now, Illeri."

She was still afraid, but she felt her heart ease, and her hands weren't shaking so badly.

"Of course," she said. "I'm sorry. I'm supposed to be taking care of you."

She pulled away, and Hikari frowned. "My burns aren't going anywhere. Take your time."

She turned her attention back to the cabinet and managed the latch this time, pulling out a box of cloth strips and a small wooden jar.

"It's an ointment for burns," she said. "Yzod has used it plenty of times." She lifted the lid and the smell of onions and aloe filled the air. "Let me see your hands."

Hikari held his hands out toward her. Both palms and every finger were red and blistered, and she was afraid to touch them.

"Illeri?" He asked.

"I don't want to hurt you."

"Oh, don't worry about that." He screwed up his face and squared his shoulders. "I can take it."

She dipped a finger in the ointment and found it felt cold to the touch. "Okay."

She noticed him wince slightly and tighten his jaw as she smeared the ointment across his hand, but he quickly relaxed.

"Almost as good as Burz," he said, forcing a smile.

She tried to be as gentle as possible, but her hands were starting to shake again. She had to stop thinking about Neveri, but all she could see was his ghastly form swiping massive claws at the chariot and plucking pegs out of the sky. She turned to Hikari's second hand, but she was shaking fully again.

Hikari opened and closed his mouth a few times as if he wanted to say something, but what could he say? They had just faced a god. And no matter how this went, she knew the others wanted to do it again.

Illeri bit her lip as she started pulling out strips of cloth, laying one against his wrist and wrapping it around. He winced.

"I'm sorry," she said softly. She tried to breathe slower, think about something else, anything to still the shaking, but every time she blinked she saw him, a monster emerging on the field with violent force.

"I couldn't do it," she blurted. "I couldn't hold those Chimera."

"Is that what you're worried about?" He asked softly. "Illeri, you *did* hold them."

She shook her head. "Not long enough."

"There was chaos, darling. You may not have noticed, but I couldn't hold the light forever either."

She stopped her wrapping and stared at the red blisters on his hands. "Because you held it so long. You found the limits of your boon. I can't even begin to find mine."

"Darling-"

"Hold still." She gently tugged his hand back and tied off the bandage. She looked up at him, and his eyes were fixed on her with such intensity that she quickly looked back down at his hand. "I don't want to talk about it anymore. I don't want to think about it."

"Do you remember the beach?"

She risked a glance back up at him. "The beach?"

He smiled. "After the Desitan festival. You may remember me at least. I made quite a memorable crab."

She giggled.

"I also did a poor job recreating the stars. Unfortunately, I became distracted and I let the stars slip from my fingers."

She frowned. "So what? The great Hikari sometimes fails his boon too? It doesn't count on a beach with no danger."

"You're entirely missing the point, darling. I let the stars slip, and they stayed there."

She raised an eyebrow.

"The waves were frozen, peaks like unmoving mountains. It was you, darling." He rested the back of his bandaged hand against her cheek. "You used your boon without even trying. It's there, inside you."

She felt a prickle of hope in her heart, but her mind quickly shut it down. "I can't call it when I need it though. Besides, the others want to go back for the orbs." She shook her head. "I appreciate it, really, but I'm not sure there's anything you can say to make me feel better."

"That's unfortunate. Well, perhaps a distraction then? I am, after all, a master performer. Poetry?"

She wrinkled her nose. "I hate poetry."

He laughed lightly. "Noted. A song then? Ah, I know, the tale of Urmash the farmer. It's a comedy, very good for lightening the mood."

She looked up at him, and she was suddenly very aware of her hand on his arm and his soft eyes fixed on her.

"Urmash was a turnip farmer outside of Den'lask, and he had a problem with this fox who-"

"Why did you stay?"

Hikari stopped abruptly and stared at her. "What?"

She felt her heart pounding. "You have friends on every world, hosts of fans... a family. So why did you stay with Yzod?"

"You mean back in Tajerim?"

She nodded.

"Well, he seemed to need help, darling." He squirmed as he answered. "I mean, of course I would have left eventually. But you know, with so many places to go…" he frowned as he locked eyes on her.

"The truth, Hikari."

"Yzod did need help. Besides, I'm a Champion now. Only a coward would run."

"Sometimes I wonder if you even know how to tell the truth, or do you always go with whatever makes the best story? Hikari the player, Hikari the storyteller."

He frowned. "That's not fair."

"Isn't it? Isn't that what you do? Put on a show?"

He grew tense, but didn't seem to have an answer, so Illeri turned her attention back to his hands, feeling a bit uncomfortable as she began wrapping the bandages around his wrist again.

"Alright then, the truth," he said. "The Champions are my family now. I didn't want to leave them." He sighed. "Gods and Chosen! I don't want to leave *you*, Illeri."

She looked up at him.

"I don't know exactly how drunk you were in Govere. I've wanted to talk to you since that night."

"Oh, I just…" she coughed.

"I wasn't really sure where we stood after that night, but I like you, and…" he grunted in frustration. "No, that's not it at all."

"Oh." She felt her heart sink.

"I couldn't leave Tajerim because I couldn't bear the thought of being away from you. I don't just like you, Illeri. I love you."

Her cheeks flushed hot. How did she even respond to that? She felt something, of course, but was it love? She kept her head down and continued wrapping his hand in silence until it was done.

He pulled his bandaged hand away and looked it over. "That's better," he said meekly. "Thank you."

"You're welcome." She pushed some stray hair behind her ear, looking anywhere but at Hikari.

He sighed. "If I scared you away, it's your own fault. You did ask me to be honest."

She glanced up at him. "You didn't scare me away."

He smiled. "Good."

They heard a clattering noise from the front of the shop followed by a yell from Yzod. "Blast it!"

Ryshi came scurrying out of the front of the shop and nestled by Illeri's ankle. She bent down and scooped him up, setting him on her shoulder.

"What's he done now, Ryshi?"

Yzod came walking through to the back with an armful of parts and tools. "It's a mess in there. I never throw anything away, apparently. I didn't realize that until I was away for a while."

"We can clean it up," Illeri said cheerfully.

"After. Assuming we don't all die."

Hikari cleared his throat. "Anything we can do to help?"

"Rest those hands of yours. Illeri can help me."

"Right." She gave one last sheepish look toward Hikari and then hurried over. She was grateful to have her mind on something else for the moment.

"Hopefully I'll heal up before we go back," Hikari said. "I'd be useless without my boon."

"At least you have a useful boon," Yzod said, dropping the parts and tools he carried into an empty crate. "I don't have much to offer."

"Of course you do!" Illeri protested. "You have the Phoenix. You're one of the smartest people I've ever met. That's as good as brawn in a fight."

He chuckled. "I'd rather have brawn."

"Me too," Hikari said with a sly smile.

Illeri crossed her arms and glared at them. Maybe she had to convince herself. Her boon wasn't reliable either. If she was going to be helpful in this battle, she had to use her mind. "You know what I mean. You're brilliant, and we can use that."

"Brilliant? You saw all my failed attempts, Illeri. The Phoenix has taken most of my life to get this far."

That was true. She thought of the large pile of failed power cores in Yzod's shop. "That's it!" She cried.

"That's what?" Hikari asked.

"How Yzod and I can help. Your old power cores."

Yzod's eyes went wide. "We hardly have the time to build anything. Besides, if you recall, they don't do well on impact."

"Exactly." She smiled.

"Exactly what?"

"What if we *impact* them on the beasts?"

Yzod furrowed his brow. "Oh my."

"What would that do?" Hikari asked. "I'm not up to speed on these cores, darling."

"They explode."

"Oh my, indeed." Hikari smiled.

Yzod shook his head. "With that many on the Phoenix, if we took a hit or went down…"

"A light show that would make Desitan monks blush?" Hikari asked.

"Basically."

"So fly carefully," Illeri suggested.

Yzod stared at her like she was crazy for a moment, and then he started to laugh. "Gods and Chosen."

Soon they were all laughing.

"It's a plan," he said. "I'll give you that."

"A good one," Hikari said, bumping her with his shoulder.

She looked over to see him smiling at her. For a moment they just stared at each other. She felt like she had a thousand things to say and yet nothing at all. Maybe she wanted to have something to say, but she wasn't sure what.

He *loved* her.

"But first we have to fix the Phoenix." Yzod picked up the crate.

"Right." She pulled her eyes away. "I'll help you."

"I'm headed to check on the others," Hikari said. "Unless you need my services."

Yzod looked him over. "Go on."

Illeri nodded her agreement.

Hikari turned and headed for the door, but she ran after him. She wasn't exactly sure why. She just hated to let him leave without saying anything. She grabbed his arm and he turned.

"What is it, darling?"

"I…"

He stared at her expectantly. "Yes?"

She pulled her hand back. "Don't die tonight."

He smiled, but his eyes looked disappointed. "I wouldn't dream of it."

As Hikari turned to leave, she sulked back to Yzod. He loved her, and all she could muster was *don't die*?

She sighed as she grabbed a tool out of the crate, and Yzod looked at her with a confused expression.

"Something wrong?"

"I don't know," she said. "Just thinking."

"Yeah." He climbed up on the Phoenix and gave Illeri a hand up. "Imminent battle, loss of life."

"Huh?"

"A lot on your mind," he said. "Who wouldn't at a time like this?"

"Right." She frowned. "Battle." She looked down at her hands. They were shaking again as she tried to steady them. She would be okay. They would all be okay. As for Hikari, she had time to figure that out.

Locin stood on the edge of Yzod's shop, watching two things at once. The first was a ragtag group of Arrajin soldiers that she wasn't entirely sure of. They shuffled more than marched. They were dirty and bleary eyed. No doubt many of them had been on the waterfront until the lines collapsed, and it didn't look like they'd slept much since. Their clothes smelled rank, and their mouths looked sour, but despite all this, the steely undergirding of their eyes said they were fated and angry. Maybe they were fated to die and angry about it, but it wasn't a combination she'd want to face in a fight.

The second thing she watched was a lone chimera rider, circling above the back field. She'd seen them on regular showings since they arrived. They'd circle a couple times, safely out of weapons range, then they'd scurry back to the North, across the Lion Agora and toward the Gods' Mount.

So far, there hadn't been any attacks from the cultists, but she wasn't sure how long that would last.

"How are you holding up?" Hikari asked.

She looked to her side as he joined her. He was watching the band of soldiers, but his eyes looked distant, like he wasn't focused on anything at all.

"Fine," she answered, not certain she wanted the company.

Since she'd come back, everything had been a blur of activity, and it made for a welcome distraction, but now, in the comparative quiet, she could feel the familiar emptiness of Nyx pulling at her insides, and she hated it.

"I saw the way you stood up to Neveri. That took some guts. I'm glad you made it out of there."

"Me too," she managed.

"To be honest, in Tajerim, when Voske said we were all coming back, I wasn't sure if he meant you, but I'm glad he did."

"Really?" She glanced at him skeptically.

"Of course. I have few enough genuine friends as it is. Can't go losing you, now can I?"

She shook her head and looked back out at the army. The drizzle of soldiers had turned into single drops. It was maybe two hundred men. Certainly it wasn't enough.

Hikari cleared his throat. "Have you talked to him yet?"

Locin immediately looked at Voske. He was pacing back and forth in front of the ranks of soldiers like he was some kind of general inspecting his troops. "Talked to who?"

"You know who. He might not show it, but he sought you out for a reason."

"Oh yeah?"

"Of course. You were his closest friend at the temple."

She shook her head. "I'm pretty sure I'm the last person he wants to talk to." She looked down at the ground and scuffed her foot. Wishing he'd just leave her alone.

"I wouldn't be so certain."

They fell into silence, and for a moment she started to feel bad for being so aloof. He was trying to bury the hatchet, and she wasn't making it easy.

"How are your hands?"

"Feel like a burner's bark at the moment, but they'll be alright."

"Burz didn't help you?"

"Rasa needed it more."

She nodded toward the assembling troop. "Are you gonna be fighting again?"

"I'm a champion, darling." He was staring over the assembled force, and his brow furrowed. "Still, I'd love to increase our odds."

"We've got eight champions, and Weylyn's even here. Sort of."

"I know that," he said, "but there's a thousand cultists, all armed with the weaponry of the Gods' Mount."

"Your point?"

"The point is we're in a city of tens of thousands, and the soldiers here are, what? Three hundred?"

Locin shrugged. "More like two."

"Alright, two. But there are tens of thousands of people. Surely someone who's not a soldier can be a fighter."

"Sure. Let's get the baker to devastate them with her baskets of bread."

He chuckled. "You know what I mean."

"Neveri has the people spooked. Good luck getting any of them to go up against that... *thing.*"

"You did it."

"That's different," she said. "I'm a champion, and..."

... I wanted to die.

"Crazy?" He offered.

She flashed a thin smile.

"Still. If there was some way to inspire them to courage, to convince them that our side not only *must* fight this battle, but that there's a chance in Nyx we can win it."

"Is there?"

Hikari ran a hand along his chin. "I think so, yes."

"Good luck convincing them." She turned away from him, and her eyes wandered back to the skies above. They were clear now, just a shining sheet of blue without a chimera in sight, and an idea suddenly started to form. "Huh."

"Are you alright?" He asked, leaning toward her.

"There might be a way," she muttered.

"And what's that?"

"First, have Burz heal those pretty hands of yours. And you need to get a speech ready."

A smile slowly grew on his face. "I'm a fabulous speaker, darling, but it's going to take more than words."

"Oh, there'll be more," she answered. "Come on. We don't have long."

Soon after, Hikari sat at a small table at the side of the Lion Agora. The afternoon heat hadn't yet relented, and he leaned into the scant shade offered by a dusty awning. The agora was still busy. Apparently life had to go on even in the face of impending doom, though the people often looked at the skies overhead, watching for any sign of the flying furnaces from the Gods' Mount.

"That's just the way it is now," grumbled the man sitting beside him.

The man was obviously a crier, and Hikari had selected his table by no mere accident, criers always knew everything that was going on in a city. That was their job after all.

"He's got everybody scared spitless," the crier continued. "Some are even going over to his side."

Hikari wrapped his gloved fingers across the table. His low cowl and gloves did little to ward off the heat, but at least his hands were feeling better since his visit to Burz. "His side," Hikari answered. "As in the Gods' Mount?"

The crier nodded and dabbed his forehead with a towel. "Can't say I blame them. Everybody knows the other shoe is gonna drop sooner or later. They figure they might as well be on the winning team when it does."

"But that's still insane. What, are they going to march on the city? Raze their own homes?"

"Better their homes than their lives, I suppose. Started out there were a few dozen a day, but yesterday I heard it was more like a hundred. People are starting to lose their minds."

"They need hope," Hikari mused, and he hung his head out past the awning to stare at the sky. Still no movement.

The crier guffawed at the word. "Hope's not really an option. Not anymore."

"Don't they believe the temple will come back for them?"

He shook his head. "Word has it, Neveri eats everyone he kills. That's why he's so huge. No one can hope to match that, and frankly," he leaned in until Hikari could smell the fish on his breath. "They'd be rotting fools to try."

Hikari concealed a coy smile as a distant roar echoed from above. "And what about the champions?"

"Killed? Eaten, maybe. Champions get a piece of the gods' power-" he held two fingers close together "-just a tiny piece. If they were smart, they ran away."

Hikari stood to his feet, letting the wry smile spread across his face. "Thank you, darling. You've been very helpful."

The old man looked confused. "You got somewhere to be?"

"In a manner of speaking."

He walked quickly to the great lion statue and swung himself onto its mighty paw, then started climbing his way to its head, drawing the eyes of many passersby. Soon, he was standing on its back, smiling as a few people in the plaza eyed him curiously. He grabbed his hood and threw it back, bracing himself against the marble mane.

"People of Arrajin! You've lived long enough under the heel of your beast tyrant. Behold, your salvation is at hand!"

More eyes turned his direction, but he focused on a sole figure on the opposite side of the agora. Locin stood in the shadow of the smithy, plying her boon toward the beast overhead.

"And who's that?" Mocked a voice. "You?"

Many recognized him though, and he saw the word 'champion' mouthed quietly from a dozen lips.

He raised a hand to the sky with impeccable timing as the chimera screeched into view. It began to circle the scene, but suddenly its left wing was wrenched downward and it floundered in the air.

"Not just I!" Hikari yelled. He drew his sword.

The rider slipped from his saddle and plummeted downward with a terrified scream, and the beast was quick on his heels, tumbling toward the center of the agora.

It landed in a cloud of dust and started kicking to right itself. Several people cried out in panic but nobody ran, as though they were too shocked to move.

Locin waved her hand his direction, and Hikari smiled. It was time to make his entrance. "The Champions of Talamh!" He yelled, and he sprang from the back of the lion.

Locin carried him in a high arc, fifteen feet higher than anyone had any business jumping, then down toward the beast in a heroic descent. He thrust his sword through the beast's neck. It gave a dying screech that echoed across the agora, then slumped to the ground, dead.

The attention of the crowd was thoroughly captured now, and they crowded in close, amazed by what they'd seen.

He held his bloodied sword up over the scene. "Behold your tyrants! Now tell me, people of Arrajin, will you stand with our army and fight for your homes?"

"What army?" A woman yelled.

"I've seen it!" Yelled a young boy. "It's over by the west field. They got pegs and soldiers, even a chariot!"

"That's right!" Locin yelled, and Hikari caught the glint in her eye from under her hood. "There's thousands of 'em! I seen it with my own two eyes! The Champions are back, and they're gonna kill that beast god!"

A roar erupted from several in the crowd.

A burly man stepped forward. "I'll fight!" A woman next to him grabbed his arm, but he nodded reassuringly. "If we don't fight, we've lost."

Soon several more were stepping up.

"Spread the word!" Hikari shouted. "Every citizen of Arrajin willing to fight gather in the west field. We march at dusk!"

Hikari recognized the blacksmith as he stepped on a crate in front of his shop and shouted over the crowd. "My arms and armor are yours, Champion! Everyone who has skill, come and take what you need."

"And what if we don't have skill," another man called, "but we want to fight?"

The blacksmith nodded. "Come."

Hikari laughed. "Yes! For Arrajin!"

The crowd echoed his cry as shouts of 'For Arrajin' and 'For Talamh' rolled through the plaza and spilled into the city.

68: At the Edge

Voske stood in the dusky interior of Yzod's workshop. One of the inventor's tables had been cleared of all paraphernalia and doodads, and all that remained was a well drawn map of the God's Mount. Around the table stood Burz, Illeri, Zengin, Endring, Sammel, Rasa, Hikari, Locin, and Yzod. All together. Finally.

He wasn't sure how they'd managed it, but Hikari and Locin had come back with a few hundred militia, and that number had been steadily growing for the past few hours until there were nearly a thousand citizens ready to fight for their homes. Leave it to Hikari and Locin to be that persuasive.

Voske leaned over the table and slowly turned his eyes to every face. He wasn't one for inspiring speeches, but he felt like he should say something. They were about to march into the biggest battle of their lives, and maybe their last. Burz' words echoed in his mind.

Fight. Bleed. Die.

The old soldier was staring over the map, arms crossed, and that same fire still smoldering in his eyes. He was certainly better at speeches than Voske, but he'd do his best.

"Here we are," he finally said. "The next battle could be won or lost right here in this room. We make the wrong call, and people die. If that makes you feel pressured, then good."

He tapped his finger against the center of the map and let his words sink in. Many of them nodded thoughtfully, but no one else spoke.

"That's the rub isn't it? If we don't act, Talamh falls. So here we are, no way but forward. So we're going forward, like it or not, and we're going to win, not because we're stronger, but because we have to." He pointed to an X crudely drawn over the Veil of Nyx. "Rasa says the orbs are here, hidden in the statue of Bei'ai."

She nodded. "Under her feet."

"That's the target. So how do we get there?"

There was a minute of silence while everyone stared at the map. If only it was so simple in real life.

"I'll start," Yzod said. "If it's just the orbs we're after, why not send him?" He pointed to Endring.

Endring cleared his throat. "It's not that easy. They know I'm against them now. They'll be watching for me."

"Then go in as a cat or something. Something they wouldn't expect."

Endring raised an eyebrow. "And how would a cat get into the Veil?"

"Then pick something smaller. A mouse or the like. Can you go that small?

Voske let out a loud cough. "This is going to take all of us," he said. "No one's doing this alone."

Sammel spoke up next. "There's another problem to consider. Even if we recover the orbs, Neveri will still be here."

Voske frowned. "Meaning?"

"Meaning still in Talamh. He'll still own the Gods' Mount, and he'll still be poised to take over the city. It's only a matter of time before Arrajin is fully his."

"And then the rest of the worlds," Hikari said gloomily.

The air seemed to be sucked from the room as everyone considered the words.

"Can he be killed?" Burz asked.

Voske nodded. "I saw him take a spear right to the neck. He bleeds well enough."

"Bleeding is one thing," Zengin answered. "Dying is another."

"Endring?"

Endring looked up sharply. There was something in his eyes, like Burz' fire, but different. Darker. More resigned. "He can die. And we need to kill him."

"Good enough for me."

"Perhaps the orbs should still be a priority?" Hikari asked. "Not that I expect us to fail, mind you. Personally, I plan to live until I'm old, fat, and gray. But let's call it a back up plan."

Voske nodded. "Reasonable."

Burz tapped his finger on the wide green fields around the Gods' Mount. "So we strike here, with everything we have. We'll send a few troops after the orbs, just to make sure, and the rest of us focus on Neveri." He looked up at Voske, waiting for a response.

Voske nodded. "It's a solid plan."

"Okay, fine," Locin said, sauntering closer to the table. "I'll do it."

"Do what?"

She grinned. "Steal those orbs. Sounds like a job for a thief. I can get in and out before those rotting cultists even know I'm there. You distract them at the front-" she pointed toward the back of the temple "-I'll sneak in the back."

Voske smiled. "Sure you're up for it, kid?"

"Oh, I'll do my job, old man. You just make sure you do yours."

"It's settled then."

"There are two more problems," Burz said, sliding his finger over to the river crossing. "First, our ground forces. We've got too many to fly them in, and if we march them over the Arrtris, they'll be serpent food."

"The hydra." Voske sighed.

"Yzod and I have a plan," Illeri said. She was wringing her hands, but she met Voske's gaze. "We'll need a peg to draw it out of the water, then we'll take care of it."

Voske squinted. "How?"

"We're going to explode it," Yzod said, and the corner of his mouth twitched in a smile like he was holding back a laugh.

Voske raised an eyebrow. "Do I want to know more?"

Illeri glanced at Yzod, and she was smiling now too. "It'll work. I'm sure."

Yzod glanced at Burz. "I'd keep your pegs clear though, 'til it's done. Just draw it out of the water, and then clear out, fast."

"I can lure it out," Sammel said.

Burz quickly nodded. "We both will."

"Fine," Voske answered. "Just don't let it snatch you out of the air. What's the second problem?"

"The chimera," Burz said. "They comprise the strength of Neveri's army. They'll turn us to cinder before we even get close to that monster."

Endring nodded. "Controlled by the bracer of Neveri."

"Leave it to me," Zengin said. He looked up with a cold stare.

"You know a way to stop the bracer?"

"Of course I do." As he answered, his eyes darkened. "By killing the wearer."

Voske shot Endring a glance and the older man nodded. "I've never seen Borroka take it off, and with good reason. She'd lose her grip on the beasts. If they turned wild, it would devastate their army."

"Nothing like a taste of their own medicine," Voske said. "Let's send enough soldiers to get it done. How many do you need, Zengin?"

"None."

They all stared at him with incredulity, but he didn't flinch. "I'll go alone."

"And if you fail?"

"I know the way she thinks," Zengin answered. "I can navigate around the battle, but anyone tagging along is going to get us both killed."

There was a long pause where nobody objected, but nobody really agreed either. When it became clear they didn't have a better plan, Voske finally relented. "Fine. Just make it fast."

He leaned back and folded his arms, looking over the map. The room was deathly quiet, and he could feel the fear that was trying to grip them, like a tangible presence in the room. He looked down at his hand where the shining sword of Jeza still blazed forth from his palm. Maybe it was a fool's errand. Maybe nobody in Talamh had any business challenging a god. But if someone was going to, it was going to be her champions.

"Alright," he said firmly. "We've got a solid plan. We've got an intimidating army out there." He looked up at them once again. "And we've got each other. We're in this to the end, and we won't fail." He forced a laugh, then his cheeks slowly cracked and the laugh traveled down into his belly until it was as genuine as it could be. "This is going to be good," he said, and he licked his lips. "Anyone object?"

At least every head around the table was raised now. Some shoulders still slumped, but it was a start.

"Alright then," he said. "We march at dusk."

They drifted out of the room as he stared back down, taking in every detail of the map, tracing their path across the Arrtris, up the green slope, and all the way to the temple. When he looked up again, everyone was gone. Everyone except Endring. He stood with his face hidden in shadows under his cowl, draped in black robes like the rotting embodiment of the Veil there to claim his soul.

"Something else?"

Endring strolled forward, coming to rest directly across from Voske, and he threw his hood back. His visage was still unsettling, and his eyes even more so. If Burz' burned with a hot flame, his burned with a cold one, like the blue spirit fire of Nyx.

"When I pulled Neveri through the Veil, he had no body. I can only assume he didn't need one."

Voske frowned. "What's your point?"

"He made one for himself."

"It's still a body, and one I intend to turn to ash."

"How?"

Voske scowled. "You doubt my strength?"

Endring leaned in, his voice rough. "He *made* himself a body. Out of nothing. You think you can kill something like that?"

Voske felt anger bubbling up inside. "Can we beat this monster or not?"

Endring straightened up. "We can. *I* can."

"Then why not explain this while they were all here."

"Because my plan is risky. And before you question me, no one will be risking more than I. I caused this, and it's only right I should fix it. I didn't want to tell the others, because we need them full of hope and ready to fight. But I think you have just the right temperament to take a chance on my plan. I'd rather the others not know." He sighed. "Sammel in particular."

Voske straightened up, meeting his gaze. "Alright. I'm listening."

Rasa stared into the nearly empty bowl in front of her. She'd eaten two entire bowls of soup, and she almost wanted a third.

Weylyn smiled. *I'm glad you have your appetite back.*

Rasa tipped the bowl, drinking the last of the salty broth.

Blue spirits seemed to be gathering around the shop, watching curiously like skittish animals peeking out of Nyx. They had lived in Neveri's shadow for a long time, and they seemed very curious about what was going on in Talamh.

"I don't remember ever seeing so many."

Spirits?

She nodded.

I think they seem to know. Whatever happens in Talamh will affect us all.

Rasa looked at Weylyn as a terrifying thought crept in. Separation of the realms. No more window into Nyx.

She grabbed Weylyn's hand and held fast. "It won't come to that."

A few spirits were staring at her intensely, and she started to feel uncomfortable. She wanted to push them away, but as she did, her hand slipped through Weylyn's. She stopped and pulled back, staring at her, and Weylyn pursed her lips thoughtfully.

Don't pick up that weight, Rasa. You're not responsible for any of this.

"But I can help."

You've helped plenty! I won't see you back in that monster's clutches.

Rasa bit her lip. "But I want to help. *We* can help!"

She let Nyx rush over her again, and the timid blue spirits seemed to draw closer, listening.

"I've done it before. I've seen the spirits affect people. If I could-"

It's too dangerous!

"But I'm a champion!" She protested.

Weylyn watched her for a moment with a pained expression. "Weylyn?"

She shook her head, and then nodded. *You're right. You're a champion, and the bravest person I know.*

Rasa smiled and then rushed off outside. The troops were gathering, and she spotted Voske and Burz marching through the ranks. She ran to catch up, drawing a smile from Burz as he spotted her.

"Glad you're up and about."

She nodded thankfully. This was the second time Burz had saved her life, and she felt almost guilty as she noted the tired lines on his face. He looked a good deal older than when they'd first met. "Yes. Th-thanks to you."

Voske turned and smiled at her. "You scared us, kid. There's a woman I'd like you to meet. The blacksmith's wife. She's agreed to watch out for you while we're gone."

Rasa's heart sank. "Gone?"

Burz rested a hand on her shoulder. "You've done more than enough, Rasa. We can handle it from here."

"But-"

"We won't have you hurt again."

"That's right," Voske said, clapping her lightly on the back. "You rest. You've earned it."

"I don't want to rest!" She protested. She remembered Weylyn vouching for her when they left for the Sacred Quarter, and she wished they could still hear her now. She glanced at the spirit, but Weylyn only shrugged.

I can't reason with them this time.

Voske and Burz kept marching on. Leaving her behind as she stood dumbfounded in their wake. There was no way she would sit back while the others fought for Talamh. She was chosen too, chosen for this. To be a champion.

"I'm going!" She said firmly.

Weylyn couldn't hide the hint of a smile. *I know.*

Rasa let Nyx close in around her, and a dozen spirits watched her expectantly like her own little army.

"Now," she said, "I just need a plan."

Endring stood in the back corner of Yzod's shop. He could hear their combined forces outside, making ready for their eventual march to the Gods' Mount. It was ill fated, but he didn't blame them for trying. They had to try something, and so did he.

He looked down at the two objects set before him on a workbench, the Crook of Bei'ai and a simple dagger, razor sharp. His was a foolish plan, but he'd been responsible for enough suffering. Perhaps the gods would think this was a reasonable sacrifice and allow him entrance to the Midding. Perhaps that was a foolish notion too.

He smelled Sammel's scent and heard the creak of the door. He quickly tucked the dagger into his belt and bundled the Crook into a cloth before turning to face his friend.

Sammel was standing just behind, scrutinizing Endring. "They're getting ready to leave."

"I know. Shouldn't you be saddled already?"

"I am, but I noticed you weren't with the men."

Endring forced a smile and shifted a bit to the side, better blocking Sammel's view of the table. "I was making some last minute preparations."

"With the Crook?"

Endring bit his lip. Sammel had keener eyes than he gave him credit for. "I'd rather not leave it lying around."

"I see." Sammel squinted, looking him over again.

He tried to relax but everything in him was on edge. Finally he just sighed and scuffed his foot against the floor. "I've been thinking, Sammel. What do you intend to do when all this is over?"

"I hadn't given it much thought."

"Live for the moment then?"

"I suppose. Maybe go back to Lakay, try to lay low for a while."

Endring smiled bitterly. "And how long would that last?"

"I suppose that depends on the outcome of the next several hours, and if I'm still alive of course."

"If you're still alive," Endring repeated, he reached back, resting a hand on the Crook. "For what it's worth, Sammel. I'm sorry."

"You have nothing to be sorry for that I'm not equally guilty of."

"That's kind of you to say, but I'm the one that dragged you into this, not the other way around."

"Be that as it may."

They fell into silence. Outside, Endring could hear someone asking after Sammel. He felt his throat suddenly catch. He had a thousand things to say to his old friend and no time to say any of them.

"Tell me about life in Lakay," he finally managed.

Sammel raised an eyebrow. "It's nothing you haven't heard."

"Then tell me something I don't know."

Sammel frowned and folded his hands behind his back. "There's fishing along the northern coast, marlin, flounder, and eel. The children like to catch minnows on the shoreline, sardines if they're lucky. We set fires on the beach that last until morning and play music from a dozen different lutes. At night you can see the water glow bright blue, as though spirits are out there playing in the waves."

Endring took a deep breath. "That's a good home."

"Yes." Sammel cocked his head to the side. "Why do you ask about it?"

"Because sometimes it's important to remember what you're fighting for, not just what you're fighting against."

Sammel slowly nodded. "True enough."

They were calling again, it wouldn't be long before Sammel would hear them.

"Just, do me a favor," Endring said.

"Of course."

"Make sure you make it back there, and put your toes in the water for me."

Sammel rocked onto his toes. "Why not do it yourself?"

Endring took a deep breath. "Just in case. This plan they've concocted. It's risky. We might not all make it back."

"That seems very likely."

"Just make sure you do." Endring reached out a hand and set it on Sammel's shoulder. "Promise me."

Sammel narrowed his eyes. "Alright," he said. "I promise."

"Good."

The door to the outside swung open, and a young soldier looked in, immediately spotting them. "Sammel," he said. "Your peg is saddled and ready."

Sammel nodded curtly and Endring watched him go, then he turned and took the Crook of Bei'ai, looping it over his shoulder. He took a deep breath, steeled himself, and walked out to join the army. There were no other words to say to anyone but the gods, and he prayed as he walked, for forgiveness, for courage, and most of all for redemption.

Voske kept his head high as he marched through the fields around Yzod's shop. There was an excitement among the troops, and a tension. Hikari and Locin had rounded up nearly a thousand men, and they milled about carrying anything they could find as a weapon. Burz had managed to round up nearly two hundred soldiers, possibly all that was left of the Arrajin guard. The newcomers seemed a little more enthusiastic, but Voske wondered how long before that began to fade. The men of Tajerim were more reserved, but then, they knew exactly what it was they were going to face.

Burz patted his belt where an empty sheath hung. "Not sure Atrius will be too pleased with me losing this sword."

Voske smiled. "You left it in the eye of a god from what your men tell me. I think he'll be pleased!"

Burz gave a slim smile. "What about you?"

Voske held up his empty hands. "I'll fight with whatever he's got. As long as I can lodge it in Neveri's face, won't make a bit of difference what shape it is."

A crowd was still milling around the smith, but when he spotted Burz and Voske, he shooed some of them away to make room.

"Champions!" He said heartily. "You need weapons?"

Burz pointed to his sheath. "Lost mine in battle."

Atrius smiled. "Not to worry! I have just the thing." He turned and snapped his fingers at a couple young men who seemed to be helping him hand out weapons, apprentices perhaps. They each grabbed a large bundle that Atrius clearly had set aside. The first was handed to Burz. Burz peeled back the cloth to reveal a gleaming bronze blade.

"It's one of the oldest in my collection. Its history isn't clear, but it was forged for a champion, that much I'm sure of."

"What makes you so sure?" Burz asked.

Atrius pulled the cloth covering free, and they could see the hilt gleaming with gold. It was expensive looking, but still simple in its design. Gold swirled from the bottom up in the form of a Pegasus and its rider.

"Thank you," Burz said with a smile.

Atrius turned his attention to Voske. "And for you, Champion."

The other boy handed Voske a large bundle of cloth. He slowly peeled back the layers, then sucked in a breath. It was the axe of Skard.

"Straznik Bram," Atrius said. "The most famed weapon in all the realm. Skard wielded it against the ancient King of the Hunt when he saved Arrajin. I want you to have it."

Voske ran his fingers delicately across the winged axe head, it was cold to the touch.

Burz laughed. "And I thought mine was special."

"Go on," Atrius urged. "Take it."

Voske felt his heart hammering as he gripped the haft and a quiver ran up his legs and through his spine, as though the history of the weapon had taken on a life of its own. He slowly turned it, studying every side. It felt perfectly natural in his hands, and his chest swelled. "I'd be honored," he said.

Atrius nodded and bowed out of the way. "My blessings go with you, Champion." He scurried off to carry on with his work.

Voske smirked at Burz who was looking thoroughly impressed. "How's that *sword of some unknown champion*, huh?"

Burz gave him a light shove, and Voske laughed.

A horn blast interrupted them, and Voske turned toward the sentry at the edge of the field. Something, or someone, was coming.

Without hesitation, Voske and Burz rushed toward the front. A force of men were heading their way, wearing the murky green robes of Neveri, their hoods hiding dark faces.

"How many?" Voske asked as they neared the sentry.

"Fifty?" He guessed. "Maybe sixty."

Burz scowled. "Against nearly thirteen hundred?"

"Maybe they're coming to talk?" The sentry guessed.

Voske grunted. "Whatever they're coming for, it's not good, and I'll have none of it." He hefted Straznik Bram on his shoulder and strode forward to meet them. As they neared, the man in front held up a hand and the others dutifully stopped. He came forward with just one other at his side.

When they were a stone's throw away, Voske called out, "That's close enough!"

The two men stopped. "You have quite an army," the leader yelled.

"Care to test it?"

"More like join it." He threw back his hood and Voske recognized him at once.

"Eprim?"

He and Burz headed forward and shook the Oracle's hand.

"How?" Burz asked.

Eprim smiled. "We've been hiding here since the temple fell. There's not much we've been able to do, but my scout here told me quite an interesting tale." He pointed to the man beside him.

"Oh?"

"It seems he was visiting the Lion when he saw a champion take down a chimera. Rather dramatically as he tells it."

Voske smiled.

"I admit," Eprim's face grew serious, "I had my doubts, but that was the second sign that you may actually be able to do this."

"Second?"

He smiled. "The first was when you cracked the Skard stone."

Voske felt his pride well up. "We'll be more than glad to have you with us." He moved toward the second man and held out a hand. "Seems we owe your scout some thanks."

The man threw his hood back to reveal Gillis smiling wildly.

"Gillis!"

Voske grabbed him and pulled him into an embrace.

"Champion!" He wheezed.

Voske laughed and pulled back, then he turned to Eprim again. "I admit, I didn't expect any help from the temple."

Eprim grew serious. "You're the Champion of Jeza. How can I claim to serve her if I reject her chosen? For too long the temple has tightened its grip on Talamh. I think it's time we remember we're here to serve. Time to restore some of the old ways." He glanced back at the troops behind him. "Warriors of Jeza!" He shouted. "Fall in!"

He waved an arm, and the ranks of men threw off their cloaks to reveal the red armor of Jeza. They marched up in dutiful rows, and stopped in front of Voske.

"The warriors of Jeza are yours to command, Champion."

Voske hefted Straznik Bram, drawing more than a few wide eyed stares from the monks. He grinned and then looked back at the men lined up behind him. Burz smirked.

Voske lifted his voice so they could all hear him. "Ready yourselves! We march in fifteen minutes!"

The men gave a cheer, and then headed off to gather their gear.

"And Master Gillis," he added.

"Yes, Champion?"

"Go see Atrius. If you're coming with us, you're going to need a weapon."

69: Battle Lines

As dusk fell over Arrajin, lines of soldiers and militia marched through the Trade Quarter. Above, pegs flew in a tight formation, and at their head, the Phoenix. Illeri stared down at her hands. They were shaking, but only slightly. They had a plan, and it didn't involve her boon, which helped set her mind at ease.

The Phoenix rattled as the pylat dipped over the streets of Arrajin. Yzod swore. The pile of old cores had him on edge. They were tucked carefully in crates near the center of the deck, and Yzod had insisted on laying down old blankets and linens under the crates to cushion them. They were rattling almost imperceptibly as the active core thrummed beside them.

"It'll be a wonder if we don't blow ourselves to Nyx before we reach the battle."

Hikari smiled. "Don't be so worried, darling. You have me on board."

"What's that got to do with anything?"

"I'm the hero. The hero never dies."

Illeri rolled her eyes, but she couldn't help but smile. It was good to see him with the bandages removed and in a good mood.

"I read *Gel'ad the Brave*," Yzod grunted. "He died in the end."

"Way to spoil the book," Hikari chided, "and bring down the mood." He winked at Illeri. "Honestly, darling, why do we bring him along?"

Below, the soldiers and monks streamed through the streets of Arrajin with nearly a thousand citizens who had come to join the fight. It was an impressive army, but it wouldn't mean anything if they couldn't cross the only bridge to the Gods' Mount. It sat ahead like a stone wall over the churning, brown Arrtris.

"Get ready!" Yzod yelled from the front. "Burz and Sammel are in position."

Illeri walked to the crate and motioned for Hikari to help her slide it to the now torn railing where the claw marks of Neveri ran in black ravines across the deck.

"Good gods," Hikari wheezed. "How heavy are these things?"

"I don't know," she confessed. "Voske loaded them."

They managed to scrape it along to the edge. Hikari leaned over as Yzod slowed the pylat to a stop, leaving them hanging in mid-air just above the river. Below, bubbles were rising, and a deep, unearthly cry echoed under the water

"Hold steady," Yzod said. "I'll get us as close as I can."

The pylat slowly lowered toward the waterline until Illeri could feel her stomach tighten. "That's close enough, don't you think?"

Yzod raised an eyebrow. "We're a hundred feet up. Just how big is this thing?"

"Very."

He pursed his lips and locked the chains. "Here it is then."

Illeri glanced toward the city. The army of Arrajin was just filing onto the shoreline, but there was no movement yet from the Gods' Mount. "So far, so good," she whispered.

She hoisted one of the cores out of the crate. It was at least thirty pounds, and the rounded surface felt slick in her hands. She set it carefully against the deck and took a deep breath, trying to settle her nerves.

"Look," Hikari said, pointing a hand down the river.

Burz and Sammel were there, rushing upstream, their pegasus' hooves only inches above the water. As they rode, Burz blew a silver trumpet, and the army let out a mighty yell.

She leaned out over the edge until her fear pulled her back. The bubbling of the water had stopped and the murky surface was still, eerily so. No fish, no creatures of any kind moving, just the steady swift current of the Arrtris. She felt Hikari tense and realized she was holding her breath.

"Come on, you menace," Hikari muttered. "Where are you hiding?"

Burz and Sammel were nearly underneath them now, and she leaned forward again, but as she did her hand brushed the core. She quickly grabbed toward it, but the slick surface slipped from her grasp, sending the explosive hurtling down toward the riders.

"No!" She yelled, and she threw her body down to the deck, watching with horror.

"There he is!" Hikari yelled.

The pegs suddenly veered skyward, bolting away from the water as a dozen immense heads erupted from below the surface, snapping at their heels.

Illeri stayed fixed on the core. It hurtled downward until it cracked against the scaly hide of the hydra, right between Burz and Sammel. A flash of searing light started to erupt, but that was as far as it got. She kept her boon wrapped around the explosion, refusing to let it happen. Not yet.

A geyser of water sprayed upward, and the roar of the hydra filled her ears as the pegasus flew past.

"What in Nyx happened!" Yzod exclaimed in wonder.

Hikari laughed. "That's Illeri! She's got it!"

The hydra recoiled, leering up at them like a snake, ready to strike a bird from the sky.

"This is for Weylyn," Illeri whispered, and she opened her hands, letting time take control of the explosion.

A shockwave ripped outward, and the air ignited, scorching the scales of the beast with burning light. It roared in pain and tossed violently, as another core from the hand of Yzod struck its body, shredding one of the coiled necks down to the bone.

Quickly it sank back below the water and the men and women of Arrajin yelled in unison then hurried to cross the river.

Illeri stood back up, feeling Yzod clap her on the back and hearing Hikari cheer her name. It was all very strange. Finally she looked toward them to smile, but instead her brow knit tightly together.

"You did it!" Hikari exclaimed. "What's wrong?"

She pointed a finger past them toward the Gods' Mount where scores of cultists were assembling on the slopes. The battle wasn't won. It hadn't even started.

"Alright then," Hikari said with a smile, rubbing his hands together. "There's more to be done." He started pulling light to them, shifting it apart and plucking out colors.

"What are you doing?"

"Well, if we're flying into that viper's nest, we're at least going to do it in style. You know, to help rally the troops. Never underestimate the power of a little drama!"

He winked at her and then threw his arms out to the sides, and flames burst across the deck and coalesced against the hull, spreading back along the sides in the form of red and orange feathers until the Phoenix had its very own pair of flaming wings.

"Not bad," Yzod said as he urged the pylat forward.

"I do try, darling."

Chaos surrounded Rasa. She was starting to regret her decision to sneak into the ranks of the militia. Now she was jostled amidst the civilians that rushed toward the slopes of the Gods' Mount. She was a Champion. She wanted to help, but maybe Voske was right. What could she do here?

A large man with a sword pushed past her, and she tripped, falling headlong into the grass. People were yelling, and she heard the war cry of the cultists ahead. A clash of blades, and anguished cries - it was all too much. Behind her the rush of untrained fighters became more jumbled, and she felt someone step on her leg. She would be trampled, and that thought brought with it panic. She instinctively reached for her boon, calling on Nyx for help as she threw her arms over her head.

But the next blow never came. The cries of the army grew distant, like voices through closed doors, and the abyss of Nyx swelled around her. Slowly she stood, turning to face the crowd. Behind her, a wall of blue spirits watched with somber faces, arms outstretched in a tangled mass, and beyond, in the land of living, the militia rushed around the spirits like an invisible dam splitting the course of a river.

Weylyn frowned. *Are you alright?*

Rasa nodded as she took it all in. She saw Spark nearby, pointing up at the Spire of Bei'ai.

Here! Come on. You'll be safe there.

The last thing Rasa wanted was to hide away and be safe. She had come to help. To fight alongside the others. But as she turned to view the battle, her heart quailed. Ahead, the soldiers clashed with the first line of cultists. She couldn't see much through the tangle of bodies, but she heard the ghastly sounds of battle, and it made her stomach turn. She pulled away from the noises, feeling the black of Nyx swallow her up until she felt she would slip right in.

Rasa?

Weylyn's hand on her arm pulled her back, and she gasped for air.

Come on. Weylyn said. *Spark is right. Let's get you to safety.*

She nodded and let herself be led toward the spire, the spirits keeping a wall between her and the fight. By the time she stood before the door, she felt her boon taking a toll, and she let it go until only Spark and Weylyn stood beside her. The spire of Bei'ai was the same height as the others, but the stone looked darker, and a narrow spine of ivory wood circled its way to the top. A field of deep purple flowers surrounded the base, and the door was painted with a deep blue skull, staring out of inky black. She pushed against the skull and the door opened to a dim room lit by a single torch in a wall sconce.

Weylyn stepped in front of her. *The tower seems clear. You should get to the top.*

"The top?"

You can see the whole field from there. Perhaps Spark can relay messages to Locin.

Rasa smiled at the thought. She could still be useful. "Right. The top!"

She plucked the torch off the wall. The bottom of the tower was covered by bowls of incense, and the bitter smell made her light headed. Nothing appeared out of place or destroyed, as though the cultists had left it alone.

She turned to the stairs and hurried up the steep path, watching as the urns of Champions past grew slowly less ornate. When she reached the top, she found a ladder leading to the upper balcony. She nestled the torch in a sconce and pushed the hatch open, letting in the fresh air. She could see the whole temple from here, and the fields that stretched to the spire. It looked like the cultists hadn't been ready for them. Cultist bodies littered the field as their reinforcements charged toward the battle line. No doubt they'd thought their hydra would buy them more time. But even now, they rallied, and chimera rose from the rooftops meeting the flight of pegasus in the sky. Archers covered the walls of the temple, raining arrows across the Champions' army.

Rasa put a hand to Weylyn's bow, slung across her back, but Weylyn held out a hand to stop her.

Not yet. You aren't ready.

"But I want to help."

You will.

She stared back at the battle, watching as more and more cultists rushed the increasingly outmatched forces of Arrajin.

An explosion to Voske's right blasted the enemy archers free of the raised portico, and debris rained across the upraised shields of Arrajin. Voske tightened his grip on Straznik Bram and glanced up. The Phoenix was aloft on the winds. Another core dropped, followed by another explosion, and finally the arrows stopped. The shields of Arrajin gradually lowered, revealing the regrouped forces of the cultists. They snarled and screamed out threats, glaring from sunken eyes.

Voske could sense the tension along their battle line and he looked down the front until he made eye contact with Locin. "You ready?"

"Yeah."

"Remember, just get to the Veil and get out, nothing stupid. We'll hold the way open for you."

She picked up a free arrow, making it spin in the air just above her hand. "Make the call, big guy."

"For Talamh!" He roared, then barreled forward, charging straight toward the enemy line.

The cultists charged in return, collapsing toward them, just inside the wings of the portico. The two sides walloped into each other like slabs of stone, but neither cracked under the pressure.

"Push them back!" Voske yelled over the din. "Push!"

Two men closed on him and he batted one aside like a ragdoll. The second swung a large iron mace straight into his hip, but his boon made the blow feel like balsa wood.

He slashed Straznik Bram upward, cleaving the man's arm at the shoulder, then he cried aloud and barreled further in, swinging the legendary weapon in wide arcs and felling opponents like he was scything wheat.

A spearman lunged toward him, finding a gap between his blows, but the head of the spear was sheared off by the razor sharp sword of Eprim.

"Champion!" Eprim called. "We need you on the portico!"

Voske looked behind him. A cluster of archers had retaken the high ground, and were firing arrows into the unshielded rear line where the militia fought.

Voske shoved his fingers in his mouth and let out a sharp whistle.

Locin spun his direction and he pointed to the archers. "Get me there!" He yelled.

She rolled her eyes and quickly raised her hands, launching him over the enemy force.

"Not that far!' He yelled as he plummeted down to the top of the portico, well behind his target.

He landed in a cloud of dust and sprang back to his feet. A few of the archers were looking back at him now, their eyes wide and knuckles white.

"Wh-who are you?" One of them asked, his voice quavering.

Voske shouldered the great axe and stepped toward them. "I'm the vengeance of the gods," he growled. "Who are you?"

The cultists turned around, drawing their pointy sticks and clustering shoulder to shoulder like a group of cornered mice.

"We're the warriors of Neveri," one of them squeaked.

Voske held up his hand, flashing the sigil of the goddess. "And I'm the chosen of Jeza. Now, which one of you will fight for the honor of your god?"

Without a word they barreled over the side, trampling each other as they fought to not be the last in line.

Voske laughed aloud, feeling his mood soar. They were going to win this.

He leapt down off the portico into the Arrajin ranks and started back toward the front, pushing past soldiers until he saw Locin again. She was working her way toward the side, to where the shadow of the sanctum hung over the portico. She was almost there.

"Just a little farther!" He yelled. "Don't let up!"

An explosion from the Phoenix rattled the enemy ranks and they broke, running back toward the top of the steps where they were trying to redraw their line. He looked for Locin again, but she'd disappeared. Hopefully that was a good sign.

"Don't let them regroup! Keep on them!"

He reached the front where Eprim fought and fell in beside him, but the advance was beginning to slow and more and more cultists nipped at the flanks, picking apart the sides of the army.

"We can't stay here forever," Eprim yelled.

"We'll hold this open," he answered, trying to muster as much fire as he could.

"How long?"

"As long as it takes."

The roar of a chimera sounded in the distance and Voske glanced skyward, noting a score of dark shadows rushing over the roof of the temple.

"Zengin better hurry."

70: High Ground

The commotion at the front of the temple was a distant echo in the chambers below the Oracles' Wing. The riverside door had proved useful for gaining surreptitious access, and the two guards at the entry had been laughably inadequate to keep it secure. Fortunately, these cultists were not only stupid, they were also impressionable, and the two guards guided Zengin through the back halls of the temple complex, the type of shadowy passageways that only servants ever really trod and that could get you from one place to another in the most inconspicuous way possible.

"Borroka's gonna be happy," one of his reluctant guides mused. "Ever since that rotting traitor Endring turned, she's been saying we don't have a champion anymore."

"Yes," Zengin agreed, his voice still rife with the honey of Metnadur. "How good that he'll be replaced when Metnadur joins the forces of Neveri."

They led him on, twisting through dark passages until they emerged in a lavish foyer, covered in gold that Zengin recognized as the guest hall for dignitaries.

"Pig slop," one of the men said. "This is where she's been."

Zengin rolled his eyes. Perhaps he'd been too optimistic in their minute intellect. "There's a battle out front," he snapped. "She's not the type to hide in her room."

The man scratched his head. "I s'pose, but she *was* here."

"Where's the closest roof access?"

"But why would-"

"The roof access," Zengin snapped. "Now!"

The dottard slowly nodded and stared back the way they'd come. "Why do you think she'd be there?"

"Because I know how she thinks."

The two men jogged back through the empty halls, winding their way to a narrow stairwell. They climbed up four stories until they emerged at the top of the temple, overlooking the sanctum and portico below. The sounds of battle were much more distinct here, and Zengin could see Yzod's chariot and a few dozen pegasus darting around the skies as they engaged Neveri's forces. Blasts of fire scorched the sky, and from the south more chimera were continuing to stream in. Their army was going to be overwhelmed.

"By Neveri," one of the guards muttered. "There she is. How'd you know that?"

Zengin followed the man's finger to where Borroka stood on the edge of the roof staring over the battle. She held her curved blade in her right hand and kept her left arm aloft, bracer glimmering in the moonlight.

"I'll go it alone from here," Zengin answered.

"But without us, she'll think you're an enemy."

Zengin glanced at the silent cultist, he seemed to be muttering to himself, as though he was having some kind of internal argument. Perhaps he wasn't as foolish as Zengin believed. "Very well," Zengin answered. "Lead on, and be quick."

The two men started across the rooftop at a brisk pace and Zengin pulled his dagger from its sheath. He'd carried this dead weight long enough.

"Hold on now!" Yzod yelled as he swung the Phoenix around, skirting just out of the range of a flurry of arrows. Hikari braced himself against the side post, staring down at the battle below and wrestling the light out of the atmosphere and down onto the battlefield. It was a swirling orange light, the glare of their pylat's wings mixed with the glow of hundreds of torches.

He gathered it close around a cluster of cultists and Illeri dropped a spark core right into their center, blasting them into fiery confusion.

"Ha!" Yzod cried. "That'll do the trick!"

Hikari swept the light to the side, searching for a new target, but it was getting harder to tell the good guys from the bad. The entire battlefield was choked with smoke and dust, and the cries of men pierced upward into the night sky, punctuated by the ringing explosions of the cores.

"Hikari!" Burz yelled.

He looked to see him atop Sauri, flying just past the Phoenix's gashed railing. "Eprim needs help in the courtyard!"

Hikari quickly swung the light to the area, illuminating a new band of cultists charging from the army's flank.

"I see it!" Yzod yelled, and he yanked at the chains, performing another sharp turn that threatened to knock Hikari off his feet.

"Move with the chariot," Illeri said.

Hikari glanced her direction and managed a smile. "Easy for you to say. You've flown on these your whole life."

"So have you."

"I've sat on these. Standing is another matter."

He refocused on the charging horde and tightened the grip on his boon, but the hotter the light grew the more his hands began to spasm, as shooting pain tore up his fingers and through his arms.

Finally, he had to relent and just held the light in place as he glanced back at the crate of cores. "How many more do we have?"

"Two," Illeri answered. "Don't worry. It'll be enough."

She looked back out over the attacking horde and staged the core on the very edge, waiting for her moment. "Three," she counted. "Two, one."

The chariot suddenly lurched to the side and the core slipped out at an angle, smashing into the ground just beside the attackers and doing little more than churning up the dirt. A blast of fire roasted across the deck, and Hikari ducked backward as the attacking chimera rushed past, roaring out its challenge.

Illeri looked up at him, wide-eyed. "Where is Zengin?"

Hikari held out a hand to help her up. "Just running a bit late, I'm sure. Don't worry, darling, he'll have that bracer dealt with in no time."

From the stables on the far side, a black mass churned toward the battlefield, shrouding the temple in shadow and wailing like banshees. Hikari could see the blistering tongues of fire churning in their mouths as they circled around the back edge of the forces of Arrajin.

He cupped his hands to his mouth, yelling down at them. "Look out! Look behind you!"

Illeri reached out toward the mass, slowing the front edge, but where ten stopped, a hundred rushed past.

"Those people need to get out of there!" Yzod yelled and he swung the Phoenix around once more, but it was already too late.

The winged horde of Neveri blanketed the force, descending on the militia and bathing the unarmored flesh in scorching fire.

The people screamed and buckled, but they had nowhere to run. They surged toward the temple, and rammed themselves into the backs of the soldiers, anything for another inch from the death that flocked behind them.

Hikari could see Burz and the riders of Tajerim battling against the flood, but what could so few do against so many?

Burz plunged into the heart of the dark swarm. He clung to his sword with a fading grip. The fury of battle had fueled him so far, but as the battle continued to rage, his strength continued to wane. Everywhere there were claws and teeth and blackened swords. His blade met a rider, and he cleaved through the man's helmet, painting the air with a spray of blood.

"Come on!" He urged. He kicked his heels into Sauri's flanks. He could see a gap in the swarm above them and shafts of moonlight shone through, lighting the path of escape. "Climb!"

He turned Sauri skyward and they surged for the gap, dipping and ducking the claws that swiped from every side. Screams of pain punctuated the air behind him. The panic of the army was all too visceral and he yelled aloud, desperate to find open skies.

He swung his sword again, but he could feel his arm burning with the effort, as though the blade weighed a thousand pounds. He'd given so much to Rasa, and he'd had hours to recover. He'd needed days. But what choice did he have?

The gap above narrowed, and he pressed Sauri on, but they were too late, and as it closed over them, his heart sank. They were surrounded. He pulled back on the reins, slowing Sauri and leveling out. The forces of Arrajin had been devastated, and they ran for cover, each man focused only on surviving.

Terror started to grip him, but he felt his heart surge against it. He couldn't go down without a fight. He turned Sauri against the swirling mass, setting his eyes on a hideous two-headed chimera that was chasing down a peg and rider. The beast seemed to swim through the air more than fly. Its fur was black as coal, and rancid tar dripped from its gaping maws.

A sudden blast drove the minions beside him back and he turned toward it with wonder. Sammel was there, still battling against the tide. The snap of his whip sowed chaos among the enemy, and they lurched away, forming a new gap in the swarm.

Burz took his chance and urged Sauri on, through the gap and toward his mark. They rose on the wind, soaring above the drooling heads of the chimera. The beast seemed more focused on the peg it was chasing, and its tongues flicked hungrily as its heads followed its movement.

Burz mustered his strength and rolled to his right. Sauri instinctively tucked in his wings and spun over, giving Burz a clean strike at the matted black fur of the creature's back. He cleaved his blade downward, feeling the bronze sink into hardened flesh. It wasn't a deep gash, but the monster let out a roar and spun upward, snapping at Sauri's heels with iron jaws.

Burz quickly doubled back, aiming for a wing that was as large as Sauri's combined. One of the heads looked back and a blast of fire exploded, igniting the air like a tinderbox. Burz pressed hard against Sauri's neck and they dove under, careening toward the jungle canopy.

The chimera was only yards behind them. It was startlingly fast, with its wings stretched up like a diving falcon.

"Faster!" He yelled.

He watched as the sword-like claws of the beast drew closer. They weren't going to make the treeline in time. He tightened his grip around his sword and steadied his knees against Sauri's flanks. "Uthando," he whispered, "guide my blade."

As the chimera came close, Burz drove his knees into Sauri hard, and he obeyed, throwing his wings out to catch the wind. The chimera couldn't slow down, and Burz drove his sword straight up toward its chest. It slashed a claw to intercept, and Burz felt the nail cut deep into his left arm, but his right arm didn't falter. He drove the blade of his sword into the matted fur, and the beast roared in pain. Immediately it broke out of its dive, flailing in the air like a fish on a hook. As it reeled back, Burz' sword wrenched free, leaving a gaping wound, but he felt the sharp claws of the chimera rip into his leg and shred through Sauri's wing. There was a moment of uncertainty while they teetered in the air, until Sauri's wing flailed violently and gave out. Burz dug his heels into the peg's flanks, bracing himself as they spiraled toward the ground.

754

"Hold still!" he shouted, pressing his hands against Sauri's withers. He called on his boon and cried out in pain as he felt the torn wing. It felt like his arm was snapped backward, bones shattered. He bit down and pressed into his boon, calling on Uthando's mercy until there was nothing left.

Sauri opened his wings for barely a moment, then they slammed into the ground. Burz felt his good leg crushed beneath Sauri's side. The pegasus rolled away, lying in a heap, and Burz' lay still, breathing hard as pain tore through his body.

He struggled to stand, fumbling to find the sword that had slipped from his grasp. All around him was chaos and death, and where was their army?

A bellowing shout sounded from behind him, and he turned to see a behemoth of a man strapped with leather armor and wielding a bloodied logger's axe. He wore the putrid green of Neveri, and his eyes were shrouded in black. He barreled toward Burz, striking with his axe, but Burz stepped inside the swing, grabbing hold of the haft.

There was a time when he could have won this fight, but now his hands stiffened, burning with the blisters of Hikari, and his ribs ached with the broken bones of Rasa. He felt anger overwhelm him as he broke under the weight of everyone else's burdens.

The man shoved him back, and his legs buckled, landing him in the dust. The brute stood over him, raising the axe high, and Burz beat at his leg, but he had no strength left. The edges of his vision began to grow dark, and in his mind's eye he could see Hadris, smiling.

He felt his hands close around the man's ankle, as something stirred within him. He could feel his boon rushing through his arms, and he tightened his grip as the brute cried out in pain. In the desperation of the moment, he felt his boon *pulling*. He wasn't giving life, he was taking it. He felt a rush like cold flame coming back down his arms, surging into his lungs. Fatigue slipped away, and his eyes shot open.

The large man looked startled. His skin was pale and his eyes wide with the look of a man facing his own death. He fell back, but Burz grabbed him tightly, climbing on top of him. His face was gaunt and wrinkled as the life poured out of him. Burz could feel it like a river now, chasing away his weariness until even the ache in his leg was unrecognizable. He felt stronger than he had in years.

The man's eyes widened in terror, and he sputtered to speak. "Wh-what is this?" He choked. "What are you doing?"

He tried to pull away, but Burz wouldn't let him go. He'd never felt this strong before. He bore down harder, drawing out every last scrap of strength until the light of the brute's eyes was extinguished, and only a hollow shell remained. He tossed the mighty man's body aside with barely a shrug and stood to his feet. The world around him was alive with blazing colors, and the power in his muscles felt surreal. He lifted the brute's axe and gazed across the battle.

Nearby, he spotted Voske fighting through a band of cultists, and he rushed to his side. A challenger with a sword swung at him, but Burz nimbly ducked aside, pivoting on his once-bad leg, and hewed the man's head from his body. He quickly snatched up the sword, brandishing the familiar weapon with a gleeful smile. Seconds later three more opponents were felled, and he looked to Voske. The big man had a nasty gash along his cheek, and dirt and blood caked his arms. He was breathing hard. Burz fell in beside him, landing a kick to his opponent that sent the man toppling back into the enemy ranks.

Voske glanced toward him with surprise. "Well!" He shouted. "Looks like someone decided to join the real fight."

"I couldn't let you have all the fun," Burz answered.

"Glad to see you're better."

Burz nodded. He could barely believe just how much better.

"This way!" Voske dove headlong back into the fray, swinging the axe of Skard as if it were a feather, and Burz set his own sight on another opponent, diving in. For the first time, he felt like a hero from the old stories. Maybe they didn't have a chance at victory, but he wouldn't trade this feeling for the worlds.

71: Vengeance

Zengin wiped the blood from his dagger. The two cultists' bodies lay in front of him near the stairwell, but his eyes were fixed on Borroka.

She was ahead at the far end, watching over the battle. It was a good vantage point, mostly obscured by the parapets and domed towers with a clear view of the temple grounds. Overhead, she watched her Chimeras as they breathed fire down on their enemies. Zengin watched as one turned on several pegs, sending them scattering.

He slowed as he approached. Borroka was transfixed by the bloody scene below, so much so that she might never notice him until he pushed her over the edge and let her body crumple against the stone garden. Something inside him said that wouldn't be enough. He wanted to see her face. He wanted to make her bleed. He stood frozen, dagger clenched in his left hand.

A pegasus swooped close overhead, pursued by a chimera, and Borroka turned as she followed it. Her eyes fell on Zengin, and she sneered.

"I remember you." She glanced at the stub where his right hand had been. "Did you come to offer me the other one?"

Zengin took a step back and kept his dagger poised. She advanced closer, and he kept backing away, safely out of range.

She laughed. "You're pathetic. You must have come here for a reason. Was it simply revenge?"

His eyes caught the glint of light off her bracer, and she followed his gaze.

"I see." She lifted her arm, and the shining bracer of Neveri seemed to glow brighter. "With every second you delay, your friends are getting eaten alive. So go ahead. Come and take it."

Zengin slowly circled, careful not to wedge himself into a corner. "Make no mistake, I'm here for one reason. To end your life."

"You're welcome to try." She lunged forward, but he leapt back, keeping plenty of distance between them.

"Let's not get ahead of ourselves," he said. "Did I ever tell you how I grew up?"

She glowered at him. "I don't care."

"I was the son of the Archon of Tajerim."

She laughed derisively. "I should have known. Soft and decadent."

"It wasn't the life you'd expect. You can't even imagine the darkness I've seen."

"I wouldn't be so sure!" She lunged again and this time the edge of her blade caught hold of his side, tearing a painful gash just under his ribs.

He winced at the pain, but he kept his wits about him and stepped back farther.

"You're going to run out of room," she mocked. "And what will you do then?"

"It was unfair," he pressed. "Difficult, but that's life. Nothing goes according to plan." He poured all the honey he could into his words, and for a moment he saw her hesitate, as though her mind was protesting the influence.

"You could struggle for decades in service to your master only to have him choose a *traitor* as his champion."

She sneered. "Endring is a fool!"

"He is, and yet he was chosen over you."

"He had access to the Veil. It was unfair. It would have been me. It *should* have been me."

"It could still be you."

She sneered in response and kept advancing.

"What if he was dead?"

"You tried this before," she spat, "and it lost you a hand."

"What if you could kill him right now?"

Borroka blinked, and her legs came to a stuttering halt.

Zengin smiled.

She trembled with anger as the thought took root. "He's here," she said in a stupor. "He's in the battle."

"I'll make you a deal," Zengin crooned. "Give me the bracer, and I will tell you exactly where he is."

She shook her head, fighting his words. "He'll die in the battle."

"At another's hand?"

Her face twisted in a pained grimace. She couldn't bear the thought of it, just as he couldn't bear the thought of another killing her.

She looked down at the bracer, then back up. "You think to control me?" She spat. She advanced again, but it was halting this time, as though she had to will every step.

"You want to take the chance that someone else finds him first? His blood is yours to spill!"

She swung toward him again, but this time he easily slid out of the way and watched as the sword drifted by like she was swinging through water.

"Give me the bracer," he said sharply, and he risked a step toward her this time. "This is your only chance to end his pitiful life and get your revenge."

Her eyes widened, and sweat dripped from her brow as she lost the fight. She slipped her sword into its sheath without a sound, then reached for the bracer's laces, picking at the knot. Zengin wasted no time lunging forward and burying his dagger in her chest.

Her eyes flickered in recognition and she grabbed hold of Zengin's hand, freezing it to the dagger as her blood ran out around his fingers.

"You found it," she said, staring at him with hatred and admiration.

"The one thing you desire most." He smiled. "And now you'll never have it. You rotting fool."

"I wanted what you wanted. Vengeance…"

Her voice fell off and her arm lost all strength. She tumbled back to the roof, and her lungs gurgled with each breath.

Zengin quickly snatched her sword from its sheath and stepped down on her right shoulder. With one quick blow, he severed her arm below the bracer, then lifted it in front of her.

"How does it feel?" he snarled.

She stared at him, gulping down her own blood.

He grabbed the front of her tunic and pulled her up. "How does it feel!?"

A cold smile curled her lips, then her head rolled to the side, and her eyes went blank, staring into the eternity of Nyx.

Zengin's hand trembled in rage as he reached down and loosened the laces. He lifted the bracer and let the bloody appendage fall with a dull thump. He walked toward the edge of the roof. Already he could tell the tenor of the battle had changed. There was more chaos, more confusion. A chimera suddenly burst into view twisting and writhing through the air as its rider screamed in terror. In moments the man was shaken free and the chimera landed atop the roof, eyeing Zengin with rage.

He quickly looped the bracer over his arm and held it up. Instantly, the beast's rage receded and it stared at him, transfixed by the sight. He reached out a hand, setting it on the chimera's nose and slowly ran his fingers over its coarse fur.

All over the battlefield, shouts erupted. The chimera were breaking formation. Some ran, others began scorching anything and everything in their path. Chaos was swallowing the cultists' ranks.

Voske felt a surge of fresh strength fill his body, and he shot a weary smile at Burz. "He did it!"

Burz nodded solemnly. The foes in the fields were retreating to the portico, but it was clear both armies were spent.

"The pegs are regrouping," Voske said. "We need to take the sanctum back. Now."

Burz nodded, whistling to the pegs above. There were only a scattered few left. Sammel swooped low, and Burz pointed toward the sanctum. "We're pushing for the temple. Cover us!"

A nod, and Sammel was back in the air, rallying what forces he could.

The men around them looked fearful, shooting hesitant glances toward the enemy. It seemed the victory over the chimeras had many ready to call it a day while they were ahead.

"Advance!" Voske called, his deep voice rolling over the field. "We're taking the sanctum!"

A score answered the call, maybe two. Most of them were soldiers, and they had the same fated look in their eyes that he felt in his own heart. He spotted Gillis among them. The young man looked shaky at best, spatters of blood dotting his face and arms. His eyes held a look of horror, and his legs trembled, but still he came forward in haltering steps. Voske smiled, slapping a hand on Gillis' shoulder as the troops regrouped behind him, stepping over the bodies of their comrades to answer the call. Above, the remaining riders circled in a loose formation, Sammel at their head.

"Fly!" Burz cried, and he gave a sharp whistle.

The pegs swooped down to the field and led the charge as the cultists fired a volley of arrows that rained across the soldiers, then another. Voske could hear the men behind him crying out, but he kept his eyes on the sanctum doors, broken and leaning behind the cultists.

Sammel raised his whip and cracked open the center of their line, and the soldiers surged through the like water through a dam, flooding toward the temple.

Voske shouted over the men as he lifted Straznik Bram. The cultists before him went pale. Their defenses were broken, their chimera scattered, the battle all but lost. Voske charged through their ranks, cutting down one after another. He was nearing the temple steps now, the broken portico looming ahead. Victory felt so close. He let his heart surge at the thought.

But his joy was short-lived. A bone chilling wail carried over the battlefield. At the sound of it the fighting came to a stand-still, and every eye turned toward the temple where a man stood on the shattered roof at the edge of the sanctum. He spoke with a voice like a mountain.

"Who is it you have come to fight against?" He challenged. "A feeble man? A quivering runt?"

The voice was deafening, shaking the ground at Voske's feet. He looked at Burz who met his gaze with worry.

"People are such fragile creatures. You scrape and claw and scratch out your lives, existing only on the whim of Sbarga."

As he spoke he slowly grew in size, bones laced his arms and legs, and his head was crowned by nine horns. The wings of a bird erupted from his back, and sharp talons sprouted from his toes. His eyes turned to pure black, and he loomed over the army, each leg like the trunk of a proud oak as he stepped into the broken remains of the portico; and the stones crumbled beneath his feet.

"Come and test your mettle," Neveri jeered. "The doors of Nyx are wide open."

A wave of terror passed over, and Voske felt despair creep in as the troops nearby began to shake and tremble. Some threw their hands over their ears and cried out, and still others turned and ran.

This couldn't be it. It couldn't end here. Voske heaved Straznik Bram onto his shoulder. His bones groaned as he summoned his boon in full force. He was weary and sore, but he bit down the ache as he felt power surge through him, and he marched through the quaking line of soldiers toward the base of the temple steps. He just had to buy Endring some time.

He glanced to the sky. The pegs were falling back, staying clear of the monstrous beast. His eyes darted to and fro, looking for any sign of Endring.

Voske looked back down at the scattering army and lifted the mighty axe of Skard in challenge. "Don't listen to him," he shouted. "Stand with me! Find your courage!"

Behind him, the scant forces of Arrajin marshaled into place, and Burz strode to his side, his sword ready, and his eyes bright.

"Together," he said sharply.

Voske smiled. "Together."

Neveri sneered. "So be it!"

The ground shook as Neveri took two large steps toward them. How could any man fight something so large?

Voske steadied himself, calling on his boon until fire filled his fingertips, then he rushed the stairs, filled with terror and fury.

Neveri laughed as they approached. "Is this it?" He mocked. "Is this your valiant last stand?" He opened his mouth, and the red-hot fire of a chimera glowed from his tongue.

"Take cover!" Voske yelled, and he dove behind the remnants of the statue of Skard, pulling Burz with him.

Fire enveloped the path, pouring between the pillars and licking at his feet. He pushed back against Skard, gritting with pain as the sweat of his body began to boil.

A sudden explosion cut the fire short and Voske quickly poked his head around the statue.

Neveri roared as he staggered backward. Part of his head was missing, and only one eye remained. Above them, the Phoenix rode the sky, light swirling around them in the form of three great dragons.

"Yes!" He yelled.

Neveri quickly righted himself, and his skull reformed, growing out blood-red skin that blossomed into bone.

"You will burn for that!"

Fire flared in his mouth again, but Voske turned and looked over the statue of Skard. The giant figure held a stone axe, as tall as six men and immeasurably heavy.

"Gods forgive me," he muttered and he wrenched the axe free, using every bit of his strength to hoist it to his shoulder. "Is that all you got, Nyxhound?"

Neveri turned sharply toward him, but before he could speak, Voske hurled the axe with all his strength.

It was a perfect throw, and the sharp edge of stone rushed toward the monster's belly with devastating force. It was just yards away when Neveri caught it. He slid backward, absorbing the blow, then dropped the stone weapon to the ground with a vile sneer. "Enough!"

He crouched low and leapt with ferocity, barreling down on top of Voske and driving his fist into his body. The impact sent Burz toppling back down the steps, and the stone of the portico shattered like glass, but Voske's bones didn't break.

He braced himself under the fist and pushed upward, driving his shoulders into the rockhard skin of Neveri.

Neveri pulled back, and Voske staggered to the ground, feeling as though his spine had turned to jelly.

"And now you see it," Neveri thundered. "Poor, mortal fool! My sister gives you the scraps of her power, and you think it's enough to challenge a god?"

Neveri heaved another fist downward, and this time Voske had nothing left to give. His head rolled back against the stone, staring upward at the sky till all he could see were the stars, beckoning him toward Sbarga. His body pulled at him, eager to let go, to slip away as the crushing weight of Neveri pummeled him into the ground, and the fire of Jeza scorched his bones from within.

Where was Endring?

72: The Edge of the Abyss

No one saw Locin. As soon as Neveri stepped out onto the field, he commanded the attention of everyone. Part of her wished she had charged that monster with Voske and Burz, and she was kicking herself for not doing it as she rounded the outer wall of the sanctum.

Her foot twisted into an unseen hole and she swore.

Careful.

"Easy for you to say." She looked over at Spark, hovering beside her. "We can't all just float around. Some of us have to work for it."

Spark smirked. *Work better.*

Locin found a place where the sanctum wall looked mostly intact, a smooth contour of stone rising toward the mangled ceiling. She took a deep breath. "Have I mentioned I liked you better before I could see you?"

You have. Spark's voice lost its humor. It wasn't cold or sarcastic. It was just sad.

Locin pushed the bubble of emotions from her mind. She had a mission to focus on. She sprang onto the wall and the sandals of Iyanu gripped against the stone, but that didn't make it easy. She ran upward, keeping up the rapid motion until she reached the lip of the roof high above, then swung over and let her sandals drag down the stonework as she descended.

"Rasa said the orbs were under the statue of Bei'ai," she whispered. "You have any more than that?"

They're in a satchel. They're actually pretty hard to see.

She reached the floor, and she felt a flood of relief. So far, so good. She quickly traced the wall toward the hall of trees until her hand scraped against a splintered shard of stone. She winced at the pain, but welcomed it. "Anybody ahead?"

No.

She ducked into the hall. Strah's tree was barren, waiting for a new Champion to be called. She suddenly felt angry. That was Weylyn's job. It shouldn't be anyone else. It couldn't be anyone else.

Locin!

She turned sharply to see Jeza's tree. The petals still clung to the branches, but they hung limp, their normally bright color faded.

"Voske?"

In a moment Spark was gone. Locin made her way to the tree, her heart racing. She had to go back and help him, but they had to get the orbs. She let her finger brush one of the delicate petals, and it broke free, drifting lazily to the ground where it crumbled to dust.

Burz is with him. He'll be okay!

"Are you sure?"

Yes. You should hurry.

She rushed forward, down the stairs, her mind still fixed on the trees behind her. They were counting on her. She'd let them all down once, and she wouldn't do it again.

The veil was still and dark, the only light came from the open door at the top of the stairs and a speckle of blue spirits. She hadn't been here since…

Are you okay?

She looked at Spark, standing beside her, a young woman about her size and age. Fully there in the world of the living. Or was she in the land of the dead? Maybe some of both. A shiver ran through her as she turned her eyes back on the black of Nyx.

Locin? The orbs?

"Do you know what happened in there? Do you know why I'm… like this?"

Like what?

She spun toward Spark with a deep scowl. "This, Spark! Why I can see you. Why I can feel Nyx on my heels! What happened?"

Spark frowned. *I don't know. I'm sorry.*

"It's like part of me is still in there!"

She swore she saw some flash of recognition flicker across Spark's face. But it was gone so fast, she couldn't be sure.

I really am sorry, Locin. I don't know how to help, but we can try to figure it out. Together. For now, you have to get the orbs! Neveri is still out there.

Someone telling her what to do only made Locin not want to, especially if they were right. But she couldn't shake the image of Jeza's tree with its drooping flowers.

"Fine. Underneath you said?"

A sound echoed down the stairs, footsteps and a voice. "Who's down there?"

Locin rushed to the side of the room, grabbing a rock with her boon and lifting it at the ready.

Two cultists burst in, looking around. They spotted her quickly, and she threw the rock hard at the first one's head. He stumbled back, but the other one rushed her, pulling her from the wall and tossing her toward the middle of the room.

"What's this?"

Spark ran behind the men and slapped the wall. They turned like there was someone there, and in their brief moment of confusion, Locin pulled her dagger and booned it toward the closer man, driving it into his shoulder. He cried out in pain as his partner rushed her, and soon he was on top of her. She felt a pull near her left side, something cold as ice reaching for her, calling her in, and she twisted to see the Veil only inches from her skin. Her heart started pounding, and panic set in. The man must have noticed, because he sneered at her.

"I've always wanted to see a soul get ripped through. I heard it feels like having your flesh peeled away with a dull blade."

"Let's find out," Locin said, and she wriggled her hands enough to pull on her boon, slinging the man hard to the side. His body impacted the Veil, and it gave softly like a pillow. For a moment he just gasped in a long breath as the air seemed to be sucked toward Nyx. And then he let out a wail, a cry of terror like she'd never heard. She tried to throw her hands over her ears, but he grabbed her wrist with an iron grip, clinging to her as a blue light seemed to drain from him and spill into the abyss. She felt those same icy tendrils through the man's hand, clawing at her wrist, and she scratched and slapped against him.

Locin!

Spark pointed to the man's sword where it hung by his side. She grabbed it with her boon and swung it down, slicing it through his wrist as the ice pulled at her soul. His arm severed and she tumbled away as the cold feeling dimmed. She peeled the still warm hand from her wrist and tossed it away as the man gave up his last breath. His lifeless body slumped against the Veil as the blue spirit frantically threw itself against the barrier, desperate to get back to Talamh.

Locin locked eyes with the other cultist, blood streaming down his shoulder where her dagger still stuck.

She lifted her hands without hesitation and flung his body into the Veil, closing her eyes and covering her ears as she fell back against the far wall, as far from Nyx as she could be. She heard the screams of pain from the second man, and she shuddered as the air moved into Nyx once more. Finally, he was silent. The pressure shifted back, and she breathed easier, but she stayed there with her eyes and ears shut fast until she heard Spark's voice.

Locin.

She forced her eyes open, and Spark stood between her and the Veil, a comforting look on her face.

It's safe now.

Locin nodded as she scrambled to her feet, but her body was shaking, and she swore her wrist still felt like ice. She hurried to the statue of Bei'ai and searched around her feet until she spotted a piece of stone that looked out of place. She pulled it until it came loose, and inside was a satchel. She pulled it out and lifted the leather flap to see the orbs glowing gold.

"That's it."

Let's go.

Locin slung the satchel over her shoulder, and then turned toward the bodies of the cultists, pale and lifeless. She shivered as she used her boon to yank the cobalt dagger from the man's shoulder and tucked it back in her belt. She turned and rushed for the stairs. She couldn't leave this place fast enough.

Rasa looked out over the temple grounds. The chimeras had all but scattered now, but the brief glimmer of victory had been swallowed by the shadow of Neveri. With every swipe of his claws men were tossed aside like chaff, and with every stomp of his feet the ground trembled.

Rasa felt fear grip her, and she ducked down, resting her back against the low balcony wall and staring toward the top of the spire.

Weylyn knelt beside her. *Rasa?*

She grabbed her knees and pulled them up under her chin. For a moment she could almost feel his claws again, and it made her stomach convulse. She felt a dry heave, but she swallowed it down and tried to focus.

"I want to help." She looked at Weylyn and saw the conviction in her eyes. "How do we help?"

Weylyn looked back out over the wall. *It's not safe here any longer.*

"I can't just leave them."

If you stay here you'll die with them.

Rasa lifted her chin. "That's what you did."

Weylyn shook her head. *I knew I could save you, but this…*

Rasa started to stand back up.

It might be better if you didn't look.

"I'm terrified," she said. "But those are my friends. They came for me. They didn't have to, but they did. And now it's my turn to help them."

Rasa mustered all her courage and stood, turning to face the battle again. The army was nearly in full retreat now, trying to stay near the temple as they circled away from Neveri. Above the battle, hundreds, maybe thousands, of blue spirits swirled curiously, but everywhere Neveri went, they ducked away, spinning around him like the eye of a storm.

Rasa felt a hand touch hers, and she looked to see Spark was back. *Locin has the orbs, but they won't last much longer.*

Rasa nodded and kept her breathing steady. "Gather the spirits," she said. "We need as many as we can get."

Weylyn raised an eyebrow. *What's your plan?*

"To bring Nyx to Talamh."

Can you hold the Veil open for that many?"

Rasa's knuckles turned white on the edge of the wall. "I have to try. You two gather as many as you can." She waved her hand toward the swirling blue storm. "All of them."

Spark nodded. *Leave it to us. Weylyn and I will spread the word. Just give us a few minutes.*

"Hurry."

The two spirits faded back into Nyx, and she steadied herself against the wall, letting the wind catch her hair and pull it back as she fixed her eyes on the temple grounds, searching for the other champions.

Endring darted through the air above the Gods' Mount in the form of a man with the wings of a raven. He had seen Voske pounded into Nyx and the rest of the army scattered by the old god. They had fled back into the fields and many hadn't stopped there. Even the pegasus were keeping their distance, flying a slow circle around the battlefield with little power to do anything but watch.

As he approached, he reached to his back, letting his hand trace the gnarled wood of the Crook of Bei'ai. The only weapon he carried was a small dagger, and only his thin tunic stood between his flesh and the ire of a god.

"Neveri!" He yelled as he approached.

Neveri looked up from the broken ground where Voske lay, motionless, and leered back at Endring. "My Champion." His voice dripped with contempt. "Betrayer."

Endring felt a shiver pass along his spine, but he did his best not to show it. "You have betrayed your people," he retorted. "You have shown yourself unworthy."

"I cannot betray *my* people. They belong to me." As he spoke he slowly rose back up, craning his neck to full height, until his face was level with Endring.

"So it was all a lie," Endring said. "You only use them, just the same as you used me."

Neveri glowered in reply. "You were always an unworthy vessel. I chose you because I had no other choice, or did you truly think I'd want such a weak willed wretch as my champion?"

Endring took a deep breath. It wasn't surprising to hear, but it still stung. "You were meant to raise them up, to free them from oppression."

"And they are free," Neveri snapped. "They are free to serve me or die."

Endring spat. "I will never serve you."

"Then die."

Neveri lunged forward, but Endring quickly shot upward, flying over Neveri's grasping hands and curling through the air. He could see a bleeding hole in Neveri's cheek, flesh that hadn't fully healed from the Phoenix's core, and he angled for it. He dodged around another blow, but a fast third caught him off guard, and he tumbled out of the sky toward Neveri's scalp.

For a moment he was out of control, falling upside down, but his reflexes sharpened as claws curled out from his hands and feet. He twisted around in the air and dug into the hardened flesh, eliciting a roar of pain from the god.

Neveri pitched forward and tried to shake Endring free, but his hold was too strong, and he leapt toward the hole in Neveri's cheek, then reached his hand back, seizing the Crook of Bei'ai. It was time to end this.

He extended the crook toward a shredded strip of flesh, but Neveri was too fast.

The god jerked his head to the side. Endring quickly flapped his wings again, desperate to adjust his aim, but it was already too late.

A colossal hand caught him mid-air and crushed the marrow from his bones. He tried to call on his boon, to transform again, but his body only convulsed in response. Everything ached and the world spun. For a moment he saw the darkened floor of the lower sanctum, where the blasphemous statues of the gods were still shrouded in shadow, and seconds later his back smashed into the granite floor.

He looked stiffly into the darkness above where the shadow of Neveri eclipsed the sky, blotting out the moon and stars, as though he had swallowed the world.

73: River of Souls

Burz stared up at the monstrous form of Neveri. He was hunched over the temple, staring in at the sanctum. The battle was all but done, every cultist or soldier either dead, gone, or standing with their eyes fixed on Neveri. Burz let his eyes dart to Voske, a crumpled form on the ground near Neveri's feet. He wasn't even sure he was alive. He edged his way around, keeping his eyes on the god, but the beast still seemed focused on Endring. Burz took the chance and ran up the stairs to Voske's body. He was limp and still, crushed into the solid rock of the portico.

"Voske," he said in a hoarse whisper.

He didn't move, but Burz could see the slight flutter of his chest as it rose and fell. He was alive, but he wouldn't stay that way without help.

Burz held out his hands toward Voske's chest, but he froze. The strength he had drained from the cultist had been slowly fading, but he still felt it coursing his veins. He was strong, and even after such a battle, his body was free of pain. His hands trembled a foot from Voske's chest, and sweat was beading on his brow.

A terrible laugh from Neveri sent him shaking, and he thrust his hands forward against Voske's skin, feeling his boon rush down his arms, pulling the strength out of him. Voske's breath came more easily, but Burz cried out as the pain overwhelmed him. He felt weak again, and his leg throbbed. When it was done, he slammed his fists against the stone beside Voske as he clenched his teeth. The fatigue of the battle had rushed back in, and he couldn't stand.

Voske's eyes drifted open. "What in Nyx happened?"

Burz shook his head, too angry and frustrated to answer. His body had given up so much, and he just wanted it back.

"You alright?" Voske sat up shaking off the dust and rubble. He was good as new, and it bothered Burz like it never had before.

But this is Voske, he reminded himself. He'd done what had to be done. He bit down his own desires and forced himself to straighten up.

"I'm fine."

Voske tried to stand, but he was still shaky, and he only managed to sit up beside Burz, nodding toward the sanctum where Neveri's attention stayed fixed. "Was that-"

"Endring. Yes."

Voske stood, holding a hand to help Burz up, but as he struggled to his feet his leg nearly gave way, and he grabbed Voske's arm with both hands.

"You sure you're okay?"

Burz clenched his jaw and forced himself to let go of Voske and stand on his own. "Fine."

Voske nodded sympathetically. "Thanks. I know it's not easy for you."

"I wasn't gonna let you die."

"Still, thanks."

There was a sincerity in Voske's eyes, a look that said he knew how near death he was. The genuineness of it disarmed Burz, and he felt the animosity drain out of him.

"You're welcome."

The ground shook under Neveri's wrath as Locin clung to the sanctum door. She heard the orbs jingling in the satchel by her side, and she clutched it instinctively. Spark was gone, off to help Rasa, and she'd just seen Endring plummet down into the lower sanctum, spinning like a carriage wheel. She bit her lip as the quaking stopped, and the shadow of Neveri loomed over the sanctum.

"Rot it," she muttered, and she rushed down the stairs to the lower sanctum, crouching in the shadows. Endring lay a broken mess in the center of the floor. Her eyes wandered from him to the Crook of Bei'ai, lying on the floor just a few feet away.

What in Nyx is that thing doing here?

His body was still, and she wondered if he was dead.

"Hey," she whispered, and she flicked a pebble from the side of the room, tapping it against Endring's foot. "You alright?"

A groan was the only response, and she glanced up nervously. She couldn't see Neveri past the lip of the broken floor, but he was still out there somewhere.

"Endring," she hissed. "Can you move?"

Another groan.

She glanced back up the stairs. She could make it. All she had to do was skirt the shadows and get around the monstrous god at the top. Easy enough. She didn't owe Endring anything, so why risk her life to help him?

He groaned again, and something inside pulled at her. Maybe some remnant of Spark. She wouldn't want Locin to leave him.

"Rot it," she muttered.

She turned and slipped away from the edge, creeping along the floor to where Endring lay. She nearly puked as she looked at him. His legs were twisted around at horrifying angles, and one of his arms was bent where there were no joints. There was blood pooling out around him, and she shook her head. She couldn't help him. Maybe nobody could.

"Locin," he rasped. "Run!"

She looked up, and her blood ran cold. Neveri was still there, and he was staring straight at her.

She stepped backward out of instinct, but before she could move, he had seized her, pinching her stomach between his thumb and fingers. He lifted her off the ground as panic gripped her. She reached out with her boon and raised a chunk of stone from the floor, then hurled it toward his eyes, but he merely blinked it away.

"I remember you," he said with amusement. "It was a pity you ran away earlier. We could have had our fun then."

"I didn't run then, and I'm not running now."

"Of course. A fighter." He squinted at her. "There is something different about you though. Ah, what am I saying, one mortal dies just as well as any other."

"You can try and-"

She didn't get another word out before he tossed her aside, and for a moment she could feel the wind rushing past her feet. The satchel flew up from her shoulder, and she drew it to herself. For as high as she was, the ground was coming up incredibly quickly.

She clutched the satchel with one hand and slung it at the remnants of the sanctum roof. The cloth caught hold of a metal bar that had separated the tiles of stained glass, and Locin swung over the old sanctum far below. A slow ripping noise started, and she heard the satchel slipping free.

"No! NO!"

As the leather tore, the orbs began spilling out, clinking on the floor far below like marbles spilling on stone. The satchel broke loose, and Locin fell face first toward the old sanctum floor. She threw her hands out, calling her boon in desperation, pushing with all her might against the stone. She slowed as she did, the force of her push shoving back against her body until she landed on the ground with a soft thud.

She glanced up to see Neveri holding one of the golden orbs, turning it over between two pointed claws.

"You," he mused. "Was it all for these? I wonder."

Locin scrambled to her feet, spotting the orbs scattered on the far side of the room. She dashed for them, but Neveri was too fast. He swatted her aside like a meddlesome ant and then scooped the rest of the orbs up in his hand.

"So much," he said, "for so little. But now you see it. You could never hope to win against me."

As he spoke, he began to pinch a single orb between his claws. He gritted his teeth and bore down, and for a moment its golden light seemed to condense, piercing outward like cracks of sunlight through the clouds.

Locin stumbled backward to the ground next to Endring. Both were spent, and both were silent. This was the world they had helped create.

As the orb cracked, the golden light intensified, but it suddenly dimmed as a blue light streaked across the sky. It looked almost like Spark, but more like a thousand Sparks, swirling over and around Neveri's hand, passing between his fingers and forcing them open.

"Rotting Nyx," Locin whispered, staring in awe at the scene.

"What's happening," Endring asked, his dim eyes barely fluttering.

"It's… spirits," Locin marveled. "They're helping. They're stopping him!"

"How?"

She shook her head. "I-I don't know."

74: The Champions of Talamh

Rasa stood on top of the spire of Bei'ai, looking straight into the face of Neveri. She had opened a rift through Nyx, and she could see the edge of the sanctum roof, the hulking form of Neveri's outstretched arm, and below, Locin and Endring laid out on the sanctum floor.

She held her arms apart, holding the rift open, but they trembled at the effort. Thousands of spirits were swarming through, perhaps tens of thousands, grabbing at Neveri's wrist and fingers. Even the air had turned vibrant blue, as more spirits than Rasa had ever seen ebbed and flowed, rolling across the temple like ocean waves.

She stepped to the very edge of the rift, and Neveri locked eyes on her.

"You worthless girl!"

Her arms trembled. How long could she even hold the rift open?

"You stare at me through Nyx? Are you too much a coward to face me?"

For a moment, fear gripped her. She felt her arms shake, and the rift started to tighten. Neveri smirked. She couldn't hold it forever. He could wait her out. He was too powerful.

She felt steady hands grab her wrists from behind. Weylyn. *I've got you. You can do this, Rasa!*

She stretched her arms to the limit, feeling Weylyn's grip steady her, and the rift spread open even further. She saw a look of surprise flash across Neveri's monstrous countenance, but she wasn't done yet. She took one large step through the rift, and she stood fully on the roof of the sanctum, feeling the stream of spirits rushing past her from behind.

"I'm not afraid of you!"

"You should be, little girl. I'm a god! Do you truly think you have enough power to hold me forever?"

"No. But I don't have to. I'm not alone!"

The wind of Nyx fluttered her hair as she shut her eyes and pulled on her boon. There was something comforting about being enveloped in the stream of spirits as they charged past her. She had done her part, now it was up to the rest of them.

Voske couldn't believe his eyes. As far as he knew, they left Rasa in Yzod's shop, but he was staring up at her on the edge of the sanctum roof, her arms spread wide, and a blue light shooting around her toward Neveri, holding his hand in place.

"What in the name of Skard is that?"

Burz stared up in wonder. "Hope."

"Hope!" Voske laughed.

He clapped Burz on the back and reached across the steps to where Straznik Bram lay, lifting it over his head. He had a second wind, and they had a chance. He gave a sharp whistle as he looked down the stairs where the huddled remains of their army stood. Most of the pegs had landed, and he could see Eprim and Gillis leaning heavily on the wall.

"Soldiers!" He yelled. "Rally your strength, and let's send this beast back to Nyx!"

Voske turned toward the temple, bounding up the stairs and scaling the broken statue of Gajah, the first champion of Desita. He could see more of the battlefield from here. His message had worked, and he saw some of the pegasus riders mounting up near the bottom of the stairs. He glanced at Rasa where she stood, her arms trembling, and he rushed along the roof until he reached the sanctum, placing himself between Rasa and Neveri. He felt a strange cold wind as the blue light streamed over him, and Neveri stared at him contemptuously.

"Didn't I kill you?"

Voske lifted his axe and held it steady. "You'll wish you had!"

Neveri began to laugh, and the sound of it rolled like thunder over the temple. "Pathetic! You can hold me at bay for a while, but your strength will fail, and mine will not. You can cut me and burn me, and I will never die! What chance do you think you have against a god!?"

As the echoes of his voice died away and the temple ceased its shaking, Voske noticed the blue light around his hand was beginning to tremble. Rasa couldn't hold him much longer. Behind Neveri, the pegs were in the air, but they were frozen in fear. They would rally, but they needed more hope. He steeled himself, and raised Straznik Bram above his head as he smiled at the beast. He let the strength of Jeza flood his body until his muscles burned, and his voice roared like thunder.

"What chance do you think you have against the Champions of Talamh!?"

Voske ran for the edge, vaulting across the gap and landing on Neveri's hand where it was frozen in place. He charged up Neveri's arm and turned, feeling the fire of Jeza engulf him until his muscles throbbed with power. He swung Straznik Bram high and brought it down with a cry, plunging it through Neveri's wrist, severing his hand. The beast cried out in pain as his hand crashed to the ground below.

As he drew his arm back, Voske dove for the portico roof, skidding across the stone. Rasa had let her arms drop now, and she sank to her knees, panting.

In another moment, Neveri had recovered, and he lifted a fist above Voske.

Voske braced himself, but instead of being crushed again under the weight of a god, he felt heat scorching the sky above him. Neveri wailed as a chimera soared overhead, Zengin riding it with a golden bracer gleaming on his wrist. Voske stood, shouting as Zengin came around for another pass. That was all they needed. The pegs soared in, emboldened by the turn of fate, as Eprim charged with his men.

Endring stared at the cacophony of lights above them. The blue of Nyx had been replaced by red blasts of fire. He'd seen Voske, rallying beyond comprehension, and the golden orbs, slipping from Neveri's grasp.

There were once again shouts of battle from outside, and the sound called Endring to stir. He pushed his hands against the floor, but the pain in his chest kept him pinned to his tomb of granite. He let out a groan, and he heard Locin's voice from beside him.

"Hang in there."

He could hear the doubt in her tone, doubt that mirrored his own certainty. He was dying, and soon.

Neveri's roar bellowed over the battlefield and he pushed past the pain this time, forcing himself up to his elbows as his eyes sharpened once more.

Neveri was beset but not bested, swiping at the air like a cat among a flock of birds. All he had to do was hit once.

Endring tried to stand upright, but his leg was wrenched backward and he couldn't get it to move, no matter how much he willed it.

"Locin," he muttered. "My leg."

"What about it?"

"Reset it."

She looked at it hesitantly. "Maybe we should wait for Burz."

"There's no time," Endring snapped. "Now do it."

She bit her lip and gave a near imperceptible nod. "Hold still."

He felt her boon condense around his leg, like the air had grown thick, then it jerked outward, snapping the bone back into place.

He cried out, but he didn't fall. He had to stand with the rest of them. Pain blazed through his bones, tearing upward through his spine and making the world grow hazy. He doubled over and gently spread his wings. They were tattered but unbroken, and his fierce eyes drifted to the Crook of Bei'ai, still glowing deep in the shadows.

"Now, give me the Crook."

Locin glanced at the relic and back. "What are you going to do?"

"End this. Now, the Crook!"

It drifted through the air and hovered in front of him. It felt like all the strength he possessed to simply reach out and take it. He looked back at her, and for a moment he wanted to say he was sorry for dragging her into the middle of this, and for her death. Instead he simply turned his eyes upward and spread his wings out wide. Whatever penance was due, he would pay it.

"It's been an honor, Champion."

He thrust his wings down and rose into the sky, making his way straight for Neveri. The old god howled in anger and batted at his foes, but his foes were champions, just like the stories of old, and they would not be felled so easily. He winged upward until he could go no farther and he could feel the dark of Nyx beginning to close around him. He could see the jagged strip of flesh in Neveri's cheek and he reached out with the Crook, setting it like a hook in the old god's mouth.

Neveri looked down with surprise, then fear. "No!"

He tried to pull away but Endring wouldn't let go. He raised a hand to strike, but the blow slowed until it was frozen in time.

"I'll do what you want," he stammered, staring at Endring with horror. "I'll give you anything you want!"

Endring felt his spirit slowly slipping away, but he clung to the Crook all the harder. "I wanted the realm to change," he answered. "A new beginning for Talamh."

"And it will," Neveri hissed. "We'll change the worlds, together."

"Yes," he answered, his voice growing faint. "Change comes when the old dies."

The darkness swallowed Endring, and for a moment he watched his body fall away, plummeting back toward the gaping sanctum, but he felt no rush of wind. He was standing in the air, surrounded by a hundred thousand souls and together they watched him. Waiting.

He sucked in an airless breath. At the bend of the crook a golden mote of light was trapped. It raged against the pull of Nyx, throwing itself against its wooden prison and cursing the names of the gods.

On instinct, Endring reached out, ghostly hands wrapping around the staff. *Neveri,* he called.

In an instant the mote swelled, and a golden form surged outward. Powerful, enraged, and caged by the relic. *Neveri,* he called again.

He could feel himself being pulled, drawn away into Nyx by the irresistible tug of death itself, but he wasn't going alone.

Neveri shrieked in anger as his golden spirit uncoiled from his body and the last thing Endring saw was the beast god's fleshly form collapsing across the portico. Dead.

75: Change

An age passed as swiftly as a moment, and the pain of Endring's body became only a distant memory. He looked down at his youthful hands with a smile.

"Welcome."

The soft female voice sent shivers up his spine, and the world around him suddenly disappeared in an undulating wave of blue. The temple below was hidden by an expanse of water and the stars above by a darkened sky that gradually brightened as it neared the horizon. All else that remained was the comforting voice that called to him.

"Endring."

"Is this Nyx?" He asked, looking around for the source.

"This is the crossroad."

A light appeared before him, brighter than the sun. It split the deep canvas until a woman stepped through. She was breathtaking. Her raven hair spilled over ivory shoulders, and her bright blue eyes told of depths unknown. A brilliant white toga draped her form, woven with amethyst thread and an amethyst diadem crowned her head.

"Bei'ai," he said, and he instinctively dropped to his knees, putting his face to the surface of the water.

"Child."

He felt her hand grace his back, and the tender touch was laced with unfathomable power. "I'm sorry," he said, feeling dread overtake his thoughts. Surely she would kill him for what he'd done. Even Nyx was too good for such a wretch as he.

"Stand."

He slowly eased to his feet, but kept his head down, scarcely daring to breathe.

"Neveri was my twin brother," she said. "I cared for him."

Endring glanced up. Bei'ai had a tear gently trailing down her cheek, and her brilliant eyes locked on his own, but there was no anger there.

"You saw the best in him, and for that, I thank you. You believed in him even more than I."

He took a deep breath, "I was naive."

"Yes, but your heart was for the lost."

Endring nodded slowly, but didn't dare speak further.

"We crafted Talamh with meticulous care, molding it until it became a beautiful world. We were all afraid of what change might bring, but my brother, he longed for it. He was determined to see the world change and grow, even if that meant destroying what we had built." She sighed. "Perhaps he was right. Perhaps change was inevitable. We held it at bay so long that when it came, it came like a tidal wave."

She stopped and locked her eyes with his. "Why did you want things to change?"

"To raise the forgotten ones," he answered. He wouldn't lie to her, but it felt as if he couldn't even if he'd wanted to. The words were drawn out of him. "It was always for them, though now that I see it clearly, it was also for me."

"And are you sorry for the way it turned out?"

"Of course I am."

"But should you be?"

She threw her arms out to her sides and suddenly they were standing in a temple with deep green draping the walls. The open archways permitted a fresh wind to blow through, carrying the scent of cherry blossoms, and in the center, a young boy held up his palm, proudly displaying a guild seal Endring had never seen. A bowl of burning incense.

"Alchemist!" He said with a smile.

Endring took a step forward staring down with disbelief. "Is this real?"

"It could be." She brought her arms back and once again the cool water rested below his feet. "All of the guildings that were lost could be restored. Would you want this fate for him?"

"Of course." Endring felt emotion welling in his chest. This was all he'd ever wanted.

"And what would you give to see it?"

Endring looked back at her, feeling as though his heart might burst. "Everything."

She looked up, and he followed her gaze to the soft blue sky. In the distance directly above them, he could see a point of shining gold.

"For something to change, it must first die," she said. "But perhaps that which never changes is destined for an even worse death. We stand now upon the brink of decision. The world can be restored back to how it was, unchanging, or it can die, and perhaps change for the better."

Endring looked down at her, "And what would that change look like?"

"I don't know," her voice quavered, but there was an intense sincerity in her eyes. "Not even Strah has seen it. I know it would not be an easy road, and I can not even say where it will lead."

Endring took a deep breath and looked up again, into the golden glow above them.

"You have been the greatest advocate of change, Endring. And we have agreed to leave the deciding vote to you."

He glanced down at her. "My lady?"

"It's a simple one. Will you break Talamh and see it remade, or leave it as it was?"

He looked at the ground, overwhelmed by the question, and yet he could feel the convictions of his heart, still strong. "Talamh is already broken," he answered.

"Very well." She brought her hands together and a golden pearl appeared, shining brilliantly against her skin. "When he crossed the Veil, we stripped my brother of his power. His transgression was too great for us to risk it happening again."

She held out her hand, as though offering the pearl to Endring. "Should you wish for change to enter the realm of the living once more, swallow this."

He took the pearl between his fingers and the power within pulsed through his arm like lightning. "What is it?"

"It's my brother's power," she answered, "should you wish to become the God of Animus in his place."

Endring held the pearl up before him, and stared at the tiny sphere.

"You have already tasted the cost," Bei'ai said. "Now choose."

76: New Beginnings

The cult fled as soon as Neveri fell, tearing off into the jungle or some other parts unknown, but there were precious few shouts of victory. Neveri's hulking form was laying down across the portico like a fallen redwood, and the temple around him had been smashed to rubble.

There was a feeling of finality that lingered in the air, and Voske breathed in the brisk night wind with wonder. No one could know what would come about as a result of this, but this at least was finished, and decidedly so.

Only minutes after the battle's end, Voske scraped and climbed over temple debris until he reached the inner sanctum, then slowly descended to the eerie stone graveyard below. Here the fractured statues of the gods were strewn about the floor, and Locin was there, kneeling beside a pile of twisted flesh and feathers that had once been Endring. He paced closer till he could see the old man's face, strangely peaceful.

"Voske," Locin said as he approached.

He paused. He had no idea what to say. "I'm glad you're alright," he ventured.

She looked back at him, and it was clear she was troubled. She wiped a sleeve across her face. "He… he did it."

Voske crossed his arms. "He really did. I didn't believe him."

Locin looked up at him. "What?"

"It was his plan, and a rotting crazy one. Giving his life to drag that beast back to Nyx."

"You knew?"

Voske looked back at the frail old man. It was strange to think he'd even been a Champion, seeing him splayed out on the ground. "He told me," he said, and he squatted down next to the body, shaking his head. "You did it, Endring. You saved the whole rotting realm."

"It cost him enough to do it," Locin said.

"There's been a lot of that going around."

"A lot of what?"

"A lot of high prices to pay. There's a thousand men in the courtyard that paid the same. I'm just…" His voice trailed off. He straightened back up and squinted at her.

"Just what?"

"I was expecting to get in here and find you…" he motioned to Endring's body.

"Dead?"

"Yes, dead," he said with exasperation. "Rot it, Locin, I'm trying not to get emotional."

She slowly stood to her feet, looking at him skeptically.

"I already saw you dead once, and that was hard enough."

She shook her head and quickly turned away, her chest gently shaking in what he assumed was a silent cry.

"I didn't mean to say it like that," he stumbled. "I mean you're alive, you didn't die, and that's good. I didn't mean to upset you."

"You didn't."

He rubbed a hand across the back of his neck, bewildered. "Then what's got you upset?"

"Nothing," she answered. "It's nothing."

He wasn't sure how to answer that. "Alright then. I uh…" He fell silent for a moment and let his eyes wander to the skies overhead. There was still a long night before the sunrise.

"I'm glad you made it too." She was looking at him again.

He smiled. "It takes more than a god to kill me. I'm too-"

"Stubborn?"

"I was gonna say good looking."

She smirked, but there was a dullness in her eyes, that belied her expression. Maybe they'd all grown a bit world-weary.

"What about his body?"

"An exaltation," Locin said. "He deserves one."

Voske blew out a deep breath. "I can't imagine the temple loving that."

"I don't care what the temple loves. We should build him a pyre out of the rotting temple."

Voske bent down and gathered the old man's body in his arms, noting the wings that drooped from his shoulder blades.

"What's wrong," Locin asked, squinting at him.

"This is the third time I've had to carry the body of a dead Champion," Voske said. "I just hope it's the last."

Hikari sat on the edge of the Phoenix where the rail was torn away, dangling his legs over the ruined world below. His shoulders slumped from the exhaustion of the battle as Yzod and Illeri worked the chariot behind him.

"Don't you two ever rest?" He yelled, keeping his eyes fixed below. The soldiers were grouping near the barracks, out of the way of the destruction. It would be a good place to set up. He found himself scanning the faces, and he had an odd sense of his own mortality as he realized he was casually taking stock of who had survived.

"I'll rest when we land," Yzod shot back.

He felt a soft thing bump into his leg and he turned to see Ryshi staring out over the field as well. The poor thing's back was bristled up in an arch, and its eyes were wide. The wyvern had been hiding below deck for the battle, and apparently ventured out now that a melancholy stillness had fallen over the field.

Hikari held a hand out, and Ryshi climbed up, straining his neck to see as he wrapped his wings around Hikari's fingers and held on.

"Pretty grim, wouldn't you say? But we made it." He let out a sigh. "Gods, did we all make it?"

Illeri's voice cut in softly from behind. "I saw Voske and Locin north. And Burz is there by the pegs." She pointed.

"We all saw Rasa. That was something, wasn't it?"

Illeri sat beside him, and Ryshi cooed softly, scrambling onto her shoulder.

"He still likes you better."

"I've seen him more."

"Hm. Fair point. I shall endeavor to win you over, Ryshi. Tell me, what do wyverns eat?"

"Hikari," she said quickly.

Her pointed tone drew his full attention, and he looked over. She looked tired and spent, and her pale skin was streaked with ash. "What is it, darling?"

"I'm sorry."

"I can't imagine what you'd have to be sorry about."

She dropped her gaze to the ground below. "I like to think. A lot actually. Probably too much."

"Well, it's a minor fault to be sure, but you don't have to feel sorry about it. I'm sure we can teach you to be as dull as the rest of us."

"Let me finish."

He nodded.

"This battle, Neveri, everything, it really changes your perspective, you know? Maybe it's just the excitement or facing your own mortality…"

He turned to face her fully as she fidgeted with her hair. "Yes, darling?"

A hint of color filled her cheeks as she stared at her knees. "I know I've been a little cold to you."

"Well not to me," he confessed. It seemed to just be who she was. She didn't open up easily, and that just piqued his interest all the more. "It's just your way, and that's alright."

She looked up, and it seemed to take some effort for her to hold his gaze. "I… oh for gods' sake!"

She leaned forward and pressed her lips against his, so quick he barely had time to taste it before she pulled away, her cheeks bright red. He smiled, lifting a hand to cup her cheek, and he pulled her close, softly kissing her. When she pulled away this time, she was smiling too.

Ryshi gave a soft coo from her shoulder as he spread out his wings and puffed up his chest.

Hikari laughed. "I think he's jealous."

She chuckled.

The sound of Yzod clearing his throat pulled Hikari's gaze up to where the inventor stood by the chains. "If you two are done now, I could use some help landing the Phoenix. It took quite a beating." A smile threatened the corners of his mouth as he watched.

"Of course, darling!"

Hikari scrambled to his feet, grabbing the chains from Yzod as he stole one more glance at Illeri. She was looking over her shoulder at him.

"Down we go."

He tugged at the chains as the pylat slowly descended toward the field. Suddenly his weariness had melted away, and he felt alive, like he could conquer the worlds.

The pyre for Endring was ignited before the sun came up. The soldiers of Arrajin built it out of the wooden beams of the temple itself. Endring's body was laid upon the wood, then ignited by chimera fire. It was truly a different sort of realm.

Burz wiped the sweat away from his eyes and stared around those assembled. It was strange to see the soldiers of Tajerim and Arrajin gathered alongside the Champions, all to honor the man that one week ago was their sworn enemy. The champions sat together at the stone tables in the outer yard, watching the blazing pyre. The occasion would have been a bleak one, but with the morning sun there was a feeling of new beginnings that permeated the air, and the Champions told stories, laughing and toasting.

Beyond that, word of Neveri's defeat had quickly spread to the people of Arrajin, and many risked the trek across the Arrtris to see the aftermath with their own eyes. They lined up in a large circle around the gathering, staring inward at the blazing pyre in reverent silence. Would they have been so reverent had they known who was burning, Burz wondered? Perhaps it was best not to speculate.

For now he leaned heavily against the table, listening as Voske retold the story of the battle they'd all just lived. A full five minstrels were there, hanging on his every word, and ready to exaggerate every detail in some heroic ballad.

Eventually the temple scribes would relive the moments and properly document what had transpired, but now was the time for legends, and Voske was a surprisingly good story-teller.

"Then," he said, lowering his voice. "As I lay dying, barely a breath left in my lungs, what do I see?" He clapped a hand on Burz' shoulder. "This face, right here, standing over me. 'Voske, are you alright?' he asks. Am I alright!? I'd have broke that pretty nose of his right then and there if I had the strength to move my arm!"

Everyone at the table laughed and Burz smiled and looked at Rasa. He knew what was coming next.

"That's when we saw her," Voske said.

Rasa blushed as every eye at the table fixed on her.

"That little girl, right there, brought all of Nyx to bear against that fiend. She challenged the strength of a god himself, and by Jeza, if she didn't win!" He shook his head and clapped his hands loudly.

Rasa looked across the table, toward the vacant seat she'd insisted on leaving for Weylyn. "I didn't do it alone," she said.

"That's fair," Voske said, raising a glass. "To those who fell."

Burz chimed in next. "To the soldiers who gave their lives."

"To the people of Arrajin," Locin added.

"Hey!" Hikari chided. "That was mine."

Locin stuck her tongue out at him.

"Fine," he said. "To friends, old and new."

"To the temple," Illeri said.

Zengin raised his glass. "To victory."

"To Weylyn," Rasa said. "And to Endring."

They all raised their glasses at his name. "To Endring," and they all drank.

Animus

Sammel stood by the pyre as the flames burned dully against the rising sun. Ten years he had been following Endring, working toward this goal. And now it was done, and he found himself feeling a strange mixture of emotions. Part of him was curious where his life would head next, perhaps even excited, but he mourned his friend, and he wasn't sure how to feel about the way things had happened. They'd succeeded, but not as they planned. It felt unfinished.

"I wish you were here," he said as he watched the flames lick the wood of the pyre.

Overhead, dark clouds gathered near the tree tops, and a distant flash of lightning sparked the sky blue. A bird soared on the wind and he smiled.

"I'm not sure what to do now that you're gone. Do I stay and help them, or go back home? It's been a long time since I had any purpose but following you in this endeavor." He lowered his gaze. "I believed in you, even when I didn't believe in the cause."

A question seemed to pull at his mind. Did he want that? Did he want to stay and help them? He had a sudden sense of clarity, two paths in front of him. One, he would stay and help the Champions rebuild. He would give his life for Talamh, and the rewards would be great, but it would be a hard road. The other, he would leave, go back to his village and live out his days free. The second path appeared to him like a clear sky and open fields. No responsibility. Nothing tying him down.

He laughed. He had done that most of his life. But Endring had come along and given him purpose, a fight. He couldn't imagine life without it now. He glanced down at the fire, the crackling sound and the smoke filling his senses, and he sighed.

"I'll stay. I don't know what I can offer them, but I think it's what you would want."

A sudden pain exploded in his hand and he doubled over, gritting his teeth. It burned like fire and spread up his arm, dulling as it went, until it filled his whole body with golden warmth. As the pain subsided, he pulled off his right glove and stared in wonder at the swirling gold sigil that greeted him. He had never seen anything like it before. It was a tree, half barren and half in bloom. A sign of change.

Endring.

His mind raced with questions. Somehow they'd succeeded. Somehow they had returned animus to Talamh, but not with the monstrous god of Neveri. He couldn't begin to guess how Endring had done this, but he had. He truly had.

Sammel laughed. He had to tell the others. But perhaps, not quite yet.

He stepped back from the pyre. The others had gone, and he was alone. He stared up at the dark rolling clouds that roiled over the western sky, and he slipped his tunic over his head, dropping it in the grass at his feet. He pulled off his other glove and stretched his bare arms out in front of him. He could feel the power inside him, beckoning him to change, and he let it take over, watching as his arms and hands transformed into the sleek black of a panther. He dropped to all four, leaping around the pyre as he felt his tail swish behind him. He could feel his muscles ready to run like never before. He set his cat eyes on the jungle, now clear in his vision, and he ran.

77: Thicker than Blood

As the pyre faded and the sun threatened the horizon, Rasa once again climbed a spire of the gods, but this time it was the spiral stair of Strah. She had Weylyn's old bow and pack slung over her shoulder and held the simple wooden box that housed Weylyn's ashes, bearing it up until she reached the last urn in line. Here she stopped and set the rough box on the shelf beside the opulent pearl urn of the last champion. The box looked out of place next to the resplendent vessels that lined the spire, but there was a nobility about its quaint nature that she thought made it look even better.

You know this wasn't necessary, Weylyn said, looking down from the step above.

Rasa smiled. "I think it was."

Why? I'm right here.

"It's not for me. It's for history."

They're just ashes. She sighed. *I always figured your legacy is people. Children, or friends. Anyone you impacted while you lived.*

"Maybe. But I want people to know who you were and what you did."

Weylyn smiled. *I think in light of all you've accomplished, my own achievements will be more of a footnote.*

"Not to me." Rasa took a step back from the box, unsure if she should say anything formal.

So tell me, Weylyn said, motioning to her old bow. *What are your plans for that?*

Rasa reached her hand up to the weathered wood. "Could you teach me?"

Gladly. Weylyn beamed in response, and her eyes traveled down to her old hunter's pack. *You might also want to conceal those better.*

Rasa quickly swung the pack off her shoulder and looked inside. The eight tethers of the gods glowed from within, and bands of light pierced out from the orb of Jeza where cracks scoured the surface. She tightened the cover before slinging the pack over her shoulder once more.

Weylyn raised an eyebrow. *What are you planning for them?*

Rasa bit her lip. "I haven't decided that yet."

But you're taking them?

She had too. She knew that somehow. It's what Bei'ai wanted, although she wasn't sure why. "Just to be safe," she said, unsure if she should even tell Weylyn.

Safe from what?

"I don't know," she answered honestly. But she knew there was still some danger, some dark road ahead. She'd sensed Bei'ai clearly after the battle, warning her, but now her warm, golden presence was gone. No matter how she reached out through Nyx, she couldn't feel the goddess. Perhaps she was back in Sbarga.

Weylyn nodded thoughtfully. *You know, Rasa, while I was alive, I was the Champion of Prudence.*

"I know."

And I don't think even I was that cautious. Who would come for them?

"Hopefully no one," Rasa answered stiffly, and then she smiled, pulling the bow off her back. "How about a lesson?"

Don't you want to rest?

"Just a quick one?"

Weylyn smiled. *Alright.*

The following day, silver trumpets announced the return of the Oracles to the temple. Aurilis stood at their head, marching forward to the top of the Gods' Mount. They had a hundred monks of Jeza, led by Eprim, marching behind their party and a thousand other servants behind them. They picked their way across the debris strewn field to the bottom of the steps, where they could see the ravaged sanctum. Here the Oracle of Strah collapsed to his knees, weeping allowed, and the Oracle of Metnadur threw up, apparently too horrified by the aftermath to hold on to her breakfast.

Burz walked beside Voske as the Champions made their way down to greet them.

"They don't look happy, do they?" Voske muttered.

"Not particularly," Burz agreed.

"Not exactly surprising," Illeri said. "This has been their home much longer than ours."

"Still," Locin huffed, "you'd think at least one of them would be grateful."

"Give them time," Burz said. "The shock is still fresh for them."

They reached the bottom of the steps, and Voske gave a courteous nod to Aurilis. "High Oracle."

Aurilis' gaze was still trained on the sanctum behind them, and when she finally did look down, her eyes were hard with displeasure. "Champions," she hissed. "I heard reports of the devastation here, but I didn't want to believe it. Now, seeing it with my own eyes…"

Burz exchanged a sidelong glance with Voske. Her tone of voice said she had nothing good to say.

"It's worse than I feared. You have, all of you, destroyed the very temple of the gods you professed to serve!"

Eprim cleared his throat from just behind her. "With all due respect, High Oracle, it was Neveri that destroyed the sanctum."

"Silence, Eprim," she snapped. "You'd do well to hope I forget your part in all this."

Burz inwardly rolled his eyes. How had he ever had respect for this woman? He leaned toward Voske, and whispered. "Has a real warmth about her doesn't she?"

Voske smirked. "Must be Uthando, such tender compassion."

"What was that," Aurilis snapped, glaring at them again.

"Eprim had nothing to do with this," Voske said. "If you need someone to blame, then blame me."

"Oh I do. I blame each and every one of you. You have let go your sacred honor, you have defiled-"

She was cut off by an exaggerated yawn from Locin, and she turned on the young woman with a fierce expression. "And you," she seethed. "You betrayed the entire realm. How dare you step foot on the temple grounds!"

Voske stepped in front of Aurilis angrily. "How dare *you* speak to a champion like that! I think you forget your place, *Oracle*."

"You defend her? That girl was the catalyst for all this!"

"You're wrong," a voice called from behind Aurilis.

They all looked beside the Oracles to where Sammel was striding forward. His clothes were rumpled and his hair was slick with dew and mud, as though he'd spent the night sleeping on the ground.

"Who are you?" Aurilis asked, clearly aghast at his appearance.

"My name is Sammel."

"Who?"

Several of the Jeza monks brandished weapons, but he ignored the motion and tromped past the procession until he reached the Champions.

Voske smiled. "Glad to see you again."

"Thank you," he said, then turned to face Aurilis. "That girl wasn't the catalyst. Endring was."

Aurilis turned up her nose at the name. "May he rot in Nyx for eternity!"

"I doubt that," Sammel mused. "The gods were more agreeable to him than you might expect."

"Agreeable to that arrogant fool? You're out of your mind."

"I don't think I am." As he spoke he raised his hand, revealing a shining golden sigil, one Burz had never seen before.

The Champions quickly crowded in, as did the Oracles, straining to see the mark.

"What is that?" Voske asked.

The Oracle of Strah grabbed Sammel's hand and touched his palm, as though the mark might rub off. "Is it real?"

"Enough!" Aurilis snapped and the procession quickly backed off, giving her their attention. "You will tell us the meaning of this, and you will tell us now."

Sammel smiled. "It's Endring."

For a moment the only sound was the quiet rustle of wind as everyone exchanged glances again. Apparently today was going to have no end of surprises.

"Endring," Burz stammered. "How is that possible?"

"For the sake of the realm," Sammel said. "He has become the god of animus and now stands in Neveri's place in the circle of nine."

"Eight!" Aurilis shrieked.

They all turned to look at her.

"Heretics," she seethed. "Lunatics! Miscreants! You profane the holy gods with your blasphemy."

Burz folded his arms. "Isn't it you who profanes them? If they've elevated Endring, who are we to disagree?"

She shook her head, but she looked less angry to Burz and more panicked. "Don't you see what you've done? You've broken the realm. This will bring war like Talamh has never known. The worlds as we knew them are gone."

"Is that so bad?" Voske asked.

"Yes," she choked out the word. "Already the city-states have been torn apart, and now this?" She straightened up and shook her head with finality. "The temple will have no part of this."

"What does that mean?"

Aurilis looked sharply at Sammel. "You are banished from these holy grounds. If I hear of you setting foot in any sanctum in Talamh, I'll have no choice but to bring the full power of the temple against you."

"Now wait just a minute-" Voske snapped.

"That goes for you as well, Champion. And the champion of Iyanu."

Locin huffed. "After we saved your rotting realm? Some thanks!"

"The rest of you can stay, help rebuild the pieces."

"Like Nyx," Burz seethed.

Aurilis turned on him now. "What?"

"I said, like Nyx." Burz stepped forward, feeling a righteous anger building in his chest. "We are the champions of Talamh. Everyone here risked their lives to save a realm you thought was lost, and I'll not stand by and watch you pillory any one of us. As far as I'm concerned. They're heroes. All of them."

He looked back across the group. Rasa, Illeri, Zengin, Hikari, Locin, Voske, even Sammel, and his chest swelled with pride.

"I will not relent, Burz. Do not make the mistake of thinking this is a negotiation."

"I'm not," he said sharply. "You've rejected some of us, so you've rejected all of us. I'll have no part in your temple."

Voske was smiling widely, and the rest of the champions circled around him, nodding their agreement.

"If they go, we all go."

Aurilis shook with anger. "So be it!"

Burz nodded to Voske, and they headed down the steps side-by-side. The Oracles parted and let the champions pass as they all marched toward the field. It felt like a weight was lifted, at least for the moment. They may be banished, but they were free, and they were together.

As they made their way toward the bottom, Burz heard Hikari shout over the group.

"Gillis!"

He looked to see the young man, staring at them with wide eyes.

"Come on then! You're with us."

Gillis smiled as he pushed his way through the crowd and marched up to the champions. Hikari patted him on the back with a laugh as they headed down the slope of the Gods' Mount.

"What now?" Illeri asked nervously.

"Now," Voske said, "we find a new home."

Sammel cleared his throat, drawing everyone's attention. "Perhaps I can help with that."

78: Home

The exile of the champions was swift and final. They were branded apostates, to be scorned by every temple on the three worlds. Of course, only time would tell if Aurilis' threats would hold sway over the entirety of Talamh. Somehow Zengin doubted it.

Still, no one was in the mood to contest the matter, so three days later they found themselves flying over the Erimos skies again. They'd booked travel to the dusty planet - no easy feat with Aurilis against them and a peg and chimera with them - and now they were bound for Sammel's home town on the Phoenix. Lakay was one of the few places in Talamh that didn't have a temple, and so one of the few places they'd be accepted.

At least that was the hope.

He looked behind the chariot, to where his chimera drifted lazily on the hot Erimos air. He hadn't decided what to name it yet. Something intimidating perhaps. He gripped the bracer of Neveri, laced to his stubbed arm. At least this was a trophy he could claim. He'd lost his position, his prestige, and his possessions, but he still had his power, and perhaps that was enough for the moment.

He glanced around the chariot and spotted the champions, Gillis, Burz' family, and Yzod all huddled near the chains. Burz' smelly pegasus was stamping nervously, taking up most of the center of the deck on one side. They were all talking and ignoring Zengin, except Yzod. The inventor was staring at him and, more specifically, staring at his distinct lack of a hand.

Zengin looked down at his stub again, and he felt a surge of anger, but he had nowhere to direct it. Borroka was dead, his father was dead, and who else could he hold a grudge against for this? The irritating thought swirled around his mind, taunting him. Maybe he just needed someone to hate. He raised an annoyed eye toward the other champions. They were laughing and smiling, as though their lives hadn't been thrown into disarray. And he was the outsider, as always.

He turned to stare over the side again. They were flying low over Erimos now, and the radiant field was down. The sun was hot on his back, but a cool breeze whipped around him. He leaned against the rail as he watched the grassy plains drift below, and beside the Phoenix a flock of hyppogryphs soared through the clear sky. He had almost managed to return to his brooding when a voice called out to him.

"Zengin."

Rasa had broken away from the champions and was standing close by.

He scowled.

"You should come join us," she said. She pointed to the rest of the Champions. "Weylyn says you're sad."

"Does she?" He looked around, uneasy at the thought of a spirit spying on him. "I'm not sad."

Rasa leaned in closer and whispered. "I know."

"You do?"

She nodded. "It's different than sad. It's like lonely, but different than that too."

Zengin narrowed his eyes. It was more like boiling rage as far as he could tell, but the word lonely needled him until he couldn't deny its reality.

"It's like you're looking for something," she said, "and you're afraid you won't find it, even though you don't know what it is. I feel that way too, but it goes away when I'm with my family."

"Family?"

She pointed to the other Champions, and he laughed.

"That's some family you've got there."

"It's a good one," she said with the kind of purity he'd only ever heard come from Rasa. "I wouldn't want a different one."

"I could think of better."

"Come on!" She grabbed hold of his arm. "It'll be good for you too."

He hesitated for a moment, then he started to haltingly follow, but as he moved, his eyes landed on Locin, standing in the opposite corner, alone. "Why don't you go get her?"

Rasa bit her lip. "She's not looking for something," she answered. "She's running. There's a difference."

Zengin took a deep breath. In fairness, he felt like running away from this conversation, but the deeper part of him compelled him forward. If this was his family now, then the least he could do was try to make it better than the last one he'd known.

As Rasa pulled him to the group, they all grew quiet and stared at him for a moment.

"Apparently I have to join you," he muttered.

Voske strolled over with a smile. "Is that so?"

"Weylyn's orders."

Voske laughed. He threw an arm around Zengin's shoulders and pulled him further into the group. "Well, come on then!"

Zengin stumbled forward. They were all staring at him. Except Yzod. He was still staring at his useless arm. For a moment the inventor looked up, and their eyes met.

"Do you have a problem?" Zengin asked.

Yzod smiled. "More like an idea."

The sun was low as they neared Lakay. The heat of it drew sweat from Voske's brow despite the sea breeze that rushed over him. The radiant field was down, and he breathed in the familiar air. They were far from Govere, but still, Erimos was home, and the familiar atmosphere brought a smile to his face.

"What's got you happy?"

He turned at Burz' voice to see him standing with a canteen of water. He held it out, and Voske gratefully gulped it down.

"Home," Voske said.

Burz nodded.

The two men turned side by side. Just north of them, the Vathys Ocean curled onto sandy beaches, and the brown grass of the shoreline waved in the swift northern breeze.

"How's the family holding up?"

Burz looked back to where his family stood, and his shoulders went rigid. "Hadris is strong."

"And the boys?"

Burz took a deep breath, and Voske could tell there was still a weight pressing down on him, though he wasn't so sure what to do about it. "They're excited."

"You bet they are," Voske chided. "They're moving next door to Uncle Voske!"

Burz groaned, but he was smiling. "I forgot about that part."

"Well, best start remembering, because we're gonna be neighbors."

"Oh?"

"Obviously. When you're old and gray and sitting on your rear, who else is gonna be there to give you a hard time?"

That at least got him to chuckle. "Fine," he said. "Neighbors, but you better not wake me up at some ungodly hour."

Voske feigned offense. "Where's the fun in that?"

He reached down to his side and pulled a scabbard and sword from under his piled belongings, the sword Atrius had given to Burz. "Here."

"What's this?" Burz took it, pulling the blade out a bit and looking at it with wonder. "Thought I lost this."

"Found it on the field after the battle. You gotta stop losing 'em."

Burz looped the sword around his waist and tightened it in place. "Thanks."

Voske shrugged, keeping his eyes fixed on the sea. "It used to be some sword of a long forgotten champion. Now, I think they'll remember it as the sword of Burz."

Burz smiled proudly.

"Of course," Voske lifted Straznik Bram to his shoulder, grinning, "this one cut off a god's hand."

Burz laughed.

Illeri shouted from the front of the chariot, waving them forward. "We're here! Lakay!"

Lakay. They'd heard nothing about this city except that Sammel grew up here, and it was secluded - a place where the gods weren't worshiped, and no one had boons. No one but them.

They crowded to the front of the chariot, looking over the simple stone homes spread around the seashore.

"That looks nice," Illeri said.

"I wonder if they have a local theater."

"Or a tavern." Locin looked back from leaning out over the rail. "What? A girl can dream, can't she?"

Voske turned his palm over, staring at the sigil of Jeza, Justice. Perhaps this was justice? They were exiled, forced to hide on the fringe of Erimos. But it felt a lot like the justice he'd gotten as a laborer. The quarry had been the place he'd always belonged. A simple place. A place he could fit in. And this felt quite the same.

"It feels like home to me," he said.

Yzod and Hikari pulled on the pylat's chains and the chariot drifted down, settling in the dry grass in the wide center of town. A central well was nestled nearby, and homes and gardens stretched around on all sides. Ahead, the sun dipped over the endless blue of the sea.

The others slowly filed off, Sammel leading them toward the well where curious villagers were gathering to see what sort of maniacs would land a pylat at a village so remote.

Voske just stayed on the deck, content to let his eyes wander the scene. *A house by the sea*, he thought. He looked out toward the lapping waves and the cries of gulls. He could build a house here with his own two hands.

He looked over to see Locin watching him.

"So… this is it?"

He nodded.

"Do you think we'll stay long?"

He locked his eyes on a stretch of land down the way, a gnarled old tree beside it, and a clear view of the ocean. He smiled. "Yes, I do."

Epilogue

Prudence

Den'rai was a beautiful city, built in the valley between two steep ravines, surrounded by life, lush and green like most of Las. The city itself was a haven of Bei'ai, a place for lost souls to gather. It had long since outgrown the confines of the narrow valley, and it stretched up the sides of the ravines with buildings of stone and wood that clung to the cliffs with wide windows, their walls covered with vines and plants flowering in an array of colors. Below, old wooden bridges spanned the river all up and down it, and at the rivers center sat an old moss covered statue of Bei'ai, her arms stretched out in welcome to the weary souls who found themselves in Den'rai.

Near the river, an old wooden tavern stood, filled with every sort of lost soul you could imagine. The desperate, the broken, the rejected. News was spreading fast. Neveri was dead, but there was a new god. A god of Animus. A god of Change. Gryph could almost feel it in the air as he sat staring at the cards in his hand. He clutched them, the brown leather of his gloves cracking as he smiled at the other men at the table. They had seedy, dishonest eyes.

"Well?" One of them said as he glared at Gryph.

Gryph was a young man, smooth faced with shaggy brown hair. He smiled as he twirled a coin in his free hand. "You cheated."

The man's eyes flashed with anger. "Idiot. You come into my house and accuse me of cheating?"

"Yeah, it's not an accusation, see? It's a fact." He glanced at the cards left face down in the deck, ten of them. "We've seen two gryphs and three lions. With ten cards left, the probability that you can beat me is zero. But you seem awfully confident, which tells me you plan to win. Either you're an idiot, and you have no chance, or you cheated."

The man snarled as he stood up from the table, drawing a dagger.

"Woah, now! I was giving you the benefit of the doubt, friend. I don't think you're an idiot. You're just a cheater. And a good one, I assume. Most people likely don't notice."

The man nodded to his friend who pulled a short curved blade out from behind his back.

"I was just leaving," Gryph dropped his cards and slowly backed away from the table when suddenly he felt his boon tug at him. It had led him here to Den'rai, tracking his mark. He could sense it. Whoever he'd been sent to kill was close. He blinked, and he saw a flash of a vision, fingers against the mossy stone of the statue and a lithe figure ducking behind it and rushing through the streets of the city.

As he opened his eyes, the first man lunged for him, and he ducked aside, kicking the leg of his chair to knock it into the man. The second man swung his curved blade out as Gryph picked up several cards from the table and jumped back to safety. He held up the cards, and the man eyed him curiously.

"Do you like magic?"

The man nodded to his gloved hands. "You don't got none."

"Ah, but don't I?"

He slipped the cards quickly into his sleeve, making it seem like they had disappeared. The other man was on his feet again now, and they both started advancing.

Gryph lifted his other hand and showed the man a stack of cards.

The man shook his head. "That ain't magic, kid."

"No, you're right. It's a distraction."

The two men stared at him for a moment confused as he lifted his other hand and tossed a smoke bomb to the dingy floor. He quickly covered his mouth as it went off, filling the tavern with smoke. By the time the two men had recovered, Gryph was long gone, pulling the hood of his cloak up as he brushed past the other travelers, his eyes fixed on the statue of Bei'ai.

He blinked, and his boon tugged at him again. He saw a lithe figure, hidden in a cloak and hood. The figure was past the statue, ducking down a side street where the shadows of the ravine blocked the bright sun. They were making it too easy.

He picked up his pace, hurrying through the crowd until he reached the street, ominous buildings rising up on either side and deep shadow ahead. He quickly ducked down the alley, hurrying along until he could see his quarry just ahead. They turned, and he saw bright eyes watching him, filled with fear. The figure took off running, but Gryph was fast. In a moment, he had grabbed them by the shoulder and spun them around, dragging them toward the end of the alley where shadow and stone was all that awaited. He tossed the figure down, noting how small and light they felt, and he stopped, slipping the worn glove off his right hand and holding up his palm. Two crossed daggers were charred against his skin, the mark of the Assassin's Guild.

"You're going to kill me?" The voice was young. Very young. It gave him pause.

"You're familiar with my guild, I assume?"

The figure nodded. "Murderers."

"No." Gryph shook his head. "Some of us, certainly. But there's still plenty who believe in justice."

"The guild stopped caring about justice a long time ago," the small voice quavered. "Now they just stamp their own seal on contracts and kill for sport."

Gryph reached in his pocket, pulling out a dagger. He tossed it to his left hand and dug out a rolled parchment, letting it fall open for the figure to see. There on the parchment was the golden signature of Jeza. "There was a time when we only took contracts that Jeza herself sealed. That's how it should still be, if you ask me. Maybe you're right. Maybe the guild isn't as honorable as it once was. But me?" He shook his head as he tucked the contract away. "I don't take a contract that isn't sealed by the goddess. That way I know it's a just kill. Whatever you've done, you've got to pay for it."

The figure stood suddenly, striding forward as Gryph lifted the dagger, ready to strike.

"Justice?" The form stopped in front of him - so much smaller than he'd thought - and pulled back the hood, letting the cloak slip from their shoulders. It was a girl, barely a cycle. She wore a plain white toga, and her dark hair was braided down her back in two braids.

"Mire."

"Would you still kill me, assassin? Is it just?"

"Jeza thinks so. What did you do that she would approve a contract against you?"

"Maybe she isn't as just as you believe."

He clutched the dagger as he stared her down, ready to strike. But something seemed off. "Who are you?"

"No one," she said. "Just a girl."

"What's your name?"

"Na'mai."

"Where's your family?"

A pained look crossed her face as she stared at him defiantly.

"I've never failed a contract." He lifted the blade, and she steeled herself. He moved closer, tossing the blade back to his right hand. Her eyes were bright blue, the brightest blue he'd ever seen, and they were filled with pain.

"Why does someone want you dead?"

"I'll tell you the truth. I'm on my way to find the Champions."

"The Champions?"

She nodded. "They were banished from the temple. They need my help."

"But you're a kid. What do they need your help for?"

"To save Talamh."

He laughed. "Haven't you heard the story? They already did that."

"Talamh wasn't saved. It was broken. The people are divided, and they can't see the truth."

"What truth?" He moved the dagger toward her neck, keeping its razor sharp edge a hair's breadth from her skin. "Why should I break this contract?"

"Because you're a good person, Gryph."

He nearly stumbled back as she spoke his name. "How do you know me?"

"You're just, even when they're not."

She lifted a hand and pressed it to his chest over his heart as he kept his dagger perfectly steady.

"You believe, Gryph. You believe in doing what's right, and good."

"Good is hard to define in my line of work."

"That doesn't make it any less real."

He slowly lowered the dagger. He needed to be sure. He needed more information.

Her eyes were suddenly slick with tears as she pulled away from him, breathing intensely. "You're letting me go?"

"I need to know this is just."

She started to duck around him, and he looked back at her. "My boon will let me track you. If I find out you deserve death, I'll come for you again, and you won't survive the next time."

She nodded gratefully, then gathered her cloak and threw it back over her head, running down the alley.

Gryph stood breathing heavily as he tucked away his dagger, listening to the clack of her footsteps down the old stone road. Suddenly a searing pain overtook him, and he cried out, dropping to his knees as a strange fiery light filled his senses. As the pain subsided, he glanced down at his hand where the burning sensation still lingered. His seal was gone, and he could no longer sense the girl, but there in its place burned the golden sigil of Strah.